SLAVE MARKET . . .

The black girl remained motionless, aloof. Her head tilted slightly. Her cameo profile seemed to taughten and angry fires raged deep in her wide-set black eyes.

With a sudden cry that chilled the blood as the scream of a lynx might, the prize Fulani wench sprang at the auctioneer. Her hands, like claws, scratched at his eyes. The auctioneer yelled. Three muscular black men, bared to the waist, captured her after a brief, fierce struggle and wrestled her back to the block where she stood rigid.

"Strip the bitch," the auctioneer ordered.

The black guards caught her dress and stripped it from her, the tearing fabric loud in the hot, breathless silence.

She stood naked—defiant. Her legs were braced apart, the triangle of hair at her pubic mound gleamed as coppery as her skin. Her marble-hard nipples stood rigid on full, high-standing breasts.

"There she is, gentlemen!" shouted the auctioneer. "Who'll open the bids on this tigress?"

Styles felt his heart sink. If he lost this, he lost everything. . . .

Fawcett Gold Medal Books
by Ashley Carter:

MASTER OF BLACKOAKS

SECRET OF BLACKOAKS

SWORD OF THE GOLDEN STUD

SECRET
OF
BLACKOAKS

Ashley Carter

A FAWCETT GOLD MEDAL BOOK

Fawcett Books, Greenwich, Connecticut

SECRET OF BLACKOAKS

© 1978 Harry Whittington

Published by Fawcett Gold Medal Books, CBS Publications, CBS
Consumer Publishing, a Division of CBS, Inc.

The material for this book has been prepared for publication by
Ashley Carter through special and exclusive arrangement with
the Kenric L. Horner Trust.

ISBN 0-449-13960-3

Printed in the United States of America

10 9 8 7 6 5 4 3 2 1

For Kathryn

"No scene of life but teems with mortal woe."
—Walter Scott

SECRET
OF
BLACKOAKS

PART ONE

The Wedding

1

"Masta. Wake up, Masta Styles. Hit's cock-crowin' time, Masta. You said for sure I was to wake you. . . . You gots to see to them ole cotton wagons, first thing this mawnin'."

Styles stirred in the down mattress and struggled upward unwillingly from warm depths of sleep toward chilled wakefulness with all its renewed apprehensions. He shivered, breaking free of the nightmare that had snared him in its persisting webbing.

A dog barked in the slave quarters. Dimly, Styles heard muted clatter of harness and gear, the snuffling of dray animals, and the creaking of iron-rimmed wheels in the predawn stillness. Negroes working down at the barns talked in subdued and cautious tones, careful not to disturb the white folks asleep in the manor house.

Across this insistent mingling of sounds rode the controlled violence of Bos Pilzer's guttural voice. The fat-bellied Dutch overseer swore in a monotone but he swore steadily, repeating himself only infrequently. Pilzer believed there were two ways to keep niggers moving—you cursed them or you stung them with the whip.

Styles writhed deeper into the sensuous warmth of the covers. He couldn't go on lying here, as devoutly as he might wish it. He had to be fully awake and in total command. This huge farm was his responsibility. Bos Pilzer's law was the rule of the whip. Yet only he, Styles Kenric, had the power of life and death over the slaves.

He flung his arm over his face. These blacks responded to any orders sluggishly and unwillingly. You stayed on their tails or you went broke. Pilzer used the lash and the slaves obeyed—for the moment. They moved when the overseer cursed them. They jumped in a way Bos found comical when he "tetched 'em up" with the lash on their tough black hides. But with every bite of the whip their resentment simmered hotter beneath the sullen surface. Only fear of greater punishment from the plantation master kept them in line. Styles cursed impotently. He had to get down there, and yet he delayed.

"Please. Wake up, Masta." Moab's hand closed on the bare flesh of Styles's shoulder. The young black shook him timidly, yet insistently. Styles hardly felt the nervous urgency in the boy's hand, but he was acutely sensitive to the heated strength in those fingers.

"Please, Masta Styles, suh. We sho' got us a lot to do this mawnin,' Masta."

Styles winced, now awake and conscious of the confusion and tensions that marked every waking hour.

His mouth twisted. He felt overwhelmed by events outside his control. The big house stirred like a broken anthill—the women and house slaves getting ready for Christmas and that damned wedding of Miz Claire's big-breasted cousin from Charleston. The thought of young Ferrell's impending return from the monastery renewed old rages. On top of this, the new head cook was uncertain and indecisive; the kitchen was chaos. There could not be a worse time for Mr. Cleatus Dennison's arrival. The slave breeder had one motive for this visit. He'd renew his offer to buy the two Fulani slaves, Blade and Moab, naming a figure in the thousands that no sane man could refuse.

"Please, Masta. You tole me you gots to get up."

Styles nodded. Sleep was out of the question, but for the moment he lay with eyes closed against the candle guttering in Moab's fist. Yawning luxuriously, Styles stretched himself languidly under the covers. His slender six-foot frame, with its golden skin, had a feline grace and the beauty of chiseled perfection. His wavy black hair, still damp with the night's sweat, toppled over his forehead. His delicately hewn features were enhanced rather than marred by the arrogantly tilted brow and an innate haughty petulance flaring his nostrils.

Styles opened his long-lashed eyes. Their trenchant blue added chill to his remote and unapproachable demeanor. He blinked against the lancing of saffron light and gazed with pleasure at his tawny body slave.

"Moab," he whispered.

Moab smiled, waiting. Moab was sixteen or seventeen plantings old. No one knew for sure, but already he was demonstrating the natural catlike grace of the sinewy, beautiful young man he would become. He was still as naked as he had been when he crept from his master's bed to his own pallet at its foot sometime during the night after Styles finally slept. This golden-brown youth was a perfect animal except for a slowly healing wale sliced across his back from shoulder to hipbone.

Styles smiled and drew the tip of his tongue across his lips. He was sensuously stirred by everything he saw in this purebred Fulani boy—the rippling cordlike muscles of his pectorals, the wide, supple shoulders, the flat belly, and that proud appendage tumescent at his pillarlike thighs. There was about this slave boy the mein of his regal ancestry—he looked to be a direct descendant of those dark-gold conquerors of tenth-century Senegal.

Styles swung one leg from beneath the hand-crafted quilts. He moved as if to get out of bed and then stopped. He sank back and lay still. His long-lashed eyes slumbrous, he gazed longingly upon Moab's bronze nakedness.

"You're beautiful. Truly beautiful, Moab."

Moab smiled unselfconsciously, pleased at his master's flattery and reassured by it. He'd heard these words often in the past few years—in hidden haylofts with pliable black girls, in bed with Bos Pilzer's wife—but from the master of Blackoaks these words assumed new and deeper

11

significance. He felt a surge of personal power, a sense of security he knew was denied every other black on this plantation.

"Them other planter-gen'mmen be 'long soon with they cotton wagons, Masta Styles." Moab's voice carried a dutiful inflection rather than any tone of conviction. He was speaking the words he knew he was expected to say.

"Yes. Yes. I know that." Styles slid his gaze downward over the boy's muscled chest and flat belly. Then he reached out, trembling slightly, and stroked Moab gently, excited by the response he aroused in his young slave.

He wanted to laugh out his exultance because Moab's enjoyment of his caress matched his own rising excitement and compulsive needs.

"Whole place. Gwine be stirrin' with folks. Mighty soon now, Masta." Moab's voice was feathered, his breathing labored. He stood perfectly still, enjoying the erotic pleasures his master's caresses aroused within him. And there was too the secret sense of power his owner's need bestowed upon him. In his way he was able to exercise a strong control over his master and he could strengthen that hold as long as his body pleased the white man.

"Yes. I must get up. Right away." But Styles said the words indolently. There were compelling reasons why he should get up at once and take command. That damned Ferrell *was* arriving momentarily. It was vital that Ferrell see how totally in charge Styles Kenric was. The way to forestall trouble with Ferrell was to let the holy bastard see who was boss here.

Moab stood erect, pulsating and rigid, in Styles's fist.

"You're a strong and handsome boy, Moab."

Styles lay and stared at Moab's gleaming body, his eyes glazing over.

"Get in, Moab." Styles turned the covers back, quivering with desire.

Moab blew out the candle and slipped into bed. Breathing raggedly, Styles reached out both arms.

"It can all wait—an hour anyway," Styles whispered. He moved his hands over Moab's heated thighs. "You

12

like this . . . don't you, Moab? . . . . You like—being—my slave?"

"Yes, Masta." Moab caught Styles's head between his hands, pushing him downward. He heard his master's frantic breathing intensify and he closed his hands tighter. "Oh, yes, Masta . . . I likes . . . being—your—slave . . . . "

2

Hunter Campbell awoke in the dark hour before dawn.

He lay in his bed for only a few moments listening to the slaves readying the cotton wagons down at the barns. Then he swung his legs over the side of the mattress, anxious to be down there. He lit a candle. Through the window he looked at the barns and the slave quarters on the incline beyond. Pine-knot torches and a roaring wood fire illumined the barnyard. Firelight glistened liquidly on sweated black bodies and in ebony eyes.

Wearing boots, whipcord trousers, linen shirt opened at the collar, and wool jacket buttoned against the winter chill, Hunt blew out the candle and let himself out the corridor door.

"Mist' Campbell . . . . Hist . . . . Hunter . . . . "

Hunt paused and gazed around in the gloom of the upper hallway. He saw a shadow slither from the darkness and a small, flower-soft hand grasped his. With surprising strength the girl drew him toward a barely cracked bedroom door.

Hunt braced just outside the door. "Jamie Lee," he whispered.

"Come in," she pleaded, tightening her fingers. "Just for a minute."

Jamie Lee pulled him through the doorway and closed it stealthily behind them. She slumped against the door facing, staring up at him, waiting. Her full-lipped mouth parted, her breath rasping across it.

Even in the vague and diffused candlelight, Hunt could see how the young girl's swollen breasts struggled against transparent fabric. She was a tiny girl, with a supple, slender body from which those breasts jutted startlingly. Her tousled curls toppled about her shoulders; she looked as if she'd lain restlessly upon her rumpled bed.

Her violet eyes accused him. "I waited for you—all night."

Hunt stared at her helplessly. "Why would you do that?"

Her smile faded. "I saw you—looking at me—last evening—"

He flushed. "You must be quite accustomed to men looking at you."

She smiled, glancing down at the high-standing breasts, so taut they looked bruised, and marble-hard nipples. She was inordinately proud—and justifiably so. "But I—looked back at you," she said.

He felt the girl's hungry eyes go over him, the dark hair, rounded forehead, and yankee-blue eyes set in a chill-burned face. His nose was straight, sharply chiseled, with flared nostrils. His mouth was tight-lipped, part of his aloofness; his aloofness had acted as a challenge to other men more than once, but he saw in Jamie Lee's eyes that she found it exciting.

"You had to know how I felt," Jamie Lee whispered. "You had to know."

"Sorry, Jamie Lee. I'm just a blue-belly Yankee. I'm not very smart."

"Don't patronize me. Don't dare patronize me. I could see you looking at me. I knew what *you* wanted. You knew *I* wanted it, too."

He winced. Was his sexual starvation so obvious? It had been a hellish long time since he'd had a woman— black or white. He'd had the slave girl Sefina, thanks to the understanding and kindness of the late Ferrell Baynard, Senior. He'd gotten Sefina pregnant and caused her to be sold as a female breeding animal to a slave breeder named Dennison. He hadn't wanted another black girl

14

since Sefina. And he didn't want this white wench. She had trouble written all over her reckless little body.

"I was entranced by you, Jamie Lee. But I also am forced to remember you are here to marry Mr. Link Tetherow."

Her eyes chilled over. Her cheeks set as hard as a ceramic glaze. Her peach-bloom complexion burned with blood hot under its flawless, translucent surface.

"Forgive me, Jamie Lee, I—"

"What are you? A molly like Uncle Styles?"

He bit back laughter but no longer attempted to answer her. "Miz Claire told me her cousin Jamie Lee Seaton was the rose of old Charleston society . . . . Are all the gentle belles as charming and winsome as you?"

"I'm what I am," Jamie Lee said without apology. "I'm a woman—"

"You're seventeen—"

"A woman—and I thought you were a man—"

He bowed. "All of us make mistakes, Jamie Lee."

Her head tilted and her mouth curled in savage disdain. "Why don't you get out of here before I scream?"

He spoke teasingly. "Does this mean you don't want me, after all?"

"Get out, you grinning bastard. And stop laughing at me."

"I could never laugh at anyone with tits like yours, my love . . . . I wonder, indeed, if Mr. Link Tetherow has any idea of just what he is getting?"

"Get out." Her voice rasped. "I will scream."

He bowed again and let himself stealthily out into the hallway. He heard something smash in Jamie Lee's bedroom, and then it was quiet in there. He exhaled heavily. He'd lost a hell of a roll in that girl's bed, but he had escaped trouble that might have swamped him.

He glanced along the corridor toward the closed bedroom door behind which Kathy slept—he hoped to God she was still asleep. He went quietly along the dark upper hallway and down the narrow rear stairs, lighted with saffron shafts from the busy kitchen below.

15

3

The girl's face came in so abruptly and so close to Morgan's that her hot breath seared his cheeks and brought him awake violently. He lay for a moment, trembling helplessly.

Before he could cry out, Jamie Lee clamped her hand tautly over his mouth. She dug her fingers into his chubby cheeks. Morgan stared up at her in anguish. The violence in her eyes warned him to remain silent.

He fought to break away from her viselike grasp on his cheeks, but he could not move. He struggled, shaking his head back and forth on his goosedown pillow.

The girl remained bent close over him, illumined only by a small candle she must have lighted on his bedside table. Her deep blue eyes glittered wildly in the candlelight. Morgan could see nothing in the darkness beyond the golden hair that framed her face and toppled warmly against him. He wanted desperately to yell for Soapy. Soapy would know what to do. Soapy wasn't afraid of girls. He wanted to call out, but she held him too fiercely. He couldn't cry aloud, either, but could make only strangled sounds deep in his throat.

"Where is Soapy?" she whispered, her heated breath fragrant against his face.

Morgan shook his head back and forth, unable to answer. He flung out his arm seeking Soapy in the bed beside him, but he found the sheets chilled and empty. He felt the old momentary dread that always incapacitated him when he couldn't immediately locate his body slave. He shook his head negatively again.

Jamie Lee released her grip on him at last.

"Why do you want Soapy?" Morgan said.

She stared at him, ill-veiling her contempt. Morgan at sixteen was a rugged youth, nearly fully grown physically, even slightly overweight. He weighed two hundred pounds

16

at least, with heavy shoulders, keg-like chest, and stocky legs. He would have been an impressive giant of a man except for the indolent fat. His gentle face, made softer with baby fat, was said to be remarkably like his deceased father's. But in his mind Morgan was childlike, and he would never be any more than that. Everybody in Charleston who knew about Miz Claire's son said it was a shame.

Jamie Lee moved her full-blown young breasts closer to Morgan's flushed face. "Would you like me to get in your bed with you, Morgan?"

He felt his heart lurch, and his face flamed red to the roots of his thick curly hair. He swallowed with difficulty. "But I got no clothes on, Cousin Jamie Lee."

"How nice," she said. "Would you like for me to take off my gown?"

He stared at her, unable to lift his bemused gaze from those breasts so clearly defined beneath the sheer silk fabric. She was going to undress, going to let him look at *them,* naked? He managed to nod, then said, troubled, "Suppose somebody comes in?"

"They won't."

"But if'n they did—"

"They won't, Morgan. I locked the door."

He felt that lurching in his heart again. He managed a wan smile, afraid he was going to be sick at his stomach. "You are hugamongus pretty, Jamie Lee. Soapy say he bet there ain't no prettier white girl in this world."

Her voice rasped and her violet-hued eyes glittered. "You want to talk about that nigra—or do you want me to get in bed with you so we can have some fun?"

He nodded, fascinated. "You can get in bed with me . . . . I'd like that a heap, Cousin Jamie Lee."

She was sliding the soft fabric of her gown upward along her body. Morgan gazed raptly, unable to breathe. He had never encountered flesh that combined the texture, color, and quality of fresh Easter lilies with the dew on them. The roundness of her hips, the splash of faint color in the triangle at her thighs, the soft planes of her belly, were all new and unknown to him. She said, "Turn the covers back for me, Morgan."

He managed to gasp, protesting. "But I'm naked."

She stopped again, chilled with frustration. "Of course you are," she said. "I want to see you naked, too, Morgan . . . . Girls like to look at boys—"

"They do?"

"Turn them back, Morgan." Jamie Lee jerked her gown up, pulling her blonde curls high so they plunged back about her pale face and naked shoulders in a golden shower.

Morgan stared at her helplessly, barely able to breathe. His chest ached so excruciatingly he thought he might die. But he was locked, unable to move, unable to pull his stupefied gaze from Jamie Lee's candlelit bosom.

Hands trembling, he turned the covers back. Jamie Lee's gaze followed the folding quilts. Her lips parted and her eyes widened in pleasure and surprise when she saw the thick, stocky mast, quivering with the pulsing of his blood. She forgot her contempt, her anger, her frustration. She gazed at the size of Morgan's manhood and knew everything was going to be all right.

She got quickly into bed beside Morgan. He did not move but lay rigid in a violent seizure of nervous shaking. "What's the matter with you?" she demanded.

Morgan shook his head, unable to speak.

"Don't be nervous," she said. She forced herself to speak tenderly, to conceal her impatience. "It's nothing to be afraid of."

He nodded, forcing an agonized caricature of a smile.

She drew her gentle fingers along his chest. She felt his thick muscles quivering in reaction to her touch. "Haven't you ever done this before?"

"Soapy—sleeps with me—sometimes," he gasped.

She laughed at him. "Dummy . . . I don't mean that. I mean—like this—with a girl."

He shook his head. "No." The word struggled up through his throat. He was afraid he was strangling.

Her hands caressed him. "Haven't you ever wanted to?"

He nodded. "Yes . . . oh, yes."

She smiled, kissing along his jaw. "Well, now you can. Now you can—touch me. Go ahead. Any way you like,

Morgan . . . anything . . . . And I'll touch you . . . like this."

She reached down, slid her satiny-smooth hand across the rise of his belly and closed her delicate fingers on him.

He managed to gasp, "Oh, God. Oh, my God." Then he ejaculated, his tool bucking violently in her fist, the hot fluid erupting, gushing, and dribbling stickily down her wrist and arm.

Jamie Lee jerked her hand away from him and sat up, staring at him, her face cold. "Why in hell did you do that?" she demanded.

"You touched me," he said.

"Of course I touched you, you ninny."

"I'm sorry. I didn't mean to—get it all over you."

She wiped her hand and arm on the gleaming white percale sheet and shook her head impatiently. "It's all right . . . . " She laughed in a rueful way. "It's not the first time that's happened . . . . What's the matter . . . . Why can't some men wait at all?"

Morgan stared at her, unable to answer because he wasn't even sure what she was talking about. His lip quivered, and he looked saddened. "Are you going now?" he asked.

Jamie Lee laughed at his tone of desolation. "You don't want me to go, do you?"

"Oh, no. I want you to stay."

She smiled and lay down again with her golden head on the pillow beside his. She whispered, "Will you try to do better—if I make you hard again?"

"Oh, it'll be hard again. In just a few minutes—if you stay here—naked like this—"

"Well, you hang on this time. You hear? Or I won't like you."

"I'll try. I'll bite my mouth real hard, Jamie Lee. Honest. I'll try."

She pulled his trembling hands over on her full breasts. "This is like teaching a baby," she teased. "A big, two-hundred-pound baby with a monster cannon."

He quivered all over. "Oh, Jamie Lee, I'm so crazy about you."

"Now, don't you go saying silly things like that. You

know I'm here at Blackoaks to marry Mr. Link Tetherow . . . . You and me—we can have fun like this, Morgan—but not if you go and get serious about an old married lady, like I'll be soon as Cousin Ferrell gets home to perform the ceremony."

His voice sank, but he nodded, despondent. "I'll do whatever you say, Jamie Lee."

"That's a good fat baby . . . . Take my nipple in your mouth, Morgan. Suck on it. Hard. Real hard. I like that."

He hesitated. "Will I get—milk?"

She laughed. "Why? Do you want to?"

"I don't know . . . . I don't know if I'd like it."

She laughed and caught his head in her hands, guiding his fevered face to her rigid nipple. "Try it and see."

Morgan took her round, rose-pink nipple hesitantly between his lips and nuzzled it, nursing. Jamie Lee lay back, sighing extravagantly. It had been a long and hellishly frustrating night, but it was going to be all right. She remained unmoving for a few silent moments enjoying the excitement and pleasures flaring through her. Then she reached down and closed her fingers on him again. "Good lord," she said, pleased and excited. "You're up and hard again—already."

"You make me ready—you drive me crazy."

Her breath quickened. "You can do it now, if you want to."

He didn't move away from her breasts.

"Do it," she told him. "I'm ready . . . . I'm more than ready . . . . I'm burning up down there."

He lifted his head. "I don't know how," he muttered. "I don't know what you want."

She exhaled violently in exasperation. Then she pulled him over upon her.

"I want you on top of me, Morgan," she said, her voice raspy. "Now . . . I want it in me . . . . I want that big thing of yours driven up in me—hard as you can, you hear me? . . . . Don't you want to do it . . . ?"

"Be careful," he moaned. "I—might let go—again."

"Damn you! Don't you dare . . . . I'm almost crazy now . . . . Now, for God's sake. What are you doing?"

He lay on top of her, resting his weight on his knees.

He had taken his engorged rod in his hand and was pressing it furiously and impotently into the dainty mat of pubic hairs at her padded mound. "What in hell are you trying to do, Morgan?"

"I'm—trying—to—put it in you," he gasped.

She stared up at him, eyes wide. She gazed, stunned with shock, chilled with disbelief, cold with rage. "Don't you know *anything*?"

"I told you," he murmured in abject misery.

"Oh, damn you. Get off me. Get away from me, you big hulking idiot . . . . You don't even know where it is . . . you don't even know . . . what to do . . . . Get away."

"Please, Jamie Lee."

She stared at him, her eyes brimmed with furious tears. "I knew you were foolish," she raged, "but I didn't know you were *stupid*!"

4

Hunt hurried across the busy, crowded kitchen. This gallery was the largest single room in the mansion at Blackoaks. It was the vital heart of the huge farm. But the thought crossed Hunt's mind that there seemed to be more confusion these days in the kitchen and less profusion of luxurious food, daintily prepared, than when this had been the domain of the *os rouge,* Jeanne d'Arc.

Such a vast operation as this satrapy needed the strong dominance of an unyielding mistress. While the elder Baynard lived, the half-Negress, half-Indian Jeanne d'Arc had ruled this kitchen as if it were her own suzerainty. Hunt wasn't sure why the intense hatred between Jeanne d'Arc and the new master of Blackoaks existed, only that the beautiful mustee despised Styles Kenric, and one of the first moves Kenric had made when he took over after Baynard's death was the quick removal of Jeanne d'Arc —from the kitchen, from the plantation. It was as if she no longer existed. One asked about her but got only shrugs, puzzled frowns, or questions in return. All Hunt knew for sure was that Jeanne d'Arc was gone and that things were not the same in the kitchen. The place needed her desperately.

Kitchens such as this one were almost unknown in the cold area from which Hunt had come. Most New England kitchens he had seen could have been set down in the pantry of this one. A massive cast-iron wood-burning stove dominated the room, but there were also great built-in brick ovens for baking, heavy spits for roasting and broiling. A thick unfinished pine table with worn benches along each side could seat eighteen and often did when the kitchen helpers gathered for meals, free periods, or when they and their smaller children huddled in near the fire-bright stove on cold days. The slaves sat along the table, joking and whispering in guarded tones, gossiping, and drinking endless cups of chickory coffee with biscuits or buns. There were always crocks of clabber, and the children and the older people ladled out great globs of it to spoon down with corn pone or pancakes.

The main kitchen was larger than the formal parlor in which the Baynards held parties and dances. It boasted a pitcher pump and a porcelain sink that drained directly to the ground beneath the flooring. A short stairway led down to the cooling room built cavernlike below ground.

A walk-in pantry with deep shelving from floor to ceiling was packed with carefully labeled preserved foods, spices, and condiments. Beyond the pantry was a broom and mop closet almost as large as one of the smaller bedrooms.

Drainboard workspace on each side of the sink was deep, as were the cupboards below it. Stained-wood cupboards, ornately carved, along the walls, had racks for heavy knives, spoons, ladles, and forks for every use.

Aunt Hattie, the slave now in charge of the kitchen and its innumerable workers, had been an assistant to Jeanne d'Arc in the old days, but had never been trusted with much authority. She was an enormous black woman with advanced lordosis. Her buttocks protruded as though she concealed a week's wet wash under her cotton shift.

She moved slowly and awkwardly on short legs, bowed by childhood rickets. She spent an inordinate amount of time sprawled, spraddled-legged in a butt-sprung wicker chair, gasping for breath and barking out orders. Many of her underlings were afraid to ask her anything because she hid her lack of knowledge under blistering vocal attacks upon the questioner.

Hunt sighed. The kitchen was one of the signs of decay about Blackoaks. But it was none of his business. He recognized that his own tenure here was shaky at best.

As he crossed the kitchen now, many of the slaves murmured his name, not really looking up at him as he walked through the heated room, redolent with odors of baking, frying, and stewing and the boiling of chicory coffee.

"Mawnin,' Masta Hunt," they said. But he had learned the hard way that it was useless and futile and, perhaps, dangerous for them for him to attempt to express any friendliness beyond returning their murmured greeting. They were embarrassed and frightened by his attention.

He exhaled heavily, feeling that old sense of guilt and impotence that had haunted him since his arrival here determined to do whatever he could to better the lot of these sad people. But he had learned to stay away from them, not because he wanted to—God knew he didn't. He wanted to help them in any way he could, but he'd found he aided them most by keeping his distance. These slaves had their own world. It didn't seem much of a world to him—a place of misery, of denied humanity—but whatever it was, he'd learned one thing for certain. They didn't want him in it.

It was still the darkest hour before the first streaking of the false dawn when Hunt reached the barns. Fires, torches, and lanterns illumined the work area in a bright-orange brilliance with strange, shapeless shadows hurled against the walls. Dozens of black men sweated under the command of the thickly built Dutch overseer, Bos Pilzer. But Hunt was there for only moments before he recognized that the man responsible for any smoothness and fluidity in the operation was the Fulani, Blade.

Hunt glanced around, looking for Styles Kenric. But

he was not surprised to find that the master of the plantation was not present. Hunt smiled grimly. Old man Baynard must be whirling in his grave at the idea of the master of Blackoaks leaving the direction of cotton loading to underlings. Rest, old man, Hunt thought in irony, there have been many changes that would curl your toes since you've been gone.

Hunt stood near a high-loaded cotton wagon and watched the operation, the likes of which he had never seen before. The work was hard, the bales were extraordinarily heavy, the dray animals obstinate. He heard the keening murmuring of the slaves as they worked. He could not understand the words; maybe they were gibberish, a plaintive counterpoint to their labors. Or maybe it was the remembered sorrowing of their ancestors leashed in faraway native villages in the African brush. It was troubling, upsetting, and yet the men worked continually and without pause. The operation seemed to have awakened every black child under the age of fifteen, and they crowded around, watching, whispering, shoving, and giggling.

Hunt's gaze wandered but kept returning admiringly to the muscular young Fulani on the gallowslike steps leading up from where the wagons were loaded one by one to the platform where the lint was pressed into bales. He supposed Blade was about twenty plantings old, as the age of the slaves was carelessly reckoned. But Blade knew every operation required in loading these wagons. He was on top of everything, keeping it moving and moving smoothly. A bale slipped its coverings; his glistening knife, sharpened beyond the keeness of a razor, appeared and effortlessly slit, chopped, and repaired. Blade moved with the grace and ease of a ballet dancer. He never made two moves when one would accomplish his task. He sweated as much as the fattest black man among them, but he never appeared to tire.

Blade was directing the last of the cotton through the presses to the waiting cotton wagons. In a fenced-in hopper, the loose clouds of cotton lint were raked and prodded into the presses. A twenty-foot cylinder, turned on graduated gear wheels powered from below by eight or ten blacks plodding in endless circles pushing a smaller pole, compacted the lint into bales that weighed up to five hundred pounds each. These bales fell out to the platform where they were covered separately with cotton bagging and secured with metal ties. Then two Negroes on the baling platform tossed each huge bale to the wagon where other black men lashed it to other high-standing cubes on flatbeds drawn by mules.

The Fulani Blade dominated this entire operation. If one of the loaders on the baling platform above him faltered or moved too slowly, he would bound up the steps easily, heft the five hundred pound bale, his sweated muscles tightening like twisted cords, and toss it out to the wagon.

Hunt watched the young Fulani, fascinated. No matter what difficulty arose—and there were innumerable troubles when sleepy men were overworked, driven, or suddenly cut with the lash of a whip—Blade handled the problem, the lights of fires glittering in his laughing, sweated face, and made it look easy.

Hunt knew the young black only vaguely. He was Moab's older brother; he lived alone, except for bed wenches who sneaked into his cabin after dark, up in the quarters; he was in charge of the plantation commissary. Obviously he was an intelligent young black, and much of the operation of this farm depended on him. Hunt had seldom seen a man he admired more than he did Blade. He grinned crookedly, wondering what his peers in the Harvard Yard would think of Hunter Campbell's admiration of an illiterate, sweated black man, moving catlike between press and cotton wagons on a backwaters farm in the remotest, God-forgotten, red-neck region of the enslaved South?

Blade was a slave and nothing more, but you wouldn't have believed it looking at him. He held himself with an inborn, splendid, and unconscious pride and self-respect, head erect, black eyes lustrous. There was undeniable stateliness in his bearing. He was slightly over six feet tall, slender, wide in the shoulders, narrow in the hips, and long-legged. There was a clear sheen in the metallic reddish tan of his skin. Sweat streaming down his sinewy body gave his flesh a coppery gloss.

His head was well shaped, with a high, straight forehead, crisp black hair slightly indented at the temples, and ears close to the head. There was something of heroic ancient Grecian sculpture about his features. His delicately hewn nose was a classic line from his forehead. His nostrils flared slightly—another touch of that regal arrogance! Bared to the waist as he was, in sweated osnaburg britches, he carried himself as though the earth beneath him were his own red carpet of royalty. His lips were full but not thick, his teeth brightly white in the firelight. His lower jaw gave the final touch to the classic beauty of the healthy young black; it was finely chiseled, squared, not jutting at all, but in no sense weak.

When he braced himself, legs apart, on those wide steps, one could visualize a long-departed Moor commander alone on some disputed parapet—savage, barbaric, but unflinching.

"He's really something, isn't he?"

At the sound of Kathy's voice, Hunt jerked his head around, staring. "What's a pretty lady like you doing awake this time of day?"

"I've always loved to watch the cotton wagons. The whole place will look like the supply depot of an army encampment when the other growers pull in with their wagons," Kathy said. She smiled. "I always love to watch Blade, too . . . . Daddy was so proud of him . . . . He had such dreams for him . . . . I guess his biggest disappointment was that he could never make his plans for Blade work out."

Hunt stood taut-drawn, looking down at Kathy, entranced. She was incredibly, blondely lovely. Her fresh and fragile beauty—she looked all new and untouched, though she was at least twenty-one and several years married—was enhanced by the firelight. The strange orange glow of the flames highlighted her delicate features and added a liquid luster to her pale blue eyes, a brilliance to her peach-bloom complexion, and glowing tints to the soft ringlets framing her face.

Though a kindly—or a malicious—providence had permitted him to be near her for well over a year, Hunt had never grown accustomed to her Dresden china fragility or the warm naturalness of the smiling that illumined her face. He'd never encountered a lovelier girl, not even among those elegant and pampered beauties sought after calculatedly by the wealthiest, most successful of his classmates at Harvard. For Styles Kenric to have married the loveliest belle in Alabama was for him to have demonstrated his own superiority among his peer landowners. By now Hunt knew Styles didn't want Kathy as a woman. But, by the same token, Styles wanted her as a startlingly lovely symbol of his primacy; Styles would never let her go; she was one of his most prized possessions—nothing more, but certainly nothing less.

"What are you staring at?" Kathy smiled up at him, teasingly, and yet gently.

"I never saw you in firelight like this before. It becomes you. Even the shadows at your cheeks and around your hair are lovelier than ordinary shadows."

She touched his hand, briefly, tautly, pressing it. She laughed. "That's why I came down here."

Hunt gazed down at her, eyes bleak. "I love you," he said.

Kathy nodded solemnly. "I know."

He found difficulty in pulling his locked gaze away from her lovely, melancholy little smile. But burning into his consciousness he felt an almost physical intensity in a gaze fixed on *him*. He jerked his head up and found Styles Kenric standing tall and aloofly immobile near the roaring fire, staring at them along his patrician nose, his crystal-blue eyes chilled and malevolent.

5

Miz Claire paused at the opened doorway of Styles's bedroom. For some moments she did not move, watching the black slave wench Shiva massage ointment into Moab's bared, muscled, and whip-scarred young back.

Miz Claire weighed less than one hundred pounds, seeming to be slowly evaporating inside herself no matter how faithfully her body slave, old Neva, forced huge amounts of healthful foods upon her. Her flesh seemed almost transparent, her small bones looking fragile. She wore floor-length gowns of expensive fabrics, designed and sewn especially for her. She favored tiered skirts, ruffles, and flounces. Her complexion, enhanced by rouges secretly scrubbed into her cheeks by Neva, was unlined. Her pale eyes appeared fixed on some middle distance, invisible to those around her.

Feeling Miz Claire's gaze on her, Shiva looked up, flustered, whining her complaint. "I left the doah open, Miz Claire, so's I wouldn't be alone in no bedroom with no trifling nigger boy . . . . I rubbin' he back 'cause Masta Styles he come and git me and say for me to do this."

Miz Claire's head tilted. "Hush, girl. Do as you're told. We want all the darkies at their best when my husband comes home . . . . "

Shiva gasped, trembling visibly. As far as Shiva was concerned, the aging woman was haunted, as are all mindless people, mindless and dangerous as witches. Shiva's eyes showed the white rims of terror. She stared at the slender white woman, like a wraith in her chiffon dress. Shiva wanted to run from Miz Claire's presence as from any haunted place. She could feel Moab's suppressed giggling through the corded muscles of his wide back. Everybody knew the old master—Miz Claire's husband— was dead, and had been dead for months.

Miz Claire glimpsed the thin grey wale raised in a jagged stripe from Moab's shoulder to his hip. She stepped into the room, her eyes stricken. "What's that?" she said. "Is that a whip wale?"

"Yes, ma'm, Miz Claire, ma'm." Moab's tone revealed the self-pity the very mention of this blemish always occasioned in him.

Miz Claire's voice sharpened. "Who did this terrible thing?"

"Oh, it were done nigh on to two years ago, Miz Claire," Shiva said, stroking the ointment into the discolored flesh.

Miz Claire gasped. "Two years? Does Mister Baynard know about this terrible thing? What does he say?"

"Oh, Masta Baynard—ole Masta Baynard—he was terrible upset when it happened," Moab said with visible pride. "And young Masta Ferrell-Junior, too. He was most kind to me. He rode out to the fields where I was just a writhin' in agony, Miz Claire, and he picked me up on Masta Pilzer's own horse and brought me right heah to the house . . . . Ole Masta and young Masta . . . they was most kind . . . . They plum scairt I ruined for life. I recall they say I a fancy nigger and that whip scar done ruint me."

"Of course," Miz Claire said. "Of course you are—ruined. An expensive animal like you . . . . How often Mister Baynard said you and your brother Blade were invaluable. You could not be replaced—a full-blooded Fulani."

Moab's golden-brown face glowed with pride. "Yes, ma'm, Miz Claire, ma'm. I am a real purentee Fulani. Me and Blade. That's a fact."

Miz Claire shook her head, deeply troubled. She appeared to be talking more to herself than to either of the slaves. "Mister Baynard must be terribly worried. How many times I've heard him say it. A Fulani must be perfect. How proud he was to own you and Blade. A perfect Fulani, Mister Baynard always says, is worth a king's ransom . . . . But once a Fulani animal has been scarred, he might as well be destroyed."

Moab caught his breath, wincing. "Oh, I don't reckon I need to be destroyed, no way, Miz Claire." Moab's red-tan skin showed sweat suddenly. "Ain't marred that bad. Ain't no way permanent, long as this no-good nigger gal keeps me oiled up good. Doctor say I gonna heal up complete."

Shiva nodded. "We puttin' medicine on it. We doin' all we can, Miz Claire."

Miz Claire seemed hardly to hear Shiva. She walked forward and drew her fingers along Moab's wealed back, as impersonally as if indeed he were an animal. "Well, I certainly hope you're doing all you can. I hope it will heal, though I don't have much hope . . . . Mister Baynard is going to be most deeply upset when he gets home and hears about this."

"I gonna be jes' fine, Miz Claire. Jes' fine," Moab said. The tone in his voice was almost pleading. No one better than he knew that Styles Kenric was the new master of Blackoaks. But the instilled habit of allegiance and enslavement to the Master and Mistress Baynard was too deep in the Blackoaks Negroes to be lightly tossed aside. "Why, I gonna be lak new."

"You're marred, Moab," Miz Claire told him in chilled conviction. "An expert breeder will certainly find that scar tissue, no matter how well it seems to heal—superficially."

"Oh, I gonna be lak a new nigger boy, Miz Claire. You jes' wait and see," Moab promised, sweating.

Miz Claire's chilled scrutiny told him she did not share his optimism. "No one would buy you—marred as you are."

Moab smiled now, slightly more at ease. "Ain't goin' to sell me, Miz Claire. Not me. I too valuable. Masta Styles done promised me that he'll never sell me."

"Well . . . . We'll see. When Mister Baynard gets home, we'll see . . . . Master Styles may not always know what's best for you darkies—or for Blackoaks."

Moab's voice shook. "Masta Styles. He the new masta of Blackoaks."

Miz Claire seemed not even to hear him. He wanted to cry out, to grab her arms, to force her to listen. But he knew he could never touch her. "Masta Styles say he got most gyascutus plans for me, Masta Styles do." Moab spoke rapidly, his panic showing in his black eyes. All his old sense of security suddenly vanished. He had seen the horrible coffle of chained blacks dragging its way past here toward the Louisiana cane fields last year; he still saw it sometimes in his nightmares, the open, bleeding sores, the straggling hopeless-eyed blacks. "Masta Styles got mighty big plans for me."

"Has he indeed? And what plans has Master Styles for you—with your back scarred like this?"

Moab looked up confidently, reassured by Master

Styles's promises, made in this same bed. "I gonna stand stud, Miz Claire."

"What?" Miz Claire retreated a step.

"Don't you talk nasty like that to a quality white lady," Shiva told Moab angrily, unable to look Miz Claire in the face.

"No. Go on," Miz Claire said. Her translucent cheeks were paler than ever, somewhat like parchment. "Is this Master Styles's plan for you?"

"Yes'm, Miz Claire. Sho' is." Some of Moab's innate self-confidence returned as he contemplated the promises Master Styles had made him in this darkened room. "Yes'm. Stand stud. I gonna do that. That's the master's plan. And for Blade, too, Masta Styles said. Masta Styles say he gonna find us purentee Fulani wenches. We gonna put the seeds in they bellies, Masta Styles say. Masta Styles say Blackoaks plantation gonna be knowed wide and far for the finest Fulani fancy niggers in this heah country. That's what I gonna do. Ain't gonna plant no cotton. Ain't gonna have to plant no corn, Masta Styles say. Masta Styles say I ain't no field nigger. I a fancy. A purentee Fulani fancy. Blackoaks gonna raise fancy Fulani niggers to sell, sired by me and Blade, Masta Styles say."

Miz Claire's bloodless face paled, starkly white, set. Her eyes glittered. "That's what Mister Styles says, is it? Plans to turn Blackoaks Plantation into a Negro stud farm, does he? Raise Negroes to sell, eh? . . . . Well, we'll just wait until Mister Baynard gets back home . . . . We'll just wait."

She turned on her heel and walked out of the room. Both Moab and Shiva wanted to tell her that Master Baynard was dead and buried up in the cemetery plot on the knoll, but they were afraid to say the words. But they were not afraid, once Miz Claire passed through the door into the corridor, to giggle about the fey and vaporous woman.

They lay giggling on the mattress until they became aware they were not alone. Shiva looked up first and she gasped in terror as though she'd been struck across the face. Moab's laughter died and he lifted his head, staring up at Neva.

The fat black woman looked like an avenging angel. Neva had been Miz Claire's body slave since the two of them had been young girls together. They had come here to Blackoaks together almost a quarter of a century ago. Neva stood between "her chile" and all the hurts of the outside world. Now she glared in rage at the two blacks on Masta Styles Kenric's bed.

"What you two trashy niggers laughin' about?" Neva said.

"Nuthin'," Shiva said. She cringed as far as she could across the bed from the stout, cottony-haired Negress. "We ain't laughin' about nuthin'."

"Tha's right. Tha's the way with empty heads. They rattle at nuthin'. They can laugh at things they cain't even understand."

"We wan't laughin', Neva," Shiva said.

Moab said tentatively, "She thinks Masta Baynard's coming home, Neva . . . . "

"No matter what that po' chile say or think, you trashy niggers don't laugh at her—to her face or ahind her back."

"No, ma'm."

"I warns you. You trashy niggers best mind yo' manners. You think they been big changes round here. You do just 'bout what you want. Some things ain't changed. I ain't changed. I here. Long as I here, you niggers gonna do like you tole."

"Yes'm, Miz Neva."

6

By daylight, half a dozen other planters arrived with their high-piled cotton wagons. Hunt stared at them, overwhelmed by the wagons lined along the lane all the way to the huge fieldstone gate out at the east-west trace.

The landowners and their sons rode their elegantly groomed horses down to the barns where long plank tables had been set up, covered with tablecloths from the house. Beyond the work area, at the sump of the incline leading up to the slave quarters, similar tables were set up for the blacks, without refinements of linen cloths or silverware. Smartly clad, scrubbed youngsters in starched shirts and pressed britches, most of them wearing polished shoes, hurried between the huge kitchen and the tables, delivering gallon containers of icy milk, steaming-hot coffee, and thick cream, along with platters of freshly prepared food.

The sun was well up beyond the pine hammock by the time the guests and the slaves sat down to breakfast. Bos Pilzer and overseers from other farms sat at a separate table with the younger sons of neighboring landowners. A bearded black man sat upon a straw-back kitchen chair on the cotton-press platform and scraped lilting tunes from a fiddle. Black boys improvised dances on the wide steps below him.

The tables were loaded with food. There were silver platters of fried ham, silver bowls of scrambled eggs. Waffles, pancakes, cinnamon buns, and yeast-risen doughnuts were set in wicker servers and covered with linen napkins. Servants came running down the incline with plates of fried chicken. There was so much food, in fact, that the planters soon were sated and amused themselves tossing scraps to the dogs and children who came as near as Thyestes, the old butler, would let them.

Indeed, the black children often fought the dogs for slivers of fried ham. They scrambled on their knees to snatch the food from the snarling animals. Many of the planters purposely threw bits of meat so that the children couldn't quite catch it. The men roared with laughter as the little blacks battled with the dogs, often getting slashed or bitten in the melee. A child brave or foolhardy enough to fight a dog for possession of a slice of ham would be rewarded by cheers from the white men at the long tables.

Hunt sat far down the table from Styles and Kathy, side by side, at its head. Hunt didn't eat much. He quickly lost his appetite, angered by the way the black children were allowed to be bitten by the dogs. Walter Roy Summerton kept remarking that the pickaninnies were happy as little monkeys. But Hunt didn't believe him.

Walter Roy peered at Hunt across the table, one brow tilted. "I'm somewhat astonished, Mr. Campbell, suh, if you'll pardon me, that you all are still down heah amongst us."

"I thought that when old man Baynard died, you'd leave this area," Gil Talmadge said. He laughed, shaking his head ruefully. "Reckon you might of, if my old man had lived—"

"Your father is dead?" Hunt said. He remembered old Fletcher Talmadge as a formidable, unyielding enemy—a man with a mind clamped steel-trap shut against him. It was hard to believe the old red-neck was dead.

Gil nodded. He went on smiling, totally unmoved by the recent death of his father. "Old man used to talk a lot about you leaving this part of the country. Got to be an obsession. Talked about using a rail, a few times—even mentioned chicken feathers and tar."

"Old Fletcher was a man didn't cotton to outsiders comin' in here to tell us white folks how to run our lives," Walter Roy said.

"My old man didn't like to listen to nobody," Gil said, laughing. "He got hisself killed 'cause he wouldn't no-way listen to nary one of us. He got killed fightin' a half-broke stallion in our horse pens over at Felicity Hall Manor. Wouldn't let nobody else get that stallion under control. We'uns tried to tell him he was gittin' too old. This just made the old fellow all the more obstinate and determined to do it his way. He said that stallion had to recognize its master. That ole horse just reared up, and Papa struck him across the nose with the bridle he had in his fist. The stallion squealed like a pig. It reared up on its hind legs, screaming and spittin'. Before a livin' soul could git in there to help Papa, that stallion had cut him to death with his hooves. Split Papa's head wide open . . . . Yeah, Mister Campbell, my papa's dead, all right." He laughed. "He shore had a strong dislike for you, suh . . . . Wasn't nuthin' really personal, neither. You was a Yankee, and that's all it took to stir his hatred."

Link Tetherow put his head back, laughing. "Seems to me that there's reason enough for hatin'. Your daddy just wa'nt never polite enough to hide his true and honest feelings."

"That's the truth," Gil said. "If Papa felt a man was wrong, Papa wanted to be the firstest to let him know he was in error. You know?" He laughed. "Seemed like he had a calling to go round settin' men right in their ways."

"I purely admired that ole fellow—yore daddy," Link Tetherow said. "A man purely knowed where he stood with ole Mr. Fletcher Talmadge."

Gil laughed, striking Link hard on the bicep. "You ought to of appreciated my old daddy. He pulled your meat out'n the fire oncet when things looked mighty hairy."

Link Tetherow's ruddy face went gray. He glanced, in almost visible panic, toward where his stern-visaged father talked with Lucas Winterkorn of Mira Vista and aging Rube Summerton of Foxwood. "Cut out that talk, Gil." Link's voice shook. "Ain't no sense bringin' that ole trouble up—you know how Papa gits."

Gil laughed again, mockingly. "What you scairt of, Link? Nuthin' can happen to you now. My daddy seen to that. You can just sleep easy at night, old son. Just like Walter Roy can—"

"I told you, Gil, I don't nevah want to talk about that no moah." Walter Roy's voice was hard and unyielding.

"What you two yellow-bellies scairt of?" Gil glanced around, pleased to have stirred up a little action. He found Hunt as his nearest auditor. He grinned and spoke in a confidential tone, but loud. "These boys an' me—an' good ole Ferrell-Junior Baynard, too, before he got the call and become Brother Alexander in the Catholic Church, for hell's sake—well, we had this little—"

Link swung out his arm suddenly and violently. He caught Gil across the face, crushing his nose.

Gil was driven backward by the force of the blow. He would have gone sprawling to the ground but a man on the other side of him caught him and supported him. Gil sat, shaking his head for some moments, regaining his reeling senses. Then, before Link could protect himself, Gil lunged at him, both hands closing on Link's throat, fingers digging in on both sides of his Adam's apple as if he meant to rip it out of Link's neck. Link fought back wildly, and they toppled from the bench, almost upsetting the table. They struck the ground, wrestling. The dogs and the black children rushed forward, yapping and screaming. Link and Gil fought savagely, Link gasping for breath and Gil refusing to release his grip on Link's throat though Tetherow was obviously strangling.

The older men at the head of the table glanced toward Styles, but when Kenric made no move to intervene, old Lucas Winterkorn lurched up to his feet. He threw his napkin to the table. His voice carried, thunderlike, above the screaming children, the yowling and snarling of the excited dogs. "Stop it, you men. Stop it . . . . Have you no respect for the mistress of Blackoaks?"

Winterkorn's savage command cut through the caterwauling to Gil Talmadge and Link Tetherow, battering at each other mercilessly on the ground. Gil released his death grip on Link's throat. Gasping for air, young Tetherow withdrew his thumb from Gil's eye socket. They stood up, muddied, wrinkled, bruised, white-faced, and sheepish.

Winterkorn said, "I suggest you boys go wash up with some good cold well water. Then come back and finish your breakfast—if Miz Kenric will permit you to return to her table."

Kathy smiled and shrugged.

"You're most tolerant and forgiving, Miz Kenric," Winterkorn said. "And lovelier'n ary burnt biscuit."

The people at the table laughed with more vigor than his small compliment deserved. Gil and Link plodded together toward the nearest well. Thyestes moved in with a cornshucks broom and batted the black children and their dogs away from the area around the white-clothed tables. Many of the black men had finished their breakfast at the rough tables, and they got up, wiping their mouths on their arms. Most of the children ran to grab up their leavings, their dogs yapping at their heels. The fiddler who had been stunned into immobility by the violence of the altercation between the young white gentlemen now took up his instrument and bow again. His music rose, brittle and tentative in the morning stillness. Dray animals whinnied along the long lines of high-stacked cotton wagons.

A fragile, self-conscious silence settled over the long table where the landowners sat. They began and abandoned short, uneasy conversations among themselves; presently the hum of talk, less boisterous than before, resumed.

Lambert Tetherow, cold with embarrassment because of his son's behavior, felt impelled to do what he could to restore a semblance of normality to the breakfast table. He said with a falsely hearty laugh of self-congratulation, "Well, Styles, I reckon we planters were right smart to hold back on our cotton last summer when they offered us five cents down at Mobile."

Styles nodded. "Yes. Prices are up. Demand is strong. Even for the lesser grades nobody wanted this summer . . . . But as I've said before, it looks as if we're never going to grow really first-grade cotton in this area any more."

The older men stared at Styles as if he'd uttered heresy. Some of them paled visibly, others looked as if they bit their lips to keep from cursing Styles Kenric—you just didn't disparage motherhood, states' rights, or the cotton economy in this company of gentlemen.

"Maybe *you* won't never grow first-grade cotton," Rube Summerton said, biting off each word carefully. "But we will—just a few miles down the road from you at Foxwood . . . . "

"We all will, suh," Winterkorn said. "It's just plain a matter of improved irrigation—of cultivation—and maybe a heartier seed stock. When we get friable earth prepared for planting—a good tilth—we'll grow the finest cotton again—just as we always have."

"I believe that day is gone for this part of Alabama, Mr. Winterkorn, sir, with all due respect—just as it passed many years ago in Maryland and in the Old

Dominion, in all the states along the coast." Styles tilted his head and peered at them along his nose as if to warn he'd meet any opposing view with the disdain it deserved.

Winterkorn met Styles's imperious gaze levelly. "I went along with you, Styles, this summer, when you felt we could get a better price by holding back our cotton. You were right then, but I part company with you now."

Rube Summerton laughed. "We brought them yankee manufacturers back with their pocketbooks opened—"

"It won't always work that way," Styles said. "I believe we ought to prepare for that contingency. This winter there's a cotton shortage. They'll meet our demands. Prices are up. Standards and gradings are relaxed. It may be many years before all these factors coincide again."

Rube Summerton leaned forward, staring at Styles along the table. He spoke loudly, almost mockingly. "Is that why you're sending so few wagons? I can tell you, young man, it's not by half what old man Baynard sent every year down to Mobile."

Styles laughed disdainfully. "Next year we'll send half this much. It costs more to plant cotton, more to grow it, more to ship it, and you end up with less profit."

The planters within the sound of Styles's voice stared at him incredulously. "Why, pore ole Ferrell Alexander Baynard must be a-whirlin' in his grave," Lucas Winterkorn said.

Styles shrugged. His voice struck out at them, cold, aloof. "Whirling. In his grave. *Grave*—that's the operative word, gentlemen. Mr. Baynard is in his grave. I'm running Blackoaks now, Mr. Winterkorn, and I'm running it my way—the way I've always felt it should have been run."

Winterkorn exhaled heavily, his exasperation showing in his ruddy, lined face. "Good God, man—you'll pardon my rough talk, Miz Kathy—taking the good Lord's name in vain like that in your lovely presence—but I just can't hardly believe I'm hearing right . . . . This lovely country is cotton land. Our economy was built and is based on cotton. Yet, you appear to plan to stop using these vast acres of Blackoaks for that staple."

"I do." Styles nodded. "This is not my opinion only. I

can tell you it is fully shared with Mr. Blanford Ware, the eminent banker from down in Tallahassee—"

"That money-vulture." Rube Summerton looked as if he'd spit.

Styles spoke directly to Summerton. "We may as well face it, sir. Cotton and sugar cane are moving to the loamy river valleys and lowlands." Styles moved his chilled gaze across their stricken faces. "I intend to raise a real money crop—I intend to supply those lowland growers with the slaves they'll need—"

"My God—a nigger stud farm." Winterkorn shook his greying head in disbelief. "You'll pardon me, Miz Kathy, but I never heard such a goddamn ugly thing in my life— turnin' lovely old Blackoaks into a breedin' farm for niggers."

Styles smiled coldly. "No matter where they grow cotton and sugar cane, they've got to have slave labor. And they've got to get slaves from somewhere. The slave import trade is banned by law—by England, and now by our Congress. Black slaves have got to come from those already on our farms. I intend to supply the market with the finest quality slaves . . . fancy blacks . . . . I refuse to cling to old ways and old habits when they are not only unprofitable—but eventually ruinous."

They all stared at Styles, but they didn't answer him. The older men were too filled with sullen rage to speak at all. They didn't trust themselves to say aloud, as Styles Kenric's guests, the things they were thinking. The younger men at the table were secretly afraid Styles Kenric might be right. He'd been totally correct about the price for cotton. Traffic in slaves went against everything they believed—it was a low, vicious, and dehumanizing trade, beneath the dignity of gentlemen. And yet, there was no doubt—money and power were passing them by, moving toward the swamps and the deltas. But—niggers? Raise niggers as your staple crop?

At this moment, and into this vibrant silence, Gil Talmadge and Link Tetherow returned from the well. They were brushed, carefully scrubbed, combed, and almost contrite. Both bowed clumsily and apologized profusely and awkwardly to Kathy Kenric. Both found it difficult to speak directly to Kathy—not because they had insulted her with their boorish behavior at her table, but simply because she was a white gentlewoman and they had never learned to be poised or at ease in such company.

Hunt watched the two young planters, his stomach taut with the contempt he felt for them and their hypocritical attitudes toward the upper-class white women. Either Talmadge or Tetherow might rape a Negress, violate a white "town" girl. But the two of them went dumb, awkward and clownlike, before plantation women.

As Gil and Link turned away from Kathy's chair at the head of the makeshift table, Miss Jamie Lee Seaton made her dramatic entrance, mincing down the incline from the manor house on the plateau.

Hunt grinned sardonically, watching her. Jamie Lee Seaton's arrival was almost a regal event—all she needed was a court in attendance and a red carpet. She wore crinolines, tiny wristlet gloves, and pointed-toed slippers that winked beneath the flounced hems of her skirt. Behind her came Shiva, stumbling and half-running in order to keep a parasol consistently at the same angle between Jamie Lee's fragile skin and the early-morning sun.

"Well, sir!" Lambert Tetherow was the first of the planters to lunge upward to his feet as Jamie Lee approached. "Will you all just look who has graced us with her lovely presence? Look who has come down heah to see us, Link boy. Yore beautiful fiancée—yore lovely goddess from Charleston."

Hunt bit back derisive smiling. Yes, here she came in all her affectation, her studied artificiality. Here was the belle of old Charleston—fresh from some early-hour assignation with the nearest available male, black or white.

Link Tetherow was transformed into a puerile dunce by the sight of Miss Jamie Lee Seaton. He took one stunned glance toward his lace-and-silk goddess and thrust both fists toward heaven and let go a yowl of exultance.

"Now, you jus' stop that carryin'-on, Mr. Link Tetherow," Jamie Lee cautioned him in mock anger, but smilingly. "You jus' embarrass me to *death*—"

"Ah, no, Miss Jamie Lee." Link looked ready to cry in desolation. "I'm just so all-fired happy to lay eyes on you I just couldn't control myself."

She blushed prettily. "Well, you're jus' goin' to have to learn to control yo'self, Mr. Link Tetherow . . . . If you go on frightenin' me in front of perfect strangers like this, I'll jus' go runnin' right back to Charleston, South Carolina!"

Link went close to Jamie Lee, flushed of face, bright of eye, looking as if he could barely restrain himself from taking her in his arms.

"Now, don't you go grabbin' at me, Mr. Link Tetherow," Jamie Lee gave him the barest touch of her lips upon his cheeks, the chastest kiss Hunt had ever witnessed, north or south of the Mason-Dixon line.

Watching her, Hunt decided he admired her. She was giving these men what they demanded of their young women, and her performance was flawless. She was good at what she did, as she was probably good in bed—when she let herself go.

He watched her tap at Link Tetherow's blushing cheek with the tip of her fan. "I declare, I jus' don't know what I'm going to do about you, Mr. Link Tetherow. You're so impulsive. You jus' sweep a pore girl off her feet . . . . You jus' grab me . . . . You're jus' so strong and big—I declare . . . . "

Link stood, awkward and helpless, speechless before his preening little coquette. Hunt looked away, shaking his head. His gaze raked across Kathy's, and he found her laughing with him . . . .

7

The climbing sun rays burned away the last blue wisps of morning mists. Even as the crews of blacks moved in to clear away the breakfast table, Bos Pilzer's guttural voice rose, shouting, "Head 'em out." The drovers moved toward their wagons and slaves hurried forward with the freshly watered, curried, and rested mounts of the land-owners. Styles chatted some moments with Lambert Tetherow, who was to represent Blackoaks in the cotton sales at the railhead. Then he spoke with Bos Pilzer, who was to accompany the cotton train as far as Mt. Zion but who would return before the auction began. Styles did not wait to watch the caravan start its trek along the trace at the foot of the plateau. He strode up the incline toward the manor house, looking neither left nor right, though everyone else stood waving and shouting noisy farewells to the drovers and to the planters astride their fine horses.

With a shock of distinct pleasure—along with a belly-tightening ache in his loins—Hunt found himself alone near the barns with Kathy. His heart lurched at the splendid truth—she had arranged it that way. God! How beautiful she was—how delicate, gentle; the ultimate re-finement of everything these landed aristocrats down here were.

Damn it! What was wrong with him? Why long and pant after a woman as unattainable as Kathy? He could never have her. He had nothing to offer her. The barriers between them were insurmountable, and yet he admitted God had never made another woman he would want as wildly as he wanted the unobtainable Kathy Kenric.

Without speaking about it, they walked slowly together up the grassy incline, away from the manor house on the plateau, toward the fieldstone chapel on the pleasant knoll beyond. Here, they could be alone, if only for a little while. And they didn't put this need into words, either. They didn't have to.

As they left the barn area, now suddenly quiet with the planters, the wagons, the children, and the dogs all gone, Blade touched his finger and thumb to his forehead as though doffing his cap to Kathy. Hunt stared at him, feeling a sense of shock. Blade's smile made his red-gold face beautiful, with that sadness from antiquity in it which gripped at Hunt and haunted him.

"Good lord," Hunt said. "He's in love with you, Kathy—"

"He loves me. He's not *in* love with me. Blade's always loved me, since we were children."

"You make it sound like something from afar—he loves you—as a slave might love his mistress—from a safe distance . . . . I suppose that's the only way you can admit it to yourself."

She laughed at him. "That's the way it is. It's not anything like you're suggesting. He is a slave . . . and stop looking like that. I've never even been alone with him—since we were seven or eight. He knows his place. And I know mine. I've known he loves me. But that's it. That's the end of it . . . . That's the way it is."

"How comfortably you people have got everything worked out . . . . As long as a black man never has a human thought, he gets along fine. Have you ever looked at him?"

"At Blade? Of course—"

"Don't you really *see* him? Don't you see the sadness in him? He looks so damned sad! Even when he's smiling like that."

She laughed again. "None of us is happy all the time . . . . And I don't think Blade is really very sad. As beautiful as he is, he probably has the wenches standing in line —outside his cabin."

Now Hunt laughed. "You know something I've learned in my misspent life, Kathy? A man can have a hundred women. But he has nothing unless he has the *one* woman he truly wants."

"How very pretty."

"Oh, I can talk beautifully. Poetically. Charm the birds off the limbs. One of the few worthwhile arts I learned in six years at Harvard."

Kathy smiled and took his hand. "I'm jealous of all those years—before I knew you."

"Don't be. I was less even than I am now. Only half-alive. Certain I knew all that was worthwhile. Opinionated. Superior. Arrogant. And I didn't even come alive until I came here—until I saw you."

Kathy laughed. "Until you stopped wearing your pince-nez."

"Ah, yes. My symbol of superiority." He drew her close against him. She shivered and drew away. "Half the people in our world are watching us," she warned.

"When in hell can I admit aloud—to all the world—that I love you?"

"I think you just did," she teased. Then abruptly she stopped smiling. Her mood altered, the way a bright day darkens when the sun is suddenly obscured by clouds. "*I* know you love me," she said. "Isn't that enough?"

He sighed heavily, chilled. "No, I don't think even you know. If you did, you wouldn't keep us apart like this when I ache—literally ache, Kathy—with need for you."

"Poor Hunt," she said. "I'm sorry—I'm what I am . . . . I almost said I'm sorry you love me. But that's not true. I'm not sorry. That's all I have—that you love me . . . . But I've sense enough to know it isn't fair to you . . . . I lie in bed at night—and I know how lonely you must be. I know how lonely I am—"

"I'm only just down the hall." He tried unsuccessfully to smile.

"It's not that simple. Or maybe it is—and I won't let it be." She took his hand and drew him down upon a fieldstone barrier beside her mother's chapel. They were concealed from the house, sheltered by a flowering bay shrub. The sweetness of the bay shrubs saddened Hunt though he could not say why, except that their gentle, fragile, and transient fragrance brought Kathy into his mind wherever he was. "I know my marriage to Styles is failed," she said. "Over. Finished . . . . And yet, until I can be free, I remain his wife. I can't have an affair with you while he and I are still married—"

"He'll never let you go."

"He must. Hunt, he doesn't want me." She shuddered. "He never has."

"He *needs* you. And that's a much more compelling reason for him to hold on to you. You are the loveliest girl any of us has ever seen—his possessing you as his wife sets him apart from ordinary mortals. You are a prized possession for the world to envy. And you are his armor."

"His armor?"

"His protective shield against those who hold unnatural men in contempt. Who would believe a man married to a woman as lovely as you—would rather be caressing young boys?"

"Oh, God." Memory—ugly as day-old dishwater flooded through her. She pressed the back of her hand over her mouth.

He drew her close. "Oh, Kathy. I'm sorry. I know it's bad enough—without my saying it aloud . . . Please forgive me."

"We can't go on being afraid of the truth."

"Why not? I can't think of anything that hurts more cruelly than the unadorned truth."

She shook her head, physically rejecting the ugly associations. "The only real truth is that I love you."

"No. That's only part of the real truth. The sad part is that you do love me, but you won't let me love you—"

"You mean—in my bed?"

He laughed. "Yours—or mine."

Kathy didn't smile. "That's what I meant when I said I was sorry you love me. Sorry for you. Because of what I am . . . . From birth I've been taught—and I've believed —that a girl like me marries one man, is faithful to him, and keeps herself only unto him—until she dies . . . . I try, Hunt . . . I swear, I try to come to you—on your terms—as other people seem able to accept love—where they find it, and when they find it, and the hell with anything else. At night, I long to get up and run to you . . . . I lie sleepless. Ill with longing. But I can't . . . . I can't . . . ."

He kissed her gently, but the irony edging his voice was less gentle. "Maybe Styles will settle it for us."

"You think he'd give me a divorce—?"

"No. I think any morning now he'll send me away— as he should have done long ago. We all know I'm not teaching Morgan anything new. I'm not earning my keep. I hang on as long as I can—only because of you . . . . I can't imagine life when I can't see you—if only for a moment on the stairway."

She caressed his face. "Then you'll never go. You'll stay—because I want you . . . . I may never let you go." She gestured helplessly. "There's so much against us. If I divorced Styles—my church would excommunicate me when I married you . . . . That doesn't seem too important right now. But it has been my church all my life. I've believed in it with all my heart. I still do."

"Hell. Why are we even talking about it? I can't ask you to give up your church . . . . For what? I don't believe in anything, except you—"

"And I, you—"

"Hell knows I can't ask you to leave Blackoaks. Your family. Your security. Your place in life . . . . I've nothing to offer—"

"There's you—"

"No. There's not even me. Let's not forget who I am . . . . I love you. But that doesn't seem miraculously to convert me into a worthwhile human being. I'm still the pusillanimous fugitive who came sneaking down here because I was unwilling to fight for—a woman—in New England . . . . I am still Hunt Campbell, too enlightened to fight even when attacked . . . . I'm the same cowardly ass who almost got your brother killed when he had the courage to fight my battle. I've never fought for anything. I've pretended it was superior intellect that placed me above common brawling. Very likely, the sordid truth is that I'm more coward than idealist. Let's not forget what a pretentious stuffed shirt I am."

She kissed him lightly, lingeringly. She offered no protest when his hand closed on the full roundness of her peach-colored breast. She felt her breast swell to his caress, every part of her body aching with need for him. It was as if every nerve were centered under his caressing palm. He bent his head, kissed the pulse at the base of her throat. She spoke in a breathless tone. "If you—want something badly enough—you'll fight for it."

He gazed at the satiny beauty of her breasts. "I know one thing—I've never fought. I've always run away from fights . . . . But if I could stand and fight—for anything —and I don't promise you I could—it would be for you."

"Please don't hate yourself."

"I don't. That's the sad truth. I've always deplored physical violence. I've always believed myself superior. Exceptional. Set apart. Until I realized what it would cost me to have you . . . . Then I am forced to face the truth about myself. I have to admit my fat-witted weaknesses . . . . I could only drag you down, Kathy . . . . I have nothing to offer you—"

"You're all I want."

"That's because you've never known anything except a life where you've been cared for, protected—"

"—and miserable. I've never been truly happy. Because I could never be truly happy unless I were loved— as I know I *must* be loved! I must be loved—or find life empty. But then I face the truth and I know you deserve better than me—"

"Better? Than you? Why, there's no beauty to match your loveliness . . . . There is no one *better*—"

"You're saying that in excitement." She smiled. "I can *see* how excited—"

"I'm in agony—that's what it really is."

"Oh, Hunt. I'm so sorry. We shouldn't have come up here alone—"

"Don't be sorry . . . . Agony is my choice. I'd rather be in agony wanting you than lying in bed with three concubines at my command."

She shook her head. "No . . . I'm not worth it. I've already failed one man."

He held her close and kissed her. "Kathy! My God! Don't torment yourself. Don't feel guilty! You haven't failed a *man* . . . . You've been tricked into marriage by a—a pervert . . . who needed to hide behind the appearance of virile manhood."

"There's no one for me but you," she whispered. "And we will find a way . . . . I'll make him let me go . . . . I will . . . ."

He laughed at her violence and took her in his arms. She turned her face up to him, her heart pounding. When his hand cupped her breast again, she quivered, her whole body quaking. In his arms she felt younger than her twenty-two years. She felt as if she were a young girl again, a very young girl with her first love, her first lover . . . .

8

Hunt was late getting to the terrace outside the sun-room where he conducted classes for Morgan. He came across the manicured plateau, sweated, slightly breathless, and in some inner agony. He found Moab and Soapy with their heads bent together over one of the reading books. Soapy patiently traced the words with his finger for Moab awkwardly to mouth after much prodding and indecision.

Soapy leapt up guiltily as the tutor approached and dropped the book as if it were fiery hot. Hunt pretended not to have seen this byplay as he ignored the fact that for months now Soapy had been secretly teaching Moab to read. He knew the boys stole off to secret places along the creek beyond the quarters where once they'd played pirates, in order to read the simple primary books Hunt had "lost" and Soapy had "recovered". Styles opposed letting any Negroes learn to read or write; besides, there was a state statute against anyone's teaching a black slave to read, write, or cipher.

"Where is Morgan?" Hunt asked.

When Soapy looked at Moab and grinned sheepishly, Hunt decided not to press the issue. Whatever had delayed Morgan both amused and dismayed his body slave, and Hunt did not pursue it. It didn't matter whether Morgan attended his daily classes or not. Morgan had learned painfully to read signs, to write his own and Soapy's names. He could not concentrate long enough to solve the simplest arithmetic problems. A day when Morgan was late to class was an easier time for all of them.

Soapy's dark face showed the blood that had flooded

upward into it and the keen embarrassment he felt in not being able to talk about Morgan. He sat with eyes averted, recalling the way he had walked into the bedroom less than an hour ago and found Morgan sprawled on his back across the mattress, masturbating furiously.

Astonished, Soapy had laughed. "What you doing, Morg?"

He knew well enough what Morgan was doing. Morgan was sweated under the savagery of his self-abuse. Soapy laughed again. "You better stop. You gonna get hair in the palm of yo' hand."

Morgan stopped long enough to curse at him. "You go to hell, Soapy."

Soapy walked slowly forward. "What's the matter, Morg?"

Morgan stopped, but continued to grip himself fiercely. "I can't help it, Soapy. It's the third time this morning I've done it . . . . I just can't seem to stop . . . . I reckon I'm going crazy, all right. But I can't stop."

Soapy sat down on the side of the bed and clucked sympathetically. "What's wrong? What happened? I always plumb loved to beat my meat. But I never knowed you to be so partial to it."

"I never was."

"What happened?"

Morgan worked his fist a few strokes. "Cousin Jamie Lee," he muttered after a moment.

"You best stay away from that white gal."

"An' you better stop talking about her. She said nigras shouldn't talk about white ladies."

Soapy shook his head. "I'm still telling you. She's bad. Badder than any black slut I ever heard tell about."

Morgan stroked himself slowly. "What'd she do to you?"

"Nothin'. Except that one time she got me in her room to fix something that didn't need fixin'. That white gal was onliest thing needed fixing. She swore she'd yell rape if I didn't do it to her."

"Did you do it?"

"Didn't enjoy it none. I was so scared I nearly peed."

"She wouldn't let me do it." Morgan's voice shook and his eyes filled with tears.

"What you mean? That white gal'll let anybody do it. She tole me I had to wait in that empty guestroom for her this morning—or she'd say I been trying to sneak looks at her when she bathin' . . . . I waited . . . . Thank Gawd she never showed up."

"She was here," Morgan said. "She wanted me to do it. But I didn't know how. Soapy, I didn't know a girl's hole was way down there between her legs like that."

"Yeah," Soapy said. "They sho' are . . . . They easy to get at if'n they want you to, but it can be pretty tough gettin' to that sweet thing if'n they don't."

"I wished you'd of tole me, Soapy."

"You never ast me, Morg. I figured you knowed."

"Well, I didn't. An' she laughed at me. An' she was all naked—the prettiest thing I ever seen in all my life. Them big tits she wanted me to suck. And her layin' there a-pantin' an' me not knowin' no way what to do. She laughed at me—and put on her gown and walked out . . . . Only I can't think about nuthin' but the way she looked —all pretty and naked—and layin' there with her legs apart—"

"She shoulda put her legs up—made it easier for you."

"What am I gonna do, Soap? I can't walk around with a hard-on all the time. I either got a hard-on, or I feel like I want to cry . . . . I either got to whip it off—or cry . . . . I can't go 'round people like that."

"What you goin' do? It's time to go to your class."

"Well, I ain't going. Not today. Not till I can stop gettin' a big hard-on. I'm gonna lay right here and beat it—till it just lay still—like it used to."

"What am I gonna tell Masta Hunt?"

"Tell that yankee I said go to hell. Go back home."

"I'll tell him you're sick," Soapy said.

"It won't be no lie," Morgan said. His fist moved faster.

Hunt was telling the boys the history of the Fulani people, those aristocratic Sudanese from whom Moab and Blade had descended. Excited, Moab strutted like an emperor, angering Soapy. The two boys were tussling when Miss Jamie Lee appeared in a riding habit.

All three of them stopped in mid-breath and held their positions, in tableau, staring at Miss Jamie Lee. Hunt felt his face flush and knew he looked as awkward and as guilty as the slave boys.

They gazed at the lovely picture Miss Jamie Lee presented. She was outfitted in a chic new habit, with black boots and a saucy hat perched on the side of her golden curls, which were pinned up becomingly at the nape of her neck. She clapped the palm of her left hand smartly with a riding crop, studying them. "I hesitated to intrude," she said with a disdainful glance at Hunt. "But I needn't have worried. Nothing very serious seems to be goin' on heah."

"How may we serve you?" Hunt inquired, awed at the voluptuous bulge of her breasts above that tiny waist. But he could see in her chilled eyes that he had made an unyielding and unforgiving little enemy.

She glanced at him imperiously. "Cousin Styles says Moab is to guide me. I'm going riding. Moab is to come along. Dear Cousin Styles says I couldn't possibly go ridin' alone."

Soapy clapped his hand over his mouth to stifle a giggle. Moab looked uncomfortable but helpless. Jamie Lee's face tinted pinkly and she hurled Soapy a brief, murderous glance. "Come along, Moab. Cousin Styles has ordered our horses brought to the front door."

Moab glanced worriedly at Hunt, appealing for help. Hunt avoided his eye. Cousin Jamie Lee had already turned on her leather heel and was striding toward the French doors at the sun room, imperiously anticipating that Moab would heel obediently. After a moment, he followed her.

Soapy sank to the fieldstone wall that enclosed the terrace. He laughed. "Pore ole Moab," he whispered. "Pore ole King Moab—he granddaddy one of the noble Fulanis . . . ."

9

Styles walked into the small downstairs office and closed the thick door after him. He sagged into the high-backed swivel chair that had belonged to his father-in-law, feeling the sense of desperation building in him. He was glad those damned wagons were gone, those stupid planters cleared out. He knew what old Rube Summerton had meant, finding fault with the comparatively few wagons of cotton he was shipping. Half the number Old Man Baynard would have shipped. Summerton was implying that the cotton sales would fail by half to meet the costs of maintaining this plantation. He had understood what Summerton was saying. The hell of it was, so had every other planter sitting at that table. The hell with them. The fact was Blackoaks had come up with less than a bale per thirty acres. Disastrous. They had pushed the Negroes. Bos Pilzer had driven them, and he had driven Pilzer. The cotton simply wasn't there—in grade, quality, or quantity. He had to find an answer, but he already knew one thing for certain—he wasn't going to find it in increased cotton acreage.

He would show Rube Summerton and those other stupid sons of bitches. Blackoaks would certainly not be the first plantation to convert to raising blacks for market. But it could offer the best stock. This was the way, first to solvency, and then to great riches—which would make all this sacrifice worthwhile.

Meantime, he stared with a growing sense of helplessness at the bills which had accumulated in the ornate pecan-wood holder on the old desk. Many of these duns had come in within weeks of Baynard's unexpected death. Styles had paid as many as he could with the money he'd discovered in the Blackoaks account at the First Bank of Mt. Zion. He'd stopped making disbursements when he saw how dangerously low the balance in that account was dropping.

He'd had no difficulty in arranging with the new president of the First Bank of Mt. Zion to transfer most of Baynard's Blackoaks account to Styles's personal account. Neither he nor bank president Luke Scroggings had questioned the legality of the transfer. Scroggings, for some reason Styles didn't understand, seemed secretly pleased to make the transfer of funds for him. As he recalled, it had been Scroggings who had suggested leaving a token balance in the Blackoaks general account.

Styles shifted in his chair. His immediate reaction had been that there *was* illegality in his appropriating plantation funds to his own account, even if he used this money to discharge current plantation obligations. Leaving a small amount of money in the general Blackoaks account would forestall any question that might have arisen had the general account been closed out totally. Neither he nor Scroggings had mentioned this fact aloud—he had not asked; Scroggings had volunteered no information.

Styles flushed, feeling faintly warm about the starched collar of his linen shirt. There would be no questions anyway from anyone but Ferrell. Yes, Ferrell Baynard would cause trouble if he probed too deeply. Luckily, in these last months, Styles had been able to keep pressure on Miz Claire until he wrested a power of attorney from her on a day when she appeared more lucid than usual. Let Ferrell try to break that. Ferrell was a Jesuit priest now—at least a novice. Let him stay there. With Miz Claire's power of attorney, Styles felt secure in his position as undisputed master of Blackoaks—even where Ferrell was concerned.

The hell of it was that even though no one questioned his authority, everything was crowding in on him: Ferrell might walk into this house at any moment! If the bastard insisted on an accounting, there would be no way to conceal the financial liabilities that were pushing the estate to the brink of disaster.

Styles stared at his clenched fists. He could work it out—if he just had time! He saw chillingly now how many times old man Baynard must have sagged in this same chair, victim to these same thoughts: I could work it out —if I just had time!

Time was his worst enemy. The growing mound of bills in arrears, the rising cost of maintaining this nine hundred square miles of feudal estate, the threat of Ferrell's imminent arrival, showed how little time remained to him. Finding accounts overdue and overwhelming would provide Ferrell the justification for assuming management of his family's farm.

Somehow, he had to buy more time!

He got up from the chair, feeling caged in the small office. He prowled its restricted space—from window to desk, from door to book shelves, small constricted paths to nowhere. He stood at the window for a long time, staring across the plateau toward the fieldstone chapel on the grassy knoll above it.

The bitter and ironic angle to his whole dilemma was that he had options. The same options the elder Baynard had faced, but resisted, all the years he had managed to outrun the marshals. Baynard could continue to draw down larger and larger amounts from Garrett Blanford Ware's bank down in Tallahassee, Florida. He could have borrowed sizable amounts from the First Bank of Mt. Zion—something Baynard would not have done under any circumstances. A landowner didn't like his neighbors to know the extent of his indebtedness. This indebtedness was something you kept concealed like a skeleton in the family closet. Baynard himself had never borrowed money from the bank in Mt. Zion; he had finally repaid Ware's bank in full just before his death.

But Baynard had had something Styles no longer possessed—the supplemental income from the large whiskey still on the property. Styles had never realized the size of that income until a devastating fire had wiped out the plant and ended the cash flow from liquor wholesalers in Mobile. Baynard had been able to meet the daily expenses of the plantation from that whiskey production operation. Yet, even with this source of cash supply, Baynard had sunk deeper into debt, so that at his death he had left the estate badly encumbered.

Another option open to Baynard—and daily more alluring to Styles as it must have been to the hard-pressed Baynard ahead of him—was the sale of slaves. Baynard had sold off slaves, one or two at a time, secretly, ashamedly. The old man had tried to hide those transactions from his family as if they were dishonorable, shameful, a mark of disgrace. Cotton had never—in the past fifteen years, at least—paid expenses of operating Blackoaks Plantation. The farm's obligations had been met, when they were not deferred as far into the future as possible, through the sale of whiskey and black slaves —two vile and commercial enterprises. Baynard's pretense was that his whiskey was exceptional, that he'd been pressured by connoisseurs of fine spirits to commercialize, and that he had done so unwillingly.

Styles was a Kenric of Winter Hill Plantation, where outwitting creditors had been refined to an art, where the shameful facts of poverty were concealed by desperate displays of gentility. He had lived through that kind of genteel poverty, pretense, and deception—he wanted no more of it. He had thought he had married great wealth until after he was already wed to Kathy Baynard. Now he had taken command of Blackoaks. The potential for great wealth was here—and he meant to realize that potential, no matter what he had to do.

First, he had to admit, as Baynard never had, that this old plantation would have gone on the auction block years ago except for whiskey sales and slave trading. But even the surreptitious sale of slaves to intinerant slave peddlers and to other planters was not the option that would have brought Baynard at least temporary satisfaction of all debts, an opportunity to establish a debt-free base to build on.

And Baynard had gone ill with an ulcerated stomach and high blood pressure, which finally killed him, rather than avail himself of his golden option—the sale of his two Fulani bucks, the fancy-grade slaves Blade and Moab.

Styles sweated, remembering the way the slave breeder Baxter Simon had come east from his stud farm in Carthage, Mississippi, to offer ten thousand in gold for each of the Fulani boys. Styles understood fully only now the terrible conflicts that must have torn old Baynard apart as he finally refused Simon's offer. And, after Simon departed, Mr. Cleatus Dennison had appeared, with his smiles and a blank-check offer for the fine Fulani animals.

"They's prime animal stock," Dennison had said repeatedly to Baynard with that unfailing, unshakeable smile. "I can afford to find—or to import—purentee Fulani women to mate—"

"You know better, suh." Baynard was flushed of face, a vein standing like a blue pencil in his temple. "The law forbids—"

"The law! Forbids!" Dennison had laughed and clapped Baynard on the shoulder. "The law is for people who can't afford to circumvent it, Baynard. The law is for people like you."

"I'll find Fulani wenches," Baynard had whispered, hoarse, sweated, driven.

Dennison had laughed again. "Not unless you are willing—or financially prepared—to go outside the law, you won't. It would require a small fortune and delicate diplomacy and dangerous personal contact to arrange to abduct and smuggle into this country a half-dozen Fulani wenches. It would mean a custom-planned adventure, old friend. It demands the right people, a lot of time, a lot of money—and no conscience."

Baynard had shook his head. "I've planned—dreamed—worked too hard—for too long . . . . I can't give up now. I won't . . . . I shall find Fulani wenches—"

"And if you find them, old friend of mine, you'll also find yourself bidding for them against resources comparable to—and far exceeding—my own . . . . Can you honestly say you're prepared to do this?"

Now, Styles prowled the office. Baynard had somehow resisted Dennison's smiling, patient, and unrelenting overtures. Baynard had believed that if he could hang on, find the Fulani wenches, he could climb from the brink of ruin to solvency and opulence breeding Fulani fancy slaves.

Styles laughed with a self-mocking bitterness. He and his deceased father-in-law had had little in common. But they shared that same irresistible dream—even when it was almost impossible of accomplishment.

Well, he had contacted the disease, or mental illness—or whatever it was that had driven Baynard to the moment of his death and that now possessed him. He had boasted to those hidebound planters, clinging by their fingernails to the status quo of the cotton economy on land no longer able to support it—he had boasted that he would market fancy blacks from this plantation. He'd make that boast a reality—if he could first steal a little time.

He stared at that stack of debts, current and past due. He thought about the impending arrival of the good Brother Alexander. And there was the charming, cordial letter from Mr. Cleatus Dennison, the gentleman slave breeder. Styles took up the letter almost reluctantly and scanned it, feeling the illness spread in the crannies of his empty belly.

"I shall be in the vicinity of your incredibly lovely residence a few days after the Christmas season. I hope I shall be welcome for a brief sojourn in the company of your esteemed family at Blackoaks Plantation. I have much to discuss with you, Styles, and look forward to seeing you again."

Styles dropped Dennison's letter back to the desk top. Not a word in it about the Fulanis. Styles's hands shook. It was there between every stilted, Spencerian-penned line of it—twelve thousand, fifteen thousand for each Fulani boy. Name your own price. Dennison would be here, smiling, unyielding, unanswerable in his logic, immovable in his avowed intention to own the Fulanis, "a few days after the Christmas season."

Styles stared helplessly at those overdue bills. Time rushed forward like a locomotive out of control on a steep downgrade. How could he resist Dennison's offers? Sale of the two black Fulani boys would buy him at least a temporary solvency, remove all threat from Ferrell's probing, and—end forever the dream that had sustained old man Baynard and now possessed Styles Kenric, mind and soul.

The timorous knocking at the corridor door was repeated a third time before Styles became aware of it. Thyestes came into the office diffidently, limping on calloused, aching feet. "A visiting white gen'mun to see you, Masta Styles."

From a habit that had been germinating in these recent months as master of Blackoaks, Styles winced under a quick stab of anxiety. Bill collector? Deputy from the sheriff? Mr. Cleatus Dennison arriving ahead of time?

"All right, Thyestes. Send him in."

Thyestes squirmed uncomfortably and spoke to the pattern woven into the carpeting. "A trashy white gen'mun, Masta Styles, suh. I tole him he should wait out at the head of the lane. I'd of sent him away, Masta, but that white man cussed me pretty good, he did—and insisted on seein' you."

Styles nodded. He shrugged his jacket up on his slender shoulders, straightened his tie, arranged his cuffs. He took one long draft of whiskey and then walked out of the house, running his hands smoothingly along the side of his dark hair.

Thyestes's estimation of his visitor set Styles's own attitude and manner toward the man. He was cordial but aloof, gracious but remote. He smiled at the stranger but tilted his head and smiled along his patrician nose.

The guest wore expensive, custom-tailored clothes that were travel-mussed, wrinkled, sweated. His broad-brimmed hat had cost dearly, but was now battered, stained. The man's beard was three days ragged—he looked to be somewhere in his forties. He slouched on the front seat of an aging coach, the rear of which had been converted to a carryall with plank benches along each side. As Styles approached, he saw spancels and shackles screwed into the carriage side boards. The man was a traveling slave trader, as low on the social ladder as one could get.

A faintly haughty and swaggering manner about the stranger angered Styles at sight. The man waited until Styles was almost to the carriage before he swung down to meet him—a petty retaliation for having been forced to await him fifty yards from the manor house. His boots were run-over and hadn't felt polish in a raccoon's age. "Howdy, suh. I'm a slave buyer. Name of Culverhouse, suh. Darwin Culverhouse from up the Piedmont country."

"Why did you wish to see me?" Styles did not extend his hand, nor did his guest. They regarded each other smilingly but warily.

"Why, I just tole you, suh. I'm a slave buyer—you got slaves." He winked. "I'm a slave buyer but with a few different wrinkles, suh. I'm from the Culverhouse family. Son of old Marshall Custis Culverhouse. And my mother was a Darwin—a fine old Piedmont family. We been Piedmont people since Colonial days. My pappy went into slave breeding, and when I grew up trained in that art, I was restless. I decided what I wanted to do was travel. Travel and trade slaves. Buy where a man needed to sell for one reason or another. And, being from a great old plantation—and a most respectable family—I have a real insight into the problems faced by us landowner-planter families. We can always use ready cash, eh?"

Insulted, Styles said, "I don't believe I have any stock for sale, Mr. Culverhouse. And obviously, you don't have any animals to offer me."

Culverhouse laughed. "Ain't selling this trip, suh. Buyin'. Price of slaves is inflatin'—if a man's got the right stock for the market. Now, I'm here to do you a real favor. I'm here to relieve you of any quality you got to offer. My plan works like this, suh. If I buy inferior stock here, I can trade it for a better grade down the road. I indeed work a special favor for you planters—I take what you don't want—and I provide you hard, ready cash—in gold—for your stock."

Styles fixed Culverhouse with an insolent smile. But his own heartbeats quickened. Was this a good omen? He needed ready cash—badly. Ready cash could buy him a little time. He'd never let this slave trader suspect, but he felt his luck was changing. He'd pick up whatever ready money Culverhouse offered—and he'd yet find some way to forestall his creditors, withstand Mr. Cleatus Dennison's incredible offers for his prize stock, and keep Brother Alexander at bay.

These thoughts flashed across his mind as Culverhouse was speaking, but the trader assumed Styles's silence was resistance and he smiled persuasively. "Listen, suh. Many gentlemen planters—like yourself—hesitate to sell their stock to these itinerant slave peddlers that run their animals beside their horses or shackle them in shameful coffles. I certify to you. You sell me a slave—it rides right in the back of my carriage. I figure these blacks are nigh human—and these days lots of them got human blood in them—they need care to keep them healthy and salable. No plodding along in mud and rain and inclement weather to get them sick and run-down. They ride. Right in my carriage. If they be docile animals, I don't use shackle or spancel. I treat them as humane as an animal can be treated—as I'm sure you do, suh."

Finally, Styles nodded. "I am Mr. Styles Kenric," he said. "I may have a few slaves I can spare you. What number do you have in mind?"

Culverhouse laughed genially. "Like to view your stock before I make that decision, suh. Let's say I won't waste your time. I'll take what the traffic will bear. You got culls, I may not wish to encumber myself with too many. On the other hand, you got a few sturdy animals, I might make a most rewarding deal—I take your culls off your hands—at a price—for the opportunity to avail myself of your best-quality stock."

They climbed into Culverhouse's carriage. Permeating the smells of horse sweat and ammonia was the strong musk of black bodies. Styles said, "I'm interested in improving bloodlines among my stock. We may not be able to agree on what I'd be willing to part with—and you to buy."

"Let's not fret the details, suh." Culverhouse glanced admiringly toward the fieldstone mansion as they drove past toward the work area in the valley and the slave quarters on the incline beyond. "Beautiful chalet, suh. Lovely. Sometimes—seeing a really fine old manor house like this, I find myself getting homesick for the gracious life at Windward Hills up in the Piedmont . . . . Windward Hills. Culverhouse family estate. Yes suh, despite all, a man gets homesick."

As the carriage approached the barns, Styles saw that the blacks who had congregated at the arrival of a visitor were suddenly nowhere in sight. A few dogs sprawled in the sunstruck lane between the slave huts. The older slaves had disappeared inside the cabins; even the children had been removed from the roadway.

"Niggers are funny animals," Culverhouse observed. "They can tell better than a human when something is amiss. They came a-runnin' when word spread a visitor had arrived. But, now, you don't own a nigger in your farthest field, I vow, that don't know you're dickering with a slave trader."

Styles called Blade out of the commissary. When Culverhouse saw the young Fulani Blade, he whistled between his teeth. "My God. A purentee Galla!"

"Fulani." Styles's pride vibrated in his voice.

"It for sale?"

Styles shook his head, wanting to laugh. Culverhouse was a dreamer, too. Styles told Blade to bring several of the families of slaves to the third slave shack on the incline. The Fulani trotted ahead of the carriage.

"Shouldn't of let me see the Fulani," Culverhouse said. "Know right where I could dispose of an animal like that for a fortune—a real retirement fortune . . . . An' no ordinary black is going to look like much to me—and culls will seem downright sickenin'."

Styles motioned the trader to pull the carriage in before the cabin where Perseus lived with his wife Poody and their offspring. Styles swung down and went up the steps. He called, "Poody. Would you come out here, please?"

Taut, brittle silence settled on the cabin as if the people inside were crouched, holding their breath. By the time the black woman Poody came through the door, Blade was walking with several other families down the incline. The slaves stood in the sun, squinting, mutely watching Styles and the slave buyer.

Culverhouse gave Poody a cursory inspection. "This here wench has got a bad harelip," he said.

"I told you the stock I have to offer you is blemished. With traits I don't want passed on. She has four colts— they range in age up to ten. You can have them all when you take Poody. As you can see, the wench is pregnant."

"Well, that at least is in her favor," Culverhouse said. "I'll look her over. If she's got no other disfigurements—

nothing that will interfere with her working—I might go up to nine hundred for her and her litter."

Culverhouse stepped closer to Poody who was openly crying now. Culverhouse spoke in a kindly but coldly firm tone. "Shut up, now. I ain't going to hurt you none. Your name is Poody, eh?"

She nodded, sniffling. She saw her man Perseus running up the incline and she reached out toward him. But Culverhouse's voice chilled. "Stand still, Poody. Don't want to have to tell you again."

The woman subsided, shivering as she stared toward Perseus. He stood, round-shouldered, impotent, at the end of the narrow stoop. Culverhouse unbuttoned the front of Poody's dress and with both hands hefted, punched, kneaded, and mashed her breasts. She winced but did not protest aloud.

"Seems sound enough. Likely twenty, twenty-two plantings old." Culverhouse spoke over his shoulder to Styles. He knelt then and ran his hands over Poody's bare feet, along her calves, and up her thighs under her skirt. "Turn around," he told her, "and bend over. Brace yourself on that chairback."

"What you gonna do, Masta?"

"You got piles, I don't want you." When Poody was bent forward, her arms braced against the back of the use-slicked kitchen chair, Culverhouse pushed her skirt over her hips, baring her buttocks. She trembled violently, but when she tried to move away from his probing hands, he spoke coldly. "Damn it, nigger. Stand still—unless you crave the back of my hand across your ugly harelip face."

He spread the cheeks of her buttocks and probed into her anus with his third finger. At last, satisfied, he jerked her dress down and, wiping his hands on his trousers, turned to face Styles. He shrugged. "Except for her harelip, she's sound enough. Got that little protrusion at her asshole like most women get child-bearing. Nine hundred —for her and her litter? That's a good price, suh. I got to get a costly increment on her just to break even—a ugly wench is not the easiest merchandise to get shed of."

Styles nodded and Culverhouse asked if he had more

stock to offer. Styles glanced toward Blade. "Is Peleg's woman Franny here?"

A young black woman, her hair in tightly pinned cornrows across her skull, came out of the crowd, gripping the hand of her man with all her strength. She looked ready to vomit.

"The buck for sale with her?" Culverhouse asked. When Styles said Peleg was not for sale at this time, Culverhouse shrugged. "Tell him to stay off this porch."

Styles inclined his head, gesturing Peleg to remain on the ground while Franny went slowly up the steps. She might have been on her way to the guillotine. Culverhouse smiled. "Why, this here is a right comely wench. What you partin' with her for? She carrying some disease?"

"She has two saplings that go along with her." Styles was casual, noncommittal. By now Culverhouse had opened the front of Franny's frock and thrust his hands in to probe her breasts. "Hell," he said over his shoulder. "So that's her flaw, huh? One tit a lot bigger than the other. One of this wench's tits hardly developed at all."

Styles merely waited silently until Culverhouse completed his examination of her teeth for sign of decay and her anus for piles. The trader shrugged then and said, "I'll pony up sixteen hundred for the lot—both wenches and their drops."

"Seventeen hundred," Styles said. He brought forward three young boys. One was badly retarded, another the victim of childhood rickets. The third was apparently healthy. Culverhouse could discover no obvious blemish on the youth. He laughed worriedly, but said, quite seriously, "I find nothing wrong with this one, but I ain't no way convinced, suh. Dealing with you, Mr. Styles, has been a real education for a long-time slave buyer."

"Mr. Kenric," Styles said. "Mr. Styles Kenric."

"Oh, I'll long remember that name, suh." Culverhouse laughed, did some mental arithmetic, and said, "If you'll take four thousand for the whole pack, I'll overlook that I don't know what in hell ails this sound-looking animal and take my chances."

Styles attempted to remain casual when he accepted

Culverhouse's offer. The slave trader laughed self-depre-catingly, paid him in gold from a thick chest built in be-neath the front seat of the carriage, even providing leather pouches for transporting the cash. "I got a notion that tells me I'm out of my depth, suh, and that this just ain't my day."

Styles thanked him and turned away without inviting the trader into the house for a drink or a meal. He walked through the sullen, silent ring of slaves. His heart leapt. He felt exultant. This *was* his day. He had done openly what old Baynard accomplished in stealth. He had sold enough slaves to buy himself brief respite from ruin. And in his mind was congealing a decision that had been germinating for weeks. He would take another bold step from which Baynard had always flinched. He was con-sidering a daring plan that might save him—something old Baynard had never had the guts to attempt, even at his most desperate. Why not borrow money right here from the bank in Mt. Zion? What the hell did he care what Summerton, Tetherow, or any of the other planters might learn of his financial condition? He could buy time, and he could save the loans possible to him from Blan-ford Ware's bank in Tallahassee for the purchase of Fulani wenches. He could make it all work. He could defeat all his enemies, including time. He could tell Mr. Cleatus Dennison to go to hell with his excessive offers for Blade and Moab.

He was smiling by the time he reached the villa on the plateau across the valley from the slave quarters. He could tell that Darwin Culverhouse was experiencing difficulty in loading his purchased stock in his carriage. From the driveway there rose the sound of hysterical sobbing. Styles did not even glance back.

At last Culverhouse had the three boys, the two women, and their brood shackled on the benches in the rear of the carriage. He climbed aboard and took up the thick-stocked buggy whip, as much a weapon of defense as an instrument to move his horses through the silent, unmoving herd of slaves.

He moved the carriage down the incline. Behind him, Poody's man Perseus had sunk to the ground at the edge of his stoop, his arms clutching at the support. He was crying openly like a child. He did not watch the carriage move down the incline, cross the workyards in the valley, and go up the rocky roadway past the big house. He struck his head against the thick post and wept. After a long time, he hit his head again, harder than before.

Franny's man had not moved from the foot of the steps before the cabin. Peleg stared after the wagon, watching it down the lane between the great trees to the formidable fieldstone gateway and the east-west trace beyond. But then he turned his head, his eyes dry and stricken. After a moment he fixed his gaze on the young wench who stood on the stoop immediately next door to Perseus's cabin. She wore a much-washed cotton dress. It was too small for her. Her breasts protruded in extraordinary firmness and fullness over her round little belly. When she saw that Peleg was staring back at her, she put her shoulders back, thrusting her voluptuous breasts forward, straining against the faded fabric. Her hardening nipples were clearly outlined under the cloth. She smiled at Peleg. He did not return her smile, but he went on staring at her breasts and did not look again toward the departing carriage.

10

Miss Jamie Lee Seaton sat the gray horse easily, gracefully, handling the animal with practiced expertise. "Why, I've been riding horses since I was three years old," she told Moab who rode respectfully just behind her. "Had my own pony when I was five."

"Why don't we ride along the trace?" Moab suggested when they came away from the horse barns.

"We'll ride where I want to," Jamie Lee told him. "Cousin Styles says it's particularly lovely along the creek —and he said you know every inch of that woodland."

Moab exhaled and said nothing more. They skirted the

slave quarters, toward which Jamie Lee did not even glance. Ascending a knoll, they approached a fieldstone house, well cared for in a carefully tended yard.

As they cantered past the house, Moab let his horse slow to a walk. He gazed toward the house in passing, for the moment lost in reverie, overwhelmed with stirring and pleasant memory. Those nights when he had lain awake awaiting the departure before dawn of the overseer Pilzer; the way he had waited in that tack room, breathless and empty-bellied with longing. In his mind he clearly saw the image of himself, bared to the waist, running across the yard, gliding like a shadow through the window and running across the room to *her* bed . . . .

Jamie Lee, well ahead of him, jerked the reins, stopping her horse. Her voice lashed back at him, shattering his thoughts. "Come on, nigger boy. Why are you dallyin' along heah?"

Moab did not reply, but sank his heels into the flanks of his tan horse, hurrying it.

At that moment a woman ran out of the front door of the fieldstone cottage. The screen door whined and slapped shut behind her like a brief, sharp clap of thunder. She was running as she came through the doorway, but she slowed as she reached the shadowed porch. She stopped and stood rigidly in the shadow of the overhang, staring after Moab and Miss Jamie Lee.

Attracted by the slamming of the front door, Jamie Lee twisted in the saddle and peered at the woman poised on the shadowed porch. As nearly as Jamie Lee could see, the woman appeared to be in her late twenties—old, yet still pretty in a tired and faded way. She said in a mocking tone, "Who's that, Moab?"

"Miz Florine," he said. "Miz Florine Pilzer."

"Do you know the old lady?"

"She ain't old," Moab answered sullenly, and then added quickly and humbly, "ma'm . . . Miz Florine is a very tol'able lady . . . ."

"You must know her pretty well," Jamie Lee persisted in a tone calculated to torment him. "She certainly seems to know you."

Moab exhaled heavily. "I lived up here on this place once . . . . Miz Florine and her husband—the overseer, Masta Pilzer—they were kind to me."

"I'll bet she was."

Moab did not reply. Jamie Lee laughed at him in a taunting and cutting way. They rode downslope into a hummock of pines where the loudest sound was the cry of yellowhammers.

"Do you really know this creek well?" she inquired.

"Every inch of it. I've played along here—long as I can remember."

"Then you must know the best place to be alone?"

"Ma'm?"

She laughed across her shoulder at him. "Ma'm?" she mocked him. "I said—if you had a black wench—and you wanted to—pester—her, only you wanted to be sure no one would find you, where would you take her on this creek?"

He did not reply and she cursed him. "Damn you, I asked you a question. Do you know a hidden place— where no one could find you?"

"Yes, ma'm, Miss Jamie Lee, ma'm. It's down the creek aways—"

"Show me the way there."

"It's kind of hard ridin', Miss Jamie Lee."

"I can ride a horse better than you can. Don't worry about me. I told you. Take me there."

Moab nodded. He urged his mount forward, going past Jamie Lee on the narrow trail. It was rough; the creek leaped across rocks, twisted suddenly back on itself like a broken snake; it spread out and oozed through swampy places. Yellowhammers and blue jays screamed at them. Small animals skittered in the underbrush. Moab did not speak, and Jamie Lee watched him with a set, chilled smile.

Jamie Lee said, "Do you know what I thought was the most beautiful thing I saw when I first got here to Blackoaks?"

"No, ma'm."

"You."

He did not speak. She said, "Aren't we nearly there? I'm certainly lost. I'll bet you are."

"We'uns can go back, if you wish, m'am."

"I didn't say anything about going back. When can we stop? You know damned good and well nobody could find us here."

"No, ma'm. We've crossed the creek three or four times. We've ridden on rocky ground where we didn't leave no track—"

"The hell with that. When can we stop?"

He drew up. "We can stop now, Miss Jamie Lee, ma'm, if you want to."

"I want to." She drew rein and then sat in her saddle, watching him. "Well, don't just sit there like a bump on a log. Help me down."

He swung out of his saddle, tied their mounts; then he reached up to take her arm, but Jamie Lee laughed and hurled herself out upon him. Her horse whinnied and reared up. Moab caught her and almost fell. He managed to brace himself against a pine and steadied himself, holding her. He tried to set her on her feet, but she twisted around, pressing her fevered thighs against him, her innominate bone cutting into him like small daggers. He tried to disengage himself, but she dug her nails savagely into his biceps.

"Stop being a damn fool. You know why I brought you here."

"No, ma'm, Miss Jamie Lee—"

"Don't give me that humble darky talk—"

"Whut you mean, ma'm, Miss Jamie Lee—?"

"Stop it! You know damned well what I mean. That '*ma'm, Miz Jamie Lee*.' Hogwash. You know why we are here. You also know about me. I know that nigra Soapy has been talking to you about me."

Moab smiled tautly but said nothing.

Her voice lashed at him. "Well, hasn't he? What'd Soapy say about me?"

"Soapy say you had him sent into yoah bedroom to repair a broken hasp on one of yoah trunks."

"And what else?"

Moab exhaled. "He say the hasp wa'n't broke."

"Oh? Did he? The damned loudmouth nigra. What else did he say?"

"Ma'm?"

"You heard me. Tell me. What else?"

Moab looked as if he had suspended breathing. "He say—you the first white woman he ever pestered."

Her face went pale, livid. "Damn him. Talking about a white lady like that. I'll have him beaten. I'll have the hide sliced right off his black ass. You, too—if one word gets to anybody—"

Now he breathed. His voice was level. "No, ma'm. I'm not goin' to say nuthin' I might know—about no white ladies—"

"Oh? Have you pestered a white woman?"

Moab smiled and shook his head. Damp beads of sweat stood on his forehead. "Le's jus' say I done felt the whip once, ma'm, Miss Jamie Lee. I don't hanker to feel it agin. No, ma'm. No way."

She laughed at him. "That means you have done it— with a white woman."

"Hit don't mean nuthin', ma'm, Miss Jamie Lee, 'ceptin' I don't crave ever to be whupped again."

She laughed again. "Then you better make up your mind right now to do what I tell you—and keep your mouth shut."

"I made up my mind to do that, ma'm, a long time ago. When you come to get me from Masta Hunter's class, I made up my mind."

"You're a smart-talkin' nigra, ain't you? You ought to be smart enough to know you can get in a peck of trouble smart-talkin' to white folks."

"I don't never do that, ma'm. Never."

"Then get your clothes off. Now. Unless you want me to scream."

"Not likely they'd hear you from here, ma'm."

"They'll hear me when I get back. I'll swear you raped me."

Moab gazed at Miss Jamie Lee, deeply troubled. She had been loosening her clothing, tossing garments behind her—all in a matter of seconds. He breathed out heavily. She had almighty big tits, all right, and she was trembling in anticipation of what she wanted him to do. It was as if she had the fever. He shuddered. He could catch that fever, fooling with her. Only the fever might be fatal for him. She didn't have sense enough to be careful, the way Miz Florine Pilzer did. Miss Jamie Lee Seaton could get a black boy's balls chopped off.

"We best head back," Moab said.

"You shut up and listen to me. You want me to tell Cousin Styles Kenric that you raped me? I'll tell them that, you black ape, and they'll hang you."

His voice was flat. "They might hang me anyhow."

"What's the matter with you? Don't you want to do it to a white girl? All niggers want white girls. What's the matter with you?" She grabbed his shirt. "You don't think I'm pretty?"

He answered softly, almost in a melancholy tone. "You gyascutus pretty, Miss Jamie Lee."

"Then take your cock out. I want to see it—"

"You down heah to git married to a white gen'mun—"

"Don't you dare talk to me like that, you nigger. It's none of your damn nevermind if I'm gittin' married ten times—"

"It matter to me. They catch us, they kill me."

"You don't stop talking, I'll scream rape and they'll kill you anyway."

He shook his head, eyes stricken. "Please don't scream, Miss Jamie Lee."

Her head tilted. "Then you do what I tell you."

Moab's wide shoulders sagged in his denim shirt. He nodded and stood immobile. She reached out and pulled his shirt hard, ripping off its buttons. "Oh, Gawd, Miz Jamie Lee, you gonna git me killed—"

"Shut up—"

"—how I gonna explain I come back from a ride with you—my shirt torn open?"

She caught his osnaburg britches and would have torn open his fly, but he retreated, shaking his head, truly afraid of her now. "I'll do it," he said. "No way in Gawd's world I explain no buttons on my pants."

He glanced both ways along the creek though he knew they were deep in the Blackoaks timberlands—few human beings ever came here. A woodpecker was noisy in a pine. A wood rodent skittered across the winter needles. Holding his breath, Moab shrugged out of his shirt.

Jamie Lee laughed, licking her tongue across her lips. "Oh, that's good, Moab. You even a prettier nigra boy than I thought. You hardly black at all. You real pretty."

"Yes'm." Moab nodded. They'd finally reached an area of agreement. With less hesitation, Moab unbuttoned his britches and stepped out of them.

Jamie Lee's violet eyes glittered. Her cheeks flushed as if she were truly fevered. Her lips drew back from her teeth. Her gaze oozed over him and her breathing quickened. "Come on, Moab," she said, breathless. "Do it to me."

"I scared, Miss Jamie Lee . . . An' it ain't up enough to do nuthin' yet."

She laughed. "Maybe this will make him stand up." She lifted her skirt and sank down upon the grass and spread her legs, knees bent, for him. She wore no drawers above her stockings; her white thighs gleamed. He hesitated, mortally afraid of her—a wilful and headstrong white girl. He faced in his mind the penalty for being caught with her. But his flesh betrayed him. She was far lovelier than any other female he had ever encountered. Even the pale mat of pubic hairs above her heated thighs was different—almost blonde, and tinted with bright red highlights in the sun. Her ragged breathing caused her full breasts to quaver. He felt the familiar ache, the emptiness in his belly, the quick rise of his penis as the blood engorged it so abruptly and with such force that the glans pulsed, bigger and brighter than a huge ripe plum. "He's ready now!" Jamie Lee cried. "Give it to me, Moab. Oh, give it to me now, you damn nigger."

Moab's mind wheeled and spun. The rest of the world was blacked out, everything else ceased to exist except that lovely peach-blossom fresh body, those legs spread wide to receive him. The rest of humanity, the laws created and administered by the inflexible white men, the scream of a yellowhammer, the sun on the water, nothing had meaning. He saw only that triangle of red-tinted hair cresting her femininity, the liquidity at her thighs, the way her hips quivered as she thrust upward impatiently toward him.

But when he fell to his knees between her widely parted legs, she caught his penis in her hand, twisting it until he bit his lip to keep from yelping in agony. Her breath was hot, her voice husky, but commanding. "You lay down," she told him. "Lay down on yore back. I want to ride you, nigger. I gonna ride you. Ride you. Ride you."

Moab sank back on the grass, the briars cutting him, the ground hard, and rocky. Eyes wide, he watched Jamie Lee sit across his hips and come down expertly upon his rigid staff. "Buck me off, nigger boy," she ordered. "See can you buck me off!"

When he didn't thrust his hips violently enough or rapidly enough to suit her, Jamie Lee bent forward and dug her nails into the soft flesh on each of his shoulders. Holding him like that, she flailed her own hips savagely. Now he bit back cries of painful ecstasy. Nothing like this had ever happened to him before. She gasped frantically for breath, her mouth parted wide. She lifted her hips as high as she could without losing the head of the pulsing shaft driven up into her vagina, and then she plunged herself downward upon it fiercely. She paused only long enough to rip open the bodice of her dress so that her voluptuous breasts bobbled crazily before his glazed eyes as she worked herself up and down . . . . White women . . . they sure as hell were strange. Crazy. Crazy as hell. Crazy. Crazy. Crazy. She was crazy, the craziest white woman of them all, and she was driving him crazy—as crazy as she was—so crazy he no longer gave a damn. Let the white men hang him. Let them shoot him full of buck shot. There were worse ways to die. He caught her full breasts in both his hands and used them to work her wildly, faster and faster, up and down upon him . . . .

11

Florine Pilzer stood for a long time on the shadowed front porch after Moab and the white girl had disappeared down the trail. Her eyes stung and filled with tears. It never occurred to Florine for one moment that Moab was simply riding as guide and groom for that white girl. She knew what that white bitch wanted. She could look at her, the way she hurried toward the pig tracks with Moab. Florine considered following them.

At last, she went back in. In the quiet house, she felt caged, as if the walls crowded in on her. She prowled from room to room, returning often to the front door to scan the trail into the Blackoaks timberlands. It grew dark and Florine knew she should eat supper, cook something for Bos to eat when he came in. She had no heart for it. She was thankful Bos and the cotton wagons would not return from Mt. Zion until late in the evening.

Darkness settled swiftly, putting the house in blackness. She sighed, thinking how wonderful it would be if Moab could get away to her for a little while tonight. She laughed bitterly. An unlikely miracle if he came because, like her, he had no idea when Bos might return from Mt. Zion. She and Moab had stayed alive so far by being too smart to take foolish chances. Bos would kill Moab if he ever found the boy in her bed, or heard a whisper that the Negro had been in it. But Bos would kill her as well: white men believed a white woman used by a black man was forever vile—and better dead.

Florine struck a sulphur match and lighted two candles, which she set near the front window as flickering aids to Bos whenever he did return. Then she went dully into the bedroom and in the darkness undressed and got ready for bed.

She slipped her cotton gown over her head, wriggled her body to shake it over her high-standing breasts and full hips. She remembered the way Moab had first caught her playing with herself. Bos had sent the boy at dawn to wash the cottage windows. How long ago, and yet it seemed only a few mornings past. Her life had begun that morning, though she hadn't realized it then. She smiled emptily, remembering. She would never forget the way Moab had stood, transfixed with shock, terror, and surprise, staring through her bedroom window at her lying sprawled, legs wide, naked on this bed, her fingers working furiously.

She could not say to this moment which of them had been more frightened—she at being so surprised by a Negro—he at having violated her privacy, knowing she had the power to cost him his life. They had stared at each other in helpless terror.

Sighing, Florine lay down on the bed. She settled upon her back and pulled her gown above her hips. She breathed raggedly, her stomach empty at what she was going to do. She closed her eyes, summoning Moab through images, heated memory, agonized need. She played with herself for a long time. She reached climaxes again and again, and each time she sagged exhausted to her pillow. But each time she lay breathless, tired and unmoving, the thought of Moab with that predatory white bitch burned into her mind again . . . .

She was still agonizedly awake when she heard Bos stomp noisily into the kitchen after midnight.

Florine pretended to be deeply asleep, rolled far to her own side of the bed. It seemed to her that Bos took forever getting undressed. She heard his growling when he found she'd left no meal covered on the kitchen table for him. He stalked the kitchen, finding food, drinking milk, and cursing because milk delivered that morning was soured already.

At last he came into the bedroom. He said, "Flo?" But when she did not respond, he undressed, grumbling. He dropped his sweated shirt and crusted trousers on the floor where he removed them. He flopped heavily on the mattress and removed his boots and stockings. He dropped each boot loudly. Florine knew he was trying to awaken her, but she continued to pretend the even, regular breathing of deep sleep. Still muttering in his guttural Dutch baritone, Bos stood up and stripped away his long underwear. He stood for some moments yawning, stretching, and scratching at his privates. Then he poured cold water from the earthenware pitcher to its large matching bowl on the washstand. He grunted, shuddering, as he washed his face, neck, armpits, and, quickly, between his legs. He was a big man, six feet tall, brawny, with fearful muscles in his shoulders, biceps, and across his back. His muscular chest was keglike. Long hours in the saddle had hardened the corded muscles in his thighs and upper legs. Drinking his own home-brewed beer had developed a thick pot belly on him, and his manhood drooped like a pendulous underhang lost in a crop of graying pubic hairs.

Finally he got noisily into bed. He said again, more insistently, "Flo . . . Flo? You awake?"

She whimpered sleepily and pressed deeper into her pillow, hoping he would give up, but he laughed and pushed his hand under her arm. Catching her by a breast, he turned her over on her back. "You miss the old man, hon?" he said.

"I'm dead for sleep, Bos." She resisted because sex with Bos Pilzer was totally without pleasure for her. It was so designed by Bos, who believed white women hated sex and merely endured it. From the first year of their marriage Bos had adhered to a set pattern. He scrubbed roughly at her breasts, ran his hand between her legs. Then he mounted her, panting and driving. He was quickly roused, quickly relieved, quickly sated. Then, without a word, he fell away from her and soon was snoring.

Perhaps an hour or two later, Bos awoke, his mind befogged, sleep numbed, certain he had heard—or dreamt!—that Florine was lying beside him, crying in the darkness. "Flo?"

"What?" Her voice sounded strangled.

"You all right, hon? You cryin', for God's sake?"

"It's all right, Bos. It's nothing. Go back to sleep."

12

Styles went up to his bedroom about nine o'clock that night. Moab was sprawled, face down on his pallet, in exhausted sleep.

Styles stared at the boy's naked body, the slowly healing wale across his back. He stood some moments, unmoving, his thoughts heating sensually as he gazed upon the red-golden body. In his imagination he recalled the nights Moab had lain in his bed with him, that beautiful body his to use as he willed. He couldn't help it; he treasured every moment he had spent with Moab. Styles's viscera tautened. That overwhelming need flooded over him. He wanted to awaken Moab, to take the boy up in his arms and carry him to his bed. But he forced himself to consider the outside pressures, and also his need to be the master in these troublesome situations.

Reluctantly, he turned away without waking the sleeping Moab. Instead, he rang for Thyestes and ordered a hot bath prepared in his dressing room. When he came out of the steaming tub, freshly shaved, his body powdered and sprinkled with cologne, he chose a fresh nightshirt, a silk dressing gown, and a white scarf which he knotted at his throat and stuffed under the dark lapels of his robe.

He studied his reflection for some moments in the full-length door mirror. He was pleased with the picture he made and he smiled tautly at himself in the mirror. He was tall, slender, and he had the look of the true patrician; this was something from the inside, something that could not be faked. He turned, strode across the room with one final glance at the naked black boy on the pallet, and let himself quietly out into the corridor.

His confident step slowed as he approached the door of the bedroom he had shared with Kathy since their wedding night. His heart lurched slightly, remembering the ugly finality of the last scene between them in that room. She had caught him with Moab; she had been violent, hysterical, unreasonable. But he knew he had been the only man in her mind for those first three years. She had been a long time alone. It shouldn't be too difficult to bend her to his will; he had always done it with such ease that even controlling her totally had grown boring.

Styles rapped on the door facing. After a brief moment the door was opened slowly, and Kathy stared at him through the slight opening. "What do you want?"

"I'd like to talk to you. May I come in?"

Her blue eyes met his squarely. "You've nothing to say to me that you cannot say from right there."

Abruptly angered, Styles caught the door in his fist and thrust it past Kathy. She caught her breath and retreated a step or two, staggered. Her face went deathly pale. She watched him coldly as he closed the door behind him.

"You look lovely. You smell pretty," she said in chilled sarcasm. "You've just entered the wrong room by mistake."

He gazed along his nose at her. "I think you'd better listen to me."

"You have nothing to say that could possibly interest me. I know what you are. I know what you've done to me. I know how you deceived me to get me to marry you. I know you never loved me. It makes it faintly endurable to know you couldn't love any woman."

"I've always loved you, Kathy. In my way."

"Your way isn't what I want. Your way is vile and perverted—and empty and ugly. I don't like to say these things, Styles. I've no wish to hurt you. But I told you—I don't want you in this room again. You bring back all the filth—the ugliness."

"I warn you, Kathy. You are my wife. Subject to my will. I warn you to consider that carefully. Now, first, there are certain conventions, appearances that must be maintained—especially when there are guests in this house. And I not only expect you to carry out your part, I demand it."

"You make me sick—"

"That may be. But this house will be crowded with guests within the next few weeks. Mr. Cleatus Dennison is one guest who especially concerns me. His estimation and regard are most important to me. He believes you and I are a happily married couple. And I require that you do all in your power to conserve and deepen his conviction about our married felicity."

"I'll sit at your dining table. I'll smile in servile adoration on key—"

"You'll do one hell of a lot more than that, madam. There is not only Mr. Cleatus Dennison to consider. There is your own brother. There is no sense burdening Ferrell with our personal problems. Any trouble between you and me is strictly between you and me, and I expect you to keep it that way."

She laughed. "Yes. Ferrell might kill you if I told him the truth about you."

His face flared red, instantly cooled. His smile twisted. "It is to forestall any chance of violence and friction between Ferrell and me that I am moving back into this bedroom with you, temporarily."

She laughed again, an octave higher, the sound uncontrolled and tinged with rage. "You're never coming back into this bedroom, not as long as I live. You'll never touch me—except accidentally."

He stared at her, shadows swirling deeply in his eyes. His brow tilted and he considered her as an unpleasant obstacle standing between him and what he meant to have—but her presence was like a reed. He would walk over her if she forced him. He hoped for her sake that she had the intelligence to realize this.

When he spoke his voice was pitched in a patient and calm tone as if he were dealing with a recalcitrant child. "You can only lose in opposing me, Kathy. You must know that by now. I've been patient with you. I've moved out of this room, not because of your will, because I wanted to. I'll also move back, because I want to . . . . But if you will be reasonable, if you will think it out, you will see it will be to your advantage before all your friends and relatives, here for the marriage of your cousin Jamie

Lee, to put on at least the appearance of a happy marriage . . . ."

"It's more than I have to give."

His voice chilled, hardened. "Then I no longer ask it. I tell you. I am temporarily moving back into this bedroom until after the Christmas season, until the wedding guests have gone."

She gazed up at him coldly. She spoke almost casually. "Go to hell."

He winced as if she'd struck him. When he remembered the way he had bent her, twisted her, used her, tormented her for his own pleasure, it stunned him that she treated him so calmly, as if he were a persistent, annoying stranger. He said, "I warn you, Kathy. I know what is going on."

She gazed at him levelly. "Stop trying to be subtle with me, Styles. Do you mean you suspect something between me and Hunt Campbell—something of the nature of what goes on in your bedroom—between you and that black boy?"

He almost hit her before he could control himself. But when he spoke, his voice had its old aloof arrogance. "I'm not blind, Kathy. Neither am I especially tolerant of infidelity."

"It doesn't matter what you profess to be or not to be. You no longer have the right to tell me what I can or cannot do."

"Kathy, you are a stupid little country girl. You have no idea what it means—in the eyes of the law—for you to be my wife. It makes you little better than chattel. I advise you to learn the truth before you ever take this tone with me again. Remember. Before the law I am your husband."

"Are you? Have you ever been?" She gazed up at him for a long beat. Then she heeled around, strode to the wall. She yanked the cord summoning a servant. Then she strolled past Styles and sat quietly in a wing chair, studying her nails. After a moment there was a rap on the door and Thyestes limped into the room. Kathy glanced up. "Master Styles is leaving, Thyestes. I would appreciate your assisting him out of my room."

The poor Thyestes looked as if he might faint. All he could do was whisper, "M'am?"

Styles peered at Kathy a moment, but she did not look at him again. Thyestes just stood inside the door, helpless. He could not leave; he was afraid to speak. Styles's mouth twisted. "This matter is not settled, Kathy."

"It is as far as I'm concerned . . . . Thyestes, please show Mr. Kenric out."

Styles turned on his heel and walked past Thyestes. He caught the door as he went and slammed it behind him.

13

Styles awoke early, refreshed and renewed. His mind felt clear and uncluttered, emptied of the passions that had agitated and driven him last night. He felt strong, no longer helpless. The hours in his bed with Moab had cooled his fury and quieted his flesh, and he had slept. He glanced at the toasted-brown body of the naked boy sprawled face down in exhausted slumber on the bed beside him. Moab's lips were parted; the boy breathed heavily and seemed to sag into the mattress in helpless fatigue. He looked very young, very vulnerable, and Styles smiled. He got out of bed quietly to permit the youth to go on sleeping, undisturbed.

He rang for house slaves and ordered a hot bath. He chose a new linen suit, a fresh, crisply pressed white shirt, and a pale blue cravat. He spent a long time dressing. He watched himself in the sun-illumined mirror but let his mind reach out to tasks demanding priority attention.

He felt reassured. His mind was free of turmoil. He could coldly and dispassionately consider the finances and the future and daily routines of the big farm and give all of it his total attention. In the back of his mind rage against Kathy still moiled, but it was a smouldering rage. He was able, in his mental clarity, to determine that she would pay, and continue to pay, for her defiance. And with this decision he could put her out of his thoughts and turn to more immediate matters.

He completed his toilet, satisfied with his reflection from the sun-lighted depths of his mirror. He looked smartly dressed, wide-shouldered, aristocratic, youthful, vigorous, successful, with that patina of arrogance that had been cultivated as a protective brand of self-confidence. When one had impeccable family background but inadequate financial resources, one traded on the currency available. And chilled arrogance was the shield of the wellborn in the straits of adversity. He smiled coldly as he strode down the corridor.

"Styles."

He had reached the head of the wide semicircular staircase, and he hesitated impatiently. His manicured hand settled on the newell post, and he turned to glance along his nose at Miz Claire. His mother-in-law wore a flowered chiffon that would have been suitable for a young girl. Her hair had been painstakingly set in tight ringlets that now blossomed riotously about her head. Her face was thinner than ever, tinted with rouge. Her smile was as bright as her dress and as inapposite.

"Styles, dear, I must speak to you—"

"Yes, Miz Claire?"

"A matter of gravest urgency. I'm sure Mister Baynard would agree if he were here—"

"Yes, Miz Claire?"

"It's about Moab. The young Fulani."

Styles flushed slightly, guiltily. He straightened his shoulders in a gesture of defiance, and his glance chilled. He was damned if this old addlepated witch would judge him or his activities. "Yes, Miz Claire?"

"The boy is ruined."

He frowned. "Ruined, Miz Claire?"

"Plainly. Oh, I understand and appreciate that you are trying to heal that whip wale across his back. But it will never heal so completely that it will pass even the most cursory inspection by an experienced slave buyer."

He exhaled. "I believe it will, Miz Claire, in time."

She shook her head, ringlets bobbling. "You know what Mr. Baynard says, Styles dear—"

"No, Miz Claire. What is that?"

"Mr. Baynard is very direct and explicit about it, dear. We've all heard him say it a hundred times—a Fulani slave must be physically flawless—unblemished—or it is worthless."

"Yes. I've heard him say that."

"I believe Mr. Baynard will want the Fulani boy destroyed."

He peered at her, stunned. "I beg your pardon?"

"It's what Mr. Baynard has always said. I'm sure it is what he'll say when he returns."

Styles stared at Miz Claire a moment in chilled rage. Then he smiled in gracious counterfeit and shrugged. "Why don't we wait then, Miz Claire—and take it up with Mr. Baynard—when he does return?"

He continued to give her his brightest smile and passed beyond her, going down the staircase. He knew she went on standing at the head of the stairs staring after him, but he did not glance back. He entered the formal dining room where a place was set for him at the head of the gleaming mahogany table. He sat alone and rang for Thyestes. When the aging butler hobbled in on painful feet, Styles ordered a carriage. Two frightened wenches in cotton dresses and heads wrapped in bandanas served his breakfast. He ate sparingly, with the same genteel fastidiousness he would have displayed had there been a dozen guests at table. It even amused him to bend his head over his plate in a mocking prayer.

He selected certain papers from his office and locked it behind him. He carried a small leather note case and a woollen topcoat, and he wore a dark planter's hat set at a precise angle on his head. He strode along the hall and went out of the front door, which a slave leaped to have opened for him when he reached it. He crossed the fieldstone veranda and went down the wide steps to the waiting carriage. He glanced briefly skyward and found the morning misted and overcast, with a slight December chill riding in on the fog. Laus, the thick-shouldered Negro driver sat on the front seat, swollen with self-importance in high hat and smartly brushed uniform. Pegasus, the coachman, similarly outfitted, stood at attention at the rear step of the open sedan with its oilcloth top. He gave Styles his most toothsome smile. "Wheah-at we headed this mawnin', Masta Styles, suh?"

"The bank in Mt. Zion." Styles deftly sidestepped the slave's helping hand and settled stiffly in the center of the rear seat. Pegasus swung up beside Laus, also sitting ramrod straight. Styles knew everyone inside the house and within sight watched his departure down the tree-lined lane.

Pegasus said, "The Masta say the bank in Mt. Zion."

Laus growled. "I heahs what the Masta say."

"He say it to me. I ast. He say to me. My job to tell you wheah-at we go, nigger."

"I gots ears. I heah Masta say."

"That's enough quibbling," Styles said. The two men fell silent and they rode in silence through the thick forests, across stretches of swampy lowlands, and along dry lanes between fields of plowed but unfenced land, into the town. The meticulously groomed horses stepped smartly, never seeming to slacken their gait or lower their high-held heads. They arrived outside the bank in little more than an hour, soon after the establishment opened its doors for the day.

The sun was up, blazing, promising a dry hot day in town. Huge trees laid shadows in bold relief across the rutted street and the planklike boardwalks. Old men lounged outside the general store chatting desultorily, covertly eyeing the distinguished looking landowner and his polished rig, uniformed niggers, and extraordinary carriage horses.

Styles entered the cool, vaultlike bank lobby, aware of the subdued commotion his arrival occasioned. The guard, clerks, and officers at their desks behind the mahogany railings looked up, smiling in his direction. There was deference in their smiles, and they were neither surprised nor abashed when Styles ignored them totally.

Luke Scroggings got up from his cluttered desk and came out of the small railed-off area. He smiled and nodded Styles through his gate and into a leather upholstered chair. He waited, but Styles did not offer to shake hands. When a man was "in commerce," there was disparity between him and a landowner, even if he held a total mortgage on the planter's property and chattel. There was currently no such blister on Styles Kenric's property.

Scroggings sat down at his desk and waited, gazing with blue eyes upon the planter. Luke was a comparatively small man—not more than five feet six in heeled boots—compact and toughly made, resembling a bulldog. His red hair, now salted with flecks of gray, was thick, straight across his freckled forehead. His nose was short and pugged, and his mouth was full, stained with freckles and cigar tobacco.

"I'm on a most unusual errand," Styles said. "I hope we can get together on an enterprise which could be mutually beneficial."

"I hope we can be of assistance."

"I am offering you a most unprecedented opportunity, Mr. Scroggings. I'm sure you know that Mr. Ferrell Baynard, while he had a checking account here, never carried a mortgage on Blackoaks Plantation with this bank?"

"You'd like to borrow money on the plantation?"

Styles winced. He would never have come to Scroggings, and would have walked out at this juncture, except that in order to make his grand-scale plans work he had to save Blanford Ware for another phase. "The way I see things, it makes fiscal sense for a plantation to maintain a drawing account in a bank situated in the immediate vicinity to make sure the cash required for routine business is always available," Styles said. "Mr. Baynard never agreed."

"How much are you looking for?"

"You understand, Scroggings, I'm here simply because I do not wish to tie up my liquid assets. By using borrowed money to satisfy current indebtedness, I'll be free to expand—as I certainly plan to do."

"What kind of expansion do you have in mind?"

It was on the tip of Styles's tongue to tell Scroggings it was none of his business. But he managed a stiff smile.

"I was thinking of curtailing cotton planting," he said. "Many plantations—especially in Virginia and Maryland —are now making fortunes raising slaves to sell to other planters. Of course this is a long-term investment—the first real payoffs might not start for fifteen years or more, unless one dealt in marketed slaves while his own crop matured."

"And you plan to do this at Blackoaks?" For the first time in the interview Scroggings's smile was genuine. He seemed to betray at least a modicum of respect for the planter. "Sounds like an excellent idea to me. What you're looking for then is a long-term, low-interest loan—something around four percent, I imagine?"

Shocked, Styles could only nod. Immediately before his sudden death, Baynard had quarreled violently with G. Blandford Ware because the Tallahassee banker was asking twelve percent on mortgage loans.

Scroggings was nodding. "I've thought for a long time that slave breeding could be a paying business. Old Forsythe always thought so. But cotton planters are mostly very hard to convert from old ideas. Difficult to convince a cotton man that times—and markets—and land quality—are changing . . . . I am surprised though that the Baynards will permit—"

"The Baynards *permit* nothing. I am master of Blackoaks."

Scroggings shrugged. "I'm quite satisfied to deal with you, Mr. Kenric. How much do you think you'll need?"

Styles drew a deep breath. The banker was far easier to do business with than he had dared to hope. And four percent interest on long-term money! God almighty, he had been caught up in a rising tide and was being swept along! "I might need—ten thousand—to start."

Scroggings nodded without hesitation. "I'll arrange to have your draws on this bank honored up to ten thousand, starting today."

Styles was nonplussed that he had found the needed cash with so little difficulty. He watched Scroggings figure on scratch paper. The banker looked up, smiling. "When you've drawn ten thousand, we can set you a new extended credit limit. There's no problem with a plantation like Blackoaks—as long as it is unencumbered."

"I assure you Blackoaks is free of any mortgage." Styles spoke stiffly and sat straighter.

Scroggings nodded. "Why don't we start by executing a simple chattel mortgage? That'll give you room to work. How many slaves do you have on Blackoaks?"

"I can't give you an exact count this morning—"

"I don't require one. A horseback estimate is good enough for me."

"We have forty families."

"At least a hundred and sixty slaves—"

"Nearer two hundred—"

"Then there will be no problem. In fact, with that many slaves, and cutting down on planting, you should be able to do some judicious marketing and trading almost at once . . . . Well, that's your decision." Scroggings found legal papers in the cubbyholes on his desk. He checked them casually, automatically. Clearly, he knew the phraseology and fine print by heart. He wrote a few figures into the blank spaces and pushed the papers across the desk. "If you'll just sign, Mr. Kenric."

Styles took up the pen, sank its nib into the inkwell, and then hesitated. "There is just one thing . . . . I have two Fulani slaves. They cannot be part of this mortgage."

Scroggings laughed and shrugged. "As you wish. I don't believe you appreciate, Mr. Kenric, that with at least two hundred slaves, a loan of ten thousand need not encumber more than fifty of your slave stock to protect you and the bank. In fact, nowadays, having niggers is just like having money in an account."

Styles signed the papers, his heart lurching. This damned clerk in his frock coat was right: he had not fully understood the value of his chattel. What Scroggings had said meant that he could borrow up to forty thousand dollars on slave chattels alone. Good God, there was no way on earth to stop him now.

His hand shook slightly as he pushed the signed papers back across the desk. Scroggings blew on the wet ink signature. "Do you need any cash at the moment?"

Styles glanced along his nose, unsmiling, putting the clerk in his place again. "That won't be necessary."

"Then we'll credit your account." Scroggings hesitated and then spoke, almost as if with tongue in cheek, as if he enjoyed some monstrous secret joke. "I suppose you want the money credited to the Blackoaks account?"

Styles stood up. He counted slowly to control his rage. He managed to smile. "I believe my own account would be more appropriate."

"Of course." Scroggings smiled faintly again as if he were hearing what he had expected to hear.

14

Ferrell Baynard laughed. He felt young, excited, and exultant, as he always had when he returned home to Blackoaks after a long time away. He was home! He was home again!

He reined in the horse he rode some yards from the huge, monolithic posts and iron gates that marked the entrance to his family's estate. As anxious as he was to be with his family again, he didn't want anyone from the house or the slave quarters to spy him yet. He wanted these few last seconds alone to savor the exquisitely bittersweet sadness of returning home after a long, self-imposed exile.

He was an exceptionally handsome youth, not yet twenty. He sat easily in the saddle, posting naturally with the gait of his mount. The flat-crowned black hat and stiff clerical collar combined with the black shirtwaist, dark suit, and aged boots, revealed him as a novice in an order that took its vows of poverty seriously.

But there was evident in his slender, muscular body the healthy exuberance of the natural athlete. In his chiseled-featured young face and Border-Scot blue eyes there lurked a touch of deviltry that poverty and secular sacrifice had not yet dimmed. His mouth was full and red-lipped; he smiled easily and engagingly. However, when he was not smiling—silent or in repose—a strange hurt stirred shadows deep in his eyes.

Delighted to be home again, he stared up at the manor house beyond the inclined lane of wintry trees on the commanding and flowered plateau. How beautiful it was! —from the fieldstone fences to the chimneys reared like proud turrets above the steep roof.

He let his gaze trail across the small chapel his father had had built for his mother on the only knoll higher than the promontory on which the chalet sat. Beyond, black men, women, and children moved desultorily in the work yards and the slave quarters, blue-misted on the rise above. How long he'd been away! How good to be back here.

He urged the tired horse forward. The zain—an aging animal neither gray nor white—seemed instinctively to sense the end of the journey, one more incline, one more lane. It tilted its head and pricked up its ears, stalking proudly up the rocky lane between the winter-bared trees.

The small black boys, appointed daily to watch the east-west trace for visitors, espied him. Their yelps of excitement and delight spread the news of his arrival to the farthest reach of the messuage.

The urchins came running, crying out, their teeth gleaming white, eyes wide and white-rimmed in glistening black faces. He was only halfway up the lane when the children reached him, leaping up on both sides of the horse. He'd taken a poke of stick candy from his saddle bag, and he handed it out as they grabbed the reins of his horse.

Ferrell swung down from the saddle, six feet tall, long-legged, and tossed his bridle to one of the lookouts.

"Masta, you home. Oh, Masta, you home."

Before he could speak, Ferrell was enveloped in a bear hug and swung up off his feet. "My God, Morgan. You'll break my back."

Morgan was sobbing and couldn't speak intelligibly. He

simply clung to his brother, blubbering, his tears hot on Ferrell's face and neck.

"I next! I next," Soapy kept saying. He circled them as if looking for an opening. Ferrell reached out his left hand and Soapy clutched it in both of his, kissing it hotly, and suddenly sobbing as volubly as Morgan.

"If you fellows are going to cry and carry on like this, I won't come home any more," Ferrell said, laughing.

"Ah, Ferrell, don't go 'way no more," Morgan pleaded, weeping. "We need you here. More'n ever now with Papa dead an' all."

"We truly needs you right heah at home, Masta." Soapy still clung to his hand.

Beyond Morgan's stout shoulder, Ferrell saw the flash of color in Kathy's bright dress, her pale golden hair glinting richly in the sun, her lovely smile, her arms extended as she ran downhill toward him.

He managed to pull free of Morgan's bear hug. Morgan seemed convinced that if he released his brother, Ferrell would depart immediately and forever.

With Morgan and Soapy close beside him, Ferrell ran up the stony incline. His round black hat blew off. He didn't even glance around. One of the urchins would retrieve it, or the hell with it. His wavy, raven-wing-dark hair, the hairline deeply indented at the temples, blew free about his ears and over his high cleric's collar.

Kathy sailed into his arms, clinging to him as he swung her around. She laughed and cried at the same time. "Didn't you know I prayed you'd come home, Simple Simon?" she wept. "What took you so long?"

"I'm here," he said. "I'm here." It was all he could trust himself to say. With Kathy embraced in Ferrell's right arm and Morgan encircled in his left, Soapy found himself euchred out. He walked closely behind them, holding possessively to the tail of Ferrell's threadbare black cloth coat. "Who are *you*?" Ferrell said to the girl standing in the sun at the head of the lane—blonde, slender, magnificent of bosom, and smiling demurely. "Don't tell me you're Cousin Jamie Lee Seaton—that sassy little brat who used to climb up in the pecan trees and spit down at us?"

She blushed becomingly and lowered her eyes. "I've grown up, Cousin Ferrell. I've changed."

Ferrell put his head back, laughing. "You sure as hell have." His blue eyes brushed over that extraordinary bust. "Cousin Jamie Lee, it's certainly time you married, for the public safety."

"Oh, Cousin Ferrell!" Jamie Lee protested, her face a bright red.

"Ferrell, you devil," Kathy said. "That collar is turned around, but it hasn't changed you one bit."

His arm tightened about her. "Oh, I've changed. But I'm still appreciative—if only from a distance." He gave Jamie Lee a brief buss on the cheek. "You must take after the Seatons, Jamie Lee. No Henry or Baynard woman I've ever seen was built like you. Were they, Kathy?"

"I don't know what you're talking about," Kathy said in mock reproof.

By the time they reached the fieldstone veranda, all the house servants were congregated there. They lined the shadowed porch between the six columns that supported the tile-roofed overhang. They shuffled, grinning but hesitant, down the two long stone steps to the cobbled driveway. It took a long time to run that gauntlet of devotion. Each black face was a welcoming wreath of smiles. Each slave wanted that single moment—a breath of time—that belonged to him alone: the young master spoke his name, recalled some pleasant or sticky incident from their mutual past. For that instant, each tendered his welcome and received in return the token of personal recognition and deep affection.

Hunt Campbell stood aside, staring at the scene. He remained leaning against the column after Ferrell had entered the house and the servants had dispersed.

Kathy came close to Hunt and touched his hand gently. Her voice was still hollow-timbered from her crying. "What's the matter with you?"

Hunt didn't smile. He shook his head, deeply puzzled, deeply concerned. "A man doesn't relinquish preconceived prejudices easily."

"What does that mean?" Kathy smiled up at him.

"It means, I came down here convinced of the evils of slavery. I'm still convinced. But when I looked at those blacks welcoming their master home, I was overwhelmed with doubt—of my own convictions. I was equally overwhelmed with sadness for those poor black bastards."

"What *are* you talking about? Or is it anything I could understand?"

"Slaves. I'm talking about slavery. The slaves will be freed—someday. Maybe their rights will in some future time be equiponderated with those of whites. But watching them greet Ferrell, and be greeted by him, I wonder what the cost will be—to the blacks themselves—in loving and being loved?"

"My God. You're becoming almost human."

"Don't you believe it. Oh, I know these black people think they're happy—because they don't know any better."

Kathy's smile was gentle and self-mocking. "There's a lot of that going around . . . . "

Ferrell went up the wide staircase, two steps at a time. At its head, his mother stood, trembling with anticipation, and immediately behind her loomed the lumpy bulk of her body slave.

"Oh, Neva!" Miz Claire wept. "My baby has come home. My baby has come home."

"Yes'm, Miz Claire. He sho' has. He sho' 'nuff has. An' prettier'n ever . . . . Lord-ee, but he's pretty—and he always was."

Ferrell came off the top step and swung Miz Claire up in his arms. She screamed. "Put me down! Put me down this instant."

"I won't let you break."

"I'm your mother!"

"What? A pretty girl like you? You can't possibly have a son that old," he teased.

"If you don't put me down this instant, I'll just tell your father—the minute he gets home."

A chill pervaded Ferrell's body and took the warmth and pleasure out of the day. He kissed his mother lightly, set her gently on her feet. He spent the next hour with her in her bedroom suite. But at his first opportunity he got Neva alone on one of the small upper balconies.

"How long has she been like that, Neva?"

"It comes and it goes, Masta Ferrell. Some days, she's jus' as ordinary as me or you. Then somethin' happens . . . . Mayhap that Mr. Styles Kenric, he upset her . . . . You jus' have to forgive a old black woman darin' to talk low-ratin' about a white man . . . . But he scare that po' chile, Masta Ferrell . . . . She jus' live in mortal terror of him . . . . Why, it started that very day when Masta Styles Kenric he forced that chile to sign over to him a power of 'turney—or somethin'. I didn't know what he wanted. She hardly did either, pore chile . . . . She was jus' sick . . . sick scairt . . . an' she started then talkin' 'bout how things gwine be all right when Mister Baynard got back home . . . . But you home now, Masta Ferrell . . . an' she do love you so. Maybe she be all right now you home."

"Yes." He nodded. He held Neva's hand tightly. "But I want you to do something for me—"

"Anything, chile. You know they ain't nobody alive means nuthin' to ole Neva but Miz Claire an' her chillun . . . . Oh, I love pore little Morgan . . . an' I purely dotes on Miss Kathy . . . . But they ain't no way nobody like you in my heart, Masta Ferrell."

"Big as you are, you're in my heart, too, Neva. You always have been. You always will be . . . . But I want you—the minute mother starts talking about father—as if he were still alive—I want you to feed her something nourishing. Maybe Jeanne d'Arc could make up little egg custards and keep them on hand—"

"Miz Jahndark, she ain't heah at Blackoaks no mo', Masta Ferrell."

He stared at her, incredulous. He had known something was amiss on the veranda. But in the excitement and the hectic movement he hadn't been able to pinpoint the wrong. Now he knew. Jeanne d'Arc had not been there to greet him. "My God, Neva. Where is she?"

"You have to ast that there Masta Styles Kenric 'bout that, Masta Ferrell."

He nodded. "Yes. I will. And I'll find Jeanne d'Arc.

But meantime you make my mother eat custards, or meat or milk, or eggs, the moment she talks of father like that —as if he were alive. In our hospital we've found that when patients are overtired or undernourished, they become confused—you watch her and make her eat."

"That chile eat like a bird."

"But you can make her eat. You can bully her . . . however you always make her do just as you want her to, you do that . . . . It's for her good, Neva. It may help to make her well again."

"That chile ain't nevah goin' be well no more—not so long as she lives in fear like she do."

He managed to force a smile. "You make her eat her egg custards. I'll take care of anything she's afraid of . . . . You know that when you and I work together, Neva, nobody can stand against us."

"Yas suh. Them's the same blessed words what I tole Gawd, Masta Ferrell, ever' night when I gits down on these ole knees and prayed. When I prayed he'd send you back home to us, that what I tole him . . . . "

15

It was ten days before Christmas.

Styles walked through the chattering and confusion of the corridors. He scowled, watching the hectic decorating, cleaning, and preparing for the arrival of guests. Soon the big manor house would be crowded with houseguests, overrun with relatives and friends crowding in from as far away as Charleston. He had dreaded their coming. But now he felt a new security; he was certain he was unassailable in his position for the first time since he'd assumed control as master of Blackoaks. He decided he would be able to entertain their guests in style and elegance. There would be an ease in his own manner that grew out of his sense of power.

He unlocked the thick oak door to his downstairs office, let himself inside, and closed the door behind him.

He sank into the swivel chair before his desk, restraining the urge to laugh in triumph. Everything was working out to his advantage. The cash provided with such alacrity by Luke Scroggings at the Bank of Mt. Zion made it possible to put into immediate action his grand scheme for converting Blackoaks from a failing cotton farm into a successful slave-breeding operation. And now the time had arrived to take a second, broader, more positive, giant step forward: he was going to invest in black female dams to mate with the best of his black studs.

He took up the letter, recently arrived from Garrett Blanford Ware of Tallahassee, and scanned the sharp Spencerian handwriting. He reread those passages that offered solid reinforcement to his ambition: " . . . I remember with interest our lengthy conversations on your plan to breed, for marketing, fancy-grade slaves at Blackoaks . . . . In view of the declining quality of cotton from your region, I sincerely hope you have by now embarked on this admirable enterprise . . . . Acknowledging that such a project is long-term, with up to fifteen or twenty years necessary before real profits can be realized, I still urge you to consider this step as most promising . . . . Please keep your humble servant and the considerable resources of our banking chain in mind if and when you need financial assistance . . . . "

Styles's hand trembled slightly as he lay aside the letter and took up the handbill.

AUCTION!
Recaptured Runaway Negro Slaves
Feb. 4, 1837
DALTONS' STABLES
Tallahassee, Florida
More than 25 valuable
young Negroes—includ-
ing purebred Mandingo,
Hausa, Fulani wenches
OTHERS

TERMS: CASH
Stock may be inspected at your
leisure—3 days preceding sale!

Styles's heart beat faster and he reread those wondrous
words: Fulani wenches!

A hesitant knock on his door-facing brought him back
to reality, to this moment. He refolded Ware's letter and
the auction notice and concealed them in a cubbyhole
on the desktop. He said, "Yes. Come in."

The door opened and Hunt Campbell entered. Styles
scowled, seeing Kathy at the young tutor's elbow. They
came into the office and Kathy closed the door behind
them.

"You wanted to see me?" Hunt said.

Styles ignored him for the moment, staring at his wife.
"Why are you here, Kathy?"

"I came with Hunt."

"Obviously. Was there something you wished to say to
me before Hunt and I get down to business?"

She shrugged and sat in a large leather chair. She
glanced around, nostrils flared slightly. "This room
doesn't smell the way it did when Daddy used it."

"Kathy . . . what do you want?"

"Hunt said he had been asked to come in to see you.
I told him I was coming with him. And here I am."

"We don't need you, Kathy."

"Perhaps not. But it looks as though you've got me,
doesn't it?"

Styles recoiled from the flat, alienated tone of Kathy's
voice. This was new and disturbing. It was one thing to
move out of her bedroom, to live separately under the
same roof—God knew how many gracious southern
marriages were lived out in this manner. But public
enmity was something he had not considered.

He kept his voice level. "This is a matter between Hunt
and me, Kathy."

She shrugged again. "Go ahead. Whatever you have to
say to Hunt won't shock me. Nothing will ever shock me
again."

He felt chilled hackles at the back of his neck. She

was warning him in no uncertain terms. "Perhaps not, Kathy. This matter is simply none of your business."

Her smile remained bright, unruffled. "Let's say I'm making it my business."

Styles gripped the arm of his chair. He fixed his gaze coldly on Kathy in the way that had always defeated her, but she merely returned his stare as if he were a casual stranger, as if she'd never lived in terror of annoying or irritating him.

"I think I know why you asked me in here," Hunt said. He sat on the thick round arm of a leather easy chair. "I could say it for you. It's about my continuing to tutor Morgan, isn't it?"

Styles pulled his enraged gaze from Kathy's face and studied Hunt a moment, looking along his chiseled nose. He spoke coldly. "Continued tutoring for Morgan is a waste of money—"

"I agree totally—"

"—money that Blackoaks can ill afford to squander at this time—"

"I'm sorry you find yourself in financial difficulties—"

"Whether I do or not, I refuse to go on spending good money when nothing tangible or worthwhile results."

"This has been my attitude, Styles, since before Mr. Baynard died. I tried to tell Mr. Baynard this, months before he died. But Mr. Baynard would not listen. He did not care how much or how little Morgan learned as long as I was making an effort to add to the boy's store of knowledge."

Styles gave the tutor a disdainful smile. "Well, maybe old man Baynard didn't care. I care. I am willing to give you whatever time you feel will be adequate to find a new position, but—"

"He's found a new position, Styles," Kathy said, her smile warm and fixed.

Styles jerked his head around. "Oh?"

"Yes." Kathy laughed. "I've decided I want to learn French. I want Hunt to stay on here to teach me."

Styles stood up. He spoke coldly. "I refuse even to consider it."

Now Kathy laughed in his face. "But I'm not asking

you, Styles. I'm telling you. Hunt is staying. As my French tutor. He is staying as long as I want him."

Styles shuddered inside. The nerves in his stomach constricted. He gazed at Kathy, raging inwardly. With Ferrell here, Styles was powerless to command Kathy or to bend her to his will. The break between them would attract Ferrell's attention, and it might lead ultimately to a church-arranged annullment of his marriage to Kathy. No matter what he had to do, he had to remain master of Blackoaks. There would be other ways to deal with Kathy.

"Damn it, Kathy," he said impotently. "It's a foolish waste of money."

"Perhaps." She gave him her most engaging smile. "But you forget the important point, my dear Styles: it is *my* money."

16

Alone in his office, Styles prowled the room as if it had become his cage. For the first time since he'd become master of Blackoaks he experienced the first stirrings of a sickening and inescapable premonition of disaster. He'd believed nothing, no one could stop him; he'd become more convinced of his strength as credit was thrust upon him; he had not really feared Ferrell. True, he had wanted to avoid a confrontation until he had strengthened his position, got debts under control, mended all fences, protected his flank. Now, he saw that defeat, if it struck, might well come from the least expected quarter of all—from Kathy!

Damn her! He stood staring out of the casement window toward the terrace where Kathy sat in the sunlight, laughing with Hunt and Morgan. She who had always been so pliable—she had been his willing chattel. This was no longer true. Her hatred made her callous toward their marriage, obdurate against his legal control of her destiny, indifferent to pleas and threats alike, unyielding in her opposition, and, because of this new hardness, dangerous to him.

He tried to laugh at his fears, to see any threat from her direction in perspective. The stakes were too high— he could amass a fortune with the resources now available to him. He would remove Kathy's fangs—in any way he could. He would not tolerate her obstinate antagonism. Her resistance would be temporary. He would see to that.

A brief rapping on his door brought him around as Ferrell entered the office and closed the door behind him. Calculatedly, Styles let Ferrell see at once that he would not bend or retreat before him: "Do you always barge into an office without waiting to be asked?"

Ferrell shrugged. "I'm glad you brought that up . . . . I find you keep this door locked when you're not here. Why?"

"This is my office. Important papers are kept here."

"It was my father's office for at least twenty-five years. He never felt it necessary to lock this door—against his family."

"Yes. Well, your father is dead. I'm running Blackoaks now."

"Is secrecy necessary to your management?"

"I value my privacy, yes."

"I'm afraid you're overlooking one fact, Styles. Your management is in the interests of the Baynard family who happen to own this property."

Styles's smile was studiedly superior. He found that after all he was enjoying this contention. Despite that turned collar, Ferrell was still a young boy and no match for him intellectually. "And I'm afraid, dear boy, you're overlooking the fact that I *am* the sole manager. I have that power of attorney from your mother, signed and delivered."

"I'm afraid we're going to have to reach some accommodation on that matter, too. I am going to ask you to approach my mother in the future only through a third party—perhaps Kathy."

"And if I refuse that request?"

"Then I'm telling you . . . Styles, we can cooperate,

or we can clash. That's your decision. But there is one area where there is no room for discussion. You are not to go directly to my mother again—on any matter concerning this farm or its operation."

"I'm afraid, my boy, that that will depend on circumstances. I feel that I am a rational, civilized human being. It is insulting to suggest I cannot discuss matters rationally—with your mother."

"You terrorize her."

Styles's face flushed, then paled. "Come now. That's a bit rough, isn't it? And unnecessary? I don't know what Kathy—"

"Kathy hasn't told me anything." Ferrell's young face tautened and he moved closer to Styles. Styles straightened, shifting his jacket on his shoulders. "Kathy hasn't had to *tell* me anything, Styles."

"Any discord between Kathy and me is certainly none of your affair."

Ferrell nodded. "As long as Kathy doesn't ask me to intervene, Styles, I won't. What I see makes me ill, but as you say, it is your affair. I only want you to understand that I am not deceived by you on any score—and this includes your most personal and intimate life."

Styles sat before his desk, apparently at ease. He peered up at Ferrell, nostrils distended. "Aren't you going pretty far? A personal attack on me now, eh? May I ask the point of your aggressive antagonism toward me?"

"I only want us to understand each other, Styles. I understand you. *All* about you. Now, for your own self-interest, I sincerely hope you will turn your attention outward long enough to understand me and my unalterable position."

Styles gazed upward, chilled. "And this is?"

"The first thing I noticed, Styles, when I returned here was the dismal decay of this place. My father kept a gang of young boys working the yards, hedges, and lawns around the big house every day except Sunday. There has not been one work crew on the plateau around the house since I've been back here."

Styles made a note, then glanced up. "A point well taken. In my own defense I can only say I have been incredibly busy. Bos Pilzer has all he can do to oversee the heavy work details. The blacks in charge of yard maintenance have become slack."

"Doesn't that suggest they're pretty sure of what they can get away with?"

"I can assure you it won't happen again."

"But I'm not asking you to defend yourself. The unkempt lawns and approaches to the house—even allowing for the winter season—are only indications of negligence and disrepair."

"Oh?"

"I was shocked, Styles. Stunned. I had no idea a place like this could deteriorate so badly in so little time. The wood trim, woodwork, columns on this house have not been scraped or painted since the death of my father."

"Money has been a problem."

"Protecting one's house is putting money in the bank. That's an old Scottish proverb of my father's. He believed that. I've heard it all my life. I happen to believe it."

Styles nodded. "I'll put painters to work on the house immediately after the Christmas season."

"It doesn't disturb you that relatives—friends—who haven't been here in five or ten years will find Blackoaks in a kind of decay?"

"As I said, money has been a factor. I had to line up everything as to priority . . . . However, we needn't clash over this. I now see my way to refurbish everything immediately."

Ferrell paced the room, deeply troubled. "It is not only the run-down condition of the house, Styles. The Negroes were provided whitewash every summer of my life, and they looked forward with pride to renewing their quarters. No one had to tell them to do it. They wanted to do it. It's now been summer before last since—"

"All right. I have been a little slow in taking the reins. I have let some things slip. All of this will be remedied—at once."

Ferrell shook his head, relentless. "You didn't even bother to replace the whiskey distillery after it was destroyed by fire. I couldn't believe it. It sits over there like a charred hulk."

"Money, Ferrell. A matter of priorities."

"Whiskey sales were always an important source of income—"

"I simply didn't have the cash to make the repairs."

"It was mostly a matter of getting work from the slaves. The lumber could have been provided from our own lands, our own mill."

"All right. Perhaps I have not been firm enough with the slaves. They were used to working for your father. Perhaps they have been testing me to see how far they could push me. Well, that's over now."

"I've seen no signs of it. The kitchen is a shambles—"

"It's easy enough to stand and tick off my lapses. I admit many of them. It's a new job, a big one, and I had to work my way into it. But what you are doing in your carping is overlooking the important matters."

Ferrell laughed helplessly. "This place falling into decay is not important?"

Styles took a stack of bills from his desk and handed them to Ferrell. "Check those, Ferrell. And check them carefully. Pay particular attention to the dates on many of them. Those bills were old—unpaid and past due— months before your father died. Your father kept Blackoaks looking like a showplace, but he might well have lost it to creditors had he lived."

Ferrell checked through the statements, each of which had been paid in full within the past three weeks. At last he nodded and managed to smile hopefully. "I congratulate you, Styles."

Styles was magnanimous in victory. "Perhaps our priorities are not identical, Ferrell. But I assure you, our goals are precisely the same. We both want to make Blackoaks self-sustaining and profitable." He straightened in the chair, face set in a cold, unsmiling mask. "I believe I can do this—with a minimum of interference."

Ferrell hesitated, and Styles felt success in his grasp. His heart slugged in its rib cage. He felt exultant. He had handled this skirmish masterfully. He had let Ferrell exhaust his ammunition and then struck back with indisputable proof of the excellence of his stewardship. Ferrell didn't inquire where the money to pay those debts came from. As long as he did not ask, the hell with him.

Let him believe the creditors had been satisfied with profits from this estate under Styles's management.

Ferrell paced the room a moment longer, the stack of bills clutched in his fist. He spoke almost apologetically. "I had no idea father had left his affairs in such a hellish mess, Styles . . . . You've done well. You have reassured me . . . . If the house, quarters and distillery are restored, I won't cavil any further. And you have helped me reach a decision that was plaguing me . . . . I had planned to leave the seminary to come back here and take over management—"

"That won't be necessary."

"I hope you are right. I feel a deep obligation to this place, to my mother, to Kathy and Morgan—"

"I have their interests at heart, precisely as you do."

Ferrell sighed heavily, almost as if half-talking to himself. "On the other hand, I have taken vows to the Church. I cannot lightly toss them aside—"

"Of course not—"

"I was almost killed—that day in Mt. Zion when Hunt Campbell arrived here on the train. By some miracle, I was spared. With the gun thrust point-blank in my face, it misfired, and I was spared . . . . I don't want to sound superstitious, but perhaps there was a reason I was spared . . . . If there was, I have not found it yet. Maybe I'll find it here at Blackoaks . . . . Maybe I'll find it in my work in the Church . . . . But as long as you manage this estate well—and respect my wishes concerning any dealings with my mother—I'll continue to look for God's will—if that's what it is—in the Church."

Styles exhaled deeply and stood up. He smiled and extended his hand. "I concur in every detail—including my approaching your mother, though I cannot believe I upset her. I will accept your decision on the matter—as deeply as it offends me, and despite the fact that I've always felt she loved me very much."

"She is emotionally delicate, Styles, and you'll just have to let it go at that."

Though Ferrell smiled faintly, he did not at once grasp Styles's proffered hand. He appeared not to see it. Styles flushed and dropped his arm to his side. Ferrell said, almost regretfully, "There's one other matter, Styles."

"Yes?"

"Jeanne d'Arc . . . . Where is she? What happened to her? I told her to get in touch with me if she needed me. I never heard from her."

Styles smiled blandly. "I tried to protect you, Ferrell, from unnecessary burdens. Naturally, when I took over as master of Blackoaks, there were certain changes, and not all of them were popular. It became the main activity around here to write whining letters to you at the seminary. I saw no sense in troubling you about Blackoaks when you had so much work to do in the order. As you say, you had taken vows. I simply refused to permit them to write complaining epistles to you."

"I regret that."

"Perhaps it was a stern measure. I might handle it differently now. But I can't apologize. A decision had to be made. I made my decision. I stood by it. It was a position I felt at the time I was forced to take."

"And Jeanne d'Arc?"

Styles shrugged. "No great mystery. She simply got tired of being where she was not wanted, Ferrell."

"Jeanne d'Arc? Not wanted here at Blackoaks?"

"Surely I don't have to remind you of the tension between that half-breed and your own mother, Ferrell. You who are so concerned about Miz Claire's well-being —and rightly—you must be aware that she hated Jeanne d'Arc. And you must know why."

17

"The house ain't there! The house is burnt down."

They sat in the carriage and stared at the charred remains of the farmhouse. A crumbling chimney reared up from the fire-struck waste. Morgan, standing up, shaking his head back and forth, spoke for all of them.

Sick, the five of them sat immobile. This excursion to find Jeanne d'Arc had begun optimistically when Ferrell announced to Kathy that he was driving over to see how the freedwoman was getting along in her new home. Kathy was enchanted at the idea of the visit and suggested they make the trip a picnic, with all the trimmings, a surprise for Jeanne d'Arc and little Scandal.

They'd laughed mile after mile on the long drive. Ferrell handled the pair of fancy-stepping carriage horses, Morgan and Soapy sharing the front seat with him. Kathy and Hunt sat in the tonneau of the open carriage, their knees touching surreptitiously. Kathy felt young, renewed, and breathless. Frequently, she clasped Hunt's hand in hers on the seat between them.

The day was brightly sunny for December; a few broken clouds scudded across a metallic sky. It had rained the night before but the sun had sucked most of the moisture from the earth. Undersides of leaves sparkled with lingering drops of rain. The threat of storm lurked along the black-scalloped horizon but had not materialized by noon as they approached their destination. Kathy was happy for the first time in recent memory; it was good to be close to Hunt; her blood pumped faster; a pleasant emptiness settled in the pit of her stomach. It was silly for a married woman, but she felt as if she were in love for the first time.

They'd had to stop and ask directions twice. They'd passed Mt. Zion and were on the trace to Chancellor. There was no point in inquiring for the farm of a freedwoman named Jeanne d'Arc. But Styles had said her place was near the estate of the abolitionist Colonel Ben Johnson.

Hunt asked Ferrell questions about the slavery-hating colonel. Ferrell remembered only what his father and countryside rumor had told him. According to legend—and local whispers—Colonel Ben Johnson had been one of the most respected land and slaveowners in the region. Then he had joined General Andrew Jackson in fighting the Creeks. It had been in these engagements that he had been brevetted Colonel. He had gone away to the army with his mind safely stored with all the accepted prejudices against inferior races—red and black. During one campaign he'd suffered what some called brain fever. Those who knew the colonel said his personality change dated from that illness. He returned from the fighting filled with a cold and abiding hatred for the man he called the greatest red-neck of the entire back country, Andrew Jackson. The colonel said Jackson's obsessive and unrelenting hatred for the Indians and his total contempt for all blacks had made Colonel Ben's service a nightmare. On his return the colonel had freed all his slaves. He had tried to farm on the same old large scale with hired hands and by working his land himself. His farm had sunk into steady decline and the colonel into disrepute among his neighbors. There was rumor that Ben Johnson helped runaway Negroes escape north along a secret trail . . . .

About noon they reached the place where Jeanne d'Arc's farmhouse should have stood, where Jeanne d'Arc was said to live with her two-year-old child.

Ferrell spoke, numb. "Maybe this is not Jeanne d'Arc's place." But, sick, he knew; this was the farm Styles had bought for her and to which Jeanne d'Arc had come to live as a free woman of color.

Kathy's voice shook. "We've got to find her, Ferrell. She must have lost everything in the fire. She must be somewhere near. Surely somebody took her and the baby in—"

"No white would take in a black—even if she were freed," Ferrell said. "If they might want to—they would be afraid—of their neighbors."

"The colonel," Hunt said.

"What?"

"You said the colonel was an abolitionist—maybe a black sympathizer . . . . If anybody would know what happened here—and where Jeanne d'Arc might be, it ought to be the colonel."

The unpainted, weatherbeaten, decaying manor house was less than a mile along the winding trace to Chancellor. Wire grass and weed clumps grew rampant in yard and fallow field. Even the long drive in from the trace was potted and weed-grown. There was a desolate sense of ruinous poverty here; one spavined horse and a cow munched grass near the dilapidated barn; there was no human being in sight.

Ferrell drove the horses up into the yard almost to the sagging front steps. A dog lunged up from the shade of a chinaberry tree; it barked a couple of times and then in complete fatigue and terror loped yelping under the front porch, quivering, with its tail between its legs.

"Colonel Ben—Colonel Ben Johnson," Ferrell called. "Anybody home?"

The silence hung oppressively for a long beat and then the front door, hanging crookedly on a loose hinge, was pulled open. A balding man with large head, massive shoulders, thick trunk, and short heavy legs in runover boots came through the doorway.

He hesitated a moment, suspicious and wary in the shade of the rotting porch. They saw he held a gun half-concealed against his right thigh. "Yeah . . . I'm Ben Johnson. What you folks want?"

"We'd like to talk to you." Ferrell smiled. "Do you know a freedwoman—part Indian, part white, and some Negro blood—a beautiful golden-tan woman—named Jeanne d'Arc?"

"She has a baby—almost two years old," Kathy added from the rear of the carriage.

Colonel Ben walked slowly to the shattered porch railing. Sparrows fluttered suddenly from the aged scroll-work above his head. His gray eyes were kindly, gentle, but harried. His wide mouth pulled down at the corners; he looked to be a man who had forgotten laughter. His hair hung shaggy about his face. His sweated shirt and coarse trousers were stained. "Might know of such a woman. Why?"

"We came to visit her," Kathy said. "All the way from Blackoaks—over beyond Mt. Zion."

Colonel Ben's disenchanted gray eyes lightened under Kathy's golden smiling. He almost smiled back at the vision Kathy made, soft gold hair rimlighted by the sun in the carriage tonneau. He nodded. "I know Blackoaks, Missy. Knew Ferrell Baynard before his untimely passin'."

Hadn't seen him though in at least ten years . . . . You his daughter, Missy?"

Kathy nodded. She hastily introduced the others in the carriage. "We planned a surprise party—for Jeanne d'Arc, at her house. We—dearly loved her . . . . We found her house burned."

Colonel Ben nodded. "Burned to the ground. Yes."

"Do you know where we might find Jeanne d'Arc?" Ferrell asked.

Colonel Ben hesitated, then: "Maybe you folks would like to take out and come in . . . . We don't have much company . . . . We live pretty rough these days . . . but I don't think you'll want to talk about Miz Jahndark out here."

Soapy remained where he was, sitting stiffly on the front seat staring into some middle distance. The others followed the colonel along the sagging, broken-boarded porch. He kept admonishing them to watch their step. "Meanin' to fix it. Meanin' to fix it," he said.

Shocked, they saw that most of the rooms were empty of furniture inside the vast old country place. Sunlight streamed in on layers of dust through soiled windows. The colonel led them along the narrow corridor to the large kitchen. This room was furnished—with odds and ends retrieved from the rest of the place—a bare kitchen table under attack from blue bottle flies, a few straight kitchen chairs, one aged, butt-sprung leather easy chair covered with a ragged quilt, an unmade bed and two cribs in the shadowed corner most distant from the huge old wood-burning stove.

All the windows were opened, but the heat in the room was intense. A woman sat on a cane-backed kitchen chair, leaning her elbow on the kitchen table. She looked to be somewhere in her thirties, already graying. Her flesh was coffee dark. Snuff stained the corner of her mouth. "My wife," the colonel said. He spoke to her. "May, these here folks come from over to Blackoaks plantation."

She nodded listlessly, peering at them apathetically. "Ask you folks to take out and eat," she said. She shook her head. "But we ain't got nuthin' fittin'. Some cold

grits, corn pone, and a crock of clabber. You're welcome
—any of you care to eat, yore welcome." She seemed to
know they would refuse.

The colonel's kind gray eyes touched at his wife. He
seemed to feel some word in her defense was required.
His brief laugh was rueful, self-deprecating. "Would you
believe May once was pretty and vivacious as you, Miss
Kathy? She were. She were a Livingstone of Green Leas
Plantation. Nice family. But she married me. For better
or for worse. She's stuck with me. Reckon she might still
be looking for the better . . . . She could of left me.
Years ago. Her folks wanted her to, God knows, when
I come back from Indian fighting, sick. But she stuck
right with me. You know they say a woman is like a fly.
You take a fly, now. It lands on a rose, it sits there happy.
Lands on a horse turd. Sits there just as happy. Women
are like that—in the men they marry."

"Ah, Colonel Ben," the woman protested. "Not afore
company."

"These folks are lookin' for Miz Jahndark, May," the
colonel said.

The woman looked up at them and shook her head.
"Miz Jahndark. Fine woman. Couldn't of been no finer
if she was purentee white. Me an' her—we'd begun to
visit back and forth. First lady friend I had in years. Both
the colonel and me. We liked her. She was always fixing
something special. She and her baby would walk through
the hammock—not far that way—and bring us delicious
dishes she'd prepared. She was a wonderful cook."

"What happened?" Ferrell said. "How did her house
burn?"

"Was set. Vicious set," the woman said. "Purpose . . . .
They burned her out."

The colonel exhaled. "The folks around here—whites—
got no more'n me and May have. Less, most of 'em. But
prideful. They didn't cotton to a Negro woman owning
her own house—and it some better than most of theirs.
And she put in a kitchen garden like none of us whites
had energy or gumption to do."

"And her house—Miz Jahndark kept her house
scrubbed and dusted and polished. Spotless," May said.

"They tried to scare her out, an' she wouldn't scare," the colonel said. "She ast me an' I thought she should stay on here in that house of her'n when plainly the white folks hereabouts resented her and didn't want her. I tole her nobody had the right to run her off her own land an' she didn't want to go . . . . She had clear, good title. She was manumitted—a freed woman. I told her to stay . . . . " He shuddered. "I reckon all what happened is my fault."

"They burned her out." Ferrell whispered it, but the sound was loud in the silent room.

The colonel nodded. "Happened on a Saturday. Them men gathered in town as they do on a Saturday. Likkered up. Drunk, they decided to run Miz Jahndark out of their country. They come to her place. Five of them. Raped her. Vicious. Robbed her. Beat her. Left her for dead in the burning house. Rode away yellin'. Right by my place. Seen 'em out on the trace. Recognized 'em. One of 'em was wavin' one of her bright skirts like a flag."

The colonel stopped talking, sickened by his memories. At last he spoke in bitter irony. "These good, decent, God-fearing people. They'll tell you, sure they run her out. She had no right livin' among 'em. Ever' blasted one of them was in church the next day—praying to Jesus God—for Christ's sake. An' all Christ ever taught was love thy neighbor as thyself." He quoted: " 'Jesus said, "Love thy God and love thy neighbor as thyself. This is the first and great commandment. And all others are like unto it . . . . " ' These good Christians, they kill, burn, rape, maim . . . in Christ's name . . . . Well, I seen the smoke billowin' up black. Rode over on my horse, fast as I could. May come running through the hammock after me. House was raging with flames when I got there. I got Miz Jahndark out. But she was badly burnt, terribly hurt and tore. Bleeding . . . . mercifully, she didn't live long . . . . I buried her—an' then May and me we come on home."

Kathy was trembling violently. Hunt put his arm about her. She said, voice hollow, "And the baby—the little girl?"

"They musta killed the baby, too," the colonel said. He stared at his wife. Their gazes locked and held for a long beat. "I didn't find the baby—the fire—too hot—I couldn't go back in . . . . I'm sorry."

Ferrell, Kathy, Hunt, and Morgan stood immobile, stunned with grief too deep for tears. There were no words.

"She had some money," Ferrell said at last. "Did they steal that, too?"

Colonel Ben peered at him. "She didn't have no money. Nuthin' to speak of. But she thought she did, even talked it around that she did—"

"She had several thousand dollars," Ferrell said.

"No . . . . The talk about the money she had might be some of the motive for them trash that robbed and burned her . . . . She thought she had a thousand or so. Told me she did. Told May. Probably told others. Proud of how she came by it. Said it was willed to her." The colonel laughed coldly. "Somebody had given her one hundred dollars. They had convinced her it was a thousand—made her believe it. Hell, she couldn't count past ten. But I counted it for her—when she ast me . . . . I know."

Ferrell bit back the bile that welled up in his throat. His hatred for Styles gorged up anew. He felt he would strangle. He wanted to kill the bastard. The lying, conniving bastard . . . . And yet, with Jeanne d'Arc dead, what did it profit to beat in his arrogant face?

A baby cried suddenly in one of the cribs near the shadowed far window. Both Colonel Ben and his wife started guiltily. They would have ignored the noise, except the baby's wailing grew louder, lustier. "It's Ethel," May said. "Pore little tike is hungry."

"Might as well take her up," the colonel said.

May got up tiredly and walked across the uncarpeted room, her shoes slapping against her heels. She took up the baby in her arms and brought it back to the table. She sat down cradling it in her arms. The child stopped screaming when the woman held it. She rocked in the chair, with the baby half-covered by a shabby quilt although the room was oppressively warm.

"May I see her?" Kathy asked.

The woman glanced up at the colonel and, after a brief

hesitation, nodded. She turned back the ragged end of the quilt. "Ethel's just under two," the colonel said. "She's a good baby—an' she's not wet or hungry, that is."

"Ain't been sickly a day," the woman said. "Not a blessed day."

The baby was fair-skinned, with blonde fringes of hair and large, round blue eyes, pretty, though somewhat underweight.

"We'uns couldn't no way afford to have a baby," the colonel said. "But if'n you can afford or not don't matter much when they decide to come . . . . An' me gittin' on in years, too."

Kathy smiled at the baby, touched its cheek with the backs of her fingers, almost yearningly. Then she straightened and turned. "I feel so terrible—about Jeanne d'Arc . . . . Ferrell, we really ought to go. It's a long ride back home."

Ferrell nodded. But as he turned, a second child, in the other crib across the room, suddenly wailed. Neither the colonel nor his wife moved. They sat locked in place, looking at each other.

"The baby is crying," Ferrell said, watching them.

"It's Emma," the colonel said. "Let her be. She ain't rightly had her nap out."

Ferrell stared at the colonel and his lady for a moment, then crossed the room and stared down at the baby kicking and crying in its crib. Something lurched in the region of his heart. He suddenly recalled the morning Jeanne d'Arc's baby had been born in the quarters at Blackoaks. He had held the child. The lovely brown-eyed child with the incredibly perfect features. He could hear their voices, filled with love, teasing Jeanne d'Arc. And the slave breeder, Simon, talking sardonically about how white the slave girl's baby was—hardly enough Negro blood in her to tell it.

Ferrell stared at this lovely child. The little girl, wearing only ragged diapers, pulled herself up in the crib. She stopped crying, staring up at Ferrell.

"She all right where-at she is," the colonel said from behind him. "Let her be."

"This is Scandal," Ferrell said.

The colonel took two long strides toward him. His voice rasped. "What you sayin'? That our own child. Flesh. Blood. Our girl Emma. Emma and Ethel. They twins."

"There's five months at least between these babies," Ferrell said. "This baby looks like—"

"Now you wait a minute, mister." The colonel straightened, face taut. "I don't know you. Don't know what you want. You say you old Ferrell Baynard's son. May be . . . . But don't come in here sayin' my flesh and my blood is some half-breed's git . . . . Emma is our baby . . . our'n . . . ain't she, May?"

His wife nodded. Her coffee-colored cheeks were pallid. "I bore 'em both. I ought to know."

"Six months apart?" Ferrell said. "That's pretty good— if true. I tell you, this looks like Jeanne d'Arc's baby."

"Emma don't look nuthin' in this world like the half-breed's git," the colonel said. "True, little Scandal was about Emma's age. But that's all. That's as close as they come. Nary bit alike. I tell you they ain't the same."

Taut, Ferrell took the baby up in his arms. The little girl smiled and touched at his cheek, stroking it. "Listen to me, Colonel Johnson . . . . I don't want to make any trouble for you—"

"Then don't. Put my baby down in her crib . . . . Just take yore folks out of my house and go along."

"If this is Jeanne d'Arc's child, I want to take it back to Blackoaks. It will be reared—as a free child. But most important, it will have everything it could want, all we can give it. I'll see to that. God knows we owe that to Jeanne d'Arc . . . . It's what I want to do for her baby."

Colonel Johnson hesitated, then spoke more sharply than ever. "Mister, don't talk that way. Runnin' down what May and me can do for our children. We can't give 'em a lot. But love we can give 'em. They be all right with us . . . . If'n this was the half-breed woman's child, I'd say to you, take her . . . . I'd have no reason to stand in yore way . . . . This here is my child . . . . I'll thank you to put her down—and go along."

Ferrell continued to hold the baby. Its diapers were sopping wet, but neither he nor the child noticed. She laughed, staring into his eyes, chattering unintelligibly. Ferrell shook his head, staring at the colonel. No matter the colonel's motives, they could do much more for Jeanne d'Arc's baby at Blackoaks than could be done for her on this subsistence farm where the other child was already one too many.

"Ferrell." Kathy's voice stopped him. "Put the baby down . . . . I want to talk to you . . . outside . . . for a minute."

Ferrell stared at Kathy, puzzled. But she appeared so calm yet so unyielding that he replaced the baby in its crib and followed her through the corridor to the front yard. The colonel said, "I don't mean to be inhospitable, but you other folks may as well go 'long to yore carriage, too."

Morgan and Hunt plodded silently from the house. They joined Soapy in the carriage. They sat silently, staring at Kathy and Ferrell in the shade of the china-berry tree. From his sagging porch, the colonel watched them, too.

Kathy's voice was low and tense. "He's got to swear that's his baby . . . . He can't let her go to us—or anybody—and go on living among these people. The colonel is already a suspected Negro sympathizer who might help runaways escape . . . . He is desperately poor . . . . This house is all they have. They must live here—among those same poor whites who have already killed Jeanne d'Arc, who already hate and mistrust the colonel—"

"But that's Jeanne d'Arc's baby. I can't abandon her here."

"Of course it's Jeanne d'Arc's baby. And you must leave her here—unless you want to cause Colonel Ben's death at the hands of his neighbors . . . . Don't you see? He has lied—to his neighbors. He had to, in order to save Scandal. He's told them—told everybody—that the baby is his . . . . They'd burn him out if they found out he'd taken in a *Negro* baby to raise as his own . . . . He can't let her go now without signing his own death warrant . . . . They'd burn him out. Just as they burned Jeanne d'Arc."

Ferrell nodded, too numbed to speak.

She clasped his hand in hers. "The important thing is, Ferrell, they loved Jeanne d'Arc, too, as we did . . . . And they'll love Scandal—or Emma. He saved that baby's life . . . but he can't ever admit that . . . for his sake . . . for Scandal's sake . . . ."

"My God. My name of God," Ferrell whispered. He closed his fingers on Kathy's arm, acquiescent. They walked slowly across the yard to where the colonel stood on the sagging porch. Ferrell said, "I'm sorry, Colonel. Truly sorry."

The colonel nodded.

Ferrell took what money he had in his pockets and gave it to the colonel. The stout man hesitated, reluctant, but finally accepted it. Morgan came across the yard from the carriage. He placed the wicker hampers of food on the porch beside the steps. He tried to smile up at the colonel and backed away awkwardly.

The colonel stood unmoving as Ferrell helped Kathy into the carriage and swung up beside Morgan in the front seat. He took up the reins, turned the horses, and set them hurrying along the weed-grown lane. Dust clouded up behind them, smoking across the man on the porch. They did not look back.

18

Link Tetherow came galloping into the lane at Blackoaks the next day before ten in the morning. They heard his hoo-rawing yell as he entered the big gate at the trace. He was outfitted in a newly tailored suit, new boots, and smart black planter's hat, which he waved as he raced up the lane. The small black carriage boys ran to meet him.

He swung down from the saddle and crossed the veranda. He gave the metal knocker a couple of fierce strokes though old Thyestes was already opening the huge front door. Link was smiling from the inside out. He was overwhelmed with his own sense of elation. Though he walked into a house tense with silences, he noticed nothing amiss.

Link strode past Thyestes into the tension that crackled in the air between Styles, his wife, and his brother-in-law. Link was insensitive to it. He saw Ferrell, Kathy, Styles, Hunt Campbell, Morgan, and Morgan's body slave Soapy, but the reason for his visit—that flower of Charleston—was missing. Politely, he replied to questions about the health of his parents, the state of the Tetherow plantation, the excitement of the coming nuptials, and he agreed that this December was indeed the mildest in his memory. But he was unable to afford more than half his mind to the present company.

Link kept shifting his weight from one stocky leg to the other and cracking his knuckles nervously. His wavy black hair glistened with perspiration. He was handsome; strongly cut features, about medium height, muscular, heavy of chest, and thick shouldered. His one defect, which might have detracted from his comeliness, was the way he walked slightly spraddle-legged, as if he were for some reason tender of crotch.

Link's gaze was like a frightened butterfly, unable to light for more than a flighty rest anywhere. Finally, he blurted out: "Where-at is my Miss Jamie Lee Seaton this mawnin'? . . . . I came a-runnin' over heah to talk over our wedding ceremony plans with her—and with Brother Alexander. I even ast Gil Talmadge to ride over—him bein' my best man, an' all. An' Walter Roy Summerton, too—him standin' up with us. I'm mighty anxious for it all to go off right. Me so nervous and all—and we Tetherows got relatives comin' from far away as Richmond . . . . An' Miss Jamie Lee has tole me of all the folks comin' from all yore family." He blushed and cracked his knuckles. "I heard you was home, Ferrell, and I just decided to ride over heah fast. I knowed we had a lot of plans to make—a-plenty of weddin' rehearsal won't hurt a thing."

An immature black servant girl was dispatched to the second floor to discover if Miss Jamie Lee were yet awake. "Jamie Lee loves to sleep late," Kathy told Link. "Sometimes she locks her door in the morning and sleeps past noon. But I know she'll want to come down if she knows you're here," Kathy assured him.

Link blushed. "She so purty—she jus' take my breath plumb away." Embarrassed by this confession and desperately self-conscious as a bridegroom soon-to-be, as well as uncomfortable in his new suit, Link sweated and cracked his knuckles.

The slave girl returned, frightened. She had been unable to find Miss Jamie Lee on the second floor. Miss Jamie Lee's bedroom was empty, the bed made. None of the upstairs servants recalled having seen her in the past hour. No one downstairs had seen her; she hadn't had breakfast. "Where can she be?" Link strode about, cracking his knuckles, fearing the worst. Jamie Lee was so fragile, so lovely. He had terrible visions of her being kidnapped, perhaps by passing gypsies.

"Don't be upset," Kathy said. "We'll find her, Link." She glanced around at the others. "Haven't any of you see Jamie Lee this morning?"

"I seen her," Morgan said. "She was walking up the knoll to the chapel." Soapy shook his head warningly, but was too late. Morgan, realizing what he had done, lapsed into sick silence.

"Why don't Masta Morgan an' me run up to the chapel and tell Miss Jamie Lee that Masta Tetherow is heah?" Soapy suggested.

Link ignored the black boy, though it did occur to him that if one of the slaves at his home plantation opened his mouth in the presence of white folks—unless he were directly addressed—he would be severely punished. Link said, "Bless her sweet innocent little heart. Up to the chapel, a-prayin' . . . . You ever heard anything lovelier in your whole life? Come on, Ferrell, walk up theah with me. That's what she is. Pure. Sweet an' innocent as a baby."

Ferrell agreed to walk upslope to the chapel on the knoll with Link. Soapy and Morgan, silent and taut, followed.

As they strode in the sun, Link said, "I know you got evil feelings toward me, Ferrell, for what happened—that day—with the Garrity girl."

116

"I've forgiven you."

"I was sure you had. You going into the Church an' all. But I feel like maybe you ain't forgot it—like I wish you would . . . . Me going to be related to you, an' all—through marriage."

"I've forgotten it."

"I hope so . . . . It was a plumb evil thing we done . . . . I never going to be able to say else than that . . . . But Gil—he kindly lied to Walter Roy and me . . . . He say you and him got it all planned . . . you takin' Lorna June out—and us takin' turns with her. Gil always was a caution. Thinkin' up things to do . . . . But nuthin' like that . . . . I hates to think back on it . . . and I goin' try to live a better life . . . . That's why I so proud to be marryin' your cousin Jamie Lee Seaton. I feel that a pure, innocent girl like that will make me a fine wife—and she'll fetch me to Jesus. I'm sure if anybody can fetch me to Jesus—and wash me clean in the blood of the lamb, Miss Jamie Lee can do it."

"I hope so," Ferrell said.

They were crossing the thick grass toward the entrance of the chapel. Suddenly, Soapy said, "Please, Masta Ferrell, can I have a word with you?"

"Ferrell, wait a minute," Morgan said.

Ferrell paused and turned in the sun. But Link Tetherow was too anxious to be with his love. He would not be delayed. He strode across the stoop and thrust open the heavy doors and entered the chapel.

"She ain't alone in there, Masta," Soapy said. His voice sounded strangled.

Ferrell frowned. In the split second it took for him to understand fully what Soapy was saying, the world wheeled, skidded, and turned upside down. From within the chapel came a howl of agony that chilled the blood of the three people outside.

They stood locked, staring toward that door. It was thrust open, and Link staggered out. His eyes were wild, stricken. His cheek muscles were pallid and rigid. He tried to speak and could not. His mouth contorted, but there were no words. He sagged against the wall and stayed there, helpless.

Ferrell strode past him, with Morgan and Soapy at his heels. As they entered the chapel they could see Jamie Lee in the priest's small cubicle off from the auditorium. She was struggling into her clothing, sobbing mindlessly.

For a moment, Ferrell hesitated. Then he walked to the door and stood staring at Moab who remained, kneeling on the floor, his fists knotted against his belly.

Link remained slumped against the chapel wall. The rough surface chewed into his shoulder, but he felt no pain. He could think only that he wanted his world to end in that moment. He wanted to dig his way with his fingers and nails into the fieldstone wall of this building, to hide, never to have to face his mother or any other human being on earth again.

"Oh, God," he whispered finally. "Oh, God. Please . . . . "

In his mind he was asking God only for one thing, for the world to end at that instant. He knew his own life was over, forever blighted. But he hadn't the strength, or the will, to face other people. He wanted them wiped off the face of this imperfect earth, too. Life as usual could not go on.

And, because this was the last thing he wanted, life did go on. Its pace was accelerated, the number of people involved increased suddenly and terrifyingly. Up the knoll came Gil Talmadge and Walter Roy Summerton. Behind them were two black slaves. Like a nightmare, the memory of a nightmare, Link saw that Gil had brought along King Arthur, the giant Negro who had been with them the day they raped Lorna June Garrity.

At this moment it didn't seem too important. Every human being was a threat to Link Tetherow. He didn't want to see anybody, he didn't want to talk to anybody.

But Gil and Walter Roy came upon him laughing and punching him, teasing him as every bridegroom was teased. The Negro slaves stood aside, but beyond them, in a continuing expansion of the horror, he saw Styles Kenric and Hunt Campbell approaching upslope from the terrace of the big house.

At last even Gil Talmadge perceived that his friend

Link Tetherow looked to be on the verge of terminal illness. He could neither speak coherently nor move his body in a coordinated way. "Hey, Link. What's wrong? What's happened to you?"

Link's mouth stretched, rubberlike, as in a bad dream. Only at last was he able to mutter, "Rape . . . . Rape . . . . Rape."

"Rape?" The word exploded across Gil's lips so loudly that Styles and Hunt heard and hastened upslope. "Who's been raped? My God, get a-holt of yourself. Tell us what happened."

Link tried to speak but could not. He was able only to shake his head from side to side. By this time Styles and Hunt had joined them. Styles saw that Link's legs were going to fail him. He caught Tetherow's arm. "Are you all right? Do you want us to send for a doctor?"

Link could only shake his head. At that moment, Ferrell pushed the door open. He was faintly disturbed to see there were so many men out there. He said, "You better come in here."

Gil and Walter Roy had to help Link into the chapel. They stood on each side, supporting him. Link could barely walk. Inside, the chapel was darkened, gray with the light through the narrow, stained-glass windows. Soapy and Morgan sat on the last row of pews at the far side of the long, rectangular room.

On the other side of the room, Jamie Lee sat, crying softly into a handkerchief Ferrell had given her. Moab remained where he was on his knees in the priest's cubicle. Eight feet above the floor was a small square window through which the sun streamed. It fell across the kneeling black boy like some kind of spotlight.

"What happened?" Styles said.

Ferrell's voice was low-pitched, chilled. "Jamie Lee. She says Moab raped her."

Link stared at the girl slumped on that pew. Everything he had dreamed and planned for them was ended. He wanted to cry. He had thought Jamie Lee was beautiful, always beautiful, and as beautiful as she was pure. And now that purity was destroyed by that black animal in there.

Link moaned, deep in his strangled throat. She was still pure! He willed himself to go on believing in her purity—against all evidence—because her copious-breasted beauty was too heartbreakingly real and undeniable to him. From the first instant he had seen her, he had been speechless and rapt. He had been unable to believe so much beauty would be his—for the world to see that it was his. How proud he would have been to walk into any church with Jamie Lee on his arm—Mrs. Link Tetherow. The women would be jealous, the men loin-sick with envy. Now, that could never be.

He leaned against the back of the pew, shaking his head. No. Now that could never be, and he would have to learn somehow to live with the loss. For he had walked in here and he had caught her with that buck Negro pumping himself furiously between her wide-spread legs.

She had been wailing—but the sound was the cry of delight he'd heard gushing from every black wench he'd ever mounted. It couldn't be true she was doing this of her own volition—and yet she had been digging her nails into the Negro's back, dragging him closer, not fighting him. But it was rape. It had to be rape.

A sob wracked in his throat. They might be fucking yet, had he not kicked that black bastard in his balls. This had brought them back to reality. This had driven them apart, the buck gasping, wretching, and curling up in a knot, and poor little Jamie Lee staring up at Link and screaming, "Rape. Oh Gawd, Link, he raped me." His eyes filled with unshed tears.

"That there the buck what raped Miss Jamie Lee?" Gil Talmadge demanded. Outrage made his voice quaver.

Link could only nod his head.

"Well, goddamn his black hide. We'll hang him. Right now." Gil's voice raged. "We'll put a fucking rope around his neck, shoot him full of buckshot for every black to see. They got to know what happens when they rape a white lady."

Moab stopped pressing his fists into his belly. He straightened slightly, staring at Jamie Lee. When she did not move, Moab shifted his terrorized gaze to Styles Kenric.

"I tell Arthur to fetch a hangrope," Gil said. He heeled around, started for the door.

"Wait a minute." Ferrell's voice stopped Gil like a fist in his belly. His eyes blazed in a way Gil remembered. "We don't need a hangrope," Ferrell said.

19

In the next hour, a besieging army was mobilized down at the huge fieldstone gates at the entrance of the lane into Blackoaks.

The belligerents gathered from east and west, riding in fast along the trace. They carried handguns or rifles. Some came on horseback, some in open wagons or carriages. All brought weapons. Word went swiftly across the countryside. Riders were dispatched from every nearby farm.

Gil sat astride his horse in the middle of the gateway, as cold and determined as an invading general. As the newcomers joined ranks, they spoke for some taut moments with Gil. Then, they either joined the swelling ranks where they passed around jugs of corn, or they rode out to round up volunteers. Gil set two men in an open wagon to fashioning hangropes.

The sun climbed steadily to the zenith of the cloudless sky. A slight breeze riffled leaves on trees but did nothing to cool the waiting combatants. At the end of the hour, new recruits were still coming in and they crowded the gate now, just behind Gil Talmadge, waiting. Gil sat easily in his saddle, staring unflinchingly toward the mansion, toward the small chapel on the knoll beyond . . . .

A knock on the chapel door brought Ferrell from the pew seat where he had been sitting between Link and Jamie Lee. Link said only, "I best be getting on down there with Gil and them others. They my friends, Ferrell."

They ignored him. Everyone was involved in his own thoughts. Hunt knew why two hangropes were being prepared—one was for him. These rednecks had wanted an opportunity to rid the countryside of the hated yankee nigger-lover. This moment would do as well as any. For some reason he was coldly resigned. The safety of Blackoaks depended solely upon what young Ferrell Baynard could do to mediate or pacify those men, drinking and growling down at the gate. His own safety was now inextricably bound up in what happened to Moab and to Blackoaks. Hunt had no real regrets—except that he wished if he were to die this morning that he had once gone to bed with Kathy Kenric. What a waste—to live so near to her radiant beauty and to die without having held her naked in his arms. He thought about Kathy instead of Gil and the rednecks gathering out on the trace.

Styles was unable to sit still. He was not deceived. Gil Talmadge meant to hang Moab—and possibly Hunt Campbell. Styles didn't give a damn about what happened to Campbell, but the loss of Moab could be ruinous. It was no longer simply a stupid matter of somebody's offended honor; if those idiots lynched Moab they would break Styles's heart and destroy his dreams and hopes. And for what? For a stupid little bitch who flung her twat at every male who came sniffing around her.

Ferrell opened the door. Soapy stood there. His fat hands shook, his eyes showed white rims of terror. But his voice was cool. "I brought Blade and Laus, Masta Ferrell . . . . I didn't know what them white trash might do . . . . I figured I best bring Blade and Laus."

Ferrell smiled and drew the stout boy into the chapel in the circle of his arm. Blade and Laus entered quietly. Laus nodded to each of the white people and retreated to the far side of the room where he leaned against the wall, waiting. Ferrell said, "Thank you, Soapy." He smiled at Blade and Laus. "I appreciate you men coming up here . . . . There's likely to be bad trouble. You don't have to stay."

Blade nodded. "Soapy has tole us how bad the trouble is—how bad it might git. Laus and me understand. We might as well be here as anywhere—if them white men gets likkered up and mean . . . . Anything you want us to do, we're ready."

Ferrell thanked him. He sent Soapy and Morgan down the slope to bring whatever arms they could find in the house.

Link mopped at his sweated face. He cracked his knuckles. He said, "I best get on down there, Ferrell. I wouldn't want my friends thinking I'm sidin' against them."

"You stay here, Link," Ferrell said. "Your friends aren't thinking. They're drinking. And it's too early in the morning for whiskey."

Link wiped the back of his hand across his mouth. "I could use a drap."

"Maybe later, Link." Ferrell turned his back on him. He went into the small unfurnished cubicle which was made comfortable on those rare occasions when a priest visited Blackoaks. He said, "How is your belly, Moab?"

"Aches something awful, Masta."

"I'm going to have to lock you in here, Moab—until this thing is settled."

Moab's eyes filled with tears. His lip quivered. "You gonna let 'em hang Moab, Masta? I sorry, Masta. Whatever I done, I truly sorry."

Ferrell smiled ruefully. "Are you? Or are you sorry you were caught?"

Moab wept openly now. "Oh, Masta Ferrell, I swear I be good the rest of my life if you jus' won't let 'em hang me this time."

"We'll settle it, Moab. One way or the other. You'll be safe in here. I'm putting Blade and Laus outside to guard the door. You know Blade won't let anybody in here to hurt you—unless they kill him first."

Now Moab's tears were totally unselfish and gushing. "I don't want to be the cause of Blade being hurt, Masta . . . . I ain't worth that."

Ferrell smiled. "Admission of sin and knowledge of our own unworthiness, Moab . . . . The beginning of redemption . . . . You've already come a long way this morning."

"I don't understand, Masta."

"Don't worry about it. Nobody will get to you—unless

they get past me and Laus and Blade first . . . . You ought to feel pretty safe in here."

"Oh, Masta, I scared. In my belly."

Ferrell closed the door slowly. "Try to think about something pleasant, Moab."

Moab gazed up from the floor. "I loves you, Masta. You. Blade. And Miz Kathy. I truly loves you. And I sorry for what I did."

Ferrell nodded. He closed the door and locked it. He heard Moab fall against it. He could hear the boy crying through the thick facing. The outer door opened. Soapy and Morgan hurried through, carrying two rifles and three handguns and ammunition.

Ferrell gave Styles a handgun. Styles took it without speaking. He sat on a pew seat, loaded the piece, and checked it.

Ferrell handed a second gun to Hunt. "I know how you feel about fighting, Hunt . . . . But it might be worth it this time."

Hunt tried to smile. "I'll never let you down again, Ferrell . . . not now, anyway . . . with my own life at stake."

Ferrell went to Laus and Blade. "A handgun and two rifles," he said. "You can take your choice. Blade, which do you want?"

"Not much for guns, Masta Ferrell. I got my pig-sticker knife . . . . Cut a boar open in one slash."

Ferrell nodded, remembering the way Blade had nutted boars with that knife, the way he kept it honed to razor sharpness, its point like a lethal needle. Laus chose a rifle and stood hefting it in his hands.

"You going to give me a gun, Ferrell?" Link said.

"You don't need a gun, Link," Ferrell said. He gave the remaining weapons to Soapy and Morgan. The two boys swelled with pride. "And I don't dare keep one . . . . I might use it . . . and Christ knows God would never forgive me for that."

Laus and Blade were stationed on either side of the wide chapel doorway. Ferrell sent Styles, Hunt, Morgan, and Soapy out to sit on the fieldstone wall that enclosed the entrance garden.

When he was alone with Link and Jamie Lee, he said, "We better talk about this. We don't have much time."

"Don't seem much to say," Link said.

Ferrell gave him a chilled glance that silenced him. "May be more than you know, Link. Why don't you just give it a chance? You're not going anywhere until Gil comes back up here."

"What if he thinks I side with you folks? Now, I ain't against you. But I do certainly feel that nigger ought to be hung."

"Should you be hung for what you did to Lorna Garrity?"

"My God, Ferrell! That ain't the same thing."

"Why not. Isn't rape rape?"

"I'm no nigger. A nigger raped Miss Jamie Lee."

Jamie Lee winced. She tried to meet Ferrell's gaze, failed. She pressed the knotted handkerchief against her mouth. She nodded.

Ferrell sighed. He got up, walked to the rear door, and let himself out of it. He walked over to the low fieldstone wall where Styles, Hunt, and the boys sat in the shade, silently watching the growing army, restive at the gate. He said, "Jamie Lee accuses Moab of raping her. She swears he raped her—against her will."

Styles bit back the bile that gorged up in his throat. He could see ruin staring him in the face. And just when he could have bought Fulani females at that auction in Florida. "Oh God, Ferrell, we can't let them hang him."

"We might not be able to stop them. If he did rape her—and Jamie Lee says he raped her."

Morgan's voice shook. "Moab never raped Jamie Lee. Jamie Lee was after him—from the first minute she saw him . . . . She came in one morning and took off all her clothes and got in my bed . . . . She wanted me to—do it—to her . . . . But I didn't know how to do it to suit her . . . . She made Moab go riding alone with her."

"That's true," Hunt said.

Ferrell glanced at Hunt, with a faint smile. "I don't think your testimony will carry much weight with these men, Hunt."

"It is true," Morgan insisted. "Moab told me and

Soapy about it. She threatened to say he raped her that day in the woods—unless he did it to her—and unless he came into her bedroom at night."

"The little bitch," Styles whispered.

Ferrell sighed. He glanced across the grassy knoll, the plateau where the house stood, the lane of winter-bared trees, and the men milling about his gate. He turned and went back through the chapel doors and closed them behind him.

Jamie Lee looked up, going pale with premonition of ruin. She said, "Did somebody lie about me?"

"About what?" Ferrell said.

Link drew a deep breath. "That nigger what raped you, Jamie Lee. Did these heah 'rapes'—did they take place more than one time?"

"Why, what a horrible thing for you to say, Link Tetherow."

Neither Link nor Ferrell spoke. Link felt something roll in his queasy stomach. He had the terrible sense that he was going to hear more than he wanted to hear, that the last barricades between the total, ruinous truth were crumbling. He cracked his knuckles. His eyes stung with tears. He watched her.

At last, Jamie Lee tilted her little blonde head defiantly. "If you two men are not going to believe me, I won't stay here. I won't let you treat me like this."

"There's a boy in that room who might be hung, Jamie Lee, unless you tell us what happened."

"Well, I'm sorry. I'm not going to lie—even to save that—that boy's life."

"He'll die, Jamie Lee," Ferrell said. "It'll be over for him. Quick. But you'll have to live with it all your life."

She burst into tears. "Oh, please, Cousin Ferrell, I can't stand any more."

Link's voice was empty, but insistent. "Did them *rapes* happen more than once, Jamie Lee?"

She jerked her head around, her lovely blonde curls bobbling. "All right! You so anxious to believe the worst about me—I'll tell you! Moab did rape me before—"

"Oh, Jesus God," Link whispered.

She seemed to gather strength from Link's total agony.

"He—raped me—three times in the past day and a half . . . once on a horseback ride, another time he came into my bedroom after everybody in the house was asleep . . . and he did it up here in this chapel—this morning."

Link slumped in the pew crying openly. Her head tilted in defiance, Jamie Lee regarded him with contempt and revulsion. She had never seen a grown white man crying before. It was a disgusting spectacle.

At last Link got himself under control. He mopped at his eyes with his handkerchief and blew his nose noisily. He said, "I best get on down to the gate now, Ferrell. Nothin' more to say between Miss Jamie Lee and me. I'm sorry. The wedding is just off."

Now Jamie Lee burst into tears—but she cried in a fit of rage. "Oh, damn you, you spineless Link Tetherow. What will I tell everybody?"

"I don't know, Miss Jamie Lee. I don't know."

Ferrell said, "Why don't you wait outside a minute, Link?"

He walked with Link to the thick door at the chapel entrance. Link said, "Nothin' more for me here, Ferrell. I best get down there—"

"You got the rest of your life, Link, to spend with your friends." Ferrell paused outside the door. He spoke to Blade in a light, easy tone of unconcern. "I want Mr. Link Tetherow to wait out here with you fellows, Blade. I wouldn't want him to leave, you understand?"

Blade said, "He be here when you want him, Masta."

Ferrell went back to the pew where Jamie Lee sat dejectedly. She had turned and was staring toward that door behind which Moab was locked. Her eyes were clouded with tears. Ferrell sat beside her and took one of her hands in his. They sat a few moments in silence. At last, Jamie Lee sniffled and moved closer to him, like a frightened little girl. "You know why I came out here to marry up with Mr. Link Tetherow, don't you, Ferrell? . . . Really why? He came to Charleston—and he was smitten. He treated me like I would melt if'n he touched me. He put me on a pedestal . . . . He ast me to marry him, and I knew I better marry him—or maybe I wouldn't never marry nobody."

"A pretty girl like you?"

"Oh, Cousin Ferrell. Gettin' married ain't all that easy —even when yore daddy has money—and you're pretty .... I was the prettiest girl in Charleston. Everybody said that."

"I know."

"Only—they said a lot of other things, too, Cousin Ferrell. Terrible things. About me. But they were true mostly. I don't know what's the matter with me. I don't know why I can't be like the other girls—those simpering, silly little fools who faint if a man touches them .... I —I've always wanted to be—touched. To be loved. Since I was a little girl, Cousin Ferrell. Did you know Uncle Jack Henry?"

"No. I'm afraid not."

"Uncle Jack—liked little girls. He liked to play with them. He liked to sit them across his lap. He used to let me play with him. He would open his pants and let me play with him .... I did everything he wanted—and finally he even put it in me .... It hurt some ... but it felt so good, I didn't care .... I just couldn't get enough after that .... I had boys and men—black and white— since Uncle Jack started doing it with me .... Oh, God, Cousin Ferrell, am I the only one who needs it so bad? Didn't you ever feel just overwhelmed, sick inside with needing somebody?"

Ferrell held her soft little hand, but he was thinking about Lorna June and the illness that drove him to her. He had been obsessed, unable to think rationally about anything else, unable to stay away from her. Willing to lie, anything, to get her naked in his arms. Dear Jesus God, *did* he understand this poor little agonized human being?

"All right, Jamie Lee. You've told me the truth. I'll do all I can to help you."

"You mean you'll make Link Tetherow go through with the wedding?"

He shrugged. "The invitations have all been sent out, haven't they?"

She sniffled. "I'm not so sure I want to marry Link now. He's so spineless. He's no good."

Ferrell smiled. "My advice to you is to shut up, Jamie Lee, and keep your mouth shut until it's time to say 'I do' at the wedding ceremony."

Ferrell walked to the door and called Link in. Tetherow was sweated down now. He felt caught in something that overwhelmed him and carried him along, whether he wanted to go or not. "You shouldn't ought to have told a nigger to keep watch on me, Ferrell. That's showing contempt for me—right in front of a nigger."

"I didn't want you to leave, Link. I had your best interests at heart."

"Yeah?" Link watched him doubtfully, suspiciously. "I tell you now, Ferrell. I ain't going to marry your cousin. She been raped by a black—she spoiled. Why it's nuthin' personal, but what white girl is not spoiled after she been raped by a nigger? . . . I got my honor to think about, Ferrell. I got to live among those men out there . . . . And by now there ain't a white man out there don't know Miss Jamie Lee's been raped by a black buck . . . . Why, they'd snub me on the street was I to marry her now."

"Have you some better plan than to go ahead with a wedding that is all set, invitations out, and folks planning to attend?" Ferrell inquired.

Link paced nervously. He stared at Ferrell, defiant. "Yes, I have. Them men out there. Let them have that black buck. They hangs him. That ends that. Miss Jamie Lee will return to Charleston. She can say to folks that she called off the marriage. She can say what she like in Charleston. I'm truly sorry, Miss Jamie Lee, but that's the way it is."

"Link, there's more to it than your good name. There's Jamie Lee's good name. There is also the matter of letting an innocent black boy hang—"

"But he raped a white lady."

"Nobody was raped, Link. You know that."

"Them folks out there don't know it . . . . And her— lettin' him do it! Oh God, Ferrell, that makes it worse."

"You're willing to send Jamie Lee back home in disgrace? Willing to let that gang out there lynch Moab?"

"I'm sorry. I'm truly sorry, Miss Jamie Lee. I got my honor to think about."

Ferrell stared coldly at Link until Tetherow mopped at his sweated face and cracked his knuckles and stared at the floor, refusing to look up. "You know, Link, if you persist in this—trying to have Moab hung to save your honor—sending Jamie Lee home to Charleston in disgrace—"

"Will you think for one minute what they have done to me?" Link raged.

"What do you think will happen to you if the truth about your part in what happened to Lorna June came to the ears of Banker Luke Scroggings? I happen to know your plantation is mortgaged to the last slave—" He looked again at Link. "Scroggings has sworn to kill all who took part in the crime against his wife, once he has proof of their involvement."

Link looked as if he might vomit. "Ferrell—I tell you I am just unable to believe that you—a southern gentleman of honor—would betray the confidence of one of his own kind."

"But you're wrong, Link. I'm no longer one of you landowners. No longer a gentleman—like you. I am now a lowly priest in the Catholic Church."

"You'd tell Scroggings?" Link shook his head, disbelieving.

Ferrell shrugged. "I never said I'd reveal anything to anyone . . . only that unless you keep your bargain with Jamie Lee—that truth will reach Luke Scroggings—without delay."

Link's eyes filled with tears and he wiped at them angrily with the back of his hand. "Damn you, Ferrell Baynard. How long could I live among them men out there if I marries a white woman who has willingly submitted her naked body to a black man?"

Ferrell spread his hands. "We'll tell them the truth. It never happened."

Link's nose was running now. He dragged his sleeve across his nostrils. "Who would ever believe such a wild and incredible story? Gil was in here. And Walter Roy Summerton. They know I know. They know Jamie Lee and that buck was caught—doing it—in *flagrante delicto.*"

"Who caught them?" Ferrell asked.

"Why, I did. You know I did. Jamie Lee know I did."

"Why should you tell anyone something that might destroy your position in society, cause you irreparable heartache? Perhaps, after all, you didn't see what you thought you saw."

"God knows I seen it. I'll see it all the rest of my life—in my nightmares."

"That's between you and God. Suppose I, as a priest, tell them Moab was helping Miss Jamie Lee decorate the chapel—for your wedding?"

Link shook his head, doubtful. "How you make them believe that?"

"If I do make them believe it, you are off the hook. You can hold your head up among them. You are going to be a laughingstock around here even if Jamie Lee is sent home to Charleston in disgrace. You'll still be the man whose bride-to-be was raped by a black . . . . But if it never happened, you and Jamie Lee could get married. You could live happily ever after—on your plantation—which you nor your folks are going to be able to do much longer unless you come up with a lot of mortgage payments—and fast—because Jamie Lee's got one thing you haven't got."

"What's that?" Link said.

"Money. Her father would be happy to pay off your mortgage on the Tetherow place—if you were married to his favorite daughter. Wouldn't he, Jamie Lee?"

"He would an' I ast him," Jamie Lee said. "He do anything I ast him . . . . He call me his own little ole eyeball . . . . I can have anything I ast him."

"Would you ast him—if we was married?" Link said.

The door opened and Styles stepped inside. He looked pale. "They are coming up the lane, Ferrell. A gang of them. They're armed. They've been drinking. They look ready for trouble."

"You stay in here, Jamie Lee," Ferrell said. "Come on out with me, Link. You've got to help me convince Gil it was all a mistake."

Link followed Ferrell out of the door, shoulders slumped round. He felt as if he were being wafted along, like a leaf caught on a torrent, and he was helpless to direct any part of his own life.

Ferrell, Styles, and Link came through the door of the chapel into the sunlight. They closed it behind them. Ferrell glanced along the slope leading from the knoll to the terrace of the manor house. In a gown of flowing chiffon, Miz Claire came upslope. She carried a handgun at her side. "Sweet Jesus," Ferrell whispered.

Miz Claire came across the lawn directly to where Ferrell stood. She spoke calmly and politely to the other men. "You've got trouble up here, Ferrell," she said. "I came up to be with you. Mr. Baynard taught me how to handle a gun."

"This is no place for a woman, Miz Claire," Link said.

"I have lived for a long time, young man," Miz Claire said. "I know now by instinct where my place is. I know it is here."

Ferrell merely smiled and nodded. He wanted to suggest that his mother would be more comfortable inside the chapel with Jamie Lee, but he knew she would refuse. His only hope was that Gil Talmadge, irrational at best, wasn't too liquored up to listen to reason.

There were at least two dozen men who came off the lane and crossed the plateau approaching the church. Many of them Ferrell had known well for most of his life. Some were invited to the wedding. Some would be guests at Blackoaks during the Christmas season. At the moment they were a posse with two sets of hangropes, following Gil Talmadge across the sunstruck lawn.

Gil held up his hand when the vigilantes were fifteen or twenty feet from the low wall enclosing the chapel. "We don't want trouble with you, Ferrell. Or your folks. Give us the nigger and the nigger-lover. We'll take them away from Blackoaks to hang them. But we mean to hang them. We're gittin' rid of the yankee abolitionist along with the nigger rapist—cleanin' up while we're at it."

Ferrell said, "Don't try to take them, Gil. If you do, there'll be bloodshed."

Gil shrugged. "So be it. That's your decision, Ferrell."

Ferrell said, "And then there's this, Gil. No matter who comes close to this chapel, it's you I'll kill . . . . You might want to think about that."

Gil hesitated. A shadow flickered across his eyes. Mostly he felt pain that his dearest friend would turn on him like this when he was doing what was his duty.

Ferrell spoke quietly over his shoulder. "Why don't you go inside with Miss Jamie Lee, Hunt?"

Hunt nodded, anxious to comply. But Gil's voice stopped him. "You stay where you are, nigger-lover. You move toward that door, you're a dead yankee." Gil glanced around. He knew better than to push Ferrell. In the confusion he had not noticed that Ferrell didn't even have a gun. Gil called his slave, the black giant. "Arthur, you go in there and bring out that black rapist. Now we got guns fixed on all of you. Don't try to stop Arthur and nobody has to git hurt."

Arthur looked ill, but he walked slowly forward, towering over all the men around him. Blade moved forward from the door of the chapel. He pulled the knife from his belt. Its blade glittered in the sunlight. "That's far enough, nigger," Blade said.

Arthur hesitated. He was head and shoulders taller than Blade; he outweighed him by at least a hundred pounds. Somehow, it looked like an equal contest. Blade stood, legs apart, waiting, the knife held negligently at his side.

"You go ahead, Arthur," Gil ordered.

Arthur winced but took another step toward the chapel. Blade stepped forward as if in some strange and ancient ritual. Their gazes were locked. Sweat rolled down from the black mat of Arthur's hair.

Miz Claire stepped forward, beside Blade. She spoke to Arthur. "Stop there. Blade can't fight you. Blade must not be harmed. Now, I can put this bullet where I want to. I warn you. Stop."

"My Gawd, Miz Claire." Gil's voice shook. "You even more unreasonable than Ferrell . . . . We only doing what we got to do. Please don't git in the way, ma'm." His voice hardened. "Go ahead in there, Arthur."

Arthur shuddered. He hunched up his shoulders, un-

133

able to turn back. He took a long step forward. Miz Claire raised the gun coolly, leveled it, and pressed the trigger.

The explosion was violent and sharp in the morning stillness. Every man in Gil's mob reacted, retreating a step. Arthur howled like an animal in agony. He slapped at the bullet hole which had ripped open his right bicep. Blood spurted between his fingers. He staggered backward under the impact of the bullet.

Gil screamed as if he, instead of Arthur, had taken Miz Claire's gunfire. Agonized, he ran forward to where Arthur stood clinging to his bleeding arm.

"My Gawd, Miz Claire!" Gil cried. "You shot my fightin' nigger."

He grabbed Arthur by the arm, turned him toward one of the wagons. "I'll git you to a vet, Arthur, soon as I settle this here business."

Ferrell had walked out to the rim of the crowd. "There's no business to settle," he said. "All a mistake. Link thought he saw something he didn't really see. The black boy was helping Miss Jamie Lee Seaton decorate the chapel for her wedding to Link . . . . Link misunderstood. Isn't that right, Link? You want to come out and tell the boys about it?"

There had been few weddings as magnificent as the ceremony at which Miss Jamie Lee Seaton plighted her troth to Mr. Link Tetherow four days after Christmas. The chapel was a riot of bright flowers. Every pew was filled with friends and relatives of the young couple. Some had come from as far away as Richmond. None had seen anything more splendid than these nuptials. Link was handsome, standing at the altar, though some might have wished he'd have held his legs closer together. Gil Talmadge, his best man, stood at his shoulder at the altar before the young priest, Brother Alexander. But the gasps and the whispers of delight were reserved for the moment the organ struck up the strains of the wedding march.

Miss Jamie Lee was a vision of virginal loveliness in white lace, white silks, white satins. Every newspaper in the state, the Charleston, Atlanta, and Mobile papers, would carry descriptions of the bride's lovely gown. But no one expressed it all as well as Morgan, standing in place beside his mother. He watched Jamie Lee approach down the aisle, sedate and ethereal, eyes becomingly lowered, face pale and set in a faint smile. But Morgan did not see her smile, her flowing dress, her white veil. He saw only the way her waist had been drawn in until she resembled a wasp; he saw only the way her stays forced her already magnificent breasts upward. Morgan gulped, biting back tears and whispered to no one, or perhaps to his own gods, "I never seen such tits on a white girl."

PART TWO

Tallahassee

1

The small black lookouts raced screaming down the tree-lined lane as the splendid caravan entered at the huge gates from the public roadway.

"Company a-comin'! Company a-comin'!"

Mr. Cleatus Dennison arrived at Blackoaks on the fifth of January in even greater pomp and elegance than he had previously displayed upon his initial appearance a year earlier. There were more and finer highly varnished coaches in escort—all with étain-blue window curtains—an increased number of gaudily uniformed slaves in attendance. Carriage horses, silver-plated harnessware glittering in the sun, stepped smartly, curried and gleaming though it was a tiring and dusty drive over execrable roadway, even from Mt. Zion. There was a grandeur about the procession worthy of any sovereign. The majestic equipage certainly accomplished its purpose, which was to guarantee homage to its master in advance: the world has been forever humbled, instanter, by the arrogance of opulence.

Routine had barely returned to the daily life of the plantation in the wake of the excitement of the showiest wedding ceremony of the season and the candlelit conviviality of the twelve days of Christmas. The reveling had flared into a climactic burst of fireworks, music, dancing on New Year's Eve . . . . Two days later most of the dozens of house guests had departed amid hasty kisses, quickly forgotten promises, and fast-drying tears. A miasmic apathy descended like an enervating fog over the entire estate in the aftermath of weeks of unrelenting feasting and festivity. Everyone reacted in his own way.

Morgan, abruptly and inexplicably—at least no one attempted to explain it to him—freed from the butt-numbing drudgery of daily tutoring, abandoned himself to that lechery implanted and fertilized in his viscera by his single abortive tryst with Jamie Lee Seaton-Tetherow. He could not expunge from his fevered mind the magnificence of his cousin's mammaries. Until she exposed to him that fresh, high-standing flesh of her peach-and-pink bosom and sweet-smelling cleavage, he had been only vaguely aware of tits as protuberant female appendages of fatty tissue. If he thought about busts at all, most had seemed like fried eggs or melons, shapeless and unlovely. Now he knew that when those nipples were nursed, reaction flushed all through *his* body. And this was only the beginning! Soapy had kindly and graphically explained to him that the vagina or cunt-hole was situated beneath and inset from the *mons pubis* or hair pad. Morgan felt himself readied in theory and disquisition on the subject now dearest to his heart. What he wanted was practical application of this erudition; he wanted to fuck.

At Blackoaks, for a Baynard to know desire was for him to achieve or acquire fulfillment. Morgan fucked. He never went to the quarters to select his wenches. Instead, he proceeded directly to that secret island in the creek where, in less enlightened times, he and Soapy had wasted their lives playing pirates. Soapy went as envoy to the quarters and chose their partners, sometimes bringing along spares, or extra participants in the orgies he liked to organize, direct, and enjoy. Sometimes, in his belly-wracking anxiety, Morgan hid in the underbrush and contented himself with his fist and fiery images while he awaited Soapy and the concubines.

They whiled away heated mornings and long, lazy afternoons at this divertissement. Except for variations he was able to arrange and stage, Soapy grew quickly exhausted and bored. But Morgan's mind was less open to extraneous detail. There was no place even for fatigue. His was a one-track mind, beautiful in its simplicity, and there was but single traffic through its roadbed since Jamie Lee had awakened his dormant libido. He didn't understand physical weariness. He grew tumescent as the wenches were brought into his presence. He undressed them, fondled their breasts, mounted them, and spent himself furiously upon them, knowing precisely at last what he wanted and where it was situated, physiologically speaking. He would lie upon his wench without withdrawing and, within minutes, was rigid and ready again. In only one aspect was Morgan disappointed: he never found tits of the color, texture, or lavish grandeur of Jamie Lee's. Most of the black teenaged wenches bared to his eyes only onion-sized, lemon-shaped, immature breasts. He was less than totally satisfied, but he was content . . . .

He took what he could get, where and as often as he could get it. Neither he nor Soapy were questioned at the manor house but were viewed with approbation: both were losing weight; their musculature appeared improved; they went to bed earlier; they slept more soundly. Morgan's recurring nightmares of the slave breeder Baxter Simon's throwing a slave girl's body to the hogs gradually abated and finally ceased.

Styles was less than receptive to the changes taking place under his very nose. With the end of Morgan's tutoring, Kathy's French lessons began. Kathy and Hunt Campbell met every morning in the sunroom. Kathy closed the doors. For an hour—and often longer—every day she was involved in her studies. Striding in the foyer, Styles felt his rage fester and luxuriate like some cancerous internal growth. The sounds emanating from the sunroom through closed doors were most disquieting to a man to whom outward appearances were the utmost consideration in his marriage. There were long silences, a little French, some music from the piano, much laughter, lowered voices, and the suggestion if not substance of whispered exchanges. Styles found this an intolerable situation; his rights as a husband were being not only challenged but openly flouted. They were making a fool of him in public, and he would not stand for it.

He became more openly disdainful and insolent in the infrequent company of his wife and her tutor. He found his hatred consuming him like some viral infection. Kathy was going too far! He would not tolerate her indecorous behavior. He would drive Campbell off the place. He was prowling his office, haunted by laughter and the cheap sentiment of a love ballad from the piano in the sunroom when Thyestes limped in and announced the arrival of the entourage of Mr. Cleatus Dennison. . . .

Hunt followed Kathy from the sunroom, and they joined the confluence of servants and family moving to the front veranda where the pageantry of Mr. Cleatus Dennison's cortege was on mind-boggling display.

Uniformed black men leaped from the carriages even before they rolled to a stop at the long veranda steps. While the coaches still rocked on their thoroughbraces, coachmen were at attention beside the gleaming paneling of coach doors.

The lead-carriage coachman swung its door open. Inside, the tonneau was darkly cool with the blue curtains drawn. Hunt gawked at dark and richly carved interior woods, vases of fresh flowers, leather seats, thickly upholstered, deeply cushioned, and spread over with silks and damasks.

Mr. Cleatus Dennison alighted, undeniably a distinguished-looking gentleman, a person of grace, charm, and noble mien. But Hunt knew Dennison was no planter, not one of the gracious cotton gentry. He owned land, but upon it he raised food and fabrics implementing his main crop: he bought, raised, bred, and sold slaves.

Hunt saw that Styles, in his own imperious way, observed a face-saving protocol. Blackoaks house servants and gathering field slaves were overwhelmed, servile, and fawning in paying homage to this last feudal lord and his retinue. With a smile that bordered on insolence, Styles remained rooted on the shadowed top step of the veranda until Mr. Cleatus Dennison came up to him, hand extended.

Hunt smiled secretively. He would have enjoyed watching the by-play between the two aristocrats, but something happened which drove them—and everything else—out of his mind. The door of the second coach was opened by a liveried footman and a dark-skinned woman alighted. Hunt retreated one full step in shock, almost as if he'd been struck in the face.

He felt his heart slip its moorings. Sickness boiled in the molten pit of his stomach. He watched the black servants help the Negress from her carriage, which was only slightly less elegant than Dennison's. What struck Hunt most forcefully was the identity of that black woman. It was Sefina!

His knees went weak and threatened to fail him. Through his mind raced the torrid memory of the last time he had seen Sefina. Pregnant, desolated, barefoot, and chained to other slaves, she had been herded into an enclosed black coach near the rear of the Dennison train. Her gaze had touched at him that day. He had thought he would never see her again, and he had reviled himself for his own evil. He had got Sefina pregnant. Because she was bearing a mustee fetus, she had been sold off to Cleatus Dennison as a breeding dam. On Dennison's Negro stud farm, the ochre pigmentation of a mulatto git would be more readily accepted and assimilated than on the cotton plantation at Blackoaks. Sefina had gone away from this place in despair. God knew, she returned in splendor!

From head to toe, Sefina was most fashionably outfitted. A small green hat and saucy feather concealed the short dark mat of curls, accentuated the liquid ebon of her eyes, the creamy smoothness of her complexion. She held herself erect, slender, and somehow almost haughty, in a traveling suit of dark green twill. Dainty slippers winked from the sweeping hem of her skirts.

Hunt exhaled heavily. In the past Christmas season Blackoaks had been visited by many lovely women, but none had been lovelier than the slave girl Sefina, and few had been as expensively or modishly attired.

Other servants, slaves, and attendants stepped down from the Dennison carriages. Except for the elegance of her toilet, Sefina was not set apart from the other blacks. Cleatus Dennison totally ignored her, and yet it was obvious to Hunt that Sefina *was* set apart from all ordinary slaves. She had come a long way from that day when she had been led away from this place in chains and a much-washed cotton shift. Hunt did not fault Dennison in any way for promoting Sefina from drudgery to concubinage— plainly, though Dennison concealed it in deference to the Blackoaks women, Sefina had become the slave breeder's favorite mistress.

Hunt stared at Sefina. Her rise in condition only proved once again what a woman could accomplish through diligence, attending to her duties, minding her master, and being the best piece of ass in all thrall.

Sefina remained standing beside the open door of the carriage until another young yellow-skinned Negress, in the white uniform of nursemaid, stepped from the same coach and was handed out, by yet another white-clad female servant, a blanket-swaddled infant.

Hunt felt his face burn—as though he were being stung by army ants. He had the unnerving sensation that everybody on the veranda and the driveway was staring at him knowingly and accusingly. That was his son there—his and Sefina's mulatto child. Wouldn't everyone who looked at it recognize its progenitor?

He watched Sefina quickly but carefully check the baby, smiling maternally. Then she turned and let her gaze move idly across the faces of the people on the veranda until her sable eyes found him. She hesitated only for the space of one quick breath, but her glance spoke volumes. She had not forgotten him. She looked into the face of their son a hundred times a day and she remembered him. She had returned to the place where she'd been born and reared, but it was him she looked for. He stood immobile, unable to move.

Hunt tried to work his face muscles into the semblance of a smile. He wanted her to know that he hadn't forgotten her either. But by the time his pallid cheeks reacted, her gaze had moved on. It was as if she had never paused to gaze upon him at all . . . .

Hunt was mentally and physically exhausted by nine o'clock that night. He was relieved when he could finally escape to his own bedroom. He had been presented to Dennison early in the afternoon—not a slave, more than a servant, less than a guest, a paid member of the household. The look the slave breeder gave him seemed to Hunt at once mocking and knowing. Hunt couldn't be sure whether or not this was his own New England conscience at work. Later, Hunt had heard Styles order Thyestes to have Jeanne d'Arc's old bedroom on the third floor prepared for Mr. Dennison's female slave Sefina. Jeanne d'Arc's room was the best on that level and its condition was improved by the scrubbing, polishing, and refurbishing given it before Sefina and her baby were moved into it. Dennison had not to this time favored the black girl with a glance, but Hunt felt it had to be obvious to everyone, as it was to him, that Sefina was Dennison's mistress whom they were being forced to accept as a guest in their house. Sefina remained sedately with the servants. The white people of the household ignored her, and yet she seemed somehow a center of all attention. At least to Hunt, the atmosphere was impregnated with tension, as it is sometimes before a fierce storm.

And if Dennison knew who had fathered Sefina's child, who else knew? Styles? Ferrell? Would Dennison make some jocular reference to the paternity of his doxy's sucker? Dennison was a man who enjoyed jokes that exposed or humiliated their victims. And if the women on the place looked at Sefina's baby—and all women enjoyed viewing infants, black or white—would there be distinguishing features that must proclaim the mustee tike as Hunt Campbell's woods colt?

Hunt sweated, unable to imagine a more horrifying development. It was no less than his transgression deserved, but the truth would totally destroy anything between him and Kathy. The others might laugh and forget —the men might even secretly envy him. Kathy would not laugh; she would never forget. Because it had happened a long time ago, she might eventually forgive him, but it would always remain a wall between them.

Unable to sit still, or to follow the thread of a simple

conversation, Hunt existed through the afternoon in a benumbed agony of apprehension. People spoke to him and he didn't hear them. He had learned that the more hurtful a potential happening, the more certain it was to transpire. They were all going to talk about Sefina's baby. Why not—she was a slave born and reared here at Blackoaks, wasn't she, now a housekeeper for the bachelor Dennison? They were going to discuss Sefina's child—and they were going to name its father . . . . Well, he could return to Cambridge and get shot by a jealous husband. It sure as hell wouldn't matter any more if he lost Kathy.

A little past nine, Hunt escaped from the living room and slunk hurriedly to his own bedchambers with a sense of release, of doom delayed at least.

He locked the corridor door and sank against it, feeling like the harried heroine in some tawdry downtown Boston melodrama so reviled by the Harvard Yard intelligensia . . . .

He forced himself at last to undress and lie down across his bed. He considered flight—immediate, now, tonight. Certainly this was the coward's way—his way. When you face trouble, meet it wisely. Run . . . .

He tried to sleep and he could not. Lights were blotted out in all the other windows of the mansion, pulling in their faint yellow shafts from the dark lawn. The quarters were long since dark. Not even a hound bayed the moon. The big old house quieted. In every room they slept serenely, and he lay awake, dry-eyed, sleepless.

He dozed at last from the fatigue generated by overspent psychic energy and the weight of sheer physical and mental exhaustion. He heard the faint, rapid tapping on his door-facing three separate times before it registered as a muted, frightened signal.

He lunged up from the bed and crossed the room. He opened the door and then retreated a staggered step. "Sefina," he whispered.

The girl wore a satin negligee over her silk-and-lace gown. She carried her baby wrapped in a light, flowered cotton coverlet. She stepped into Hunt's room and moving numbly, he closed the door. To conceal his nervous anxiety and discomfort, he lit candles and was going to light a lamp but her gentle voice stopped him. "I only hoped . . . thought . . . you might want to see . . . my son . . . Masta."

He winced and blew out the match before it singed his fingers. Looking at Sefina for permission, he went close and turned back the coverlet.

He exhaled heavily, staring down at his son. The baby was lighter in color than other babies Hunt had seen at Blackoaks. Shaken, he gazed down at the tiny half-breed —the mulatto offspring of himself and this slave girl. He told himself he should feel something besides fear of exposure and guilt for his sin. This was *his* son. He had begotten him, but again there was no exultance or pride, only the puritan ethic of depressive guilt at work. His quick, passionate, all-night coupling with Sefina had produced this small human being—his son. He could feel no paternal affection, though he wanted to with all his heart.

He touched the child's cheek with the backs of his fingers. The flesh was warm; he withdrew his hand quickly, troubled. Surely, he should somehow pay for what he had done to Sefina—and, through her, for his crime against this beautiful little male being who was doomed to spend his life between the two worlds of white and black—despised by one, ostracized by the other.

He shivered as if chilled. This was *his* son doomed to a living purgatory. It occurred to him that he could take the child, return north, and rear it as his own— which it was!

His face burned. He couldn't do that. He was too cowardly. He could never face the questions, the leers, the secret laughter roused by the child's dark skin. And even if he possessed the courage—which he did not!—he saw that Sefina truly loved their son. He had hurt her enough. He couldn't break her heart now by tearing her baby from her arms—as any white slaveowner might! He couldn't abuse her further simply to still a fearful New England lashing of conscience. And there was no way he could take both of them with him to New England, even if he'd wanted to—and he did not! Face it, New England for all its loud cries of outrage against slavery, its abolitionist fever, its ears for the plight of the black, was not ready for miscegenation. He wasn't ready for it . . . .

He sweated, seeing himself for the hypocrite he was, condemning these southerners for secretly mating with black wenches and then casually rejecting responsibility for any product of that coupling. He was tarred with the same stick, painted with the same brush, cut from the same cloth! He was worse, because he had ranted against just such inhumanity.

He stared at the baby, praying he would feel a positive, warm, and redeeming response. He tried to thrust all this mind-numbing guilt from his consciousness and to concentrate on the natural, instinctive, and normal feelings of paternal love and pride. Every man was popularly believed to experience such exalting sensations upon beholding his own progeny for the first time. It was not there. Fear was there. Guilt was there. There was simply no room in his mind for the sacred, warm, humane feelings of family love and delight.

Instead, his mind wheeled with panic.

He looked at the baby's turned-up nose, his lips pursing and sucking, his hair brushed and curled so lovingly on his pate, but instead of thinking about his son, he thought in terms of loss and cost. What if Kathy found out? What if Cleatus Dennison made some joke that got him laughed at? Would Miz Claire permit him to stay on at Blackoaks if she knew the truth—that he had sired a mustee—with one of her own servants-for-life? If he were forced out of Blackoaks, how would he see Kathy? How would he live without her?

His mind whirled.

"He's a pretty baby," Sefina said. "And so good. You never saw a better baby . . . . I prayed you'd want to see him . . . . "

"Of course I do, Sefina . . . . I know—he's *my* son, too . . . . I've never forgotten you."

"Nor me you, Masta—"

He winced. "I know how you must hate me." He gazed down at the child which Sefina held with such pride for his approval. The baby was nude, perfectly formed, beautiful, its flesh a pale tan. He exhaled because he could find no resemblance to himself. The child resembled only another infant. All babies looked alike to him. He inhaled as if he had not truly breathed since her arrival at Blackoaks this morning. "I don't blame you for hating me."

"I bear you no hatred, Masta. No drop of hatred."

He gazed down into her gentle, calm face, soft and almost serene in its resignation. Clearly she was telling him the truth. She did not hate him.

He laughed self-deprecatingly. "It's all right . . . . I hate myself enough for both of us." He stared down at his sleeping son, doomed to a half-life between two unyielding worlds. "I hate myself enough—for all three of us."

2

Moab awoke suddenly and lunged upward on his pallet, chilled with terror.

He held his breath, afraid he had screamed in his sleep. In fact he was certain he'd been awakened by his own helpless, strangled shouting as the hangrope closed about his throat.

Seeing that Masta Styles had not stirred in the big bed, Moab sighed heavily. If he'd cried out, he'd have wakened his master.

Moab shivered. He would almost have welcomed an order from his master to get into the big bed with him. Sometimes he disliked the things he was forced to do when Styles was driven by compulsive passions. Often he hated the actions forced upon him whether he wanted them or not. He drew none of the thrill from being in his master's embrace that drove Styles to mindless ecstasy. But he didn't care what Masta Styles did to him—anything was better than working ten hours a day, in the sunstruck fields. Still, he was required to pretend the arousal and excitement Styles expected and demanded from him. Sometimes he let his mind picture a wench in his arms instead of Styles. This made excitement come easier. He never sought sexual contact from Styles any more than he dared to shrink from it. He had to make his master believe he *wanted* to submit, that he enjoyed their lovemaking as much as Styles did. This was not too difficult—a man in the rage of passion believes what he wants to believe. As long as Styles had an object for his sexual release, he could believe it was ecstasy shared—if he bothered to consider it at all. Still, being used—sometimes cruelly and painfully—was better than lying on this pallet night after night in sleepless terror and loneliness or caught in mindless nightmare.

During the month after the fearful threat of hanging at the hands of white men who cared nothing for his life, Moab lived in terror that died only slowly. Night after sweated night, he lay sleepless reliving that horrible, endless day. His fears grew after the actual danger was over and past.

He had sagged in a state of shock while the white men deliberated over whether he was to die by lynching. All that day while Masta Ferrell struggled to prevent the hanging, Moab crouched benumbed by terror on the cement floor of the priest's crib in the chapel. He was too deeply steeped in shock to react to peril. The shudders and the cold sweats came later—in the night—to haunt him and drive everything else from his mind.

Try as he would, Moab could not escape the horrifying nightmares of being lynched by white vigilantes. He felt abandoned even when he recognized he had not been deserted by the men of Blackoaks. Alone in the dark nights he found no sense of security. Rather than the knowledge that Masta Ferrell had been ready to fight to save his life, there was instead only a total sense of desolation, of that helplessness singular to a black whose life white men were determined to take.

He could not say at what moment in those agonized weeks he found escape from horror in remembering Miz Florine Pilzer. If he could only summon her into his mind, he could drive out the dread, temporarily at least.

At first, Miz Florine's presence burned its way slowly, like caustic acid, through the thick residue of terror that numbed his mind to all but the repeated images of his dangling, neck broken and twisted, at the end of a white man's hangrope. At first, recalling Miz Florine, her lovely body and her fiery needs, her anxiety to please him, he would grab at the memory only to have it dissolve in the more pervasive and destructive escharotic of terror.

But a month is a long time. Moab was young; his reproductive drives were far more potent than his fear of death, even when the fear had come so abruptly and threateningly close.

Each night he dreamed more of Miz Florine and less of dying violently.

But, almighty God, that Miz Jamie Lee! It was almost as exalting to escape her as to cheat the hangrope! That white girl was bad, and Miz Jamie Lee was somehow blanked from his mind, part of a tragedy too terrible to recall. But Miz Florine belonged to a better time—a day when he had known Masta Styles only as some figure of white authority distantly removed above him. Miz Florine had wanted him from that first morning, almost as fiercely and helplessly as he'd desired her. Miz Florine had taken him into her bed; she had gone down on her knees to him. She had implanted within his mind that first rebellious seed: he was not a slave; he could not go on being a slave. Slavery meant submitting, as she submitted to him. With her crouched so before him, he'd indeed felt like an emperor—a direct descendant of those nobles of ancient Senegal that Masta Hunt Campbell later told him about.

He gradually overcame his nightmares by dreaming of Miz Florine. Slowly, his manhood returned. For weeks, unmanned by terror, he'd been physically incapable of erection. It was as if his terrified mind associated horror and death with a rigid penis, with sexual gratification. This disabling condition altered as he dreamed of Miz Florine. Dreams of Miz Florine boiled up in a cauldron and scalded out his fears.

He longed desperately to see her again. He warned

himself that he had to stay away from her. Hadn't he come near enough one hangrope because of a white woman? He had to have better sense. What kind of fool learned nothing from fearful experience? But the more his mind played with Florine—and the overheated hours they'd spent together—the more his wish became a driving need, and then an obsession. He could think only that she was alone up there in that cool fieldstone cottage, remote on the shadowed knoll above the slave quarters. She must be thinking about him. She must want him. Could he crave her so terribly unless she shared that compulsive need?

Then one morning at daybreak he found himself creeping stealthily upon the Pilzer cottage from the misty creek bottom lands. It seemed to him something planned and approved by providence. Last night he had fallen asleep at last, dreaming of Miz Florine and not of a hangrope; thanks to his memories of her he was recovering from an agony of terror. Then something had wakened him in the earliest dawn.

He had lain on his pallet listening to the work gang shuffling along the roadway past the manor house, heading toward the fields. He had listened to their mournful keening that was almost a heartbroken melody as old as their race. Then he had heard the familiar clop of hooves of Bos Pilzer's big gray horse. How well he knew that sound! How many mornings had he lain on his cot in the tack room waiting to hear the overseer ride out of the yard?

The overwhelming desire had started then, simmering as if in a cauldron, boiling up until at last, unable to resist those primal urges another instant, he had slipped silently from his bed. Holding his breath, he had stepped into his osnaburg britches. He didn't care that he might be caught. He didn't care that he might be killed. She was up there. She was waiting for him. He had to go to her. He had gone out the corridor door and down the rear stairs, across the busy, overheated kitchen, and out of the house, almost running. The kitchen workers had called to him, had spoken his name, giggling and teasing. There was no mystery in their minds about his mission; he was on his way to ride some wild-bucking wench. He hadn't answered them. He hadn't heard them.

He had walked past the whiskey distillery, which stood on a long-angled path leading away from Bos Pilzer's cottage in the park above the quarters. No one must suspect his destination! He had had only slight fear that Styles would waken, calling him. With Mr. Cleatus Dennison as house guest, Masta Styles had little time for Moab. For this, Moab thanked the ancient gods who'd guided his people to splendor and dominance east of Senegal. This was all meant to be!

He had barely noticed that a crew of workers was erecting the final framing to restore the burned-out distillery. Some of the younger bucks who knew Moab had called his name. He had waved casually, absently, and kept walking . . . .

Then he came up from the timberlands and the creek bottom to the Pilzer house. But she saw him as he emerged into the cleared park surrounding her house. The front door slammed behind her. Breathless, Moab saw her standing on the shadowed porch, waiting. He ran . . . .

"You've come. You've come back to me." Florine caught his hands and drew him after her into the house. She locked both the screened and wooden doors. No one ever came up here—she existed in a nebulous nowhere, neither part of the world of the slaves nor of their owners. She locked the doors in an almost symbolic gesture, though she didn't think of it that way—to secure them, together, behind it. It was a kind of faith that she would never have to let him go again, even when she knew better. "Let me look at you. Let me look at you." She was laughing and crying at the same time.

Now that he was with her, in the quiet house where he'd been happiest, a frightening reaction set in. He seemed to go dead in his loins—as if fear and guilt destroyed his manhood. God help him if he wasn't even going to be able to get a hard-on. A shudder wracked him as if he were cold.

Florine wore only the cotton smock he remembered, buttoned at the throat. Under it she was naked. She pressed against him, caressed the swollen muscle-cords which raised the copper-penny paps upon his chest. She cried out, "Moab. What is it? What's the matter?"

"I scared."

"Of what? Why?"

"I got no excuse—no reason why I'm up here."

"No one will know."

"If they catch me, Masta Styles have me whupped—"

"Oh, no. They wouldn't dare scar you again." She drew her hand along the healing wale down his back. She writhed with the sensual thrill that went through her like a flare of lightning.

"Masta Styles done warned. I make trouble—I go back to the field gang—"

She drew a deep breath, studying him. "Oh, Moab, do you—can you—truly care for that unnatural creature? Men aren't supposed to lust after other men, Moab."

"I reckon I got to do what he tells me." His wide shoulders sagged. "He kindly. He gimme what I want. Anything I want, he gimme. He make life easy for me."

"Oh, Moab—"

"I don't have to do nuthin'—'cept what he wants done . . . . Don't sleep in no barns no more. Don't have to care for the stock, or the garden, or the flowers or the yard—"

"Oh, Moab, was it so terrible up here with me? Was it?"

Now he put his arms about her, drew her tightly against him, feeling the soft cushions of her full breasts. "Wasn't no way terrible . . . . Happiest time I ever knowed—up here with you."

"Oh, Moab." If he had heaped diamonds upon her, he could not have pleased her more. Trembling, she reached down, loosened the button at the top of his fly.

He caught her hand. "But I jus' see. Plain. It scares me . . . . I belonged up heah . . . now I don't . . . . I could be kilt . . . . I could git you kilt . . . . I got no right—no matter how much I want it."

"Oh, Moab, I don't care! I have no life without you anyway."

He trembled violently. "Suppose Masta Bos was to walk in?"

"I don't care . . . . Oh, Moab, I don't care . . . . You are here . . . . We mustn't waste it—not a minute . . . . I've wanted you so terribly. Like this, Moab." Her hand pulled free of his and she tore at the buttons of his britches. They toppled about his ankles upon the floor. She caught his tumescent rod in her fist. Holding it, she sank slowly to the floor on her knees before him. He stood, watching her part her lips, come closer, closer. But he listened tautly for any sound from outside, ready to bolt in terror. But his flesh betrayed him. He was overwhelmed by desire that fulgurated from brain center to gonads in one dazzling split second. Her heated mouth drove him insane. It was reality when he had existed so long on dreams alone. She nursed hungrily as if she'd been literally starved for him all these months.

He took her up in his arms though she whimpered in protest as he pulled her to a standing position. He stepped out of his britches wadded on the floor and carried her into her bedroom. He laid her down gently across the mattress and for a moment stood gazing down upon her.

She smiled up at him, clinging to his rigid penis. When she moved, the small gold and diamond cross suspended on a dainty chain about her throat danced between her taut-standing breasts, winking at him in the morning sunlight.

She saw him gazing at the cross, which had been a gift from Bos. "Do you like it?" she said, smiling. "Do you want it?"

"My God. What would I do with it?"

"You can have it . . . if you'll just come to me like this—even once in a while . . . . You can have it." She reached up and caught the expensive cross negligently in her fingers. "If you want it—"

"I don't want it." He laughed and came down upon her, pushing her legs wide apart to receive him. "I don't want anything—right now—but you . . . . "

3

Ferrell spent most of the waking hours of his final days at Blackoaks walking alone across its broad acres. A knot of despair formed in the pit of his stomach at the thought of returning to the seminary in Charleston. Once he had been certain that the hypocritical life of the slaveowner was not for him. He was unable to believe in the divine right of a white man, or any man, to own slaves. Other young men, born to slave-holding families, accepted their position without question. The bondage of one man to another was older than recorded history. But that an evil was an old evil didn't make it right. It was evil, an evil he could never condone, and he found it almost impossible to live with it. On the other hand, in a long and desperate year behind the high, cloistered walls of the seminary, he had learned that that life held no answers for him. Slavery was evil, and a life dedicated to service to others had to be right. But he felt suffocated behind those walls, strangled. The blood that coursed through his veins was hot, passionate, and the deadly burden of the brotherhood had not yet cooled it one degree. He needed to be among the living, the vitally alive . . . .

He prowled the deep hammocks, crossed the humid swamps, climbed the sand hills where only snakes and loblolly pines could grow. Walking, he prayed silently, but no answer was offered him. There was no burning bush, no crooked stick wriggling suddenly into a serpent. The clouds didn't erupt with lightning and a voice to solve his dilemma for him.

He found the answer in an odd way, and finding it didn't make him happier; it saddened him. In a few days his leave from the seminary would be ended; before that deadline he would have to be back in Charleston. And the knot of agony distended, and he felt fevered, helpless. He admitted he had sinned, but, God knew, this penance was excessive—to be walled in with young men capable only of loving God or each other—the one openly, the other secretly.

The only answer vouchsafed him was that he was not needed here at Blackoaks. Perhaps there was no real place for him in the priesthood; this would have to be tested by time. But he saw that Styles was making a hard, concerted effort to bring the handling of the huge estate under control. He would have to give him time. He didn't like many of the things Styles did; he despised what Styles was doing to Kathy. But this was their affair and would remain so until Kathy asked him for aid. Meantime, running a vast farm was a tough job. Given time, Styles might meet its demands.

The argument between them had paid immediate dividends. Styles had put the fear of God in the slaves immediately. Ferrell was astonished at how quickly the distillery was restored. Within days it would be in operation again. He found it odd that Styles would have neglected it so long. Labor and materials were in excessive supply at Blackoaks. The gangs of workers, the stacks of lumber, the work supervised by young Blade, and the distillery reared again against the sky as it had when it was his father's pride.

The yards were improved overnight, and each morning dozens of young blacks could be seen diligently sweeping with twig brooms, hoeing, pruning, trimming. Almost overnight, the appearance of the lawns, flower beds, trellises, gravel driveways was restored to the absolute tidiness that resulted only from constant care. In the quarters, Blade, Laus, and others doled out the whitewash and broom-handled brushes. The blacks made the painting a nonstop party with barbecued pigs, chickens, turnip greens, collards, and other delicacies dear to their hearts. They were singing down there and laughing aloud again. He smiled when he heard them and turned away from the reflected glare of the whitewashed cabins. No sign of litter remained in the roadway that climbed through the quarters or around the yards. The whole area gleamed with cleanliness and hummed with a sense of well-being.

The determining factor in his decision to return to the

seminary was the improvement in his mother's condition. Under the regime he set for her—and zealously overseen by Neva—Miz Claire's vapors lifted. She carried flowers each morning to Mr. Baynard's grave in the cemetery above her chapel. She did not speak of his returning; she had no memory that she had done so. She was going to be all right. He had held her illness as the matter that would make up his mind for him, secretly certain she would improve with terrible slowness if at all.

He met Kathy on the upper stairway and kissed her cheek lightly. She laughed at him. "The Ferrell-Junior I remember would have died before he would have kissed his own sister."

"The Ferrell-Junior I know has learned a lot—in spite of himself."

"Listen. Don't you say bad things about Ferrell-Junior. If ever there was a lovelier person in this world, I've never seen him—nor hope to."

Now he laughed at her. "And who would ever have expected you to speak even a kind word about him?"

She put her arm about him and they walked along the corridor toward Miz Claire's private sitting room. "I've missed you. Every night, I thank God you're back."

"Yes. Well, that's it. It's time for me to return to the seminary."

She stopped cold. Her face paled. "Oh, Ferrell, no. Please. You aren't going back? . . . I believed you'd come home to stay."

"I hadn't made up my mind, Kathy. Now I have. I'm going back."

"Don't you know how badly we need you, Ferrell? How I need you?"

"No. Things are going well. They seem to be."

She sagged, her face pallid. "Oh, Ferrell, the whole place needs you. Only you—or father—could keep it all together."

"Styles is making an effort."

Kathy hesitated outside her mother's door, her eyes anguished. But she didn't speak of Styles as he expected her to. Instead she said, "Oh, Ferrell, how can you go back to that place—if you hate it so terribly?"

He kissed her lightly and opened the door. She preceded him into the ornately furnished living room. Its laciness, frills, and rococo furniture totally reflected Miz Claire's tastes. She was sitting in a wing chair near the French doors and the balcony, which overlooked the lawns, knoll, and chapel. Neva was unhurriedly brushing Miz Claire's hair.

Ferrell touched his lips to Neva's cheek and bent down to kiss his mother. When Kathy remained standing a few feet from her chair, Miz Claire looked up, troubled. "There are tears in your eyes, Kathy. Why are you crying?"

"It's Ferrell. He's going back. To that seminary."

Miz Claire sighed and smiled expansively. "I'm so proud, Ferrell. It makes me so proud that you have given yourself to Christ."

Ferrell almost replied but bit his lip and smiled instead. There was no sense in trying to make her understand in a million years that he had not given himself to Christ in going into the brotherhood. He had run to the society as an escape—from himself as much as anything else. But he could not tell her he had not found Christ behind those ivied walls, or any more conscious attempt to live according to Christ's teachings, than one would find in downtown Charleston. The brotherhood was like any other institution; it had become a bureaucracy dedicated to perpetuating itself and on a personal scale to satisfying ambition at any cost. He could not tell her anything like that. She would be unable to believe it—or if she believed it, it might destroy her.

Kathy said, "Why should he go back there? He hates it there—and we need him so badly here."

"Amen," Neva said in a barely audible whisper.

Ferrell laughed and put his arm about the stout woman's shoulder. Miz Claire gave Kathy a frozen smile. "Hate it? Working in Christ's vineyards? How could he hate it, Kathy?"

"He manages," Kathy said.

Miz Claire's hands fluttered. "What is there about that beautiful work to hate?"

Ferrell drew Kathy against him. "Try to understand,

Kathy . . . . I'm going back because I can't keep running away from life that doesn't please me. I ran away from here to escape pain too great to bear."

"We loved you. We would have helped you, if you'd let us."

"But I could think only how I had failed Lorna . . . . I know now. I'll never love anyone else—"

"Oh, Ferrell—"

"Don't blame yourself, Kathy. I failed. I couldn't stand against family and friends for her. I thought I couldn't—the person I was then couldn't simply stand up and tell the world to go to hell and marry her . . . . I—destroyed her and I ran into the Church because my life became unbearable."

"You've paid. Whatever you've done, you've paid a thousand times."

"Maybe you can never pay off a wrong. Now I find life in the order is the last thing I want. But I can't keep running away."

"You wouldn't be running away to come back—where we need you—and love you so."

"Amen," Neva said.

"I know you'll find peace and happiness in the service of God," Miz Claire said.

"And what's to become of us?" Kathy said.

"Things are running better now, Kathy. The quarters are painted, cleaned, the yards glisten again, the field gangs—"

"Have you considered it might be because of you?"

"Amen." Neva spoke slightly louder this time.

"You're back home, Ferrell," Kathy said. "Maybe even the slaves believed you were going to stay."

"Amen."

"No. It hasn't anything to do with me. Give Styles credit—"

"I give Styles credit for nothing."

"—the slaves only need something to do that restores some pride in themselves."

"Pride? In a slave?" Miz Claire said. "They have no pride. They're like little children. They only know to do what you tell them. Nigras are what they are. Like animals with some human intelligence."

Ferrell laughed at her. "Mother, you know you don't believe that. How can you believe that—knowing Neva as you do?" He winked at Neva. "Have you ever seen a more prideful woman in your life than Neva?"

Miz Claire reached up and patted the stout black hand. "You're a wonderful person, Neva."

"I black. But Masta Ferrell right. I'm prideful, 'bout what I am. I Miz Claire's black girl. That's what I am. I'm past fifty. I lived at Blackoaks every year of the past twenty-five and more. It my home. I know I belong to Blackoaks, and that make me proud. Oh, you right, Masta Ferrell. I black, but I got pride. Terrible pride."

4

A thick pall of depression settled over Blackoaks in the days after Ferrell rode away, returning to the seminary. Rain pummeled the earth from leaden skies. The sound of laughter and spontaneous song died from the quarters across the valley from the big house. Tasks that might be postponed were delayed, thrust aside and forgotten in an atmosphere of gloom.

One who shared not at all in the general melancholy at Ferrell's departure, Styles managed to conceal his triumph and jubilation by pressing forward in the achievement of his avowed goals—one of which was to restore the old superior-inferior relationship that had informed his marriage to Kathy.

He sought Kathy the evening of Ferrell's departure. He found her alone in her shadowed bedchamber. A small fire crackled on the hearth against the gloom and chill of the room. A single candle guttered on a bedside table. Kathy huddled in a wing chair near the rain-dulled windows.

"Kathy?"

She turned slightly in the chair glancing at him, eyes cold and dark as the rain-swept night.

"We must have an understanding, Kathy. You've been —flaunting—your relationship with this—this tutor. I won't have it."

"I'm afraid there's nothing you can say about what I do, Styles. And I'm too unhappy to discuss your problems with you tonight."

"I'm afraid you will have to discuss them. I resent your behavior. I won't tolerate it."

She shrugged. "Divorce courts must be open eight hours every day, Styles." Her voice was dead, devoid of emotion.

"If you think you can solve any of your own problems by divorcing me, Kathy, you'd better disabuse your mind at once. Unless you want to give up your Church—"

"The Church got me into this marriage. I don't feel much for the Church right now."

"Even if I'd let you go—and I don't intend to. You'd be a divorced woman—an outcast, and excommunicated from your Church . . . . This won't happen, because I don't intend to divorce you, Kathy. You are my wife. In the eyes of the law. In the Church. You will behave as a wife should behave because you will remain my wife as long as we live."

Kathy peered at him through the musky gloom as if he were some particularly vile insect. She did not answer. Her lips curled and he saw her tiny fists clenched in her lap, but she did not speak again. He felt a chill at the nape of his neck. There was a strength and rigidity about her he had never even suspected. She had loved with all her heart, and now her hatred was equally intense. He experienced a distinct sense of discomfort, and he knew she would not speak again no matter what he said. Uncomfortable, he shrugged his jacket up on his shoulders. He could not leave without the last word. He said, voice hard with disdainful chill, "I've warned you, Kathy. I hope you are intelligent enough to understand my meaning."

She appeared not even to hear him . . . .

He walked, chilled, along the corridor and down the

wide staircase, somehow feeling as if he were in retreat. Ridiculous. A man's wife was his chattel, as was his furniture, as were his slaves. She didn't understand this, but she would before he was through.

He found Mr. Cleatus Dennison relaxed in one of the deep leather chairs in his office. He winced, wishing he didn't have to face the eternally smiling man at this moment. Dennison had poured himself a tall drink of whiskey from the fast-dwindling stock left behind by old Baynard.

"Well, Styles, I'm going to do you a favor this visit. I'm not going to beat about any bushes. We both know I want your Fulani fancies—Blade and young Moab. Eh? We're friends by now. Friends should not try to mislead. I'm prepared to pay you twenty thousand dollars for those two boys. Right now. Tonight."

Styles managed a chilled smile. He walked around the desk and sat down. He poured himself a short drink. Dennison had managed to knock Kathy from his mind. He considered what he could do with twenty thousand dollars—a small fortune in these times.

"I take both the boys tonight. I assume the risk. From tonight. You know, Styles, as well as I do, the ethnic diseases that affect Negroes. Some of them are as old as the race itself. One disease lives inside them—they grow up to full maturity, beautiful and healthy animals. Suddenly the very bone marrow is diseased—in a few years they are dead. Kwashiorkor is a nutritional disease of infants and children. Came from a heavy corn diet in Africa originally—edema, pot belly, and changes in skin pigmentation. You got a slave on your hands that you can't sell. Kwashiorkor is rare over here. But what is not rare is the weakness inherited from the slaves who came out of the holds of slave ships—with that native disease. I only bring up these matters to warn you that I've found in twenty years of raising niggers for market it ain't all gravy. There's a terrible risk. I can't think of a higher-risk undertaking in the raising of any other animal."

"I appreciate your concern," Styles said with some irony.

"Oh, I'm sure you think I'm playing the alarmist. But

I'm not. Suppose you are foolish enough to refuse my offer. Tomorrow either or both those boys can be dropped by fever or epizootic. It happens among niggers all the time."

Silently, Styles thanked the gods for the loans he had arranged with Luke Scroggings and with Garrett Blanford Ware down in Tallahassee. He said, "Anything that promises a big profit carries a big risk factor."

Dennison took a long drink and opened his mouth wide, exhaling the heat from his mouth and throat. Styles watched him, proud that he was able to remain calm without that old gut-tightening apprehension. Dennison was not exaggerating the risks. Dennison laughed. "Well, I see I'm to fail again . . . . Tell me, Styles. You've been in recent communication with Blanford Ware down in Tallahassee, haven't you?"

"Should I have been?"

"Never try to outbluff an old poker player like me, Styles. I was afraid Ware would write to you and send along that flyer promising Fulani wenches for sale at auction in Tallahassee."

"I believe I got such a notice."

Dennison laughed, enjoying himself now that he was reconciled to failure in his bid for the Fulani slave boys. "You believe you did! Don't you know that even if there are Fulani wenches of sucker-bearing age, you are going to be up against men with resources exceeding mine when you bid?"

"I'll have to take that chance."

"All right. Suppose you do bid in one of the wenches. Tallahassee is not Mobile or New Orleans. It's not even Natchez . . . . It is a small wild town in a lawless territory. You know what niggers are down there? Runaway niggers. This auction offers black runners. Niggers that have maybe killed and run—or just run. You won't know until you own them. Renegade blacks are bad niggers."

Styles laughed. "But you'll be there?"

"Oh, I'll be there."

"And you'll be bidding?"

"If there is stock that looks as if it might add something to my herd, yes I'll bid. But I'll have my barred-windowed coaches. I'll have my strong blacks to keep any stock I buy under control. Everything is in my favor, few things are in yours."

"I plan to take Blade and Moab with me. I should have little trouble."

Dennison's face paled. He looked as if he might drop his glass. "Don't be an utter ass, Kenric. My God! Do you realize that to get to Tallahassee you'll cross some of the wildest country east of the Mississippi—or west of it. Florida Territory is where the renegades run when it's too hot for them anywhere else. Why, you take two Fulanis into Florida Territory, you'll get your throat cut —and you'll lose your slaves. No, sir. You leave those boys right here."

Styles exhaled heavily and took a deep drink. No sense in doubting the slave breeder. For once at least, Dennison was being completely honest. "Dregs of humanity—that's what lives in the Florida Territory. A hot, wild country where a man's strength is about the only law. They'd kill you for those two boys. Hell, they'd kill you for a gold dollar."

Styles tried to smile. "What you're trying to tell me is to stay home."

"No. I know better than to waste my breath trying to convince you of that. You smell a Fulani wench all the way from Tallahassee. No. You'll go. And you'll bid beyond your resources. That's your affair . . . . But there is the matter of common sense. Since you insist on making the journey, you'd better prepare well—and wisely."

"I'm listening."

"Take strong black men. Your strongest. The crudest bozal you got is your best protection. I'd say take two of your best black bucks. Armed. Let them understand they are leaving Alabama and what civilization we boast here. They are to shoot first when approached and ask questions later, on the trail. How much money you plan to take?"

"I figure a few thousand."

"You take more than enough to pay board at the ordinaries or taverns you find along your trail, you're insane. Take almost no cash with you. When you win a bid at the auction—if you do, they'll accept drafts on banks. That's what they mean by cash. They don't want cash any more than you do. If you'll take my advice, you'll dress plainly—the more you look like a dirt farmer, the easier your passage is going to be."

"I can't see you arriving in Tallahassee looking like a dirt farmer."

"No. I'll go there in style—as I came here. But my protection is in plain sight. My blacks are trained, armed, equipped. I'll have no trouble."

Styles smiled. He nodded, accepting Dennison's advice. His heart beat faster and his imagination flared at the excitement of the mission to Florida Territory. "Thanks for your advice. I'll heed it carefully—and I'll see you in Tallahassee."

Dennison put his head back laughing. "Yes. We'll meet in Tallahassee. But here's my last friendly warning —I'll see you in Tallahassee, but not as your friendly adviser."

Styles undressed, prepared for bed, but found himself too tautly wound for sleep. He could not lie still on the big bed. He was on his way to Tallahassee. His dream of owning Fulani wenches was about to come true. Men like Dennison might well have greater funds behind them —undoubtedly, they all did. But he alone owned the two fine young bucks. There were no more beautiful animals in the South.

He swung out of bed, slipped into a silk robe, and, knotting it about his flat waist, went out into the corridor. He struck a match to a candle in his office, poured himself a drink, and quaffed it in one long pull. He had hoped the whiskey might tranquilize him, but he blew out the candle watching the flame flare with the alcohol on his breath. He stood a moment in the darkness, wider awake than ever.

On the dimly-lit upper corridor, he saw a line of light under the closed door at Hunter Campbell's bedroom. He remembered their friendliness when Campbell had first come to Blackoaks. Campbell was the first man he'd met in years with an education even approaching his own. They had spent hours conversing in French. They had fenced out on the terrace. That was all past. Chilled, Styles rapped on the door-facing. Hunter Campbell was nothing more than one last chore to which he had to attend before he departed for Tallahassee.

Hunt opened the door after a brief pause. His brow tilted when he saw his guest.

Their gazes clashed for the space of a heartbeat, held, cold. "May I come in?" Styles said.

"It's your house, Styles." Hunt retreated a step, bowing slightly.

"I'd begun to believe perhaps you'd forgotten this slight detail," Styles said, entering the room.

Hunt straightened. "Ah? So it's one of those visits, is it?"

Styles closed the door behind him. He said, "We're both educated men, Hunt. Subtle—"

"You're none too subtle, Styles, as a matter of fact. There is the air about you of the jealous husband."

"Is there? Perhaps you're reaching unjustified conclusions. I don't believe I've mentioned my wife's name."

Hunt shrugged and waited.

Styles said, "There is much difference between New England and the South, Hunt. In the South, a gentleman is required by his code to take any steps, no matter how violent, to wipe out a stain on his honor."

"Violent, eh?"

"I assure you, Hunt, I'm not here to make jokes."

"Then what do you want—and try not to be too subtle. It's after ten and I'm not at my best."

"I am making a trip to Tallahassee. In Florida. It's a trip of some weeks' duration."

"May I wish you a pleasant journey?"

"I hope this will provide ample time for you to make contacts, arrangements, plans for removal. I do not want you to be here at Blackoaks when I return from Tallahassee. Is that clear?"

"I don't see how it could be any clearer unless you held a gun at my head."

5

Styles's converted carriage reached the red-clay hills of Tallahassee only after thirteen days of miserable travel across treacherous trails, unmarked roads, and almost impassable swamp traces. Styles himself couldn't count how many times they lost their way, following a promising road south until it dwindled to a dim path and expired in the bare yard of some farmer who came out to meet them with a gun across his chest.

He rode alone on the back seat. He wore battered clothing and a weatherbeaten planter's hat. Behind him, in the wagon bed into which spancels and shackles had been welded, Perseus crouched silently, watching the back trail. On the front boot, the huge-shouldered Laus and the young giant Pegasus rode, armed and alert. By the time they came into the capital village of the Territory of Florida, they were all fatigued and mud-splattered.

By the tenth day Styles had reached that state of exhaustion in which he looked forward to nothing more than a hot bath, a full meal, and a comfortable bed at the home of the banker Garrett Blanford Ware.

He was surprised to find Tallahassee more than an ordinary frontier village. About the town was a rough touch of France—a flavor that spilled into city limits from the settlement on a land grant given to Lafayette. The territorial capital site had been chosen because it lay an equal distance—about 200 miles—from Pensacola in the far-west panhandle and from St. Augustine on the Atlantic. Finding a centrally located seat of government was the most important consideration of the first territorial delegation. These men spent twenty-eight frightful days crossing the territory from Pensacola to the east coast. Among the terrifying perils they encountered were attacks by savage Indians and runaway Negroes. They agreed to meet with the east-coast representatives, but they would meet them only half-way.

Florida had been recognized as a refuge for runaway Negroes from the adjoining southern states since before the War of 1812. Colonel Nichols, an English commander, when driven out of Pensacola by General Andrew Jackson, had established a territory on the Apalachicola River for red men and black runners. This fifty-mile settlement persisted until Colonel Duncan Clinch of the U. S. Army reduced its fortifications to rubble, killing over two hundred black men, women, and children by blowing up one of the fort's magazines.

Tallahassee was an Indian word for Old Town—so called because the place was flourishing as a settlement when DeSoto had reached it in 1539. About half a mile south of the old Oclocknee and Tallahassi Trail, the area was originally the Indian fields of Tallahassi, shaded by huge groves of live oaks and magnolias. The seat of government for the Territory of Florida was established on these red-clay hills in 1823. Settlement was delayed because of stubborn Indian resistance to white encroachment. Under the former mild, paternalistic, and nominal control of the Spanish, the Indians had lived unthreatened, as they wished. Their existence in those years was described as the picture of perfect happiness—inner content, tender love, and generous friendship. The Americans soon taught them a more progressive and enlightened way of life as they encroached upon their lands and dominated their existence. The Indians were slow to understand the sudden, willfully cruel, and unyielding harassment doled out upon them under General Jackson. But, by burning their villages as he came upon them, slaughtering and driving off their cattle, raping their women, and executing their leaders via kangaroo courts, Jackson in his uncompromising way considerably broke their spirit, diminished their power, destroyed their livelihood, decimated their numbers, and got himself elected President of the United States for his heroic activity in the territory. By 1822, there were less than four thousand Indians in the entire wild land, comprising an area about the size of the state of New York.

However, even this scant number of Indians, scattered in small villages across the wild territory, were too many and too threateningly close for the white people in neighboring states. They demanded that all savages—red and black—be driven or transferred to the deep swamps at the southern tip of the peninsula. The U.S. Army spent the next forty years attempting to effect this arrangement. But the savages were cleared from the hills and farmland surrounding Tallahassee within months, and a capitol building was begun on a ridge downtown in 1823.

The town itself was laid out on the quarter-section donated by the federal government. The streets—Monroe, Calhoun, Jefferson—were named for prominent Americans by the grateful town fathers. More than fifty houses, churches, commercial buildings, schools, and a hotel—noisy and dirty, but well-patronized—were built in 1830, when the population reached almost fifteen hundred.

Each new landmark was constructed upon a hilltop, and all were linked by magnolia and oak-shaded red clay streets. A farming center, seat of government, railroad terminus, the town grew rapidly and was a haven for land speculators, politicians, and other desperadoes. Almost from the first there was a steadily growing and segregated section for "freed" Negroes who preferred performing menial labor for rich whites to sharing the uncertain fortunes of the harried Indians.

One factor that accounted for the steady growth of the town was its freedom from epidemic disease—the plague of cities such as New Orleans. Tallahassee was never molested by those terrible maladies that annually almost decimated the seaports, river towns, and swamp settlements during the hot summer months.

Laus drove the carriage across the tracks of the Tallahassee-St. Marks Railroad. The line, built between 1834 and 1836, was the third railway line completed in the United States and the first in the territory.

Laus, Pegasus, and Perseus stared bug-eyed at the strange sights of the town. They came into the business section—laid out on a ridge northward from the capitol square. Adams and Monroe Streets were noisy, busy, and crowded. Farmers, cattlemen, fugitives, and gamblers jostled business men and politcos on the walk. Styles's black slaves stared unbelievingly at the black men walking those streets as freely and openly as the whites. Once in a while only was a black forced to step off a walk into the clay to make way for a white man. Mostly, they all went about their business in the heat without paying much attention one to the other.

Styles tapped Laus on the shoulder with the tip of his cane. "The Commercial Bank. Over there. The red brick building. That's Mr. Ware's bank. Pull up in front of it."

Laus nodded. He turned the wagon across the street against the flow of carriage traffic. A white man in a flatbed wagon cursed him volubly. Laus held his head high, eyes straight ahead, and ignored him.

Pegasus leaped down, exhaustion forgotten in the excitement of their arrival in this vast center of activity. He waited to aid Styles in alighting from the carriage. But Styles remained on the seat, staring at the locked doors of the bank. Though it was no more than two hours past noon, the bank was closed for the day.

Styles felt a slight flutter of disappointment. He was almost overwhelmed by fatigue, the need for a bath and a cold drink of water. He called out to a man lounging against the front of the bank. "Do you know where Mr. G. Blanford Ware lives?"

"Shore do."

"Would you mind telling us how we might find his home?" Styles asked.

"No. Don't mind. Ever'body knows the Banker Ware's house. Big old place—showy—with columns and gables, on Park. Can't miss it."

6

"Well, land sakes! I do declare! I don't believe it! Styles Kenric of Blackoaks! So you finally come down heah to God's country, eh, my boy? We finally got Styles

Kenric of Blackoaks, Alabama, all the way down to the Territory of Florida." Garrett Blanford Ware beamed in genial welcome. There had been a slight delay when the black servant had retreated into the old porticoed home to announce Styles. But finally Ware had come bounding along the foyer from some inner room, his thin face wreathed in smiles. Extremely tall, gaunt as a wire-grass steer, the banker wrung Styles's hands and called back across his own bony shoulders, "Margaret, oh, Margaret, come and see. One of your very favored young men of all has kindly consented to drop by when he comes into our town. Fine! Yes, suh. Fine. I can't begin to tell you, Styles, how good it is to see you! Uh . . . . How long you plan to be in our fair city?"

Styles frowned slightly. "Why, I came in response to your letter, Mr. Ware."

"My letter?" Ware frowned, apparently puzzled. "Oh, yes! Of course. My letter about the auction. Should of known that flyer with the notice of a purentee Fulani wench would bring you a-runnin' from up there in Alabama . . . . Uh . . . . Did you have a nice trip?"

Styles glanced beyond the banker toward the cool interior of the vast old house. "A fatiguing trip, sir. Had no idea it would be so exhausting."

Ware laughed heartily. "Yes, suh. You do look a mite peaked. Like you been drawn through a keyhole. Reckon a good hot bath, a hearty meal, and a few hours in a bed will change all that, eh? Have you ready to get down to that barracoon to inspect them Fulanis."

"Yes. That will be fine. How do they look?"

"They?"

"The Fulani wenches. I haven't wasted a trip, have I?"

"Well, now! We'll talk about the quality of the Fulani later. Whether you have wasted a trip or not depends on what you plan to spend. I can tell you, my boy, this town is crowded with potential buyers. Haven't seen anything stir up the excitement of this slave auction in all the years I've been here."

Margaret Ware had by now come along the foyer, squeezed past the servant who held the door angled open only far enough to permit her to join her husband between the wooden door and the outer screen. They stood side by side, and despite their smiles they appeared to Styles to be somehow barring the door to him. Trying to be fair, he supposed he did smell rank, he was muddy, almost disreputable looking. But he could not keep down the rage that rose up inside him when they did not invite him inside the front doorway.

She put out her hand and barely let Styles touch it. He felt as if he were more than exhausted and travel-wrinkled, as if he were somehow diseased. "It's so good to see you, Styles," Margaret said. She was as tall as her gaunt husband but twenty pounds heavier, with the raw-boned look of a backwoods woman. It was difficult to look at her and reconcile the unlikely consideration of her extremely delicate health, which was often mentioned. "How long do you plan to be in Tallahassee?"

Styles frowned again. "Well, until after the auction on the fourth. Certainly no longer than that."

"How nice. I do hope we shall see a great deal of you."

Styles felt his jaw sag. What in hell was this? He had assumed he would be welcomed as their guest. These people had spent weeks and months annually at Blackoaks over the past twelve years. They had been demanding, arrogant, often overbearing. Styles began to understand some of the chilled hatred old Baynard had developed toward them in the last couple of years of his life. They had come in expecting the best of everything, making extraordinary demands on the family as well as the house servants.

"Where had you planned to stay?" Margaret said.

"I hadn't made any plans," Styles said in chilled honesty and waited, meeting their gazes levelly.

Blanford Ware had the sensitivity to flush slightly. Holding his gaze was more than difficult, it was impossible; Ware seldom looked anyone straight in the eye for more than a few seconds. He always explained that it put people at ease when a banker didn't stare at them, didn't probe, as it were, with his eyes. Ware said, "Well, you know we'd love to have you as our guest, Styles. Lord knows, I'd insist on it at any other time."

"Oh?"

"Margaret's health, Styles. I'm sure you understand. Her health is so delicate. Strangers in the house simply upset her until she is physically ill. We just can't have that, can we?"

Styles bowed slightly. He did not bother to smile. The money he was able to spend at the auction depended upon this man, but at the moment Styles could only contain his rage. He would borrow his money—at whatever interest the bastard demanded—but wait until they presented themselves next at Blackoaks. He looked forward to that moment with almost passionate anticipation. "I do understand," he said. "I'll undoubtedly be able to find lodging for myself and my servants."

"I'll see to that," Ware said with an expansive gesture. "Let me get my hat and jacket. I'll ride down to the hotel with you. Town is overrun just now with out-of-towners. They might turn you away—a stranger and all. But they'll find a place for you with my endorsement. Yes, sir." He spoke over his shoulder. "Malcolm, bring my hat and light jacket." He smiled at his wife, his eyes darting. "And don't bother to wait dinner for me, Margaret."

"Why not?" Her voice quavered with the emotions suppressed under it.

He shrugged. "Because I'll be busy, my dear. I'll eat downtown."

Ware walked out to the carriage at the curb with Styles. Styles was aware that big, rawboned Margaret remained in the doorway, staring after them. Neither he nor the banker looked back. Ware strode swiftly, like a man making his escape. Pegasus said, "Howdy, Masta Ware, suh. It sho' pleasant to see you again, Masta, suh."

"Hello, Pegasus. Why are you wearing a gun?"

Seated in the carriage, Styles explained why he and his three black attendants were armed. Dennison had warned him of the dangers of the trail, not the least of which were highway desperadoes who haunted the long and lonely trails. Ware agreed that Dennison's advice had been correct. "But," he said, "I would remove the guns from your slaves while you're in Tallahassee. None of you will need guns in our town—and it might create some unpleasantness if our people came upon niggers armed this way."

Styles took the guns from the black men. They surrendered them reluctantly. He placed their guns in a strongbox secured under the front seat. Laus, Pegasus, and Perseus had worn their guns proudly. They had been set apart these past thirteen days from all other slaves they had ever encountered: they had been permitted to bear arms.

Ware said, "Drive back downtown to the town house, Laus. I'll soon have a place for you fellows to sleep and the best cooking this side of the Georgia line."

As the carriage rolled along the inclined clay street, Styles listened to Ware extoll the virtues of life in the territorial capital. "As you can see, the folks who are fortunate enough to live here because of their legislative duties or other business have built lovely old Georgian homes. We have a beautiful town. And—though we do have a quarters where freed niggers congregate—we have little crime. No need for guns or bodyguards."

The foyer of the hotel was crowded, stirring with men in a way that resembled a molested beehive. There were elegantly dressed gentlemen—obviously landowners—in town either for the auction or the legislative meetings. Elegance, of course, is relative, and the best of them would have been assimilated without notice in a crowd at the St. Louis Hotel in New Orleans. But in a rough frontier village on the edge of Indian country they were colorful. Most of them knew Banker Ware and greeted him warmly. In the crowd were men who appeared to be gamblers, card sharps, cattlemen, railroad people. But most of them were at least in clean clothes, and Styles knew that he looked like a tramp and that his disreputable appearance was exaggerated as he walked beside the expensively attired banker.

The hotel was overcrowded, but within minutes after Ware had drawn the manager aside in whispered conversation, Styles was invited to sign the register. "A front suite," the clerk told him with an obsequious smile. "Overlooking the street and the capitol square. Cool at night, too."

"I'll need accomodations for three slaves," Styles said.

The stout-faced clerk smiled again. "Yes indeed, sir. That's all taken care of, sir. Will they need to be shackled at night?"

"No. I want them to have a good place to sleep. And plenty to eat."

Ware clapped him on the shoulder and laughed. "Don't give it another thought, my boy. This hotel has catered to hundreds of fine gentlemen and their slaves just like you. I promise you they'll take care of your stock and your slaves just as the owner of Blackoaks Plantation has every right to expect."

At the sound of Ware's voice many of the men—especially the dandily dressed landowners—glanced at Styles. Styles flushed slightly, feeling more than ever like a tramp. "Is there any place I could get a bath?"

"Next door at the barber shop, sir. We'll send one of our black boys over to prepare your bath and help you lay out your clothes."

As they turned away from the desk, Ware said, "Why don't I wait in the bar? I'll have a couple of drinks while you bathe and freshen up. Then we'll have dinner in the hotel dining room—you'll be my guest. They serve a steak that plain melts right in your mouth." Then Ware lowered his voice. "Then, later, if you wish, we could drop by and call on Orange."

"Orange?"

Ware smiled and nudged Styles with his elbow. "Let's say Orange is an octoroon friend of mine. Lady friend, eh? She has some girls there that will take your mind off your woes."

"No," Styles said. "I don't think so."

Ware hesitated, then gave him an odd glance as if at last some lingering doubt had been cleared up in his mind. "I understand," the banker said. "Well, I'll drop by Orange's place on my way home. She'll be expecting me. You know?"

7

The Dalton Stables barracoon, built to house the slaves for the first Tallahassee auction, was new. Only the stench was old—the ammoniac, sick-sweet odors of human offal, urine, vomit, garbage, and spoiled food strewn among litter in the compound. Ancient smells—all old odors—as aged as man's inhumanity to man. The place was a mere stockade, two open spaces enclosed by new-felled pine logs and separated by feeding troughs and lean-to enclosures, one opened upon the male area and the other upon the female yard. The shelter had been hastily thrown up with its barbette where the auction would be held in an open field behind the barns, stables, smithy, and corrals of Dalton's Stables.

By nine o'clock the next morning Styles was striding across Adams toward Dalton's Stables, which were located conveniently near the hotel and the capitol square.

The stables, blacksmith shop, and feeding barns were busy and overcrowded. It was easy to believe that Dalton had the most profitable business in the vicinity. He cared for the animals and many of the slaves belonging to the legislators and business men of the town. When Styles arrived there were already at least a dozen well-dressed men inspecting the slaves who would be offered on the auction vendue.

Dalton was a twisted man, a victim of kyphosis. Despite the abnormal curvature of his spine, he was a spry man who moved rapidly and purposefully among his customers. Only his sun-bleached eyes betrayed any trace of the inner agony he had come to accept as his normal state of existence.

"I am Styles Kenric of Blackoaks. From up Alabama way," Styles told Dalton.

The twisted little man nodded and smiled. "Blan Ware

told me you might drop by ahead of the auction. Welcome, suh. What can I do to serve you?"

"Your flyer," Styles said, "offered Fulani wenches."

"Wench. We got one purentee Fulani wench. But I'll tell you honest, Mr. Styles—uh, Kenric. I tell you honest, a man would have to be guillible as a fly-swallower to pay more'n ten dollars for her."

"A pure-blooded Fulani wench? You must be joking."

"No, suh, I ain't joking. We got bad niggers. I see you are a man knows a hawk from a handsaw. I won't try to deceive you—they're all bad niggers. They was tracked down and captured one way or another. But they is bad inside. My ole grandpa always said once a nigger was bad—he was forever bad. I believe it since we set up that barracoon out there."

"Do you mind if I look at her?"

Dalton's agonized eyes lighted in something almost resembling a delighted smile. "You want to inspect her? Shuck her down and inspect her?" He laughed. "No, suh. I don't mind one whit. Let me call three or four niggers to help you hold her."

With Dalton springing along awkwardly beside him and three heavy-muscled blacks in their wake, Styles entered the female yard of the barracoon. Because of Dalton's odd attitude, he felt a sense of dread—a certainty that he had wasted time and money coming south from Blackoaks. A single pure-bred Fulani wench among all these runaways and Dalton's first words were to warn him against her!

Dalton locked the pineboard gate behind them. Styles felt the cold and insolent gazes of the black women appraising him. There was none of the humility that characterized every slave he had even seen—these were fugitives, runners, slaves gone wild. Some of the women called obscenities as they approached. One or two spread their legs wide as invitation to the black bucks. All of them wore soiled cotton shifts, nothing beneath them.

Dalton limped into the lean-to, kicking at the women sprawled on the ground. "Get out of here," he said. "We gonna have a shuck-down inspection." He glanced around. "You, Ahma, come here, you black bitch."

The girl Dalton had spoken to was sprawled against a shadowed wall. She unwound her long legs and stood up, taking her time.

Styles gasped, staring at her. He had never seen a lovelier girl in his life, black or white. She was at least six feet tall in her bare feet, statuesque and perfectly proportioned. Her crisp black hair, almost as straight as an Indian's, was parted severely in the middle and worn in braids on each side of her head.

"She purentee," Dalton said, as if following the train of Styles's thoughts. "An' I tell you somethin' else. She purentee bitch."

The woman called Ahma walked slowly toward them. The other women, giggling, or watching silently, crowded in a semicircle in the brilliant sunshine just beyond the roofing of the lean-to. Ahma held her head high with a chilled arrogance. Her breasts strained the rotting fabric of her cotton shift.

"She purely hates anything with a white skin," Dalton said, watching her. "Know how she was cotched? She was running with the Indians. But she got snake-bit. Rattler. They left her to die and some white people took her in, cut the venom out, nursed her back to health. How'd you repay them white folks for they kindness to you, Ahma?"

Ahma stared down at the twisted little man in hatred, unrepentant. "I burnt down they shack—and I ran."

Dalton laughed. "She purentee bitch, I warn you."

"How old are you?" Styles said.

Ahma looked at Styles for the first time. Her eyes met his almost levelly. Sunlight touched at her skin, giving it the same coppery cast that set Blade apart from other Negroes. Her forehead was high, her nose cameo-perfect; her black eyes, widely set, blazed with hatred. Her full-lipped mouth twisted, revealing white, strong teeth. "What do you care, white ass?" she said.

"You keep a civil tongue, Ahma. This gentleman might buy you—if he's still fool enough to want to by auction time."

Ahma spoke directly into Styles's face, her tone chilled.

"You buy me, white ass, and I make you only one promise. I'll kill you. First chance I get."

Dalton shook his head. "She ain't going to give you no straight answers, Mr. Styles. We got papers on her—she appears to be no more than sixteen years old. They tell me she run all the way from the Carolinas. Killed her master up there and ran south—all by herself."

Styles managed to smile, keeping his poise. "You don't sound real promising, Ahma. But I still want to look at you."

"Shuck down, Ahma," Dalton ordered.

"Fuck you," Ahma said. She remained standing tall, braced like a lynx, ready to spring.

Dalton wasted no time, he jerked his head. The three bucks bounded past Styles and grabbed Ahma. She fought furiously. The women in the sun screamed, yelling with laughter, begging the bucks to undress them. "I won't fight you, honey. You can shuck me down all day, you want to."

"Shit," Dalton said when the three men wrestled Ahma to the ground but could not subdue her long enough to strip off her dress. She clawed their faces and bared chests until they were bleeding. Dalton brought shackles. The men held her still long enough that Dalton got her ankle in the metal restraint.

Panting then, Ahma lay still, staring at them, face flushed. The bucks pulled her dress over her head. She remained crouched on the ground, naked. Her breasts were full, perfectly proportioned for her body. Her stomach was flat and the coppery hairs at her rounded pad glittered in the sun. Her legs were sculpted to elegantly turned perfection, thighs, calves, ankles, and feet; she was unblemished. Her body bore no welts, no signs of beatings, no whip weals. There were no belly striae—she had not borne children.

"Stand up, Ahma," Dalton ordered. "Let Mr. Styles Kenric here examine you."

Ahma merely stared at them and refused to move until Dalton jerked his head toward the bucks again. Then she got slowly to her feet and stood with her arms at her sides, her head tilted, eyes fixed upon some distant cloud.

Styles advanced toward her slowly, speaking softly. "I have no wish to harm you, Ahma. I don't want you harmed at all. I'd like to take you home to my plantation. I have two pure-blooded Fulani youths there waiting for you, Ahma. Blade is about twenty now—and Moab, he's about your age. You're bigger than Moab. But you aren't bigger than Blade. We'll treat you kindly, Ahma. Now will you let me check your teeth?"

He was close to her now. She tried to kick him, but the shackles restrained her. She remained unmoving. Cautiously, as if dealing with a caged tigress, Styles extended his hand toward her. When his hand touched her, a shudder wracked her body. She screamed suddenly, and before anyone could move, she butted him with her head.

Staggered, for a moment dizzy, Styles stumbled backward. Dalton caught his arm supporting him. "She a purentee bitch, suh. If you smart, you put this one out of your mind."

Styles shook his head to clear it. His head ached painfully, but Ahma seemed unaffected by her vicious butting.

His voice remained level. "I'm going to take you home with me, Ahma. One way or another. If you want to go two hundred miles in chains and shackles, that's up to you. But you are going."

She gazed at him unblinkingly for the space of a long heartbeat and then she coldly spat in his face.

8

The story of Styles Kenric's first encounter with the purentee Fulani wench Ahma reached the hotel ahead of him. Men were laughing—some of them sympathetically—when he walked into the bar just before noon, nursing a bruise the size and color of a guinea-hen egg on his forehead.

Between a sense of distaste and a grudging pleasure, Styles found himself something of a celebrity as he crossed the hotel foyer toward the bar. Men bowed, smiled, and spoke his name with some deference and empathetic grins.

"Howdy, Mista Kenric, suh."

Styles hesitated and recognized the slave trader Darwin Culverhouse after only a moment of sorting through the litter of his discarded memories. The tall, disreputable man, the self-confessed black-sheep son of the Culverhouses from up in the Piedmont, had not changed from the day he'd arrived at Blackoaks looking for slaves for sale. He looked as if he wore the same stained suit and battered Panama planter's hat. His beard had the ragged three-day look—as it had upon their first meeting. His run-over boots were still unpolished, and yet he carried himself with the self-confident manner of the well-born. Another factor which remained constant was the aggressively haughty and swaggering mannerism which Styles had found particularly offensive in the lowest of white professionals, the itinerant slave peddler.

"Recall me, do you, Mr. Kenric? I'm the slicker that you outslicked on a slave deal."

"Did I?" Styles stared at Culverhouse along his nose.

Culverhouse laughed. "Feel no animus toward you, suh. None whatsoever. Made no real profit from the transaction I had with you. But over the years I've learned a great patience—forebearance. You can't win all the time. You were simply too clever for me. I admit it and no hard feelings. Down here looking for bargains—and a Fulani wench, eh?"

Styles nodded, looking about for an escape. He was a center of attention and he would not have wanted to be seen with a man like Darwin Culverhouse under any circumstances.

"I'm buying," Culverhouse said. "But like many another man from the states down here, I'm looking for lost or stolen property. If I can locate a runner, or a stolen slave, and prove the animal belongs to a landowner, I can rake down a bigger profit than I can by blocking out a coffle of culls."

"Yes." Styles nodded and tried to step beyond Culverhouse, but the man caught his arm. "Have a drink with me, Cousin. I think I got a business proposition that you'll want to hear about."

Styles shook his head, without smiling. He glanced around with a sense of desperation, seeking an escape from the aggressive slave trader. He certainly didn't want to be considered in a class with this man.

Someone called his name from within the bar. Styles recognized Baxter Simon. In his middle thirties, Simon was heavy-shouldered, barrel chested. He was handsome in a tough, disciplined way. He was flat-bellied, narrow-hipped, with strongly hewn features, unyielding brown eyes, and squared jaw. He was fashionably dressed. Though Simon was not one of the landed gentry, he was certainly many stations above Darwin Culverhouse in social position. Though both men dealt in slaves, Simon was a breeder, far more acceptable in society than a peddler who owned only his wagons and shackles.

Styles said brusquely, "Excuse me, Culverhouse." He stepped around him and walked toward where Simon awaited him, grinning, his brow tilted. Styles felt his face grow heated, remembering the way Simon had defamed him, practically naming him a homosexual in public. Damn him. Styles felt the renewal of that old hatred. But at the moment he wanted to escape Culverhouse. He was shaking hands with Bax Simon before he realized that Culverhouse was standing at his shoulder, like a leech.

Simon extended his hand and smiled. He seemed to have forgotten completely the incident of Styles's fingering the Fulani Blade at Blackoaks two years ago. Styles wished to God he could put the nasty scene from his own mind and forget it.

"Got a table. Right over here," Simon said. "Come have a drink with us."

"Howdy, Mr. Simon," Culverhouse said.

Simon's swarthy face pulled into a look of contempt which quickly altered into a false smile. "Oh, hello, Culverhouse. What you doing down here?"

"Same as you and Styles," Culverhouse said. "As I was telling Styles, I might have a real buy for him—"

"Come along, have a drink with us," Simon invited. He looked none too happy to include Culverhouse in his party, but he seemed to accept that Darwin was with Styles. Styles simply ignored the slave peddler who walked closely behind him as if warmed by reflected glory.

Simon introduced Styles to half a dozen men before they reached his table. He did not bother to introduce Culverhouse. Most of the men ignored the peddler, but Culverhouse continued to smile, undismayed.

When they reached Simon's table near a double window overlooking the main street, two men stood up. "Cleatus Dennison," Styles said.

"That's right," Dennison said. "We're all here. Looks like you wasted a long trip. Eh?"

"Did I?"

"Surely you ain't gobemouche enough to buy a hellion like that."

Styles smiled. "Most perfect woman I ever saw."

Dennison laughed. "Physically, yes. But it's inside—in her mind—where she's rotten. You'll never break her. A man would be a fool to pay good money for a bad negress like that."

"Dennison is right," the other man at the table said. "I'm Alvah Eastin, Mr. Kenric. I know how savage nigras git once they go bad. You may not believe this, but I was one of the hundred and thirty-nine men under Dade in that massacre down on the Withlacoochee River."

They sat down in the loud chattering of the room. They made a place for Culverhouse, shifting their chairs around for him, but they did not include him in the conversation. Nevertheless, as they talked, Culverhouse nodded and smiled, following the conversation as if content. Simon ordered drinks around. The soldier, Alvah Eastin, persisted with his story of the massacre.

"Reason I tell you about this massacre is that it was the nigras who was the savage animals, not the Indians."

Dennison laughed. "Alvah tells that story because it's the biggest thing in his life. It's the only story he's got."

"Well, I did git out alive. One of the onliest ones what did. We marched into the swamp and was trapped. Them Indians fought like wild, and they beat us clear and certain. Most of us that warn't dead was bad wounded.

We thought the skirmish had been hell. But we didn't know what hell was.

"Immediately after the Indians cut us down and retreated, and before we who lived could regroup, forty or fifty nigras on horseback galloped up and alighted in the midst of our dead and wounded. Them blacks tied their beasts and commenced with horrid bloodthirsty shouts and yells, the butcherin' of our wounded and the plunderin'. They stripped the bodies of our dead of their clothing, watches, and money. Then they began splitting open with axes and huge knives the heads of all soldiers what showed the least signs of life. And accompanying their bloody work with obscene and taunting screams of derision. And they kept yelling at each other, 'What'd you git to sell?'

"One soldier got up and asked the nigras to spare his life. They met him with the blows of their axes and their fiendish laughter. They shot down the army oxen in their shafts and burned the last of our wagons."

"And how did you escape?" Dennison said with a note of irony in his voice. "Somebody has got to ask Alvah or it stalls his story."

Alvah Eastin smiled absently, reliving the old horror. "I was layin' sprawled half under blackberry vines. I was covered with blood with open gashes in the head that gave me the look of having been shot through the brain. One nigra come close, took what money I had, stripped me. He even started to lay my skull open with his axe. I was too near dead to care really. But then he said with the most horrible contempt I ever heard in a human voice—if them black animals is considered human—he said, 'Damn him. He's dead enough.' He kicked me, and when I didn't even react, he walked away and left me.

"Now, the reason why I tell you that story is to compare in your mind the savage red man and the savage black. They ain't no way to compare them. A Creek or a Muskogee Indian on the warpath is an angel of mercy compared to a black that has reverted to the bush—to his own old cannibal ways from Africa. They minds can't even contain the word mercy. Like mindless animals, all they know is kill."

"There you are, Styles," Dennison said. "Alvah went into all that detail to tell you what I said at first, no sane man buys a nigger or Negress that has reverted."

Styles shrugged. "I've followed your advice till today, Cleatus. I'll give a lot of thought to what you say, of course. But I believe I will stay through the auction, no matter my decision."

"Of course. I want you to be my guest for dinner before the auction."

"Are you here in the hotel?"

Dennison gave him an odd look, then shook his head. "No. I'm not. I rented a ten-room mansion over on Park. Tell you why. I have my housekeeper along—"

"Sefina," Styles said.

Dennison smiled knowingly and nodded. "That's right. In New Orleans, I can rent adjoining suites at the St. Louis Hotel for my black housekeeper. But they aren't yet that broadminded here in Tallahassee."

Styles said nothing and Dennison laughed. "Don't tell me you're as prudish as these other old maids, Styles. A man has got to have a woman. Eh?"

Styles nodded. He did not glance toward Simon but felt that memory of illness. But Simon seemed completely to have forgotten the day Styles had grown hard and breathless with excitement milking down Blade in an inspection of the Fulani. Simon said, "Now, Kenric here has a lovely wife. I'd envy him if I envied any man with a white wife. A white-skinned woman makes me want to puke, tell you the truth."

"I prefer dark meat myself," Alvah Eastin agreed.

"Amen," Darwin Culverhouse said.

"Not only is a white woman ugly to look at—especially when she begins to sag in the tits and the belly. But they so goddamn hard to live with. I was married to a white woman for a while. I thought I had plumb gone down to hell. The good lord in his kindness took her off in childbirth, and I don't contemplate marriage again—no more than I contemplate kissing a black woman full on the mouth. I couldn't do that neither." Bax Simon shuddered.

"Nor I," said Eastin.

"Amen," Culverhouse said.

"When my wife was alive, she was so religious you wanted to vomit when she started spoutin' the Bible at you," Simon said. "She railed at me about my visits to the quarters and the way I was pestering the black women down there. Hell, I plain asked her right out what she intended to do about it. She herself hated sex, and I hated worse burdenin' her with it. She told me I would never share her bed again—tracking in the mud of the quarters on my boots and the slime of black cunt on my cock. She liked to talk that way—she'd scream all that stuff at you—as long as she was condemnin' you. But she was too prim to say shit otherwise."

"Lot of that among white women," Eastin observed.

"Amen." Culverhouse capped it.

Simon took a long drink of his mint toddy. "I got enraged. I completely quit our wedded bed. But I didn't make it easy on her. I had her watched constantly. She wasn't goin' to take on some other man secret-like—or ever relieve herself with her finger if I could keep her from it."

"Hot damn," said Eastin.

"You always was a man knowed how to handle a woman," Culverhouse said.

"Well, we lived like strangers in that big old house at Willow Oaks. She acted like she was going insane. I started bringing the wenches up to the house and into my bedroom to service me.

"Finally, she comes to me, pleading with me to take her back in my bed. She don't care any more that I have black wenches, too. I laughed at her and agreed. She rips off her clothes and gets in my bed. She was wilder than 'ary black wench I had. Nine months later, she was dead, in childbirth. I had one wife, and I wouldn't of taken a million dollars for her. But I wouldn't give you ten cents for another one."

"Amen," said Darwin Culverhouse.

Dennison ordered drinks around. They discussed the Indian wars, the price of cotton, the best trails north into Alabama. They did not mention Ahma again. But though they talked of everything else, Styles had the gut feeling that both Dennison and Bax Simon were here to buy the

Fulani wench. What man could pass up such a perfect creature? You had to believe you could break her. He was certain they believed they could control her. They had the know-how, the life-long training. But most of all, they had the resources. They could bid until they did own her. He felt ill with the threat of loss . . . .

9

A carnival atmosphere rose from the slave auction at Dalton's Stables. Crowds spilled out of the compound, along the corrals, and in knots under the shaded barn overhang. Hawkers sold drinks, cigars, souvenirs, boiled and roasted peanuts. There were at least two hundred men milling about the stables and the barracoon. The stockade had been freshly swept, washed down, and carefully policed. The sick-sour aroma was replaced by the rancid odor of disinfectant and black human musk. The herd to be auctioned had been outfitted in cotton shifts and new osnaburg britches.

Styles moved through the crowds of gawkers, sightseers, the curious, and the serious buyers. Among these latter were the landowners who classed themselves as avid collectors of perfect animal flesh.

A drumroll summoned the buyers to the parapetlike mound where a long wooden table had been set up under a canvas stretched to provide shelter for the auctioneer and his assistants against the blazing Florida sun.

His heart battering raggedly, Styles worked his way as near to the front of the crowd as possible. Plankings had been set up on long sections for rough benches. Most of the men stood up, sweating and pressing forward, seeking the animals they had previously chosen. Styles heard the repeated complaint, "Hell, they ought to have these animals numbered. It ain't easy recollectin' a nigger you fingered a couple days back. Hell, all nigras look alike to me."

But the parade of black, brown, ochre, and yellow humanity proved that few if any of the blacks truly resembled one another. They passed up to the block singly and infrequently in pairs—there were no Florida laws concerning condition-of-slaves sales. They were the African bush Negro—flat nose, slant forehead, underslung jaw. There were the griffo, the zambo, the octoroon, and some obviously with three-quarters Indian blood.

They were sullen, withdrawn, sick with resentment and hatred. Some had been running free with the Indians for as long as ten years. They were hostile, defiant. These people followed orders only when a guard's whip lashed their bare legs or cracked across their backs. One could easily recognize the newly escaped slave—the frightened, timid, quick to obey an order, eyes always downcast.

Styles let the long parade pass without any real interest. He saw no stock to compare with anything he owned at Blackoaks. And there was the additional negative aspect: these were the runners, the dangerous, the maniacs. The strongest and finest-built were not as outstanding as Laus or Pegasus. No field hand compared to the rugged Perseus.

Bidding was brisk. Styles found himself surprised at how often Bax Simon and Mr. Cleatus Dennison signaled their bids. Darwin Culverhouse bid often, but dropped out when the bidding rose above three hundred—he had to count in his profit when he resold the stock.

Styles watched Dennison and Baxter Simon. They were intense, studying notes they'd jotted down earlier, concentrating deeply. Few of the blacks brought as much as one thousand dollars, although Styles had seen spirited bidding go well above three or four thousand at vendues in New Orleans. Most of the blacks sold for around five hundred. Even the auctioneer, imported from the huge vendues at New Orleans, admitted these animals posed great risks to buyers. Still, even at five hundred average, the auction was a financial bonanza for the backers—these runaways had been reared by someone else, captured and purchased for a few dollars' bounty.

At last, the culls were dispensed with. Styles felt the nerves tighten in his belly at the gasps and sudden sharp intake of breath among the men around him as Ahma was prodded up on the auction block. None of the women had been forced to strip up there on the stage—inspections were over; buyers were assumed to have made their choices before the stock went on sale.

The arrogant defiance of this splendid young female acted as a challenge to the auctioneer. She gazed at him in a contempt that included every man in the audience. She stood taut, rimlighted by the sun, a resplendent young Fulah wench, her skin like burnished copper, her legs delicate pillars.

"Here she is, gentlemen. *Our pièce de résistance.* Ahma. A purebred Fulani. Not a gentleman among you who knows African bloodlines who doesn't also know and appreciate how rare a prize Ahma is. Most beautiful wench I have ever seen in more'n twenty years of auctioning Negro flesh in the finest slave markets of New Orleans. Look at her! I don't exaggerate—I don't lie to you—when I swear to you there are Creole gentlemen in New Orleans who'd pay ten thousand for her—unblinking—as she stands there. Just look at her! Who among you can doubt she descends directly from queens?"

"What'd you do with a wench that big?" someone called from the audience. Hoots of laughter rose around the stage.

"Brother, if you didn't do no more'n just look at her, she'd be worth whatever she cost you," the auctioneer said when the laughter subsided.

The man in the audience hooted, calling out, "You know black flesh, Mister Auction-Man. I give you that. But you don't know my wife."

The auctioneer gazed at the lovely wench. He drew his tongue across his lips and the frayed tips of his mustache, deciding in that instant to put into this auction that extra charge of excitement these affairs always demanded—the shocking moment that would be talked about in the months to come and would guarantee ever larger audiences at the next vendue. He said, "Take off that dress, Ahma. Let these gentlemen see what all you got to offer."

Ahma stared defiantly at the auctioneer for the full

period in which the audience clapped and yelled its enthusiastic endorsement of the seller's order.

Ahma remained motionless, aloof. Her head tilted slightly. Her cameo profile seemed to tauten and angry fires raged deep in her wide-set black eyes. But she did not move to comply, nor speak.

Angered, the auctioneer ordered her for a second time to shuck down. She remained unmoving. He came around the table and approached her, face pallid. He was not accustomed to black defiance.

With a sudden cry that chilled the blood as the scream of a lynx might do, Ahma sprang at the auctioneer. Her hands, like claws, scratched at his eyes. The auctioneer yelled—a highpitched sound, almost womanlike. He fell back, retreating. He ordered the guards to subdue her. Three muscular black men, bared to the waist, captured Ahma after a brief, fierce struggle and wrestled her back to the block where she stood rigid.

"Strip the bitch," the auctioneer ordered.

The black guards caught her dress and stripped it from her, the tearing fabric loud in the hot, breathless silence.

Ahma stood naked—defiant. She stared straight across the heads of the shouting, panting men, into infinity. Her columnlike legs were braced apart. The triangle of hair at her pubic mound gleamed as coppery as her skin. Her marble-hard nipples stood rigid on full, high-standing breasts.

The auctioneer recovered his poise. He said, "There she is, gentlemen! Who'll open the bids on this tigress?"

Styles felt his heart sink. He didn't want to lose Ahma. He wanted to call out a bid well above anything quoted during the long day. He forced himself to wait. There was a pause and finally the bidding was begun half-heartedly at three hundred.

"Gentlemen! Gentlemen!" the auctioneer reproved them. "Don't let the spirit in this wench deter you. A good whip and she'll come around. This is pureblood Fulani. Don't insult me with such bids. Don't insult yourselves."

"Five hundred," said Mr. Cleatus Dennison.

"Six hundred," called Baxter Simon.

"Seven hundred—and fifty." Styles barely recognized the cawing voice as his own.

Neither Dennison nor Simon bid again until others raised the price to one thousand. The auctioneer laughed. "Now, gentlemen, we can get serious. We can get down to business. Do I hear twelve-fifty?"

"Twelve-fifty," Dennison said.

"Fifteen hundred," Baxter Simon called.

His stomach nerves tied in knots, Styles said, "Two thousand."

He had prayed inwardly that the bidding would cease. After all, even if Ahma were a purebred Fulani, the highest bid of the day had been only seven hundred on the other stock.

Again, neither Simon nor Dennison upped Styles's bid. But when a man from Louisiana bid twenty-five hundred, Dennison raised the ante to twenty-seven and Simon made it an even three thousand.

Styles was afraid he was going to be sick at his stomach. He saw now that he had lost Ahma. It was almost as if these flesh breeders were toying with him, waiting for him to withdraw. His face taut and pale, Styles glanced around. He found G. Blanford Ware in the crowd. For a moment their gazes met. Ware nodded, a barely perceptible affirmative movement of his head.

Styles felt better. Ware was encouraging him, putting the resources of the Commercial Bank behind him. Ware believed—as he did—in what he was trying to do. Ware meant to help him take home this strange prize. He lifted his arm in the air. His voice was controlled for the first time. It was good to know you were not alone against odds like this.

"Thirty-five hundred dollars," Styles said.

The breathless pause between bids was longer this time. Perhaps the Louisiana planter had seen the little by-play between Styles and the Florida banker. And there was always the wildness of the wench to consider. Finally, the Louisiana planter raised the bid to thirty-six hundred.

The bidding against Styles abruptly ceased at an even four thousand dollars. The Louisiana man said, "Hell, there ain't no cunt worth four thousand dollars." Neither Dennison nor Bax Simon bid again.

When Laus, Pegasus, and Perseus arrived in the carriage, two black guards marched Ahma out, her arms shackled behind her. She wore the dirty cotton shift she had had on the first time Styles saw her.

Dennison, Baxter Simon, and Darwin Culverhouse pushed through the crowd to where Styles stood. Dennison carried a steel chain, the type of choke collar one used on vicious dogs. "Put that around her neck. Whips might quiet her. Fists might calm her. But when you cut off her breath, she'll follow you eagerly."

Styles took the chain, thanking him.

"Me and Simon. We could have bid your ass off, Styles. I hope you understand that. We decided not to."

"Why?"

Dennison smiled. "Several reasons. One, you got that other perfect Fulani—Blade. You got that younger boy, Moab, coming along. Almost a pleasure for both Bax and me to know you finally got a mate for the Fulani Blade."

"Too," Simon said, "she a runaway. She a bad nigger."

Dennison laughed, nodding. "A proved troublemaker. Neither of us needed that on our stud farms. And last, I did it as a kind of salute to old Ferrell Alexander Baynard, Senior. A Fulani mate for Blade was his dream. And a real brass-tailed gentleman he was."

Simon smiled. "Tell Miss Kathy, this wench is my gift to her—loveliness for the lovely."

Darwin Culverhouse waited until the Fulani wench was shackled in the rear bed of the carriage. Perseus was moved up to share the front seat with Laus and Pegasus. Dennison and Simon shook hands with Styles, wished him the kind of luck they were convinced he was going to need, and then they drifted away.

Culverhouse caught Styles's sleeve. "Mr. Kenric. Admirable thing you done in there. Had no idea you were situated to outbid some of them rich men in there. I got a proposition for you. I know where I can find two Fulani wenches. They ain't beauties like this wench you got here. But they should be a hell of a lot more malleable. I'll deliver them to Blackoaks—as soon as I can."

"What will they cost me?"

"That's what I don't know. All I ask is your word as a gentleman that you will buy them off me once I invest in them. Whatever they cost, I want one thousand dollars for each one—above their cost and my expenses . . . . But if you want purebred Fulani wenches, I can deliver."

Styles nodded, agreeing. Darwin Culverhouse extended his hand. Styles hesitated before he touched it. Then he realized this was the way Culverhouse intended to seal their bargain. They shook hands.

10

The February sun was cresting across the cloudless roof of heaven when Laus turned the horses north and headed out of Tallahassee. Though it was midwinter, the world was greening up for spring and the first dogwood showed white in the copse of trees. The rutted trail slowed the carriage. Riding alone on the back seat, Styles had to fight against the urge to check over his shoulder. Though the wench was shackled, he felt nervous, vulnerable, as if he rode with an uncaged panther in the wagon bed.

Styles was never afterwards sure what caused him to lurch forward suddenly and jerk around on the seat, supporting himself against its backrest. He gasped and yelled, "Laus! Stop the carriage."

Luckily, the carriage was moving at a slow clip or the girl would have been dead. Though she was shackled, wrists and ankles, she had lunged over the tailboard of the converted carriage. She hung there, head down, her black hair dragging on the rutted road.

Her face was pallid and she was fighting for breath, almost unconscious when Laus, Perseus, and Styles ran back and lifted her again into the carriage. Styles poured her a cup of water from the canteen. She stared at him, refused to touch it. "Why do you want to kill yourself?" he demanded.

She did not answer, merely stared at him, her eyes bleak with hatred.

"We gonna need us a cage for that nigger wench," Laus said.

Ahma made a snarling sound, baring her teeth. Laus shook his head and retreated a step. "I don't want nuthin' to do with a woman like that," he said. "She worse'n ary wild animal."

"Somehow, we've got to keep her from jumping off the back and strangling herself," Styles said. He took up the choke chain which Dennison had given him as a gift. "This is your own doing, Ahma. These men will tell you. We don't want to hurt you. But if we've got to use chains, we'll use them." He formed a slip loop and dropped the chain over the girl's proudly tilted head. She made no protest. The chain settled about the smooth ceramiclike flesh of her throat. Styles secured the other end of the chain about his wrist. "We'll be kind, Ahma. Or we'll be rough. That's up to you. But you are going home with us." He tried to force a smile. "The hell of it is, if you'd only stop fighting—you're going to be happy where we're taking you—maybe truly happy for the first time in your life."

The Fulani girl's lovely face twisted, and she spat at him.

He shrugged, looped the chain over the rear seat backrest, and told Laus to drive on. He sat at an angle on the seat. From the corner of his eye he could watch her. She stared backtrail, her face going soft with sadness. She appeared near tears. For the first time she looked like what she was, a sixteen-year-old girl.

They spent the night at an ordinary near the Georgia line. The surrounding area was swampland; mosquitoes, frogs, and nightbirds screeched out the long, dark hours. Under mosquito netting, Styles was finally able to sleep. They bought corn pone, eggs, and clabber for breakfast. Ahma refused to touch her food. When they removed the shackles from her wrists, she clawed at the nearest of them, hands like talons. She was rather badly bitten by mosquitoes, her cheeks and eyelids swollen and puffy.

When Laus had their carriage horses hitched and ready

to move out, Styles said, "Perseus, why don't you ride in back with Ahma? You can tell her about Blackoaks. Wouldn't you like that, Ahma?"

The girl merely stared at him, eyes malevolent.

"Please, suh, Masta. I don't crave to sit back there close to that gal. She dangerous."

"Are you scared of her?" Styles said. "My God, Perseus, she's shackled and wearing a choke chain."

"Just the same, I scairt. She like a conjure woman, Masta. She don't have to touch you. She evil. She got evil eyes."

"For Christ's sake, she's just a young girl."

"Please, Masta." Perseus looked ready to cry.

Styles spread his hands helplessly. "Pegasus. How about you? You're not afraid of her eyes, are you?"

Pegasus exhaled heavily. "I sits with her you say so, Masta. But I got no wish to git near her . . . . Had a woman in our cabin once what went insane. Her eyes . . . just like this gal's eyes . . . . She'd kill you, and not even know she done it . . . . She got the madness, all right."

"The hell with it," Styles said. "Head them out, Laus. Let's go. I'll watch her."

It was almost one o'clock in the afternoon before they reached a weatherbeaten farm shack enclosed behind a weed-choked snake fence. Laus pulled the carriage into the yard. A lanky, string-throated man in overalls and denim shirt came out on a stoop, carrying a gun. "What you folks want?" He called. When Styles moved to swing down from the carriage, he said, "Jes' stay where you are, mister. State your business."

"We'd like to buy some food."

The farmer studied them, slightly mollified. "Can you pay?" He called over his shoulder. "Maw. Come out chere." A woman, even thinner than the farmer, her flesh burned the color of old coffee, her straight hair lank about her sunken cheeks, come out on the stoop, two naked children clinging to her tattered skirts. "We got some food we might sell these folks?"

The woman stared at them a moment, then whispered

194

something to her husband. "That a crazy woman you got shackled up there?" the farmer asked.

"No. She's not crazy," Styles said.

"She a conjure woman?" the farmer persisted when his wife whispered to him again. "We got our chillun to think about. We don't want no conjure woman on our place, even she shackled."

"She's a runner," Styles said, exasperated. "She ran away. We're taking her home. Can you sell us food or not?"

"We got some side meat, corn pone, and some clabber. Cost you—" the farmer hesitated, naming an impossible price. "Cost you a dollar for the five of you."

Styles nodded. The farmer permitted the three black men to sit on a use-slicked bench under a chinaberry tree. He brought food out to them in broken plates. "Ain't lettin' niggers eat off our good plates," he said.

Laus, Perseus, and Pegasus fell to, eating silently. Styles took a bit of the food and found it so greasy he was unable to swallow it. He ate a little of the clabber. When the farmer brought out a bowl of clabber for Ahma, Styles took it from him, thanked him. He called Laus, gave him his own unfinished meal. Laus thanked him and wolfed it down hungrily.

Styles went around the carriage. Ahma slumped against the back seat, her long legs curled under her. Her face was serene. She seemed not to see him. "Are you hungry, Ahma?"

Finally she shook her head.

"Please, Ahma. Try to eat. Just a little of this clabber. I don't want you to get sick."

She met his gaze. She neither agreed nor refused. Taking up a full spoon of the clabber, he held it out to her. After a brief hesitation, still gazing unblinkingly at him, she opened her mouth. He put the spoon between her lips and she accepted it docilely.

Styles sighed expansively. He felt he had come a long way on their journey. "That's better." He smiled. "You don't want cracker people like these thinking you're a madwoman or a conjure woman."

She spat the clabber full into his face. The coagulated milk struck him between the eyes and trickled down on each side of his nose. Rage gorged up through him. Almost in reflex, he threw up his hand to backhand her across the head. But he controlled himself. He called Perseus over, gave him the girl's food. Then, with great calm, he wiped his face with his handkerchief.

She continued to stare at him unblinkingly. Her face remained stonelike, but deep within her ebony eyes he could see the raging laughter swirl in savage shadows. He forced himself to smile. "You aren't a conjure woman, are you?"

She stared at him silently.

He continued to smile though his face muscles ached. "You're going to be hellish hungry before we get home, Ahma. It took us thirteen days to come down here. A four- or five-day trip—but if we get lost as we did before . . . . You know, you're a smart girl. You ought to think about it. Clabber in your belly will keep you alive. It won't do a thing in my face."

Her head tilted. Faint hints of moisture formed in those black eyes, but she did not speak.

"Two beautiful Fulani boys are waiting for you up at Blackoaks, Ahma. Blade and Moab. They will belong to you alone. You'll live with them. You'll have good food —none of this cracker hog-swill. Good food, a nice soft bed. Long nights with Blade in your arms. You'll want him, Ahma. No matter how much you hate me, that's how much you're going to love Blade. Why don't you behave and eat so you'll look beautiful for Blade? You'll make babies together, Ahma. You and Blade. Beautiful pure-blood Fulani children."

Now she spoke, moaning, a savage sound of heartbreak. "Babies? For you to sell, white Masta? Sell like you bought me yesterday?" She raged, fighting at her bonds, tears streaming down her cheeks . . . .

Styles's shoulders sagged. He walked slowly around the carriage and swung up into the seat, waiting for the black men to climb in. It looked like a long, hard journey home . . . .

11

Styles kept his carriage moving steadily north and west into Alabama. Often the roads were no more than faint, weed-choked traces through deep forests. There were tough decisions where rough roads forked. Only a few such sites were marked by road signs; usually where signs hung, the lettering had been obliterated by time, weather, or buckshot. Overall, Styles admitted he had no way of knowing if he were completely off the road to Montgomery, which Banker Ware had laid out on a rough map for him to follow. Both Dennison and Bax Simon had confirmed the banker's directions. Travel was slow, often interrupted by trouble when Ahma was taken from the carriage and led into the underbrush at the side of the road to relieve herself. Once, she broke free and ran. Only Perseus had been able to overtake her in a pine hammock. He lunged, tackling her. She was mauling him as a panther might by the time Laus and Pegasus twisted her arms up her back and pulled her away. For the remainder of the trip, Perseus was assigned to lead Ahma into the underbrush on the choke chain secured to his wrist when she answered calls of nature.

In the middle of the afternoon of the fifth day they rode into a settlement in southeast Alabama clearly marked with a large X on Banker Ware's map. The village was an anaemic sprawl of clapboard houses with a general store and stables where the east-west trace intersected the north-south trail. Styles felt like weeping in relief and delight. Preston, Alabama. Here, according to Ware's map, he turned north on the roadway which eventually ran past Blackoaks and west into Mt. Zion.

Styles's eyes burned. He wanted to laugh in exhausted exultance. Until this moment, he had not fully realized how taut-drawn with tension and fatigue he was. He had been unable to relax for a moment during the last five days. In fact, his stomach nerves were drawn tighter than wire, burning and quivering.

12

A light, persistent late-winter rain dogged them all morning. The roads were muddy and pot holes were concealed in black water. But none of them cared. They were almost home to Blackoaks. Only Ahma grew more silent and withdrawn as they approached the plantation.

"Yay, Masta!" Pegasus shouted. "Gates of Blackoaks yonder. We home, Masta. We home."

Styles's heart beat faster. There was an unexplained emptiness in the pit of his stomach. There was something, after all, about coming home again, something that stirred your emotions. His mouth pulled into a twisted smile; it was all right, he was looking forward to seeing Moab more than to being with Kathy. He had not changed that much, after all.

Laus laid the whip across the lathered horses. It was a little after one in the afternoon, the sun was hot, the roads had been rough. But the tired horses responded; they, too, sensed how near they were to home.

The carriage wheeled into the lane between the huge fieldstone gate posts. The small black lookouts came running to meet them under the lane of trees, but they were not yelling as they usually did. A strange pall of silence seemed to pervade the estate. Styles supposed it was no quieter than usual—there was always a heavy pastoral quiet at Blackoaks—returning from the outside world merely intensified the impact of quietness.

"Go on past the house," Styles told Laus. "Drive into the quarters."

The small black boys retreated at each side of the lane as the carriage sped past them, went beyond the manor house on the plateau and down the incline into the valley below.

Blade leaned against an upright outside the commissary. He straightened as the carriage passed, moving up the incline into the quarters. At Styles's signal, Blade leapt off the commissary stoop and loped up the incline toward his cabin.

Laus pulled the carriage in before the whitewashed shack where Blade lived. Tired, Styles swung down and went around the wagon. He released the shackles on Ahma's wrists and ankles but let the choke chain dangle from its loop about her throat.

When they tried to help her alight, she batted their hands away.

"Get down, Ahma," Styles said. "You're home."

She unwound her long legs and leaped down over the rear of the carriage. Instinctively, Styles caught the dangling choke chain and gripped it tightly in his fist. Her head tilted proudly, Ahma ignored the other blacks who came from their cabins and stared at her. Styles nodded toward the stoop of Blade's cabin, and she preceded him up the steps. Her shoulders were erect, her Junoesque body straight, but there was about her such a sense of dejection that Styles felt an unwilling stirring of pity for her. Looking at her, one could easily forget she was little more than a child—a child who had been through hell.

When they paused on the stoop, Blade pushed through the crowd of people gawking in the sun. Styles silently signaled Laus who turned the carriage and drove it back down slope to the stables, Pegasus beside him. Pegasus turned on the seat, staring back at them until they turned at the barn. Styles supposed Pegasus was waiting for the moment when Ahma would break and run.

Blade came up the steps. He bobbed his head toward Styles but did not take his eyes off Ahma. Barefooted, the girl was almost as tall as he. Their eyes met levelly. He smiled gently and his smile made him beautiful. His gaze touched at her wide-set eyes, the delicate perfection of her nose, the full, dark-red lips. He had never seen anyone as lovely, and he was struck dumb. He could only smile, moving his wondering gaze across her large breasts, her flat stomach, the rounded curve at her pelvis, the columnlike legs, braced apart. He brought his eyes back to the coppery tan of her face. His smile spread into a grin and at last he spoke. "You a big 'un, honey."

Something happened in Ahma's rigid face. For an instant her cheeks paled and then flushed faintly with color. Her eyes struck against Blade's and fell away. Her tooth sank into her underlip. She drew a deep, ragged breath. Clearly she had never seen anything like Blade before either, nor had she anticipated encountering anything like him in this vale of tears. Her smile was small and tight, tentative. "You sho' big yo'self," she said.

He nodded, smiling. "I gittin' bigger ever minute I looks at you."

Her face paled, she did not meet his gaze. He extended his hand, holding in it a large red apple. She hesitated a long moment and then took it.

"You're a purentee beauty," Blade said.

She took a big bite of the apple, stood chewing it with some savagery. She would meet his eyes, look quickly away.

"You come to stay with me?" Blade said. "You like to stay here with me?"

She took another bite of the apple, chewing faster. Blade extended his foot and kicked open the front door of his cabin. People surrounding his shack moved closer to the stoop, giggling and nudging each other.

"I treat you mighty good," Blade said.

She bit the apple again, dispensing with it, chewing up the core and seeds. "I might kill you," she said at last. "I already killed one man."

"I'm not scairt," Blade said. He continued to smile warmly. "An' I got lots of apples."

"I like apples," she said at last.

"Sure you do." Blade nodded. He laughed. He reached out slowly. She trembled slightly but did not move. "I don't really care for your necklace."

She smiled and let him remove it over her head. Styles said, "For God's sake, Blade. Don't let her run away. We went through hell getting her here. She cost more'n

200

that big house up there. If she runs away, I'm ruined—and so are you."

Blade glanced at Styles and smiled reassuringly. He tossed the choke chain behind him. It clattered briefly when it struck the ground. "She ain't gonna run nowhere. Are you, honey?"

She met his gaze. "My name is Ahma," she said. "An' I did kill a man."

Blade grinned. "My name is Blade. An' I bigger than you. Stronger. I can lift you with one hand. Hold you right up over my head I want to. An'—if you want to kill me, I let's you try, Ahma, honey—every night."

The people crowded around the porch laughed and shoved each other. Ahma did not even look toward them. She bit her lip but smiled faintly, despite herself. "I might stay—awhile," she allowed. "If you truly as big as you say you is."

Blade put his head back laughing. "I bigger. I just don't likes to brag."

Styles went down the steps of the cabin. The slaves standing in the yard bobbed their heads and retreated, making a path for him. He paused in the blaze of afternoon sunlight and glanced back toward the cabin. Ahma had followed Blade inside. Styles heard her ask what kind of furnitude Blade had. He told her it didn't matter because he could make for her anything she wanted. She wanted a new chair, he'd make it. She wanted a new bed, he'd make it for her. She paused inside the door, already finding fault.

Styles exhaled heavily and walked down the incline and across the valley toward the house. He found himself praying to somebody, something, that Blade could handle Ahma. He found no excitement in the charge that flared instantly between them, although he had been aware of it and was somewhat reassured. But it seemed to him that women were bitches. Some of them were violent bitches. Ahma had already proved her violence. She needed a good fucking—the kind the Mt. Zion louts called "a good horse-fucking."

Thyestes awaited Styles on the front veranda of the

mansion. Styles said, "Hello, Thyestes. It's good to see you. Good to be home. How are your corns?"

Thyestes bobbed his head but did not meet Styles's eyes. He opened the front door and held it for him. Inside, the house was pervaded by a funereal silence. "Where is everybody?" Styles said.

"They round, Masta. They round. You like a nice hot bath, Masta, while they prepares you a nice lunch?"

Styles frowned, glancing at him. "Yes. That will be fine. Will you tell Miss Kathy I'm home?"

Thyestes swallowed hard. Styles had started toward the wide staircase leading to the second floor. He paused and glanced across his shoulder, his face taut. "Damn it, Thyestes, what's the matter?"

"Miss Kathy, Masta. She ain't heah."

"Is she in town? In Mt. Zion? Where is she?"

"I plain don't know, Masta. I shorely don't know." Now Thyestes did cry. His eyes brimmed with tears and they streaked down his dark cheeks. "Maybe if you ast Miz Claire, she'll tell you all about it."

"All right. Have them prepare my bath—and lay out fresh clothing."

"Yes, Masta . . . . Welcome home, Masta."

Styles climbed the stairs slowly. His legs felt tired. Mounting these stairs was like wading in hip-deep water. He supported himself on the railing. At the head of the stairs he turned first toward his own room, then instead heeled around and strode in the opposite direction.

At the corridor door of Miz Claire's upstairs suite, he rapped. After a moment, the door opened and huge Neva let herself through and closed it after her. Her eyes widened at the sight of Styles and she winced. But she did not retreat. "You jes' git home, Masta?"

"I'd like to speak with Miz Claire. Will you tell her I'm here?"

Neva hesitated. Her eyes showed pain. "That chile is jes' this minute gone to sleep, Masta. I cain't wake her. She ain't slept for two nights—crying and sick—"

"Why is she crying? Why is she sick?"

"We had bad trouble after you went away to Florida Territory, Masta Styles. It's just about broke Miz Claire's

202

pore little heart. It's more this time than that chile can bear."

"All right, damn it. What is it?"

"It's Miss Kathy, Masta. And that Masta Hunter Campbell."

He spent a leisurely hour in the tub, with the water frequently warmed by buckets rushed up by houseboys from the kitchen. Afterwards he shaved and then lay down across his bed. His eyes were dry, hot. But after the long trip, the sleepless night, the tension, he was exhausted. But he did sink into sleep. They awakened him at seven for dinner.

The meal was set in the formal dining room, in honor of his return home, he supposed. The best china, silver goblets, and gleaming flatware glittered in the lamplight. Miz Claire sat at one end of the long table. Morgan sat mutely in the middle, and Styles's place was set at the head. Thyestes pulled back the chair and then pushed it forward as Styles sat down.

Styles shook out his gleaming white linen napkin and spread it across his knees. He saw that Miz Claire was sitting tautly at the end of the table, holding herself together by some supreme effort of will. Morgan stared into his plate and did not look up.

Styles said, "Who knows about this?"

Miz Claire looked up, eyes bleak. "About what, Styles?"

"Who is aware that Kathy has run away with the yankee?"

She spread her hands helplessly, but Morgan looked up and spoke. "Everybody knows."

"Everybody? The people in the next town? The people on the nearest plantation? Everybody knows?"

"Oh, I'm sure not, Styles," Miz Claire said. "We've kept it as quite as we could . . . . But the household knows—all the slaves. There's no way to keep the slaves from gossiping among themselves."

"I'm talking about outside the family," Styles said. "Who has visited here? Who has heard about Kathy's flight?"

"No. Nobody outside the family. Not yet."

Styles waited until Thyestes served his soup, the steam rising from the bowl of lentels and white acre peas. "Then that's the way it will be. No one off this plantation will know that Kathy is gone—until I say differently."

Claire dabbed at her eyes with her napkin. "Oh, Styles, I do understand you. I do pity you. But how can we keep a thing—a terrible thing like this quiet?"

"Pity has nothing to do with it," Styles said. "I don't want your pity, because I don't need it."

"Oh, Styles, I am so sorry."

"I don't want your sorrow or your compassion. I simply want you both to understand. We will keep this matter quiet as long as I say we will. We'll damn well keep it quiet, or you'll all answer to me."

Miz Claire nodded. "Whatever you say, Styles."

He took up his soup spoon and ladled up soup to his lips. He took one taste, dropped the spoon. He dabbed roughly at his lips. "Thyestes."

"Yes, Masta."

"This stuff tastes like swill. Take it back to the kitchen. Tell that woman in there that either she learns to cook, or I sell her to the first coffle that passes."

Styles went into his office after dinner. He tried to concentrate on the business matters which had piled up in his absence. But he could not keep his mind on it. He poured himself a glass of whiskey, and another, and a third. He staggered slightly, going up to bed at ten, but when Thyestes attempted to support him at his elbow, he cursed him and shook his hand away.

Moab was on his pallet when Styles entered the bedroom. Moab wore only a pair of cotton underpants. Styles gazed at him a moment as if he were a stranger. "Welcome home, Masta."

Styles shook his head as if trying to clear it. "Go down to Morgan's room. Tell Morgan and Soapy you are to sleep there for a while. Then I'm going to send you out to live with Blade and his new wench."

Moab sensed his easy world crumbling around him. He tried to smile, writhing on the bed so the thick muscles of his chest caught the lamplight. "Don't you want me to stay with you—just tonight, Masta?"

Styles waved his arm. "Go on. Get out of here. I've got too much on my mind. I don't want to be bothered with you."

"Masta don't love Moab no more?" The boy stood up, trembling. He looked ready to cry.

Styles drew his arm across his eyes, blinked hard. "I hate everybody in God's world right now, Moab. If you're smart, you'll get out of here."

When Moab went out at last, Styles locked the corridor door. Even in his confused state, Styles understood Moab's misery. The boy had been happy living with Blade. This had ended abruptly. Again, he had found life pleasant up at the overseer's cottage. Most of all, he had enjoyed the ease and luxury here in the mansion as Styles's personal houseboy.

Styles laughed savagely and spoke aloud as though the boy were still in the room. "You've got to learn, Moab. Nothing lasts. In this world, nothing lasts."

He prowled the room until after three in the morning. He vacillated between rage against Kathy and Campbell and maudlin self-pity. He tried to lie down but could not stay on the bed. He sweated. He threw open all the windows, but the night breeze was too weak to penetrate into his room. He sprawled with a glass of straight whiskey in a high-backed overstuffed chair. But this was like a bed of rocks. His skin felt too tight, as if he could no longer endure living inside it. His flesh stung as if he were being chewed mercilessly by fire ants.

He prowled the room because he could not lie down, he could not sit still. He drank because when he was sober, he thought, and thinking led him only in savage circles. He wanted answers and there were no answers except in straight bourbon. He passed out a little past three, falling on the floor because he misjudged the distance to his bed.

He came down to breakfast at nine the next morning. He was freshly bathed and attired. About him was the kind of calm that rides in the eye of a devastating hurricane.

He entered the breakfast room where Miz Claire and Morgan awaited him, grimly silent. He gave them both brief, chilled smiles and sat down at the head of the table. He drank iced water from the silver goblet. He sighed heavily. "I'm pleased to be able to tell you that my wife has gone to visit relatives in Charleston. She is visiting with Jamie Lee Seaton's parents."

Miz Claire's head jerked up and it was as if clouds lifted from her cheeks. "Oh, thank God," she said. She smiled in sick relief. "Did Kathy leave you a note? Where? I had the house girls check everywhere for a note of some kind."

Styles hesitated for a long beat. At last, he nodded. "Yes. She left me a note . . . . "

"How wonderful, Styles. Where did she leave it?"

"She left it, Miz Claire." Then his voice softened. "In a secret place we have."

"Oh, thank God. You've heard from my baby."

Styles nodded. "Yes. I've heard from her. She's gone to Charleston for a visit—an extended visit, she said."

"I wonder why she didn't tell me about it?" Miz Claire said. "She didn't even mention her plans to me."

"I don't know," Styles said. "I only know she says she's all right—in Charleston."

"Well, that's all that really matters, isn't it?" Miz Claire said.

Morgan looked up, his cheeks bulging with ham and scrambled eggs. "Where's Mr. Hunter Campbell?"

Styles's face paled slightly. He straightened his shoulders in his jacket. He spoke coldly. "Don't talk with your mouth full, Morgan. That's extremely bad manners."

Morgan swallowed hard. "But where is he? Do you know?"

Styles's jaw was taut, a muscle working in it. But his voice was icily calm. "I don't know where he is, Morgan. Precisely. I believe he returned north. Before I left for Florida, I told him to make a decision. Either he was to stop preaching abolition to our slaves, or he was to get out. I suppose he left because of that. I had told him I expected him to be off the place when I returned from Florida. I'm sure he returned north. It was simply a coincidence that Kathy left about the same time."

"She left the same day," Morgan said.

Styles kept his voice cold and level. "Perhaps she did, Morgan. But she went east to Charleston. To visit relatives. The yankee went back north. To his home. Is that clear to you?"

"Yes, sir. It just seems funny, that's all. That they would leave together in Ferrell's single-seater when they wasn't even going the same way."

"We won't worry about that, will we, Morgan? As long as we understand they went separate ways. That's all that matters, isn't it? That we understand this." His voice hardened. "He went north to his home. She went east to visit in Charleston. That's what we must understand, Morgan. We must remember that—if anyone asks us."

PART THREE

New Orleans

1

In the Hotel St. Louis in New Orleans, Hunt Campbell winced, acutely and unpleasantly aware of the attention being accorded to him and Kathy. People across the lobby stared at them, whispering and nudging each other. Hunt took off his soft, wide-brimmed hat—which once had belonged to Styles Kenric—and mopped his heat-sweated forehead.

Kathy stood a few feet from the registration desk, waiting. With mixed feelings of annoyance and distress, she recognized two women, wreathed in smiles, bearing down upon her. Her first thought was to run. She stood her ground, dismayed at never being able to escape acquaintances anywhere, even this far from home. Sickly, she watched the two old maid Bretherton sisters, Miss Ethel and Miss May Ellen, swoop down upon her with smiles like talons to impale her.

"Kathy Kenric! What a surprise!"

"What a pleasant surprise, Kathy! How are you, dearest child?"

"What are you doing in New Orleans?"

"On another shopping spree, aren't you?"

"And dear Styles—" pointedly searching the area with darting eyes—"where is dear Styles?"

Kathy managed finally to answer. "I am here—

shopping." She hated lies. She hated herself for lying. "No. Styles isn't with me."

The smiles on the prim faces faltered, but then renewed. At this moment, Hunt turned from the registration desk, carrying a huge brass key on an even larger carved disk, and followed by a black uniformed bellboy with their bags. "Our room is ready, Kathy," he said before he realized the two women were staring, bug-eyed and pale of face, at him. "Our rooms," he added lamely.

Neither of them spoke on the way up the stairs to their room.

"Who were those old crows?" Hunt asked.

"The Bretherton sisters. Old maids—"

"I could see that."

"—from The Briars—"

"Ten miles from Blackoaks?" His jaw tightened and he exhaled heavily. "Oh, Christ."

"It doesn't matter, Hunt. We can't spend our lives hiding. People have got to know. Sooner or later."

"Yes. Damn it. But those crones. We might as well send a fast dispatch message directly to Styles, telling him where we are."

She tightened her fingers on his arm. "Do you really care?"

"No. I guess not. But I know sooner or later Styles is coming looking for us. I would have liked a few days of making love to you before he arrives to kill me."

"Oh, darling, we'll make love forever—the rest of our lives."

His dry, white lips twisted into a wry smile. "Yes. That's what I mean."

She stopped him at the head of the stairs, letting the porter go ahead of them along the corridor. She drew Hunt's head down and kissed him, her mouth parted. "We're together, darling. That's what matters. And I love you. More, probably, than you can even understand . . . . No one can part us. Ever. Don't you see?"

Her kiss, her voice, her eyes, and the gentle pressure of her hands inflamed him. He kissed both her hands and, putting his arm about her waist, strode along the corridor

toward the room where the bellboy stood holding the heavy door open for them.

When they were alone in their room, Kathy sank into an overstuffed chair and stared at the high double bed, the damask drapes at the balcony doorway, the French painting of a girl and a doe. Hunt strode about shedding his jacket and shirt. He stood holding the linen shirt in his fist; its collar was almost black with soot and grime. "I figured we needed a bath first. I ordered water sent up —and then lunch . . . . I didn't think we'd want to go out—yet."

She blushed and then laughed and kissed him. "Do you realize—I'm in a hotel room—with a stranger?"

"Strangers make the best lovers—they're more demanding," he told her, stepping out of his tight-fitting linen trousers.

"What are you doing?"

"I hate to make love with my clothes on. Actually, I refuse to."

She gestured meaninglessly. "Aren't you going into the other room?"

"For what? I'm proud of my manhood. I've nothing to hide." He tossed his trousers over the back of a straight chair and unbuttoned his underpants. Kathy gasped and fell across the bed, face down. She heard the knocking at the door. She remained where she was, hearing buckets of hot water poured into the huge tile tub in the adjoining room. She could hear Hunt splashing as he washed in there. Finally, she sat up on the side of the bed. At that moment, he walked into the room from the steaming bath, pink and naked, toweling himself.

She stared at him, unable to speak. She tried but coul' not withdraw her fascinated gaze from the rigid, hig' standing staff. She had never seen anything like it. She sat trembling, unable to look away, scarcely breathing. She felt a hot flooding of desire inside her.

"For hell's sake," he said. "Aren't you undressed yet?"

"In here? In front of you?"

"You don't think I brought you to New Orlean' look at that stupid dress, do you?"

211

"I'm sorry. I'm too shy . . . . You'll have to give me time."

"Time? Look at me. I can't give you time—"

"Oh, Hunt. I can't undress in front of you—in the daytime—"

"Didn't you undress in front of Styles?"

She spread her hands, let them drop. "No . . . . Yes—once—but we'd been married a long time."

He strode back and forth before her, waving the towel, that rigid *thing* jutting tilted and ludicrous before him. But he was not laughing and she dared not laugh. Besides, he was beautiful—like a warrior striding into battle, lance at the ready, needing only the sounds of trumpets and the furling of banners. "Good God. I'm aching—yes, damn it, miserable and aching—with need for you, and you're not going to undress."

"Oh, I am. I am. But can't you be patient—a little patient—?"

He stood directly before her, his face flushed. "I'm patient, but—" Hunt suddenly slapped his rigid staff with the backs of his fingers and it quivered, engorged with blood, trembling with passion. "I'm patient. He's not."

She moved her fingers tentatively to the front of her dress. "I do want to. I'm just too shy."

He advanced a menacing step, glaring down at her. "Are you joking? You've nothing to be shy about . . . . Damn it," he glanced involuntarily toward the locked corridor door as if Styles might be standing, armed, beyond it, "we don't have time to be shy."

Her face paled and she found herself glancing toward that door. "We have—the rest of our lives, don't we?" Her eyes pleaded with him, deeply troubled.

He laughed. "Of course we do." He caught the front of her dress, and with ease that stunned her, he ripped it down the front and then with both hands peeled frock and underthings from her breasts and shoulders. He lifted her, shook the dress away, and then swung her up in his arms, heading toward the hot bath awaiting her in the tiled tub. "But the rest of our lives—what's that? No matter what it is, it's not time enough."

He placed her in the hot water. She still wore her

stockings and shoes. She managed to work them off and toss them across the room while he soaped her body, lingering at her armpits, her breasts, the soft down at her pelvic eminence, the curve of her ankles . . . .

They did not sleep that night, nor go out of their room the next day. Their meals were brought in to them by black men, sophisticated and blasé, who had seen everything and who saw nothing. Late, on their third night, Hunt awoke exhausted to find a candle burning beside their bed. Kathy lay with her head on the inside of his upper leg. She held his limp penis in her hand, working it, studying it wondrously. When she saw he was awake, she smiled across the expanse of his belly and chest at him. "Why are men so beautiful?"

"To make beautiful women want us, I guess." He yawned.

"You drive this lady crazy. I can't sleep for thinking about you. If I sleep, I wake up, wanting you . . . . Have you loved many girls?"

He stifled a yawn and caressed the full taut globes of her breasts, not answering.

"That's right—don't tell me," she said, and laughed.

She pressed her lips upon the tumescent head of his rod. "You're so beautiful—and so sinful—I want to eat you! I hope you're not fattening."

On their fourth morning at the Hotel St. Louis, Kathy awakened at ten and found herself alone in their bed. They had wakened first with the false dawn that shown through their window at five. Hunt had mumbled something about seeing the men selected by the executor of his mother's trust as his New Orlean's banker-adviser. She had barely heard him, wriggling her body beneath him and wrapping her legs about his waist and locking her ankles fiercely. How quickly she'd recovered from her shyness and her timidity! She pumped her hips in passionate abandon. She heard his rising tempo of breathing, felt the hammering of his heart over hers, the thrust of his manhood deeper and deeper inside her. And then, when she wanted this agonizing ecstasy to last forever, it was over and she slumped beneath him. In moments she was asleep, and five hours later when she wakened, reaching for him, he was gone . . . .

She lay on the bed watching the shadows chase themselves across the high ceiling of her room. She heard the street sounds, but they did not entice her. She was content here—as contented as she had been sick with misery at Blackoaks.

She shivered, thinking how nearly she had come to letting Hunt leave the plantation without her. By midnight, she'd resolved she could pay the price of living unmarried as Hunt's mistress; she could not endure losing him and remaining suffocated and starved as Styles's wife. By four o'clock she was packed and had sent the whining Shiva running to the barns to order Ferrell's runabout buggy hitched to a fast carriage horse and brought to the front door—in stealth and silence.

She had seen the light under Hunt's door and knew he was packing to leave after breakfast. She had hesitated, lifted her hand to knock, then turned the knob instead. The door was unlocked. She had let herself inside and closed the door quietly behind her. He had heeled around, eyes widening when he saw she was dressed, wearing a tiny hat, ready to travel. "I'm going with you," she had said.

"You'll break your mother's heart."

"Yes." She had gone on standing just inside the door. He was packed, ready to leave.

"He'll come after us. Styles. He'll kill me—if he can. He may kill you."

"Yes."

"I'm nobody, Kathy. I've nothing to offer you."

"I don't care. Do you want me?"

"Of course I do. I've always wanted you. I've prayed you'd come through that door—it's been unlocked, just like that, for two years."

"Then I'm going with you."

"Do you have any idea where I'm going?"

"No."

"Neither do I."

"I don't care."

He had strode across to her then and took her in his

arms. She had turned up her face to him and opened her mouth for his kiss, trying to show him how completely she surrendered to him . . . .

Ferrell's horse was racing in the shafts of his buggy. It was as if the animal had longed for a road and early-morning chill, with the first dawn to light the path. They had been in Mt. Zion before the first store was opened. There, Kathy had felt her first indecision, her dread of being recognized. At the hotel, rail agents had told Hunt that the train south to Mobile wouldn't come through until noon of the following day. But there had been a stagecoach due, headed toward Montgomery in less than an hour. Having arranged to have the carriage and horse cared for at the stables until they were called for by Blackoaks people, Hunt had bought two tickets to Montgomery.

After half a day in a hotel in Montgomery, they had caught a train south to Mobile. Kathy was still mixed up inside, torn between her need to stay with Hunt and the total disruption of her life up to this moment. Nothing had prepared her to be a fancy woman or an adultress.

She had sat clinging to Hunt's hand, the cinders stinging her cheeks and her eyes. "Those people keep watching us. Do you suppose they recognize us?"

Hunt had closed his fingers on her hand and he spoke gently. "It's too late to worry about things like that now."

She had moved nearer to him on the uncomfortable seat, needing to be within the circle of his arm. Outside its warmth, she shook with cold on the hot, breathless train. She had gone back in her mind to the passion for Hunt she had felt and denied so long, the way they found moments together in the long afternoons, the anguished desire she could read in his eyes. In her memory she had considered all that had happened to her after her break with Styles. That break had been clean and total and final. No sense feeling shame, or regret about that—and she had felt none. Until she had learned what Styles really was, what he really wanted, she had fought against that growing passion for Hunt; she had tried to make a life for herself and her husband, even when she'd known he didn't want it. When everything else had failed, she had pleaded for divorce, only to be answered with threats. She had taken the only course open to her, she had run away with her lover. It was evil, perhaps, but it was her sole hope of escape—and, as Hunt said, she could swim or drown in her Rubicon, but she could not go back. She would not go back . . . .

She writhed in the bed, seeking a cool place but knowing her body heated the sheets and the mattress. She wanted Hunt with her, she was hot and liquid with need for him. She felt she would never tire of making love with Hunt. The world had its cynical maxim that whatever burns intensely and white-hot most quickly burns itself out. This did not have to be true! Looking ahead, she found life entirely too brief for all the excitement she could foresee in their consuming passion one for the other. Strange, Styles had used her as an object to debase —in this perverted way he derived the only pleasure possible to him in their bed. She smiled now and drew the backs of her fingers slowly and gently across her parted lips. Hunt did all the same things Styles had done! Sex, she supposed, was limited in scope; it had its form, discipline, and rules—with far fewer moves than chess!— but in Hunt's arms, there was love and *shared* excitement where before there had been only pain and acute discomfort at Styles's cruel and uncaring hands. Where Styles could respond to sex only if he hurt and debased her, Hunt acted in desire and tenderness and a compulsion to see that she was satisfied and exalted first. Styles had inflicted pain. Hunt inflicted pleasure.

When she could stay in bed without Hunt no longer, she dressed carefully and ventured down to the lobby, fresh, cool, and exalted with the love she felt for Hunt— and for the whole universe! The Bretherton sisters sat together in the lobby. She thought their smiles fixed beckoningly upon her, and they let her think so—like praying mantises—to lure her close enough to destroy. When she was within feet of them, her smile froze, died.

The Bretherton sisters looked through her, around her, their faces dead and white and set against her. Unsmiling, they stared at her as if they had never seen her, refusing even to acknowledge her. Crushed, she almost fled back to her room. She wandered about it, feeling the walls crowding in upon her, her world shriveling beneath her feet. She went out on the balcony and huddled, staring, at the street below her and seeing none of it.

Hunt walked out of the offices of the J.M. Frobisher Banking & Shipping Company, Ltd., in the business district on Carondelet. The New Orleans branch of the Boston Frobisher Company had reassured him on the matter of finances, at least. There were sound stocks in the portfolio willed to him by his father, more than one thousand dollars available in cash at his disposal from his mother's trust. There were several hundred dollars in his own savings from his two years employment as tutor at Blackoaks Plantation. His advisers' suggestion was that he leave all his money in his account at interest except small amounts of cash, and they would make inquiries about suitable employment that might interest him.

He walked slowly along the busy walk in the humid sunlight. His cash resources provided the good news: he and Kathy could continue in their unreal world for perhaps a year, then he would be forced to find work. He tried to assure himself he had only the present; therefore he should relax and enjoy it. He could not look ahead even one year in his affair with Kathy. At present, they burned white-hot, and yet even in their most passionate moments, a part of him listened for Styles's step behind him. For him and Kathy there was only this present and the fulfillment of everything he had desired so hungrily and helplessly for so long. But there were coldly defined limits imposed upon them by circumstances over which neither he nor Kathy had any control. You believed that if you got precisely what you wanted, you would be content. He had got Kathy. From her early shyness she had come a long way and now was awaiting him naked on the bare bed when he walked in. But that moment would arrive—and the hell of it was he had no idea how soon —when the bills would all come due. In these past days he had had love and delights beyond his wildest fantasies, and yet he remained haunted by the threat of violence that hung over them. Styles was emotional, vengeful, unforgiving. And Styles needed his marriage to Kathy to conceal the secret that could destroy him. A landowner could whip his slaves, beat his wife, and cheat his neighbors, but he had to be a *man,* nothing less was tolerated. Styles would come looking for him. He and Kathy had one chance—to hide. And this course was demanding too much of Kathy, asking her to avoid public places, plays, dances, restaurants, and social relations with acquaintances, new, casual, or from the past. It was unfair to her and might well destroy her love for him. And yet to hide was their only real hope of escaping Styles's vengeance— of prolonging their make-believe world even for a little while. Hell, ever since he had left Blackoaks he had felt irresistible urges to check across his shoulder as he walked in the open street.

At that instant, a man tapped Hunt on the shoulder. In panic, Hunt almost bolted. By an extreme effort of will, he managed to remain standing on the corner. A carriage rolled past with three gaudily attired octoroon women laughing in its tonneau. Taking a deep breath, Hunt turned slowly.

A black freedman, a sharply dressed "man of color," smiled at him. "You like some hot entertainment, young Masta?"

"What?"

"Got you a fancy high-yaller wench down near Congo Square, young Masta. She French. She French in the way it counts."

"Congo Square?"

"Where the black folks *live*! Why, Masta, come along with me. Was you evah a black man jus' one night down on Congo Square, you nevah want to be a white man again."

"No. No. Thank you." Hunt shook his head, only barely aware of what the man had said. He crossed the street, hurrying.

He found Kathy huddled, gaze turned inward, upon a wicker chair on the balcony overlooking the street. He poured himself a drink, added water. Sipping it, he walked out to her, the street noises loud below him. He leaned against the iron grille railing. She gave him a bleak smile. "Where've you been?"

He told her briefly. She continued to gaze bleakly at the building across the street. He saw that she didn't see the brick, stone, mortar, or the sun reflected in its windows. "What's the matter, you tired of me already?" he asked.

In a flat voice she told him about the sisters Bretherton. "I ran," she said. "All the way back up here."

"Damn them." He tightened his fist on his whiskey glass. "Well, we're not going to hide from women like that. We've a right to our lives—a right to go where we like . . . . Come on, we'll go to the art gallery before dinner."

She attempted a smile, failed. Then she shook her head as if clearing the old maids and all other evil and defeatist thoughts from her mind. "Yes. I'll get my hat."

She got up and kissed him fiercely as she went into their room. He stood in the balcony doorway watching her with a tender smile.

Under his warm smiling, her good humor returned and she took his arm. They laughed going out of the door. "How right you are," she said. "We'll forget them. And everyone like them from now on." Her lovely little head held high, they crossed the lobby. She was pleased to glimpse the way every man turned to look at her—the young, the old, even those escorting ladies. If they thought her lovely, she longed to tell them, it was because love made her lovelier.

Hunt recognized with mixed emotions the adulation accorded her. She was incredibly gentle and fresh and lovely—with the look of untouched beauty—the loveliest female New Orleans had seen in years. How would you hide a girl who was so hearbreakingly lovely that every man turned his head to stare after her and watched her, agonized, wherever she went?

They spent two enchanted hours in the art gallery. Kathy had forgotten that such huge collections of masterpieces were gathered in one place. This was such a lovely city! So much to do! And they were together. They would be happy—no matter what people tried to do to them.

2

Styles could not sit for more than five minutes in any chair. He could not find space enough to prowl, room enough to breathe. He walked the house, going up and down the wide stairs, along the corridors, out to the terrace, and back to the sunroom. He stalked the fields, the lanes, the timberland. More than ever he withdrew, answering anyone who spoke to him with sarcasm, sneering, or ridicule. He was infected with hatred, he was obsessed with it.

No one on the big farm could say when or if he slept at all. From the slave quarters, across the valley, Blade could stand on his stoop at any hour in the dark after midnight and see the tall man striding back and forth in his dimly lit bedroom. At dawn, the field hands on their way to chop cotton could see him standing at his window, staring outward but seeing nothing. At first, stout Bos Pilzer on his gray horse would lift his blacksnake whip in salute, but Kenric gave no indication he saw him, and Bos shrugged.

One night, Miz Claire rapped on Styles's bedroom door after two. At length he opened it and gazed at her, lips twisted, eyes surly. She was astonished to find him impeccably dressed. Only his eyes had the frantic wildness of a forest animal. "Yes, Miz Claire. What is it?"

"I just worry about you, Styles. You don't sleep. You don't rest. Have you heard from Kathy?"

He opened his lips to answer, changed his mind, shrugged. "No."

"I am so sorry. I hate to see Kathy break your heart."

"Heartbreak is not even germane, Miz Claire. But I am not a man who submits lightly to betrayal."

His torment festered inside him. He dreaded that day when the whispers and gossip spread out from this plantation to the neighboring farms and estates and towns. He did not see how he could live with the dishonor, the disgrace, the shame and humiliation that would be hurled upon him like slime once the hidden scandal became common knowledge. The expressions of condolence and sympathy like masks over the secretive, sardonic smiles.

He knew they waited for him to order a fast carriage, sturdy horses, and loaded guns. Yet as the days passed he became less anxious to rush out on a wild-eyed pursuit of the lovers. But inaction was unbearable, too. He began to sit for long hours at his desk with a whiskey bottle beside him writing letters which he sealed and rode in to Mt. Zion to post personally.

One morning in the second week after Kathy and Hunt had eloped, a seedy-looking man in whipcord suit, string tie, and felt hat presented himself at the front door. He told Thyestes, "My name is Joe Bullock, boy. Yore master ast me to come out from Montgomery to see him. Will you tell him I'm here?"

Thyestes studied the man a moment, the stubby hands decorated with black nails, the tattoo on the back of his left hand, the dusty shoes. But there was a chilled air of strength and cruelty and determination about Mr. Joe Bullock. Thyestes invited him into the foyer and then limped to the locked door at Kenric's office. He rapped, and after a long moment, Styles opened the door.

Bullock limped across the foyer on tender feet, much as Thyestes walked, as if trying to touch the earth as lightly as possible. Styles did not offer to shake hands. He jerked his head, motioning Bullock into his office, then he closed the door and locked it. He refilled his glass with whiskey, offered Bullock a drink.

Bullock shook his head without smiling. "Not this time of the morning."

"As I told you in my letter, I have a matter of extreme confidence I wish you to handle for me."

"Yes. You want me to find your wife."

Styles's head jerked up, his cheeks pallid. "How did you know that?"

"Only a guess, Mr. Kenric. Ninety-five times out of a hundred when I'm called that's what the caller wants—his wife has run away."

"This is in complete confidence. If you whisper a word of this—to anyone, God help you."

Bullock almost smiled. "I have only one loyalty, Mr. Kenric. That's to the man who pays me. I can keep my mouth shut. And I'm good at my job. You can trust me. I'll find her."

Styles showed Bullock a small painting of Kathy. The detective whistled almost involuntarily. "She's a lovely girl." Styles's mouth twisted and Bullock shrugged. "No problem finding a girl what stands out like Mrs. Kenric, is all I meant."

Styles described Hunter Campbell in as complete detail as possible—the frozen-north look about his mouth and cheeks that had not yet relaxed after two years in the South. "Don't worry, if he's with the girl, I'll find him," Bullock said. "You want I should bring her back?"

"I want you to return here and tell me where she is."

The detective nodded.

Five days passed and Styles heard nothing from Bullock. But the detective had warned him he worked slowly, carefully, with attention to every little detail. "When you hear from me, I'll have the final news for you."

Knowing that Bullock was trailing the pair had a calming effect upon the torment raging in Styles's mind, and his thinking processes improved. Cerebration was possible without chasing the same fruitless agony on the same old mental treadmill.

He was out on the front lawn watching the crew of black boys pruning, chopping, and cutting when a buggy wheeled into the lane between the huge fieldstone gates. The black lookouts raced between the overhanging trees to greet the visitors. Lambert Tetherow of Pinewood Forest Plantation and old Lucas Winterkorn of Mira Vista swung down from the carriage and joined Styles in the cross-hatching of shadow from the magnolia tree.

Styles watched them approach with the air about them of men on condolence calls. The expressions on their faces were the looks hypocritical men wear to funerals of old enemies, sadness with the secret smirking that lurks just behind the gray shroud of grief. His heart slipped its moorings. The rumor had spread beyond the boundaries of Blackoaks. A slave from one plantation had met a slave from another, and the whispers had begun. His fists tightened involuntarily. Damn them. They had not really forgiven him for being right about the price of cotton or for daring to propose turning Blackoaks from cotton culture to a Negro stud farm. He had not seen either of them recently. Nor had he wanted to. He wished to Old Harry he never had to see them again; in that moment he wanted nothing more than to obliterate their perfidious faces.

"Styles, I want you to know right off," Lambert Tetherow said, "me and Lucas have come on a matter of your own best interest. Since my boy Link married Miss Jamie Lee, I feel family-like toward you and the Baynards. What hurts your family, hurts mine."

"And I always wished the best for you, Styles," Winterkorn said in that tone one uses to console the bereaved. "We hear Miss Kathy is not here at Blackoaks . . . . Is that true, my boy?"

"That's true." Styles's voice was icily cold. "She is visiting with Jamie Lee's people in Charleston."

Winterkorn and Tetherow glanced at each other, faces pale. Tetherow said, "We have it on good authority—eye-witnesses, Styles, though I wouldn't like to say who, since I swore not to reveal my source and the ladies have no wish to harm you—we have been told that somebody saw Miss Kathy at the Hotel St. Louis in New Orleans."

His heart pumping oddly, Styles merely shrugged. "Impossible."

"Impossible? They saw *her*. They saw her with the tutor, Styles. I know you want to trust in the fidelity of your lovely young wife. I am equally sure you have never before this moment had reason to doubt her true faithfulness. But there can be no mistake, Styles."

Styles forced a cold smile. The rage was packed so tautly under his level voice that both the planters understood his implied warning. If either of them pursued this matter further, he would kill them. If they besmirched his wife's good name, or his honor, he would kill them. He merely said, "Whoever told you that is mistaken. My wife is visiting in Charleston. The tutor—he had already returned north to his home before I left for Florida." Those were his words. He said nothing about killing either of them, but they got his message.

Winterkorn was deathly pale. Tetherow winced, looking miserable. They glanced at each other, but said nothing.

Styles's smile lightened. He clapped Tetherow on the shoulder and spoke with a false heartiness. "Don't you know, Lambert, if that damnable lie had an iota of truth in it, I would be in New Orleans personally at this moment to attend to the matter?"

Tetherow swallowed with difficulty. "I said that, Styles. I said that knowing you as I do—you can ask anybody—I said Styles Kenric would be down there in New Orleans defending his honor and the sanctity of his home."

Styles nodded. "And I would be. A man without honor has nothing. But as you see, I am here. To put your minds at ease, let me tell you I have letters from Kathy posted from her aunt's home in Charleston. She could scarcely be in two places at once, eh, gentlemen?"

"No, Styles."

"Would you care to have me read you Kathy's latest letter, gentlemen? It is intimate, but I will do anything to allay your suspicions of my wife's character."

The two men retreated a step, shaking their heads. Again, the coldly savage formality was all the warning they needed.

"My God, no, Styles," Winterkorn said. "Why, I felt all along there was some mistake."

"It's just rumors and lies," Lambert added quickly. "You know how them things start—even about a girl as lovely and pure as Miss Kathy."

Styles gazed at them, his eyes glittering like the cold steel of rapiers. "Well, the next time you hear that rumor, you might well remind the gossip that Styles Kenric will invite them out if that lie is repeated once more. If a woman is at fault, her husband—or her father—will answer to me. If a man dirties my wife's name with this lie, I will kill him on sight. You might even inform your secret source that Kathy may well want to face them with their lies—when I return her, and her aunt, here from Charleston."

Styles walked across the fields into the timberland. His fists were clenched as were the nerves in the pit of his stomach. Once deep in a pine hammock, he sagged against a tree bole and vomited. He stayed there for a long time, his mouth sour. But when he straightened, he no longer wanted to kill Kathy and her lover. Toward the tutor he felt only a searing contempt. He knew what Campbell was, a cowardly, hollow man, existing on surface values, unable to discharge his smallest obligations or responsibilities. He did not deceive himself. Hunt Campbell had run away with Kathy. In time, Hunt would run away from her because it would take more guts than Campbell possessed to stay with her. No. To hell with that mendacious bastard. It was Kathy against whom his total rage was directed. It was Kathy who would suffer retribution, slow and lifelong. Death was too quick, too easy. He wanted Kathy to live, to pay every day of her life for what she had done to him.

He would have his own brand of vengeance. He had wanted to kill her because she had betrayed and disgraced him, because now she was forever soiled, tarnished, tainted with the stigma of the faithless harlot. Until this moment he had not wanted her back. But he saw this was because he was too shattered to think straight. His battered pride was less important than an irreconcilable need for an eternal vengeance that would cripple her spirit and eventually destroy her mind and soul. Nothing else would satisfy him.

Thinking with cold clarity, he saw, too, that he had to have her back here at Blackoaks. He held control of this plantation only through his marriage to her. He would bring her home, and with something to hold over her that would keep her quiet and obedient. She would come back, and she would live out her life under his thumb.

He walked faster, beginning to see how it would be.

Moab glimpsed Styles walking alone through the pine hammock. The boy quickly concealed himself in the undergrowth, holding his breath until his master passed out of sight over a knoll.

He got up then and ran all the rest of the way to Florine Pilzer's fieldstone cottage in the park above the quarters. Scary! He had carefully gone miles out of the way to avoid being caught approaching Bos Pilzer's house and had almost been found out by Styles Kenric! He whistled between his teeth, empty-bellied.

He was still breathing raggedly when Florine came through the screen door and met him on her shadowed front porch. She wore that smock he knew so well, buttoned only at the throat. As he came up the steps, he saw she'd not buttoned it at all today! It folded back to reveal her full bare breasts, the flat planes of her belly, the dark mat of hair at her thighs. He responded instantly, desire flaring through him.

He ran to her and caught her in his arms, sliding his hands in under her smock, caressing her, pressing her body against him. "Oh, Moab, I've missed you. So terribly."

"I come. Quick as I could. I tole you. I'll always come —quick as I can."

"I keep thinking you've got another girl—some black wench."

"I never want anybody like I want you . . . . Nobody else knows jus' what I want, like you."

She kissed his mouth, his chin, his throat, licking at his sweat-salty flesh with her tongue. "Oh, Moab, anything . . . anything you want."

He laughed. "I wants—everything . . . . I wants you to start—on yore knees to me and give me—everything."

She nodded, panting as if she, instead of Moab, had raced through the forest. "Yes." She took his hand in hers and drew him after her into the silent house.

He said, "I don't live with Masta Styles no more . . . . They done sent me back to the quarters—to stay with Blade and his new woman . . . . But mostly Blade makes me sleep in the commissary."

"Oh, Moab, now you can come to me—every morning —after Bos leaves. Like old times, Moab."

Moab peeled away her smock, dropping it to the floor behind her. He stood and gazed at her nakedness, stroking her breasts, moving his hands over her body. Florine's eyes glazed over. Her breathing was labored. He swung her up in his arms and carried her into the bedroom. She sank down upon him with a little cry of need, wrapping her arms frantically about him, able for the moment to forget the future, content in mindless ravening with this sensuous present . . . .

The sun was climbing with unmerciful heat up the wall of heaven. Blade watched the sun shaft shrink across the floor toward the window of his shack. "Gawd," he thought, "I got to get me down to that commissary. Masta Kenric, he gone kill me, I don't get down there."

Ahma writhed against him, pressing her face into the softness at the base of his neck. She drew her tongue along his throat, feeling as gentle as a kitten but trembling with desire. In his exhaustion, Blade had toppled over on his back. She gazed at him, feeling uncontrollable needing. He was so beautiful! "Blade. Blade, honey. Do it to me again. Once more, Blade, 'fore you go off to work."

"My God, Ahma. You gone kill me."

She laughed. "I warned you."

"I got to git down to that commissary. Mornin' half gone, and I layin' here a-pesterin' you . . . or you a-pesterin' me . . . . I got work to do, gal."

"I don't want you to leave me."

"You know I got to."

"I don't know you got to. Let's run away . . . just you an' me. We could make it, Blade. Then you'd never be a slave again."

He stared down at her. His voice was flat. "I don't want to run away from Blackoaks, Ahma. This heah my home . . . since I was a little boy."

She jerked her hand away. "You a slave. A white man's slave. Ain't you got sense enough to see that?"

"I see that. I see I don't know nuthin' else."

"You smart. You could learn."

"Yeah. An' I could run—and git us both killed."

"We gits kilt, we die free."

"I in no hurry to die, gal—that's why I lettin' you kill me . . . nice an' slow." He gazed into her eyes. "Listen, Ahma. I has had a good life with the Baynards—and with Masta Styles . . . . Maybe I don't like him too much. But he been good to me. They all has. I'se had what I wanted, I been happy as most folks I see. Hell, I always been like a hog in warm mud. Now I got you, I in high cotton."

"I hate anything with a white skin. Whites beats you. Sells you. They treat you like they animals."

"I ain't never been beat. I a nigger. But I a Blackoaks nigger. Someday—when you been heah a while, you see what that means . . . you forgit all the old hurt."

"I forgit nuthin' . . . . I stays heah only long as *you* wants me—"

He laughed. "Then you die heah—less'n you kills me off . . . . You got to stop fightin' white people, Ahma. They too strong. They own everything. We black, our skin black. To them that makes us folks different. But that's the way life is for us—way it's always been. But you and me—we beautiful black folks. Reckon nobody on earth prettier'n you and me—unless maybe that sucker you gone bear me."

"I gwine bear no chile—let that white man sell it—like he bought me."

Sick, Blade lay silent for a moment. He swallowed back the illness. "We won't no way think about that now, Ahma. No. We'uns won't think about that now."

"You bes' think about it, 'cause nobody—white or god —gwine sell my baby."

Blade covered Ahma's mouth with his own and rolled over upon her, pressing his body between her heated thighs, trying desperately to blot the ugly images from both their minds. She caught him inside her long legs, locking her ankles at the base of his spine, flailing her hips and moaning—a keening wail that rose to a paean of unbearable joy, so that the dogs barked in the street and the neighbors laughed, nudging each other and smiling toward the cabin where Blade lived—where Blade *truly* lived.

Morgan ran ahead of Soapy, awkward and stumbling, going down the incline from the manor house toward the stables.

"Laus," Morgan called. "Laus, would you hitch Patches up to the buggy real fast? We got to go into Mt. Zion."

Laus swung up, his shirt sweated and stuck to his massive shoulders and barrel chest. "You in a mighty big rush, Masta Morgan. What you got to get into Mt. Zion for? I can't think of nothing in Mt. Zion worth ridin' in there in a hurry for."

Morgan dogged the big slave's steps, nodding, stumbling, hurrying him. Laus laughed indulgently and finally led the horse and single-seater that once had been Ferrell's runabout into the sunlight outside the barn. "Theah you is, Masta. But I still don't know why you in such a rush to git in that little ole town."

Morgan leaped up in the carriage and took up the reins. He barely waited for Soapy to clamber in beside him before he slapped the leathers on the rump of the horse, sending him lurching up the incline. Laus yelled after them, laughing, "You be careful with that hoss he don't run away with you."

Soapy clung to the iron seat rails as the wagon clattered down the tree-lined lane and wheeled west, racing toward Mt. Zion. He yelled, "Why *is* we in such a rush to git into Mt. Zion?"

Morgan let the animal slow to a steady trot and sat back, smiling. "We goin' to meet the train fum New Orleans."

Soapy stared at Morgan, shaking his head in disbelief. "Now why is we goin' do that?"

"We goin' do that ever' time the train comes through Mt. Zion . . . . I likes to watch that old train go through. I likes the way everybody in town stops everything to watch . . . . It's like a circus in town when that ole train goes through. Anyways, Hunt gonna come back on that train."

"You said something about Masta Hunt."

"That's right." Morgan nodded eagerly. "Mr. Hunt tole me something that I didn't tell Styles. No sense making Styles mad."

"What Masta Hunt tell you?" Soapy was doubtful.

"He coming back."

"What?"

"That's what he tole me. He told me the day before he left—and the day before Kathy went to Charleston— he told me he had to. go. Shit, Soapy, I like to cried. Hunt always good to me. He was my friend. He didn't try to teach me too hard or bother me 'cause I talk like a nigger."

"Masta Hunt was always good to me." Soapy nodded, remembering the books Hunt had "lost" for Soapy to find after he'd been ordered to desist teaching the slave boy to read or write. "Always mos' kindly."

"So we goin' to meet his train . . . . Ever train comes in, we be there in Mt. Zion waiting. The day he does come back, we be there."

Soapy laughed. "That sounds fine." He somehow doubted that Masta Hunt would ever come back to Black-oaks. But he did not say this aloud because he knew it would depress Morgan. It was better to let Morgan have something to believe in, even if that something was very unlikely ever to come to pass. Besides, Soapy loved to watch the train come puffing into town and then go storming out of it to all the strange, faraway places he'd never seen and never would.

They arrived in Mt. Zion an hour before train time. They tied up the rig in the shade of an ancient oak near the station. "We walk up town and git us something to eat," Morgan said. "My ole stomach's growling."

The bartender's voice stopped them at the door of the tavern. "You can't bring that nigger boy in here."

Soapy hesitated, retreating, but Morgan caught his arm. Morgan said coldly, "Soapy is my body slave. He go where I go."

The bartender smiled. "You the youngest Baynard

boy? . . . All right, come on in and buy what you want. But the nigger can't eat in here."

Soapy and Morgan stood uncomfortably near the shadowed bar, feeling the hard gazes of the townsmen on them, as the bartender prepared them a lunch of sandwiches, chicken, cheese, and strawberry drink. He wrapped the food in paper, collected fifty cents. Soapy and Morgan returned to the station and sat on the end of the platform, eating and watching for the train. Long before they heard its approaching whistle, townspeople were gathering from every direction like ants converging on an outdoor chicken fry.

When the train rolled into the station, Morgan leaped up. He ran awkwardly, stumbling often, bent over and searching the open windows of all the cars. He ran all the way to the coal car and back again, rechecking. He sagged beside Soapy, panting. They remained there in the sun until the conductor waved his arm and the train got up steam, bucking forward along the converging rails. .

"They wasn't on that ole train," Soapy said.

"Maybe they be on the next one. Anyhow, we be here."

"Yeah. That's fun. I like that, Morgan. I purely like being right here watching that ole train come in and go out—and all the time Miz Kathy or Masta Hunt might step off that train. And we be here to meet 'em . . . . We really comin' in on Thursday?"

Morgan nodded emphatically, watching the train disappear in the distance. "We be here," he said.

Exhausted, Blade had fallen asleep in the heated morning cabin with Ahma in his arms. Their bodies adhered with sweat, but Ahma smiled and could not have cared less. She watched the beautiful lines of Blade's classic profile, thinking she was happy for the first time in her life. There was no roiling hatred within her, no fires that would not be quenched, no driving compulsion to claw and destroy everything she hated. Blade had made her as calm as a kitten. She asked no more of her gods than to be permitted to stay like this in Blade's arms.

"Blade . . . . " Someone called from outside the shack.

231

Ahma sat up in bed, struck with a sense of terror, though it was bright daylight. Blade wakened slowly, yawning and stretching.

"Blade . . . . You in there, Blade?"

"Oh, my Gawd," Blade whispered. "That's Masta Styles. He gonna skin my tail for layin' abed with you this time of day."

He swung out of bed, wide awake now, and stepped into a pair of osnaburg britches. He gave Ahma a quick, calming kiss and strode out on the stoop, squinting against the brilliance of the sun, and staggering slightly because the backs of his legs were still weak. A man didn't recover from Ahma in a few minutes.

"Howdy, Masta."

"You sick, Blade?"

"No, Masta. I fine. I sorry I ain't down there workin' like I know I ought to be." He tried to smile and glanced meaningfully across his shoulder toward the girl on the bed inside his cabin. "I been gentlin' my kitten, Masta."

Styles forced himself to smile though his gray face ached with the effort. "You mind takin' a little walk with me, Blade?"

"Oh, no, Masta. I wants to do anything you wants me to do."

Styles nodded his head up the incline toward the lane that led past Bos Pilzer's place and into the timberlands beyond. "I'd like to talk to you, Blade. I might have a job I'd want you to do for me."

"You know I can do anything you want Blade to do, Masta."

"Yes. You've always been a good boy, Blade. That's why I hope I can trust you."

Blade's smile faded, the tone of Masta Styles's voice suggested that he was not to be trusted. "When I evah failed you, Masta?"

"Never, Blade. Not yet. But you see, I might need for you to take our finest carriage and go to bring Miss Kathy back home. Would you like that?"

"Miss Kathy? Where is she, Masta?"

"She's in Charleston." Styles's tone hardened. "But by

232

the time I'm ready to send you for her, she may be in another town. She might be as far away as New Orleans."

"I never been to N'Awleans, Masta. I never been to Charleston. Don't think I ever been farther than Mt. Zion since I four, five years old."

"I'm not worried about that. I know that you can do what I need you to do. You'd want to help Miss Kathy— if she needed you to come and bring her home?"

"I do anything for Miss Kathy, Masta."

"Yes. I know that . . . . But if I send you, you'd be maybe four or five days on the road with Miss Kathy. Just the two of you."

Blade shook his head. "Miss Kathy as safe with me, Masta, as any china doll what might break if you touch it."

"Perhaps." He gave Blade a leer of forced camaraderie. "Still, I've seen the way you look at white ladies—when you think nobody is noticing."

"Ah, no suh, I wouldn't do that."

By now they had passed the last whitewashed cabin of the quarters and were following the lane across the tree-studded park where Bos Pilzer lived in a fieldstone cottage. Styles forced a faint laugh. "How about it, Blade? You ever pestered Bos Pilzer's woman?"

Shocked, Blade shook his head. "Aw, Masta, no. I a black boy. I know my place. I don't touch no white lady. Special not Masta Bos Pilzer's white lady. I got no wish to have the hide peeled off my body with a snake whip."

"But you have thought about it? You've thought about mounting her, haven't you? If you could get away with it?"

Blade stopped, his face bleak. His eyes were stricken. His bronzed body was beaded with sweat. "Masta, no. What you tryin' to do to me? What you trying to git me to say?"

Styles forced a warm smile. He saw that he had frightened Blade, set him to trembling with fear. He had believed he could stride into the subject of women, white women, and white women's bodies, without subtlety. He saw that he would never win Blade's confidence without the subtleness of Iago.

At that moment, they heard Mrs. Pilzer's voice lifted in a half-singing cry. They might have run to check on her safety, but there was pleasure, not fear or distress in her voice. Styles laughed. "Sounds like somebody's pestering the overseer's wife right now."

He walked forward along the lane again, and after a hesitant moment Blade followed, troubled, slack-shouldered.

Styles laughed. "Come on, Blade. I'm just trying to be your friend. If you humped the overseer's wife, I'd never say anything."

"I nevah did, Masta. Naw, suh, I wouldn't do that."

"Don't lie to me." But Styles smiled as he said it.

"Naw, suh. I wouldn't evah do that."

Styles forced a hearty laugh. "The hell you wouldn't. The hell any man wouldn't, Blade. Black or white. I guess the color of a man's skin doesn't matter where a hair trap is concerned. You know you'd like to cover a white woman and sink that old snake of yours up into her. I've seen what a mast you've got."

"I got me all the bed wench I needs, Masta Styles. I don't need no other woman but Ahma. I admit I use to pester maybe two, three different black wenches a day. But now you brought me Ahma—I ain't got strength for nobody but her. I don't *want* nobody but her."

"That's fine . . . . I was just talking to you . . . trying to find out if maybe you hadn't thought about crawlin' a white woman."

Blade drew a deep breath, but he did not speak.

Styles said in a gentle, serious tone, "I know you've always loved Miss Kathy."

Blade did not speak. Sweat flooded down from his crisp black hair across his straight, high forehead. "Not like that, Masta. Not like that."

"But if she were in trouble somewhere, you'd want to go and bring her home?"

"Oh, yes, Masta." Empty-bellied without fully under-standing why, Blade glanced back across his shoulder toward his cabin where he'd known his first complete happiness with Ahma. Without being able to say why, he

234

felt that happiness was somehow terribly imperiled. But he nodded, his voice strong. "Oh, yes. If Miss Kathy need me, I go anywhere. I do anything for Miss Kathy."

3

Fifty dollars for an evening gown that Kathy might wear twice—in the extremity of an emergency? Benumbed, incredulous, Hunt asked the salesgirl to repeat the price, believing he'd heard wrong. The withering glance the saleswoman gave him would have humbled him had he not been in a state of shock. It was not that he was parsimonious, stingy. He certainly was not. God knew he didn't begrudge Kathy the loveliest apparel they could find. He wanted her to have the nicest of everything, as long as they could afford it, but that wouldn't be very long at this rate. His frugal soul was outraged. His was a lifelong training of thrift, economy, prudence. One thought twice before one spent a dollar. Why, bread was five cents a loaf, milk ten cents a quart, a suit of excellent quality could be purchased in Boston for twelve dollars—with two pairs of pants—a suit a man might wear for years. He didn't believe in a pinchfisted existence; it was not a matter of cheese parings and candle ends. One simply didn't waste one's substance. Fifty dollars for an evening gown?

Sweated, aware that the haughty saleswoman's contemptuous smile was fixed on him, Hunt fished in his pocket and brought out his snap-purse. Still not believing it, he counted out the money.

Kathy had not even noticed his discomfiture. She had never been denied anything in her life any more than she had ever inquired the price. She spun on her toes before the full-length mirror. He admitted that the ice-blue gown, with its simplicity of line flowing to her toes, wasp-waisted, and flaunting a charming décolletage, caught all the light in the small, *haute-monde* shop Kathy had discovered on Ursulines Street near Royal in the *Vieux Carré*.

He felt repaid a thousand times by Kathy's delight in the gossamer gown. Ten dollars for fragile dancing slippers, new crinolines, underthings, and hoisery, and when she was finally dressed by nine that night, she was incredibly lovely.

The hotel room was a shambles by the time she had finally completed her toilet. Underthings, slips, crinolines, stockings, papers, shoes littered the room. Not a chair but was covered with discarded clothing. Her dresser was a heap of perfumes, powders, and lotions, lost in tissues. Kathy gave the havoc a regretful glance and sighed. "I need a maid—I never did this for myself before."

He winced, wondering at the cost of a freed black woman in New Orleans. "I think you've done quite well," he said, trying to smile. "It looks as if the Battle of New Orleans were fought in this room."

She laughed and kissed him lightly. He was transported by the faint, haunting cloud of her cologne. "I don't need anything but you, darling."

"Certainly not." He smiled, surveying the carnage. "Somebody will clean it up. We'll just leave it here until they do."

A draft of stunned silence preceded them across the hotel lobby. Men stared, women's lips parted, and their eyes widened. Hunt swelled with pride, glad now that he'd spent the whole fifty dollars. Kathy was lovelier, rarer than an orchid—and as striking.

His heart slipped slightly, however, in reaction to the attention she garnered simply by walking across a public room. Going out with Kathy in public places was like setting up a huge beacon light beckoning Styles Kenric on a direct course. The hell with it! They couldn't hide in their room. Those damned old maid Bretherton bitches must have returned to the Briars weeks ago. By now the sisters had undoubtedly informed the countryside that Kathy Kenric was living flagrantly in an adulterous relationship at the Hotel St. Louis. Where could they hide when Kathy was the most breathtakingly lovely young girl these people had ever seen, when even the faint traces of her cologne were unforgettable?

Kathy floated down the entrance steps to the banquette. The hotel doorman abandoned a couple on the walk and strode toward Kathy, bowing and smiling. He whistled up a carriage.

Antoine's Restaurant, their destination, had just been established on St. Louis Street. As their carriage rattled across the cobblestones on Royal, they could see the gleaming carriages, the glittering diamonds, furs, and evening clothes of the town's smartest and richest socialites.

No attendant, slave or freed could have been more attentive and courteous than was their black cabbie. He got into the line of fine landaus and sedans, refusing to halt one inch away from the decorative grille outside the new restaurant. He swung down with the agility of a monkey from his high seat. He touched Kathy's elbow with the lightest and most respectful gesture, helping her to alight to the banquette. Hunt paid him and the aging black man bowed them across the walk to the entrance where the doorman obsequiously parted the glass doors for them.

Kathy's eyes glowed with awe at the elegance of the dining room. But her delight in the sparkling surroundings was dimmed by the impact she made upon New Orleans's most sophisticated citizenry. The bored forgot their attitude of boredom; *ennui* suddenly dissipated. The blasé stared openly. The unamazed were impressed. In a room glittering with diamonds, resplendent with sable and mink, Kathy was the sensation of the season. The undeniable homage of a brief, impregnated silence in the first view of her, followed by buzzing chatter, greeted her and persisted as they were placed in one of the most public of tables by the maître d'hôtel.

Hunt writhed uncomfortably in this most conspicuous site. Had all the lights in the restaurant been directed upon them, they could not have elicited more attention and curious gazes. Hunt wanted a more secluded table in a less exposed area, but after a few moments he admitted that Kathy would have drawn all eyes had they been seated in a corner behind a palm. He ordered *huîtres, crevettes,* and a *filet de boeuf avec légumes,* to be followed by *fromage* and *café brûlot.* The waiter, without taking his hooded eyes from the decollete bodice of Kathy's gown, smiled and nodded. "And, *m'sieu',* may I suggest a cup at least of gumbo creole—"

When the waiter returned, he placed a card beside Hunt's plate. He inclined his head almost imperceptibly toward a man sitting alone half across the room. The man bowed and gave Hunt a warm and eager smile. He looked to be somewhere between forty and sixty. His face was gray with a look of dissipation, and his salt-and-pepper hair was brushed carefully across his bald patch. Adding to Hunt's immediate reaction of distaste was the small gold and diamond earring the man wore in his left ear.

Hunt hesitated, considering returning the note unread. But as the man continued to smile, Hunt at last took up the paper and read the griffonage scrawled across its face.

According to the *carte de visite,* the man's name was Julien-Jacques Gischairn. This meant nothing to Hunt, less than nothing. He deciphered the scribbled message: *"Ma'm'selle, M'sieu',* May I visit for one moment at your table? I am an old and close friend of your respected father, Major Baynard."

Scowling, Hunt handed the card across the table to Kathy. She scanned it and glanced up, smiling openly and unreservedly toward Julien-Jacques Gischairn. Inwardly, Hunt raged. Kathy smiled as if she'd known this intruder forever. Obviously the old lecher wanted nothing more than to be closer to Kathy's half-bared breasts. While one couldn't blame him, one didn't have to encourage him. Hunt watched Kathy incline her head in a nod. Gischairn leaped up, almost upsetting his chair. He came bounding with springing steps between the tables, beaming, still carrying his huge linen napkin.

He gave Hunt a brief nod, bent over Kathy's hand and touched his mustached lips to her fingers. "May I sit down?" he pleaded.

"Of course." Kathy smiled, as guileless as a child. She watched Gischairn with a pleased little smile tilting her lovely lips. He pulled out a chair for himself, edged it fractionally closer to Kathy's, and sat down toying with his napkin.

"Let me say at first who I am," Gischairn suggested.

"Please do." Hunt did not smile.

Gischairn never took his eyes from Kathy. "I am no one, really. Not in the sense that old John McDonogh came here and made a fortune selling plantations, lumber, and slaves, then spent those millions building this city." He shrugged. "But I too sold slaves and cotton in the Exchange until I had the millions I need to do what I always wanted to do—enjoy the beauties of McDonogh's city. Eh?"

"The female beauties?" Hunt inquired with some irony.

"Of course, my dear young friend. What else? I am indeed a connoisseur of beauty, a collector of the lovely. And I must say, most humbly, and with tears, *ma'mselle,* I've never seen your equal in the fifty years of my life in this town."

"How delightful of you to say that," Kathy said, and her tone added, teasing, "And so nice you knew my father—the illustrious *Major* Baynard."

He chewed at his lip and tried to look contrite. "I'm sorry my little ruse was so transparent, *ma'mselle.*"

She laughed with him. "It's all right. My father was never a major, you see."

Gischairn shrugged. "My *gaffe,* my dear. But I felt so secure, once I learned he belonged to the landed gentry of Alabama. Most landowners are majors or colonels, at least."

"You're forgiven," Kathy said, "only because you are so delightful."

"I am afraid, my dear, that your—husband?—" he managed to glance toward Hunt, "has already pigeon-holed me as a voluptuary, debaucher, *paillard.*"

"Oh, Hunt is most observant," Kathy said, without giving him title or rank.

"But I am more than a libertine, my dear. I am not only one of the richest men in this city, I am its social arbiter. No, I don't exaggerate at all. My frown can destroy a man or a woman socially. Sometimes, it amuses me to foist some clod upon our best people, and then abandon them, midair. I am really an evil person. My single redeeming quality is my respectful awed appreciation of beauty such as yours . . . . That's why I asked to be permitted to join you. Already you are a long step up in New Orleans's society, because you have appeared to know Julien-Jacques Gischairn, to be an intimate of mine. Frankly, because you recognized me, there are people in this room who would be afraid not to pay you the homage of exchanged greetings."

"Why are you telling me all this?" Kathy inquired.

Gischairn laughed, putting his head back and spreading his hands in delight at her candor. "Because, my child, I thought you'd be pleased to know that were I to sponsor you—and your husband?—I could assure you entrée into the very best homes on St. Charles Avenue."

"And you—what would you expect in return?" Hunt inquired.

Gischairn glanced at him in mock agony. "My dear young man, *nothing!*"

"Altruism was one of the first indefensible virtues I learned to discard—in the nursery," Hunt said.

"I would have every reward—as virtue is a reward. I would have you and Miss Baynard as my guests at the Absinthe House, the Hotel St. Louis, here—several times a week. The ballet. The opera. You would be my guests. My reward would be to be near enough to bask in the gentle beauty of your young lady. To glow in the reflected glory of her loveliness."

"All of that," Kathy said with a bright laugh that turnéd every head in the place. "But I couldn't let you waste your time, *M'sieu'* Gischairn, delightful as you are."

He looked genuinely crushed. "And why not? Don't you want entrée into the upper circles of society? Don't you want to be accepted by the best families?"

She shrugged. "It's most kind of you, but all I really want is to go to bed."

"Bed?" His mouth drooped open. "What is in bed?"

"Hunt," she replied, laughing at him. "You see, I love Hunt with a kind of madness that you wouldn't understand, that delights me—and that frightens him."

"I'm a congenital coward," Hunt said.

Julien-Jacques Gischairn pushed back in his chair. "May I say that I hope, sir, you never grow insensitive to this treasure you have here?"

Afterwards they walked along the banquettes of the Quarter, which were lighted by the ornate streetlamps copied from those in Paris. The town vibrated with life, even at this late hour. Kathy stared, incredulous as the mixture of races, colors, classes—Frenchmen, Spaniards, Creoles, mustees, yankees, river men, priests and nuns— passed them on the walks.

Kathy was yawning helplessly by the time they stepped out of the cab before the Hotel St. Louis. Her ten-dollar slippers were frayed, soles worn through. She took them off, clinging to Hunt's arm on the hotel steps to brace herself, and carried them. The night clerk and sleepy bellhops smiled indulgently in her wake. A deep stillness pervaded the building. Kathy sagged, looking somehow crushed by fatigue, like a faintly wilted gardenia.

Hunt felt overwhelmed by his love for Kathy—a wild passion all mixed with the tenderest devotion. Sadly, he wondered if they might not look back on this night as their happiest time of all. He shook the thought away. His problem was that he had no faith in the future.

Inside their door, Kathy peeled off her evening gown, letting it fall at her ankles and dropping her ruined slippers atop the wrinkled fabric. She walked on the dress, crushing it under her feet on her way to the bathroom. Hunt, stopped in the act of removing his tie, stood immobile, staring, shocked at the crumpled gown, discarded among the other litter strewn across the floor.

He heard her humming the tune she'd bribed the violinist to play half a dozen times tonight for them alone. She'd danced close in his arms and he could feel the frantic pounding of her heart through the fullness of her breast.

He sighed heavily, mouth warped into a wry smile. He undressed and fell across their bed, throwing pieces of her discarded undergarments and a shoe to the floor. He lay there, struggling to unravel the bedsheet.

She came, naked and completely unselfconscious, from the bathroom. Her body gleamed in the saffron lamplight, and she absently massaged herself, yawning sleepily. But, beside him on the mattress, she was not sleepy. She reached for him. She slid her heated hand across his flat belly, stroking him lovingly. "Oh," she whispered. "It's been such a long, long evening . . . . Love me, Hunt. Please. Love me . . . . "

He took her in his arms. As he thrust himself to her, he sensed a cold spot, like the bull's-eye of a target, between his shoulder blades. He was shaken by an overwhelming urge to leap up and check the darkened room. Had he locked that damned corridor door? Damned if he wanted Styles to come raging in upon them right now. Breathing hollowly and quivering with pleasure, Kathy locked her ankles at his waist and drew him down to her. He thrust himself closer with all his strength, all his passionate longing. The hell with Styles Kenric . . . . What better way to die?

Hunt located a second-floor apartment in a walled house on Dauphine Street in the *Vieux Carré*. The rent was less by the month than he currently paid for each night at the Hotel St. Louis. But he did not mention this aspect to Kathy. He had no wish to burden her with economics. His banker, ensconced in his plush office on Carondelet, had not yet been able to find suitable employment for him. Hunt was pragmatically certain the banker would never find work for which Hunter Campbell, Master of Arts, *summa cum laude,* Harvard, was prepared. Anyhow, he preferred to spend all the time he had with Kathy. He still believed they could subsist on the fifty dollars a month income from his mother's estate, dipping into his savings as sparingly as possible.

He soon learned to his dismay that they must hire a cook if they expected ever to eat their meals at home. Two maids would be a minimal necessity if Kathy were to be kept clothed and served and the apartment cleared for navigation.

Kathy chatted blithely, enthralled by the sights enlivening the narrow walled streets, the delicate lacelike iron grillwork balconies of the *Vieux Carré*. She promenaded beside him, peeking through grillwork gates at beflowered patios beyond arched carriageways. Their own patio was hidden from Dauphine Street by an eight-foot wall covered with ivy and fig vines that lunged limberly in every breeze and splayed fantastic shadow patterns across the flagstone pavement. They entered this willow-curtained central yard through the *porte cochère*. A fountain cooled the bright square of hibiscus, wistaria, jasmine, and bougainvillaea.

Kathy exclaimed delightedly at the stairway and the wide veranda that overlooked the patio and ran the length of their apartment. She had not dared hope there existed so perfect a haven for them—Italian-marble mantelpiece, twelve-foot ceilings, in her bedroom a full-length mirror in a gilt frame, a crystal chandelier that tinkled belllike with every breeze through the dining alcove. "So perfect," she cried, kissing Hunt. "Oh, darling, do people die of happiness?"

He exhaled, thankful he hadn't admitted having chosen this place simply because it was cheap.

They were happy on Dauphine Street. The maid and cook were even more expensive than Hunt had feared, but he told himself they could manage. Kathy desired only the smallest outlays for entertainment. She'd rather sit beside him on their balcony eating shrimp salad than go to Broussard's for dinner. They'd make ends meet, somehow.

Their first evening, when he returned from hiring a cook and maid, Kathy met him inside their front door naked except for a sheer gossamer negligee she'd bought that afternoon in the French boutique on Ursulines. He'd stopped by the St. Louis Hotel bar for a drink because he'd thought he saw Styles striding ahead of him on Bourbon Street. He had been shaken when he walked into the bar. Three drinks quieted him and braced him for the hurried walk through the darkling streets to his apartment. He'd bought a bottle of Plantation Choice— the whiskey Kathy's father had distilled with such inordinate satisfaction. "Stuff's gettin' hard to come by," the bartender told him. Hunt nodded. "Yes. I know." He carried the bottle under his arm, and strode toward Dauphine Street, refusing to surrender to the fearful urge to wheel around and check the street behind him.

Kathy held out her arms to him. Her beautiful, full breasts with faintly pink nipples and the dainty triangle of her femininity were not concealed at all by the fragile fabric but were enhanced by it. She kissed him, frowning slightly at the strong alcoholic smell of his breath. Then she smiled. "You want to do it to me before supper, or after supper—or both?"

He shook his head, unable to believe this girl was related to the timid Kathy Kenric who had been too shy to undress before him when they arrived in New Orleans. He laughed, teasing her. "Do I want to do what?"

Her head tilted and she let the negligee fall apart. She drew a deep breath and he watched her face and throat bloom as pink as her nipples. "Do you want to—fuck me?" she said.

Now he did laugh. "Where'd you hear a word like that?"

"When I was four years old." She smiled. "But I didn't know what it really meant until you showed me."

He laughed and pulled her close against him. "Do we have to eat supper?"

She kissed his throat, moving her hands down to his fly and the erection bulging there. "You are supper," she told him.

Kathy drew him after her into the bedroom and he sagged across the bed, allowing her to undress him. The drinks at the Hotel St. Louis bar, the talk of the men around him about the sixty lovely whores putting on shows before they took on their customers at the French Riding Academy, had roused him. He had been incredulous at the proven statistic that two thousand women worked in the twelve hundred whorehouses in the redlight district. An older man had laughed. "We became the New World mecca for whores when old General Jackson paid off his troops in New Orleans. The soldiers had money and the girls flocked in here to earn it, their way." Several men had invited him to accompany them to the

French Riding Academy, but he had felt guilty about whoring while Kathy awaited him alone. The experience of her naked freshness burned the last wisps of alcohol out of his brain, and he throbbed with desire for her. But even as he locked his mouth over hers and thrust his tongue as deeply as he could into her throat, he was thinking with half his mind, what's the best way to get out of here if Kenric shows up at that door? He could leap from the balcony. That was the only chance he would have. He'd jump to those cobbles below and run. He'd run if he didn't break his leg in the jumping. Hell, he'd run even if he broke his leg. Suddenly, loving her with all his strength, he found himself weeping bitterly, overcome with self-hatred . . . .

Hunt had left no forwarding address when he and Kathy moved from the Hotel St. Louis to Dauphine Street. There was no doubt, Styles's trail would lead him directly to the St. Louis. But New Orleans was a big city —they should be able to lose themselves in it. But when he returned home the second afternoon, Julien-Jacques Gischairn was having tea with Kathy on their veranda. He had brought them a house-warming gift, a sterling-silver carafe and glasses. Hunt dropped into a chair. If Gischairn could find them, Styles Kenric would be along any day now.

Hunt awoke every morning unnerved by the paralyzing thought that this might be that day when Kenric showed up. It had been weeks now, months. This didn't make sense. Kenric wasn't the kind of man to permit his wife to run away from him. Pride and public opinion motivated Kenric's life. And Kenric had no claim on that plantation, which obsessed him, without Kathy there as his wife. Oh, Kenric was coming. But when? When? Hunt felt as if a perfect marksman had aimed an arrow at his heart, pulled back the bow, and let it fly. It could not miss, the only question was one of time.

Gischairn visited Kathy at least four afternoons a week. Hunt found him there when he came in from the bar. He disliked the aging lecher intensely and would have warned him to stay the hell away, but Kathy enjoyed the old gossip there. Kathy laughed when Gischairn visited.

She was always telling him gossip of the town's renowned and infamous, retailed to her by Gischairn. She became an encyclopedia on the old roué's beloved city. "Did you know all the streets in the Quarter are twenty-five *French* feet wide?" she asked. "You know what a French foot is?"

Hunt was only fuzzily aware of each separate day—they blurred and ran together. He began to drink rum moments after waking. He waited, tense, for footsteps on that stairway outside their veranda. A servant's sudden rapping on a door unmanned him. He drank to calm his nerves. His stomach remained tied in knots and burned savagely when he ate the rich foods for which every damned restaurant in the Quarter was famous. A glass of milk made him vomit. Whiskey he could hold on his stomach, thank God.

He spent more and more time at the bar in the Hotel St. Louis. Here, he needed one quick drink to screw up even enough courage to stand and converse casually with the men around him. He was a good conversationalist; his education provided him a hundred subjects for dissertation. He was a good listener when these dissolute southerners talked about their mistresses and their trips to the whorehouses.

He was continually amazed at the way these men openly discussed the most intimate details of their lives with their women. Hunt could laugh and enjoy their stories, but he could not talk about sex or mention Kathy's name. He realized he was so wholeheartedly accepted because he possessed the loveliest young woman in New Orleans. This made him a celebrity in a way, as it made hiding impossible.

When time came to leave the bar, he needed two stiff shots of straight whiskey to force himself out into the street. Once there, he skulked along, hurrying, taut-bellied at shadows, moving swiftly past alleys, staying close to the buildings, like a cutpurse. When he strode into the apartment, he immediately poured himself a drink, and he yelled at Kathy when she told him he drank too much.

Failing Kathy, he drank. Despising himself for his cowardice, he drank. To find the courage to face each new day, he drank. And so the weeks and the months slipped past in an alcoholic fog. There were nights when he was too deep in a drunken stupor to love Kathy, nights when he escaped her loving arms by holding up a bottle between them. And the hell of it was, all he wanted was Kathy—and he was destroying her, and he was destroying himself, and he could see what he was doing, but he could not stop.

Kathy was too happy to be afraid of Styles's finding them. If he found them, she could envision nothing except the final break between them. Even Styles must know she would never return to him. Perhaps he did know that. Perhaps this was why he did not follow her. Only Hunt's unreasoning fear of Styles troubled her. Only his increasing drinking disturbed her. She wished he could see what he was doing to himself. Mornings, his hands shook visibly when he lifted his cup of *café-au-lait*. Many nights now she had been heartbroken to see Hunt come stumbling in so drunk he scarcely recognized her, eyes wild with animal fear.

She was so happy with Hunt—when he was sober, when he would stay in the apartment with her—that she felt sinful. Her exultant happiness made her feel guilty. She had all she would ever ask of life, she loved Hunt, and he loved her. To ask more was blasphemy. She knew she was wicked—an adultress who had deserted her husband—she should suffer, but she was not suffering. She felt no shame. She was in love for the first time in her life—truly in love with a man who could return that love.

Looking at him, she felt warm and quivering with a physical need that could not be sated. The desire for his love grew stronger every day, more intense, newer, and more pleasant. She felt sinfully, passionately happy. The better she knew Hunt, the more she loved him. She loved him for his strengths as much as for the weaknesses that made him vulnerable. His fear and his drinking were transient—they would pass. Once this business with

Styles was satisfactorily settled, their lives could be serene.

This present unhappiness was to her like a furious rain cloud set against the face of a blazing sun. When he insisted upon going to his banker, she knew he really meant he was headed for the St. Louis Hotel. She understood his fears and she smiled. But as soon as he was out of the house she missed him, and longed for him, and counted the hours until he returned.

In the afternoon, she went nervously out upon the balcony and searched the street both ways for Hunt. How long and empty were the hours when he was away. Why did men have to go in to town, even when there was no reason, no commerce, no profession? They had to drink with other men, exchange lies, laugh with them, or they felt less than manly. Laughter, with women, she supposed, was good. But it was different—it was not enough for a woman. She lived for her man. She sighed because she caught no glimpse of Hunt in the narrow, cobbled avenue. Unhappily, she returned inside the living room.

The afternoon settled into lazy stillness. The street beyond the courtyard grew very quiet, with a droning silence more appropriate to a forest. It was as if in the heat of afternoon the town itself slept, stunned, and those who moved, half-awake, held their breath and trod on their toes for fear of waking the sleepers. A carriage rattled over the cobblestones, but, rather than shattering the quiet, the vehicle intensified it.

Kathy wandered about the apartment as if caged. Perhaps if she took a bath and then splashed her body with a new cologne she might rouse Hunt despite his preoccupation with fear. She removed her housedress and stood naked before the mirror of her *table à toilette*. Her vague reflection pleased her. Her hair showed a soft golden glow. Only her eyes disturbed her—anxious, even in the dark mirror, as if Hunt's fears infected her. Her pupils were too large, were set too deeply in the ceramic pink glaze of her face. Her full lips were too red, blood red. Her gaze fondled her breasts. They were full, shapely. She might wish them larger if this would please Hunt.

She wished anything that would please Hunt and insure his increased devotion, as her own desire for him mounted higher every time he touched her. She willed him to know how passionately and furiously she loved him, how every day was pointed toward that moment when he took her in his arms. Breathless, she felt heated liquidity forming inside her at the thought of his loving her. She touched her breasts, the nipples growing hard like small pink marbles.

Yes, she'd have a bath, quickly. The fresh tang of the *eau de cologne* would soothe and invigorate her. And she must stay away from thoughts of Hunt when he was away from her! The very idea of his loving her brought back that wild ecstasy he'd taught her. She wanted to lock him in her arms, to secure him tightly against her— and keep him close inside her forever. Only then would she be complete. But unless she had a cool bath quickly she wouldn't be able to wait. She felt her skin prickling. She was restless, quivering with need, aroused with dreams about him that she dared not allow inside her conscious mind.

She stood in the doorway of the balcony, naked, watching the street, praying he would come home sober. Please, God, don't let him stumble coming up those stairs. Don't let him sprawl unconscious across our bed. I need him so terribly. She did not know how to deal with his desire for her, which could not overcome the lifelong pattern of his fears . . . .

4

Blade shucked his clothing as Styles had ordered. Styles lounged in a high-backed overstuffed chair, watching the slender, bronzed young body exposed to his gaze. His heart slugged arrhythmically. Only the obsessive desire for vengeance against Kathy kept him from thrusting aside every other consideration and throwing himself on his knees before the naked, godlike youth. Even consumed with hatred, he stared hungrily at Blade's long, heavy-headed penis, the hanging scrotum, the muscled legs like pillars carved from cedar.

"All right, Blade," Styles said, "into the bath tub."

The three houseboys who had been enlisted to supply hot water and lye soap and to scrub Blade down looked at each other and giggled as the "field" nigger let himself gingerly into the cramped quarters of the tiled tub. Blade looked miserable, as if he might be letting himself down in the stewpot of some ancient cannibal tribe from his dark past.

"You'll like it once you become accustomed it to," Styles said, leaning against the wall. "You're going to like everything I teach you, Blade. Everything."

Blade nodded doubtfully. "Yes, suh, Masta." He could not understand what his becoming accustomed to daily hot baths had to do with his finding Miss Kathy in some distant city and returning her to Blackoaks. But he'd long ago learned that white masters were gods who moved in mysterious ways.

Just the same, he despised the clutching hands of the houseboys as they scrubbed him. When one of them reached to wash his crotch, Blade shoved him, hard. "Watch yo'self, black boy."

The houseboy glanced toward Styles, appealing to the master for support. Styles laughed. "Let them wash you down there, Blade—gets sweated."

Blade stood unmoving until he was bathed. Two boys scrubbed his body with thick fresh-smelling towels. Blade found this pleasant. His body glowed. A boy splashed a sweet-scented after-bath cologne over Blade's shoulders. Blade winced, offended by the strong musk. "Splash it under your armpits, Blade," Styles ordered, "and put some around your crotch. It might sting slightly. But it'll make you smell better . . . . When you spend five days in a carriage with Miss Kathy, she's going to want you to smell good—not like a nigger."

Blade wanted to remind his master that he *was* a nigger, but he said nothing. He realized by now that Styles was being kind, trying to be kind. And it was pleasant to be the center of so much attention. He supposed eventually he would get used to these fat-assed houseboys jumping to attend his least need. He wondered if they wiped your tail for you? One thing, he'd have a hell of a lot to tell Ahma tonight.

But when he walked into their cabin she greeted him with a savage cry of protest. "You stink, Blade!" she cried. "You stink worse than a white man."

"I stink *like* a white man," Blade said. "White people likes this smell."

She swore. "Well, I don't like it, and you ain't trackin' that smell into my bed. If'n you got any wish to bed down with me tonight, you best git down to the barn and wash that stink off. And don't come back till you smell like a man—my man."

"Oh, hell," Blade said. "What I gonna do? I please my masta and my woman hates me . . . . Hell, Ahma, you got me between a rock and a hard place."

"You go scrub off that white-folk smell. Then we be all right—then we think about your hard place."

He laughed and kissed her. But she held her breath and shoved him toward the door.

Each morning, Blade went up to the big house. His day began with a hot tub, with the houseboys scrubbing and massaging him, and Styles watching. Then breakfast was served, and Styles taught him the correct way to use a knife and a fork. All Blade could think was, how was he to live in the quarters after he learned to live like his white master? If he held a fork like that, they'd laugh him off the hill. And as long as he smelled of cologne, Ahma wouldn't even let him in her bed.

And every afternoon when Styles finally released him, Blade went hurrying to Ahma, loins aching, a bulge at his crotch. He could deny the sensuous things Masta Styles spoke to him of, but they got inside him, and they infected him, and he found release only when he could push Ahma over on her back, spread her lovely legs, and mount her. At least his ardor pleased and enthralled Ahma. She never complained about his lovemaking.

Styles taught him to read and write. "Warn you,

Blade. It's going to tax you. You're nineteen—and you never went to school, you've never been taught anything from a book. I'm going to teach you. You'll be able to read signs, directions, hotel bills, anything you need to read. But you're going to learn in weeks what many people take years to master. Think you can do it?"

Blade nodded. "Blade can do anything, Masta. Anything you want him to do."

Styles sank languidly into the tall-backed overstuffed chair and crossed his knees. He smiled gently. "But how about the things I might not want you to do, Blade?"

Blade felt his face grow heated. "Like what, Masta?"

Styles smiled, wanting to reassure Blade, to gain his confidence. He intended teaching the young Negro another lesson even more important to his schemes than reading or writing. He wanted to instill in the Fulani the thought that he might pester a white woman as he did the black wenches—that she might be *more* than receptive, no matter what Blade had been taught all his life.

Styles spoke in a bland yet heated tone, consciously aimed at arousing the young black's desires. One fact made his task easier. Blacks were simple, direct, and honest in their approach to sex—much like the aroused stallion: to desire was to take. His job was to arouse Blade's desires to a fever pitch, to diminish his old fears until, no matter the youth's innate will power, he would not be able to resist those needs during five days alone on the trail with Kathy.

Styles drew a deep breath, feeling faint. When Kathy was returned to him, used by a black man, her last defenses would be demolished. The rest of their lives together would be a time of retribution, the only vengeance that could appease the rages obsessing him. He asked no more than this; he would accept no less. And to accomplish it, he would arouse this boy's desires beyond human strength to resist. Before he was through, no matter what Blade had believed before, he would deeply implant in the boy's mind the overwhelming fantasy that Kathy had always secretly and passionately wanted him.

To Blade the white man's insinuations were frightening threats to his essential notions about things. To Blade,

Kathy was part of the stone chapel. Blade had small feeling for religion, one way or another. Sometimes, when a priest came to Blackoaks, Miz Claire had invited all the slaves who wished to share the services. Sometimes Blade had gone, but not because he understood the strange ceremonies conducted in some alien tongue, or because he found the small sip of wine worth the tiresome waiting and kneeling. Blade's own religion lived in some primal memory of his ethnic heritage—the bad medicine and the good medicine that were all mixed up with the trees and the water and the sun and earth of a dark continent Blade dimly recalled from childhood stories related in horror by slaves who had endured the terrible middle passage.

No, the reason he had attended those infrequent Sunday services in Miz Claire's chapel was because he had wanted the aching sense of pleasure on those rare occasions when he could secretly watch Miss Kathy on that front-row pew, gathering all the light in the place—from the candles, the polished candlesticks, and the sunlight coming through the stained glass windows.

Watching her in the only adoration he felt, he could forget the suffering figure on that cross. He stared from beneath lowered lids at Miss Kathy's gentle blondeness, and he was happy. He had forgotten the backbreaking labor of the long week, the days under the merciless sun. He was young. He was strong. He could endure all of that. Seeing Miss Kathy so close, even as rarely as he did, had made it all worthwhile . . . .

—Blade's mistrust of all white people completely excluded Miss Kathy—and in extension through her, his devotion encompassed young Ferrell, and poor clumsy Morgan, Miz Claire, and the old master of Blackoaks. It could reach no further, but this was enough, this was his world. He respected young Master Styles, but he had never liked him. All other white people were enveloped in a haze of distaste seen through half-lidded eyes. But he had loved Miss Kathy since they were toddlers. They used to crack his hand when he was five, with knife blade, pot, or anything handy, when he reached out tentatively to touch the white shine of sunlight illumining her yellow baby curls. His hard lesson of the gulf between them began there with punishment if he touched her—as if he would ever harm her! Or let anyone harm her! Sometimes she had cried as he howled with pain when they hit him, her baby tears twisting her lovely little face. And they would hit him again—the black nurses—scorning him: "You see, now you'se made Miss Kathy cry. Bad boy. Bad nigger boy, you made little Missy cry." He had learned to hold back his own tears because he hated so terribly to see her cry . . . .

—As they grew up and were no longer permitted to play together, whenever he chanced to meet Miss Kathy, his young mistress always remembered him warmly and spoke his name with a gentle smile. He would feel his heart pound at those far-spaced moments, and his chest swelled, his shoulders straightened. He wanted somehow to die in some fearful battle to prove to her how much he adored her. Her smile made him feel taller. Sometimes he was so affected by her smile that he could not answer her, but he always matched her smile and bobbed his head and clung to the memory like a miser with a piece of gold . . . .

One time he had been sitting in the chapel pew, gazing in rapt obsession at the sunlight glowing around Miss Kathy, when something had snagged his attention, troubling him. He had turned his head slightly and started, shocked, to find Master Styles Kenric staring at *him*. Blade's gaze had fallen away, and he had felt sick, bereft. But he had never looked at Miss Kathy in the way Masta Styles suggested now. Never, and he said so. "Oh, no, Masta, I never looked at her except with mos' deep respect."

Styles laughed indulgently. "All right, Blade. But I think you're lying. And that's too bad, I'm your friend, or I want to be—and you don't ever have to lie to me . . . . "

The reading went well. Styles was incredulous at how quickly Blade learned the basics. An "a" was an "a" no matter where Blade found it, as was a "z" and an "m." Styles could put the letters together and Blade could painfully decipher them: "New Orleans, Masta. N-e-w O-r-l-e-a-n-s."

"You're a brilliant boy, Blade," Styles said. "No wonder Miss Kathy always said you were different—better than the other Negroes."

Blade winced, knowing Styles was going to bring up what had become a hateful subject to him, though it aroused him until he could not hide the bulge at his crotch, his secret desiring for a white woman, for Miss Kathy. Blade liked all the lessons, the attention, but he wished Styles would not bring up this fearful subject to set him in conflict with a lifetime of rules and values he'd been painfully taught. "Yes, Masta. I better than other Negroes. I a Fulani."

Styles laughed, pleased and nodded. "Yes. But that's not what I meant. Not what Miss Kathy meant. One night, in our bed, she told me you were the most beautiful man she had ever seen, Blade."

Blade flushed, feeling exalted, frightened, and confused in the same instant. "Suh, Masta?"

"That's right. You never knew this, Blade. But one time a couple years ago you were swimming down in the creek. Miss Kathy was out riding. Did you see her?"

"No, suh. I never did. I don't recall that."

Styles nodded, smiling. "That's what Kathy said at the time. She didn't believe you saw her. But she saw *you*. You were swimming naked in the creek. You know what she said? She said she nearly fainted at the sight and size of that black snake between your legs." He saw that Blade believed his lie, wanted to believe it.

Blade swallowed hard, empty-bellied. As difficult as it was for him to believe that Miss Kathy ever talked like that, even to her own husband, in the privacy of their own bedroom, he was pleased. He was proud of his manhood. It was good to know Miss Kathy appreciated it.

—An hour later, he walked into his cabin in the quarters with a hard bulging at his osnaburg britches. Ahma was preparing supper. "Moab gonna come in here any minute to eat," she protested, but her hand was massaging that huge bulge at his fly.

"The hell with that, girl. I wants you. Now." He

trembled, hardly able to wait for her to jerk the cotton shift over her head and throw herself, laughing, upon him on the bed.

"Lord," she cried. "I really got me a man."

Blade nodded, panting, but in his mind he saw Miss Kathy concealed behind underbrush, watching him splash naked in the creek. The anguished pleasure almost made him sick at his stomach . . . .

Styles was pleasantly surprised to find Blade adept in addition and subtraction. Years of working in the plantation commissary had taught Blade the basics of simple arithmetic. Styles had only to hone those rudiments. Blade would handle money better than most white farmers.

"Kathy and I used to talk about you at night in our bed, Blade." Styles relaxed in a wingback chair and told Blade to make himself comfortable. "Can you believe that? She liked to talk about you."

Blade's face burned; the emptiness spread in the pit of his stomach.

Styles watched Blade, narrowly assessing the youth's reaction to his lies. "She told me she kept thinking about that big staff of yours, Blade."

"Ah, no, Masta—"

"Yes. But she did. Why would I lie to you?"

"I reckon you wouldn't lie to me, Masta."

"I'd have no reason to lie to you." Styles shrugged. "I just think you ought to know. She would get excited and talk about riding that huge rod of yours . . . . You know why she never let you suspect how she felt?"

Blade's eyes grew moist. "Miss Kathy too good, too gentle."

Kenric's mouth twisted, but he forced a smile. "Oh, no. She wanted you . . . more than she wanted any other man—"

"Ah no, Masta—"

"What are you afraid of? We're alone here. Talking—friend to friend, eh? It's the truth. But it's also the truth that you are black—"

"Yes, Masta."

"And Kathy was afraid you might tell somebody—if she let you near her. Oh, she wanted to. She would tell me how badly she wanted to—if only she had believed you could keep your mouth shut."

By now, Blade was unable to conceal the great bulging at his crotch. He ached fiercely, torn between sickness and savage need.

Striding back to his cabin across the valley, Blade tried to sort it out in his mind. He could not believe the things Styles said to him, and yet he could not think why his master would want to lie to him. The thought that Miss Kathy had seen his tool, had dreamed of it, had wanted it inside her. No! He couldn't believe it, but he ran, crossing the valley and going up the incline to his cabin. He only prayed that Ahma was lying across their bed, naked. He didn't see how he could wait for her to undress . . . .

Every night, long after Ahma was sprawled face down, exhausted and deep asleep, Blade lay awake, torn up and confused inside. Styles was friendly, he was good to him, and yet the sensual ideas he kept throwing at him had his mind whirling.

Since childhood, Blade had been taught the long cruel lesson that white people were superior and white women untouchable. They were like enemies, but most of all they were his betters. Even the most militant Negro he encountered accepted this as a fact ground into the slave mentality over two hundred years in servitude, white people were superior. They were more than an enemy—an enemy might be an equal, or an inferior—whites were not, whites held some elevated position, a special coign of vantage. There was some unscalable inequity between the races. He had come to accept the wide, inaccessible gap between him and every white man—and with white women the distance was twice as great, as the faintest star is deep beyond the moon. He saw the white women, and there was a desirable beauty in their faces, the fragile line of profile, the throat, the thrust of milky breasts revealed at low-cut bodice, the scent of musk they covered themselves with. This got into a man's nostrils, and it cut deep. But for years he had learned to put them out of his mind. He had a good life, many black wenches, and he wanted no trouble with white men.

Suddenly, now, Styles was telling him that everything he had been taught, everything he had believed, was all wrong, that it was possible to possess the body of a white woman—that, indeed, she wanted you as badly, even though both of you had had to hide your guilty need.

God help him, his world was turned upside down. He didn't know what to believe . . . .

5

Julien-Jacques Gischairn came to the little apartment on Dauphine Street to say goodbye to Kathy. She heard the thunder of cannon from the esplanade as Gischairn came up the steps. She heard him whimpering petulantly. "Those damn cannons. Those damn cannons."

When Kathy's maid Alexi, a savagely black girl with flat nostrils, ridged brow, and underslung jaw, announced that M'sieu' Julien-Jacques Gischairn was in her parlor, Kathy brushed at her tears, dabbed spots of rouge on her lips, and patted at her hair as she went out to greet her visitor.

Gischairn clutched both her hands in his, turned them up, and kissed them frantically. Kathy looked at him in alarm. She had never seen him so rumpled, less than impeccable. When he attempted to smile at her, he almost burst into tears. His poise had been razed, replaced by panic, his *savoir-faire* had deteriorated into petulant terror. There was no laughter in his face, no memory of laughter. He had no petty hearsay to retail, no gossip about the town's famous and infamous. His hands shook. He could speak only of the plague which had struck so suddenly that he, and hundreds of the best people like himself, had been caught inside the city and unable to book immediate passage north.

"You're leaving town?" she said. She had to force herself to turn her miserable thoughts outward to him and his problems. She did not see how she could pretend an interest in anything he had to say. For three nights now, Hunt had been unable to copulate with her. He had wanted to; he had sweated in desperation. But no matter what they tried, he remained limp, useless. "Impotent," he had moaned. "My God, Kathy, fear has destroyed my manhood. I'm impotent." She had barely understood him. He had always been so quickly roused, rigid and waiting. Suddenly nothing she could do could rouse him enough to penetrate her. He talked of fear, but she was desolated. He was tired of her. He had found another girl in this great city. He didn't want her any more. "My God, Kathy . . . I want you more than life. But that's it, don't you understand, I'm dead inside. Stewing in my own cowardice has killed me, Kathy. Try to understand." She had whispered she understood, but she hadn't. She had pleaded with him to believe she didn't care whether he could do it to her or not—but she lied about that, too. She forced herself to concentrate on Gischairn: "You're leaving town?"

He burst into tears. "Of course I'm leaving town. Our beautiful city infested—with the yellow jack. My God, Kathy, aren't you leaving?"

She shrugged. "I don't know. Hunt has talked about the plague— I know he is in terror of it—"

"Child, anyone with a grain of intelligence is in terror. A thousand people dead in three days! And I can't get passage on a river boat. I can't even hire a Negro to drive me north to Natchez."

"I'm sure you'll find some way."

"Oh, I will. What good is all my money, if I get the yellow fever? I'll get a way out of here—no matter what it costs me." He could not speak of light matters, gossip was forgotten. The cannons thundered farther along on the esplanade, and he visibly trembled. He could speak only of the epidemic, and to add incredible discomfort to the terror, the clouds of mosquitoes blown in on every wind across the river. "It came upon us so suddenly this year. We had no chance to escape . . . . It's all *their* fault—" he didn't bother to give *them* names or titles, "—they laid out our beautiful city in the center of the densest swampland. Seventy-two inches of rain a year! More than one hundred miles of open canals. Canals—it's like having sixty open cesspools to breed disease. And so contagious! My dear, you can't even get another human being to come near you for all the gold in the world when you have it. They leave you for dead. They run . . . . And there's only the Dead Church for you then—"

"The Dead Church?"

"Why, my dear, its the second oldest church in this poor, dear, doomed city. They built it in 1826—just to bury the dead who had died of yellow fever."

"Poor Julien. You'll be all right. I know you will."

He tried to laugh, wagging his head so that the diamond earring sparkled. "Yes. I'll outrun the plague. I will. I've done it before, and I'll do it now. Somehow . . . . But I had to see you one last time. I told myself I could not leave my beloved city, I could not expose myself to death, without looking one last time on Beauty—"

"You should be a poet," she managed to smile. Another distant cannon sounded, rattling the walls like thunder.

"Oh, my dearest, beautiful child! Don't you realize the peril? Come away with me. I'll buy passage for us. To Cincinnati. Chicago. New York. We'll sail to Europe."

"I'll be here when you get back." She sighed. "I couldn't leave Hunt—as long as he wants me. Not even to travel across Europe with you, dear Julien. Come to see me when you return. I'll be here."

"I pray you will. I pray to the gods of beauty to protect you. No. I must see Hunt. I must beseech him to take you away from this pesthole."

"Hunt will take me—if we must go."

"It's not a matter of wanting to take you. You must find a way to get out of town. Roadways are blocked. Trains are overcrowded. Ships won't book one more passenger. Oh, God, my darling, we're abandoned in hell." He looked around, trembling. "Make Hunt take you away. Until then, stay inside—don't get near anyone —you can't tell they have the plague until they have fever, begin to vomit. Avoid people. Sleep under mosquito netting. Protect your sweet and gentle face from disfigurement by those swarms of mosquitoes. Yellow fever *and* mosquitoes. When God strikes Sodom, He has no mercy."

Another cannon blasted. Shaken, Gischairn clutched up her hands, covering them with kisses. And then, weeping openly, he took his leave. He walked slowly to the door, staring back at her. But by the time he reached the steps, he was running . . . .

Kathy hurried through the apartment, went out on the small balcony overlooking Dauphine Street to wave goodbye. She watched Gischairn dart out from her *porte cochère* and run across the flagstones to his waiting carriage. He opened the rear door and lunged inside. Two white men grabbed at the shafts, trying to take the carriage. She heard Gischairn's scream from the enclosed carriage. The driver whipped the white men until they fell away from the wagon. Then he sent the horses racing along the cobbles and around the corner going toward Bourbon.

Hunt had left the house an hour before Gischairn arrived. He lived in horror of the plague, but he could not endure sitting helpless—and impotent!—in that apartment and looking at Kathy's sad, uncomplaining little face. It was more accusing than the most heartless grand jury. He had ruined her life, stolen her from her family, brought her to a strange town stricken with the plague, and he wasn't even man enough to make love to her. Drunk. Impotent. A despoiler. Styles had been clever as hell. He had let Hunt stew in his own terror until he was dead inside and haunted by the face of a man he'd never seen before.

"I must go to the bank," he told Kathy. He saw in her face that she knew he was lying. He wanted a drink—in a bar downtown somewhere. He wanted to get away from her. She bit her lip and sank into a chair, crushed. If Hunt didn't want her, she didn't want to live.

His eyes stinging with tears, he stood for a long moment, staring down at her. He wanted to stay with her. He wanted to hold her in his arms and try to tell her how much he loved her. But he could not show her, because he could not even get a hard-on. The kindest thing he could do was to get away from her. He wiped the back of his hand across his mouth. He had to have a drink.

When he came out of the *porte cochère* to the street, he looked both ways, but he didn't see the seedy-looking man. He hurried, going downtown.

He walked through Carondelet with a handkerchief pressed against his nose. He passed half a dozen dead wagons—two-wheeled carts each pulled by a horse and piled with the black, strangled bodies of yellow fever victims. God, they had to get out of this pesthole where all the authorities knew to combat the plague was to pound drums all night and fire cannon all day. And people crumpled on the street in front of you, gasping and suddenly spilling the black vomitus while bystanders fought to get away.

When he paused outside Frobisher's, he went taut. There stood the man who had haunted him for almost a week now. In fact, he could count back to the first night he had been physically unable to love Kathy. That was the day he saw this fellow standing near the entrance to the St. Louis Hotel bar. The man walked as if his feet hurt. He wore a cheap, wrinkled suit. He stared at Hunt as Hunt had seen vultures watch a sick animal, unblinking.

Hunt swallowed hard. The man's cold eyes were fixed on him. Hunt clutched his cane in his fist, but somehow he knew he would be helpless against the man, though he was at least a foot taller, twenty years younger. There was a look of controlled violence about that man—as if he delivered death for a price. Hunt wanted to confront him. *You're from Styles Kenric, aren't you? You've come to kill me, haven't you?* They were questions he wanted to ask but could not ask. He could not endure the answers. He stared at the man a moment and then almost ran into the bank.

He got himself under control in the offices of Frobisher & Company. When he came out, the man had moved from his position near the entrance. Hunt wanted to laugh with relief. He yelled for a hack. A cabbie stopped for him. "The St. Louis Hotel," Hunt said and fell into its tonneau, sinking deep in the seat, pulling down his hat.

When he stepped out of the cab, paid the black hack driver and turned to enter the St. Louis bar, his anus contracted violently. The seedy-looking man in the derby lounged a foot from the door. Hunt had to pass him to enter the bar. The cold, dead eyes were fixed on him, like the angel of death. That's what he was, the hired angel of death. As stupid as that thought was, Hunt could not shake it. Superstition? A man with his education? In this enlightened time? And yet, no amount of intellect could deny that the man was there, his gaze fixed on Hunt, watching him cross the banquette, push open the door, and enter, almost running.

He had two quick drinks. He found himself surrounded by congenial young men who had been attracted to him because they had seen him escorting Kathy, but who liked to chat with him and drink with him.

Hunt tried to ignore the seedy-looking man who limped in on aching feet and sat alone at a small table against the wall. It was hard to ignore that unblinking gaze. Hunt ordered another drink, sweating.

The men standing at the bar around Hunt had been talking about the plague, about the chances of getting out of town alive. But one of them said something about San Xavier, and all the other men stopped talking, listening.

"Did Xavier kill his wife?" somebody asked.

"He could have. And I believe he could have got away with it," said a dark-haired gentleman. "No jury of men in this parish would convict a husband for killing a faithless wife."

"Amen."

"Xavier caught Rousseau with his wife Christyn. Xavier shot Rousseau, once, Rousseau didn't die immediately. We all believe Xavier wanted it that way. He's an expert marksman and duelist. He's killed in duels—more than once. We think he could have killed Rousseau on the spot if he'd wanted to."

"Why didn't he?"

"Damnedest thing I ever heard. Xavier impaled the bleeding Rousseau on a pointed pole, carried him in the rear of his carriage, and tossed his impaled body out before his own house—for his wife and children to find."

"An incredible man, Xavier."

"Obviously not one to tinker with. Eh, Campbell? You're a New England puritan. Do you feel Xavier was justified in such barbaric violence?"

Hunt glanced toward the hard-eyed man at that small table. He licked at his lips and shook his head. "A man must protect his own home," he said.

"Amen."

"A man has his honor. His honor is everything. A man without honor is nothing. Less than nothing."

"But is a gentleman ever a barbarian?"

One of the men laughed. "Obviously—when he is driven far enough. Xavier proves that, doesn't he?"

"Yes." A man laughed and struck the bar with his fist, laughing with his head back. "Yes. But poor Rousseau. There but for the grace of God goes any of us."

The others smiled guiltily. A youthful man at the edge of the group said, "It's nothing to joke about—"

"Who's joking, Petit Pierre?"

"I hope you are. A man must protect his home. A man has a right to kill under such circumstances. A right, suh? He has the duty."

"Oh, Jesus, Pierre. Wait until you're old enough to shave. Wait until you've violated some uncaring bastard's nest, cuckolded some man who has not touched his own wife in two years, but wants to kill you because you have." He laughed and clapped Pierre on the shoulder. "Come back and tell us what you believe then."

Hunt swallowed back bile. He fervently needed another drink. But he knew if he drank whiskey, he'd throw up. If he vomited, they'd throw him in the pesthouse with the yellow fever victims, not realizing his was a sickness of the soul.

He said goodnight and left the bar, hurrying. He was conscious of the seedy man's gaze fixed on him until he reached the banquette. He turned toward Dauphine

Street and strode swiftly, almost running, glancing back over his shoulder.

He stepped into the entranceway at his courtyard and for a moment pressed against the wall, exhausted. He breathed heavily through his parted lips. Kathy called down from their second-floor veranda. "Hunt? Are you all right?"

He waved his arm impatiently. "I'm all right. I'm all right."

He went slowly up the steps, sweated. He mopped his face with his handkerchief. His stomach roiled. Kathy met him at the door. She tried to kiss him, but he straightened, avoiding her lips. "Kathy, I've made a decision. You must go back home."

"To Blackoaks?"

"Yes. At once. As soon as we can get you on a train or a stage. I'll hire a carriage if I have to."

"I won't leave you."

"Don't talk like that, Kathy. I have dragged you down as far as I will allow. I won't drag you any further."

He strode past her, going into the bedroom. She followed, watching in taut silence. He loosened his tie, dropped his jacket on the floor. Unbuttoning his shirt at the chest and cuffs, he went to the window, pinked the curtains, and stared down at Dauphine Street. The man was down there, leaning against a wall across the way.

He was down there, waiting. The angel of death. The hired angel.

6

Styles said, watching Blade's face narrowly, "You will admit, Blade, that Kathy has always been particularly kind to you?"

"She always kind. Mr. Ferrell always kind. She most kind because she a most kind lady."

Styles laughed. "How wonderful to be so innocent! Didn't you ever notice a black wench who paid more attention to you than she should? You knew what *she* wanted, didn't you?"

Blade was forced to grin. "A man can tell about a wench."

Styles laughed and nodded. "A man can tell about a woman. Kathy was kind to you. Don't you think maybe she was trying to tell you something?"

"Lawdy, I don't know, Masta. Seems like nowadays I don't know nothin' for sure. Why you want me to think all these things—if I got to go alone to bring Miss Kathy back home?"

"Because I want you to face the truth, Blade. I want you to know things as they are."

Blade frowned, more puzzled than ever. But each time Styles spoke to him of mounting a white woman, he protested less, his denials weakened. He admitted that once Miz Florine Pilzer had tried to get him inside her house. He'd gotten a hell of a hard-on, but he'd been afraid. He'd gotten away. "But maybe now, knowing what you know, you wouldn't fight so hard, eh?" Styles said.

Blade exhaled heavily. He believed now what Styles wanted him to believe. Styles had always held that a superior intellect could control the mind of a lesser human being. He smiled in grim satisfaction: he had warped Blade's mind into the shape he wanted, into a shape that he could control.

Blade was confused and deeply troubled, but he could not doubt Styles's kindness; he could not doubt his motives.

It was as if Blade's lifelong beliefs were a diseased covering that Styles skillfully desquamated—peeling and scaling them away—until the youth stood renewed—in Styles's image.

"It's almost time, Blade," Styles told him. "Soon now, I'll send you for Kathy. Now that you know the truth—what a weak vessel a woman is—no matter the color of her skin, you'll want to bring Kathy home safely—you'll want to protect her."

This was involved reasoning, and Blade made no effort to follow it. He merely nodded.

Blade's anticipation grew as Banipal, the black tailor from the plantation craft shops, cut and resewed Master Styles's new suits to fit him. He wanted to laugh aloud with the physical sense of pleasure the fine materials roused against his skin, the way his shoulders socked into place. He stared with pride at the beautiful man reflected in that mirror. He'd had hand-me-downs before. This had been the way of his life until he had outgrown every man at Blackoaks. But these were new suits. Styles had worn one or two of them perhaps twice. A couple came out of the crackling bags in which the New Orleans tailor had packed them. He glimpsed the admiring gazes of the black seamstresses as their fingers flew, basting and putting in the final stitches where the tailor had marked the suits to be let out—under the armpits, across the chest, and in the spine to relieve the slight pull at the lapels. Banipal was a tired-looking old black man with a cottony cap of wiry hair. He suffered failing eyesight and splitting headaches, but Blade kept telling him he was one hell of a tailor. The old man never smiled. "Shut up, black boy, and stan' still," was all he ever said. But smiling, Blade saw his words of praise pleased the old fellow. Banipal *was* a hell of a tailor. He might have been a rich man had he not been a slave.

As the suits were refinished, pressed, and fitted for the last time, the panic spread in Blade's belly. The suits might make him look like a powerful black man of the world; he had conquered reading and writing; he could handle money and not be cheated; but he reminded himself he was just a confused nigger boy who had never been more than a few miles from Blackoaks in all his life. Why was his master choosing him for this mission? Why shouldn't he go himself? How would he find New Orleans? And how to find Miss Kathy in a city that huge, with the river snaking through its maze of streets, its blur of strange faces? And how could he look Miss Kathy in the face after the intimate things Master Styles had been saying to him about her? All the suppressed, inhibited, prohibited, forbidden desires boiled upward as if he were in an overheated cauldron. He could not believe Miss Kathy could ever go against generations of values and prejudices that forbade a white woman's looking at a Negro carnally and made his own life forfeit if he were caught returning even her most fleeting glance. Oh, God, he was mixed up inside, torn between a need to run away and an urgency to gather up these fine clothes Master Styles was so kindly showering upon him and hurry, racing to find Miss Kathy.

Common sense told him that Master Styles had left much unsaid. Common sense told him that Master Styles pretended to believe Blade followed his involved reasoning and puzzling motivation, but that the master of Blackoaks didn't really give a damn whether he did or not. He had to trust Master Styles because he had come to feel a devotion toward him because of his kindnesses. No one had ever been kinder to Blade. He would try to understand what his master wanted; he would try to follow his instructions, even when he scarcely understood them at all.

At least he would find Miss Kathy. He would bring her back home. And, kindly God, he'd be alone with her on the trail for five or six days. He felt sweated, strangled, deeply troubled, violently aroused.

There came that wondrous morning when Banipal ordered the final fittings. The suits were beautiful in gray, olive, and off-white.

"You washed?" Banipal wanted to know.

"I'se scrubbed, Uncle Banipal," Blade said.

Banipal sniffed. "Yo' armpits still smell like a goat. You gwine ruin these fine clothes Mas' Kenric is givin' you."

Styles came into the room. He seemed taller this morning, thinner, icier, and more aloof. He smiled at Blade, but his smile was remote, taut, and he was more withdrawn than ever.

Styles flopped into an overstuffed chair, slouching down in it with his long legs extended before him. His nod was the signal to Banipal to proceed with the final fitting.

"Shuck down, boy," Banipal ordered.

Blade hesitated. He glanced toward Master Styles, but Kenric was staring at the steeple he'd made of his fingers.

"Hurry up, Blade," Banipal ordered. "Mast' Styles bein' mighty kind to you, nigger. Doan' you waste his time."

Blade unbuttoned his pants. They fell about his ankles and he stepped out of them, feeling as if literally he was stepping out of his old way of life. He did not see how he could go back. He unbuttoned his shirt, aware that Master Styles had closed his eyes tightly. Now, Styles opened his eyes and watched him, expressionless, unblinking.

Blade tossed his shirt over a chair. Banipal handed him a set of underclothes, a single suit of cotton with quarter-length legs, a buttoned rear flap, and no sleeves. "What's this, Banipal?"

"These here are underclothes, nigger," Banipal said.

"Why I need 'em? I got these pretty new suits."

"That's why you need underthings. You got to protect yo' new suits from yo'self. Now shut up and git in 'em."

"He needn't wear them this time—if he doesn't want to," Styles said. His voice sounded oddly hollow.

"Yas, suh, Masta," Banipal said. Under his breath, he mumbled, "Nigger got to learn to wear 'em. Might as well start learnin'. He sho' gonna foul up them beautiful clothes I work so hard on."

Styles managed a faint, taut smile. "You listen to Banipal, Blade," he said. "You put on those underclothes while you're on this trip. Fresh. Every morning—before you put on your new suits."

"And after you *wash*—and wash good—with lye soap," Banipal said. Blade bobbed his head in agreement, promising to remember, promising to wash, promising to obey.

The oxford-gray suit with a white linen shirt and an ascot with a touch of red in it fit Blade perfectly. Styles tilted a wide, soft-brimmed hat on Blade's head. Only the outline of Blade's manhood at the crotch of the skin-tight trousers troubled him, but neither Banipal nor Master Styles mentioned it or appeared concerned, though both had to be aware of it. He decided to say nothing. He felt slightly naked but not ashamed. There was even a sense of pride. The chest and shoulders were not the only places where he was well built. He was anxious to show Ahma how beautiful he looked, though he could not escape the thought that Ahma belonged to a part of his life that was over, whether he wanted it that way or not.

Banipal brought out two pairs of old Master Baynard's boots. One pair was highly polished brown, the other a gleaming black.

"Them boots is big enough for you," Banipal said, answering the question before Blade could ask it aloud. "You think you such a big man. You ain't the onliest big man in this heah world. Master Baynard, he war bigger than you. Bigger in the feet, too. If'n they doan fit you, it cause you gone barefoot so much you flatted out yo' feet like a duck . . . . You git used to 'em."

Blade sat cautiously in a chair. When Banipal snarled at him, he remembered to flick up the tail of his coat. Styles awarded him with a taut, chilled smile. "You're learning fast, Blade . . . very fast."

Banipal helped Blade pull the boots over his big feet. Blade stood up carefully as if he were stepping on eggs. He expected pain to explode in the crown of his skull from the unaccustomed agony of boots. But the soft innerlining and glove leather hugged his feet. Banipal had not lied. Old Master Baynard's feet had been big, slightly bigger than Blade's. He glanced at the bulge at his crotch and wondered how the Old Masta would have measured up in this area?

He took long strides in the boots as he had seen Mr. Styles walk back and forth across the room. A glimpse showed him a faint smiling had lightened Styles's tormented face. He felt a swelling of love for Master Kenric. He had loved only Kathy—from afar—and through her, her immediate family. Now, he knew he loved this strange white man who had been so kind to him, and so honest. He would do anything Styles Kenric asked of him. Styles had been kind, generous, and patient with him. He had painted a side of life he had dared not believe existed. He had opened a whole new world to him, and outfitted him to stride into it as if he owned it. Somehow, he would show Master Styles his gratitude, he would repay with devotion the love Styles had so selflessly extended to him . . . .

7

At seven o'clock the next morning, Hunt stole stealthily from their bed. Scarcely breathing, he dressed quickly, watching Kathy nervously. She'd cried most of the night, swearing she would never leave him; she would die if he did not want her; she had no life if he did not want her. She'd fallen asleep only sometime in the dark hours before dawn. Lying beside her in the bed, he had made the final decision, which he told himself was in her best interests as well as his. She had to get out of New Orleans, away from the plague, away from this city where she was alone and a stranger. She could return home to Blackoaks. She could send for Styles. He would come for her. As for himself, he had less now than ever to offer Kathy. He had nothing, for he was dead inside. He lived in a state of sweated anxiety that could only intensify until he got away from here—he had to run. If he took her with him, she would only slow him down, and he would in time destroy her. God knew he should never have brought her away from Blackoaks.

He stared at his pale, haggard face and the frantic eyes in the mirror. Why should he prolong this affair? Sometimes the greatest kindness was an act of immediate cruelty. He had to break away from her before he was a stumblebum, staggering and falling in gutters. What was to happen to their love, which had been the complete fulfillment of what both of them had so hungrily desired for so long? If he broke away clean now, wouldn't this action alone preserve their love in the only way it could possibly endure in this imperfect world—forever fresh and fiery, in their memories? It was not that he had tired of her as she had accused him of being, weeping last night. No. He still loved her. Despite the fact he was leaving her, it was her welfare that was foremost in his mind.

Kathy whimpered in her sleep and Hunt hesitated, his eyes suddenly burning with tears. How could he leave her? She looked so young, so vulnerable, so helpless.

Dressed, in soured shirt and unpressed suit, he stood for one moment, staring down at Kathy. Perhaps if he confronted that man—that angel of death who trailed him like a buzzard—and told him that he had left Kathy totally, that he could come up here and take her away, perhaps the fellow would stop dogging his steps, let him go in peace. He cursed himself. This was .the most despicable thought he'd permitted in his pickled brain—trading Kathy for his own safety.

Hunt let himself out the front door. By the time he reached the courtyard, he wavered, irresolute. He had never loved anyone but Kathy—perhaps he would never love again. If he lost her, what had he to live for? He would delay another day. Perhaps this would make it easier for Kathy. Perhaps he could make arrangements for her. The morning cannon boomed across on the esplanade and he shuddered and thought he had to get her out of this pestilence-contaminated town. But there was only one place for her—she had to return to Blackoaks. If he left her here, with servants, the rent paid, they would come for her. If he hung around here, she would refuse to go home, even though for both of them this was the only reasonable solution. Damn it. He would only get himself killed by delaying. In what way would his death help Kathy? He was sorry. He loved her, but, in the real world, love was not enough. It never had been. It never would be. He couldn't go on like this, like an ass between two bundles of hay, until somebody shot him. He wasn't thinking straight. He needed a drink. A drink would clear his mind.

As he stepped out of the *porte cochère* of the patio, he stopped. He staggered trying to retrace his steps to the safety within the walled courtyard. The derbied man stood, slouched against the rough wall, standing as if the banquette flagstones chewed at his tender feet.

Hunt gripped his cane, thinking he would use it for

whatever it bought him. He'd confront the bastard, demand to know what right he had to hound him like this. Then he saw that the street was vacant except for the two of them. There was no one to help him. This man had him at his mercy. It would be smarter to walk swiftly past him, to get to a crowded street where he might be safer.

"Your name Hunt Campbell?" the man said.

Hunt trembled visibly. Sweat leaked from his hatband. If only he'd had sense enough to have taken one drink before he left the house, he could have faced this with some semblance of courage. His voice sounded like the caw of a strangled crow. "Why?"

The man gave him a dead smile that did not reach his flat gray eyes. "My name is Joe Bullock. From Montgomery—"

"Well, Mr. Bullock, what do you want with me?"

The cold mouth twisted, pulled down at the corner. "Friend of mine. Asked me to look you up—if you are Hunt Campbell?"

"I'm afraid I don't know anyone in Montgomery, Mr. Bullock. If you'll excuse me—"

"Styles Kenric," Joe Bullock said.

Hunt stopped as if he'd been poled.

"Kenric?" he whispered.

"That's right, friend. Styles Kenric. Of Blackoaks Plantation. Do you know him, Mr. Campbell?"

"I am sorry, Mr. Bullock. There must be some mistake. I am in a hurry."

Hunt strode toward the corner. He did not look back. A chilled place the size of a quarter tingled in the middle of his back until he went hurrying around a building. Out of sight of Bullock, he ran. Sweating, he came out on Bourbon Street where men were washing down the banquettes before their shops. A horse-drawn hack clopped unhurriedly past. Hunt called out. The driver pulled up on the reins and Hunt leaped up into the tonneau. "Carondelet," he whispered. He glanced back toward Dauphine Street. Bullock was not in sight.

He sat tensely, unable to relax. It was out in the open now. Joe Bullock of Montgomery. Styles Kenric had hired him to trace his wife. And even more to the point, he was certain now Styles had hired the man to kill him. There was the casual attitude of death about Bullock. He could kill as easily as he could smile. Easier.

Frobisher and Company didn't open until eight. Hunt had coffee in a corner cafe. He could hardly keep the hot liquid on his stomach, but he remained there, afraid to stand alone in the street.

Inside the bank, he withdrew a thousand dollars. He borrowed an unused desk. He sat down and scribbled a brief line. "I am sorry, Kathy. This is best for you. Hunt." He counted out five hundred dollars, folded it in the note paper, sealed it in a bank envelope and left it with a bank officer to be sent out to Dauphine Street by bank messenger later in the day. *Best for you.* The words spun in his mind. Hypocricy beyond belief. Shakespeare had been right: The devil can cite scripture for his purpose.

When he came out of the bank, he stood hard against the pillars at the entrance studying Carondelet Street in both directions. He heard the boom of the cannon. He ran across the banquette and got into an open cab. "The train depot," he ordered.

The black driver stared at him, shaking his head. "No sense goin' down there, Masta. You ain't goin' to buy no train ticket—they's bought up for a month."

"I didn't ask you that," Hunt told him, raging. The black man shrugged and slapped his reins across the rump of his horse.

The depot was crowded, every bench occupied, people sitting on the floors, slouched against the walls. The smell of human sweat and fear was oppressive. The lines before the two ticket windows were long. Hunt got in line. He knew he was not thinking clearly, but his was a single-mindedness of purpose. He had to have a ticket. He had to get out of here.

An aging man, round of shoulders, sparse-haired, his sallow face twisted with some inner grief, touched the arm of the woman in line ahead of Hunt. He said, "Ma'm, you want to buy a ticket to Atlanta? I bought two. One for my wife. She was struck by the plague. She died last night. If you want to buy her ticket."

Hunt spoke quickly. "I'll buy it," he said. "I'll give you—three hundred dollars."

The woman burst into tears. The old man shook his head. "I'm sorry, ma'm."

Clutching his ticket, Hunt went out on the platform to await the train north. Inside, he was laughing exultantly. The sun blazed down, but the heat was better than the smells inside the waiting room. The train was due in an hour. He looked in every cranny of the depot, the baggage area, the long platform. There was no sign of Joe Bullock. He was going to make it. One hour . . . .

Kathy awoke at ten. She reached out her arm, knowing Hunt was not going to be in bed beside her. Her eyes brimmed with tears. She got up in her sheer gown. His suitcase was still in the closet, as were all his clothes. He'd even worn the soiled shirt from yesterday. She felt better. He had said he was leaving, but he had not gone yet. There was still time. She could make him stay. There had to be something she could do.

She did not feel like getting dressed. She wandered into the kitchen. She was not hungry. She wanted nothing to eat. Alexi offered her coffee. Kathy shook her head. "Did you see Mr. Hunt this morning?" she asked.

Alexi shook her head. "He war gone out when I come, Missy."

Kathy nodded. She went back to the bedroom and lay down across the mattress. She stared at the wall. On the esplanade the cannons boomed. She heard someone knocking at the front door, and then after a moment Alexi came in. "A letter for you, Missy. From a bank."

Kathy took the letter. She got up and walked into the shadowed living room. She sank down in an overstuffed chair. She opened the envelope, unfolded the single sheet of paper. The paper money fluttered to her lap. She did not look at it. She read the single, scrawled line: "I'm sorry, Kathy. This is best for you. Hunt." She went on sitting there, holding the letter in her fist. She did not cry. The hurt and loss were too deep for tears.

PART FOUR

The Fulani Blade

1

Blade's carriage ground almost to a halt. He managed only tortuously slow progress against the out-flooding tide of people and vehicles fleeing New Orleans's built-up area. His horses plodded through the sloughs, sawgrass, and mangrove of the lowlands. He caught his first glimpse of distant rooftops of the city; he heard puzzling intermittent blasts of cannon. The further he penetrated the dense swamp, the deeper the ruts of the narrow passage, the soupier the broken shoulders of the roadway, the heavier the glut of outgoing traffic. A rural Negro taught to defer to others, his peers as well as his superiors, Blade at first pulled politely out of the roadbed as he met oncoming travelers. But after he'd been left to dig himself out of bogs above his axles and had been forced to hang aslant over a canal for more than an hour while high-piled wagons, surreys, carriages, and smart landaus rolled past him, he surrendered to inner rages. Not one driver even glanced his way to nod any suggestion of gratitude. He laid the whip to his horses and slogged tenaciously forward. Now they looked at him! White men—and women—hailed him maliciously as black son of a bitch, nigger bastard, whore-hopping ape and mother-fucking coon. Some leveled guns at him, some threw globs of putrid mud. He kept his eyes forward, his jaw set, his buggy whip poised, his fists gripping the reins. Miss Kathy was up ahead. He could see the town. He had made it at last. It had not been easy; it didn't look as if it would become easier . . . .

His carriage was the most dazzling part of the accoutrements setting him apart as a distinguished man of color. The vehicle was not the largest in the Blackoaks livery, but it was the finest. An enclosed coach, it honored the Hungarian village of Kocs, for which all such vehicles were named.

This fashionable equipage represented the zenith of ever-improving construction and creativity among dedicated cartwrights. One gazed in awe at its gleaming exterior paneling, its soft calf-leather interiors. Its glass windows lowered or raised at a touch. Its damask curtains shielded against road dust or prying eye. One looked and marveled and wondered how further advances in the art of coach-crafting could possibly evolve. Was not this the epitome of travel elegance? How could one hope to move from one place to another with greater comfort, quiet, and speed? Two deeply padded seats of glove-quality leather faced each other, with lower panels that could be lifted and set in place making a bed so that one, or two, could sleep during long and tiring journeys. Doors opened on noiseless hinges, with small steps that folded outward for ease in alighting. A glass partition between the driver's area forward and the cab interior could be lowered. The front boot was protected by an overhang and by half a framed windshield of simulated silver set above the splashboard. Also, isinglass and water-resistant oilcloth curtains could be snapped around the exposed seat in inclement weather. This sedan had been designed by experts who recognized that a comfortable and alert coachman is as important to a pleasant outing as fine horses and unborn-calf-leather upholstery or rocking thoroughbraces. One stood awed at the quality and thoughtful craftsmanship. One said, here is a worthy vehicle for the return of Miss Kathy to Blackoaks. And if he lived, Blade meant to bring his lady home . . . .

Blade was totally stunned by the careful attention Styles Kenric had devoted to every detail of his odyssey. Late into the night, Master Kenric had sat at his desk and had written letters of reference ahead to managers of ordinaries along the route to New Orleans. He had painstakingly marked each ordinary and the miles Blade should plan to cover during daylight hours. He had arranged for reservations at these taverns for Blade Baynard of Blackoaks, as Styles's agent—a man of color.

Kenric had never once stated that his representative was a black freedman, but he let the travern-keeps and others to whom he wrote assume this. He was well aware that the excellence of his conveyance, the fine cut and rich quality of Blade's clothing would be the convincing stroke. At least ten percent of the black population of the South was free by the years of the second Jackson administration. These free blacks lived precarious lives— some remained semislaves, some were sharecroppers, semiskilled craftsmen, some became slaveowners. Most freed blacks were women. They lived in towns and sections of cities like New Orleans rather than in the rural areas. Most were octoroons, quadroons, or mustees, rather than the pure African black; some were racially mixed with Indians. But "free persons of color" in the Deep South were so few in number and so closely related to the planter class by financial interest, birth, or blackmail that they held an "accepted" position in the establishment. Only in rural areas were they harassed, hounded, or slain for "passing through." The landowner believed only the "freed African Negro" was potentially disruptive. For all these reasons—and for the distinguished figure Blade presented in wide-brimmed planter's hat, tailored suits, and polished boots, and for the glitter of his coach— Styles was convinced his agent would be accepted and tolerated, if not fawned over, on the route south.

Blade was provided a detailed map with every rest stop, night stop, and town clearly indicated. Styles vividly recalled his own thirteen-day jaunt south to Tallahassee. But that was frontier country. The roads to New Orleans were well traveled, clearly marked.

On the morning Blade was to depart, Styles fit a heavy

flat belt between his underclothes and outer garments. The belt fit snugly and Styles assured him he would soon become so accustomed to it he would forget he was wearing it. "Guard it well," he said. "There are enough golden eagles there to buy your way to Europe and back. They're worth almost twenty paper dollars each. Use them as you need them, but don't let somebody steal them from you."

"Naw, suh, Masta, nobody steals nuthin' from Blade." He grinned and showed Styles the razor-sharp knife sheathed inconspicuously along his belt. "Any man come at me, I cut him so quick and so easy with my pig-sticker, he be two days running befoah he realizes he cut daid."

Styles laughed tautly and clapped the tall, slender black man on the shoulder. "Bring her home," he said. Then, cryptically, disturbing Blade even more, he added, "And remember everything I told you."

Blade swung up into the beautiful carriage. He was troubled now with that confusion over "everything Masta Styles had told him." This added to his anxiety at taking this long trip alone, his sadness at leaving Ahma, and his mistrust of his ability to carry out the assignment Master Kenric had given him. For the first time he doubted his ability to accomplish any goal he set for himself. This was stepping into the unknown. It was the first time he'd ventured alone overnight from this farm. And there were his haunting fantasies. It had come to pass under Master Styles's prodding voice that Blade saw Miss Kathy's lovely face and soft golden hair even when he was pestering Ahma in their bed. The journey itself was frightening enough, but he was all mixed up and deeply troubled inside . . . .

The slaves at the barn shouted warnings, called farewells, and wished him luck. Blade glanced one final time toward the cabin where he and Ahma had just entered their own Eden. His eyes brimmed with tears and his heart slipped, battering irregularly. Nor did his depression lift as he rolled past the familiar old manor house and down the incline between the rows of black trees to the fieldstone gate.

He looked back one last time and headed west on the

trace. He'd gone only a few yards when Ahma sprang up and ran out of the underbrush. He pulled hard on the reins. Ahma clambered up to the seat beside him. He laughed through his tears. "Thought I tole you goodbye once, gal."

"Take me with you, Blade."

"You know I can't. I got my orders. You know I can't."

"Please, Blade. Take me with you. I'se had these terrible visions of what will happen if you go off and leave me alone."

"You ain't really one of them conjure women, are you?" he teased. He put his arm about her and kissed her.

She wept, her voice passionate and intense. "Let's take his carriage—and his money, Blade. No, don't shake yo' head. Listen to me! We could run north. They'd never catch us. They'd never find us up there."

"I can't do that, girl. Even if I wanted to, I couldn't do that. Masta Styles trusts me and I cain't fail him—no more than he'd fail me, or do me dirty."

"He'll do you dirty! When it's your turn, you'll see. He'll turn on you. Yoah skin is black and his is white—and he don't care about you. He'll kill you—or sell you —or beat you—quick as he'd look at you."

"He a kind man, Ahma. A good man. He been good to me. He'd nevah do none of that . . . . Anyhow, I got to bring Miss Kathy home."

"Oh, damn you." She burst into tears, crying openly, tears streaking her golden-brown cheeks, her nose running, her lips swollen. "Ah gon' run away. You leave me, I gon' run away."

"Now you shut up that talk, girl. You ain't goin' to run away. You goin' wait heah for me. You my woman now."

"I wants to be yo' woman. But I can't be yo' woman with you off in some New Awleans place—and me dyin' here."

He kissed her gently. "I comin' back to you, Ahma. I swear. I comin' back. Quick as ever I can."

He lifted her in his arms as though she were a child, though she was almost as big as he. He stepped down to the ground with her and placed her on her feet. She clung to him fiercely. At last he broke away and got back into the carriage.

He swallowed back his own tears, triggered and increased by Ahma's helpless crying at the side of the road. He forced himself to smile. He took off his soft, wide-brimmed white hat and waved it to her. For a long time she ran after the carriage. Crying openly, Blade whipped the horses into a run. When he looked back he saw Ahma where she had fallen, sobbing in the middle of the trace.

Blade arrived at his first scheduled night stop about an hour before sundown. The settlement was little more than a casual toss of slab buildings and shacks. The ordinary was dark wood, two storied, on a crossroads. People sat up on their porch rocking chairs to ogle the fine carriage. They walked out to the road in the waning sunlight to inspect its magnificence as Blade pulled into the area before the ordinary.

When they saw a black man—attired in gentleman's clothing—alight from the carriage, they stared, wide-eyed, silent, and then they whispered, nodding and watching him warily and hostilely.

Blade took the letter of reference—which was also his pass if he were halted by slave patrollers—from his inner pocket as he entered the musty lobby of the tavern. The owner, slouched in sweated denim shirt and streaked white pants, set his bare feet apart, stopped fanning himself, and began to shake his head as Blade entered the front door.

"Sorry," he said in deference to Blade's elegance of dress and the rich vehicle outside the ordinary door. "We can't allow Negroes in here."

"Mr. Kenric—" Blade had been carefully taught never to call him *Masta* Kenric in speaking to anyone on this trip—"Mr. Kenric has sent you this note about me for you to read."

The fat man looked at the letter of reference, but didn't take it. "Oh, you the man Mr. Styles Kenric of Blackoaks wrote to me about?"

"Yes. He said he had paid for my lodging here. Tonight —and for one night when I return."

"Well, that's right. That's true. But you see, boy, what happened is that before I got his letter and draft payin' for your board and lodgin', I was all booked up for tonight. You understand?"

Blade knew he was lying. Obviously, he was the single transient to have stopped here at this hour. But Blade was a gentle Negro by nature. He wanted to laugh at the white man's transparent lying, but he did not. "I got to have some place to stay. And he did pay for my supper."

"Oh, he did. Supper and breakfast for you. It's just that they ain't no place open in my dinin' room, boy, and I got no place for you to sleep here in the house. You want to bed down out in the stable with your carriage, that's fine with me. I'm truly sorry. But that's the best I got to offer. An' you can set yo'self in the kitchen and Minnie Bell—she's my cook—she'll feed you all the vittles your belly can hold. And she'll have yo' bre'kfus' ready for you come mawnin'. Sorry about the mix-up, boy. But these things happen sometime."

Minnie Bell was a fat-assed black woman, somewhere in her thirties, with bulbous tits and protuberant belly. Like her master, the owner of the ordinary, she wore no shoes, padding about the large pine-floored kitchen in her bare feet. She was an excellent cook—she spooned out succulent sweet potatoes, black-eyed peas, pork roast, and hot apple sauce with homemade bread. She fed him two extra helpings of rice custard for dessert. She watched him eat, admiringly. "Ah shore dearly loves to see a man what's got a healthy appetite. Shows me, he's a big man— in every way . . . . Reckon I might sneak out to the stables later on—after my man Washington is asleep—if you'd like that."

"I'd purely favor it," Blade lied, "any other night. But I had a rough trip. I purely skin-tired, and I got to get up 'fore sunup tomorrow."

Minnie Bell did not smile. "I'll have your bre'kfus' ready," she said.

On the way out, Blade nuzzled the back of her sweated neck, squeezed her left breast tightly, and stroked her buttocks lovingly. She was mollified and laughed as he went out the door. "Sleep well, you purty devil you."

When he was "permitted" to sleep in the stables on the second and third nights because the ordinaries and taverns where Styles had reserved lodging for him were unexpectedly "overflowing with important white folks," Blade was resigned to this reception and treatment. But when he came at last to a town on the Mississippi Gulf coast, the tavern owner ran out to meet him as he swung down from his coach.

"Wait a minute, nigger," the man said. He was an orange-haired man in his fifties, his sun-baked face seamed with wrinkles, his eyes blue and coldly hostile. "Jus' don' even bother to get down from that there seat. We don't take niggers here—even if you are one of them 'freed gentlemen of color.' Nigger blood is nigger blood. Niggers are niggers and they don't sleep nor eat in white folks' houses."

Blade swung down from the coach but remained beside the front wheel and he removed his hat, holding it at his side. He was aware that half a dozen white men, most of them with beer mugs in their fists, had crowded, grinning in the doorway to watch.

Blade said, "Ain't this Stubbs's Tavern?"

"That's right, boy. Stubbs's Tavern. For white folks. An' I Mister Eakins Stubbs. Now we got that all settled, boy, you can climb back in your fancy rig and haul ass out of here."

"Didn't you get a letter, Mr. Stubbs, from a Mr. Styles Kenric of Blackoaks, saying I'd be here tonight?"

"Oh? That? Well, Jesus Christ, boy, Kenric didn't say you was a nigger. If he'd of told me you was a nigger, I'd of sent his draft back to him. He said his 'agent' would be coming through."

"That's me," Blade said.

"Well, you're still a nigger. Now, I am fair. I got nuthin' against a nigger. Long as he stays in his place. I hire niggers right here in my tavern. I treats them right. But by God, they knows they place. They ain't uppity."

"I ain't uppity, Mister," Blade said.

"You sho's hell puttin' on airs, boy. Fine clothes.

Fancy carriage like I could not afford for my family in a hundred years. Don't tell *me* you ain't uppity."

"I need some place to stay the night, that's all."

The men in the doorway laughed and nudged each other. Eakins Stubbs grinned in a way he did not expect Blade to share, encouraged by the laughter and grunts of approval from behind him. "Well, if you was half as smart as you is uppity, nigger boy, you'd spend this night driving them fine horses toward wherever it is yo' headed."

"They're tired. They've got to have water and food and rest . . . sir," Blade said.

"Well, don't take that smart tone to me, boy. I got a place out back. You can feed them horses, rest 'em, water 'em. Won't cost you a dime. Yoah nigger-lovin' fren, *Mister* Styles Kenric done paid for it."

"Could I get some food?"

The men nudged each other, laughing, waiting. Eakins Stubbs glanced over his shoulder and then shook his head. "Nope. Not in my place. Not out in back of it. Got no food for uppity niggers. You wants to sleep out there with yo' horses, you take yo' chances, you do it."

The men in the doorway laughed, and shoved each other, roaring their approval. Sick, Blade stood undecided a moment. Then he shrugged and kept his tone low and thick with humility. "Thank you, Mister Stubbs. I reckon I'll sleep out there—if that's all right with you."

One of the men in the doorway, grinning, shouted, "Sleep tight, nigger." The others went into paroxysms of laughter.

Blade climbed back into the coach seat and urged the horses to the stables at the rear of the tavern. Stubbs and his customers came to the back door, spilled out into the yard, watching him. He unhitched the horses. Then, glancing toward the men, he removed his jacket, hat, shirt, and tie. The blade of his knife was raised in relief against his wide belt. He led the horses out to the trough to drink and washed himself while the animals snuffed up water.

The viewers laughed loudly, contemptuously, and made jokes about uppity nigger boys. But they remained where they were. He was aware they measured the breadth of his shoulders, the bands of muscles corded across his back and rising on his chest. Finally, they lost interest and returned to the bar. His nerves were taut in the pit of his belly. He wished devoutly that the horses could have stood a night's ride; he wanted nothing more than to keep moving.

He fed the horses, rubbed them down, and poured out the rations of mixed oats, corn, and hay. He set up the padded panels and lay down inside the coach tonneau. Darkness closed in. He opened the door against the wall to get a breath of air. He took the razor-sharp knife from his belt and clutched it in his fist. Those white boys, getting drunker, might decide to have some fun with the uppity nigger, despite the fact that he was in better physical condition than any three of them had ever been. He considered the odds. He was badly outnumbered, and he wanted no trouble with backwoods whites. But they would be besotted with wine, and this knife in his hand was a terrible equalizer. If he were going to hang for the murder of one white red-neck, he would hang no higher for killing five . . . .

He could not sleep. Fear drove the thought of Ahma, Styles, Blackoaks, and even Miss Kathy from his mind. But fear is exhausting. Sometime, long after midnight, it grew quiet in the tavern. He listened, but there were no sounds in the stables but the snuffling of the horses and the whistling of rats in the hay. Fatigue clouded his mind, numbed him. Gripping the knife, he fell asleep. His hand relaxed and the pig-cutter rolled away on the soft leather.

He dreamed he was in some sort of steam bath where he was being massaged by moist, heated hands. Those hands closed on his penis, and gently stroked his testes. He struggled awake, aware that his cock stood rigid and quivering. Then he saw the dark shadow between his legs. Gasping, he slapped around in panic, seeking his knife. He could not find it at once and he bit hard on his underlip to stifle a yell.

"Hush. Hush." It was a female voice, whispering gently. "It's me. I is Trumpet. I seed you when you was washing up. I watched you from the kitchen. I nevah saw nothing like you . . . . I couldn't git you out of my head . . . . I snuk out here soon's I could get me away."

"Did you bring me something to eat?"

Her fist tightened on his distended staff. "I brought you something better than food." She covered the plum-colored head of his penis with her mouth, nursing it furiously.

He tried to resist her, but he could not. The hungry way she nuzzled him set him afire inside. He forgot fear—he forgot everything except her sucking mouth, the heat of her tongue and throat, and the fact that he'd been almost four days on the road without a woman with nothing to keep him company and provide release from those over-whelming dreams about Miss Kathy except his fist.

He reached down, lifted her up. "What about them—white men out there?"

She seemed disoriented for a moment, wild with desire. She shook her head, clearing it. "They all gone home. They talked about ridin' you out of town. But I knowed. You was a *little* nigger, they would have killed you and throwed your body in the river. But they seen you out there today, too. They might of kilt you, but they knowed one or two of them was goin to die along with you—and they didn't like them odds." She laughed. "You safe from everything 'round heah, purty boy, but me. I goin' eat you up like a cannibal, less'n you climbs me pretty fast."

Blade laughed and rolled her over on the soft leather under him. She spread her legs wide and then gasped in exquisite pain as he drove himself inside her. "Oh Gawd, purty boy. You is plenty built . . . . Oh, man, you could git to be a habit with a gal—in one hell of a hurry . . . . "

2

Hunt was in physical agony. Having battled his way aboard the train at New Orleans, his fear giving him fantastic strength, he had spent, it seemed, an eternity on the overcrowded wooden seat. And now, since realizing the train must stop at Mt. Zion, Hunt's terror had multiplied tenfold.

Six hours before the incredibly crowded train pulled into Mt. Zion, Hunt was growing ill with dread. The train would stop for only a few minutes; he recalled that from his arrival there two years ago. But sometimes a few minutes can seem forever. Every rube in the community turned out to watch the new-fangled steam train pass through twice a week; it was their most popular entertainment. Only a few people in the dirty little village knew him, but the hell of it was it only took one pair of prying eyes and one big mouth to set Styles on his trail. He tried to think how he might cope with the brief stop. If only there were some compartment aboard the train where he could hide. Hell, he had no compunction about hiding. He no longer lied to himself about his personal courage or integrity. He was a son of a bitch, but at least he was still among the quick.

Long before he was prepared, the conductor walked through, swaying with the motion of the train racing along at twenty miles an hour. "Mt. Zion. Next stop. Mt. Zion, Alabama. Next stop. Mt. Zion."

Hunt pulled his soft, wide-brimmed hat down to cover as much of the right side of his head and face as possible. He turned up his jacket collar and leaned against the window framing as if he were sleeping. As the train slowed to enter the station, his heart speeded up, racing. Sweat rolled down from his hair and stung his eyes.

The train puffed and rattled to a stop before the Mt. Zion platform.

Hunt was aware that several people were gathering their belongings and leaving the train. His armpits were sopped with sweat, and the chilled marbles of moisture ran in separate balls down his rib cage. The more people there were to debark, the longer they'd be delayed here. What if they took on water, or firewood? That could delay their departure almost an hour. An hour of sitting exposed when no one out on that platform was going to budge away from here until the train took off again. Hunt sagged lower in the seat.

He didn't know when he first heard Morgan's voice. There was the battering of a fist against the window across the aisle, and then Morgan, yelling, "Mister Hunter! Mister Hunter Campbell! Mister Campbell! It's me. It's Morgan, Mister Campbell!"

Hunt sank lower, pressed harder against the window framing. Oh, the poor retarded son of a bitch. Why in hell did he have to do this? Through his mind flashed his memory of his telling Morgan he would return to Blackoaks. Hell, he'd done this simply because the kid had taken his leaving so badly, choking back the tears. His words had relieved the boy, and, he remembered now, Morgan had promised to be down at the depot to meet his train when he came back. Jesus Christ! Who'd think the backward boy would actually keep such a promise?

He heard Morgan yelling outside the train on the platform. "Hey, Soapy! Down here, Soapy! I found him. It's Mr. Campbell, Soapy."

Sliding down as far as he could on the painful bench, Hunt prayed for the train to get into forward motion.

"Mr. Campbell! Hunt! Wake up, Mister Campbell. It's Mt. Zion. It's me, Morgan."

And then Morgan's voice raised higher, alerting the farthest outpost of the village: "Down here, Soapy. It's Mister Hunter!"

At that moment, the train started up.

Hunt stayed where he was, crouched low in the seat. His fists were clenched until his knuckles had grayed out. His shirt was sopping wet with sweat. "Thank you, God," he whispered. "Thank you, God. Thank you, God."

Morgan almost wept when the train started out of the station before he could attract Hunt's attention. As the train moved, he moved with it, lumbering along awkwardly, shouting over the increasing sound of engine and wheels and clattering cars.

The train picked up speed. Running beside it, Morgan shouted over his shoulder, "Come on, Soapy. It's him."

He ran faster, ungainly, awkward, not even looking to see where he was going. Bent over, he was trying to see

Mr. Campbell on the far side of the car. Clumsy, he stumbled. "Hunt!" he screamed.

He began to cry, running faster, gawky and ungainly. He could see Hunt in that seat across the car, but Hunt never turned around; he remained staring straight ahead no matter how loudly Morgan yelled.

Lumbering along, Morgan tripped in a broken space between the platform boards. He fell hard against a baggage cart, rebounded from it in a clownish, graceless way. He hung for a moment, awkward and lumpy at the brink of the platform. And then suddenly he was gone. He fell between the platform and the moving train. The monstrous car struck him, rolled him over, crushed him, and moved faster down the track, gathering up steam.

In horror, everybody on the platform ran to the place where Morgan's body lay like a discarded straw doll beside the tracks. Soapy, walking numbly, pushed through the crowd and went slowly to where Morgan lay dead. He sank to his knees beside him, weeping, crying for Morgan.

3

Yellow jack . . .

New Orleans was a harlot cast into the lowest reaches of hell. She denied her contagion with her dying breath. Annually, city and parish authorities attempted to conceal or minimize the arrival of the epidemic, which came like a grim human exterminator, until deaths increased to sensational proportions—almost one thousand deaths in the week Hunt fled north via train. Often, officials permitted vacationers to debark from river steamers, stagecoaches, or trains when the plague was already raging out of control. These men were not motivated by malicious desire to invite outsiders to see New Orleans and die—it was just that when word of epidemic spread, it destroyed a million-dollar tourist business, and the town suffered irreparable damage to its reputation for months, even years, though the yellow jack came abruptly in the hot, steaming summer nights and ended as suddenly and inexplicably. But now the truth was rampant—hundreds were dying daily in an epidemic of yellow fever as mysterious in its origins as it was uncontrollable in its destructiveness.

The best medical minds asseverated that yellow fever was spread from the putrefaction of the swamps and canals and cesspools on night vapors. They advised anyone who could not escape the stricken city to close and seal windows and blinds every night. Sleeping in airtight bedrooms was almost unbearable because of the summer heat and humidity and because of the stifling sweatiness in subtropical rains. There were those cursed with a gallows sense of humor who insisted that the health authorities ordered cannon fired and drums pounded, not to alter the atmosphere and burn out the night vapors as advertised, but to warrant that every man was awake, sleepless, and wide-eyed when Bronze John came for him.

There wasn't much cause for laughter in the depths of pestilence.

Someone in the public medical bureaucracy ordered huge bonfires set in street intersections at sunset and kept stoked until dawn. It was argued that the flames would burn out of the night vapors any yellow-fever germs not destroyed by the cannon blasts and drumbeats. Opponents disagreed, but since no one could authoritatively disprove the efficacy of fires, the project was instituted on one of the hottest nights in July, heat and smoke adding to the discomfort of frightened, dying, trapped, and harried citizenry. Fire tenders sat all night as far from the fires as possible, drinking and slapping at the clouds of mosquitoes. All day long, men with horse-drawn carts plodded into the mosquito-infested wetlands to haul out logs. Nothing seemed to discourage or diminish Bronze John. People stumbled to their knees in the middle of the street, faces darkening hideously, and vomited the black fluid. Those who made it through one more night ran from death. They cursed the goddamn mosquitoes, which added to their agony. Some even prayed, but many were afraid to fall to their knees for fear they would not get up.

The brutally insensitive sorts who never believed there was anything personal in death by epidemic, robbed the dead bodies, looted abandoned stores, and pillaged closed homes. The governor ordered the militia sent in with orders to shoot to kill these stiff-robbers and pillagers on sight. When investigation showed that the governor owned the land from which logs were being hauled at inflated prices to burn in downtown streets, nobody suggested the militia call on him. Venality in high places at public expense is nothing more than clever business; street crime is a felony. The fires raged, the dead carts rumbled toward churches and cemeteries with their grotesque corpses kissed by Bronze John, like tumbrels rolling from an assembly-line guillotine.

The lowest slave died along with the most distinguished master—victims of the same fever, identically delirious with febrility, face blackening, and foul blood oozing from mouth and nostrils. Bronze John recognized no caste.

Kathy passed the days and nights after Hunt abandoned her in complete depression. Desolated in spirit, she was unable to eat or sleep. She lay wide-eyed and unmoving across her rumpled bed all day, wandered the apartment all night, dragging her sheer negligee in her wake as if it were some sort of talisman. At first, she kept waiting for Hunt to return. Even when he had told her he was leaving her, she did not believe it; she had no life but him; she did not believe he could walk away from her.

One morning, she threw open the windows and blinds in her bedroom and stood in the balcony doorway watching Dauphine Street. She willed Hunt to turn the corner and come hurrying toward the walled patio below. She pleaded with God to send him back to her. She kept going over the same vaguely remembered line from somewhere in the Bible: "And I sought him whom my soul loveth . . . . "

Standing there, she watched a well-dressed woman leave a shop and walk slowly along the banquette toward her. Suddenly the woman grasped her throat, doubled as if someone had struck her in the stomach, and, bent over, retched. Horrified, Kathy watched. For that instant, something so ugly and terrible that it drove her loss from her mind, consumed her. She screamed, "Alexi!"

The black girl came running from within the house. They stood together and watched the woman trying to crawl away from her own vomit.

"Alexi. Go down there and help her."

"You crazy, Missy? That woman got yellowjack. She dyin'. She contagious. For God's sake close them blinds and them doors. Come inside. Get away from that balcony."

Alexi was so shaken, so visibly terrified that Kathy obeyed her wordlessly. Alexi closed the blinds, the tall doors, and drew the drapes. The room darkened, and in the dim stillness Kathy forgot the woman crawling on the walkway and remembered Hunt. She sank crying to her bed.

Alone in the apartment that night after Alexi left, Kathy wandered the empty rooms. She heard the drums, the cannon, the clatter of dead-cart wheels on the cobblestones. She smelled the smoke from the sodden woodfires. She pinked the drapes and looked for the woman on the banquette. She was not out there. Kathy wondered if the poor woman were dead. "If she's dead, I envy her . . . . Your heart doesn't break when you're dead . . . ."

She stood in her sweated, wrinkled gown and gazed at herself in her framed, full-length mirror. She had not brushed her hair in the days since Hunt had deserted her. She had not changed her gown. She had not washed her armpits. She remembered drinking coffee, but she had not eaten anything.

She could not stand to look at the thin, sallow-faced creature in that glass. She looked around, found a heavy statuette of naked lovers. She hurled it and smashed the mirror. She couldn't help being hideous in her grief, but she didn't have to look at herself.

She stared down at the shards of glass littering the floor. One foot-long sliver fascinated her. It somehow resembled a dagger. She knelt and took it up in her hand.

Holding it, she stared at the white flesh of her inner wrist. The curved shard was needle-sharp. How easy to scratch that white flesh until the artery ruptured. How quick. How much easier than the poor woman vomiting out her life on the street.

She nodded. She had found the answer. She would cut her wrist—this was the quickest way, if only she didn't botch it. She lifted her right hand and her eyes widened. Blood leaked between her fingers. She had gripped the shard so tightly she had sliced her palm. Sickened, she threw the shard, and it smashed on the parquet flooring.

Crying, she sank across the bed, thinking about the long, empty night ahead of her, all the long, empty nights . . . .

She lay staring at the shadowed ceiling, wishing Hunt would come back, if only for a little while. He would need his suits. He hadn't even taken his pince-nez. If he would came back, she would tell him, "I forgive you, Hunt. I know. I failed you, and I was not worth the price of staying here with me." He was deathly afraid of yellow fever. Gischairn had said anyone with an ounce of intelligence dreaded the fever. And, too, Hunt feared Styles's vengeance. His fear of Styles had unmanned him. He did love her—not in the mindless way she loved him, not enough to stay and fight for her and expose himself to the dread epidemic, but he did love her. Oh God, he did love her!

She fell asleep at last. She was lying on the bed, the sheet streaked with blood from her palm, when Alexi came in the next morning. Alexi's angered muttering wakened her. "Now why she have to break that nice mirror? Just make work for me. That's all she do. Just make work for me. More work."

Alexi got a dust pan and broom and cleaned up the floor. Kathy kept her eyes tightly closed until the black girl had gone back to the kitchen, complaining.

She didn't want Alexi to think she was awake because Alexi would want her to eat breakfast, at least to drink café-au-lait. She did not feel like eating. She pressed the back of her hand against her forehead. She had a slight fever, and her head ached. She would lie quietly in bed and pray that Alexi let her alone.

Her fever didn't diminish as she'd believed it would. Her face and body grew hotter. The mattress was heated from her febrility. Her mouth was dry. Her head ached miserably. When she blinked her eyelids, pain lanced to the crown of her head. She would get up for a glass of water. She was dehydrated. She would feel better when she had a cool glass of water.

She sat up, and suddenly she felt her stomach gripping her, roiling with unbearable pain. She tried to cry out. When she opened her mouth, vomitus gushed from her lips and splashed down the front of her gown.

She toppled over on her side, her head hanging over the foot of the mattress. She retched, vomited involuntarily. All she could think was that now she had vomited on her gown, she would have to change it.

The sick-sour smell of vomitus rose from the floor, and she gagged but was too weak to lift her head back to the bed. She called, terrorized, "Alexi!"

The maid came to the door. The smell of vomitus assailed her wide, flat nostrils, and she stopped as if poled.

Kathy tried to tilt her head to look up. "Alexi . . . . "

Alexi stared at Kathy, at the pool of vomitus spreading across the parquet flooring. She retreated, shaking her head. She whispered, "Lawd help us! She got de yellow jack!" She heeled around and ran.

"Alexi!" Kathy cried. But Alexi ran across the front room. Kathy heard the front screen door slam behind her.

Alexi went three steps down the stairway toward the patio. She stopped, came slowly up the steps. She opened the screen door stealthily and entered the front room. The letter from Hunt still lay open on the table where Kathy had laid it with the five hundred dollars in paper money atop it. The money had winked at Alexi for days now, grabbing her eyes every time she walked through the room. A dozen times she would have taken it, but no one else came up here. It would be too obvious she had stolen it. She thought about the girl lying in her own vomitus on that bed in there. It didn't matter any more who took the money, that girl in there wasn't going to need it. Alexi took up the bills, folded them in her fist, and went out of the house again, letting the door slam behind her. Then she ran down the steps, across the patio, and out into the street. She did not look back.

Joe Bullock walked on tender feet across the patio and climbed the stairs. He heard no sound from within the apartment. He rapped on the door with his knuckles.
"Missy?"
He waited and then knocked again on the door framing. There was no response. He tried the door, found it unlocked. He limped inside the long veranda. There was an eerie silence about the place. He walked the length of the veranda, returned to the door of the living room.
"Missy? Mrs. Kenric? You in there?"
There was only the dread silence. He went into the living room. From old habit he took up the note and envelope from Frobisher's. He read Hunt's quickly scrawled message. He dropped the paper on the floor in disdain. "Fucking coward," he said to himself.
He glanced into the small kitchen where unwashed dishes were stacked in the sink. He went along the small corridor to the bedroom. As he approached, the stench of vomitus struck him.
He paused at the bedroom door. He stared at Kathy for a long time. She lay sprawled in her own vomitus. Her face looked fevered, one hand was cut and scribbled with dried blood. She was asleep.
"You poor little bitch," he said.
He exhaled heavily, turned on sore feet and walked out of the house.

4

Blade maneuvered the coach deeper and deeper into the stricken city. His exhausted horses, nervous in unaccustomed crowds and spooked by every blast of cannon, fought their harness and reared inside the shafts. Blade was as skittish and troubled as they, but he managed to quiet the frightened animals and to control his own growing sense of anxiety and terror.

Blade soon knew he was hopelessly lost. He had never imagined in his wildest nightmare a city as huge and sprawling as this—a confusion of stores, houses, and buildings crowded against each other in a maze of streets that promised one direction and led you another, or simply ended at a river that seemed to break its own back and flow against itself, retracing its way through the bewildering jungle of brick and stone. He most hated an incredible cathedral reared against the sky to dwarf all trees, houses, stores, and, especially, a lost Negro youth in a miniscule carriage.

He rode past this same cathedral three times before his sweated frustrations led him to cut his carriage suddenly in front of a white man's dray. The white man cursed him and might have lashed out with his bullwhip, but Blade's size and the implacable rage in the boy's brown face dissuaded him. "Dauphine Street, sir?" Blade called, pleading.

The drayman relaxed slightly and pointed west. "Yonder. Back of town," he said. "Watch how you cut in front of a man. A good way to get yourself kilt."

Blade nodded and thanked the drayman. He pulled his team around, turning the coach in the street. He made the right turn and was soon deep in narrow, shadowed streets which twisted between high walls and overhanging balconies trimmed with ironwork grilles. Every time he relaxed his grip on the reins to read a street sign, a hospital wagon or police buggy raced past, or cannon erupted and his horses reared, threatening to bolt.

Trembling with fatigue, drawn taut, Blade pulled up on the reins and sat slump-shouldered, ready to surrender to defeat. He could wander forever in this tricky maze of streets. People willing to stop long enough to hear his questions, invariably replied with a vague gesture and a brief "yonder." His horses were ready to bolt. He could see himself killed in this strange, delirium-like place. He'd never find Miss Kathy. He'd never get home again.

Sweated, he gazed around him. Ahead, he espied a livery stable. He slapped the reins and the horses responded. He pulled into the wide doors of the hay-and-amonia-smelling barn. A white man got up from a butt-sprung kitchen chair and walked toward him, his small eyes studying the animals and the sleek coach. "I'd like to leave my coach and horses here. Can you have them watered, fed, and stabled?"

"Cost you a dollar a day."

Blade drew a golden eagle from his pocket. The white man's deep-set eyes widened, then narrowed, and he inspected Blade carefully—from expensive leather boots to wide-brimmed planter's hat. "Got no change for that kind of money."

The gold eagle had no value to Blade, except to buy him temporary release from handling the fractious horses and rig while he searched out Dauphine Street and Miss Kathy. He extended his hand. "Take it," he said. "You can give me change when I come back."

"How long you figure to be gone?"

"I don't know. Not long. I've got to find this number on Dauphine Street. I figure I'll do better walking."

"You sure's hell will. Somebody'll kill you for them horses and that coach. Lot of people desperate to get out of this town. Where you from? You a stranger in town?" The hostler pocketed the golden eagle, clutching it tightly in his fist inside his pocket.

"Can you tell me how to get to Dauphine Street?"

The stable owner nodded, walked with Blade to the wide doors, blinking as if bat-blind against the saffron sunlight. "You go yonder. Past that cemetery. You turn west and you cross Rampart. Can you read?"

"Yes."

"Then look for Conti where it crosses Rampart Street. Go east yonder two blocks down Conti. Conti crosses Dauphine. Hell, you miss it, you walk on to the river, count five blocks back and you got Dauphine. You turn on Dauphine—this here number you want is to your left from Conti as you walk from here."

Overwhelmed with a sense of relief and release, Blade exhaled heavily. The white man made it sound so easy, as if his long journey were almost over. He smiled. "Never mind no change. You keep that eagle, Mister."

The man whistled between his teeth, then shrugged and nodded. "One thing, friend—"

"Yes, suh?"

"We can't no way be responsible for your rig—or horses. Not with things crazy like they are."

Blade's shoulders sagged. He hesitated, then turned and started back to his coach.

"What you goin' do, friend?"

"I can't keep anybody from stealin' my horses and rig, I'll take 'em with me, after all."

"That ain't smart. No offense, friend, but that will be a stupid move. We'll do all we can to protect your property. We got to stay in business. And you done bought yo'self twenty bucks worth of my friendship. I'll cover the rig with canvas and we'll put them horses in safe, inside stables. Out on the street, with night coming on, you got jus' two chances of keeping 'em—slim—and none."

Blade stared down at his hands. They shook. His voice was level, pleading as much as threatening, though the threat was there under every word. "They best be here when I get back . . . . I got to git my lady out of this town . . . . I got no way but that coach and them horses . . . . They gone, I got nothing . . . and then I don't care about nuthin', including killing somebody."

The hostler tried to smile. "Go on, friend. Find yoah lady."

Blade walked reluctantly away from the livery. He was prey to the sick sensation that the white man would give him that same false smile and empty words when he returned—and found his property "stolen."

Involuntarily, his hand touched the knife handle at his belt. God help the man who caused him to fail Miss Kathy. He was, from birth and youth on the farm, an easygoing, compliant man, submissive. He found it possible and rewarding to get what he wanted through smiling, compromise, and accommodation. But something new had been burned deep into his guts on the long journey from Blackoaks to New Orleans. Perhaps it began with Master Styles's revelation that white people lied and dissembled and tried to hide their true feelings, just as slaves did. Perhaps it began with Ahma and her rebellious, militant nature. He'd laughed at her and kissed her mouth closed on her treason, discontent, and disloyalty. But he'd recognized truth in her virulent words, though they'd stunned his deeply ingrained sense of servility and his carefully nurtured slave mentality. All she said went against everything he'd been taught. Now, he felt some of her rebellion choking up inside him. It was as if he'd not traveled across only three states—he had made a pilgrimage to the dark side of the moon. He wondered if he could ever return to his old way of life. He'd endured mendacity, insult, theft, petty malice, and racial mockery at every stop on the road. At first, he'd accepted the indignity as the condign fate of any black man in the white man's world, but the longer he traveled, the more exhausted he became, and the shorter burned his fuse of tolerance. Those red-necked whites had outraged even his poorly developed sense of justice. Not even the total superiority of the whites could justify the petty and wretched mistreatment doled out to him. His resentment simmered, flared, and boiled into virulence. Infuriated, he held himself on a short leash, ready to strike out in fury.

Taut, empty-bellied, he passed the cemetery and turned again away from the westering sun. A cannon boomed. He trembled involuntarily, hesitating, the earth rumbling beneath his feet.

While he stood, indecisive and desolated, a man ran past him. But what a strange and incredible man! Blade stared at the colorful figure—the man was more a peacock than an ordinary Negro. Blade had never seen such plumage, such colors in hat, feather, and brilliant green suit over ruffled pink shirt. Despite his fatigue, Blade smiled faintly at the garish brightness of the man's garb. Immediately behind this man came a miniature version of the first—gaudy suit, pink shirt, green shoes—all sharply tailored clothes. The second man, little larger than a dwarf, galloped on short, stubby legs. Fascinated,

Blade stopped in the middle of the banquette, staring after them.

A third man—in rough clothes and workboots—bowled into Blade and sent him sprawling face first against the wall of a building. The man was almost half a foot taller than Blade, broad in the shoulders, huge in the chest, long-legged.

Blade struck the wall, feeling the roughness bite into his face. It was like flint striking flint—fires of rage flared inside him. He'd been kicked, thrust aside, mishandled, and spat upon as long as he'd endure it. Without stopping to consider consequences, the size of his adversary, Conti Street, or how lost he could get, he wheeled around and raced after the huge man.

The big man easily overtook the brilliantly plumed dwarf. He caught the little fellow at the scruff of his neck, hoisted him three feet off the ground and hurled him like a sack of meal against a wall. The dwarf struck with the sickening thud of a thrown watermelon. He seemed to slide in terrible slow motion down the rough concrete to the banquette where he lay face down, unmoving.

The gaudily plumaged man up ahead could have escaped when the big fellow stopped to attack the dwarf. He was half a block out front and gaining. But, glancing over his shoulder, he saw the little man hurled viciously against the wall by the giant attacker.

The green-suited man stopped running and spun around, as lithe as a ballet dancer on his feet. His eyes showed white rims in his dark face. His mouth contorted, twisting. He screamed like a macaw. Though he was no more than of medium height, underweight, and outclassed in every other way physically, he ran back toward the big man, wailing like a banshee.

This was exactly the reaction the giant devoutly desired. He set himself. In a flash of color, the green-suited youth flew at the big man like a fighting bantam in a senseless, one-sided cockfight.

The big man caught Green Suit by the throat. The youth gouged at the big man's eyes, caught his fingers in the man's nostrils and yanked upward, kicked violently at his groin. But the giant held him at arm's length, closing his fist mercilessly on the smaller man's throat. The boy gasped for breath, his arms flailing, his kicking diminishing.

Blade lowered his head and crashed into the small of the giant's back, sending his shoulder like a battering ram into the fellow's spine.

The giant grunted in shock and agony. His grip on the green-suited youth relaxed. The boy lurched away, gulping in draughts of air. Stunned, the giant heeled around, sobbing for breath. He stared in amazement and rage at Blade, and then he charged, growling.

Blade waited until the last possible moment before he was smothered under the huge body, then he drove his left fist upward, deep under the big man's belt. The man staggered, retching, but recovered as though from the bite of a mosquito. As the giant lunged toward Blade, Green Suit tackled him from behind. The giant delayed long enough to chop downward with his hamlike fist across the back of the boy's neck. Green Suit went limp, sliding to the walk as boneless as a jellyfish.

Blade was attacking as the giant wheeled to face him. Blade's wild-swinging right was deflected on the man's huge left arm. A right, driven straight into Blade's face, stopped him as if he'd been poled. Stunned, Blade went reeling against the face of a building.

He shook his head to clear it. As he straightened, the big man was pulling a thick-butted gun from beneath his wide belt. His face contorted and his voice shook with rage. "Now, you goddamn purty nigger, I gonna teach you."

Blade stared at that gun coming out of the man's belt, at the twisted face. The man meant to kill him. Blade grabbed his pig-nutter knife from its belt sheath while he was lunging forward. The knife blade whisked across the back of the giant's gun hand, slicing it. Blood spurted. The big man jerked his hand up and away from the gunbutt, growling. He reached out, trying to catch Blade in the circle of his loglike arms. But Blade's knife flashed and sliced the man's belt, and ripped down along his fly. The giant retreated.

Backing away, his hand bleeding profusely, the giant grabbed for his gun again. He pulled it from beneath his belt and moved forward. Suddenly his pants fell about his ankles, tripping him. He staggered and toppled helplessly to his knees.

Around them a wailing of laughter swirled. But neither the fallen giant nor Blade was aware of people around them.

Blade brought the knife up under the man's chin. The point dug into the chin bone. Blade's voice shook as the giant's had a moment before. "Stay there, nigger. On your knees. Stay where you is, or I send this knife up through your chin and out through your eyes."

The giant opened his mouth to speak, but the faintest pressure of the glittering knife blade made him bite his lips closed. He stared wide-eyed up at Blade, tilting his head backward.

Blade said, "You stay where you are. You almost dead, nigger . . . . You nevah gonna be nearer dead . . . . I could of ripped your belly, easy as I ripped yoah belt. Easier . . . . I hope you got sense enough to know that."

Terrified, the big man tried to nod without impaling himself on the point of Blade's knife. His eyes blinked frantically. He understood.

Blade watched the youth get up, brushing at his green suit and setting his rakish hat at an angle on his head. Then he helped the dazed dwarf to his feet. He spoke to Blade. "Come on. Less'n you want to kill him, we best up and on."

Blade stared into the big man's white-rimmed eyes. "You move, big nigger, 'fore us is two blocks from here, I will kill you—you hear?"

The big man tried to nod again. He seemed to understand by what narrow miracle he still breathed rather than lying sprawled, a disemboweled corpse.

Blade withdrew the knife, returned it to his sheath. Green Suit caught his arm and the three of them raced to the corner and rounded it. As they glanced back, the big man was pulling up his pants in a hail of raucous, hate-riddled laughter. They did not stop running for three long blocks.

They stopped at last, breathless. Green Suit stared at Blade and grinned widely. "You know who that was you cut down to size back there?"

Blade shook his head. The thought raced through his mind that his fury had been directed against the men who'd victimized and injured him along the road as much as against the huge stranger.

"Man, that there was Achilles Clayton . . . . Man, Flider and me are deep in yore debt. You saved my life—and I don't pretend nuthin' less. If Achilles didn't throttle me on the spot, he'd of throwed me in jail—and, man, I die in jail . . . . I'm a bird, man, I got to fly free."

"Put you in jail?"

"Man, don't you know nothin'? Don't you know who that bad enemy you made was? Achilles Clayton. He a undercover policeman."

"Police? Then who are you?"

The boy smiled and bowed deeply. "Name of Peter-Dick Penury, man. Leading pimp of New Orleans. Also knowed as Big Peter, Big Dick, Big Pen, and Big Ury. But most known for the best-looking whores any pimp ever owned."

"Pimp?"

"Gawd, boy, don't you know nuthin'? How deep in the country you from? Man, I bet the sun purentee sets between yo' farm and the nearest town! . . . You got a hell of a lot to learn—lucky you met up with the right people —good ole Flider and me, Peter-Dick Penury."

5

Blade walked beside his two new-found friends in the lowering sunlight. They moved across a shabby area. Somehow Blade was sure Miss Kathy didn't live down here, but he said nothing. It seemed impolite to question a man kind enough to volunteer to put aside everything else and see that he got where he wanted to go. He had been lost and he had found a friend, two friends, counting the grinning little Flider who smiled and nodded a lot but didn't say much. He didn't want to alienate his new friends, but he was far more lost within the vast city than he had been when they set out. They walked along a walled street and turned abruptly into an open space full of caterwauling sounds, of bongoes, voices, horns, and piano.

Blade stopped walking and stared, eyes wide and unable to credit what he saw before him. Accustomed to rural life, he'd found the city itself unbelievable; this place was a demon's miracle, a kind of sprawling party spawned in hell. The area, on the west side of Rampart Street, extended roughly between St. Peter and St. Ann Streets. It was all light and noise and raucous laughter. After his long, tiring journey, his inner rages and the encounter with Achilles Clayton, this place exploded across his senses, unreal, a mirage or fantasy seen in mind-boggling fever.

A mindless jumbling of booths and stands, stores and cribs, of crowds of laughing black people, well dressed compared with plantation slaves, some even gaudily attired, the scene exuded a carnival atmosphere that pervaded the waning day. Yet the bright gaiety was a sense of tension that was almost tangible. It was as if all life and good living were crowded into this square and distilled into this immediate present.

The swarming of people, the likes of which Blade had never encountered before, seemed to emerge out of nowhere, to swirl in currents and floods and eddies, all hurrying nowhere.

He gazed breathlessly at the wonders and excitement laid out before him. Everything else was forgotten—shoved deep in his mind—Miss Kathy, Ahma, his gut-aching rages, his fatigue and anxiety. He was lifted out of himself and transported into a new existence by the sights and sounds and smells of this demiworld.

While he stood breathless trying to drink in all the visual marvels of a black world without slavery, agony, or fear, strange dark people flowed past him. They strolled absolutely free, chattering among themselves, moving with laughter and freedom and happiness that Blade could not credit. The men's suits were not as handsomely cut as his, but they were brighter, as Peter-Dick Penury's was—wide-brimmed hats plumed with saucy parrot feathers, jackets a gaudy purple or splash of orange, deep forest green touched with bright pinks.

And the women! Aye God, the women! They were painted, lips red and eyes shadowed in pastel blues and greens and yellows. All were incredibly lovely compared to the drab and overworked wenches of the farm country. Some were glitteringly black, a flaunting, radiant black, and some were almost white, and others glowed with a lucent high yellow. And most remarkable of all, the dresses they wore—as if their bodies were merchandise on display. Skirts slit above the knees, exposing heated thighs. Ankles ornamented and sparkling with bracelets. Bodices cut so low that only the nipples of full, upthrust breasts were tentatively concealed. Even the nails of their fingers and toes were flagrantly reddened. They were, Blade decided, the most exciting and elegant-looking women this world's bazaar had to offer.

Flider and Peter-Dick Penury watched his face with the same pleasure he displayed in witnessing the wonders before him. "How 'bout this, Brother?" Peter-Dick clapped him on the shoulder. "Ain't this the place you asked me to bring you?"

"Where is this?" Blade's eyes followed the swinging hips of a wench along the banquette. "Is we died and gone to nigger heaven?"

"Almost, Brother, amen!" Peter-Dick said. "Man, this here's Congo Square. You see what you want, and we gets it for you. Right, Brother Flider?"

Flider grinned widely and nodded his outsized head so vigorously he had to grab his green hat to keep from losing it.

"I want one of them women," Blade said, swinging his arm in no particular direction. "Any of them. All of them."

Peter-Dick laughed. "You forgit these cheap tramps, Brother. I savin' you for something special. These nigger girls ain't good enough for nuthin' but white men."

"I didn't know they was no place on earth like this," Blade said as they moved forward again through the booths.

Now his nostrils were assailed by the smells of food—cooking, simmering, boiling, barbecueing, frying, every booth offered something different. Catfish fried with the eyes popping and juicy in the heads, pickled pig knuckles, spare ribs and ham hocks, huge cauldrons bubbling with creole gumbo, and stacks of crisply fried chicken wings, backs, and necks, three for a copper penny. Pies cooled on counters, ten inches across and two inches deep for five pennies—cherry, pecan, apple, yam, or pumpkin. Every booth, no matter its main merchandise, held kegs of sugar-cane stalks for a penny each that a man could peel down and munch the sweet juices as he walked, spitting out the cottony residue on the littered banquettes. Shrimp prepared every way known to the palate of the blacks and creoles; oysters steaming in vats, fried in corn meal, or lying open on the half-shell. Blade walked slowly, drooling over chitterlings, red beans, and rice.

Peter-Dick bought gumbo, French bread, and shrimp. They sat at a rough table and wolfed down the food, watching the parade of women. Blade frowned, watching Peter-Dick, who was relaxed, totally at ease, though less than thirty minutes earlier he had stared death in the eyes, "Ain't you worried?"

" 'Bout what, Brother?"

"Achilles Clayton. He found you on yonder street. Couldn't he find you just as easy here?"

"He could. The bastard stool pigeon. But it ain't his job to come into the Square after me. And big as he is, he ain't got the guts. Right, Brother Flider?"

Flider grinned and nodded, slurping up the okra, shrimp, and juices of the gumbo.

"You see, Brother," Peter-Dick said, thrusting a wad of bread into his gumbo and stirring it around until it was sodden and dripping yellow juices, "Achilles is a cop. Leastwise, the police pay him. But he ain't no more honest than a white cop. He don't care that I a pimp—he care where-at I pimp. I got out of my territory today—in streets he is paid off to protect."

Blade stared at Peter-Dick, puzzled. The slender, green-suited youth laughed. "Achilles wasn't after me and Flider for breaking ary law. Hell, he breaks more of 'em than I knows about. You see, I got me a territory where my whores are allowed to walk. I pays the police for protection, and I is protected and my ladies is protected. But, a man like me—I can't be satisfied with a little ole area—I needs to spread out. Needs to spread my wings. Needs to fly. Amen, Brother!" He clapped Flider on the back, laughing. "I was trying to do that today—get me some new streets. Got into territory that Achilles is paid to protect. He'd of killed us if you hadn't come along with that pig-sticker of yours. I eternal grateful, Brother. Amen!"

"Amen!" Flider echoed.

Blade took a huge spoonful of gumbo. "You could of gotten away—but you come back when Achilles jumped Flider."

Peter-Dick shrugged. "Flider, he my brother."

Blade stared, unable to believe it. "Your brother?"

"Not blood, man. Best way they is. Love. I chose him for my brother. Amen. Right, Flider? Flider love me. He think I a great man—and I love him for thinkin' it. That make him my brother. Like the way you cut old Achilles' pants today make you my brother!" He put his head back, roaring with laughter so people stopped and turned, staring at them. He suddenly remembered something. "Come on, my brothers, finish yo' gumbo. You still hungry, I buy you a catfish to eat on the way. We got to see the conjure woman."

"Amen," said Flider.

Night closed down on the Square as they crossed it, Blade munching the hot catfish wrapped in newspaper.

They reached an old building of Moorish origin. Peter-Dick rapped on the door.

After a moment the door was opened and saffron lamplight spilled out past a tall, angular woman. When she recognized Peter-Dick her wide mouth spread in a warm smile, revealing glittering white, diamond-studded teeth. Blade's mouth sagged. A woman, but what a woman. At first, he figured her to be the ugliest female creature he'd ever had the misfortune to encounter. But this mistaken impression was quickly dissipated. Indeed she wore a bright bandana over hair pinned in tight corn-rows upon a long, narrow skull. Her ears protruded extraordinarily, and her face resembled a horse Blade had once known. Her nose was long, wide at the nostrils. Her jaw was underslung. But when she smiled she was beautiful, and later, as Blade saw, when she went into a trance she was upsettingly lovely.

"Ruhmar, want you to meet a new friend of mine. More'n ary friend, he a brother. He saved my life today when your spell run out. I figured I best come in and get that spell renewed. Brother Blade, he might not always be around."

Ruhmar smiled at Blade, but then her eyes darkened. "Achilles Clayton," she said.

"That's right!" Peter-Dick clapped Blade on the back. "I tell you they no conjure woman in the bayou country that can hold a candle to Ruhmar . . . . You don't even have to tell her when you got trouble—she already seen it."

Ruhmar nodded. "I seen Achilles had attacked you when I opened the door. I seen this young boy helping you and pore little Flider bad hurt. We got to do conjure on Achilles Clayton. You was right to come straight here—soon as you filled your gut with gumbo and catfish."

Ruhmar told them to sit down at the table. "Don't nobody talk," she said. "I got to get in touch with Damballah and Ayda . . . . You still got the *ouango* I give you to carry to protect you from gods of death?"

Peter-Dick nodded and laid the small ornament on the table beside the golden eagle. Ruhmar closed her eyes tightly shut. "The gods say I must give you a gri-gri against the black evil. You must carry it as you will the *ouango* once I have restored its powers."

She fumbled in the mesh bag at her side and brought up a small object that resembled a fish-lure to Blade. It was made of tail feathers from a bird, rattles from a snake, eyes of a lizard, tied with bright thread.

She began a long, muted-voiced incantation over the gri-gri. Listening to her voice, Blade began to lose contact with everything except the sound of her speaking; nothing else could penetrate his consciousness. He felt himself grow dizzy, and then his whole body became as light as a feather. He knew he remained seated in his chair, but it was as if he floated on a cloud. He was vaguely aware of what happened, but it was as if vari-colored lights flashed in the room or behind his own eyes, he was never afterwards sure which. He saw the woman take up a long, lanky doll that amazingly resembled Achilles Clayton as Blade remembered him. She laid the doll on the table and took a six-inch hatpin from the mesh bag. She dedicated the pin to Damballah, to the gods of pain, the gods of death. She slowly shoved the pin through the right hand of the doll, through its wrist, its inner elbow, its shoulder. The lights flashed weirdly. Dimly, he heard her voice. "You are safe from a gun, or a knife, or any object of death in the hand of Achilles Clayton. His bullets will go astray, his knife will fail him. You have the strength of Damballah against him. You have the protection and love of Ayda. You may go forth, secure against evil, as long as you love Damballah, swear allegiance to Ayda, and follow the laws of our gods in dealing with those you love."

The strange flashing lights diminished, disappeared. Gradually, Blade came awake, rested and restored, but once again conscious of his weight on the chair. Ruhmar smiled at him. "I am sorry to have had to put you under a spell, my son. But your mind—it questioned, it was deeply troubled—it disturbed me."

Peter-Dick gave the woman a brief kiss, and she ushered them out the door. He carried the gri-gri and the *ouango* in his jacket pockets. He was withdrawn and silent for some blocks. Blade walked quietly between him and Flider, his mind aswarm with questions, doubts, exalting thoughts.

Suddenly a gaudily dressed young girl stepped from the shadows. She spoke Peter-Dick's name and they stopped. He shook his head, clearing it. Then he walked over to where the girl waited in the shadows. She was round in the hips, her thighs seeming to strain the fabric of her skirt. Her breasts were full in a low-bodiced blouse. Her green slippers glittered in the lamplight.

They talked for a long time. Blade could not hear what they said. But he was shocked when Peter-Dick suddenly struck the girl across the face. She burst into tears and retreated into the shadows. Peter-Dick returned to where Blade and Flider stood.

Blade said, "Why you hit her?"

Peter-Dick glanced at him as if he'd never seen him before. Then he smiled. "She one of my girls . . . like I was telling you . . . . I had to hit her. If I didn't she leaves me and gits herself a man who will . . . . She better off with me."

Peter-Dick exhaled heavily. He glanced around. "Hey, Brothers, we got to turn it in for the night. Huh? I know it's early, but I weary."

"I think I got a broken rib, Brother," Flider said.

"Well, why in hell didn't you say so?"

"Don't hurt that bad, an' we got other things on our mind."

"We git Dr. Sofrono to look at you on the way home," Peter-Dick said. "Then we gits a bath, and hits the hay for the night. Right, Brothers?"

"How about my lady?" Blade protested. "You promised me you help me find Dauphine Street."

"Yeah. Sure." Peter-Dick nodded absently. "We do that tomorrow, Brother. First thing tomorrow."

He was yawning as they stopped in the dark, smelly crib which Dr. Sofrono used as an office off his medicinal smelling apartment. Sofrono was an aging white man, thin and stoop-shouldered. He examined Flider's ribs, bound his chest tightly, and gave him a pint bottle of medicine. "Mostly laudanum," he said to the dwarf. "You'll like it. You'll start crackin' your ribs every day."

Peter-Dick's apartment near Congo Square was a revelation to Blade. He had no idea that many whites lived in such splendor, and he had not suspected any blacks were so blessed. The apartment boasted an iron-grille balcony, a veranda overlooking a walled patio, a living room, dining alcove, kitchen, two bedrooms, and a small bath with earthenware commode and tiled square tub.

But the size and appointments were not as startling as the furnishings. Couches, chairs, oversized bolsters, and carpeting were all bright, contrasting splashes of color— Peter-Dick had used everything in decorating his apartment except good taste. The walls of the living room boasted murals of overly endowed lesbians in every known and suspected position of passionate embrace.

"What you think?" Peter-Dick said.

"I don't know what to think. I never seen nothin' to match it. I didn't know folks lived like this—less'n they kings."

Penury crossed the room and yanked a cord. Blade heard nothing, but Peter-Dick went about the apartment shedding his clothing. His schedule, he said, was for himself to take the first bath, then one would be prepared for Blade and lastly for Flider who'd have to be carefully laved in order not to wet his bandages. He was standing bare except for bright cotton underpants when the veranda doors opened and three black girls entered bearing hot water. "They slave girls," Peter-Dick said. "Ain't mine. But they belongs to the house. Come on and watch me take my bath."

Flider and Blade stood in the doorway while the three girls soaped, massaged, stroked, and pampered Peter-Dick in the tub. Then they dried him and covered his body with a scented powder, followed by toilet water splashed under his arms and about his privates. Yawning, he headed toward his bed. "You next, Brother Blade. An' give those girls your underclothes and shirt and suit. They bring them back in the morning, fresh and pressed."

Blade removed his moneybelt and laid it across a chair in the second bedroom which Peter-Dick had assigned to him. By this time fresh water was brought, the downspout closed off, the tub filled. Self-consciously, Blade stepped into the water. He was nervous and when the girls first touched him he trembled, ticklish. But they soon lathered him with soap, rinsed him, and he forgot to be self-conscious. His penis stood rigid, quivering. The girls stared at it, pleased and excited. They whispered, "Hope Mr. Big Dick don't see this. He gonna feel mighty faint."

They scrubbed him with the towel, spending much time and tender attention upon his penis and scrotum.

Poor little Flider had to sit naked, swathed in chest bandages on the side of the tub, his feet in Blade's wash water while the three girls accompanied Blade into his bed. He lay down on the mattress. The girls slipped out of their shifts and lay down beside him, one on each side and the third between his legs, with her head on his right pelvis. He felt as if he were caught in a wild fantasy, six full and rounded breasts to fondle, three overheated mouths to kiss, nurse and nuzzle him, three liquid-hot vaginas to encase and strip him down until he was too weak too move, too exhausted to stir, hardly aware of when they slipped out of his bed . . . .

Blade awoke at daybreak from old habit. There was deep stillness inside the garishly furnished apartment, accented by Peter-Dick's deep breathing in the other bedroom, and Flider's offbeat, odd-sounding snores from the living-room couch. Blade was anxious to be up and on his way to Dauphine Street. With a grin he admitted a man couldn't loiter in an atmosphere like this without becoming totally addicted to it. He saw his clothing had been washed, clean, pressed, polished, and laid out for him during the night as his host had promised. His moneybelt lay undisturbed on the chair where he'd thrown it. He reached out, picked it up and secured it about his waist. One might mistrust strangers, but not his brothers. He grinned, thinking about Peter-Dick and his easy laughter, and the way Flider grinned, perfect audience for every move Peter-Dick made.

At nine, he heard them stirring. He got up then and dressed. The full-length mirror showed him a smartly tailored, impressive-looking young black man. He set his soft-brimmed hat at an angle on his head as he had seen Peter-Dick do last night.

He found Peter-Dick and Flider having cinnamon buns and steaming coffee at the breakfast table. They looked up, smiled, commenting on his sharp appearance.

"Hear them girls took care of you last night, put you right to sleep," Peter-Dick said with a smile.

Blade bit his underlip. "You mind?"

"Hell, no. Glad you was accommodated. It's all right, if you don't mind slave wenches."

"I never knowed no other kind," Blade said.

"We gonna change all that," Peter-Dick said. "Going to introduce you to a lady today worthy of you."

"I got to get me on to Dauphine Street."

"Sure. Sure. Plenty of time for that."

Blade drank his coffee. The buns were so light they almost melted in his mouth. "You really know how to live, Brother Peter-Dick," he said. "You do live like a king for a fact."

Peter-Dick smiled. "White folks got no idea what goes on down here in Congo Square . . . . If they did, they'd be down here."

"Amen," Flider said.

"White folks such fools, really," Peter-Dick said. "All they want is to have a good time. But they don't know how. They either tax or outlaw anything they truly enjoy. It's like they 'fraid to admit their honest needs."

After breakfast, Peter-Dick shed his bathrobe, enjoyed a bath with three new slave girls to lave him, then dressed in an orange suit, matching shoes, and green shirt. His large tie was blood red. His orange hat had a brilliant green parrot plume in its band. Flider dressed similarly. Then, Peter-Dick was restless, anxious to be out on the street.

They walked a few blocks on Rampart and turned into a narrow, walled lane.

At an inset doorway in a wall, Peter-Dick rang a bell. As they waited, Flider kept hopping from one foot to the other, in a frenzy of excitement, grinning up first at Peter-Dick and then at Blade.

The door was opened by a formally dressed black man. He stared coldly at Peter-Dick. Peter-Dick merely looked through the servant, "Tell Mam'selle Moseby that Peter-Dick Penury is calling," he ordered.

"*Mam'selle* never gits up before noon, boy. And she sees no guest 'fore two in the afternoon."

Peter-Dick stepped forward, putting the flat of his hand

hard into the starched dickey of the servant. "She'll see me. You go up there and tell her I here, or I'll do it."

The servant retreated. His face twisted, but he said, "If you *gentlemen* will wait in the parlor, I'll see if *Mam'-selle* can see you." He made something vile of the word gentlemen.

Peter-Dick grinned, Flider giggled. Peter-Dick jerked his head and Blade followed him in the wake of the mincing butler. They were shown into a shadowy, overstuffed living room, heavy with rococo furnishings. Blade and Flider sat down, but Peter-Dick wandered, restless, unable to sit still.

After what seemed an hour but may have been only half that, the butler returned and said that Mam'selle Moseby would see them now in her upstairs sitting room. They climbed the stairs, went along a carpeted corridor. The butler rapped on a closed door. The woman inside the room said, "Come. *Entrez-vous.*"

Blade hesitated just inside the doorway. For a moment, overwhelmed by the faint yet heady and almost intoxicating perfume, he believed the woman, seated on a chaise lounge, rimlighted by the sun through delicate draperies, was not real but an ideal of all women. She was a quadroon, almost white, but with the soft, smooth skin of her black forebears.

From her rich, luxuriant black hair, touched with red lights in the scrimmed sunlight, to her manicured toes, she was exquisite. Lying among the soft pillows, she was regal, even with that fragrant hair tousled and framing her alabaster face. In her sheer gown and even more transparent negligee, she was practically naked. Her arms and breasts were golden, tipped with rubies. Her full red lips, her grape-black eyes, slanted slightly beneath tilted brows, were set like rare jewels to ornament the classic lines of her features.

Blade stared at her slack-jawed, realizing that both Peter-Dick and Flider were watching his reaction rather than looking at the lovely young woman—she was somewhere between seventeen and twenty-seven. She was a woman to whom age was not going to play any part for at least a quarter of a century. By then, all her other talents would be so developed that when she died no one would have realized she was not still as lovely as at this moment.

He felt his face grow hot, realizing that she was studying him with interest. Something passed between them —something that was like static in the air before a storm, something Blade had no words for. Her eyes undressed him, appraised him—the wide shoulders, muscular chest, flat belly, narrow hips and long legs. She liked what she saw and drew the crimson tip of her tongue across her full lips in a slow, licking motion that disturbed and aroused Blade as total nakedness in another woman might not have done.

"You should have sent word you were calling, Peter-Dick, you bad boy," Mam'selle Moseby chided him without taking her gaze from the natural bulge destroying the symmetry of Blade's trousers at the crotch.

"No time. This all happened so suddenly. I knew you'd want to see him."

"He is nice." She nodded, licking her lips again. "By far the nicest you've brought to me so far. I'm quite pleased, and I forgive you for this ungodly hour."

Peter-Dick said, "Mam'selle Moseby is one of my dearest friends, Brother Blade. I owe her—well, almost as much as I owe you. An old debt. Perhaps I can dispose of it today by presenting you to her."

"You owe me nothing, Peter-Dick," Mam'selle Moseby said with a crooked smile. "After today, our accounts are cleared."

Peter-Dick laughed. "I knew you'd say that, the moment I laid eyes on him."

"Would you leave us alone—for a little while?" Mam'selle clapped her lovely, long-fingered hands. The butler moved closer, bowed. "You will serve M'sieu' Penury and M'sieu' Flider my best wine—in the sun-room."

Peter-Dick clapped Blade on the shoulder and walked out with Flider and the butler. Blade heard the door closed.

Alone, Mam'selle Moseby did not take her eyes from him. Her gaze devoured him. She took her time, calmly appraising the perfection of his old-coin profile, the depth of his chest, and always returning to the rising bulge at his fly. She smiled faintly. "Would you undress for me—Blade? Is that your name? Poor Peter-Dick, he will never learn the amenities."

"Undress?"

"Please."

He hesitated, but when his own gaze moved over the dark triangle ill-concealed at her thighs, the fullness of her ruby-tipped breasts, he saw that he could be no less accommodating than she. She went on reclining on the lounge, but the tempo of her breathing increased as he tossed his jacket behind him, loosed his tie, and unbuttoned the frilled front of his shirt.

He laid his shirt over a chair back, unbuttoned his underclothing. Then he stepped out of his trousers. When he removed his boots and took off his trousers, the girl sat up slightly on the lounge, her face growing warm.

He removed his underclothing and stood naked on the soft carpeting before her. He recalled all the times he had been required to shuck down for slave breeders visiting old Master Baynard at Blackoaks. He had never enjoyed showing off his body to those men. He enjoyed it here.

For a long time the girl on the divan said nothing. She let her eyes feast on the golden brown of his body, the corded musculature, the high-standing member at his thighs. His legs were like perfectly carved pillars. She felt herself responding, growing hotly liquid inside, aroused as she had not believed she could ever be stirred again.

"You are a beautiful man, Blade."

He nodded. "You're beautiful, too."

"Come here." She sat up straight and extended her arm. He walked close to the chaise longue. She closed her long, delicate fingers like talons upon him. She breathed between parted lips now. "I want to taste you," she said.

"Ma'm?"

He drew a deep breath, held it. She milked back the foreskin, revealing the plum-colored glans. Smiling faintly, she drew it to her lips and slipped it between her teeth. She nursed at it, and he ached exquisitely in his prostate.

She appeared to remain coolly aloof. She drew away for a moment, then suddenly abandoned herself to over-powering desires. She thrust herself forward upon him. Her teeth raked him.

He trembled visibly, his whole body quivering.

Whimpering unintelligibly, she clutched his hips in her hands and shook him furiously. "Oh, God," he whispered. "Oh, my God."

She held him fiercely for a long time. Then she sighed and lay back, allowing him to withdraw.

She sagged back among the pillows, gazing up at him sleepily, warmly. Her negligee parted, her breasts and *mons veneris* stood in sharp relief against the delicate fabric of her gown. "Do you want me to do it?" he asked.

She shook her head. "Not now. Despite what you may think, I went as wild as you—wilder. My orgasm was as real as yours even though you didn't touch me down there. I've been hungry for a man like you all my life."

The backs of his knees felt weak, but she let him go on standing there while she gazed at him lingeringly and told him briefly about herself. She was the mistress of a white man, the chairman of the board of the largest bank-ing corporation in the state. Politically and financially he was powerful. In the bedroom, he was something less than adequate at sixty-five. He had arranged for a lifetime income of fifty thousand a year, even when he died. Often, she was afraid he would die when he became so excited in her bed where his ejaculations were always premature and always left him exhausted, with herself in a state of frenzy.

"I need you," she said. "Did Peter-Dick suggest any— arrangement?"

"He didn't even tell me about you. But I reckon no-body could."

"Would you like to be my man? My total man, I mean. I would be yours whenever you wished, except for those brief stupid times when my lover was in my bed. If I had you, I would not care what he did and what he failed to do."

"I'm sorry—"

"Wait. I know a strong young man like you wouldn't want to be a pampered kitten. I will set you up in any business you wish. I will buy you clothes which will make those fine suits you now wear look like rags. I will give you everything—everything—"

"I'm sorry."

"How can you refuse such a totally unselfish proposition, giving you everything I have, asking nothing except your loving arms, your body, your kindness."

His eyes bleak, his face muscles rigid, Blade shook his head again. "I am sorry." Mother of Mary, she would never know how sorry . . . .

"You turned her down?" Peter-Dick strode along beside him in the sunlight. He was stunned, shaken, and incredulous. Flider could only shake his head and kick at the banquette. "How in hell could you turn her down?"

"I told you. My lady. On Dauphine Street—"

"Oh, shit! You're through with that stuff. That life is behind you. You're going to stay here in Congo Square where a black man can live like a king. You go back there and tell Mam'selle—"

"No. You got to help me find Dauphine Street, or I has to find it alone."

Peter-Dick laughed at him. "I can't do that to you, Brother. You go back to that plantation, you go back to slavery. Man, you walking free right now. Don't that feel good? And you don't know what life is ahead of you here—"

"God knows, I can see how it might be. And I know it would be even better. But I is what I is, Brother Peter-Dick. I can't turn my back—I couldn't live with myself, even down here—"

"Oh, hell," Peter-Dick was laughing when a man yelled hoarsely behind them.

"Stop. This is the law. Stop."

Peter-Dick jerked his head around. He saw Achilles Clayton, gun in hand, running toward him. "Son of a bitch," Peter-Dick said. "What's that bastard doing in the Square looking for me?"

"Stop. This is the law. Stop."

"Up anchor," was all Peter-Dick said. On each side of the dwarf, they caught Flider's little hands in theirs, lifted him from the walk and ran.

Behind them, a gun exploded. Peter-Dick cursed. "That son of a bitch. He gonna kill somebody. Can't kill me—I hexed against him."

"Peter-Dick." The words struggled up through Blade's strangled throat. He was aware that little Flider had sagged, dead weight. When he looked down, he saw the bullet hole in Flider's cranium, the blood spurting from it. "It's Flider. He's shot Flider."

Sobbing suddenly, Peter-Dick swung the little man up in his arms. He ran, slowed, with Achilles yelling at them to halt. Flider was dead, part of his skull blown away, his eyes staring, sightless.

Blade caught Peter-Dick's arm. Peter-Dick was crying openly, tears streaking down his face, his nose running, his mouth swollen. Blade led them into a narrow alley. He grabbed Flider's body from Peter-Dick's arms and carried it as they raced along the alley toward the splash of sunlight at the end.

They heard Achilles Clayton's shout as he ran into the alley. They came out into the sunlight. A barn door was opened diagonally across the cobbled lane. Blade ran into it and Peter-Dick followed him.

Blade placed the small body against a stack of hay. He heard chickens clucking, he saw the ropes, lines, and gear of animal handling, but the barn was empty. Peter-Dick knelt beside the dead Flider, crying helplessly.

"He dead, Peter-Dick," Blade said. "I sorry. But he dead. That man gonna git us, we ain't smart."

"The bastard," Peter-Dick looked up. "I know why he's after us, Brother. Why he came into the Square. He's looking for you. You humbled him in front of people. When you could of killed him, you cut his belt and his pants opened. People laughed at him. He wants to kill you."

"I waitin'."

"No. You ain't waitin'." Peter-Dick stopped crying and wiped his sleeve across his running nose. "No. I got to git you out of the Square. And you got to stay out. Don't never come back—or that man kill you. He evil."

6

"I'll kill the son of a bitch," Blade said.

"No you won't." Peter-Dick Penury shook his head vehemently. He wiped at his leaking nose again. "If it was that easy, you think we wouldn't have fed him to the 'gators long ago?"

They crouched in the deep shadows and watched Achilles run past in the sunlit lane. He carried his gun ready at his side. He checked every cranny and alley. In a moment, he would come back on their side of the street.

Blade said, "I know's how we can put him out of his meanness—jus' temporary. Jus' long enough for you and me to get out of this hen house . . . . But you got to be brave enough to show yo'self out there. Then you duck back in here—and you run all the way to that courtyard door—"

Peter-Dick stared doubtfully at the patio entranceway. "It bolted."

"That ain't no nevah-mind. You ain't goin' to have to run through it. You jus' run to it—less'n you rather not show yo'self in the lane?"

Peter-Dick laughed. "Hell, what I got to be scairt of? Achilles can't kill me. I hexed against him."

He drew a deep breath, caught Blade's hand tightly, gave him a cocky grin, and ran across to the barn door. Cautiously, he peered beyond it. He grinned and nodded. But Blade was already grabbing up a small line. He secured it between two uprights on a line between the lane entrance and the patio door. He measured the rope at the tip of his own nose and nodded, satisfied. The line was knotted so tautly that it almost twanged when he strummed it with his finger.

Peter-Dick had stepped outside the barn door. Blade could see his shadow through the doorway. Blade retreated to the darkness. He wasn't too concerned about Achilles's seeing him when the police officer ran into the barn—in that first moment the big man would be bat-blind.

Peter-Dick yelled. "I'm down here, you nigger son of a bitch!"

His voice rattled windows and set the chickens inside the barn to clucking. Blade heard the blast of Achilles's gun, and then Peter-Dick lunged through the doorway. "Bastard missed me," he whispered as he ran, well beneath the rope.

Blade pressed against the darkness of the plank walls, waiting. The flustered chickens clucked and flew nervously on their perches. At that moment, his gun up before him, Achilles ran into the barn. He said, "Where-at is you, you—" And then the rope caught him across the Adam's apple, almost decapitating him. He took two long steps forward and was hurled flat on his back.

As Peter-Dick and Blade moved past him, Achilles was writhing on the floor like an insect, gasping for breath, his eyes bulging. He had dropped his gun. Peter-Dick took it up and smashed it against the upright.

Blade knelt down and took the little dead drawf's body in his arms. Peter-Dick said, "Thanks, Brother. We can leave Flider down at the bar on the corner. He'd like that."

When they came out of the bar, Peter-Dick said, "Now, where'd you say you left your coach and horses?"

"Stables called Apollon's."

Peter-Dick shook his head doubtfully. "Well, if the coach and horses is gone, we'll carve some cash, or somebody else's animals—of equal value, Brother—out of them."

"Amen," Blade said.

The same white man was in the same butt-sprung kitchen chair when Blade and Peter-Dick walked in. His face whitened under his freckles. He looked ready to cry.

"Oh, man, have I got bad news for you, sir," he said to Blade. "We had a robbery last night—"

"And his coach and horses was taken. Right?" Peter-Dick said.

The hostler nodded, but as the two black men stepped closer, one on each side of him, he weakened slightly. "Now. We did all we could. We think the police might recover—"

Peter-Dick laughed. "The police might recover, but I don't think you gonna recover, Mr. 'Pollon."

"Now, wait a minute. What kind of talk is this "

"I figure you gonna sound funny, talking high—like them men sopranos down at the Cathedral," Peter-Dick said. "My friend didn't tell you. But I sent word when he come here. Them horses was valuable. I tole him to tell you. If you lost 'em, we ain't gonna try to collect. We jus' gonna cut your balls out."

"Now, hold it. Goddamn it, just hold it."

"You lost our horses and coach, mister, we didn't. Right, Brother?"

"Amen," Blade said. He took out his pig-nutting knife. It glittered even in the cavernous density of the huge barn.

"I yell for help, they put you black boys away for life," Apollon said.

"You should of yelled last night, Mr. Apollon," Peter-Dick said. "Even if you yell now, you too late to save your balls. We cut fast, and we cut deep. Amen, Brother?"

"Amen."

Peter-Dick moved with that ballet-dancer litheness. Before the hostler could set himself, Peter-Dick had leaped behind him, pinned his arms, and scissored his own arm across the hostler's windpipe. "Go ahead, Brother, cut him."

"Wait a minute. Before God, wait." The hostler gasped for breath. "Maybe they ain't stole. Some things was stole last night. But maybe—maybe they got changed around."

Peter-Dick said, "Sounds reasonable. You mind waitin' a couple minutes 'fore you cut out his nuts?"

Blade nodded.

Peter-Dick continued to hold the man's arms pinned

behind him, his grip tight on the man's throat, allowing him just enough air to remain conscious. "Show us."

"Let me go."

"We ain't making a lot of talk with you, Mister," Peter-Dick said. "You crave to show us? Or you want us to cut —and then you show us? It don't matter to us—they your balls you're playin' with."

"I'll show you. Maybe the stalls in back. We'll look back there."

"Sure we will."

They led the two Blackoaks carriage horses out from the rear of the barn. From a barred door built to look like a closed wall, they allowed Apollon to pull the coach. "Now hitch 'em up, Mister Apollon," Peter-Dick said.

Cursing, his rage making his face a deathly white mask, his eyes murderous, Apollon backed the animals into the shafts, hitched them to the carriage. "Now, you git out of here, you black bastards," he said.

Peter-Dick said, "Man, I sorry you take that tone. I was feelin' almost friendly toward you. Now, I see you got to learn not to try this again—on nobody."

"You keep away from me. Goddamn you, keep away from me. You got your fuckin' property, now git out of here."

"Just want to kiss you goodbye, honey-man. Jus' want you to remember what can happen to dishonest white folks."

Apollon retreated. Peter-Dick let him take a couple of steps, allowed him to wheel around and grab for a pitchfork. Then he brought his coupled fists down on the back of Apollon's neck. The hostler crumpled forward as if kissing the rough planking of the barn wall. He slid slowly down it. Pitilessly, Peter-Dick caught him by the ankles, hoisted him up, and tied him to feed-bale lines, pulled him a couple feet from the flooring, and left him there. As he turned away, loose change fell from Apollon's pockets. Pleased, Peter-Dick turned back. He took all the money Apollon had, turning all his pockets inside out. They were surprised at the amount the hostler carried on him. "Hell, his business is almost as good as pimping," Peter-Dick said, swinging up into the carriage beside

Blade. Apollon was screaming for help as they rode out to the street.

Peter-Dick looked at the change and gold pieces mixed with paper money in his fists. "You want this money? Think you might need it 'fore you git home?"

"I don't want his filthy money."

"I don't either." Peter-Dick yelled at children playing in the streets as they rode past. He threw money into the street and laughing, watched the scramble. As they crossed Rampart onto Conti, the last of the money was gone and grabbed up.

They turned left on Dauphine Street. Blade was filled with a sense of exultance. He had made it. Somehow, God—in his great wisdom—had delayed him long enough for him to learn to deal with life. He'd had a lot to learn and he'd been lucky to meet the right two teachers—Peter-Dick Penury and little Flider.

"When we get to your place, Blade," Peter-Dick said, "you drive this carriage into the patio, and you bolt the outer gates. Then you put these horses in a stable inside the yard. You understand me?"

"You teach good, Brother, and I learns fast," Blade said.

"Amen, Brother . . . . Now, when I leaves you this time, Brother Blade, I won't see you no more—"

"I sorry 'bout that. Truly sorry."

"So am I. But I want you to know, you my brother. I love you. You my family. An' I love you. Ain't never had no family 'cept I had Flider and my girls. My father abandoned me 'fore I was born, and my ma followed him soon after. I never even got titty milk from my family . . . . I growed up on these streets. Right here in New Orleans. I slept in doorways, and I learned to steal, 'fore I could walk good. But long as I know I got a brother like you somewhere, I proud. Mighty proud."

Peter-Dick nodded toward a walled house. Blade slowed the horses, stopped them. There was an eerie pall of quiet over the street, broken only by the cannon from the esplanade. Peter-Dick leaped down, opened the *porte cochere* gates. Blade drove the wagon in, already looking for Miss Kathy on the veranda, at one of the windows.

The sight of her face, her golden hair, would repay him for all the evil he'd endured on the long journey here. But the house was as quiet as the street.

Peter-Dick helped him unhitch the horses and lead them into an unused stable. There was neither feed nor water for the animals. The silence was oppressive.

"Man, you sure this the place?" Peter-Dick said.

"Upstairs apartment," Blade said. Peter-Dick shrugged and followed Blade up the steps. Blade rapped sharply on the screen door. He waited, but there was no reply.

"It's unlocked," Peter-Dick said.

Blade opened the door and they stepped inside the veranda. It was cool in the apartment, but the stillness was deep, taut.

"We might as well look around," Peter-Dick said.

Blade nodded. They paused in the doorway of the bedroom. Miss Kathy lay sprawled face down in dried, caked vomit. Her face was flushed with fever, her hair damp, the bed soaked. "I send Dr. Sofrono," Peter-Dick said.

Blade thanked him. Peter-Dick touched his arm. "A white woman," he said. "A sick white woman. Man, you got trouble. Goodbye, Blade—and God help you, Brother."

7

In less than an hour, Blade had mopped up the vomit from the floor, changed the bed clothes, and removed the stinking, sodden gown from Miss Kathy's body. He stood a moment, looking at her nakedness. Her breasts were beautifully cupped, her nipples palely pink, the hairs at her *mons veneris* dainty and light. His eyes filled with tears. But he felt no sexual arousal. He remembered what an old black man had told him once, "It's great to want a woman's body, and to take it. But what's truly great in this life is for a woman to want you to have her body, and her give it to you." He found a fresh gown, worked it down over her head and arms, covered her body. Then he pulled the fresh sheet up over her. She opened her eyes, smiled bleakly, but he saw she didn't believe she truly saw him. She thought he was part of her latest fevered dream.

Blade prowled the apartment, awaiting Dr. Sofrono. He strode to the end of the veranda and stared down at the street. He saw no sign of the doctor. But he saw a man fall in the street, vomiting black fluid. He retreated, his nostrils distended, eyes wide. On the street, the ill man begged passersby for help. They looked at him, shaking their heads, hurrying past, running. Blade wanted to hate those people, but he understood their fear. It gripped him. He had seen the fever strike since he'd arrived in this town; the cannon boomed as a constant reminder of death. His was an ingrained and superstitious fear of disease—a heritage from the river of the past from which all of us dip. He shuddered and returned to the living room as if, hiding from sight of the plague, he might escape it.

He was not afraid of Miss Kathy. He went into the bedroom, bathed her face with cool water. She did not open her eyes but whimpered once and reached out her fevered, trembling hand. He took it, held it gently. How pale it looked against the darkness of his own skin. She cried out—something unintelligible to Blade—and sank deep into fevered sleep again.

He heard a rapping at the screened veranda door. He strode through the house. Dr. Sofrono stood there, carrying his bag. He said, "Hello, Blade. Peter-Dick asked me to come."

"Yes, thank you, Doctor."

The doctor stepped inside the screen door and no further. "She's got the yellow jack, eh?"

"I don't know. I guess so."

"Nothing I can do for yellow jack. Nothing anyone can do. I'm sorry."

"Then why did you come?"

"Don't hate me, son. It won't help any. I came because

Peter-Dick asked me. I do a lot of business because of Peter-Dick—and his girls. He asked me to come."

The doctor shook his head and turned to leave. "Wait a minute. You come. Can't you see her? Might be they's something you can do," Blade said.

"There's nothing, my boy. I'm sorry. Yellow jack is deathly contagious."

"You scairt? A doctor? You scairt?"

"Yes. I'm afraid. If you had sense enough to know how terrible yellow jack death is, you'd be afraid. All I can do is tell you to get out of here. There's nothing you can do for her."

"How you know, Doctor? You ain't seen her."

"I don't need to, my boy. I've seen them dying with yellow jack. By the thousands. Looking at one more won't help her, and it won't help me."

"Doctor. You go on down them stairs if you want to. But you hear me first. My lady is all that means anything on God's earth to me—if I got to die, tendin' her, from contagion, I as soon die for murder—tryin' to get her some help."

The doctor sighed and shrugged. "Where is she? I'll look at her. You can't say I didn't look at her."

"Thank you, Doctor."

Almost as if holding his breath, the round-shouldered little medic entered the bedroom where Kathy lay in a delirious state between nightmare and consciousness. The doctor pulled down her eyelids, studied her pupils. He straightened and shook his head. "I can give you some laudanum, Blade. Won't help—but will ease her until—"

"Laudanum? You give little Flider laudanum when he broke a rib. Is you some laudanum doctor?"

"Don't bad-mouth laudanum, my boy. It makes death easier, and that's no small matter . . . . And I'm far more contemptuous of myself—and desolated—that there is nothing I can do for—your lady."

"All right, Doctor. I takes the laudanum."

Blade walked with the doctor to the door at the head of the stairs leading down to the patio. The doctor said, "There's nothing you can do, my boy. You're not affected yet. My advice to you is get out of town. You can't help her. You can only forfeit your own life."

Blade nodded.

When the tired little medic was gone, Blade shook himself as if to rid himself of fear, superstition, despair. He walked slowly back to the bedroom. He pulled a chair close beside the bed and stared at Miss Kathy. His eyes brimmed with tears. He had come so far, and he had been too late. Maybe if he had not met Peter-Dick and Flider, had not delayed at the swank apartment of Mam'selle Moseby, or wasted the long hours in the house of the conjure woman . . . .

Suddenly he stood up, knocking over the chair. The conjure woman. Ruhmar! She had hexed Peter-Dick against violent death. Why couldn't she hex Miss Kathy against the terror of death by plague?

He found a workshirt hanging on a hook in a closet. He unbuttoned his own fancy laced shirt and tossed it over a chair. He put on the old blue shirt and rolled the cuffs back almost to his elbows. He stood one long moment gazing down at Miss Kathy. Then he left the house, almost running. At a bazaar he bought a wide-brimmed straw hat and pulled it down upon his head. If Achilles Clayton were looking for an elegantly tailored man, Blade might be able to get to Peter-Dick's apartment.

Running toward Conti Street, which was the only way he knew to get back in the area of Congo Square, he crossed St. Peter. That street led directly into the Square. He turned back and ran along St. Peter.

At the building where Peter-Dick had his garish apartment, Blade looked both ways and then let himself into the patio. The three slave girls who had serviced him were working in the courtyard. They looked up at him, giggling, and lowering their gazes.

"Got to see Mr. Peter-Dick," he told them.

One of the girls shook her head. "He ain't up there, honey. He ain't nevah here 'cept late at night when they ain't nowhere else to go."

Desolated, Blade looked around helplessly. A sure way to get himself killed was to stalk the Square looking for Peter-Dick. And yet every moment counted. A girl said,

"You want to wait upstairs, maybe I could find him
. . . . I know some of the places he goes in the daytime."

"Please," Blade said. If only he knew where Ruhmar
lived, he could go directly to her. But if he did—without
Peter-Dick as intermediary—would she help him? He
couldn't take that chance, any more than he could wander
the alleyways looking for her door in this vast town—with
Achilles Clayton on his trail.

He climbed the stairs. He heard the girls tittering and
whispering at the foot of the steps. He recognized the
invitation. He had only to turn and smile, and they would
follow him up to the bedroom. But he did not turn. He did
not smile. He was too deeply worried, too torn up inside.
He could not arouse images of naked bodies writhing to
please him. He could see only the deathly pale mask of
Miss Kathy lying alone in that apartment on Dauphine
Street.

He sagged into a wicker chair on the veranda. He heard
the distant cannon, the girls talking as they worked in the
courtyard below. Time passed with maddening slowness.
It seemed hours when he saw Peter-Dick stride into the
patio below and come bounding up the steps. Peter-Dick's
face contorted with the rages roiling inside him. "Goddamn. What you doin' here? You beggin' to git kilt?"

"I need your help, Brother. I never come otherwise.
But I need you. My lady need you."

"Nothing I can do for her. Nothing the doctors can do."

"You can git Ruhmar for me."

Peter-Dick stared at him, mouth twisted. "You gone
loco? You think I ast that conjure woman to go into a
room where a white woman has yellow jack? You think
I'd even ast her?"

"You could ast her. I won't never ask nothing else of
you." Blade's eyes were brimmed with tears. His lips
quivered.

"Oh, shit," Peter-Dick said. "All right. I'll go see
Ruhmar. I'll ast her. But what about you? If you gits
killed—what good you goin' be to your white lady then?"

"Please, Peter-Dick. Get her. Please. I know how you
loved little Flider . . . . Please. That's the way I loves
my lady. I can't no-way live unless I do all I can for her."

"Sure. And let her take you back to some fuckin' plantation where you'll be a black slave again. Jesus. You one stupid country boy." He stared at Blade, raging, and then he managed a faint smile. "I'll try to git Ruhmar. You wait inside my place. Inside. Don't you let nobody but me in. Not even one of them hot-assed little slave girls. That damn Achilles got ways of forcing women to do what he wants—or they in trouble. You waits quiet."

. . . Another incredibly interminable hour. Standing at the balcony window, Blade heard a closed hack clop along the street. He saw it turn through the carriage entrance into the patio below. He ran across the room and out on the porch. He saw Peter-Dick swing down from the hack. Peter-Dick stared up at the apartment. When he saw Blade, he signaled, summoning him to the patio. Blade ran . . . .

It was breathless and hot inside the closed hack. Ruhmar sat rigid and silent between Peter-Dick and Blade. He saw she had her mesh bag filled with her paraphernalia, including a live lizard.

"I met yore friend Achilles three times today already. He can't talk yet. But I could tell he was looking for you. We had a funeral for Flider. Achilles followed us all the way to the river," Peter-Dick said.

"The river?"

"We weighted Flider's body and throwed it in the river. He never liked a lot of fuss about nothing. We had some music."

The hack stopped. Peter-Dick pinked a curtain. "We here," he said. "I opens the gate." He swung out of the hack and opened the gate, and the carriage pulled into the courtyard. Peter-Dick bolted the entrance gate. He returned to the hack as Blade helped Ruhmar alight. "I wait down here," Peter-Dick told her. She nodded.

Blade followed Ruhmar up the steps. She stopped in the living room and said to him, "You got to follow me, boy?"

Blade nodded. "I got to."

She shrugged. "So be it." She entered the bedroom and hesitated, staring at the girl on the bed. Blade saw the horse-featured face of the woman grow taut. This was the only sign of her inner fears. She walked to the bed and knelt beside it. From her mesh bag, she drew a small mirror. She wiped it on her checked skirt and placed it close against Kathy's lips. She removed it, found moisture. She nodded. "She still breathing. But scarcely. I don't know, boy. But we try. Build a fire."

Blade went into the kitchen, put wood and kindling in the iron stove, struck a match. The fire faltered, and he sweated, waiting for it to catch. When the weak blue flame rose, guttering orange around the turpentine-moist pine slivers, he returned to the bedroom. Ruhmar was kneeling beside the bed, talking in strange singsong words. "God in Zanbesia—God in Zanbesia—Zombi in hell—Zombi in hell, hear my prayer."

Ruhmar's muted chanting seemed to continue interminably. Trembling, Blade stood watching her. There was a beauty and radiance about her he had first seen as she prayed in her own room for Peter-Dick's safety. That glow had returned. She prayed to God in heaven and to satan in hell. She was a healer of ills; she was a caster of spells, a diviner, a maker of hexes, a lifter of evil spirits— all of which returned to healing of ills, spiritual, mental, physical, moral, internal and external, in this world and out of it.

Ruhmar turned her face upward—her ugly, beautiful, radiant face. "Help me cleanse the liver of this girl, oh mighty Zombi. Take back your evil from her, Zombi. I ask you, Zombi. Cleanse her liver. Man's liver cannot refuse what poisons it, cannot reject and force back in vomit what violates it as the stomach can . . . . The liver can accept and clean itself . . . . The liver accepts —and cleanses—or it dies . . . . Oh, mighty God of the good, looking down from Zanbesia . . . . please leave this child to those who love her . . . . Take her to Bamboulaland when she has lived out her days of love on this earth . . . . Help me, God in Zanbesia. Help me, Zombi."

At last, when Blade was completely sweated down, Ruhmar rose from her knees. She seemed remote, removed from this time and place. She walked toward him, her eyes flat, looking through him, or turned in upon herself. "Come. We prepare the potion."

He followed her into the kitchen. She moved in that odd, unworldly manner, as if she were walking in her sleep. From her mesh bag she took the cleaned shell of a turtle and placed it on the cupboard counter. She told him to put the largest pot in the kitchen on the stove and to place in it a quart of water to boil. He did as she directed, watching every move she made. Her first move shocked him. She caught the lizard running inside her mesh bag, placed it in the turtle shell and smashed it with a pestle. As she worked, she chanted in a low tone.

He realized with a sense of shock that she was not praying. She was asking for guidance. She was reaching out to the supernatural for direction in preparing this brew. She talked for a long time. She would listen for what appeared an eternity to Blade, then she would nod and mix herbs, roots, goofer dust—gathered from the grave of some root doctor—snake venom, powder pounded from the swollen and dried liver of a bloated lizard, fruit from the castor plant. By the time she had stirred this potion in the turtle shell and called down the blessings of the god of the night—the evil Zombi—upon it, the water in the pot had boiled down to little more than vapor.

She did not appear to notice. She poured her mixture into the heated pot, wiping out the last drop of it with the palm of her hand. Then she placed her hand in the liquid to cleanse it. Blade watched the fluid bubble around her black fingers. She did not wince and seemed unaware of heat or pain.

She glanced at him. "We must let this boil and simmer to thickness, so it almost congeals. She must drink it while it steams hot. Hot. It must burn its way past the fever, past the stomach . . . ."

Blade nodded, completely mystified, terrorized, and confused. The conjure woman kept stoking the fire. The iron plates on the stove top glowed red. At last, with her bare hands, the woman took up the pot by its handles and poured the thickened residue again into the turtle shell. She took down a teacup from a cabinet shelf. Carrying both and talking in a mumbling whisper, she returned to the bedroom.

She placed the turtle shell on the table. It steamed and stunk—an odor that turned Blade's stomach. He bit back the bile that rose in his throat.

She hesitated, glanced at Blade standing nervous, fidgeting at the foot of the bed. She turned back the cover on the unconscious girl and lifted her gown above her breasts. "Part her legs," she ordered. "You will sit there. You will thrust the third finger of your right hand as deeply into her vagina as you can. You will keep it there until I tell you to move."

Blade nodded. He sat on the end of the mattress. He parted her legs and pushed his finger between her fevered labia. Ruhmar had not lied, Miss Kathy was burning with a raging fever.

Now, Ruhmar poured the teacup full of the steaming liquid. It was blistering hot. Ruhmar placed her fingers hard over Kathy's closed eyelids and spoke softly, flatly for some moments. Then she jerked her hand away. She sat on the edge of the mattress, lifted Kathy's head in her arms. Cradling her, she placed the cup of foul-smelling fluid to Kathy's lips. Obediently, as if obeying a will outside her own, and fantastically more powerful than her own, Kathy drank the potion. Blade stared, unbelieving. Kathy's pallid cheeks gave no sign that the mixture was almost boiling hot.

Ruhmar waited, but Kathy did not retch or vomit back the fluid. The conjure woman exhaled heavily. Then she laid Kathy's head back on the pillow. "You can stop that now," Ruhmar said to Blade. He jerked his finger away.

Ruhmar replaced Kathy's gown, covered her first with the sheet and then with every blanket she could find in the place. She sent Blade for the largest washtub he could find. When he brought it, she placed it beside the bed. "She going to vomit—soon. Vomit like she never vomit and pass black fluid like she never did. I done what I can. I can't do no more. It is up to Zombi now. If he take her, so be it."

Ruhmar knelt one last time beside the bed. She placed a long-fingered hand gently on Kathy's flushed, fevered forehead. She intoned in that muted voice, "Let this child waken, cleansed of evil, cleansed of the filth and vile of plague. Let her live. Let her go forth from this place—in faith, in watchfulness, or in lust. In faith she finds her way in time to Bamboulaland. In watchfulness, she finds peace on earth—to the time of atonement. Only in lust does one fall into oblivion . . . . Protect her . . . . "

Ruhmar stood up then, all business. She took up her turtle shell, her mesh bag. She said, "I reckon you wonder why I had you hold her like that?"

"Yes, ma'm?"

"To give you something to do. To occupy your mind. To keep you from fretting and disturbing me—and driving away Zombi when we needed him so bad. You got nuthin' to do now but wait. Wait and keep her clean . . . . You gonna have plenty to do." She smiled and touched his face. "You a good boy. A purty boy. I done what I could for you . . . .That be ten dollars."

Blade nodded eagerly and gave her a golden eagle. "You a real purty boy," she told him. "Even us conjure women got to eat."

He followed her to the closed hack. Peter-Dick was sweated. He had smoked a half-dozen cigars. He shook hands with Blade. He did not smile, but he said, "God watch you, Brother."

Blade clung to Peter-Dick's hand a moment. There was much he wanted to say. But there were no words. Then they were gone. He closed the entrance gates and went back up the steps. When he reached the bedroom, he almost passed out—the bed was covered with black fluid and the foul odor was sickening . . . .

It lasted two days. Blade mopped and washed, wiped, cleaned, and immediately it was all to be done again. He boiled bed clothes and gowns; he washed and hung linen out to dry. He bathed Kathy with cool well water, and the cloth grew hot in his hand from her fevered flesh. She rolled and tossed all night, crying out in delirium. But she did not die; she grew stronger. He slept, if at all, for only a few minutes at a time. He grinned—sometimes he slept walking down the steps and while he hung clothes on the line in the patio. He lost track of days and nights—

there was only a continuous nightmare of time. Miss Kathy was in hell, and he was beside her every moment . . . .

One morning—or perhaps the sun blazed at midnight, he could not say since everything was turned upside down in his fatigued mind—he walked into the bedroom carrying an armful of fresh sheets, gowns, pillow cases. He wore the workshirt, opened to the belt, and he had slipped into a tight-fitting pair of old trousers he'd found in the closet. He wore no shoes—Styles's carefully molded facade of the handsome young black, the man of color, was eroded. He looked like a slave. He was with Miss Kathy. He was working for her. He was exhausted, but he was content.

Kathy's eyes were opened. She looked wan. She gazed at him and smiled weakly. "Oh, Blade, is it really you?"

"It really me, Miss Kathy."

"I thought I dreamed you."

"No. It's me, Miss Kathy. It's Blade. I here now. I come for you."

She wept suddenly, helplessly. "Oh, thank God . . . . Take me home, Blade. Please . . . take me home to Blackoaks."

8

Kathy slept. Overwhelmed with fatigue, Blade walked drunkenly out of her bedroom.

He staggered and sank to his knees in the shadowed living room. Before his eyes he could see the anguished figure of the crucifixion in Miss Claire's chapel. All mixed in with the agony of the statue was Ruhmar's beautiful horse-face. He tried to pray. All he could say was, "Zombi. Zombi. Zombi."

Then he sank forward on his face. From half around the world he heard the faint, muffled boom of cannon. It was a welcomed and soothing sound. He tried to push up to his knees. Miss Kathy would awaken, she would need him. He toppled forward helplessly and was asleep before his face struck the rough fabric of the carpeting.

It was two days before Kathy was ready to travel. Sometimes, like a fevered child, she cried and begged Blade to take her home. He agreed, but he delayed. She was debilitated, far from well. He tried to feed her—grits, fish, boiled shrimp, and creole gumbo from the nearest restaurant. But she never ate more than a few bites, a few sips. She looked as if she might throw it all up, and Blade took the food away.

With the worn-looking Kathy watching him, he carefully packed her clothing in a steamer trunk so that, pleased, she laughed and said, "You're better than a maid, Blade. You're faster. You're neater. You never complain—yes, and you're prettier."

He nodded, not looking at her because he knew she would see the terrible desires in his face inflamed by her voice, her words, her gentle beauty. "Yes'm, Miss Kathy."

He asked what she wished done with the clothing in the other closet. "Throw it away," she said. "Burn it." She bit her lip and her eyes filled with tears. "Take any of it you want, Blade. Some things should fit you—good enough to work in. Leave the rest."

He found a few garments he wanted and he placed them in the carpetbag Styles had given him. He lashed the steamer trunk to the rear of the coach and threw his own bag under the front seat. Then he lifted the kick-panels and set them in place between the padded seats of the coach, making a bed. He brought down pillows—all he could find in the apartment, sheets and blankets. He made up the tonneau of the coach as a bed for Miss Kathy. Satisfied that everything was ready, he brought the horses from the stables, backed them into the shafts, and hitched them into harness.

In the trough inside the stables, he washed himself as thoroughly as possible. Then he went up the steps, with only a towel tucked about his waist. In the living room, he donned fresh underwear, a new lace-front shirt with frilled cuffs, and one of the suits Styles had had tailored for him. He felt a flare of warmth toward Styles. He had been kind! He did love him—as a loyal slave loved his master. He despised enslavement, he had tasted freedom briefly, he was torn inside, but he loved Kathy and Styles above all other people on earth.

He pulled on another pair of polished boots, gleaming so they caught all the light in the dimly lit room. He splashed cologne on then—another gift from Styles!—and set his wide-brimmed planter's hat at the jaunty angle he'd learned from Peter-Dick. Then he walked into the bedroom. He was pleased and excited at the way Miss Kathy's eyes widened and her lips parted. She stared at him incredulously. "Blade, is that really you?"

He nodded, smiling, pleased and happy.

"Oh, how handsome. You're the best-looking man I ever saw, Blade. Truly you are."

To cover his embarrassment and discomfiture, he said, "I ready to carry you down to the coach now."

"Oh, Blade! Are we going now? Are we really going home?"

He nodded, but he could not share her exultant anticipation. His heart seemed to slip and his belly was empty in a way that food could never satisfy.

He bent down and slipped his arms under her legs and around her back. He was shocked at how light she was. "You gonna have to start eatin' biscuits, hamback, and grits," he told her.

She laughed, laying her head against his broad shoulders, as secure as she would have been in Ferrell's arms. "I'll get fat and sassy again—as soon as we're home at Blackoaks."

His hand closed just at the upward cup of her left breast. He felt as if he'd stuck his fingers into fire. She said nothing, and he did not move his hand. He wanted to sob in despair. She was not aware of his hand cupping her breast. She was not aware of him—except as a slave.

Why was he doing this? Why was he going back to a place where he and all the other black people were like the animals? Lower than the animals. Beasts of the field.

She closed her eyes as he carried her through the apartment and down the stairway. She did not look back at the place where she'd been happiest and saddest and at the lowest ebb of her life. She had been happy here with Hunt. She would have been content with him forever. She was glad to escape it.

Blade walked in silence, despairing. He laid her down in the tonneau of the coach. She caught his dark-brown hand, squeezing it. "It's so perfect, Blade. You're so thoughtful."

"Yes," he said. He sighed. "You want anything, you reach through the front window and poke me."

He closed the door and swung up into the driver's seat. He turned the animals slowly and went out the entranceway to the street. Dauphine Street looked desolated in the morning. He drove slowly, seeing the dead-carts piled high with new corpses, seeing the people fleeing from the plague and those victims of it who had fallen and were not yet dead, but were shunned by the people who walked wide around them, in terror.

He pulled the coach into the slowly moving traffic headed east and north. He crossed a bridge, and glanced back toward the stricken city. It seemed an eternity, rather than a matter of days, since he had crossed this bridge on his way to find Miss Kathy. He was leaving the town, a different person—older, wiser to the wicked-ness and cruelty of the world, and filled with a sadness that would not lift. Distantly, behind him, a cannon boomed a last, faint farewell. Blade laid the whip across the rumps of the horses, moving them out.

Lying down in the tonneau of the carriage, Kathy heard the sounds of unseen people, wagons, carts. She could hear disembodied voices, the clop of horses' shoes on cobbles. She stared at Blade's broad back, his wide shoulders, his tilted hat. She smiled, secure, and she slept.

Sometime in the afternoon, Blade pulled in under the shade of a magnificent magnolia. Kathy wakened. He brought a tray of food from a tavern. He opened the door and sat on the edge of the seat eating bread and barbecued spareribs. She did not want to eat. The thought of food nauseated her, but Blade said, "Eat some-thing. You gone sicken again if you don't eat something."

She smiled and ate because he asked her to. She could not disregard his thoughtfulness. She ate the fresh bread, chewing it a long time before she dared to swallow it. The coffee was good and she drank it all. The chicken and dumplings were excellently prepared. She ate more of them than she thought she would. She smiled at Blade again. "You were right. I feel better."

He nodded and shook out her robe for her, placed her slippers on her feet. Tying the robe about her waist she went out to the privvy behind the tavern. When she returned, Blade was leaning against the side of the coach. He helped her back inside and closed the door.

"Where will we spend the night?" she said.

He shrugged. "We find a place. I find something nice for you."

She laughed. "Oh, I'm sure you will. You spoil me, Blade."

"Yes'm," he said. "Yes'm. I want to, Missy."

She sank back on the pillows as the coach pulled back onto the deep-rutted road. She knew they would be welcome in many of the estates between New Orleans and Biloxi and on the road north from Mobile, once they came into Alabama. Her father had been well known in the state, well liked, and for a little while she had reigned as a "belle" of the balls in Montgomery. Such a long time ago! She did not suggest to Blade that they enter any of the gates at the plantations they passed. She felt ugly—thin, sallow, and unwholesome with the effects of her illness. And there was her loss of Hunt. She was weak and she found it easier to cry than to laugh. She could not have made the effort required to be good company, act the vivacious belle as she'd be remembered in most of those old homes. The inns, taverns, and ordinaries they would find along the way were poor and rough, but she could sleep. In her debilitated state, sleep came easily when she could blot Hunt from her mind. At an inn, she would not have to make conversation or be pleasant, or attempt any of the other social graces, which she would have found impossible and intolerable in her present convalescence.

The first night en route they spent at a large and drafty old ordinary near the Louisiana-Mississippi line. Perhaps once there had been grace and gentility about the place, but it was now unpainted, barely swept, seldom dusted, shabby, and threadbare. The rustic owner of the inn was overcome by Miss Kathy's obvious social status and her gentle blonde loveliness. He was awed by the splendor of her coach, puzzled by the extraordinary good looks and tailored quality of her servant. The innkeeper bowed to Kathy, sent slatterns to clean and polish her room. Then he set a table for her in his dining room. He spread a fine linen cloth with only one cigar burn in it and silverware that once had graced elegant tables in a better world.

After dinner, Blade came in from the kitchen where he had been served. She tried to walk up the steep steps to her second-floor room. She was too weak and faltered. He swung her up in his arms and carried her easily. The innkeeper stood, slack-jawed at the foot of the steps, watching.

Blade laid her gently across the bed, turned to leave. He was shocked to find her eyes brimmed with tears. "Why you cryin', Miss Kathy?"

"You," she said. "You, Blade. What would I have done without you? What would have become of me? . . . And only you . . . . I cannot believe such a big man can be so tender, so gentle."

He nodded, letting his little bow of acknowledgement thank her. Then he went out the door, closing it behind him. For a long time he stood immobile, staring at his trembling hands.

9

Kathy awoke the next morning sometime after sunup. She felt better, refreshed. She had slept well, despite some stinging bites that she feared were bedbugs. She bathed as fully as possible with a washcloth at the earthenware basin to be sure she removed any lingering mites she might have picked up from the thick old mattress.

She sent for Blade, had him bring the steamer trunk up to her room. She chose a light and flowered dress. It was far from ideal for travel, but it would be cool in the oppressive heat. She went down to breakfast. The innkeeper bowed her to a table with a fresh linen tablecloth and a single magnolia bloom in a vase. She thanked him. "Your man, Blade, ast me to put the flower there, ma'm."

She thanked Blade when she went out to the courtyard where he was lashing her steamer trunk to the rear of the coach. He nodded but said nothing. He would have helped her into the carriage, but she said she wanted to sit with him for a while. "I'm tired being an invalid," she said. "I'm sick of feeling sorry for myself."

He made her as comfortable as possible in the front seat. The innkeeper and his help came out and stood squinting in the sun to wave goodbye.

The road was open and lonely for most of the morning. The summer sun blazed pitilessly. The farms they passed were mostly poverty-ridden subsistence tracts. There was little difference between the shacks whether whites lived in them or freed blacks. Occasionally, they would meet a lone man riding a mule or driving a cart loaded with watermelons, tobacco, or corn. These people, white or black, pulled aside for the grand coach and touched their hats, nodding them past. A lovely girl escorted in a splendid coach by a well-dressed young black servant was as near aristocracy as existed in the South in those years. No one neglected to pay passing homage.

Blade was aware of nothing outside the overhung front of the coach. Kathy's nearness was like a charge that raced through him and burned everything else from his consciousness. He watched her as much as he could without being caught staring at her. There was something heartbreakingly fragile about her beauty—it broke his heart. He looked at her, and he felt as he had when they were children together, that she was a golden doll that would break if you touched her.

He wanted nothing more than to touch her, to caress her, the soft tendrils at the nape of her neck, the cupped breasts, the long and shapely legs. In the back of his mind, Styles's overheated voice prodded him. 'She has always wanted you. She would love for you to take her —if no one ever knew. She was thrilled at the sight and size of your cock one day when she saw you naked. She wants you. She has always wanted you.' The thoughts whipped back and forth across his mind. His head ached, and he gripped the reins until his knuckles grayed to guarantee he did not reach for her.

No one rejected his lifetime of training, not even in gut-tightening passion. She was his lady. But he was a slave. A black slave. He had Kenric's word that she secretly longed for him, but she had given him no sign. And God knew he had waited dry-eyed for that sign, any sign. There had been none. He ached, but he knew he had to wait for her to make the first move. She would make that first move if she wanted him, and somehow he must hold his passions in leash, he must wait. Rape never entered his mind because rape has nothing to do with desire or love. Rape is the perverted need of a sick mind to maim, hurt, debase, or kill. He wanted her love. He wanted her lips lifted to him, her thighs open to him. Somehow, he must wait.

He glanced at her fragile profile, feeling exalted by this gentle beauty so close to him. Her faint cologne attacked his nostrils, inebriated him.

Deep in his heated brain, he heard Styles's voice, muted, fevered: She had watched him swim naked. Concealed, she had stared at his long cock, at his balls, at his wide shoulders and pillarlike legs. She had grown hot with desire. She had never after been able to get him out of her mind.

From the corner of his eye, Blade saw that her face was fevered, that she had pressed her wisp of kerchief against her lips. "You all right, Missy?"

She nodded. After a moment, she spoke haltingly. "Blade . . . may I ask you something?"

"Anything, Missy." His heart battered erratically against his ribs.

She hesitated even longer this time. She spoke at last to the trees on her side of the carriage. "Did you have any help—when I was most ill—vomiting, spoiling the bed . . . when my gown and the bed had to be changed a dozen times a day?"

"Two dozen," he said, trying to put her at ease.

"You did it all yourself. You washed me. You . . . ." Her voice trailed off.

"There wasn't nobody else, Missy." He turned and looked at her, hoping her eyes would meet his. But she kept her head averted. Her face was flushed.

Somehow, he told himself, they had reached one of the moments Kenric had suggested would come, here on this empty road. He could hear Kenric's voice prodding him —"she talked constantly of you—she saw you naked— she wished for you—if only no one would know" . . . .

He had pulled the coach in before Stubbs's Tavern about seven that night before he recalled this infamous site from his trip out. As the horses slowed, Eakins Stubbs himself was bounding out of his tavern, wiping his hands on his soiled apron, and shaking his head, motioning Blade on past.

Then Eakins Stubbs saw Miss Kathy and he lowered his arm. He said, "Oh, I figgered you was alone ag'in, nigger."

Kathy said, "I won't permit you to talk to my boy like that, sir. He represents me. When you are disrespectful and evil to him, you dishonor me."

Blade felt his face flush. The last thing on earth he wanted to hear Miss Kathy call him was "my boy." Though she spoke protectively, his stomach roiled. She might have been saying, "You kicked my dog. I won't permit you to kick my dog."

His jaw tightened, a muscle working in it. He had been a man until now. Suddenly she had castrated him. He was a beast of the field. He was her slave.

Eakins Stubbs bobbed his head, bowed, and gave Miss Kathy his widest, falsest smile. "I do apologize, ma'm. No slight to you intended. No, suh . . . . It just that we been havin' trouble with freed niggers. They come through here on their way to New Orleans, or out of there—and they act like they human. They want to come right in my place like a white man. I won't have it. I won't have no blacks runnin' my white trade away. It ain't that I got anythin' against a nigger—long as he stays in his place. But I can't have them driving my trade away. No, suh. Not with times as hard as they are."

Miss Kathy humbled the innkeeper with a chilled glance. She said, "You may help me down, Blade."

Blade swung down and went around the rear of the coach. Carefully, he avoided looking at Stubbs. It was not setting well with the white man to have been humiliated and put in his place with a black as witness. Blade reached up and touched Miss Kathy's elbow lightly. She set her dainty foot on the step and came to the ground as a butterfly might, with grace and beauty.

Stubbs backed toward the entrance of the inn, bowing ahead of Kathy. Blade followed at her shoulder. As Blade crossed the threshold in Kathy's wake, the innkeeper hesitated, almost ordered him out. Something in Kathy's manner stopped him, and he permitted Blade to stand behind Kathy's chair.

The room was large; it might once have been three rooms. It was dominated by a fieldstone fireplace as huge as the north wall, with a mantel stacked with ornaments, mementoes, hunting knives, and aged guns. Along the rear wall a mahogany bar had been set. Behind it were rows of liquor and wine bottles and a frosty mirror which provided no reflection except to the brightest light. There were many rude pine tables with straight chairs placed around them. More than a dozen men drank beer, at the bar, at the tables. They fell silent, gazing at Miss Kathy, grinning secretively and nudging the man nearest them.

Blade felt the emptiness spread in the pit of his belly. He wished they had not stopped here. He had no idea how far ahead was the next hotel, but even if they'd not found one before midnight, he would have preferred it. He touched the knife sheathed on his belt to reassure himself. These rednecks had never seen anything as lovely as Miss Kathy. They were liquored up. They were bored with the ugly routine of their rustic and illiterate lives.

"I want your best room," Kathy told Eakins Stubbs, remembering the bug bites she had endured last night.

"Yes, ma'm, I got a fine room at the front, upstairs.

All quality folks what stop here like that room. They tell me how they like it. Comfortable. A good cross ventilation. I think you'll like it."

"I hope you sleep well, pretty Missy," one of the customers said. He was a man of medium height in black shirt and black pants, black boots. His balding head was a mass of curls. They grew over his ears and spilled over his collar. He laughed loudly. "You git scairt—or anything—you jus' call out. An' I'll shore come a-running. I'll even run a-coming!" He threw back his head and slapped his table, choking with laughter.

"Now, Gribbs, you take it easy," Eakins Stubbs said. "This here is a quality lady. Can't you see that?"

Gribbs leaned forward on the edge of his chair, peering at Kathy as if looking for something he'd never seen. "I bet she goes to the privy just like us ordinary folks. How about that, honey?"

Kathy ignored him. She spoke directly to Stubbs. "I'll go to my room now. If you can guarantee my safety."

"Oh, honey, I'll guarantee you'll be safe. You a quality lady? Hell, I'm a quality man. Me and you ought to get together." Gribbs yelled.

Kathy stood up. She said, coldly, "I'll have my dinner served in my room."

"Yes, ma'm. We'll sure have it sent up to you. And I do hope you won't take offense at Gribbs. He don't mean no harm."

"You let Gribbs talk for hisself," Gribbs said. He stood up. "Honey, you don't want to go through Biloxi without seein' the main sight of ole Mississippi—Farris Gribbs! Best when seen up close."

Kathy's face was chilled. The men in the room roared with laughter, nudging each other. "You will serve food for my man up in my room also," she said.

"Can't serve niggers indoors, ma'm," Eakins Stubbs protested. "Can't have 'em eatin' off my good plates."

"Don't black people prepare the food and serve it?" Kathy demanded. Her head tilted. Her eyes showed her rage. "Don't *they* touch those plates?"

"Ain't the same thing, ma'm. Ain't the same thing at

all," Eakins Stubbs said. "We'll feed your boy—out in the stables where he can sleep."

She stared straight at Stubbs. "Blade is going to sleep in my room," she said coldly and loudly so that she could be heard by the farthest drinker at the bar. Eakins opened his mouth to protest, but her glare silenced him effectively. "You'll bring a pallet and have it placed at the foot of my bed," she ordered.

"Yes'm. Your boy can sleep up there. If that's the way you'll have it."

"It's the only way I'll stay in this place." Kathy's face was taut.

"We'll fix the pallet, but we can't feed him."

Kathy started to speak, but rage made her hesitate. Blade said quickly, "It's all right, Miss Kathy. I ain't hungry."

She looked at Stubbs, moved her gaze to Blade, and then raked her eyes savagely across the faces of the white backwoodsmen. None had ever owned a slave. But each knew a white woman could have a black man sleep on the floor inside her room or just outside its door. It was the same as having a dog in the room, for protection.

The Negress who had serviced Blade on his first stop at Stubbs's Tavern brought the huge tray of food and hot tea. Blade watched her, ready to speak, but she acted as if she had never seen him. She set the tray on a table, removed the napkin, and then retreated. Kathy had just seated herself at the table when there was another knock. Blade, standing beside the window, gestured to her to remain seated. He walked across the room and opened the door. It was Eakins Stubbs carrying a palliasse. He threw the narrow mattress filled with straw at the foot of the bed. Kathy thanked him. Blade said, "I'll see to the horses."

He followed Stubbs into the narrow corridor and showily locked the door to Miss Kathy's room. He dropped the key into his jacket pocket. Stubbs stared at him, but Blade kept his own gaze lowered. He followed Stubbs quietly down the stairs. Stubbs mumbled to himself, but loud enough for Blade to hear. "Get nigger stink in that room. Take me a week to git it out. Dollar's

347

worth of scouring soap an' you'll still be able to smell the nigger."

Blade went out to the coach. He hefted the trunk on his shoulder. It was extremely heavy, but he walked through the barroom and up the stairs carrying it casually.

He placed the trunk in Miss Kathy's room. She held out a chicken drumstick to him. Smiling, he ate it hungrily, wiped his hands on a napkin and dropped the bone on an empty plate. "There's plenty for you," she said. "I could never eat all this."

Blade smiled, remembering Trumpet and her hot mouth, her wildly flailing hips. "I think I've got friends in the kitchen," he said.

He went out again, locking the door behind him. He led the horses out to the stable. He took his time watering, feeding, and rubbing them down. When he returned to the bedroom, Kathy had undressed, put on a gown, and gone to her bed. She had thrown a blanket over the flat palliasse at the foot of her bed.

Darkness pressed in at the windows of the big room. From below, they could hear the boisterous laughter, the shouts, and, infrequently, the rage and cursing of the men in the bar.

Kathy turned down the lamp. The room was plunged into darkness. Blade sat on a padded wing chair and removed his boots. He folded his trousers and placed them with his hat and jacket on a straight chair. He removed his shirt and undershirt. Wearing only the tight-fitting underpants, he lay down on the palliasse.

Kathy said, "Good night, Blade."

"Good night, Missy."

They were silent. After a while, men rode away from the tavern on horseback, shouting in the darkness. It grew quieter downstairs. The blackness in the large bedroom dissipated into a deep gray.

10

Blade sweated. He was in hell. The slave mind was conditioned to accept unquestioningly what could not be changed. A black slave could not look at his white mistress—this could not be changed. Master Styles had altered all that in his thinking and had left him in a fevered state of flux. Now, he had fallen back into that old world of enslaved sequacity, compliant acceptance of his fate. But his body remained wild with passionate need in a dark world in which he lay indurated by inner heat, only inches from her bed.

Kathy whispered, "Blade, are you all right?"

He managed to control his breathing, to keep his voice calm. "Yes'm. I'm all right."

"I heard you moving around."

"I'm all right." He writhed in physical agony on the straw pallet.

She was quiet for a long time; time passed slowly, like the intervening seconds in a Chinese water torture. Suddenly, Blade heard her muffled sob. She had been crying for a long time, trying to keep him from hearing. He got up from the pallet. He walked to the side of her bed, as aware of the bulge of his engorged penis against the fabric of his underpants as of her uncontrollable grief. "Missy Kathy," he whispered. "Are you all right?"

She burst into tears, crying openly. "Oh, Blade, I'm not all right. I'll never be all right again."

He sat on the side of the thick mattress beside her. He leaned against the carved headboard, feeling the sharp curls and raised lines chew into his bare back. He did not feel it except as a minor irritant. He was aware of nothing except her golden body, like a shadowed wraith on the bed beside him. "It's all right, Missy. Blade's here. Blade's here."

She sobbed aloud. He half lifted her and enclosed her

in his arm. She pressed her face into the soft flesh at the top of his shoulder. Her tears splashed on his bare chest; her moist hot breath burned his neck. He held her gently. He wondered if she noticed the tumid ridge bulging his underpants at the fly. He knew she did not. Kathy was lost inside her own grief.

Her body was heated, almost as when she'd had fever in that apartment on Dauphine Street. She no longer had any but the lingering aftereffects of the yellow jack— her ills now came from her heartbreak. She was depressed, shattered in spirit. But this didn't mean her illness was any less severe than the disease of her body. She shuddered, crying and clinging to Blade, feeling alone, forsaken, abandoned. She had given her love with all her mind and soul, and she had been rejected. She saw no life ahead for herself.

"Oh, Blade, what's to become of me? I'm going back home—to 'what? To Styles? Oh, Blade, the thought strangles me . . . . I lie here unable to stand the thought of returning to him—and yet I've nowhere else to go . . . . He's not a man, Blade . . . not as you are. Not as other men are . . . . He doesn't want me—he doesn't want any woman . . . . Maybe you can't even understand that—"

"It happens, Missy, even to black men—"

"—you've never wanted anyone with all your heart, and then found they consider you less than dirt! That's the way Styles treated me. He didn't want me. He hated having to sleep with me, he was repulsed when he had to touch me . . . . The only way he could enjoy—having me—was to hurt me . . . . If he could hurt me, he could get some pleasure. Do you even understand that, Blade?"

"I understand, Missy."

She pressed closer, the heated outline of her body etched itself upon his body. His hand had slipped beneath her upper arm in the fevered heat from her breasts, her armpits, her soft bicep. The room spun in the darkness. He tried to hear what she was saying above the pounding blood in his temples.

"You can't know," she wept. "I was in hell, Blade . . . . I found Styles—with a young boy. A young naked black boy . . . . I finally understood what Styles wanted, what he had to have to respond, to come alive, to feel passion. A young boy! And I hadn't even known there were men like that. And I was married to one. . . . I went into hell, Blade . . . and I lived in hell until I ran away from him . . . . I don't know what he told you—"

Through Blade's mind raced some of the rousing things Styles had told him—"she watched you swim naked, she went wild with desire; she wants you—if only no one would ever know." She had lain in her bed with Styles and she had told him how deeply she wanted Blade—if only no one ever knew. He said nothing.

"—but that's why I ran away from him. I had to leave him, or go insane," Kathy was saying, crying. He pressed her closer, and whether he intended to or not his hand closed on her breast. "I thought Hunt loved me. I believed it. He acted as if he did. He told me he did. I thought I would be happy. I had failed once, but at last I thought I would spend the rest of my life with a man I could love—with a man who would love me . . . . Poor Hunt. He was so afraid—inside. He was afraid of everything. He lived in terror of the moment when Styles found us. All he could think was that Styles would kill him . . . . He got so—he couldn't love me, either. He ran away. He abandoned me. I lived—depressed—all I could think was should I pull all my hair out, stand screaming until I was put away somewhere—or commit suicide and end it all, quickly."

His hand closed on the lovely globe of her breast. He tried to be gentle, but passion burned through him and all sensation in his body was concentrated, centered in the palm of his hand against the sheer fabric of her gown, the full soft rise of her breast. He trembled, and Kathy stopped talking, aware that he was caressing her breast, but also that she had raised her own thigh so that her *mons veneris* rested, pressed against his hip. She caught her breath, tried to draw away, but Blade could not let her go. With his free hand, he cupped the cheek of her behind, holding her against him.

For the first time she saw the huge rise in his underpants. As she stared, the glans pressed through the fly like a fist and his penis sprang upward. For some seconds she stared at the size and quivering rigidity of it. Terror flashed through her, but she could never feel terror because of Blade. She tried to keep her voice level, she tried to keep her fascinated gaze from his high-standing rod. "Please, Blade, you better go back to your mat now."

"Missy, I can't. You know I can't."

She struggled, but she was helpless even in his gentle embrace.

Blade drew her hand down upon that cartilaginous rigidity. He closed her fingers on it, clasped them there. She felt him pulsing, trembling, and quivering. She held it longer than she meant to—she didn't mean to hold it at all! Her mind ordered her hand to jerk itself away immediately, but she let him move her hand along its hardness and heat.

She drew her hand away, but Blade had released her some moments before. He slipped his hand under her gown, caressing her dainty pelvic eminence. She writhed, trying to stop him. A thought erupted through her mind: he'd done this to her before, he'd done this many times before. She had to stop him. She had to let him know he could never do it again. He had to be put back in his place. He was a slave. He was black. She was white.

"Don't, Blade." Her hand gripped his wrist. "Please. We can't." His fingers moved between her thighs to her clitoris and whirled in circles against the marblelike erection he found there. Her head rolled back and forth on his shoulder. "We can't . . . . we can't."

"I got to, Missy . . . . Can't you tell I got to?"

"Blade." She raised her head from the heat and unnerving hardness of his chest. She spoke more calmly. "It's my fault. I lay in your arms. I let you hold me. . . . I was stupid . . . but I wasn't thinking, Blade. I was so alone . . . . You were kind. That was all I saw . . . all I knew."

"And you—you're all I see, Missy, all I know." He whispered against her ear. His hand spun swifter and she felt sick with shame when her whole body responded, quivering at his touch.

"All right! I led you on, Blade." She trembled. How could she deny her emotions when her hot liquidity flowed around his fingers and she was powerless to stop his caressing her? "Oh God—we can't do this . . . . If I were to give myself to you, I'd be ruined . . . . I could never hold my head up again." She sobbed helplessly and tears streaked hot along her cheeks, stabbing him.

"It's gone past *can't*, Missy . . . far past can't . . . . I want you so terrible. More than anything in the world . . . . All these days—all them long nights—holding you. Taking care of you. Looking at you . . . . I wanted nuthin' else."

Kathy nodded, trying to writhe away from his hand on her breasts, his fingers working at her thighs. "I—felt your touch, Blade . . . even when I was only partly conscious . . . . At first—I thought I was—dreaming. But then—I knew . . . oh, Blade, I knew . . . . But you don't understand . . . . That doesn't change who I am, who you are . . . you and I . . . . We can't ever do this . . . . Please see that."

Now his eyes too filled with tears. His voice sounded odd, fragmented. "Nobody ever know, Missy."

"I'll know . . . ."

If he could have stopped, this would have stopped him. In this moment, he knew finally that everything Styles Kenric had told him about Miss Kathy was lies. He had suspected before, but now it was brilliantly, heartbreakingly clear. The myth. White mistress yearning for her handsome black buck. Lies—as far as Miss Kathy was concerned.

She reached down, caught his hand, stopped him. She was breathing as raggedly as he. "Please, Blade. I love you too much to fight you—to scream out. Not love— like this—you and I like this—but as I've always loved you . . . . Can't you understand? I love you too dearly to cause you to be killed—or hurt . . . . If I cry out, they'll kill you, Blade."

"Please don't cry out, Missy . . . not now . . . . You wants it . . . God knows, I can tell . . . . I a stupid nigger . . . but I can tell."

"All right! I'm insane with need! Is that what you

want to hear? You're a beautiful boy—a handsome man—beautiful. ... You're bigger—down there— than anyone I ever knew ... This room ... this darkness ... my loneliness .... Oh, God, Blade, everything's against me .... You *must* be strong .... *You* must help me .... We cannot .... We must not."

He kissed her swollen lips gently. She felt his firm mouth upon hers. For a moment she shuddered in that instilled reaction of shocked revulsion. A Negro kissed her, in passion, on the lips. How often she'd heard the sensational, incredible whispers about white women and their black bucks! She had not believed those stories any more than she could believe what was happening to her now. Blade lived in one world and she in another.

She pressed her head upward, returning his kiss passionately. Her mouth parted. She struggled but then sank in unwilling surrender against the mattress. She felt her full breasts crushed under the corded muscles of his chest. She shivered in fear, in horror—in a savage and overwhelming flare of desire. She wanted to repel him, but she was betrayed by her own emotions.

In agony she saw the ruin that faced her tomorrow—and in all the days ahead. But in a strange, giddy mindlessness, she saw she didn't live for tomorrow—nobody did. She could live only in this moment, this present, in which she lay helpless to resist, prone beneath him, driven wild by the strength and heat and hardness of his body.

His muscled legs pressed her own legs open. His hands slid her fragile gown up under her armpits. He came closer. He thrust himself into her. If his mouth had not been clamped over hers, his tongue deeply thrust into her mouth, she would have screamed—not in terror but ecstasy.

His hugeness filled her, probing deep into her where she'd never been touched. She felt herself quiver, and as he worked, she responded again and again, unable to control herself, no longer wanting to. She felt exalted. Blade drove out all memory of Styles's flaccid failures, Hunt's weaknesses. Blade made her whole. She locked her ankles about him.

Kathy clung to him fiercely. She whispered breathlessly against his mouth. "Oh, Blade . . . I've—never . . . really done—done it before . . . never . . . never . . . never." Her voice rose with her passions and her body shuddered in sensual gratification.

Exhausted, she sank deeper into the mattress, transported by his loving her, her insides stroked, caressed, and inflamed. When she could resist no longer, she thrust her hips unward against him in abandon. He clutched her tighter with uncontrolled savagery. His very fury drove her beyond reason.

They sagged upon the bed in physical collapse. He lay heavily upon her. He rested upon the support of her inner thighs. She smiled, thinking for the first time how clever nature had been to mold a woman to hold her man like this, his weight agreeable, his nearness exquisitely unbearable. He did not withdraw from her and she lay under him, breathing in exhausted gasps.

She whispered against the soft texture of his throat. "Blade . . . what is to become of me? . . . I've learned —what loving is—been driven wild—for the first time . . . by a—black man—by a slave . . . . Oh God, Blade, what have we done?"

"We'se loved, Miss Kathy. Loved."

"We've broken every law. We've ruined our lives . . . yours as much as mine."

"We loved—like God meant it, Miss Kathy . . . that's all."

"We've got to live among people—who know what we did was—wrong."

"Listen to me, Miss Kathy." His voice was as gentle as her memory of his hands in all those days and nights he tended her through her illness. "Pleasurin' is what God gives two people who truly need each other . . . . Pleasurin' is what God gives people when they *right*—one for the other . . . . Pleasurin' don't know color of skin . . . or money in the bank . . . or laws. Pleasurin' is God-given right and natural between a man and a woman . . . . Wasn't never *evil,* till *man* said it was evil . . . . God meant pesterin' to be *good* . . . ."

As he talked, he grew rigid inside her again. Kathy felt

her own hot and viscid fluids flowing. She wanted to laugh in delight and exultance.

In that moment she could not care about tomorrow. She was mindless. She did not deceive herself. Her agony was ahead of her. But for this present, need burned fear from her mind. She lashed her body upward, wanting with all her heart to thrill Blade as he exalted her, to give ultimately of herself as she was transported in her delight.

She found herself become enslaved, his slave, as he got his own emotions more under control. He drove her out of her mind, purposely. He thrust slowly, increasing the speed until she rolled her head back and forth on her sweated pillow, helpless, mindless, enraptured. Then he would move slowly again, leaving her in midpassage, making her fight for him, driving herself frantically against him.

He brought them to a peak of pleasure, but lost control. He chewed at his mouth, gasping. He battered at her and clung to her. He covered her mouth with his and thrust his tongue deep into her throat. She gasped and sagged, supine, beyond the ability to respond any more, exhausted.

He lay still beside her. She reached over and caressed his face, his ears, his hair, his neck and shoulders. He sank unwillingly into deep sleep, giddy with need for sleep. His ankles ached, the backs of his knees felt stringy, pain flared jaggedly across the small of his back, and his eyes burned. He kissed her lightly, mumbled something unintelligible, and sagged face down into the pillow.

Kathy turned from him, and he did not know whether she slept or not. He came awake abruptly when he heard her crying. He lifted his head, found she'd buried her face in the thick pillow to muffle her sobs.

Anguished, Blade forgot his own fatigue. He'd never felt so sorry for anyone in his life. Gently, he kissed the soft tendrils that grew wispily at the nape of her neck. He felt a tremor wrack her body. "Did you hate it that much?" he whispered. "Was it that terrible, Missy?"

"Oh, Blade, don't say that. Don't ever blame yourself . . . . You were so wonderful, so wonderful."

She turned slowly toward him. She tried to smile through

her crying. Her eyes were as red as her nose and her lips were damp and swollen from her sobbing. A final sob shook her and then she put her arms about him and pulled his head down to her warmly fragrant breasts. "You are my first love, Blade . . . my only true love . . . . "

He lay for a moment in the valley between the bruised mounds of her peach-hued breasts. He stayed there until he couldn't breathe any more, listening to the ragged thunder of her heart. He raised his head and suckled her nipples. Her body quivered and her hips vibrated, almost involuntarily.

He felt himself grow erect again. Excitement erupted through him and he held her tightly to him. She shuddered, trembling, but dug her nails into his back.

"You drive me wild," she whispered.

He thrust himself to her. She gasped and bit her lip. She responded in frantic abandon. Her desires were in violent conflict with her mind, but reason had no chance. Blade felt himself lifted out of his own body, unable to control the wildness erupting through him. It poured out of him, all the secret, hidden, and repressed dreams, the years of need, the weeks of agony, the moment's ecstasy. He did not know what terror lay beyond this night, but for this moment she belonged to him . . . as God must have meant it in the beginning.

This time Blade was unable to fight off exhausted sleep. It was as if he were stunned. He never remembered when his head struck the pillow and he slept throughout the rest of the night as if drugged. He sprawled face down, his forehead and one arm dangling helplessly over the side of the mattress. He was overwhelmed by the wild and fantastic moments locked against Kathy and beaten into unconsciousness by the cataclysmic forces of release and the quiet peace that followed in the wake of their fierce and lovely passion. He smiled, thinking he and Kathy had something together neither of them would ever find with any other person. He was sated. He was complete. For this moment he was content. He sank deep into the warmth of mindless sleep . . . .

11

Kathy lay on the bed beside Blade. She was as exhausted as he, but she could not sleep. She turned her head and through her tears stared at his wide shoulders, the lean hips, the long legs—the incredibly lovely body—of a black man. A slave.

For someone else, what had happened might have existed in this night and been put aside in the bright light of tomorrow morning. But it went deeper than that with Kathy—as Blade had gone deeper into her than she had ever supposed any man could drive himself. It could have been easy—it should have been. What had Blade said in his natural wisdom? God made fucking beautiful. Man named it ugly and evil. What else had Blade said? Nobody will ever know. She would know . . . .

From birth she'd been taught, as she'd tried once an eternity ago to tell Hunt. A girl like her married one man, kept herself only unto him. Some people could take love or sex where they found it and forget it, and put it behind them. God, how she envied such people. But she could never be one of them.

The stifling stillness of the rural night pressed in upon her; the darkness was like a soft coverlet that nevertheless suffocated her. But in the darkness she was for the moment content.

She looked forward with dread to the dawn. What possible good could come to her with the glaring brilliance of daylight? With the end of this night came the end of her first true happiness—she had found what she had once foolishly believed as a young girl that all men and women found together as lovers. Dawn would begin a new existence, that terrible unknown life to which she was now condemned: a white woman, enslaved and driven beyond reason by desire for a black slave. An impossible situation—to contemplate any existence at all beyond day-break.

She looked at the wide shoulders of the young sleeping giant. No man—of any color or condition of life—had ever been gentler, better, more loving, more concerned about her enjoyment and satisfaction in their lovemaking. He was man enough to control himself, to assure her fulfillment. He wanted, more than his own gratification, her full pleasure. For the first time she had been loved by a man who wanted to share the ecstasy possible to them and not to grab for himself what satisfaction he could. She had never been loved as she had this night. But this was not good in the world they would walk into together after daybreak—everything she'd been taught from birth, everything she had lived by for twenty-two years had been violated.

Her eyes brimmed with helpless tears. If only there were some answer, some way out for them. But she knew better. There was no way for them to be happy—in the same world. They would not be tolerated in the South; they would not be accepted in the North. There was nowhere for them to go together.

They had to part or there was nothing but heartbreak ahead for them. It was easy to say they would stay away from each other—but what about when desire overwhelmed reason?

She had to look ahead honestly to those hot mornings or steamy afternoons when she would see Blade, tall, slender, a bronzed young god, and memory of this night flooded through her. What power on earth could keep her from running to his arms?

They could not run away together—except into final heartbreak. There was nowhere to go. Hurt awaited them in Haiti, Jamaica—the black man and his white woman, belonging to neither world and despised by both.

There was nothing but harassment and horror for them in the world she knew. White men would kill Blade, but they would not permit him to go on loving her. And it was as impossible for her to go into his world with him.

There was no place on earth for them together.

She bit her lip. Could she return to Blackoaks, the

young mistress, hiding her secret love? She knew better. There was no way to meet Blade secretly, and if there were, she could not because the inner conflict would soon destroy her. Perhaps she could deceive her family and the people who came to Blackoaks. But if she kept her fearful secret, she lived in intolerable guilt. If the truth about her and Blade became known, she would be scorned, villified, despised. She would be an outcast among her own people. Those good, church-going, upstanding people who at this moment did not care if a woman named Kathy Kenric and a Fulani slave named Blade lived or died, would force them apart, or they would kill Blade as a matter of white honor.

She had to restrain herself to keep from reaching out to touch the heated, corded muscles of Blade's shoulders. Because of him, his gentleness, power, and understanding, she had known one night of sublime happiness.

Eyes blinded with tears, she stared upward into the darkness. Perhaps this single moment of happiness was more than most dull, frightened little people knew in seventy years of existence. Everyone else, everything else, had been driven from her mind as Blade loved her. This was their happiness. The only place that happiness could exist would be in their memory of it.

It could not exist in the world they lived in. If she went home, she honestly admitted she could not stay away from him, though she would try. There had been the long pattern of her life, and she would try to adhere to it. But the heat of her memory would burn away everything except her need for Blade, his love for her.

This merely exposed them to agony—she would get him killed, herself despised among her own people.

She swallowed hard through her aching throat. She could not go on pretending Blade was nothing more to her than another of the slaves at Blackoaks. And in the same thought, she knew she could not live admitting ahead of time that she would be running to his arms, begging for his love, hiding with him, planning secret rendezvous, lying . . . .

She had never been created to live like that. She could not live. That was the final answer. She could not live with

Blade, the world would not let her. She could not live without him. She would not want to.

She wanted only to die—in this moment—while her memory of their exultant happiness filled her, before what she and Blade had had together was soiled and made vile by the evil minds of the people they would meet when dawn came.

She got stealthfully from the bed, careful the mattress did not rustle, that the bedropes did not squeal. Holding her breath, she tiptoed across to the small table against the wall. She found a match, struck it, and watched its flame rise yellow and orange and blue and cerise. She lit a candle. Then she sat down, taking up a pencil and sheets of paper from among her things.

She wrote two notes. The first was to Styles. It was brief:

Styles,
When you read this, I will be dead. Poor Blade wants to bring me home to you. I have chosen to go to hell instead. I found life unbearably unhappy, though happiness was all I ever wanted. I once could have been happy with you, Styles, if you would have let me, if you had wanted me. I could have spent my life with Hunt—if he had wanted me enough. But my last words to you on this earth are these: I found ecstasy only with your Negro slave.

K.

Her note to Blade was a single line. She wrote,

Blade,
This is all I can give you to prove to you that you are the only true lover in my heart. Please forgive me.

K.

She worked her wedding ring off her third finger, left hand, and dropped it into an envelope with the note to Blade. Then she addressed it, "Blade." She put it into the jacket of his suit.

Returning to the desk, she sealed her note to Styles in another envelope. She wrote "Styles" across its face and sealed it with wax from the candle. She placed the letter on top of her clothing in her steamer trunk, knowing that it would be delivered to Styles and that someone would have to go through it.

She found Blade's trousers across the back of the chair. She took up the wide leather belt, found the sheath and the thick handle of his knife. She closed her fingers over its rough texture—and somehow remembered the way Blade had drawn her clasped hand up and down the rigidity of his own staff.

12

Blade awakened with the first pink flush of false dawn through the wide casement window. He awoke smiling and turned on the bed, thinking they could have each other one last time before they went back to the coach to begin the rest of the journey home. He did not care how long it took them to reach Blackoaks. He did not care if they spent the rest of their lives in that coach, moving forward, stopping for the night, stopping all day in some secluded glen, going nowhere, going everywhere—together.

He saw his knife at once. His gaze leaped to focus on her hands clasping the knife between her breasts. She had driven it to the hilt. She was dead.

He sat staring at the ceramic glaze of her face, the soft tendrils about her forehead, the fullness of her sweet and gentle lips. His mind was numbed. He could not even cry aloud, though inwardly he raged mindlessly, wandering lost in the deepest jungles of eternity without her, screaming out the magnitude of his loss, his fearful hatred of this world and its people and all its gods.

He stayed crouched there over her. The room grew lighter. Sounds of movement rose from the stables, the barnyard, the kitchen, from adjoining rooms as people, animals, and fowls stirred to wakefulness in the early morning—as life went on.

Life went on . . . with this thought came the first dim realization of his own immediate danger. This flashed at once through his mind, but he could not care—not yet.

He stared with horror and despair and loss at the beautiful body dead beside him on their bed. She was like a lovely golden statue—too beautiful to be real. She lay desecrated and destroyed—dead, by his knife, driven upward into her heart. Aiee! He hated himself with a savage, unspeakable loathing that enveloped everything he had ever done, everything he had ever touched.

Tears welled at last in his eyes and ran unchecked down his rigid cheeks. For a long time he cried helplessly, like a child. This was the end, Blade felt. His life ended at the moment it had truly just begun. He had saved her from the plague in New Orleans, but he had slain her himself by forcing himself into her, by demanding to possess her body.

Aiee! God, how would he live without her? He had found—for one brief moment in time—an ecstasy, a fulfillment, a reason for standing against all the cruelties of this existence, and then he had lost it and with it any hope or faith or reason for going on living.

He crouched there thinking only one thing—his own death. Kathy was dead and he did not want to live without her. He had killed her—he had done something to her she could not accept and live. He had caused her death. How could he go on living knowing this? He pressed the back of his right fist hard against his mouth to stifle the sound of his sobbing, the animal cry of distress.

"I'm sorry," he whispered. "I'm sorry."

She was like a waxen figure, and it was too late. His words could never reach her, never change anything, never relieve the agony that had caused her to kill herself.

But staring at her, he found a faint reason for living, for staying alive. Looking at her fragile loveliness, he knew the truth. For whatever motive, Styles Kenric had lied to him—maybe for no better reason than Kenric's perverted hatred of her womanhood. The truth was that Kathy had never, in all the years she was married to Kenric, looked Blade's way, except as a warmly regarded part of the family—a slave, but loved. She had never spoken to Kenric of him in passion.

He saw the full truth only at last. He had been used as a tool of vengeance by Kenric. Kathy had hated her husband, deserted him for another man, and he had to repay her in the most vicious way his filthy, perverted mind could invent—send a Negro to mount her, to force himself upon the fragile and gentle girl.

His throat aching so terribly he could barely swallow, he saw that he had one last chore to perform for Kathy. He had to stay alive. He had to return to Blackoaks. He had to kill Styles Kenric for the evil they had done to her. He had to repay Kenric before he himself could die.

"God help me," he whispered. "Please God help me."

Realizing he had to stay alive, now brought fully into his consciousness how difficult—how impossible—that might be. Kathy had committed suicide. But she had used his knife. He had spent the night locked in her room with her. Who was going to believe a young girl like Miss Kathy had killed herself when they had a Negro to charge, to convict, to execute for the crime?

He had had a white woman's body. A coroner's inquest might prove conclusively enough for his white superiors that her vagina had been penetrated, that she'd had sexual intercourse—in a locked room with a black man. Even if she had killed herself after such rape, he was guilty of her murder in any white man's eyes.

He sweated. He had covered Miss Kathy, mounted, penetrated, and *known* her in a land where for a Negro as much as to touch a white woman's hand, even accidentally, could be an automatic death warrant.

In his mind he could see them coming up the steps, entering the room. He was as good as dead. He could see himself, neck broken by the hangrope noose, swinging limply from a tree, his body riddled with bullets. Except for the terrible flood of old fears that made him want to vomit, he could not care. What could those white men do to hurt him now? Miss Kathy was dead. His own beautiful, golden, gentle, and laughing Miss Kathy was dead. He could not care about anything else—not even what happened to him. It didn't matter any more. . . . but staying alive long enough to get his hands on

Styles Kenric's throat, this did matter. To get out of this room, to get on the trail, to cover the long miles between Biloxi, Mississippi, and Mt. Zion, Alabama, he was going to have to be smarter than he had ever been in his life, smarter than all the white men he would meet, prepared to take actions nothing in his existence had in the least prepared him for.

He forced himself to stand up and look about the room, to think coldly and calmly. His stomach roiled, empty. The backs of his legs were so weak he was afraid he would fall. The noise of rising people and stirring animals penetrated his consciousness. He had to get out of here, away from the suspicious and prejudiced Eakins Stubbs. He had to get Miss Kathy's body out of here.

He went to the chair and took up his clothing. He put on his undershirt, shirt, tight-fitting trousers, stockings. He pulled on his boots and stood up, buckling his belt and buttoning his fly. He went to the earthenware basin and washed his face, conscious of the sweat breaking out on his body.

He walked to the bed and looked down at Kathy. The front of her gown was crusted with blood, but most of her bleeding had been internal, the slice of his knife was that sharp and certain. He found a flowered dress and pulled it on over her gown. He removed his knife and tied a flat cloth pad over the incision. He put her stockings and shoes on her. Then he looked about the room, gathered up her belongings, packed her steamer trunk, and closed it.

He stood one more moment, checking the room. Then he went out of the door, and locked it behind him. The front steps led down to the lobby and the bar. He glanced along the rear corridor and found a stairwell. He walked along the corridor and went down the steps, hurrying.

When he came off the stairs into the kitchen, Trumpet looked up from the stove and smiled. "Mornin', handsome. You hungry? You want breakfast?"

"What?"

"I said, you hungry? You want breakfast?"

"Oh, no. Only make that white man boss of yours mad."

"Hell with him. I know how to handle him. I cuts

him off—won't let him have none till he ready to flog me, or give in. When he give in, I get what I want."

Blade barely heard her. He crossed the kitchen as she spoke and paused at the rear screen door. She said, "You want I should take a tray up to your lady?"

He heard that all right, loud and clear. "No. She sick. She say she don't feel like eatin' this mornin'. No sense taking nothing up to her."

"You got a few minutes, I take something to you—out in the stables."

He forced himself to smile, even as he shook his head. Sweated, he went down the steps, crossed the soap-scabbed yard to the stables. Trying to work calmly, he hitched the animals to the coach, led them around the buildings to the front door of the tavern.

He drew a deep breath, trying to compose himself, to control the way his hands shook. He entered the lobby, sighed with an almost aching sense of relief when it was empty. He went up the stairs two at a time, stopped, stepped sedately off the stairs into the upper corridor. He brought the steamer trunk from the room and lashed it on the back of the coach.

He was setting up the panels to make a rear bed when someone spoke at his shoulder. He started, shaking all over at the sound of Eakins Stubbs's voice.

Stubbs laughed, pleased that Blade reacted like an ordinary Negro—he jumped when a white man spoke to him. "You and the Missy leavin' kind of early, huh? My cook say she don't even want nuthin' to eat."

Blade turned to face the innkeeper. His eyes were bleak, his face muscles taut. He spoke as though unable to get a full breath. "My lady—she daid."

"What?" Stubbs staggered, retreating a step. "What the hell you say, nigger?"

"She die, Masta. Las' night. She was sick when we got here—"

"Yeah. She looked peaked. I saw that. But daid? Where'd you people come from yestidy, nigger?"

"New Orleans," Blade said.

"Yellow jack," Stubbs whispered in horror, retreating another step.

"I don't know," Blade said. "She was sick—before we left."

"Oh, shit." The innkeeper spread his hands and spoke in frustration to the chinaberry tree, the sky, to infinity. His hands shook. He could hardly hold back the tears. "My God. My good Jesus Christ God. She got the plague. God damn it. She had the yellow jack when she come in here. You knowed it, you goddamn black son of a bitch. You knowed it. I saw her face and knowed she was sick. But yellow jack? You brought her here sick with plague."

"I sorry, Masta—but I needs a coffin—"

"Never mind that. You just get that body out of here —and get to hell away from here now. You carry her out of there, and don't you let nobody see she daid. You hear me, nigger?"

Blade nodded. He walked past the innkeeper and entered the ordinary. He went up the steps. In the front bedroom, he put on his jacket and set his planter's hat on his head. Then he took Miss Kathy up gently in his arms and carried her body down the steps and out to the coach.

Eakins Stubbs leaned against the front of his tavern, looking as if he were ready to vomit but was afraid to because vomiting was a deadly symptom of the plague. His eyes wild, he watched Blade place her body in the coach and close the door. "Go on, nigger," he said. "Get her out of here—and don't you never come back this way. So help me God, don't you ever come back."

The coach was five miles along the trail east before Blade drew a normal breath. He exhaled heavily, feeling as if he had not breathed since Stubbs spoke to him outside the ordinary. He had taken the first step. He was on the way home.

He passed the funeral parlor less than thirty minutes later. He painfully spelled out the words, pulled up on the reins. He turned the coach, went back, and, after heading the horses east once more, halted outside the mortuary.

He knocked on the door. The bald man who answered it shook his head when he glimpsed the color of Blade's skin. "This here is a white funeral parlor, boy," he said.

"My lady is white—she is in my coach. She daid."

"Dead?"

"We comin' home from New Orleans, Masta. She sick when we left there—"

"The plague! Jesus Christ. Get away from here, boy. Right now."

"Masta. I needs a coffin. Yoah best coffin." Blade's breathless voice hardened. The bald man hesitated, enraged at Blade's tone. Blade knew what could happen to a black man in Mississippi for speaking disrespectfully to a white man. That didn't matter now that Miss Kathy was dead. He wanted a fine coffin for her. He meant to get one. How in hell could a white man's hangrope hurt him now? He repeated in that cold tone, "I need a coffin for my lady."

"Don't dare take that tone to me, nigger."

Blade's eyes filled with tears—agony mixed with a rage he dared not show. His squared jaw thrust out slightly. "Listen to me, Masta. She my lady. She daid. I got a long journey home—two, three more days. I got to have me a coffin—a fine coffin."

Some of the anger subsided in the mortician's eyes, and his face relaxed. He understood the agony in Blade's eyes. He was nothing but a nigger, but his agony couldn't have been deeper even if he'd been human. The mortician nodded.

"I got a fine coffin. But you can't bring her in here—not and her dead of yellow jack."

"Just sells me the coffin. I put her body in it. I seals it."

"I can sell you my best, boy." He glanced at the splendid coach and sleek horses. "Cost you two hundred—and fifty—dollars. You got that much?"

Blade pulled out his money belt. The mortician beckoned him into the lobby. Blade poured out the stack of gold eagles on a dark table top. The coins glittered, reflected in the mortician's eyes.

"Oh, yes, we'll provide a fine coffin. Silk and satin lining. Something your lady's folks will be proud of." The man nodded and nodded again. He smiled. The golden eagles glittering on the counter made all the difference. He counted it, estimating the number of golden eagles as nearly as he could without staring openly at them. "We'll just have a coffin brought out to the walk . . . . You'll have to put it in the carriage . . . . I can't expose any of my boys to a contagious disease, you understand?"

Blade nodded. The mortician counted out twelve of the golden eagles and pocketed them. Then, certain the Negro was illiterate, unable to count, he took up another one. He was gouging the poor bastard at a moment of grief. Well, the yellow jack was hell, and the nigger had brought it up here. Life went on. You took what you could get, no matter how sorry you might be for the poor devil.

Blade passed the inns and ordinaries along the trail without glancing toward them, and he sought hospitality in none. He was icy inside with rage. He felt he had endured all the white contumely he could stand. He had heard other blacks talk about white viciousness, but he'd never seen it so clearly in action. He let the horses plod slowly, but he kept them moving, north and east on the trail.

He stopped just before dark at a tavern. He bought hay and grain for the horses. He removed them from the traces, took off their harness. He watered, fed, and rubbed them down. But though darkness was closing in, he hitched the animals again, and pulled out on the trail.

He had been driving less than an hour when he saw the lanterns swinging in the roadway ahead. He pulled in on the reins beside the black wagon. The two young white men approached from either side of the coach. One held a lantern aloft, illumining Blade's set, grief-stricken face and the sealed coffin.

"We slave patrollers," the man told him. "You got your pass?"

Blade nodded. He reached in to the inside jacket pocket and found, rather than the one letter of reference he expected to find, two envelopes. The man on the other side of the coach said, "What you got there, boy, a coffin?"

"It's my lady," Blade said. "We was coming home from New Orleans. She was sick—she died back a ways."

"Jesus," the slave patroller said. He shook his head, waiving the letter of reference. Blade's grief-stricken face, the fine cut of his clothes, the excellence of the team, and the splendid coach, along with the brass-ornamented coffin impressed and convinced him. "Go ahead, boy."

"Thank you, Masta," Blade said. He shoved the envelopes back in his pocket. He drove through the rest of the night, his eyes fixed on the dark trail ahead. The horses followed the ruts in the road. Blade was not sleepy. He felt no hunger. He did not hurry the horses, let them plod at their own pace.

His thoughts were murderous. All he could think was that Miss Kathy was dead. She needed to rest no more, she knew hunger no more. For a brief flickering of time they had been two people overwhelmed with the joy of discovering each other. Tonight they returned to their old roles. She was the white mistress—going home in a sealed casket. He had tasted a moment of freedom. Tonight he was a slave again, as dead inside as Miss Kathy was dead, kept alive only by murderous hatred.

He was returning to Blackoaks, to slavery, but he was heading there not in obedience but in bitterness, and the need to kill. He was Styles Kenric's slave. But his white master had betrayed him.

A little past dawn, he pulled into a stable behind an ordinary. He swung down from the coach and kicked a Negro stable boy awake. While the boy fed, watered, and rubbed down the pair of horses, Blade sat on the edge of the water trough. He removed the two envelopes from his pocket. One was addressed only to Blade. Instinctively, he knew it was from Miss Kathy.

His heart battering, he tore open the envelope. Her wedding ring fell out into his hand. Eyes bleak and tear-filled, he stared at the little golden circle. It was too small for his little finger. He found a strip of leather cord, looped it and wore the ring about his neck. He leaned against the coach while the stable boy hitched the horses in the traces.

Slowly, he spelled out the words until he could read her message to him:

Blade,
This is all I can give you to prove to you that you are the only true lover in my heart. Please forgive me.

K.

His throat aching with the lump in it, he reread the short note a dozen times. She didn't hate him. He felt as if a terrible burden had been lifted from his shoulders. He nodded toward the sealed casket, extending through the right front window from the tonneau of the carriage. "Thank you, Miss Kathy. Thank you. We're going home now. We're going home."

The wind rose out of the south and it began to rain, at first in a gusty drizzle and then pelting down in a shower that darkened the dreary afternoon, a blinding sheet of wind-riven water. The storm continued after nightfall. But Blade, after feeding and watering the team at an ordinary stable, moved them at once out on the trail again. He was unaware of the blast of rain that blew in across him. He scarcely saw the flashes of lightning that seared the sky, sent the horses into panic in their traces, and illumined the forest in stark blacks and deathly whites. He was truly aware of nothing except his own grief and hatred, the small circle of gold at his throat, and Miss Kathy's sealed casket.

Ignoring the rising waters at the shoulders of the road, he kept the tired, spooked horses plodding through the rain, sometimes through sodden mud where only water-covered ruts marked a roadbed. He drove as if possessed, not by a fear of death or the fear of being apprehended by the law now, but by a kind of animal savagery, a need to kill as old as the jungle, older than retribution. He hated the rain, though he hardly felt it. But the rain slowed him. His horses had to mince, stumbling, picking their way in the wet, black night through a driving rain.

Holding the reins tightly enough to remind the animals

he was controlling them and was contemptuous of their fears, their stumbling, their panic at every flare of lightning and peal of thunder, their exhaustion, he felt the rage building in him, and he wanted to drive faster and faster.

The horses plodded slowly. He knew he was living in a void of fury and dread and mindless hatred. If he were going to be smarter than a white man, he should be coldly devising a plan for when he came to Blackoaks and faced Styles Kenric. He was still a slave, and at any overt action, Styles could kill him or order him killed. Perhaps the moment he lived for would be delayed. But it would come. Sooner or later he would be able to think again without numbing hatred, and that moment would come. It would come. He sobbed suddenly in the darkness.

When the rain ceased just after daybreak and the sun came out, brassy in a sweated and humid heat, Blade halted the coach and pulled into a clearing some one hundred yards from the road.

He swung down from the carriage seat and took out of his carpet bags the suits and shirts Styles Kenric had given him and that poor Banipal had worked so devotedly to make perfect for him.

Perfect? Perfect for what? For ugliness. For diseased evil. For lies. For vengeance. For something that never could be, never should have been.

He took each of the suits in turn in his fists and ripped them into shreds. He tore them savagely, not content with ripping the seams or with destroying the shape of them. He tore them across, ripped at them until nothing remained but the shirt and white pantaloons he wore. Strips of useless cloth and lint piled about his boots.

He strode about the thicket, gathering the driest limbs, sticks and small logs he could find. He carried them back to the clearing near the carriage. He worked for a long time building the fire of bits of sticks, pine needles, and then damp, finger-length branches. The fire flickered damply, flared up, orange and blue and sickly gray. He knelt over the pyre, blowing hard on it until the larger limbs caught and flamed. Then he laid larger branches across the fire. When it was blazing, he went to the wagon and gathered up strips of cloth in his fists—the gray, the olive, the white—the last filthy remnants of what that white man had given him along with his lies and his horror. He had loved Kenric for the kind gift of these suits, and now he hated him more terribly for the truth about those gifts.

He threw the cloth on the fire, watching it burn. He stood numbly, letting his gaze follow the leaping flames and upcurling smoke. The fire died back and he fed it more cloth. He stood at the fire until the last strip of cloth was consumed in flames, and he wore only the shirt, pants, and boots Kenric had given him.

He looked down at himself. The shirt, pantaloons, and boots were too clean even though damp with rain and discolored with the sweat and agony that had oozed from his pores. He kicked the fire to pieces, stomped it with his boots until it was black and dead. Then he knelt in the ashes. He scooped them up in his hands along with wet earth and sodden leaves and smeared the muck along his tailored pantaloons. Even this wasn't enough, and he rolled in the bed of the dead fire, rolled and smeared himself until he was covered with filth, splotched with ashes and soot and wet earth—until he was sure he was a dirty nigger again, a field nigger, but clean inside; a slave, but his own man.

He looked up, staring toward Blackoaks far ahead of him in the distance. His face twisted savagely. He gripped his fists at his sides, his nails digging into his palms. God damn you, Mister White Man, live happy, because I'm coming for you, white man. I'm coming to get you. This nigger is coming to get you.

PART FIVE

An Uprising of Slaves

1

The dreary summer weeks that followed Morgan's tragic accidental death, and the lachrymose funeral services that brought in every plantation family within a fifty-mile radius and involved even the slaves in an orgy of mournful hymns, lamentations, and sobbing, left as its residue a pall of desolation. A stunned sense of sorrow enshrouded Blackoaks.

Styles found himself impotent against the wasteful inactivity, the undue period of mourning accorded Morgan's death. He would walk into the kitchen to find a house girl ironing one of Morgan's shirts—and sobbing. He watched the bills mount from the services, the food, and materials consumed by the guests. Miz Claire saw to it that Morgan's funeral was one of the most expensive affairs in Blackoaks's history of openhanded hospitality. She and Neva wept about the untimely death of their baby. To Styles, the whole business was acutely, embarrassingly sodden. It frustrated and annoyed him to have to listen to effusive expressions of regrets at Morgan's death "in the flower of his boyhood" from people who should have had the minimal intelligence that would have told them the backward boy was no loss to anyone—except perhaps to the addled Miz Claire and the fat body slave Soapy who now moped about the house like a lost dog.

Worse than the waste of time and money and emotions was the almost superstitious sense, to Styles—who was far too well educated to be in any way superstitious—that Morgan's funeral somehow marked the moment when an irreversible decline settled like an evil mist to erode his power and authority as master of Blackoaks.

Styles strode about the vast farm, trying to find answers where there were none. Of course, Morgan's funeral had nothing to do with the financial predicament in which he now found the estate. Perhaps that began long before old man Baynard had died. But one thing was certain as death and taxes—the bills were coming due, growing overdue, and he was unable to scrounge up the resources to satisfy them. He had cleared away a mountainous stack of debts once, many of the obligations hanging over from Baynard's years as administrator of the estate. But he saw now that liquidation of obligations with borrowed money was nothing more than a stopgap. It had never occurred to him, even though he had been reared in a mortgaged home, that bank interest could mount so swiftly, so ruinously. If a man had only to pay the interest on nine and ten percent loans, he might make it. But when that rapidly multiplying interest was added to the daily cost of maintaining and supplying a huge farm and its almost two hundred slaves, it became an impossibility. He found himself going into Mt. Zion two and three times a month to visit Luke Scroggings at the bank. Scroggings's affability and unchecked willingness to extend more and more credit disturbed him and frightened him. But as long as he could get the cash there, he had to take it.

He found the costs of daily expenses ruinous. He had bought Petit Gulf seeds and planted a cotton crop one-third the size old man Baynard had always broadcast. The crop had been excellent, but by the time it was picked, baled, and sent by cotton wagons to market, there was no profit. None. Bos Pilzer had glared at him, without sympathy. "Hell, Styles, I tried to tell you."

Styles cut the overseer off sharply. One damned thing

he didn't have to do was to listen to his employees spout gratuitous advice. Who the hell did Pilzer think he was? Seneca had said in ancient Rome, let no man presume to give advice to others who has not first given good counsel to himself. Where did Pilzer get the right to speak? He was a little higher in status than the Negro slaves—only a little.

Daily, tensions mounted between the master and the overseer, and Styles found that as Pilzer showed less respect for his authority, he discovered the slaves to be less tractable. Styles learned, too, that Miz Claire in her vapors and vagueness—intensified since Morgan's death—incited the slaves to disrespect for him, probably without even realizing she did it. Whenever she was asked about "the Masta", Miz Claire invariably replied, not that Styles was their new master and that they should obey him on the pain of death, but rather, in her vague way, smiling, "Your master is away. We must be patient. We must wait until he and Morgan come home."

Styles sat in his office, staring, seeing nothing, his mind engrossed in all these frustrations. The knock on his door was repeated three or four times before he even heard it. When he did hear the timid rapping, he felt a flash of rage at any intrusion. His voice rasped, cutting and forbidding. "Who is it? What do you want?"

"It's Soapy, Masta. I'd most appreciate talking to you."

Soapy entered the office diffidently. He was terrified of Masta Styles. He had come in contact with him only as infrequently as possible while Morgan was alive. Morgan had been his bulwark and shield against any outside attacks. As long as Morgan lived, Soapy could look at Styles Kenric as a distant and remote danger, someone to avoid but not a present peril.

"All right, boy, what do you want?" Styles made no effort to conceal his distaste for the fat-bellied, sagging-breasted slave.

"I gots to talk to you, Masta—about my freedom."

Styles laughed, a bitter and angry sound. "Your what?"

Soapy trembled but stood his ground. From his shirt pocket he extracted a folded sheet of ruled paper. He opened it and extended it toward Styles. "Masta Morgan writ that. Writ by his own hand. And signed with Masta Morgan's blood."

Styles read the note aloud. "To whom it may concern, I Morgan Baynard, of sound mind and good morals, do decree that my body slave, Sophocles of Blackoaks, shall be freed forever upon my death. Signed, Morgan Baynard." Styles looked up. "Did you know what this note said?"

Soapy nodded.

Styles persisted. "How did you know?"

"I knowed Masta Morgan writ it. I was there. I read it."

"Do you know it is against the law for you to read or write—that you could go to jail for that crime?"

Soapy swallowed hard. "Not no more, Masta Styles. I a free nigger now. Freed niggers can read and write—without breakin' no law."

Styles waved the paper, his mouth twisted. "You're not free, Soapy. You are a Blackoaks slave. You merely worked for Morgan—while he lived."

"Nah, sah. I belonged to Masta Morgan. I he body slave. I he boy. They always tole me that. I belong to nobody but Masta Morgan—and if Masta Morgan want to set me free—he kin."

"Listen to me. I don't want to hear any more of this. Morgan was a retarded boy. That means he was not of sound mind. That means he did not know what he was doing. This piece of paper is worthless. It means nothing."

"It means I free—"

"It means you're an impudent, fat-assed Negro boy who has lived like a pet for seventeen years. It means you have become so uppity and so insolent that you walk in here and make demands—"

"No, suh. I not make demands. I jus' come in to tell you. I free, that letter say I free."

Styles stood up. "Listen, you black son of a bitch. You are no more free than you ever were." He stared down at Soapy who looked ready to dissolve like hot tallow. He took up a long-stemmed sulphur match and struck it.

When the flame caught, he held it to the corner of Morgan's note.

"No. Oh, Gawd no, Masta. That my freedom paper! Oh Gawd, Masta!"

Unthinking, mindless with terror and loss, Soapy leaped toward the burning paper, grabbing at it. Styles let the boy's hand brush his and then he backhanded him across the face. Soapy went stumbling back to the wall. He sagged there, crying helplessly. Styles dropped the ashes into a tray. He rang for Thyestes. When the butler came in, Styles said, "Send for Laus. I want this black bastard taken to the barn and given fifteen lashes—for insubordination, and for daring to attack me."

"Oh, no, Masta," Soapy wept.

Disturbed, his face growing rigid, Thyestes nodded and limped from the room. Styles sat down at his desk and coldly ignored the sobbing fat Negro boy as if Soapy had ceased to exist. When Laus appeared after what seemed a chilled eternity to Soapy, Styles repeated his orders about whipping Soapy. "When he's been lashed until he knows his place, send him to live with one of the families in the quarters—"

"Oh, Gawd, Masta Styles. I sorry. Whup me for touchin' you . . . . But don't send me to the quarters. I ain't nevah lived in the quarters. I a house boy."

"You *were* a house boy, you insolent son of a bitch," Styles said. Inside his own mind he admitted he was venting all the rages and frustrations that had been building for months, taking them all out on the fat and helpless body of the slave boy. He didn't give a damn why he was doing it. It would show these blacks who was in charge at Blackoaks. "Tomorrow, you report to the field gang."

"But I can't, Masta. Fore Gawd, Masta. Have some mercy. I a house boy—I ain't no field nigger."

Styles waved his hand, motioning them to take Soapy out. He went without fighting, but Styles could hear his sobbing even after the front door was closed on him for the last time.

2

Florine Pilzer awoke while Bos was preparing his breakfast, plodding noisily in the kitchen. She lay breathless, her heart pounding. For no good reason she was convinced that Moab would come stealthily through that window as soon as Bos had ridden off to oversee the field crews. She had not seen Moab often; he had gotten up to her one day as late as noon. He had told her he had been placed in charge of the commissary while Blade was away in New Orleans, but he would come when he could.

She heard Bos go out the back door, letting it slam after him. He did not care whether he woke her or not. He hated having to get up in the darkest hour before dawn; he hated anyone who didn't have to get up. She heard him in the tack room, in the stables, and she lay counting the minutes until she would hear the heavy clop of his horse's hooves crossing the yard, heading down into the quarters.

She was trembling by the time Bos was gone. The silence washed back over the house and yard when Bos was gone. Holding her breath, crossing her fingers at her sides, she waited.

She felt perspiration break out in small beads across her forehead. Suppose he didn't come? He had to come. He was young and as horny as a billy goat—it had been a week for him the same as for her. He would come.

She smiled, thinking how she might surprise and excite him. They had first met when he looked in that window and caught her playing with herself. Her gown had been rolled up under her armpits, her breasts had stood taut, nipples hard, her legs had been spread, her fingers fighting at her clitoris. What if she were playing with herself when Moab came now to her window?

She felt her skin grow flushed and overheated at the

thought of this added fillip of excitement she could offer Moab—proof of how deeply she surrendered, submissive, to his every whim. Smiling, she kicked off the covers. She lifted her hips, resting her weight on her shoulder blades and heels. She pulled her long gown up above her breasts and tucked it under her armpits. Her heart battered against her own hand. She let her fingers fondle her breast, feeling its taut firmness—how young it was! How young Moab made her feel!—and the sweetly painful rigidity of the nipple. She wanted him so badly she quivered in anticipation.

She slid her hand down across the slight bulge at her stomach, the rise at her soft mound. She pushed her fingers downward and moved them in a circular motion, faster and faster. Come *now,* Moab, she whispered deep inside her mind, come through that window and see what I am doing for you.

Sick at her stomach, Florine remained in bed until nine. She could no longer stay there—she had to see Moab. She would walk down into the quarters. She would go to Blade's shack and call for Moab. As the overseer's wife she had every right to request Moab to do chores for her at this house. That's what she would do. And she'd tell Bos what she'd done—she wanted Moab to handles the chores Bos found so onerous after a long, sun-blasted day in the fields overseeing work crews. No one could fault her for this. She felt better and she wished she'd devised this ruse weeks ago.

She dressed hurriedly and went, empty-bellied, into the brilliant summer morning sun. The sunlight cast sharp deep shadows of trees and houses across the parched earth. She walked, head up, purposefully, into the quarters and down the incline toward the cabin where Blade lived with the new Fulani wench.

Florine stopped outside the cabin. She was aware that dozens of eyes were fixed on her from darkened interiors of the shacks on both sides of the lane. She had intended to go up on the stoop, knock on the door, and ask for Moab. Now, with all the blacks watching, she wanted them all to know the purity and legality of her expressed intentions.

She called, "Moab. You home, Moab? I got some chores Master Bos says for you to handle up at my place." There, that was loud enough. It bought passage for both her and Moab, up the lane and into her bedroom. What these blacks could not see was none of their business.

The door of the shack opened and Ahma stepped through it. Florine's mouth parted at the size and beauty of the elegantly built girl. She was indeed beautiful enough for the beautiful Blade. But the girl had a wild, savage look about her, and though Florine smiled up at her, Ahma merely stared back, intently, and she did not smile.

"I'm looking for Moab. I've got some chores for him," Florine said.

Ahma shook her head. "Moab ain't here. He gone to work. He can't leave that work for you."

"Master Bos said—"

"I don't care, lady, what Master Bos said. Moab, he working in Blade's stead at the commissary. He only git off little while at noon. That's all. He can't be workin' round no white woman's house."

The gazes of the two women clashed and held. They stared at each other, neither deceived by the other for an instant. Feeling her heart sink, Florine knew defeat. She couldn't make a scene, that would destroy the credibility she had as Bos Pilzer's wife. But she wanted to see Moab. She wanted to go directly to the commissary and call him out, but she felt guilt at the idea. This would be too transparent. Even the most ignorant black understood the sexual urges that forced men and women into foolish and extreme actions. She said, coldly, and loudly, "When Moab comes home at lunch, you tell him what I said."

Ahma shrugged. Her jaw hardened, and her eyes chilled. She had news for Blade when he came home, other than the wondrous, dreadful, fearful news that he had impregnated her. She was going to have their baby. But now she had other disturbing news. The white overseer's wife was hot after Moab—as plain as a bitch in heat. She said casually. "I tells him . . . Miz Pilzer."

Florine thanked her in a loud, warm voice, but she let her murderous gaze bore into Ahma's bronze-gold face. Let the big amazon know she hated her. She had ruined something perfect. She could have come here as often as she wished and ordered Moab to perform chores at Bos Pilzer's place, under Bos's relayed commands. But Ahma had spoiled that. Florine knew she could never come back here calling for Moab. She turned and walked slowly up the incline toward the lonely fieldstone house in the high park.

When the black youth ran past the commissary porch where Moab sat leaning back in a straight chair against the shadowed wall, Moab called out to him, "What's your hurry, Stom?" The youth paused, breathing hard. "A whuppin' goin' on over to the stables."

Moab sat down forward on all four legs of the chair. "Who is it?"

"Think it Soapy," the boy said. He lingered no longer, running toward the smithy and the barn directly across from it.

Soapy? Morgan's body slave? Moab scowled, unable to believe this. He got up, closed the door of the commissary and ran across the sunstruck valley. Slaves were gathering from all directions, homing in on the barn as if the news of the flogging traveled on the wind. Black men came from the fields, the distillery, the shops, the animal pens. Often a lashing was a time of almost carnival atmosphere. In the days of Master Baynard, when a slave was meted corporal punishment, everyone agreed it was deserved. Master Baynard—the old master—bent over backwards to be fair and impartial. Under such conditions, the slaves had assembled to watch, to see a culprit receive his just deserts.

Moab slowed at the doorway of the barn, troubled. The interior was hot, dusky, cavernous, smelling of hay and leather. There was tension in the atmosphere. There was no sense of justice served here today. The slaves who had gathered to witness the whipping were dour-faced, grumbling, angry and hard-eyed.

Moab pushed through the solemn ring of witnesses.

He winced, seeing Soapy, stripped bare and secured by ropes on pulleys, which were tied off when the fat boy's toes were raised an inch or so from the straw-littered plankings of the floor. Spancels, ordinarily used to hobble or clog a horse or cow, were set about Soapy's flabby ankles, and he was fettered, spread-eagled between two uprights, his fat buttocks exposed to the whip.

Moab did not look around; he went directly to Soapy. By now he knew that Master Styles had ordered this punishment, and he realized what could happen to him if Styles's rage were turned upon him. And this might happen if he were caught showing sympathy to Soapy.

The hell with that. He'd take his punishment. Soapy was his friend. Soapy had exposed himself to reprisals by teaching him to read and write. Moab did feel pity for his old and dear friend. He could not conceive of anything Soapy might have done to deserve fifteen lashes with a buggy whip.

He knelt beside Soapy. Soapy was no longer crying. He waited in numb horror. He saw Moab and tried to smile. "Soap," Moab whispered. "What happened?"

"I reach—I grab for my freedom paper, Moab. Masta Styles, he burnt it. I went kinda crazy. I grabbed at it. He say I attack him. Oh Gawd, Moab, they gwine hurt me bad—I ain't toughed my skin none . . . . I ain't nevah been hurt like this . . . ."

Moab could think of nothing to say. There were no words. He touched Soapy's flabby shoulder gently. "I try to find something to put on it," Moab promised. "We use the same salve Miz Pilzer used to rub on me . . . . Jus' don't hope for too much, Soap . . . . I do what I can."

"I know you will, Moab." He tried to laugh. "I glad you come. Wouldn't want you to miss the fun."

"Stand back, Moab," Laus said. Moab glanced up at the huge Negro. The slablike shoulders were welted with muscles, and thick cords stood in sweated relief along his chest and back. Laus was so damned big, Moab thought, the only man he would bet on against Blade. Not even Blade could stand against that terrible strength—in a man who was ordinarily gentle as a kitten.

"I got no moah belly for this than you has," Laus said. "Hit's Masta's orders this nigger be whupped. I'm doin' orders."

Moab pressed Soapy's shoulder one more time to try to reassure him that he was not alone, and then he stepped back.

Rage gorged up in Moab as Laus tested the buggy whip in his hamlike fist. There had seemed, even to Moab, a mean brand of justice when Bos Pilzer laid the blacksnake whip across his own back. He'd been stealing time from the work gang, sitting on a log in the shade, beating his meat. And Pilzer had struck him only once. Fifteen lashes administered by the huge Laus across that doughy skin of Soapy's was a kind of murder.

Moab drew a deep breath. He decided to run to Styles, to beg for leniency for Soapy. After all, Styles had never denied him anything. He would let his master know he would come to his bed when asked. Styles might relent if he approached him. But as he turned, he saw Styles standing tall and rigid, just inside the barn doorway, his face a set, emotionless mask. Moab's heart sank. Asking Styles anything just now was hopeless. He retreated, the dread and fury building in him as the whip snapped across Soapy's fat buttocks, upper legs, and back.

Laus glanced toward Styles, almost as if pleading for a reprieve. There was none. "Make him feel it," Styles ordered.

Laus wondered at the man who had been thoughtful and considerate and kind on the long trip to Tallahassee and back. He had seen to every comfort possible for his three slaves. He had seen that they were fed, bedded down, sheltered. He permitted no one to reproach them except through him. Now, he seemed a stranger to that man, remote and unapproachable, cold with evil. The grumbling opposition of the gathered slaves only infuriated Styles and hardened him in his purpose, which was to see Soapy flogged as an example to all the slaves.

"Whip him," Styles ordered.

Laus nodded, sick at his stomach. He laid the narrow ribbon of the buggy whip in cutting strokes across the fat boy's buttocks. Soapy moaned and then he screamed. Laus hesitated, brought the whip down, methodically, regularly, resigned to his hated task.

The leather cut the soggy flesh deeper each time. Blood bubbled at first and then spurted from the open wounds. The blood spattered the floor and the walls. Soapy screamed, crying and begging for mercy. He was on fire. He was bleeding to death. God save him. Morgan save him. Morgan. Morgan. Morgan.

Styles coldly watched ten strokes of the buggy whip, then he turned, as if losing interest, and walked out.

From the assembled slaves rose a guttural growl of hatred and disapprobation.

"That's 'nuff, Laus," Perseus said. "He jus' a fat young boy . . . . You gwine kill him."

Laus hesitated, whip raised aloft. "I doan give him the full lashin'—I gits 'em," Laus protested, agonized.

"Who gwine tell that white man?" Perseus glowered around the ring of black faces. Some met his gaze, but most lowered their eyes, studying the plankings.

Laus breathed in deeply, waiting. He drew his gaze across the cold, set faces of the encircling black men. Suddenly, he threw the whip behind him. "Oh, the hell with it," he said. "That boy bleedin' to death now."

Moab and Perseus cut Soapy down. With horse blankets they formed a quick stretcher on broken wagon shafts. They laid Soapy face down on the blankets and four of them carried him out of the barn. Perseus was chilled with hatred and outrage. "That son-of-a-bitchin' white man," he said. The slaves near him, trained from birth in the divine rights of the white master, shuddered. "He sell my wife like she a cow—now this pore boy see his young masta die—and he whups him till he bleeds like a stuck pig."

"Masta Styles, he good to us on our trip to Florida," Pegasus said in a fearful tone. He would have preferred that Perseus blaspheme against God—God was a vengeful tyrant, but Pegasus had never *seen* him. Styles and his vengeance was near at hand.

"He ain't never done nuthin' to make me hate him

less," Perseus said. "We take this boy to my place. Nobody there since my woman was sold—and my kids."

Moab went to fetch salve from the commissary. When he returned, Perseus had blotted the blood from Soapy's buttocks and legs. The boy's rear looked like flayed meat. Moab spread the salve as gently as he could. Soapy cried out. Moab spoke softly, working quietly. Perseus leaned against the wall, watching them. Moab sat in a rocking chair until Soapy slept at last. Perseus remained standing, propped against the wall, his face a mask of hatred. Moab stood up, whispered. "He sleepin'. Reckon I run on now."

Perseus seemed not even to hear him . . . .

Moab pushed the door open at Blade's cabin and stepped inside. As he cleared the threshold, something struck him on the side of the head. For the moment stunned, he toppled against a table, almost upset a chair. He set himself, regained his balance and heeled around, snarling.

His gaze clashed against the murderous eyes of Ahma. She stood beside the door, her fist still clenched, ready to strike him again.

"You dumb nigger boy." Her voice flayed him.

"What the hell's the matter?" Moab demanded.

"You. That's what's the matter. You and that stupid cock-crazy white woman."

"What're you talking about?"

"Don't you come in heah playin' the fool with me, you stupid nigger boy. You don't fool Ahma, no more than that white slut does. Here she comes, prancing down here, with that white innocent face of hers callin' Moab! Moab!" She minced across the room, her falsetto voice mocking Florine. "You bettah stay away from that white woman."

"You mean Miz Florine Pilzer?"

"How many white sluts you pesterin' this week, big dumb cock?"

"What about her?"

"She come callin' for you. That's what about her. She prancin' down here, trying to get you killed."

"You're crazy."

"I nevah said I wasn't crazy. But I ain't crazy enough to go pesterin' around a cock-crazy white woman what's going to get me killed. I'm telling you, boy. You bettah stay away from that white woman—"

"Keep your voice down, Ahma. For God's sake, you want some of these people to tell her husband?"

Ahma laughed mockingly at him. "Makes no nevah-mind who tells her husband. Word gonna get to that sucker anyhow." She hummed, taunting him: "Who overseers the overseer's wife, while the overseer's busy overseeing?"

In panic, Moab cried out, "Stop that. My God, you do want to git me killed?"

Her mouth twisted. "Looks to me if it don't matter if I gits you killed or you gits yo'self killed. You dead, either way."

"I careful. I been careful."

"More dead people has said them words than any others—"

"I don't care. She's been good to me. Better than anybody else—better than my own mother."

"I bet she has."

"I was sent up there. I lived up there for almost a year. Wasn't never nobody as kind to me as she was."

Her mouth contorted out of shape. "That real touchin'. That's a real sad story. Pore little orphan boy. Nice white lady takes him in like stray cat. She jus' opens her legs wide—and takes him right in."

"Stop that."

"I gone tell Blade when he gits home. If he don't beat the hell out of you, I will myself. Pregnant an' all like I am, I'll whop you, you don't git good sense."

Moab sighed and sank into a chair. He sweated and wiped the back of his hand across his face. "It ain't that easy, Ahma. Sure, you laugh an' make fun. But she lonely —and she *has* been good to me."

"Fine. Then you jus' write her a letter and thank her for being so kind. And you *send* it to her."

Moab laughed. "I don't know if she can read."

Ahma's voice remained unrelenting. "You write it. She know what you mean—if'n she can read or not."

3

The days passed slowly at Blackoaks in the drowsy summer heat, each like another burden hoisted upon Styles's slender shoulders. He spent the nights sleeplessly, pacing in his room. Night rains flared up suddenly and whipped against his window. He stood at the casement, watching the fury of the driving rain against the panes, the sharp crack of lightning, the overwhelming rumble of thunder—feeling inside himself the fury of the night storm. By day he wandered the estate, feeling the cold and malevolent eyes of some of the slaves. He challenged them, openly staring them down, daring them to make any move against him. Pilzer suggested he should carry a pistol with him, but he did not, as much because Pilzer suggested it as because he didn't want to frighten away the vengeful hatred in some of those ebony eyes. He hated them as they hated him; he wanted them to know where they stood with him; he hoped they would make any move against him so he could show them clearly just where they stood with him. He would order them whipped, he would kill them, or he would sell them to the Louisiana cane fields and certain death, and not think twice about it.

At ten o'clock one humid morning, with no traces visible to the casual eye of his sleepless night spent pacing in his room, Styles left his office and mounted the wide staircase. Despite the sweated heat, he looked cool and fresh, scrubbed and shaven, wearing sweet-smelling and carefully tailored clothing, with polished boots and just the sharp tang of cologne to define his immaculate freshness. He carried several sheets of legal foolscap which had arrived in the morning mail. The paper was from the bank and required both his and Miz Claire's signature. The document was in effect the final argument against incarcerating Miz Claire—at least until Kathy was returned from New Orleans. If everything went as planned, he would have Kathy totally under control—she would do as he told her, she would accept his decisions, and this might well include sending her mother away to an institution for the insane.

Until that moment, despite the power of attorney he had prevailed upon Miz Claire to sign and turn over to him, he often needed her signature on papers such as this.

Luke Scroggings's accompanying letter—obviously dictated to a secretary who had etched the words in slanting Spencerian on watermarked bond paper—was apologetic. He hoped Styles would understand. Since the amount of the mortgage against chattel and lands at Blackoaks had reached the new total of thirty thousand, for the estate's protection, as well as the bank's, he required both Styles's and Miz Claire Baynard's signature on the note. As soon as this executed paper was received in the bank, Styles could rest assured the money he required would be deposited to his personal account.

Styles came off the stairs and strode along the sunlit upper corridor toward Miz Claire's private suite. It was urgent to get these papers signed and returned to the bank. He wanted that money in order to satisfy that lien against the estate held by the Commercial Bank of Tallahassee. It would exult and please him as few things did any more to be able to say to Garrett Blanford Ware that if the old trust were gone from between them, please accept his regrets—and full and final payment on his mortgage. God, he'd love to see the look on that hypocritical bastard's face when he read that letter. Well, as soon as Miz Claire managed to scribble her name, he would send Pegasus riding to the bank with the papers. Besides the satisfaction of smiling when he called Ware a son of a bitch, he needed resources, capital to meet daily expenses of this place.

He rapped on the corridor door of Miz Claire's suite. The door was quickly opened wide enough to permit the bulky body of Neva to sidle through and as quickly closed behind her. Her eyes hardened as she stared at Styles. He might be the most beautiful white man Miz Claire had ever seen, but Neva was not impressed—she saw the small, tight mouth, the mean eyes, the chilled, self-important arrogance. That man was ugly, chile . . . .

"What you want, knockin' on this doah like that?" she said.

Styles peered at her along his nose. His voice chilled. "First, I want you to get a civil tongue in that fat black head of yours, Neva. I don't want you ever to speak to me like that again."

"What you want?"

Styles felt the rage rise up in him. His hand clasping the foolscap tightened, shaking. He kept his voice icily cold. "I want to see Miz Claire."

"What about?"

"It's none of your business. Now, do you want to tell her I want to talk to her, or do I go in there and tell her myself?"

She laughed, a cold, venomous sound. "Sho' nuff, honey. You walk right in there and tell her. Right ovah my dead body, go ahead."

He gazed at her savagely, a look that had sent self-important white people into cold sweats. "That can be arranged, too, Neva. I don't know who you think you are—"

"I don't think who I are, Mister Styles. I know who I are. I ain't like some white folks what marries into money, and puts on airs—"

"You black slut—"

"I knows who I am. I am Neva of Blackoaks. I born here. I *belongs* here. I am Miz Claire's slave. I know who I am. I know I got to protect that chile—from being disturbed, from being frightened by self-centered people who don't care what they do to her, long as they gits what they wants."

"Tell her I want to see her, you fat bitch. This instant."

"Calling me dirty names ain't gwine buy you nothing. You acts fancy and mighty as you wants round folks that believes you fancy and mighty . . . . I know you upset my chile—she scairt of you—an' I know Masta Ferrell done warn you to stay away from her. Now, you got something you want she to see, you leave it with me and I see that she gits it."

Styles's tone did not alter. "You tell I am here, Neva. Now. I am out of patience with you."

Neva set herself in the doorway. "That chile sleepin' after a terrible night of cryin' about her chile in N'awleans, and her chile in he grave . . . . She sleepin', and ain't you—ain't nobody going to disturb her."

"She can go back to sleep."

"Naw, suh, she cain't. It ain't that easy. Sleep come harder and harder to her all the time. And wakin', that chile in hell . . . . Now, you can stand here and cuss me till you black in the face as I am, but I ain't waking her."

Styles stared down at his clenched fist. When he spoke his voice was calmly and deadly quiet. "All right, Neva. I'll wait. But you haven't heard the end of this. You are a fat, old, and useless black woman. You eat like a hog— and you're of no earthly value on this place any more. I can tell you this. The first passing coffle, you will be part of it. I'll sell you, you old harridan. We'll see who runs Blackoaks."

Her eyes met his, unflinching. Her voice was as quiet as his. "Yes, suh. We see . . . . "

Moab paced the shaded stoop outside the commissary. He was empty-bellied with fright. He was shaking with need to get to Miz Florine. He had to protect her. He had to tell her that Ahma threatened to expose them to Blade the moment he returned from New Orleans. Being careful was no longer enough. He had to stay away from her. He sweated. He would have closed the commissary and raced through the timberlands, taking the long way to come up from the creek to the high park where Miz Florine lived, but he knew better. A long absence would have to be explained. The more questions people began to ask about him, the sooner he and Miz Florine stood revealed before Master Styles, Bos Pilzer and the people of Blackoaks.

Moab watched Soapy limp haltingly down the incline toward him. This was the first time since his flogging that

Soapy had ventured outside Perseus's shack. Moab was glad to see his friend up and able to stagger along. But he was too mixed up inside, too worried to talk with him.

Soapy managed to lift himself to the first plank step, and then up to the commissary stoop by gripping the upright supports and pulling. He grimaced, sweating. "Howdy, Moab. Came down to visit with you. You got some pillows or soft blankets—I could sit in that rocking chair."

Moab managed to smile. He brought two folded blankets and two goosedown pillows and placed them in the rocking chair for Soapy. Soapy eased himself down upon them, biting at his lower lip. Then he exhaled and smiled. "You looked kinda fretted, Moab. What's the matter?"

"Listen, Soapy. How'd you like to do something for me?"

"I do anything for you, Moab. You know that."

Moab forced a sick smile and nodded. "You a good boy, Soap. I want you to sit here and watch the commissary for me—just for a little while . . . . You don't have to know nuthin', or do nuthin'. Ain't likely this time of the mawnin' that anybody will come heah, but they got to be somebody round in case they do."

He patted Soapy's shoulder, thanking him and almost ran, going beyond the barns and stables, in the direct opposite way from Miz Pilzer's house. He passed the whiskey distillery, and the loitering workers there shouted and hooted. "Got yourself a wench waiting in the woods, Moab?" "Want me to come along to show you what to do?" "You need help, Moab, you take a man along—me. . . . ." They roared with laughter and Moab tried to grin in response. But there was nothing amusing in this situation. Talk about his disappearing into the woods would get back to the quarters and to Ahma. The others might be fooled by his going directly away from the overseer's cottage, but Ahma would not be deceived for a moment.

He wanted to weep, and his eyes did brim with helpless tears as he entered the pine hammock and turned, hurrying through the trees toward the creek. She saw him coming up the incline from the swamp and she ran out on the porch to meet him. Today, even this frightened and disturbed Moab. Suppose someone passed and saw her waiting there like that? Couldn't you look at them—her waiting on her toes and him running toward her across the knoll—and know they were lovers? Unholy lovers. Adulterers.

He caught her hand and drew her quickly into the house after him. She tried to kiss him, to caress him. He was too nervous, withdrawn. He shook his head. "Moab, what's the matter?"

"Everything's wrong, Miz Florine . . . . I loves you. Like I never loved nobody on this earth—"

"And I you, Moab. You know that. Don't I try to show you—?"

"It ain't us, Miz Florine. It's Mister Bos, and Ahma—"

"What about Ahma?"

"She knows about us."

"That nigger bitch."

He winced. "I a nigger, too, Miz Florine."

She dissolved into tears. She looked as if she would fall. "Oh, God, Moab. I was just cursing her. I didn't think. You know I don't want to hurt you—you know I love you—your beautiful body—all dark and lovely—I love it most."

He shrugged, his shoulders sagged round. "It don't matter. We can't see each other no more."

"Oh, Moab. I've got to see you—"

"They kill us if we do. That for sure."

"Moab, I don't care! I'm dead without you. You think I have any life—but waiting for you—watching that park out there for you? Moab, we'll be careful."

"It won't help. He gonna find out. It gonna kill him —but first, he gone kill us."

"I tell you, I don't care. Damn it, Moab, I'll tell him—"

"What?"

"I will . . . I swear I will. If you won't see me, I'll tell him. Because I don't want to live without you."

"Oh, Jesus Christ, Miz Florine. Ain't no sense in gittin' yo'self killed—gittin' me killed—"

"I want to see you, Moab. I want to love you." She sank crying to her knees and clasped her arms about his hips. "I want to love you like this, or I want to die."

"Please Gawd, Miz Florine, don't—"

"I want to love you," she whispered, distracted. "Like this." She fought open his fly and thrust his penis deep into her mouth. She nursed him furiously, feeling him grow distended, feeling his resistance fade. Then he caught her head in both his hands, thrusting her harder upon him. His fists closed over her ears. She heard his moan. At least for this moment they were together . . . . it would not end. He would come back . . . he would have to come back . . . just as she would always be here waiting for him.

"Oh Gawd," she heard Moab whisper. "Oh, my Gawd. What I gonna do?"

Styles was at his desk when someone rapped on his closed, locked door. He still seethed with the rage that black Neva had stirred in him. He felt impotent against her—nothing but smashing that fat face, that cold mask of implacable hatred and contempt for him, would ever relieve the fury inside him.

He got up and crossed the office. Miz Claire stood there. He frowned, seeing something altered in her manner but for the moment unable to understand or name it. Her hair was done in the ringlets Neva painstakingly formed for her each morning. She wore the usual floor-length satin dress, but over it she wore an odd kind of colorful apron with a large pocket in front. But it was in her face, in her bearing, in her eyes, that the change had occurred.

"May I come in, Styles?" Her voice was firm; there was no hint of vagueness.

"Yes. I'd like to have you sign some papers for me."

Her head tilted slightly, and she glanced at him in a chilled way. "We'll talk about that later, Styles."

"But it's most important, Miz Claire."

"Later, Styles. I said later. I am most upset. I came directly to talk to you about what I have heard, what has upset me. I'm afraid anything else—anything else —will simply have to wait."

He shrugged and motioned her toward the big overstuffed chair beside the desk. He felt a chill, a sense of dread. He saw clearly what was different about Miz Claire. She was as coldly sane as he had ever seen her. Rage tightened the prune lines about her mouth, hardened the pale blue of her eyes. Obviously, Neva had gone directly to her with his threat to sell her, and as obviously the news had shocked Miz Claire out of that unreality in which she passed most of her days.

Styles waited, but Miz Claire did not sit down. She remained standing, taut, her hand thrust into the huge apron pocket, which he now saw bulged thickly. He tried to smile, "What is it that troubles you, Miz Claire?"

"This." Miz Claire withdrew her hand from the apron pocket. She held the gun steadily in her slender, unwavering hand. "I suppose you know that Mr. Baynard taught me to use this. He wanted me to be able to protect myself when he was forced to be away on business—when the children were younger, and I was here alone—except for the servants."

He nodded. "I'm quite aware, Miz Claire." He decided he had misread her. She was as mad as a guinea hen. "I saw you shoot Gil Talmadge's servant up at the chapel."

"Yes. I shot the slave in the arm, Styles. I could as easily have shot him in the heart."

"I've never for an instant doubted that, Miz Claire."

"I expect to carry this gun with me at all times from this day, Styles," she said. "In this apron. Or another like it. I think it fair to tell you, I shall never be without it . . . . It is also fair to tell you that one of the most important things about using a gun, which Mr. Baynard taught me, is never to point it unless you mean to use it . . . . I shall certainly use it without hesitation if I am driven to pointing it."

Looking at her, he knew she had never been more honest. She was like a reed, but, like a reed, she persisted. She could be walked upon, pushed over, trampled, and she would persist. She was an extremely gentle woman, but she had a streak of courage and stubborn will that made her a formidable foe. He knew this, too. He smiled, "What has this to do with me, Miz Claire?" He kept his voice calm, letting her know he found her unreasonable, irrational.

"It has to do with you—and with my body slave."

"Why, Miz Claire! What lies has that woman been telling you?"

"Neva doesn't lie to me, Styles. I must advise you, as calmly and seriously as I can speak. If you ever threaten Neva with sale, or in any other way, I will protect her—with this gun. Do you understand me, Styles? She is my property. She is not for sale. Whatever jurisdiction you have been granted in administering this estate, it does not extend to Neva. I hope—for your sake, Styles, that you do not take me lightly. If you come near Neva again, upset her again, frighten her again, I will not shoot at your arm."

"Miz Claire. Miz Claire. This is all a mistake. A foolish old woman's imagination." It occurred to Styles to wrest the gun from her. But two things stopped him. First, she *was* an expert marksman. She was coldly angry. She might well press that trigger before he got the gun away from her. But the most compelling reason why he made no effort to take it was that he wanted her to carry a gun. When the time came to put her in an institution for the insane, her gun-toting and her threats against him would certify her as irrational and mentally incompetent. He smiled at her and went on smiling. At last she looked down at the gun and at Styles, and slipped the weapon back into the big pocket. Then she turned and walked out of the room. He exhaled heavily, realizing he had been holding his breath and that his sweated hands shook.

4

Styles stared at the unsigned contract and cursed aloud. That damned paper had to be signed. Repaying Ware's bank was important, but getting cash to meet daily expenses was urgent, and that stupid woman was blocking everything. Damn her, he'd see her in the nearest snake pit if it was the last thing he did.

Miz Claire had walked out of his office and left his foyer door ajar. It remained open. Thyestes limped through it, and hesitated just inside the threshold. "Masta? A gen'mun to see you. Say he name is Alvah Eastin. Say he from down in Floridy. Say he meet you in Tallahassee."

Though the name Alvah Eastin was vaguely familiar, it was not until Thyestes tied him in with Tallahassee that Styles recalled the Indian fighter who had lived through the Dade Massacre on the Withlacoochee River a few years back. Styles was in no mood to entertain any guests, but he did not see how he could turn away the man he had met in the company of Cleatus Dennison and Bax Simon. He nodded. "Send him in, Thyestes."

"Yes, suh." Thyestes hesitated. "Masta?"

"All right. What is it?"

"This Masta Alvah Eastin. He a slave peddler . . . . I'd of made him wait at the head of the lane, but he say he friend of yours."

Styles frowned. He had not recalled that Eastin was a slave peddler. In fact, Eastin and Dennison had treated Darwin Culverhouse with an overt contempt, as if he were far below them socially and tolerated only in the mistaken assumption that he was a friend of Styles Kenric. Alvah Eastin entered, walking with head forward and shoulders hunched, as a man accustomed to following a plowhorse might do. "You a slave trader?" Styles greeted him.

"I do what might make me a buck," Eastin said, sagging into a chair and accepting a full glass of uncut whiskey. He sipped at it thirstily. "I picked up a few head of likely animals at the Tallahassee auction. Was plannin' to work them on my grove near Micanopy. Got some Indian trouble in that belt—the government has just abandoned that whole area to the Seminoles. Mr. Cleatus Dennison suggested I might make in a few months what my grove wouldn't provide me in a couple years—starting with my coffle in Georgia and workin' toward the Louisiana canefields, selling, buying, trading as I go—and dumping my culls in Louisiana."

"I wish you luck." Styles lifted his glass in a toast. He asked about the health of Bax Simon and Dennison.

"Reckon Mr. Simon went on back out to Carthage, Mississippi. May head that way if they's time 'fore cane cutting season in the Louisiana delta. Both he and Mr. Dennison mighty interested in your Fulani wench—name of Ahma?"

"Raising Fulani fancies is a slow business," Styles said. "My only hope for any profit is that Darwin Culverhouse can keep the promise he made to me in Tallahassee. Said he knew where he could find two or even three more Fulani wenches—if I was willing to pay his expenses, profit, and the tariff. I told him I was. I been waiting, but I haven't heard from him."

"Darwin Culverhouse?" Eastin said. "You ain't gonna hear from that scudder. He was kilt—down in Tallahassee. Got in a card game at a kind of whorehouse run by a woman named Orange—and somebody cut his throat. Real messy . . . . But Darwin is dead. Too bad, too. Think he came from a good family—up the Piedmont way . . . ."

Mounted on a spirited quarter horse, Styles rode out to the fields where Bos Pilzer had the field hands clearing land. Eastin rode a tired gray gelding that was road-weary and mud-splotched. He had seen the coffle Eastin had blocked out and with which he had been wheeling and dealing east into Georgia. They were a sorry-looking lot. At a glance, Styles estimated most of them were culls. He did not foresee Alvah Eastin unloading them this side of the canefields, which was the last stop for the blacks—most of them died within a year or so in the stifling, breathless cane swamps.

"Got me no pity for blacks," Alvah said as they rode toward the cleared field. "They stay in line for me or I lay the lash on them. This don't straighten them out, I plain shoot 'em like mad dogs. I see what they did at the Massacre."

Afraid Eastin might launch into his favorite horror story, even on horseback, Styles cut in, "Don't see how

I can let you have top quality field hands for under one thousand, Alvah."

"Can't pay more'n eight hundred. Ought to have them for seven-fifty in this market . . . . I admit to getting a thousand for a good-quality field hand at the vendues in New Orleans. They's a lot of expense and risk twixt here and that city. I got to git me a profit or they ain't worth killin' to me . . . . I got no love for nigger flesh. I ain't like ole Cleatus Dennison—breedin' them to improve the stock." He laughed coldly. "Far as I'm concerned, a black ape is a black ape, no matter what cross-breedin' you do to him."

Styles didn't bother to argue with him, though the excellent quality of the Fulani wench Ahma should have shown Eastin his error. But a man with prejudices was never convinced of the falsity of his beliefs; they could not be altered except to be reinforced. He didn't give a damn what Eastin believed as long as he could pick up a fast four thousand dollars for five field hands. This was a low price for quality men, but he couldn't haggle. Four thousand would give him some breathing room. He could keep the farm in operation until some money crop came through.

Bos Pilzer sagged in his saddle. He looked up and touched the wide brim of his planter's hat when Styles and Alvah Eastin joined him. Pilzer's sweated shirt hung on his outthrust midriff over his belt. His guts felt squashed together after a day in the saddle. He belched and nodded when Styles introduced him to Eastin. When Styles said, "Mr. Eastin wants to look over the stock. He might be buying four or five hands," Bos belched again. His face paled under the deep tan, and his eyes glittered. He did not speak because the sharp chill of Styles's glance stopped him. Styles said, "You want to bring those niggers over here and line them up?"

Inwardly raging, Bos rode out into the sunswept fields and herded the sweated workers to the rim of shade at the edge of the hammock. They came willingly, glad to escape the blaze of sun and the unbroken chopping. They lined up, grinning and nodding timidly at Styles and the stranger.

Eastin rode close to them. He said, "You boys listen to me. I need four or five real strong studs. You know what I mean? They's a big market right now for you black boys that can crawl two or three wenches a night." He let them laugh and nudge each other for a moment, then he added, "But jus' gittin' a hard-on ain't enough. That's why I'm looking for the best. That's why I come heah to Blackoaks." They looked at each other, smiling, puzzled, but anxious to hear more. "A boy has got to have the juices to impregnate a wench every time. They got to get yore seed in they bellies so they can bring in a healthy drop."

"I'se jus' yo' boy," one black said. "I ain't nevah missed yet . . . . You can jes' ast anybody what knows, Masta . . . . and a few round here I ain't missed with that nobody don't know 'bout."

Eastin laughed. "I like a black boy that's sure of himself. Any of you boys would like to go along with me, step out of that line and I'll look you over . . . . You look good I'll take you along—you'll git plenty to eat—and plenty of wenches."

"How 'bout workin' in de fields?" somebody called.

Eastin laughed. "I ain't gonna lie to you, boys. You might have to do some field work, too. But then, I nevah said I was taking' you to heaven—I jus' said your main job would be studdin' them wenches."

The men in the lines looked at each other, at Alvah Eastin and his road-worn horse. A few said they reckoned they'd stay at Blackoaks—his promises was something like dying, maybe you'd cross the Jordan to a land of milk and honey. But nobody knowed for sure. They knowed what they had at Blackoaks.

At last, after some delay, only three of the boys stepped forward from the line. They were young—they had come into the work crews since old Master Baynard had died. They had not found working for Styles Kenric at Blackoaks anything like the land of milk and honey. They liked the wenches here, but the prospect of unlimited sleeping-around privileges was too inviting to be refused.

Looking at the three stalwarts, Bos felt his rage deepen.

These boys were the best of the lot. They were young—they had many productive years ahead of them. They were healthy. He gripped the reins of his horse until his knuckles whitened. This was one of the stupidest things Styles Kenric had pulled in a remarkably stupid administration.

Eastin swung down. He inspected the boys' teeth, their chests and backs. He told them to drop their pants and spread the cheeks of their asses. He bent down looking for signs of piles. "First one of you boys that farts feels my whip," he said. All the men in the line laughed, and the young boys roared. They were pleased with themselves and the choice they'd made. "I'll take these three," Eastin said. "But I'll need a couple more to block out my coffle. Two more I need, or no deal."

"Why not pass up this deal, Mr. Kenric?" Bos suggested.

Styles's glance slashed like a whip across Bos's face. He said, "All right. Two more of you boys step forward. I don't give a damn which two, but move, or I'll choose the two."

They looked at each other, frightened, disturbed. Styles knew what the biggest problem was. It was what Bax Simon had warned old man Baynard against more than two years ago now—letting these black animals live in family groups. These bucks had wenches, and some of them had drops they didn't want to leave behind. Nobody stepped forward.

Enraged, Styles urged his horse forward. He rode down the sagging line of black men, reining his horse in so close to them they had to retreat or be walked on by the horse. With the end of his riding crop, Styles struck two young field Negroes on the shoulder. "You," he said. "And you. Step out there." He turned and spoke to Eastin. "These two look all right?" He knew Eastin would agree. He had selected men the slave trader could not afford to pass up at eight hundred each . . . .

Styles and Eastin rode beside the five field hands, across the plateau and down into the valley to the barns where shackles would be welded to their ankles at the smithy.

Three of the youths were silent, walking calmly, but two of the boys cried openly.

Styles cursed them, but Eastin said, "Hell, let 'em git it out'n they system. Before we're five miles down the road they'll forget what they was a-crying about. A nigger's memory ain't half as long as his pecker."

Behind them, Bos had to ride among the remaining field hands swinging his bullwhip to make them return to their chopping. They were savage in their protests. The last two boys Styles had arbitrarily chosen had big families, women they were truly attached to. They did not want to leave Blackoaks. The other blacks who knew them well did not want them sent away without even being allowed to speak to their women. "Who gwine tell they women tonight? Who gwine tell they babies that they daddy ain't comin' home no more?"

The older men mumbled. Things had not been like this in the old days when Master Baynard was alive. There had been an infrequent sale of a slave, but one could see that the master himself was deeply concerned and would never have made the transaction had there been any alternative open to him. It broke their hearts sometimes, but it broke the old master's heart, too. This new master didn't care a damn. He had no heart. No feelings.

"Git to work and stop that goddamn grumbling," Bos raged, "or I lay my whip across the backs of the last one of you." His savagery worked; they fell silent; they stared at the new-turned earth; they chopped slowly but steadily. The hell of it was, Bos's heart was not in his savage commands and heartless threats. Their grumbling expressed his own feelings, only with but an atom of the fury Styles's short-sighted crime had erupted in him . . . .

Styles saw Soapy perched like some black potentate on pillows and blankets in a rocking chair on the commissary stoop. The sight of the fat boy sent the rage surging up in Styles—the bastard, coming to him with demands for freedom. He kept his voice casual. "Got a boy there you might be interested in. He's learned to read and write—"

"That's against the law here in Alabama, ain't it?"

"The law was broke before we could do anything about it. A lot of planters need a black that can count bales, bags, and write simple stuff. You might get a good price for him."

Thoughtfully, Eastin reined in before the commissary stoop. He shifted in his saddle and sat looking the fat black boy over. "Why you sittin' on pillows, boy?"

"Got whupped, Masta."

Eastin shrugged. "Well, I always say, a whupped nigger is a better nigger. How'd you like to come down from there and come along with me?"

"Where at you goin', Masta?"

"Down the road. You'll see the sights. We'll find a good place for you. Would you like that?"

Soapy shuddered. It was in his thoughts to tell the man that he was free, he had been freed by his master, but he felt Styles's malicious gaze on him and he was afraid.

Soapy said, "I sorry, Masta. Much as I likes to 'ccommodate you—I gots to stay heah. I watchin' this place for Moab."

Styles's voice flicked at him like the lash of a whip. "Get down from there, damn it. You're going with this man."

Soapy got up, shaken. He began to cry helplessly. He stared at the five young field hands. "I ain't no field nigger, Masta." He gazed up at Alvah Eastin. "Please, suh, Masta. I a house boy. I ain't no field nigger."

Eastin said, "For Christ's sake, boy. Stop that snivelin'. Git over there in that line. Any black baboon can learn to be a field nigger." He laughed. "Hell, ain't nuthin' to it. You jus' keep your black mouth shut and your black ass moving."

Moab rounded the barn an hour later, returning by way of the distillery. When he saw the dozen Negro women, men—and Ahma—standing on the commissary stoop, his bowels turned to buttermilk.

He looked around, wanting to run. Only there was no place to run. All he could think was that Ahma had spread his secret across the quarters. He walked sickly forward.

"Where you been?" Ahma demanded. "You lef' Soapy

here alone. Your master Kenric wants to see you in his office. You in trouble, boy."

Perseus said, "Don't go yet. He in some kind of anger. He might sell you to that coffle."

"That coffle gone down the road toward Mt. Zion," somebody said.

Moab swallowed hard. "Masta ain't gwine sell me. He promised."

"Nobody thinks he sells pore little Soapy, either," Perseus said. "But he did."

Stunned, Moab could only stand, shaking his head.

Then he saw that three of the young black women—two of them obviously far-gone pregnant—were weeping helplessly and were being comforted by the other women. Moab felt he had walked into the aftermath of some disaster. "What happened?" he managed to say.

"What happened is what I been telling you people is going to happen as long as you let that white man up there—" Ahma swung her lovely arm toward the house on the plateau—"as long as you let your fine *Masta* Kenric sell yo' husbands, yo' wives, yo' chillun like you animals. You ain't animals. Ain't none of you animals. He the animal. He the heartless animal what thinks he so great he can sell us, and whip us, and kill us."

"Ahma, you shouldn't talk like that about the master," an older woman said, terror making her voice quaver.

"Why not?" Ahma raged. "Am I lying to you? Am I telling you something you have not seen yourselves? You got to stop him—before it's yore turn to be sold—to see your babies sold."

"How we goin' stop him?" Perseus said. "He sold my woman—my babies. Nuthin' I could do."

Ahma's look of contempt should have withered the broad-shouldered black man. "No. Nuthin' you can do—long as you don't do nuthin' . . . . When you stand up on yore hind legs and say to him, 'Stop! You ain't sellin' me. You ain't sellin' my wife—not if I has to kill you to stop you.' "

The women and the men on the commissary gasped at this blasphemy. They looked at Ahma in true terror, afraid of her.

Ahma wept suddenly. But they saw her tears were of rage, not weakness. "Damn you all," she said. "You go like sheep to the slaughter. You go like hogs to be castrated . . . . Damn you. You deserve what he does to you . . . . You got no guts. You got no gumption."

"Masta feeds us, Ahma. He plan for us. He gives us a house to live in. Clothes to wear."

"And the right to bear children for him to sell, or whip, or work to death," she answered, eyes bleak. She hesitated, watching big Pegasus walk across the dry, hard earth from the barn. The big Negro hesitated in the sun at the edge of the stoop. He touched at his hat and said, "Howdy, Miz Ahma. I been sent heah by Masta Styles. I got a message. I no way agree with the message. He ain't say I got to. He say I got to say to you—if you don't stop talkin' against him, he gonna put you in shackles."

To the surprise and shock of the gathered slaves, Ahma put her head back, laughing. The sound rose, mockingly, like a curse flung toward the manor house on the plateau. Her long legs apart, her hands on her rounded hips, Ahma stared at Pegasus until his eyes faltered under hers and were lowered. Then she jerked her head, staring at the others. "There. You hear that? Shackles if I don't shut my black mouth. What more do you need to know I'm right? If your dear master is so good and kind—why is he so scairt of anything I might say about him?"

Bos Pilzer rapped on the foyer door of Styles's office. Without waiting for an invitation, he walked in and closed the door behind him. He held his wide-brimmed hat in his hand. His eyes were raging.

Styles glanced up. "Why are you barging in here in the middle of the afternoon?"

"It's for your own good I'm here."

Styles stared upward along his nose. "I'll tell you now. There is one thing I won't tolerate from you, Pilzer. And that is interference in my affairs."

"You don't know how to run a cotton farm, Mr. Kenric. You done proved that—surely to your own satisfaction—

in these past two years. It ain't time to cut off expert advice. And that's what I got for you . . . . You got to stop selling off our best young field hands. We got to have money crops. We got to bring in a huge cotton yield next year—we don't do that without the strongest and best young bucks."

"You through? I told you more than once, Pilzer. I've got to run this farm. You order the Negroes around. You think this makes you an expert. Well, I have to come up with the money to make it possible. Sometimes I might have to sell off field hands—"

"We don't have field hands to be sold like that. My God, with the crops we're planning, you've crippled me."

"I bleed for you. I've told you that cotton is no longer the important crop on this farm—"

"You also found out this year—the hard way—that this farm can't exist without the best possible cotton yield we can get."

Styles's smile twisted his mouth. "That's where you're the expert. I expect you to bring in the best possible yield—with the people you've got to work with."

"You don't make that possible—"

"Then, my advice to you is to get your pay and clear out."

They glared at each other a moment. Bos swore. The stupid son of a bitch was so arrogant that he would destroy himself rather than back down an inch. It didn't matter that both of them knew he couldn't run this farm a week without Pilzer. Kenric was willing to let him go rather than accept advice and counsel.

Bos Pilzer shook his head.

"No, sir. I'll just let that pass like you didn't say it. I see you're angry and you're upset by problems you can't handle. You're willing to take that rage out on me . . . . Well, sir, I was here long before you came here. I owe this farm and the Baynards more loyalty than that. I didn't come in here asking nothing for myself. I got nothing but the best interests of this farm in my mind. No, sir, I'm to be fired, I think you'll have to bring home young Mr. Ferrell to do that."

"Ferrell doesn't run this farm, Pilzer. I do."

"No, sir, you don't run this farm. I do. You couldn't run this place a week if I was to walk out on you. Don't think I don't want to. Don't think it don't make me sick to my guts to see what you're doing to this beautiful and great old farm . . . . I go along that you're the boss. I'll do what you say—even when I get sick at some of it."

"Then you stick to your job. You keep your mouth shut. You do your work and let me handle the running of my estate." Styles stared up at Pilzer for a moment, intently, then he pointedly turned back to the papers on his desk—the top one of which was the bank note demanding Miz Claire's signature and as yet unsigned. When Pilzer went on standing there, Styles glanced up, face pallid. "That's all, Pilzer."

"No, sir. That ain't quite all. I follow your orders. But I reserve the right to tell you when you're wrong. Somebody's got to have the guts to do that."

"Thank you," Styles's smile was bitter and mordant. "Thank you for your deep concern for my affairs."

"No, sir. It's just that you make my job impossible, I got to stop you if I can. You've sold them prime young field hands. Nothing we can do about that. But there is something else. Every time you whip a poor, defenseless kid like Soapy—or sell black men away from their women— you get them riled up, hating you."

Styles's mouth twisted. "Well, that's too goddamn bad."

"Yes, sir, it is." Pilzer's voice remained cold and flat. "I don't give a damn about the niggers or what happens to them—except where it makes my job harder to do. Every time you make them blacks hate you and growl against you, the harder it is for me to handle them. And I do care about that. I got a job to do—and I'm damned if I'm gonna let you keep me from doing it because you won't listen to common sense."

Styles stared up at him. Finally he said, "The next time you want to talk to me, Pilzer, send a Negro boy to the back door and Thyestes will relay your message. I'll come down to the barns to see you. I don't want you tracking mud in this house on your filthy boots again . . . . "

5

The summer had been wet and the black trees lining the driveway from the fieldstone gateposts up the incline to the manor house on the plateau at Blackoaks were damp and dripped raindrops like tears. Since Morgan's funeral, there had been little laughter. The small black boys set as lookouts no longer screamed and ran to meet incoming carriages. They stood in the driveway, sedate and solemn, until the guests pulled up and alighted. When they spied the fine coach with Blade on the front seat, they cried out joyously among themselves and ran along the rocky lane to meet him. But they recognized the coffin, protruding through the front window from the inside of the coach. They saw, without understanding, the murderous set of Blade's dark face. They fell back, retreating as the coach plodded past, and Blade did not even lift his hand in greeting. They knew that Blade had brought more sorrow to Blackoaks, a world already steeped in woe.

Blade sat like a zombie, clutching the reins, letting the tired horses plod up the rocky incline between the dismal trees. He was only vaguely aware of the children running beside the carriage, cheerless and somber. His gaze was turned inward.

He barely saw the drive that circled before the columned veranda. A sombre mist enshrouded the lawns, fields, hammocks, hanging darkly, deepening the melancholy sense of grief, of *tristesse*.

As if the doleful message of his arrival had gone out simultaneously from the lane to every cranny of the plantation, black men, women, and children converged on the plateau, walking silently in a funeral hush. As the mud-crusted coach pulled in before the wide fieldstone steps, the doors of the house opened. From within came the younger girl servants, hurrying and then slowing and retreating to stare numbly at the brass-ornamented coffin.

Thyestes came quickly through the doorway but hesitated at the head of the steps, staring at Blade. Neva waddled through the door behind Miz Claire, and finally Blade, his stomach knotted, saw Styles Kenric stride out to the columned veranda and then stand, silent and incredulous, his sharply chiseled face a pallid mask.

No one spoke or moved. The slaves came into the driveway and stood hollow-eyed in a semicircle. At last Blade swung down from the coach. Those who had seen him elegantly attired, jaunty and handsome in tailored suit and planter's hat, stared disbelievingly at the barefooted man, sodden and streaked with dirt. He went to the steps. Miz Claire came forward to meet him. In afflicted times, she was always the one who kept her poise as if life itself had somehow conditioned her to grief.

She said, "What happened, Blade?"

Blade nodded, bowing slightly. His eyes brimmed with tears. He shook his head. "I don't know, Miz Claire . . . . they was a yellow fever epidemic in New Orleans . . . . Miss Kathy was very ill . . . . She died—on the way home."

Miz Claire buckled slightly under the impact of his words. Neva stood close behind her. "My baby," Miz Claire whispered. Neva supported her with her stout arm about Miz Claire's slender waist. "My poor baby."

"I sorry, Miz Claire," Blade said. His voice broke. "Ain't no words to say my sorrow—for you."

Blade's grief, the choked words, the tears spilling along his mud-glazed cheeks, seemed to restore Miz Claire, to remind her of her duty.

She nodded, tilting her head slightly. "Thank you, Blade . . . . If you will please drive up to the chapel. Leave Miss Kathy's coffin up there—before the altar . . . . We'll have the funeral ceremony as quickly as I can get word to Father Anthony . . . . Oh, my . . . . So many people will be coming to the services . . . . Oh, Neva, what shall I wear?"

"We find you something, Miz Claire honey," Neva whispered. Her full lips quivered and she stared toward the heavens, eyes filled with tears and hatred. It was as if she prayed for strength to support Miz Claire when she wanted to fall sobbing and roll on the ground crying for the beautiful little Kathy whom she had held in her arms, rocking her and drying her tears.

Suddenly, Miz Claire swung her arm out in a meaningless gesture. She shook her head and spoke in an empty, obstinate tone. "Well, we just can't have the funeral until Mr. Baynard and Morgan return home . . . . What would people think if we didn't wait for Mr. Baynard?"

Despairingly, Blade gazed at Miz Claire a moment. Neva drew her closer, against her shoulder, and shook her head at Blade, motioning him to drive on up to the chapel. Blade hesitated one more moment, looking beyond Neva and Miz Claire toward where Styles Kenric stood. Styles did not move. His legs were apart as if he were braced against the stunning impact of Kathy's death. There was no look of loss in his overly handsome face, nor any trace of grief. His was the stony look of a man who has been cheated . . . .

6

Blade drove the coach downslope from the chapel, going past the silent manor house, across the plateau, and down to the barns and stables in the valley. The slaves had dispersed, going silently back to their cabins. The death so soon of another of the Baynards disturbed and frightened them and stirred old superstitions of doom from the deepest wells of their forgotten pasts.

At the barns, Blade halted the team and swung down from the coach. He turned the reins over to Pegasus. Pegasus said, "Howdy, Blade. Welcome. How was N'Awleans? Was it like they say—with niggers laughing and walking free?"

Blade gazed at the big man. "You wouldn't believe it," he said.

Pegasus called after him. "Man, you must had yo'self a

high old time. You shore 'nuff ruint all them purty clothes."

Blade walked across the blue-misted valley and plodded up the incline toward his cabin. His throat felt tight and painful with unshed tears. His mind swirled with hatred. He could not look forward with any pleasure to seeing Ahma again. He felt his life—except for one last violent chore—was ended. He had no desire to live. For the first time he could not look beyond tomorrow. He did not want to.

He came up the steps. The front door was thrown open and Ahma bounded through it. She caught him in her arms, kissing his mouth, his nose, his eyes, the base of his throat. She clutched up his hands and kissed them, holding them tightly against her parted lips. "Oh, Blade," she whispered. "I love you so. I missed you so terrible . . . . I'd of waited for you—inside the cabin and naked—but I wanted all these folks to see how much I love you, how much I've missed you, how happy I is to have you back— how much you love me . . . . "

"I love you, Ahma," he said.

Troubled, feeling somehow repulsed, Ahma caught his hand and drew him through the front door. Loudly, she kicked it shut behind her. "What the matter, Blade? You ain't happy to see me?"

"Miss Kathy died, Ahma. I'm sorry. I've knowed her— I've loved her all my life. I'm sorry. I do love you, and I've missed you. It's jus' that I'm all beat up inside. I ache and hurt like I didn't know a man could hurt."

Ahma laughed. She jerked her cotton shift over her head and shoulders, tossing the much-washed frock behind her. She wore nothing beneath it. "I was dressed fo' yo' homecomin'," she said. "Oh, Blade, I got so much to tell you. So much to say. But it gotta wait. First gotta come first. I ain't dreamed about nuthin' but you comin' in that door and grabbin' me and throwing off our clothes . . . . ain't quite like that, but it close enough."

He stared at the full breasts, the rounded hips, the long legs like golden sculpted pillars, her black eyes alive with anticipation and adoration. What evil had destroyed the simple happiness he and Ahma had found together? He wanted to love her, he wanted her to love him, he wanted her to have all the excitement and pleasure that had made it easier to await his return. But he was empty inside.

She kissed him and drew him to the bed with her. "Man, I nevah seen such filthy clothes. You been wallering in some pig pen?"

"Yes," he said.

She laughed. "Don't you care. I been a lot filthier than you. When I run away from South Carolina and headed for Indian country—I was thick with briars and mud, and mosquito bites . . . . You ought to of seen me, Blade."

"I wish I had seen you, Ahma. I would have loved you."

She had unbuttoned his shirt. Making a face she threw it against a far wall. "You know when I loved you? That first minute I saw you . . . . I wanted to laugh . . . . I sixteen—seventeen—been through hell. But all of a sudden it didn't make no nevah-mind . . . 'cause I had woke me up in heaven, and you standin' there in front of me with a hard-on."

He smiled. "I didn't have any hard-on."

"You did the way I recollect you." She unbuttoned his muddy pantaloons and he shed them, kicking them away. He looked down at his limp member. "Gawd, I sorry, Ahma."

Ahma laughed and kissed him greedily. "It don't matter. You tired and plumb tuckered out . . . . I excited—and burnin' hot 'nuff for both of us . . . . I soon make you forget you tired and all the bad things that happened to you." She kissed him and drew her tongue across his lips and up the squared line of his jaw. "How come you so all-fired purty? I bet—before—you was a king—in some far-off land—and all the girls in your kingdom come in and went down on they knees when they see you."

He kissed her and smiled. "You been talking to Moab."

She went on kissing his face selectively, his closed

eyes, the tip of his nose, along the old-coin line of his profile. "Moab say the Fulanis ruled a huge land for nigh on seven hundred years . . . . I forgit . . . The Yankee teacher tole him that. . . . But we a great people—when them whites was mewling and wettin' theyselves . . . . You a great people." She had caressed his chest, pinching his paps. She drew her hand over his flat belly and through the crisp hairs at his pelvic area. She took his rod in her fist, feeling it engorge with blood. "See? It ain't so tired after all."

"If it was dead it would come up, all you doin' to it."

She went on caressing him. She whispered, breathless. "Oh, Blade, I missed you so terrible . . . . I felt like I'd go crazy nights layin' here without you . . . . I knowed I never lived until I come to you. I was wild and raging inside and full of hate—and you quieted me . . . and I know I got to have yo' or I go wild again. It's a kind of craziness, Blade, without you. Nuthin' real but screaming and scratching and hating . . . without you."

She lay down on her back and gazed up at him, ebon eyes liquid yet unblinking. She drew him over upon her, her skin tingling when his heated flesh touched hers, adhering. "Oh, do it, Blade," she cried. He thrust deeply inside her. She clasped her ankles together about his waist, locking them possessively. She screamed, wailing at the top of her voice, "Oh Gawd, Blade, do it!"

He stopped pumping and stared down at her. She laughed up at him mischievously. "I know I yelled louder'n I had to," she said. "But I wants all them women folks out there to know how *good* you is."

He laughed. "Most of them already know."

She raged in mock anger, catching his head and drawing it down to her. She kissed him fiercely, pumping her hips rapidly, driving herself upward. The bed ropes squealed. She felt herself wracked with exquisite furies. She clung to him, dizzy, not even sure for the moment where she was. Then she began to move her hips anew, in rhythm with his strokes—anything to keep him from leaving her, even for a little while. She felt herself being carried upward helplessly again and she bit his hand savagely. Pain stabbed through him, but he worked, faster and faster, saying nothing, trying to drive out all the devils that haunted him . . . .

Ahma lay quietly beside him, her head resting on the fleshy inside of his wide shoulder. She held his hand to her mouth, kissing each of his fingers separately. She was exhausted, but she was wide awake. She whispered, "You sleeping, Blade?"

"How can I sleep with you talking every minute?"

"I missed you, Blade."

"You done proved that, honey."

"I—got some—news for you. It kind of good. Kind of bad. It make me feel all happy. It make me feel like I want to *kill*."

"That do sound serious."

She lifted her head, gazing into his eyes. "Would you run away with me, Blade? Run north?"

"Right now I couldn't walk north. I couldn't crawl north."

"I'm talking serious, Blade. We got to git us away from here."

"Ahma, oh gawd, Ahma, don't start that. I all beat. I all beat inside. Now you got me whupped—and you start talkin' runnin' again. Where we gonna find a house like this? Where we find a bed like this?"

"I don't care. I didn't have no place like this before. I got along."

"You didn't have me before. And you got along."

She wept suddenly. Her hot tears splashed on his face, struck his lips. He put his arm about her gently. "Oh, Blade, don't . . . . I know I been pestering you to run away. But now it more than that. We got to go, Blade. I gone have your baby. I gone have our baby."

He stared at her in disbelief. He laughed suddenly, the pleasure eating through the agony that distracted him. "Ahma! You talking true?"

She kissed him. "You planted deep, Blade. I ain't come a-bleedin' three months now. I cotched. That's for sure. But I knowed. I knowed the first time you did it to me that I was cotched. Nothing could go that deep, feel that good, and me not be cotched." She drew kisses, like scribbled marks across his face.

He laughed, holding her close, feeling excited, tender, protective—and with it all, dead inside.

"But that's what I been goin' over and over in my mind layin' here without you," Ahma said. "I havin' *our* baby—I not havin' no sucker—for that white man to take from me—and sell."

"He won't ever sell our baby," Blade said.

7

Styles returned to his office from the front veranda. He did not speak to anyone. None of the servants spoke to him. He entered his office, closed and locked the door. Distracted, he crossed the small room, aware of the sunlight at the window, a humming bird fluttering around the gardenias beyond the panes, the bank note unsigned on the top of his desk. He poured himself a drink.

Kathy dead. The very words inside his mind stunned him. He did not love her, he supposed he never had. Her loss would not be too important, but the terrible void remained. There was no balm for his outraged honor. She had deserted him for another man. She had died, but she had not suffered. Whatever he had anticipated, it was not this.

A knock at his door roused him. He took another long gulp of whiskey and crossed the room, patting at his mouth with the handkerchief. He stuffed it in his breast pocket and unlocked the door. Thyestes stood in the corridor with an envelope in his hand. Shiva stood at his elbow. "Pardon, Masta," Thystes said. "This gal was going through Miz Kathy's steamer trunk. This letter was on top of the dresses. We thought we best bring it to you."

Shiva nodded, shivering with fear behind the butler.

Styles took the envelope. It was addressed simply "Styles" in Kathy's rounded handwriting. "Yes," he said. "It's for me. Thank you, Thyestes. Thank you, Shiva." He closed the door in their faces.

He sat down, took up a letter opener and slit the envelope. He unfolded the letter, held it, staring at it, focusing upon it only with difficulty, hatred forming a hazy red film across his eyes. Finally, haltingly, he read the note Kathy had written.

Fever washed through him in agonizing waves. He reread the brief note a dozen times looking for one word of regret, self-reproach, the qualm of conscience, acknowledgement of wrongdoing, of repentance for what she had done to him. Nothing. Not a word. Far from being contrite, she had ended her note on an obdurate theme of hatred, a thought for him to live out his life with; "I found ecstasy only with your Negro slave."

He took another drink of whiskey, finishing off the glass. He took up the bottle and filled the glass to the brim again, spilling it on the papers on his desk. Damned little bitch. She had gone to hell, thumbing her nose at him, writing down on paper—paper that might have fallen into any hands—that her last act on earth had been to take a black man as her lover. She could not live with her guilt, but she made damned sure that he had to.

Styles finished off the second tumbler of whiskey. The world wheeled slightly before him, but he attributed this to his rage, his sense of outrage, his need for reparations for the evil done him.

He strode out of his office, leaving the door flung wide. He crossed the foyer, went out the huge front door and left it open behind him. As he crossed the fieldstone veranda, he saw Miz Claire, her arms loaded with magnolias, gardenias, and lilies. She said, "I am going up to the chapel to be with Kathy, Styles. To take some flowers. She loved flowers. I am going to pray for her. Won't you come with me?"

He gestured sharply, swinging his arm cuttingly downward. "Go to hell." He strode off the veranda. She stopped, shocked, and stared after him. He walked swiftly along the drive, going around the house, across the

plateau, and into the valley where slaves worked desultorily in the oppressive heat about the barns, shops,
and stables.

Blacks bobbed their heads as he passed, but he ignored
them. He strode past the horse barn and the smithy,
going directly to the commissary. Moab was seated on
the stoop in the shade, his kitchen chair resting on two
hind legs against the clapboard wall. Moab forced himself to smile.

"Where's Blade?" Styles demanded.

Moab said, "I don't know. Up at his cabin, I reckon."

"You get up there. Tell him I want to see him. Down
here. Now."

Moab nodded. He straightened the chair, got up, and
stepped off the stoop and went up the incline into the
quarters. Styles remained where he was, standing in the
sunlight, unconscious of its heat or glare. After a few
minutes Moab returned. "Blade say he be right along,"
he said.

Styles did not answer. He stood, taut, watching the lane
from the quarters. When Blade appeared, he stiffened,
feeling the hackles on the back of his neck.

Styles felt overwhelmed with hatred. He could not even
admit to himself that his sensual passion for Blade had
been transformed through his jealousy into murderous
loathing. He had never admitted, even in his own mind,
that he had transferred his own feelings about Blade to
Kathy in building the Negro youth's desires for her to
a fever pitch. Since that morning, more than two years
ago, when he had seen Bax Simon fondling, caressing,
touching Blade, he had been shocked into an awareness
of his true desires. He had changed from that moment
forward. His repressed desire for Blade had never been
far beneath his conscious mind. Now, knowing as he had
secretly feared all along, that Blade would never return
his passionate adulation, would never want to make love
to another man, that he had brought to Kathy her only
ecstasy, he was shaken with hatred.

Styles watched Blade approach. He wore only a pair of
osnaburg britches, no shirt or shoes. A leather string was
looped about his neck with something like a charm—a

gri-gri the Negroes called the trinkets—bouncing on his chest. When Blade stopped before him, Styles saw the ornament was a gold ring. It was the wedding ring he had given Kathy.

"You said Miss Kathy died—of yellow fever?" Styles said, holding himself in leash.

Blade shook his head. "She had yellow fever."

"But she didn't die of yellow fever?"

Their gazes clashed, Styles's arrogant loathing against Blade's unmitigable hatred.

"Did she die of yellow fever?" Styles demanded.

"No."

"She didn't die at all, did she? Did she? You killed her, and you stole her ring." Styles's arm flashed out. He grabbed the leather string and broke it. "You lied, damn you . . . . She didn't die, you killed her."

Blade growled deep in his throat. He forgot enslavement, obedience. He was filled with rage as old as his forebears, rising against their enemies. He fled back in time, past the parapets of the Moors, the kingdoms of Senegal, the jungles, to the caves where there were only two conditions—life and death. Life to the stronger, death to the weaker.

"I didn't lie," he said, agonized. "No. Damn you. You lied. You lied to me. About Miss Kathy. About everything. You lied. You killed her."

· "How dare you speak to me like that." Styles grew livid. He turned his head. "Laus. Pegasus. Saul. I want this man shackled. I want him whipped."

"No." The word raged across Blade's lips. "No more. No more. You don't whip me. You don't lie to me. You don't kill. Not any more."

He lunged for Styles. Styles retreated, staggering backward, yelling for help. Blade's fist struck him in the mouth and staggered him. Blade kept crowding in like a jungle animal for the kill. His talonlike fists closed on Styles's throat, and they went down, striking the ground, Blade's knee in Styles's belly, his hands closing on his neck.

Moab stood on the stoop, immobilized by shock. He saw Styles strike the ground, saw Blade's muscles tighten like steel wires as his hands closed on the master's throat. Moab felt nothing except that Blade was going to kill Styles Kenric, and if Blade was driven to murder, there was right in what Blade was doing.

Laus, Pegasus, and several other men including Saul the smithy came running from the barns. Laus yelled at Blade. It had never entered Laus's mind to attack a white man. All he could see was the terrible criminality of what Blade was doing, the fearful price Blade would have to pay for this attack.

Laus reached them first. Styles's face was turning blue, his eyes bulged, his mouth lolled open. He struck weakly, but impotently, trying to get one breath of air rather than to protect himself. His hands closed on Blade's wrists, but he could not pry him loose.

Laus caught Blade about the bare waist and bodily hoisted him in one fearful backward lunge. Sobbing, fighting, Blade still held his arms extended, his fists clawing for Styles's throat.

Pegasus knelt and helped Styles to his feet. Styles bent over for some seconds, gasping and retching with the dry heaves. Blade fought loose, but Laus caught his wrist and twisted his arm up between his shoulder blades. Anguished, Blade knelt in the dust, face contorted.

Styles straightened at last. "I want him shackled. I want him flogged."

"No." Blade struggled again. Laus almost had to twist his arm from the socket to keep him on his knees.

Laus jerked his head and Saul caught Blade's free arm. They let him get to his feet. They half-carried him, fighting and struggling against them to the upright outside the smithy.

By now the slaves—men and women—had gathered from the quarters, from the shops and stables. Walking rigidly, mindless as a zombie, Ahma came down the lane as Blade was spanceled and shackled to the four-by-six upright outside the smithy.

Styles told Laus to get the bullwhip. Ahma screamed, "No." She ran forward, raging. Styles jerked his head. "Shackle her."

Pegasus caught her. He held her until shackles were

brought from the barn and closed on her ankles and wrists. Moab ran to her. He put his arm about her, comforting her, restraining her.

Laus brought the bullwhip from the barn. At the sight of the thick leather lash, Ahma screamed again. Styles jerked his head and the whip cracked, cutting across Blade's shoulders.

The red welt rose on his golden flesh. Blade seemed unaware of it. His murderous gaze was fixed on Styles and he did not blink. "Kill me," he said, gasping as the lash cut him again. "You got to kill me, white man, or you can't never let me free again."

Ahma screamed, "No. No. Blade, no."

The bullwhip struck again, slicing the flesh, the blood pouring along Blade's shoulders and chest. He sagged, but he continued to stare at Styles. "You bastard," he said. "You white bastard. You got to kill me."

Styles suddenly signaled Laus to cease the flogging. He walked close to Blade. He drew the back of his hand across the red welts Blade's fingers had left on his throat and neck. "I don't have to kill you," he said. "I can tame you, Negro. You'll live. But you'll wish to God you were dead. You'll never attack anybody again. I'll mark you—for as long as you live."

Blade spat in his face, hanging from the upright. Styles calmly removed his handkerchief, wiped away the spittle.

He turned his back on Blade then and entered the smithy. The slaves watched, locked in numb horror. None spoke. Moab kept his arm tight about Ahma. She remained on her knees in the dust, her gaze fixed on Blade, tears streaming down her face.

Inside the smithy, Styles said in a chilled calm to Saul, "Where is the big 'R'? The runaway branding iron. Get it for me."

Saul brought the branding iron. He could not remember the last time it had been used. It was dust-covered, rusted. Only incorrigible runners were ever branded, and there had been none at Blackoaks in many years—Saul could not even remember the last one. An R branded in a black back forever marked him.

Styles took the branding iron and hefted it in his fist.

He said, "Pump the bellows, Saul. I want this iron red hot."

Saul nodded. He pumped the bellows until the coals on the forge glowed. Styles thrust the branding iron into the white-hot coals. He held his head back to escape the intensity of the rising heat. "Keep pumping," he ordered.

"It hot," Saul said. "It blazing hot, Masta."

Styles nodded. He withdrew the iron from the coals. He walked out of the smithy. The slaves crowded in closer, but none spoke. Perseus had moved up beside Ahma and Moab, but he said nothing. He stared, his eyes bleak.

Laus said, "You want I should turn him, so you can git his back?"

"No." Styles spoke sharply. He approached. Blade stared at the iron, and struggled furiously.

"Wait a minute, Styles." Bos Pilzer rode through the silent, sullen ring of slaves. He remained on his horse. "You're destroying a valuable nigger there. Do you know what you're doing?"

"Unless you want the same thing, Pilzer, you stay out of this."

"Listen to me, Styles . . . . Don't do something in your stiff-necked, unbending obstinacy that you'll regret to the day you die."

"Stay out of this, Pilzer. This black bastard raped my wife. He killed her. He stole her ring. He tried to kill me. Well, I'm going to show him that I am his master, and he'll never dare rise against me again."

"Styles, don't be a fool."

Styles lifted the branding iron and advanced toward Blade. Ahma screamed and tried to fight free. Perseus and Moab held her. But Blade did not move. When the huge R was inches from Blade's face, Styles hesitated, waiting for Blade to whimper, to plead.

Suddenly Styles thrust the branding iron with all his strength into Blade's face. Ahma's raging, animal screams were the only sound. It was as if not a man or woman breathed while that branding iron seared Blade's face. The sharp, sizzling sound of fried flesh was loud in the silence. Blade's left eye melted under the heat, its socket seared, red hot and empty. The flesh was burned away to the bone from his forehead, foreskull, and nose. His mouth cooked and split like broiled meat. His teeth were bared through the break in his lips in a permanent horrible grimace. His right eye broiled, gray, lying like an oyster in the heat-seared socket. He was completely blind.

Styles withdrew the brand and threw it to the ground. Behind him, Moab vomited, suddenly and fiercely, spilling his insides down the front of his clothing.

Blade screamed once. He howled mindlessly and then did not make another sound. Ahma had thrown herself prostrate on the ground, crying and moaning. The other slaves remained immobile. Some sank to their knees. Other fixed sullen gazes on Styles Kenric, watching him unblinkingly.

Arms stretched high above him by the shackles and ropes, Blade had sagged as far as he could. The ropes cut into his wrists, blood streaming down his arms. Styles stood over him, raging. "You're no perfect Fulani now, Goddamn you. You're not a perfect anything. Now you are nothing. Now you are just a *nigger*. Just one more *nigger*."

Styles turned and let his gaze travel slowly across the morose faces of the slaves. His voice was thick with that same contempt and sarcasm he'd heaped upon Blade. "Heed this well. It could have been a hangrope . . . . This is the payment for any black man who touches a white woman."

No one spoke. Their sullenness and morosity was like a shield against him. Nothing he could have said would have reached them.

Styles turned, glanced again at Blade. Blade had sunk into unconsciousness, sagged against the shackles and ropes. He was disfigured. He was destroyed. But he lived. Styles felt that old inner flare of frustration that Blade could escape him by passing out.

He heeled around to leave. Ahma pushed up from the dirt. She screamed, "Kill me—or I'll kill you . . . . I'll kill you." Her voice rose to an agonised howl.

Styles glanced toward Laus. "Get her to her cabin. Shackle her—to the floor and to the walls."

Ahma crouched on her knees. She struggled up to her

feet and tried to run toward Styles, her clawing hands outstretched. She shrieked like a mortally wounded animal. Her shackles tripped her and she plunged face first to the earth. Rolling on the ground in helpless, mindless rage, she howled like a she-wolf. Her ululation stirred something old and nameless in the slaves. They trembled in paroxysms of repressed savagery, but slavery was too deeply inculcated in the most embittered of them. They grumbled and keened in impotent wrath, but they stayed where they were.

Styles turned his back on Ahma, on the fuming slaves, on the disfigured hulk of Blade. From his horse, Pilzer stared at Styles incredulously. Styles ignored the stout overseer, walked past the barn, and went up the incline to the grassy plateau. He crossed the lawn, entered the French doors at the sunroom. He strode through the silent room and went up the stairs, striding swiftly. He bit back his own gorge. He reached his own bedroom, opened the door, stepped inside, and slammed it behind him. He took one more step and then stumbled to his knees, vomiting. He vomited until he was heaving drily in anguish, but he stayed crouched on his knees, unmoving.

8

Moab walked stiffly forward to where Blade slouched, unconscious, against the smithy upright. He bit his mouth, looking at Blade's marred and mutilated face. He took the knife from the sheath on Blade's osnaburg britches and severed the ropes securing Blade's outstretched arms to the shackles high on the post. He caught Blade in his arms, let him down gently to the ground. He stayed there, kneeling beside him, holding him while the slaves slowly backed away and he was alone with him.

Blade stirred in his arms. Moab said, "It's all right, Blade. Don't try to move. We'll get you to the cabin."

"No." Blade could barely speak through his broiled, split lips.

"Pegasus, Laus. They be back soon. They help me git you home," Moab said.

"No." The word was stronger, the agony behind it fearful. "Laud 'num."

"What?"

Blade gripped Moab's arm tightly. "Laud'num, Moab. God's sake. Laud'num. Doctor. Give me. For. Miss Kathy . . . . Pain . . . in my carpet bag . . . get laud'num . . . in God's name."

"Yes." Moab was not sure what Blade wanted, but he understood it was some remedy to ease his brother's intolerable pain. He laid Blade gently against the upright and then ran across the valley and up the incline into the quarters.

Laus and Pegasus were sinking pegs into the walls and floors on which to hook the shackles and spancels to hobble Ahma. She lay sprawled face down on the floor, weeping. Moab went to her. He knelt beside her. But when he touched her shoulder, she snarled mindlessly at him and sobbed louder.

Moab, watching her in pity, found the carpet bag. He opened it and inside found a small bottle marked "Laudanum." Gripping it in his fist, Moab went out the door and ran downslope, returning to the smithy.

He winced. Blade was writhing on the ground, rolling his head back and forth, insensate with pain. Moab ran, knelt beside him. "Blade. Blade. Listen. It's me. Moab. I got the laudanum."

Blade slowly stopped rolling his head back and forth. He allowed Moab to support him against his shoulder. He opened his mouth as wide as he could. Moab placed the mouth of the bottle between his teeth. Blade bit down. Moab poured the liquid into Blade's mouth. Blade swallowed. When Moab tried to remove the bottle, Blade bit down hard. Moab poured more liquid. After a moment, Blade released the bottle. Moab recapped it and put it in his pocket.

"Moab." Though he was holding Blade in his arms,

Moab heard his brother speak painfully, loudly as if calling him from the dark distance.

"I here, Blade."

"Chapel."

"Oh Gawd, Blade. Let me git a wagon. I'll get you home."

"No." The word was a growl of savagery and protest. "Git wagon, Moab. Chapel. Chapel."

"Nothin' up there, Blade. My Gawd, nothin' up there."

"Chapel. Damn you. Chapel."

"All right, Blade. All right. I'll get a wagon."

He ran across the road and entered the barn where a wood-hauling wagon stood, mule hitched, wood only partly unloaded, forgotten. Moab caught the mule's harness at the cheekpiece and led the animal from the barn as near to Blade as he could get him. He helped Blade stand. Blade's legs were free, but his arms were still linked at the shackles on his wrist.

Moab helped Blade climb up the wagon spokes and ease one leg over the side of the wagon. Blade fell forward then against the seat. He pulled himself up and sat, head back, lolling on his shoulders, moving back and forth in a mindless rhythm of unbearable pain. "Chapel," he muttered.

"Yes, Blade." Moab slapped the reins across the mule. It lumbered forward, going upslope. Moab gripped the lines. What if Styles came out to stop them? He touched the thick handle of Blade's knife which he had thrust under his belt. He found himself praying Styles Kenric would come out to stop them. There was no way help could get to Kenric before he stabbed him to death and sliced him and cut him until all the blood ran out of Kenric, and the unholy agony out of Moab.

The wagon lumbered past the manor house, oppressively silent in the waning afternoon. Moab turned the cart upslope to the chapel on the knoll. When he halted the mule before the fieldstone building, Blade said, "Help me down."

Moab swung down from the wagon. Empty-bellied, he walked around to where Blade, swaying under the burning impact of pain, was reaching blindly for the metal wheelrim. Moab reached up, caught Blade's hands and arms, and helped him step down. Deep inside him, Blade was mewling in agony, but when Moab said, "Let me help you git home, Blade," Blade swore, his mutilated mouth twisting. He said, "You see if Miz Claire in there, Moab."

Moab opened the door. Candles illumined the small chapel. Miz Claire knelt on a fabric-covered prayer stool beside Miss Kathy's coffin. Moab's eyes touched the slumped, agonized figure of the crucifixion, and he swallowed back hot bile, retreating. "She there, Blade," he said.

Blade nodded. Holding his hand before him, Blade stumbled toward the door. Moab guided him. When his hand closed on the door-framing, Blade stopped. He said, "Go home, Moab . . . . Damn you . . . . Go . . . . Comfort Ahma . . . . You all she got . . . now."

"Please, Blade—"

"Damn you. Go. I in agony, boy. Go."

Moab nodded. He backed away from Blade, crying. Blinded by his tears, he crawled into the wagon and turned it, rattling back down the knoll.

Blade sank to his knees in the doorway of the chapel. He called, "Miz Claire . . . . Miz Claire . . . . "

Claire had heard the voices at the chapel door and had already gotten up from her knees beside the coffin. She opened the door, then stopped, stunned. She shook her head, her face contorting. "Oh, my God . . . . Blade . . . what have they done to you?"

"They—ruint me, Miz Claire."

She stared in sick disbelief at the raw, savage striae of branding-iron marks, the bloody, empty socket, the gray sightless eye, the exposed skull.

"Oh, God, Blade. They've ruined you . . . . oh, poor Mr. Baynard . . . . What will he say? . . . his perfect Fulani—"

"Please, Miz Claire . . . . Please . . . . I in misery . . . . I ruint . . . . I in pain. Like I on fire . . . . Gawd,

Miz Claire . . . . help me . . . kill me, Miz Claire . . . kill me . . . . "

She stared at him, her eyes brimming with tears. At last she nodded. She drew the gun Baynard had taught her to use when Ferrell and Kathy were only children. She held it out before her, less than three feet from the agonized black man kneeling before her. She pressed the trigger.

9

For a long time after Blade's body had been placed in a cypress coffin and removed for burial in the slaves' cemetery, Moab remained alone, huddled on the blood-stained chapel foyer floor.

He did not know how long he stayed crouched there, or what finally roused him. Everyone had gone away. A fearful quiet had closed in upon the plantation as if physically isolating it from the rest of the world. His hand touched the handle of Blade's knife. It was his now. It was all he had of Blade. Thinking of Blade recalled Ahma to his mind and Blade's concern for her, even in his dying agony. He thought of her alone in that cabin. He got up and ran blindly across the plateau, downslope through the work valley and up the incline into the quarters. He heard her crying hysterically before he reached the cabin. He went in to her. He whispered her name softly, over and over, and sank on the floor where she was shackled, drawn up in a knot of terror and loss, shaking from head to foot with physical paroxysms. He thought impotently, "God, let me help her! Please, God, let me help her!" But she would not listen to him; she was hardly aware of him. She sobbed in that mindless wailing way until she at last fell silent in emotional exhaustion.

"Blade!" she screamed. "Blade!" again and again. When no one answered, she fell silent, as if listening, staring emptily, deserted, terrified, alone.

He remained on the floor beside her until she cried herself to sleep. He pulled a pillow from the bed, laid his head on it and after a long, eternal time, he slept. She awoke him a little after dawn the next morning, rolling her head back and forth on the floor, mewling and crying.

By the end of the second day, Ahma's eyes were dry. She no longer wept wildly, in delirium, shrieking like a soul in torment. She lay silently, consumed by virulent hatred. After hours of silence, she whispered, pleading, "Moab . . . . cut me loose. Get me out of these shackles."

"He'll just have you shackled again . . . . He might beat you first."

"No. He won't do nuthin' to me. Not any more. I know now what I got to do . . . . I'll wait till night . . . . They won't know I free . . . . I'll take Blade's knife—I'll castrate him—as Blade used to castrate the hogs . . . . We'll let him live—without his balls. And we'll run."

He shook his head. "They'll kill you."

"God, boy. I'm dead. Don't you know I'm dead—?"

"You bad hurt—you ain't dead."

"All I live for is to cut him . . . . I'll be so careful— God knows I don't want to kill him . . . . I want him to live—crippled and stewin' in his evil . . . . to think about his evil . . . . every day of his life."

"Ahma, I can't help you free—to kill yourself."

"You want me to live in torment?"

"I don't know . . . . I know Blade wants you to live . . . . He told me to—take care of you. He say I'm all you got now."

"Then help me cut that evil man."

"I hate him, Ahma. Worse than you ever can . . . . But Blade's dead . . . . There's enough death, Ahma . . . ."

She stared at him coldly. "If I live to get free, I got to kill him—or I got no reason to live."

"You got Blade's baby."

She shuddered, her mouth quivered, and she gasped helplessly, almost shattering into torment again, but she remained rigid and did not cry.

10

The uprising at Blackoaks grew as a thunderstorm, a hurricane, a tornado comes up from the smouldering horizon—the unrest is out there, the destructive wrath, the uncontrollable passion, even if it can't always be seen. The revolt of the blacks grew out of Styles's arrogant mismanagement. It came from the unrelieved distress of people with ancient hatreds tamped down deeply to explosive tension. It erupted from desperation out of control. It flared in retaliation for Styles's casual sale of slaves—from the broken families and broken hearts left behind. It exploded from those fuming daily frustrations for which there was no redress except violence. It blazed up out of stored angers from when embittered people saw Soapy whipped until his body bled like raw, chopped meat. It was triggered by the horror of Blade's disfigurement and the uselessness of his death. But it still might have misfired except Ahma's broken weeping, her incessant ululations, which would not let them sleep, or rest, or forget . . . .

Moab tried to fix food for Ahma, but she refused to eat. She sat morosely, staring at the floor, once in a while tugging, helpless, at her shackles.

They heard the men grumbling in the lane, the heavy tread on the plank steps, across the pine-slab stoop. Moab went to the door. He saw Perseus there, bare to the waist, his face streaked with some atavistic garish orange grease. Behind Perseus on the stoop and steps he saw Peleg, Saul, Paint, and in the dark lane five or six others he could not recognize in the darkness.

Perseus said, "Ahma . . . . "

She spoke from the floor where she was crouched, shackled. Her voice was dead but underlined with hatred. "What you want?"

Perseus stood beside Moab in the doorway. He was

faintly illumined in the candlelight, the jungle markings on his face glowing faintly. "We ain't gwine wait no more . . . . Some of us . . . . not too many . . . . we tied up Laus and Pegasus . . . . Others won't come along, but swear they stay out . . . . They say they stay in they cabins no matter what we'uns do."

Ahma sat up straighter. She tugged at the shackles, moaning, keening. "Cut me loose . . . . "

"No, Ahma," Perseus said. "It's for us to do . . . . But . . . . what us do?"

She stared up at him, her heart pounding violently, her mind swarming with horrors against the evil white master. "You make him hurt, Perseus . . . that what you do . . . . Fire . . . fire make him hurt—in the grain storage—fire in the distillery—the commissary—fire—in the animal barns . . . . Fire to gut his big house . . . fire make him hurt in the balls."

Perseus nodded, then spoke in doubt. "We burn the house—we hurt Miz Claire—"

Ahma's voice scourged him. "The hell with her . . . . Her skin white ain't it—same as his?"

At last, Perseus spoke in an accommodating tone. "We make him hurt, Ahma . . . . " Perseus nodded and retreated, going across the stoop and down the steps.

Moab said, "I'll go with you."

Ahma's voice, sharp and lashlike, stopped him. "Moab. Fore you go. Come here."

He returned to the interior of the candlelit cabin. She jerked her head, motioning him to close the door. "You let them go . . . . They scairt . . . . they stupid niggers . . . they don't know they got to kill all the whites or they dead . . . they leave one white alive to say they name—they gets killed."

"You wanted to go with them—"

"I could of been sure nobody lived to name us. Maybe I could of kept them from gettin' killed . . . . We gone break loose. You and me. While they's fire—and killing—and people runnin' around wild—we gone run north . . you and me."

"Where we go?"

"Away from here, boy. North."

"Yes," he said. "We'll go."

Her voice hardened. "We might not make it. You better think on that . . . . "

"I've thought about it. I'd rather die than go on being a slave."

She nodded. "Somehow, you got to get the key. I got to get free of these shackles. Cuttin' won't do . . . . I got to run free—run fast . . . . "

"Laus keeps a key at the smithy. I know where. I get it."

She caught his arm. "Not yet. Wait. They time. When the fires start . . . . "

11

Florine Pilzer was among the very first to see the sky flare into furious pinks that settled swiftly into blood-red clouds of smoke that seemed to spread across the sky. It was sometime after midnight. Bos had mounted her, pumped furiously, ejaculated prematurely, and left her in a state of sleepless misery. She lay there thinking about Moab, knowing she had to see him, even though she risked both their lives. She had no life without him.

She threw off the covers and lunged out of bed. The support ropes squealed. She ran across the room to the window. Behind her, disturbed, Bos sat up, sleep-drugged. "What? What's the matter?"

"Jesus Christ, Bos, the whole plantation is on fire."

He awoke instantly, fighting the covers. He lumbered across the room. The reflection from the infernal fires beyond the quarters lighted the inside of his house. "Oh, shit," he said. "Them black jungle bastards. They turned."

He heeled around, feeling rage, horror, and the terrible sense of waste that the appalling fires set by ignorant blacks would destroy their very hope of livelihood. And he kept seeing Miz Claire. He had to get across there to her. He prayed the house wasn't burning yet.

He fought his legs into his trousers, pulled on his boots. He got a gun, brought a rifle to her. "Lock them doors. They try to get in, you shoot, and shoot as fast as you can."

She had not moved from the window. She was transfixed. She turned her head. "Where you going?"

"Jesus, I got to see if there's something I can do. I got to try to stop them."

"They'll kill you. You know you'll be one of the first ones they want to kill."

"Yes. Well, fuck 'em. They got to kill me first. And if I go down there to them, maybe they won't come up here."

He strode across the kitchen, bared to the waist. He called back from the door. "Keep these doors locked. Stay in here. Don't let nobody in."

She followed him to the rear door, locking it after him. She stood at the window, watched him come out of the barn, his big horse saddled, his gun shoved into the saddle holster. The distant fires illumined him. He was already sweating. She watched him ride across the yard, kicking the gray in the flanks to hurry the animal.

She went on standing at the window, watching the patterns of lurid flame and smoke against the night sky. She clutched the gun, the metal chilled against her sweated palms, gunoil strong and pungent in her nostrils. Distantly, she heard explosions and the crashing of falling buildings. She felt as if she were looking into the mouth of hell. She wondered where Moab was . . . .

Skirting the edge of the quarters, Pilzer rode the gray downslope into the valley where most of the fires crackled, raging and blazing out of control. He saw the figures of black slaves running from the deep shadows, picked out for a moment in the vivid light of the fires, etched in the sudden bursting of combustion, and then lost in the darkness again. He heard the wild shouts and cries. From the quarters arose a sickening keening.

He saw that the newly restored distillery was in flames —the fires and smoke blazing upward. Nearer, the animal barns, the storage barns, the stables were burning. Animals squealed, men yelled, that sobbing wail rose from behind him.

He rode as close to the fires as possible. Men ran out of the shadows. Without stopping his horse, he moved in close to them. He reached for the gun in the saddle scabbard. He shouted, his voice raging above the roar of flames. "Hold it, you black bastards. What the hell you think you're doing here?"

Three of the blacks who had run toward him, with torch and pitchforks, stopped under the impact of his authoritative voice. They stood glistening with sweat, reflecting the fires in their eyes, their wet bodies, and in the paint streaking their cheeks. "Jesus," he thought. "The black bastards have reverted . . . . They've gone all the way back . . . . Painted savages . . . . Shit . . . . They've turned, all right . . . . "

He jerked at the gun. For a moment it caught on the leather, and he concentrated on wrenching it free. The painted slaves stood in the firelight, tongue-tied and immobile. As he straightened, a looped length of cowrope settled over his head. Before he could react and grasp it it was yanked tightly about his neck, cutting the skin and stopping his breath.

The rope tautened and he was pulled from the saddle. He struck the ground hard, the last atom of breath driven from his body. The black with the rope was fast and expert. Before Bos could straighten, the choking noose had been set, the line run down his back, and his wrists snagged. He wondered who was handling that rope. The only Negro capable of such rapid, faultless action was the Fulani Blade—and God knew, that poor bastard was dead.

His wrists were tied so swiftly and so mercilessly that the circulation to his hands and fingers was cut off, and he felt his sun-and-labor-toughened skin slicing. The rope was brought up under his crotch, run through the noose, and carried down his legs to secure his ankles.

He lay helpless on his back and stared up at the sweated, contorted face. The black had a twelve-inch butcher knife. He would have disemboweled Pilzer on the spot; he wanted to, he intended to, but whoever was in charge was after bigger fish. "Drag him to the smithy," he heard the voice say from the darkness. "We gots to git up to the big house 'fore that Kenric can get away."

Two of the black men caught the ropes along Pilzer's back and dragged him across the rocky ground to the smithy. He didn't believe he would make it. The tightened noose strangled and choked him, the rope at his testes crushed him agonizingly. The world skidded and bumped and everything spun in front of his eyes. Just as he passed out, he was rolled to an upright at the smithy. He lay, gasping for breath.

After a long time, Bos saw two other figures, roped and secured a few feet from him in the smithy. He recognized the huge bulk of Laus, rendered helpless as he was, secured with ropes. Beyond Laus, he heard Pegasus choking, sobbing, and making incomprehensible noises in his anguish as if he alone were responsible for this fiery holocaust.

"The bloody bastards," Pilzer said. "They'll get themselves hung. That's all they'll do. They won't get away with this. People will see these fires—they'll hunt 'em down and hang 'em."

"That gwine be too late for you, white man," Laus said.

Pilzer caught his breath, staring at the huge man in the darkness. He did not say anything else . . . .

In the manor house the violent explosions and crackling of the fires woke the white people and the servants. When the fierce flames burst up in the distillery, the walls of the house shook. The terrified servants ran to the kitchen, streaming down the rear stairs. They gathered at the huge pine table without knowing why. Those who wanted to escape ran from the rear doors of the house and across the plateau in the direction of the road. But most of them—the majority—remained huddled together in the kitchen. Some sank to their knees trying to remember the prayers Miz Claire had tried diligently to teach them. "Now I lay me down to sleep . . . . As it is on earth and heaven . . . . Give us this day . . . . Oh, Gawd . . . . I have sinned . . . help me, Gawd . . . . My soul to take . . . ."

Wearing a silk housecoat over the fine satin of her gown, Miz Claire came out of her bedroom hearing the mindless screams of the house servants. "Fire!" Neva waddled beside her, her bulky body covered with a heavy wraparound that resembled a horse blanket in color and texture.

Wearing boots and trousers, shirttails flying, Styles came out of his bedroom. He saw Miz Claire hurrying toward the staircase with bulky Neva plodding at her heels.

"Where are you going?" Styles demanded.

"Oh, Styles, the Negroes are burning everything."

"Them niggers gone blood crazy," Neva said. "They gwine kill us all."

"Never mind, Neva," Miz Claire said. "I'll have to stop them."

Styles strode to the staircase and went down it at an angle, intercepting her. "Where in hell do you think you're going?"

"I'm going to stop them."

"How in hell do you expect to stop them?"

"I am their mistress. They will listen to me—"

"Chile, they won't," Neva said. "They ain't gwine listen to nobody."

"I'll handle this, Neva," Miz Claire said sharply. "We can't have this—what on earth will poor Mr. Baynard say when he and Morgan get home—to find everything burned to the ground?"

Styles caught her arm. "You stay in this house as long as you can. You keep her in here, Neva. Stay downstairs so you can get out if—when the fires start."

He went down the steps then. He got a handgun and a rifle from his office. He shoved the pistol under his belt and carried the big gun. Thyestes limped, half-running from the rear of the house. "Don't go out there, Masta Styles," he said. "It you they after . . . . They say they gone git you—if they has to burn you out of this house."

"You black bastard. If you knew that, why didn't you tell me?"

Thyestes cried suddenly, helplessly. "I didn't know

when, Masta . . . . They talk . . . lot of time them niggers talk big."

"All right. You stay in here and try to take care of Miz Claire and Neva. And stop sniveling. They won't hurt you."

"Then niggers gone crazy, Masta. They hurt anybody— even they own folks like me." Thyestes was shaking visibly.

When Styles stepped out on the veranda, the night was bright with fire and smoke. He could hear the wild cries and yells of the arsonists. And from the quarters rose a keening wail that disturbed him more than the screams of rage. He stepped off the end of the veranda, went between the clustered gardenia bushes, incongruously sweet-scented in the hellish-red night.

He crossed a patch of lawn to the road which led down to the barns in the work valley. He hesitated, his hands gripping the rifle. He saw the four black figures stalking up the incline toward him. Two carried torches and two were armed with knives and pitchforks. In the torchlight he saw the paint-smeared faces and dread flashed through him.

As they approached, without speaking, but as if at a signal, they separated, putting several yards between each man. He was dismayed by this. He'd had no chance to kill them all, but he had felt he could kill at least two of them before they got to him. If they'd stayed close together, the immediate death of the man at another's side could have taken the heart out of the survivor. He hesitated but continued walking forward, watching the men widen the distance between them, their weird faces glittering in the strange light.

Suddenly he heard movement from the deepest shadows to his left. He swung around, brought the gun up. Two bare-chested black men leaped at him from the hedge. He cursed, grasping at the trigger of the gun. He fired, but the shot went harmlessly into the sky. From behind him two more men lunged from the blackness while those four figures from a nightmare continued to stalk forward. Something caught Styles across the skull, and he went to his knees. He dropped the gun and it fell on the flinty roadway. He was barely conscious. He managed to stay on his knees though he swayed convulsively. Too fragmented to be a thought, a myth or ethnic legend flared through his mind. The jungle warriors especially favored the testes and penis of their bravest foes, believing that to eat these parts gave them the dead man's courage.

He was not unconscious, but neither was he fully aware of what was happening around him. There were guttural growls that added up to a decision to disembowel him. And then he heard a harsh, pitiless voice ride over the others. "Do killing him hurt him? How he hurt when he dead? You cut out he guts, he dead."

"Then what you do? We got him like this, we can't let him live."

Perseus laughed. "We can lets him live—if we lets him live—our way . . . . Drag him in the grass . . . . Strip him down . . . . Hold him . . . . This white man wish he dead 'fore I through with him."

Styles was aware of hands grabbing his arms. He was dragged across the flint-pocked roadway to the grass. His shirt, pants, and boots were stripped away. He struggled, but they held him face down in the grass. Perseus knelt behind him. "You two holdin' his legs . . . spread 'em wide."

The other black men raged with laughter at this. The sound of their raging was unreal in Styles's mind. The sound got inside his head and spun there wildly. Two men, grasping his ankles, held him spread-eagle. He felt the first driving thrust into his anus. He bucked forward, yelling. Perseus caught his hips, digging his fingers into his pelvis. Holding him locked immobile, Perseus thrust again. This time, Styles screamed. It felt as if a huge torch had been thrust far up into his rectum. He felt his flesh tear, and he screamed. He kept screaming until Perseus caught his hair in his fist and battered his face into the earth, again and again. Styles bit the dirt, chewed the grass, moaning, and then, when Perseus thrust once more with more power than ever, he sprawled forward in an ecstasy of agony.

Styles lay still. It went on in a scorching, agonizing orgy of pain. He lost consciousness. When he woke up they were gone. He shook his head, looking around. The buildings in the valley below still flamed, and smoke rose, billowing in pink clouds, but the big manor house remained. He shuddered. They hadn't killed him because they wanted him alive, the object of their raging scorn and ridicule, the white man who had screamed like a woman as he was being sodomized in the grass.

PART SIX

Runaway Blacks

1

The fires burned furiously. The distillery glittered beyond the pine hammock, an inferno rocked with intermittent explosions that splattered the night sky with lurid
oranges, pinks, and greens. Roofing at the storage barns
imploded, the dried cypress shingles tumbling into the
flames, renewing them. Sparks circled upward on fiery
updrafts and threatened the tinder-dry slave cabins. If one
cabin were ignited by the sparks, they would all go in a
fast-rushing, gutting blaze. The slaves crept out of their
shacks timidly. Pausing on their stoops, they stood enthralled at the reddened skies, the lunging flames. Some
ventured down the steps to the lane. They congregated,
herded close together. They could feel their faces
scorched by the burn of the terrible conflagration all the
way down in the valley. Their frantic, almost rhythmic
praying and keening rose unintelligibly.

Moab came out of Blade's cabin as soon as the fires
erupted. He paused in the shadows and watched the confusion. He walked out into the lane and went along it and
into the smithy.

When he ran inside the open, stone-hearthed smithy, he
stopped, frustrated. Laus, Pegasus and—for hell's sake—
Bos Pilzer sprawled fettered like rams awaiting slaughter.
The rioters would get back to them later—the white over-

441

seer and two loyal slaves. Moab felt a surge of sick regret. They had been good to him, all of them. He would never again see them alive.

"What you want in heah?" Laus said.

Moab paused, then shrugged. "I want the key. Can't leave Ahma shackled in that cabin. That wood terrible dry—and sparks a-fallin, up there, big as horseturds." •

"Yes," Laus said. "Git her out of there."

"Cut us loose, Moab," Bos said.

Moab hesitated. He owed Bos Pilzer a great deal. The overseer *had* sliced his back with a bullwhip, but since that unhappy moment over two years ago, no man had been kinder to him. It seemed hellish to leave a human being to be disemboweled when you had been pestering his wife steadily. Somehow, this made Pilzer almost family . . . . At the thought of Miz Florine, another sense of emptiness and loss attacked him.

Laus made the decision for him. "Leave Mas' Pilzer here, Moab . . . . You doin' this white man no favor cuttin' him loose now . . . . He go out there now, them niggers kill him this time for sure . . . . They gwine git him soon enough . . . . He got one shitty little chance to stay alive . . . that's stayin' right here on his back. You stay yoah ass away from heah—or they gits you too," Laus said.

Moab nodded and retreated from the smithy. The last thing he heard was Pegasus's helpless sobbing from the deep shadows near the forge.

Clutching the brass key, Moab ran out of the smithy and up the incline into the quarters. Around him, the night was brilliantly illumined. He was only one of many figures darting along the lane, running between the houses. Many of the men and women were looting the smokehouse, saving what they could from the fire.

Empty-bellied, Moab ran past Blade's shack where Ahma awaited him. Following his inmost instincts, he ran from the quarters and crossed the park, racing toward the fieldstone house where he had known his moments of greatest happiness. Suddenly, a warning flashed in his mind, slowing him. Miz Florine was alone and she must be in terror. She'd be watching at the windows, ready to shoot at any shadow that moved toward the house. Damned if he wanted her to kill him now when he was almost free. Throwing away caution, he yelled loudly, "Miz Florine! Miz Florine!"

He slowly crossed the grass-plotted yard to the porch. He heard the front door whine open and slam behind her as she ran out to meet him.

"You all right, Miz Florine?" he said.

Florine sagged against his chest, sobbing. "Oh God, I could have killed you. I almost shot you." Sobs wracked her body.

"Well, don't cry. You didn't. I here. I ain't got much time—please don't cry anymore."

"I can't help it. You're here. I almost killed you. I can't help crying."

"Listen to me, I come to say goodbye. I gwine run . . . . Tonight. I ain't tole nobody but you."

She cried even harder now, her tears hot against his flesh. "Please, Moab, don't. They'll run you down. They'll kill you."

"We got one chance. Tonight. While the fires are keepin' everybody runnin' around—"

"We?" She swallowed a sob, going tense.

"Ahma. Blade's woman and me. We gwine run north."

She wept inconsolably. "You'll find it no better there. The whites up north will hate you—just like the rednecks down here—only they won't help you at all."

He drew a deep breath. "We made up our minds. Hate us or not—we be free."

"I'll tell them—I've got to stop you. Before they kill you."

He tightened his arms about her. He kissed her gently. He turned her face up. "You know I know better than that. You won't tell nobody . . . . You been good to me—from the first, better than anybody else . . . . You ain't going to change now."

"Oh, Moab, Moab. What will I do without you?"

"You know I wouldn't never leave you—if they was any way on this earth we could be together. They ain't. You know they ain't—even if you won't admit it. You know they ain't . . . . I can't go on like this—being a slave. Not any more. They something in me. I'd rather die . . . . Blade told me a long time ago—our papa was killed by dogs when he tried to run. I know why he run—I know I got to run."

She wept suddenly, helplessly. He clung to her and his eyes brimmed with tears and spilled against her cheeks. His crying made her feel better, stronger, and she sniffled, straightening. She reached up and placed her palm against his cheek. "You got to take care of yourself, Moab."

"An' you, too."

"I'll be all right." Her voice was dead. She reached up and caught the gold and diamond cross on the gold chain about her neck. She jerked it, breaking the tiny links. She pressed it into his hand. "Take this with you . . . . It's worth—a few hundred, I don't know . . . . it'll help you . . . . You won't get no help unless you can pay for it . . . . Black or white—nobody is going to help you unless they can make something out of it. You can trust whites as much as blacks—if you've got money . . . . you can't trust either one if they can't make a profit out of helping you—because they might always turn a dollar out of betraying you."

He kissed her. She wept, clinging to him. He did not cry again. He drew away from her, with her gripping his arms, his wrists, his hands until he was outside the door. He went close once more and kissed her. Then he heeled and ran. She whispered, "Moab," after him. But he did not slow down.

Returning through the babbling and confusion of the quarters, he made another decision. The gold cross gripped in his right fist determined him. Florine had given him her most valuable possession, her only valuable possession. He could not leave until he had done all he could for her. He pocketed the diamond and gold cross along with the brass key, and walked past Blade's shack again, returning to the smithy.

He let himself into the big open room as quickly and quietly as possible. Laus saw him first. His voice was hard, bitter. "Why you back heah, boy?"

"Masta Pilzer," Moab answered as honestly as he could.

"He been good to me. Better'n any man 'ceptin' Blade . . . . I gone cut him loose."

Laus cursed him. "You cut him loose, he try to stop them fool niggers, he gits his belly slit."

"No," Moab said. "Because I'm only going to cut him loose so he can go back up there and protect his home— Miz Pilzer . . . . Somebody got to."

Laus hesitated a moment as the wheels meshed slowly in his burr head. "That make sense."

"How about it, Masta Pilzer?" Moab begged.

Pilzer didn't hesitate. "Yeah. I'll git back up to my place . . . . Shoulda never left her up there by herself . . . . I pray to God she's still alive."

"So do I," Moab said, slitting the ropes with Blade's knife.

"You go up by the pigpens, Masta Pilzer," Laus said. "They ain't nobody up that way—and they won't look for you there . . . . You can cut through to your place."

Moab waited until Pilzer shook free of the ropes and stood up. Pilzer stared at him a moment. Then he reached out and caught both Moab's arms in his hands, gripping them fiercely. "If I'd of had a son, Moab," he said, his voice tight, "I'd of wanted him just like you—only I wouldn'a minded him being white."

Moab nodded. "You all right, too, Masta—for a white man."

Pilzer laughed and turned, lumbering out of the smithy and hurrying up the path toward the pigstys. Moab watched until he could no longer see the bulky figure in the darkness. Then he said, "You want me to cut you loose?"

Pegasus almost sobbed. "Yeah, boy. Cut me loose—and I go out there and I take a wagon shaft and I kill them filthy niggers."

"Let him alone," Laus said. "Even if he ain't got sense enough to know when he well off, I know. Git out of heah fore somebody find out it you what cut Pilzer loose. Go on, boy. Git."

Moab went out the rear of the smithy as Pilzer had. Then he cut back along the lane into the quarters above where the commissary was burning fiercely. When he entered Blade's shack, Ahma snarled at him like a whelping lynx.

"You been up to that bitch, ain't you?" she said.

He knelt beside her, using the key in the shackles. "I done everything you want done, Ahma . . . . I'm ready to go . . . . Now. They ain't no horses. No carriage. Everything is burnt or run off . . . . We got to run for it."

She threw aside the shackles. She slipped her arms into an old work jacket that had belonged to Blade, set one of his straw sun hats on her head. "I ready . . . . You got that letter what Kenric wrote so Blade could get past the slave patrollers?"

Moab got the letter. He folded it, put it in a jacket pocket. He put on work shoes, a denim shirt, the jacket. He carried Blade's knife. "We walk out alone—I meet you up there on the road past the Pilzer house—it's the best way out."

She nodded. She started toward the door, hesitated, then heeled around and caught him against her. She kissed him roughly. "I don't really hate you, Moab."

He laughed. "You will—'fore we gits north."

Naked in the grass across the hard-packed gravel lane from the manor house, Styles lay bleeding and agonized, hands clawing at the earth. The red and orange of the fire was as lurid and furious inside his head. He was on fire. He was in hell.

He saw three figures running on the road near him. He lifted his head, wanting to call out for help, but he did not speak. He was afraid to—these blacks might finish him off. His mouth twisted bitterly between savage pain and savage self-hatred. He didn't see that it mattered much if these blacks killed him now. Perseus and those thugs with him hadn't left him much to live for. He was no longer master of anything in their eyes. He had known he would have to endure the crocodile tears of those who pretended to regret with him that another man had taken his wife from him. Now he would be a figure of scorn, ridicule, filthy jokes.

One of the three men stopped near him. "Wait a minute, boys."

Styles lifted his head. He recognized Thyestes's voice. He said, "Thyestes. Help me."

Thyestes limped to him, knelt beside him. The elderly Negro moaned in sympathy. "My Gawd. My Gawd. Them rotten niggers . . . . Here, you boys, helps me lift him. Easy now, an' we takes him in the house and up to he bed . . . . Don't you worry, Masta, we gits you a doctor jus' as soon as we can."

Styles bit back bitter laughter. As soon as they could? Those rioters wouldn't let anyone leave this place alive, for any reason.

The four blacks carried Styles as gently as they could, across the fire-flushed yard to the front door of the manor house. Thyestes opened the huge door, and they sidled carefully through it with Thyestes rasping orders they could not have followed had they been listening to his unhinged chattering.

Styles let his head sag. He knew he left a trail of blood with every step they took. A fastidious man who despised above everything else being the object of pity or recipient of aid from anyone, he found this emotional pain almost physical and more tormenting than his torn and ruptured anus.

With Thyestes dogging their heels, the houseboys carried Styles, face down, up the wide staircase, along the upper hallway to his bedroom. The crackling and exploding fires were more distant now, though the walls, floors, and ceiling of the cavernous upper corridor were garishly lit.

They laid him on his bed, still face down. Thyestes, less hysterical with obligations to discharge, reacted in old habit. He sent one of the houseboys to set maids working with mops and pails and clear water to remove all traces of blood from veranda, foyer, stairs, corridor, and bedroom flooring. He dispatched another boy to fetch a doctor from Mt. Zion. This youth, mind frozen with terror, got as far as the wide veranda steps where he sank down with his head between his knees and wept helplessly.

Thyestes himself tried to stanch the flush of blood from Styles's rectum. But Thyestes quickly learned that he could not check the seepage, he could only aggravate it. In a kind of sick horror, he covered pads with grease and set them in place as gently as he could.

"God damn it, Thyestes, you're killing me," Styles muttered between gritted teeth.

"Yassuh, Masta, suh. I doin' the best I can."

"Goddamn it. No wonder I'm bleeding to death."

Fighting back nausea, Thyestes only nodded. "Yassuh." But he felt better when the pads were set in place. When he could no longer see the seeping blood, he was relieved, if not satisfied with his work.

Styles sank into the warmth of semiconsciousness—it was like sliding out of conscious agony down into a pool of tepid water where blissful unawareness was the last and only hope of heaven.

At last, leaving only a candle lit on the table beside his bed, Thyestes and his houseboys retired from the room.

Slowly, Styles swam back up to reality. He lay unmoving. He stared at the fluid patterns of light and shadow cascading along his walls in streams of red and gold and cerise. Locked in numbing agony, he gazed unblinking into an unknown depth, the same thoughts chasing themselves on the dark treadmill of his mind. He lay immobile, thinking, overwhelmed with his thoughts, until dawn.

2

Led by Perseus, the rioters had erred first in following Ahma's savage advice to Perseus. Ahma was thinking in terms of terrorizing revenge, of total vengeance. She had not stopped to consider actually striking against the hated white enemy and perhaps succeeding in the insurrection. She hadn't taken that much time. She had seen the destruction the U.S. Army fires had caused in the food bins of the Florida Seminoles. Fire brought immediate terror, but its devastation was complete because starvation followed inevitably in its wake. Perseus had asked her how to hurt Styles worst and she had raged at him, "Fire!"

"Fire," Perseus had relayed to his followers, and they had agreed in fury. Yet, oddly, neither Perseus nor the most rabid rioter in his small band had wanted to burn the main house if this meant endangering Miz Claire. So inculcated were their minds with reverence for the mistress of Blackoaks that they could not, even in raging hatred, put the torch to her home. They had talked about burning down the house. They would burn it down—if they could not get at Styles Kenric any other way. But they were confused in their minds—torn between routing the hated Kenric and harming the revered Miz Claire. They had delayed. They had put off razing the manor house until the last. Four men were on their way there with torches when they had met Styles in the roadway, and so the big old house was spared. When dawn came, the manor house stood, alone and untouched in the midst of charred devastation, the shells of fieldstone foundations, bodies of slaughtered horses, cows, fowl.

Fire brought terror, but it also brought white men riding in to help within the first two hours. Fire was the single most feared disaster faced by these rural people, the plantation owner as well as the dirt farmer. Fire in a pine grove or an oak scrub could spread out of control, wipe out crops, homes, and outbuildings in one greedy swipe. Few rustics went in to bed at night without checking the dark sky for some telltale sign of fire—a wisp of smoke, the smell of heated turpentine, the stink of a fire in the swamplands, the glow against a night cloud.

Fires could not be hidden. Fire at night was a spectacular signal crying for help across the countryside. Fires brought half-dressed men from their beds on quickly saddled horses. Fires heated the crucible where old enmities were melted, temporarily at least, and fused into frantic cooperation.

A fire at night could be spotted as much as five miles away. A fire lightened the horizon like summer lightning, it blazed across night clouds, it roared, sending panic through every man who viewed it—there but for the grace of God is my place, my life, my hopes . . . .

Men were already riding toward Blackoaks as the first buildings flared up and imploded. They started out on horseback, racing along the traces, joined by their neighbors. They clattered in wagons, the beds loaded with shovels, picks, anything that might help subdue a walking fire, and guns.

They raced toward Blackoaks from the nearest thirty-acre subsistence farms where the red-neck farmers disparaged the arrogant plantation owners all week and scorned their uppity manners on Sunday. The dirt farmers despised the landowners because all life seemed loaded in their favor, something like a crooked wheel of fortune. Blacks toiled in their fields while they sat on shaded verandas and sipped mint drinks based in expensive whiskey or rode fast horses across the countryside as if they owned the world. But the crackling of fire extinguished even the memory of envious hatred. One thing most of them had learned, the big landowner turned out first to help his neighbor in time of disaster—working shoulder to shoulder with him. You couldn't hate a man very fiercely who was being wiped out by fire.

The plantation people came from as far away as The Brairs. At The Briars, the Brethertons had sworn an eternal hatred against Styles Kenric—and in his name, his in-laws, the Baynards—because Kenric had called the Bretherton girls liars when they had reported meeting Kathy Kenric in New Orleans. Kenric had threatened to call out to duel the Bretherton men if the Bretherton sisters persisted in their slanderous lie. The Brethertons had waited, trembling with rage, for that call. They had argued among themselves as to which of them would have the pleasure of cleansing their honor and the good name of the Bretherton ladies—angels, all!—by slaying Styles Kenric in a duel. But fire changed all that—or, if it was not altered, the hatred could be hung in suspension, the satisfaction of honor delayed. Ferrell Alexander Baynard had more than once, in the years past, raced to The Briars in time of disaster. They owed him and his memory a great deal—they could not stand by and let his land be destroyed by fire. They rode to help . . . .

The Tetherows came, whipping their horses to lathered fury, from Pinewood Forest Estate. Gil Talmadge routed out his best and youngest slaves, piled them in the bed of an open wagon and led them on his own horse, bouncing and rattling from Felicity Hall Manor. There was no great love for Styles Kenric felt by the people at Pinewood Forest—the Baynard cousin, Jamie Lee Seaton Tetherow, had proven herself to be unprincipled baggage. This secret would die behind the sealed lips of the Tetherow men and women, but they felt nevertheless that they had been sold a spavined horse by their friends and neighbors of two generations, the Baynards. Link especially saw how he had been gulled by—of all people—a man of the cloth, the young embryo priest Ferrell-Junior. Ferrell had lied to him that day about what Jamie Lee and that black slave-boy had been doing in the chapel. Ferrell had let him believe lies, had, in fact, used the duress of threat and blackmail to encourage his capitulation to a scheme which he'd somehow believed all along to be spurious. Jamie Lee had been proffered to him as a chaste virgin. All the time the Baynards had known better—hell, the Baynard servants and slaves had known better.

Still, in a way, because of the Tetherow-Seaton marriage, the Baynards were family—and with fire raging at Blackoaks, all malice had to be put aside. The Tetherow men came riding hard.

Gil Talmadge had not been back to Blackoaks since the day Miz Claire had so cruelly shot his prize fighting black, King Arthur, in the bicep. They had treated him as an enemy over at Blackoaks that day, even Ferrell-Junior, whom he loved as he could never have loved a blood brother, admired, revered, prized—even Ferrell had behaved as if he hated him. Gil was unable to see what he had done to rouse such enmity in the hearts of his dearest friends. Hurt to the quick, he had sworn to stay forever away from Blackoaks except in the event of weddings, funerals, disasters, or direct invitation. Disaster flared in that conflagration visible across miles of forest, and he came racing.

The first flush of false dawn struggled against the lurid brightness of the variegated blazes as the first riders raced up the lane between the overhanging black trees. These were the dirt farmers from the nearest sites. They slowed their horses even before they reached the manor house, eyes widening, mouths sagging. Few had ever witnessed such conflagration! God knew, the rich had it better in easy times, but disaster was vaster for them, too. They rode into the drive before the house and swung down from their saddles, gazing helplessly at the holocaust. None had anticipated such violent and widespread devastation. What good was a handful of men against inextinguishable fires in half a dozen places at once? They needed a leader, someone to tell them what to do first. Meanwhile, they could only stand, incredulous and overwhelmed. If one of the landowners would have come riding up on his finest horse at that moment, they would have welcomed him with cheers—he would not have hesitated in shouting orders that they would have executed, even when they were wrong.

Thyestes came out of the house, carrying a lantern held aloft over his head. He wept with joy at the sight of the white farmers. Passing, he glimpsed the weeping houseboy huddled on the steps, and he kicked him viciously in the side and muttered from the corner of his mouth, "Thought I tole you to git a doctor from Mt. Zion!" Without waiting to hear the boy's gasped reply, he strode down the steps to the farmers. "Thank Gawd! Thank Gawd!" Thyestes cried. "Thank Gawd you folks have come. Niggers is uprising! They burning down our place."

"Uprising!" The word burst across the mouths of the farmers. They had not anticipated anything like this, though now that they saw the wild fires raging out of control in so many places, it was plain to see the niggers had turned, all right. "Uprising? God almighty. Where-at is Mister Styles?"

"That po' man lying—assaulted—helpless up in his bed. Ain't nobody to stop them niggers. They burnin'—killin'—thank Gawd you come." Thyestes wept.

A black wagon bearing two black-suited slave patrollers rattled up the tree-lined incline from the gate. They leaped from the wagon, offering to help in any way they could. Just somebody tell them what to do. Sure's hell, those fires had to be contained.

"That may not be so easy," a farmer said. "We got a nigger uprising here."

"Uprising!" one of the patrollers said. He locked his gaze on Thyestes. "Is this here one of the uprisers? By God, we'll hang him."

"Oh, law, Masta. I a house nigger. I ain't no burning, killing nigger," Thyestes moaned.

"If we got an uprising," the second patroller said, "you fellows better stay here and keep them niggers from puttin' the torch to this house—"

"That's right," a farmer agreed.

"Looks to be all that can be saved," another agreed.

The patroller continued, "Me an' Freddy Lee will ride in to Mt. Zion and fetch Sheriff Steelright and a posse . . . . we ride them rioting niggers into the ground and hang 'em."

"Please, suh, Masta suh," Thyestes said. "If you be goin' into Mt. Zion, please ast Dr. Townsend to ride fast as he can out here. Masta Styles Kennric is most porely . . . . He layin' this minute assaulted—and bleedin' up on his bed."

"Yeah. We do that," Freddy Lee said. "Soon as we alert Sheriff Steelright, and git some help to chase down them niggers." He clambered back up on the wagon. His partner leaped up beside him, and they went thundering down the lane, swinging the wagon wildly out on the trace, heading toward Mt. Zion.

"Reckon we best keep a lookout for some of them niggers tryin' to get up heah to set this ole house afire," one of the farmers said. "Hits about all them blacks has left standing."

More farmers came riding up the lane to stop beside their neighbors, locked and stunned by the extent of the devastation, the size of the conflagration, their own help-lessness in the face of an insurrection of blacks.

The first large landowners arrived immediately behind them, and concerted action was instituted. The Winter-korn men rode in first from Mira Vista. Old Winterkorn yelled at the farmers, "What the fuck you standin' around with your fingers up your ass for? Let's get to fightin' them fires. We can't save much—but we got to keep it from spreading."

"It's more'n fires, Mr. Winterkorn," a farmer ventured. "Hit's a nigger uprising. All them fires been set by them black devils."

"Uprising? Well, by God, that's one thing we won't tolerate from no niggers. No, by God. You fellows got your guns?"

No farmer had a gun. Winterkorn spoke loudly to Thyestes. "Thyestes, you and that sniveling black boy there. Git in there and bring out old Baynard's guns to these fellows. We'll march down there and blow the black skulls off every black bastard that stands up before us."

The farmers cheered this. Winterkorn glanced around, satisfied with the reaction of his troops. Thyestes kicked the black houseboy again. The boy leaped to his feet, and in a few moments Thyestes and the youth returned, their arms loaded with guns. Thyestes sent the boy back into the house for ammunition. Winterkorn ordered one of his sons to distribute the guns among the farmers.

Thyestes said timidly, "Them slave patrollers went in to Mt. Zion lookin' for the sheriff and a posse to chase down them uprisin' niggers, Masta Winterkorn, suh."

Winterkorn glanced over his shoulder. "The hell with them. Them niggers be in the next county before Steelright rounds up a posse. You let me handle this, Thyestes—if you'll be so kind." These last words, though softly spoken, reduced Thyestes to dread silence.

Winterkorn assumed command. This was an action that met with instant approval from the farmers. Armed now with Baynard guns and ammunition, they awaited orders from their self-appointed commander. Astride his wide-rumped gelding, Winterkorn was an imposing figure— with gray beard, sad but resolute of face, unyielding blue eyes, and an almost arrogant tilt to his gray head. At that moment, these men would have followed him anywhere—including into yankee territory.

Before Winterkorn could line up his men and deploy

them, Gil Talmadge rode in, his horse winded, trembling with fatigue, spilling lather. Behind him came his open-bed wagon filled with Felicity slaves.

"Riot?" he said. "Them black bastards uprising? Hell, let's git down there and rout 'em out."

"Just what we was planning sir, when you rode up," Winterkorn told him. "I was just giving out the orders to our people."

Gil hesitated. He was constitutionally opposed to being told what to do by any human being—a trait directly inherited from his late lamented father. But he was anxious to get into action. The thought of riding in upon niggers and shooting them point blank overcame any of his natural dislike of being ordered about by even so distinguished a man as old Winterkorn. He said, "Hell, let's git started."

"What about them niggers of yours?" Winterkorn asked.

"What about 'em?" Gil said.

"We got niggers riotin'. Hadn't you better git these blacks shackled?"

Gil hooted with laughter. "My niggers? Hell, don't shackle 'em. Arm 'em. They'll fight right with us. I don't have no disorderly blacks on my place. My blacks do what I tells them."

The Tetherow men rode in, followed closely by the Brethertons. They had anticipated some tensions when they first met with Styles, but they discovered he lay helpless, assaulted by the rioters, and would not be part of the armed peacemakers. The Brethertons relaxed, and one of them told Winterkorn to lead on.

Thyestes said, "I gits our cook to rustle up a big bre'kfus' for you gen'mun. I knows you gen'mun be rousing up and hangin' them riotin' niggers."

The darkness before dawn, the dawn, and the early morning itself formed a time of unreality to Styles. He swam up, feeling as if his lungs must burst before he cleared the warm thick liquid in which he was drowning, to find Dr. Townsend bent over his posterior. Doctor Towsend said, "You been used pretty bad, Styles. I'll give you a big dose of laudanum to see you through the pain."

Styles remembered taking the laudanum from a large spoon. His swallowing the liquid was followed by an expanding sense of warmth that flowed outward through his body, even stilling the fires searing his rectum. Then he was aware that Dr. Townsend was working with a needle and gut of some kind, and he screamed, as much in outrage as pain. The needle sank into his flesh. He gasped, and then he passed out. When he awoke, the doctor was washing his hands at the earthenware basin, and rolling down his sleeves.

The doctor walked back across the room and bent over Styles. He said, "I'm leaving laudanum with Thyestes. When the pain is bad, I won't have to tell you to call for the laudanum—you'll yell . . . . And, I'm afraid you're going to have an outsized asshole, Styles, even when them stitches and tucks I made heal up."

The aging doctor laughed and Styles cursed him; this was the last Styles remembered for a long time.

It was a long day in the Pilzer house above the quarters. There was silence, but it was a silence that intensified with daybreak, rather than dissipating. There was a tension in the atmosphere that was almost tangible. It broke only when the posse, led by old Winterkorn, paused to enlist Pilzer in a manhunt. Florine's touch on his arm reminded him of his vow to Moab. He owed his life to the black boy. He would keep his promise. He had no real desire to chase down niggers—he saw enough black faces every day in the fields, too many. Besides, among the rioters were sure to be a few of his best men—the workers on whom he could depend. He hated to witness the waste when those blacks were shot, beaten to death, or hung. "I best stay with the little woman," Pilzer said. "She's had a bad night."

Winterkorn nodded and the mounted men spread out, riding downslope toward the creek.

"I'm glad you didn't go," Florine said. "You did promise Moab."

"Yes. Them niggers would have killed me when they

got back—if it wasn't for Moab." But Pilzer was staring at Florine oddly. She felt her face flush red to the roots of her hair. Had Pilzer heard something about her and Moab? Had he finally heard about their affair when it was over and forever ended? She found herself fretting with her hair, brushing nervously at her dress, uncomfortable under his puzzled gaze.

"Well, what is it, Bos?" she demanded at last. She really didn't want to know. But there was no sense in waiting, either. He had been eyeing her strangely ever since he returned from the smithy. It might as well be brought out into the open.

Pilzer shook his head and frowned. "I don't know. Something's wrong about you. I can't place it—but something's wrong."

She tried to laugh. "Maybe I'm relieved because you're still alive," she said. "It could be that, you know."

"No. It's nothing like that. It's something about the way you're dressed."

"You've seen this old dress a hundred times."

"Maybe you've fixed your hair different." He frowned but went on staring at her, moving his gaze over her.

Florine felt the blood flood upward into her face again. She said, trying to change the subject, "Why, Bos Pilzer, I never knew you to pay so much attention to the way I look since we was first married." She laughed at him and patted his face. She would not have believed it possible. In fact, when she had given Moab the locket from about her neck, she had laughed at his fears. She'd promised Moab that Bos would never notice, that he never looked that closely at her any more.

But he would not be laughed off the subject. His was a stolid, determined mind. Once an idea was fixed in it, he could only grind away until he found the answer he sought. "Something different—about you—you—not your hair or that dress. You. Hey! I know what it is. You ain't wearing that diamond and gold cross I brought you from New Orleans."

Her face pallid, Florine reached up and touched at the base of her throat. All she felt was the irregular pounding of the pulse there. The missing trinket was the first thing Bos had noticed. He had been troubled when he walked in and looked at her; it had taken all these hours for him to figure what was missing. "I took it off," she said. "I laid it down somewhere—and I lost it."

"Some nigger stole it."

"Bos! No nigger comes near this place. Moab is the only Negro who has been in this house."

Pilzer's ruddy face grayed out. He looked as if he might cry. His big mouth quivered, and his heavy jaw tightened, a muscle working in it savagely. "Moab," he whispered. "He was up here. You said he was up here."

"For just a minute—looking for you."

"That's it. He came—*after* he saw me tied up in the smithy—"

"Oh, no, Bos. Don't go making yourself sick with hatred when you know Moab wouldn't do a thing like steal— from me and you . . . . He worships—you."

"My God, woman. Do you think I want to believe it any more than you do? I don't. Moab saved my skin, as sure as I'm standing here talking to you. He knowed I was good to him, and he repaid me . . . . But it got to be Moab what took your cross—"

"No, Bos! No!"

"Couldn't of been nobody else. He the only one knew you had it—or had any idea what it was worth . . . . Goddamn it, that just goes to prove what I has always said—no matter how good you treat a nigra, you can't trust him. Even Moab . . . a nigra will steal from you any chance he gits."

When Styles swam up from the warmth of laudanum-induced unconsciousness, the sun was bright in his room. Thyestes and Sheriff Thurmond Steelright stood over him. "Masta, suh," Thyestes was whispering. "Please, masta, suh, could you wake up a minute?"

Styles opened his eyes and stared up at the butler and the sheriff.

Sheriff Thurmond Steelright was a bulky man in khaki clothes and snake boots. He held his sweated trooper's hat in his hand, turning it uncomfortably in his stubby fingers. "Mr. Kenric, suh, we wonder if you feel well enough to come down. We caught some of them niggers—the ringleaders—all we need is for you to identify the ones that assaulted you."

"My God," Styles protested. "I can't walk—anywhere."

"You don't has to walk, suh," Thyestes said. "We done fixed up a wicker chair with pillows and four boys will carry you down to the front yard where the sheriff has them niggers shackled an' waiting."

As Styles was transported in the heavily pillowed wicker chair by four houseboys, Sheriff Steelright plodded beside the entourage. "We had no trouble roundin' them niggers up. No, sir. Mr. Winterkorn and his people had most of them when we got out here. The farthest any nigra run was to the thickets in the creek. Wasn't none of them more'n a mile from the quarters when we caught 'em."

According to the sheriff, five of the arsonists had been caught hiding, one of them under a house in the quarters. The sixth, a black named Thumb, was caught with his arms loaded with hams from the smokehouse. "This yere seemed like primy facey evidence to us," Steelright said. "He cried and carried on. Said he wasn't one of them riotin' niggers, that he was jus' gettin' food before it went up in fire. Hell, nobody believes a nigra like that."

Thumb was still crying when Styles was carried out to confront the culprits. Gil Talmadge, the Tetherows, the Winterkorns, and the other neighbors—both from small farms and slaveowning plantations—stood ringed behind the blacks. They were blistered, briar-scratched, sooty. All but Thumb stood silent and defiant.

"You recognize these as the men who assaulted you?" the sheriff asked Styles.

Styles moved his gaze across the faces of the mutineers. None looked at him except Perseus. Perseus met his gaze levelly, and it was Styles who looked away, flushing slightly.

"It was dark," he said. "But I recognize some of them."

"That's fine, Mr. Kenric," the sheriff said. He spoke loudly so that the accused heard him clearly. "Your identification is all we need—it's the only trial these men will git. We hang 'em—on your word."

"Right," Gil Talmadge said. "We hang 'em so other

niggers can see what happens when a black slave goes bad and rises up against his white owners."

"Hanging is the answer," Winterkorn agreed. "Not only as punishment, and they deserve punishment for what they've done to this great old estate—but as an example."

"You point them out, Mr. Kenric," Sheriff Thurmond Steelright said, "an' we do the rest."

Styles nodded toward Paint. "That's one of them. Paint. Yes, he was one of them." Paint was yanked backward out of the line by one of the posse. Styles moved his gaze. "Saul . . . . Yes, I was shocked to see Saul . . . . I thought Saul was loyal."

"You can't tell when a nigra will go bad, sir," the sheriff said as Saul was hauled from the line.

Styles name Peleg and Mercury as his attackers.

"And this man Thumb?" Steelright said.

Styles shrugged. "I was jumped from behind—from the dark. I didn't see him. He might have been one."

Thumb howled like a wounded animal. "Oh lawdy, Masta. How can I be one? I was at the smokehouse—I ain't been near up here. Ask these boys. Ask them."

A deputy sheriff struck Thumb with the butt of his gun full in the face. Thumb staggered but was not allowed to fall. He was lined up with the others. Only Perseus remained standing alone. His legs were apart, his shoulders back, his head held defiant. Plainly, he had his vengeance, his exultant moment of revenge, he had made the white bastard hurt. He was ready to die.

"How about this one—this uppity nigger Perseus?" the sheriff said.

Styles hesitated. "I don't know. I didn't see him."

"These other boys say he was the leader—"

Styles shook his head, raising his hand to stop the sheriff. "All I know is that Perseus was a loyal boy. He went with Laus and Pegasus as my servant to Tallahassee. I never had a complaint to make against Perseus."

"You making a big mistake you don't name him and let us take him along," the sheriff warned.

Styles said, "No. Let Laus keep him shackled in a cabin in the quarters—until we know for sure . . . . He was loyal—as loyal as Laus . . . . I want to be more sure."

The sheriff shook his head, but shrugged. "It's your decision, suh . . . . I jus' hope it ain't your mistake."

"No," Styles said, "I wouldn't want to make a mistake."

He sat and watched as the five slaves were marched, ankles shackled, down the lane. The long procession of posse, landowners, and farmers turned and headed west toward Mt. Zion. They marched the Negroes two miles from Blackoaks. They looped hangropes over limbs of oak trees. The five slaves were set on horses bareback with nooses tight about their throats. At a signal, the horses were struck sharply in the rumps and they lunged forward. The bodies swung, kicked, and twisted for a good ten minutes, some of them. The plantation men stayed on after the sheriff and his posse retired and the farmers returned to their homes. The plantation men spent the next three hours shooting the suspended bodies and watching them wheel and turn comically when struck by the bullets, dangling at rope end. And so finished the uprising of slaves at Blackoaks.

3

Ferrell delayed making the final preparations for accepting the Church and the priesthood as his life. He found himself growing impatient with existence behind cloistered walls. He could not put out of his mind the temptations of the world. He did find a contentment during the long silent periods when the brothers did not speak, even at meals. He found himself going over in his mind the path he'd followed which had led him to the seminary and to the priesthood. It was as if everything in his life had pointed him in this direction. He hated the hypocrisy, the mendacity, the casual cruelty he found among people of his own class. He had not believed he could be one of them. He had run away from them. He thought about Lorna Garrity with a terrible longing. He knew now that he had loved her—that he loved her still! —as many of the brothers around him loved the Church and its life. He had hurt Lorna—he had lost her through eternity. And it was this realization that finally brought him to the decision to take the vows of the society—to immerse his life in service to the Church. It was not what he wanted, but there was nothing in the world outside for him, either.

A headline in the seminary library reading room caught his attention, and sent his life on another wild and tangential course. He stood beside the polished table and stared down at the Charleston *Post*. The headline snagged his attention, but it was the lead of the second paragraph that clutched at him, left him sweated and empty-bellied:

AN UPRISING OF SLAVES

Quelled in Alabama

5 Mutinous Blacks Hanged

A recent revolt by five mutinous black slaves caused extensive property damage but no loss of life at an old and respected Alabama cotton plantation, according to reports of the Alabama Governor's office which have been received by the *Post*.

Blackoaks Plantation, owned by the highly regarded Baynards of Alabama, was the scene of destruction by fire. Reports say only the estate manor house and the slave quarters survived the flaming holocaust.

The five perpetrators of the arson were captured and hanged by a posse led by Sheriff Thurmond C. Steelright, the report states.

It was pointed out by the Governor's office that Blackoaks Plantation has a black slave population of over 200. The malcontents numbered fewer than half a dozen.

The revolt was quelled and order restored the same morning. Property damage included storage and work barns, animal enclosures and craft shops, according to the report.

That same day, his clerical collar forever removed, his

black shirtwaist doffed, Ferrell resigned from the order and started home. He had made the trip once by horseback across Georgia and eastern Alabama, and he felt this experience had aged him. It had certainly given him the wisdom to buy a buggy and a sound horse. This last journey was a long trip over execrable roads and places where the roads became faintly marked traces and even paths. The nights were stunningly cold. Rain pummelled him, and by the time he reached the Chattahoochee River to cross into Alabama, he shook his head wryly. "You've given me one hell of a send-off from the seminary, God."

He was glad for the long, lonely ride, even with all its discomforts and rough hardship. It gave him time to think. In a way it was like the silent retreats at the seminary—one thought whether he wanted to or not.

He thought about Blackoaks. The story on the uprising made him understand as nothing else could have what his father had meant about his being destined to take over the management of Blackoaks. He had only the accounts of the newspaper, writing from the sketchy bureaucratic reports, about a distant slave revolt, and yet he was certain the five hanged men were less to blame for what had happened than was Styles Kenric. And Styles could not be saddled with the final blame—that belonged to him, Ferrell Baynard, Junior. His father had known Styles was not the man to manage the huge estate. Ferrell himself had known it. But he had been willing to set aside his convictions because it was convenient to leave Styles in charge while he ran into the protection and seclusion of the society.

It was a bitter thing to admit that the trouble at Blackoaks could be laid at his feet—and him in a seminary hundreds of miles away. He had been badly hurt. He wanted to escape. He had tried to say to hell with the family lands and the family properties and the family fortune—he had been ill-used by life, and he wanted to escape the terrible risks a man faced everyday in the normal routine of living. He'd endured heartbreak, and he didn't want it again. He had been victimized by friends, betrayed by his peers, and he wasn't going to let that happen again. He had run into the Church—not for anything he might offer the Church, but because the Church was his way out, an escape this side of suicide.

He stared ahead on the narrow trail, looking toward home. He had run because he was cowardly. He had left Styles Kenric in charge when Styles had no qualifications for the job. Styles had failed—this was in every line of the *Post* story—but the blame for that failure belonged with him, not with Styles.

"Give me a chance to make it up, God," he said aloud. "I'll make it up, somehow. I failed my family at Blackoaks. I sure as hell failed you in the Church . . . . I don't ask anything for myself . . . . The only thing I could ever want was Lorna. I lost her. Hell, I threw her away . . . . All I want is the chance to restore the damage I have caused by my selfishness . . . . Please God . . . ." Then his hands gripped the reins tighter. "And please, God, help me to remember that all that has happened at Blackoaks was my fault—and not Styles Kenric's fault. It is easy for me to remember that now—out here on the trail. But please, God, help me remember it when I meet him face to face."

Wearing a bathrobe, Styles sat up in bed when sheriff Thurmond Steelright was ushered into his bedchamber. Styles had not expected the sheriff to be accompanied by a deputy whom he introduced as Hawkins Calkerson, and by Gil Talmadge, Link Tetherow, and Walter Roy Summerton. "We was in town, me and Walter Roy and Link, when we heard you sent for the sheriff. We figured if they was more trouble, Walter Roy, Link, and me ought to ride along," Gil said.

"We got your message, Mr. Kenric," the sheriff said. "We come out as soon as we could."

"Thank you." Styles nodded. "I would have sent for your sooner, Sheriff. But I was just told. I can tell you there's going to be meat peeled off some black hides when I learn who failed to get word to me as soon as possible . . . . Two of my prize blacks—Fulani fancies—are missing."

"You reckon them killed in the revolt?" the sheriff said.

"No. We know better than that. No. They ran. We figure they must have run during the riots. While everybody was busy with the fires and the rioters, they took off running."

"That gives them one hell of a start on us," the deputy said.

"I was not told for a couple of days," Styles said. "These damned blacks. You can't trust them."

"No, sir, that's a fact," the sheriff agreed.

"Hell, don't worry, Styles." Gil leaned forward, bubbling with enthusiasm and anticipation of action. "We'll run the black bastards down."

"Wait a minute, Gil," Styles said. "The reason I sent for the sheriff—the reason it was important for me to talk to him personally, I want to impress upon all of you just how valuable these blacks are. They're about as valuable as black animals can be. I don't want them killed."

"Run down, captured, and returned," the sheriff said.

"That's right, and I'll pay a handsome reward," Styles said. "I'll do anything to insure they're returned to me alive. That girl cost me a fortune in an auction down in Tallahassee, Florida. And the word is she's carrying a sucker. That makes her twice as valuable. You just can't buy a purebred Fulani in this country any more—not unless you're willing to pay a small fortune. I want her back—alive, and well."

"We'll take every precaution," the sheriff said. "But when we send out a flyer on them, we can't guarantee what some slave patrol might do."

"Then don't send out a flyer. Run them down—"

"That's not as easy as it sounds, Mr. Kenric. My jurisdiction only extends in this county—"

"Me and Walter Roy and Link could get up some hunters in a party—to take over when the sheriff has to turn back. I'd cotton to a little exercise like runnin' down a couple of runaway blacks," Gil said. "How about it, Walter Roy?"

"Sounds all right," Walter Roy said.

"You remember one thing, Gil," Styles said. "That boy. Moab. He could bring up to ten thousand dollars in certain slave auctions."

The sheriff whistled. "Animals that valuable. Likely they didn't run at all. Probably they were stolen—during the fire an' all."

"No." Styles looked down at his clenched hands. "No. They ran. The girl is a runner. I was warned when I bought her that she would run on me. I thought she'd be content here at Blackoaks. But she talked Moab into running—and her pregnant."

"Can you give us some kind of description?" the sheriff asked.

"You won't be able to miss those two," Styles said.

"All nigras look alike to me," the sheriff said. "I'm sorry, sir. They got any distinguishing marks?"

"I told you. They are not black—not in color. They are a light chocolate color. Very light, more tan even than chocolate. And neither of them has kinky hair like most Negroes. Their hair is very black and crisp—but straight. The girl is very nearly six feet tall in her bare feet. She has an extraordinary figure—she's big in proportion to her height—large breasts, rounded hips, and long, shapely legs. Her name is Ahma . . . . Now, the boy may not be quite as tall as Ahma. He hasn't his full growth yet. He's about sixteen or seventeen years old. He is a very handsome boy—with a profile that is more white than black— no flat nostrils or ridged brows . . . . No, you'll have no trouble spotting them in a crowd of blacks. The only problem is the two- or three-day lead they've got because I was not informed any sooner that they had run."

The sheriff shrugged. "If they are as easy to spot as you say, it might not be a terrible problem, running them down. People will recall them."

"That's true." Styles nodded. "They won't be able to run anywhere that people won't remember them."

"And, too," the sheriff said, "they're scairt, they niggers, and, niggerlike, they stupid. They likely spent more'n half their time runnin' in circles. We'll get 'em back."

"Right," Gil echoed.

"I want them back," Styles said. He sank back on the bed after the sheriff and his posse were gone. He thought about Moab, and his heart seemed to slip in an agony of loss. Yet, even if Moab were returned to Blackoaks, he would never resume the old liaison with the boy. No. He took a deep breath, released it. That phase of his life was over and past . . . .

When he could walk again, aided by a cane and not twisted by excruciating pain, Styles got out of bed about ten one morning. He perambulated painfully, bent forward slightly. There was the unremitting sensation of an iron bar driven on the bias far up his colon. He called two houseboys, had them shave, bathe, and sprinkle him with cologne. Then he chose his finest suit, a pale pearl-gray. When he was dressed, he sat—on a goosedown pillow—in one of the high-backed wing chairs near his bedroom window. He told Thyestes to send word that Laus was to deliver Perseus to his private rooms.

Thyestes looked ill. He opened his thick-lipped mouth to object, even on pain of punishment from his master, but Styles waved him imperiously from the room.

Waiting, Styles felt his heart beat oddly, irregularly. He sat, hands locked over the rounded head of the malacca cane he used when he walked even short distances. His face paled, turning his cheeks an unhealthy gray, and his eyes glazed over. His mouth was pursed in hard, tight lines when Thyestes knocked and Laus entered, leading Perseus by a chain secured to metal wrist cuffs.

"Thank you, Laus," Styles said. He did not bother to look at Perseus. "You may go, Laus—and you, Thyestes."

"Please, Masta." Laus shook his head. "I best stay in heah and keep an eye on this nigger."

"Wait in the hall, Laus."

"—Masta, this nigger was the ringleader of them revolters. He might of fooled you. But I tell you—" Laus looked ready to cry.

Styles's voice sharpened. "You may wait in the hall, Laus. Close the door. But I assure you, I won't need you."

"Yassuh." Laus bowed and retreated. He closed the bedroom door. For the first time, Styles looked up at Perseus, staring at him along his nose.

"Go ahead, Perseus," he said. "You better kill me right now. It may be your last chance."

Perseus remained standing, straight and wide-shouldered. Styles had never realized Perseus was so well built, with thick muscles rippling across his chest, his paps standing dark, his belly flat, his legs long and muscular. He was not handsome as Blade had been, and he was as black as any Congo Ovimbundu Negro. But he was something Blade never was, an aggressive, angry Negro, driven by hatred and unafraid of death or torture. Perseus shook his head. "I don't want to kill you . . . . I never wanted to *kill* you—"

"You almost did—"

"I wanted to make you hurt. As you made me hurt. As you made my woman hurt. As you made my children."

"I never knew you hated me, Perseus."

"Now you know."

"Yes, now I know. I've known for almost two weeks . . . . I could have had you hung—with the rest of them—that morning. I hope you know that."

"You should have. I lives in hell. I cause the brutal death of five good men."

"That's very touching. But it is not important. No sense in crying for the dead. Those men are dead. You are not. Not yet."

"I not afraid to die."

Styles smiled coldly. "Maybe you are afraid to live?"

Perseus stared at him, puzzled.

Styles spoke in sardonic chill. "I'm going to give you a chance to cheat the hangrope. One chance. I've been thinking about it since the night they brought me in here bleeding when you reamed me out the biggest asshole south of the Mason-Dixon line . . . . Well, maybe I found out that for me the way to heaven is through hell. You taught me that, you black stud. And you have a choice. You can stay here—sleep in this room—as my body slave, or you can go to the hangrope. I've only to send for the sheriff . . . . "

Perseus shook his head. "Why would you want me to stay here—with you?"

Styles smiled. "Don't you know?"

Perseus shook his head again.

"You can hang—or you can give it to me—like you

did that night of the revolt . . . every night . . . every time I want it . . . till one of us drops dead . . . . And I can tell you now, it's not going to be me."

Perseus stared at him, revolted, ill, incredulous. He shook his head, retreating a step. "Gawd almighty, you're crazy."

Styles shrugged. "Perhaps. But you better be thankful I am—my insane desire is all that is saving you from a hangrope noose."

4

Bos Pilzer had gangs of black men, women, and boys breaking up, raking, and carting away the debris, which remained stark and black after the fire. Mr. Luke Scroggings arrived about ten one morning in a new carriage with leather-upholstered seats and a fringed roof. His wife sat beside him on the front seat. Now that she had delivered her baby, people gazed at her in awe, saying that, at eighteen and over two years married, Lorna June Scroggings was even lovelier than she had been at sixteen when she'd had all the young men in the region baying outside her window night after night.

There were those who whispered that a certain chill in Lorna's face, a tautness about her cheeks and her lovely lips, and an undeniable disenchantment shadowing her violet-gray eyes made her seen much older than eighteen. These people also said that though Lorna had been unhappy and had suffered agonizing experiences, the good lord knew nobody had had it easier than she since her husband had been named president of the only bank in Mt. Zion.

She sat without talking, steadying herself by clinging to the metal side guards of her seat as the team pranced into the lane and up the rocky incline at Blackoaks. The small boys ran out to meet the carriage, but Luke waved them away with his buggy whip. He did not turn in at the driveway that circled before the columned veranda at the manor house. Instead, he headed the team toward the valley where he hoped to inspect the fire damage.

"Jesus God," Luke said. He pulled hard on the reins, halting his horses. Both he and Lorna stared, appalled at devastation. Luke was stunned at the extent of the destruction. He had heard wild rumors at the bank of the fire damage, but he had discounted the stories as just rumors. He saw now that the error had been on the conservative side. As a farm, Blackoaks was out of business for the foreseeable future.

"God almighty," Luke whispered. He was not speaking to Lorna. He had long since learned that she was interested in little he had to say and never showed the least concern with his business matters. And this was a business matter. He sweated, thinking about the mortgage the bank held on this place, the increased capital he had pledged to Blackoaks and Styles Kenric. His mind rattled like an abacus, adding, subtracting—dividing—retreating. He took out a handkerchief and mopped his freckled face.

Bos Pilzer rode up the incline to where Luke had halted the buggy. He removed his planter's hat and bowed toward them. "Mornin' Mrs. Scroggings, Mr. Scroggings. Welcome to Blackoaks."

Luke smiled and nodded. He leaned out of the new carriage and extended his hand, which Pilzer shook warmly. Luke liked and admired Pilzer. The Blackoaks overseer was one of the best, steadiest, and most solid customers of the bank. Few people realized how wealthy Pilzer was. Luke admired this trait most. It seemed to him that Pilzer personified the most admirable Teutonic traits—thrift, ambition, energy, and caution. Pilzer added substantially to his savings account each month when he was paid his salary. The Pilzers obviously lived frugally and they were furnished a house rent free, were supplied with fresh vegetables, smoked hams, and milk. Clothing was one of their only expenses, and Pilzer had told him that Mrs. Pilzer made all her own dresses, his shirts, and his underclothing.

Luke understood the unique position into which the Pilzers were thrust in the caste system of the South.

There were two worlds—the rich upper heights where the landowners and slaveholders dwelled, and the wretched world of the poor. Pilzer and his wife belonged in neither of these two widely separated worlds and were accepted in neither. Luke felt nothing but sympathy for Pilzer and his wife, because Luke had struggled, clawing all the way, self-made and self-taught, from the depths of that second world to the fringes of the first.

"Come out to inspect our damage, Mr. Scroggings?" Pilzer inquired.

"I thought I ought to see it for myself." Luke nodded and smiled. "The bank does hold considerable of a blister on this place."

Pilzer exhaled. "Well, we been in hell—excuse me, Miz Scroggings—" He waited, but Lorna Scroggings appeared to have heard neither his expletive nor his apology. "We are burned out. The really sad part is the waste. You know, when people ignorant as darkies riot, they hurt themselves worse than the people they hate. They burned down the food and storage barns first. Now that was where the stuff they eat was stored. Their own food they burned. They set fire to the chicken pens. I bet you not half a dozen hens got out of the fire alive—and they already been stolen and cooked by the nigras. Then they set fire to the barns and stables where the animals they work with were kept. Horses were either burned to death or they killed themselves in terror trying to get away from the fire. So the work animals are dead. The fowl are dead. The cows that wasn't out to pasture were either killed or went dry. They trampled their own calves to death. Yes, sir, we been right there—in hell." He apologized again to Mrs. Scroggings who gazed at him, through him.

"It really looks sad," Luke said. "I was only out here once before. But this was my idea of one of the most beautiful, best-run farms I had ever seen."

"Would you like me to show you around—I reckon you want to see just how bad it is?" Pilzer said.

Luke agreed, then hesitated. "Perhaps we ought to see if Mrs. Scroggings couldn't be made comfortable in the house."

"Yes, sir," Pilzer agreed. "You just follow me to the

veranda entrance. I'll call Thyestes and have Mrs. Scroggings made most comfortable."

Pilzer was rattling the door knocker when Luke helped Lorna alight from the carriage.

Thyestes opened the door. He looked first at Pilzer, his ashes and mud-splattered boots, his sweated clothes. Then his gaze touched at Luke Scroggings—the freckled, shanty-Irish face, the red hair, the ferretlike blue eyes—and moved on to Mrs. Scroggings. The chilled manner of the banker's wife put Thyestes in a quandary. His quarter-century as keeper of this door had trained him to detect the fake and the false and to recognize quality. In Luke he saw trashy white, perhaps new-rich, but certainly not quality. On the other hand, though she in no way resembled the gardenia-fresh loveliness of Miss Kathy, Mrs. Scroggings brought to his mind Miss Kathy's casual acceptance of her place in life. There had been an unself-conscious sense of position about Miss Kathy that was unmistakable. This lovely young woman had it, too. Thyestes bowed and smiled. "Mornin' folks. Welcome to Blackoaks."

"Thyestes, this is Banker Lucas Scroggings and Mrs. Scroggings," Pilzer said. "Mrs. Scroggings would like to wait inside while I show Mr. Scroggings around the fire damage."

Thyestes's smile widened. He nodded again and opened the door wide. "Do come in, ma'm," he said. "I do all I can to make you mos' comfortable."

Lorna followed Thyestes across the large foyer to the bright sunroom. He bowed her into the most comfortable wing chair and went about, pulling open the draperies at the ceiling-length windows and doors. Sitting there, Lorna felt a strange emptiness, the first weakness she'd experienced in two years. This lovely room, this beautiful old house, the quiet and the dignity. Once, to be part of this world had been the alpha and omega of her existence. In her mind she could see Kathy Baynard moving through this room, and Ferrell-Junior—and, in fantasy—herself. She had never been in this room before, and yet it was almost like *déjà vu*. She had known what it would be like. She had wanted it all so badly.

"You jus' compose yo'self, Miz Scroggings, ma'm. I gits you something nice an' cool to drink, and then I informs Miz Claire that you are here in the sunroom."

"It's all right, Thyestes. You don't have to."

The musical softness of her voice filled Thyestes with a desire to cry for no good reason, only that it recalled Miss Kathy so vividly. He had not suspected there was another girl as lovely as Miss Kathy within a thousand miles. Lorna's gentleness made Thyestes want to please her, to make her smile—though she had not smiled yet. "No. Miz Claire will want to know she got such lovely company, Miz Scroggings. You jes' make yo'self com'fortable. Miz Claire been tol'able ill lately—and she may be restin'. But I see. I see."

Alone, Lorna sat as if listening for something. She had a haunting sense of uneasiness, as though if she listened she would hear Ferrell-Junior's remembered voice, his unforgotten, unforgettable laughter. He had run through these rooms, sat in these chairs, climbed those stairs, walked in these yards, sprawled on those couches. He was gone. She told herself she did not care. Sometimes now, busy with the baby, she went as much as a whole day without once thinking about Ferrell-Junior.

She tilted her head slightly. She would not change the course her life had taken. She had been brutally misused by Ferrell and his friends. She wakened in her nightmares, remembering the terror of it, but remembering most of all, the way Gil Talmadge had yelled at Ferrell, "I'm gonna have her. Like I told you I was gonna have her." Ferrell had known Gil and his friends were going to find them in the forest, find her naked, helpless. She closed her eyes tightly, shutting out the hateful memory, shutting out Ferrell. She pressed her small lace kerchief hard against her mouth.

When she opened her eyes, Miz Claire stood before her. She had come in like a waith from the terrace beyond the French doors. Lorna shivered involuntarily.

"Are you all right, my dear?" Miz Claire inquired in a soft, vague voice. She carried fresh gardenias and green fern in a basket. "Shall I ring for Thyestes? Perhaps a whiff of camphor?"

"No." Lorna straightened. "I'm all right." Inwardly, she thought bitterly, 'I'm one of the walking crippled, but I'm all right. Your son destroyed me, but I'm all right. I'd believed a girl could love many men—but I learned I could never love anyone but your son. But I'm all right. He destroyed my love for him. But I'm all right. He destroyed my capacity to love—to care. But I'm alive, and I'm all right.' "I'm all right," she said aloud again. "Thank you, Miz Claire."

"I'm sorry, I don't know you, my dear. Getting old, I guess. I just can't recall you."

"I'm Lorna June Scroggings, ma'm. I was Lorna Garrity."

"Oh, Garrity, of course. The Garritys of Autumn Glades Plantation. Are you a member of that lovely old family?"

Lorna June shrugged. Once, the fact that she was a cousin to the Garritys of Autumn Glades Plantation had been her entrée—her only hope of entry—into the world where Miz Claire and her family lived. All of this was like ancient history to Lorna, trivial and unimportant. Ferrell had destroyed her capacity to care any more.

"Kathy will be delighted you're here," Miz Claire said, smiling.

Lorna shivered, staring up at the painted, waxlike face, the vacant blue eyes, the fey movement of the fragile-looking hands. My God, she thought. She doesn't even know where she is! But this did not frighten Lorna—she had endured it in her own family after Ferrell had returned her—raped and unconscious—to her doting parents. Her father had retreated into a vaporous world, inhabited by people like himself and Miz Claire, unable and unwilling to go on enduring reality.

She didn't even blame them. She would have joined them if she could, but that escape would have been too easy. She had a chilled theory that the mindless are God's truly chosen people in the modern world. The Bible said God made man in His image. The first man had been mindless. Perhaps that was the answer. If you didn't *know*—you couldn't hurt. Her own mother had been unable to retreat into her own mind, but she had drawn the shades in their big old house in Mt. Zion and passed her days hidden from the public, unable to face people because her only child had been misused and made vile by evil and uncaring young men from the highest reaches of the upper class. Her mother and father had escaped, in their own ways, but she had not been permitted to escape.

She forced a wan smile and said, "Thank you, Miz Claire."

Miz Claire waved her hand in a meaningless, vaporous gesture. "We've had so much trouble here at Blackoaks recently. The poor nigras revolted and burned all the barns and work buildings . . . . Poor Mr. Baynard. He will be heartbroken when he and Morgan return . . . . They are away for a while, you know . . . . But Mr. Baynard will straighten all those nigras out in a hurry when he returns."

"I'm sure he will, Miz Claire." Lorna had no problem in following Miz Claire's convoluted fantasies. She felt as if she were at home, nodding and agreeing and smiling at her own poor father.

Thyestes hurried, limping in from the foyer. At his heels padded a stout black woman, with thick hips, heavy legs, a keglike belly and bulbous breasts. She went to Miz Claire and put her arm about her. Neva smiled at Lorna and spoke gently to Miz Claire. "Time fo' yo' rest, chile. I thought you was restin'—and you out gatherin' flowers . . . . I sure our guest will excuse us."

"Yes," Lorna said.

"You make yourself comfortable, Miss Garrity," Miz Claire said. "I'm sure Kathy will be in soon—and do remember me to your dear family at Autumn Glades."

"Yes," Lorna said.

Luke pulled a chair as near to Styles Kenric's bed as possible and sat down, trying at appear at ease. He said, "Bos Pilzer was kind enough to show me around the work area, Mr. Kenric. You've suffered extensive damage."

"Nothing that can't be repaired."

"Repairs are going to take a long time—considerable cash," Luke suggested.

"Well, we've always got a good friend in at the bank in Mt. Zion, eh?" Styles said. He laughed and waited.

Luke did not smile. "We've gone along with you, Styles. Perhaps to an extent beyond wisdom. This was a mammoth farm. A big operation. Thirty thousand did not seem an unreasonable mortgage—when slaves, storage barns, craft shops, and animals were included. Most of that has been wiped out by the fire."

"We'll rebuild," Styles said coldly.

"You're talking about two—three—five years," Luke said. "I'm thinking in terms of the bank. In terms of meeting mortgage payments—interest and principal. Also, we may as well be realistic. With your craftsmen at work full time, your field laborers totally employed, your storage barns filled, you still required a heavy cash outlay to meet daily expenses here at Blackoaks. You still have this house—and two hundred blacks—to feed and care for. The outlook is less than promising, Mr. Kenric."

"I'll make it. With the new loan. As soon as I can get Miz Claire's signature. We'll pay off the Florida bank, and we'll start rebuilding. I'll be on my feet again."

"Yes. Well, that's the problem. It's just as well you did not get that loan application completed. Our bank will not—will not be able to go through with that loan."

"Now wait a minute. You've already confirmed that loan—"

"I'm sorry. It was committed under totally different circumstances."

"But I'm obligated to pay off that bank in Florida. You agreed. You said I had the money. Why, hell, they'll foreclose."

"I don't think they will. But we at the bank are naturally interested in any such development. We'll cross that bridge when we get to it. It will simply be a matter of discussing it—between ourselves. As to the rest of the stipulated loan, I'm sorry. Until you are rebuilt, operating again—well," Luke shrugged and spread his hands. "I'm helpless, Mr. Kenric. I'd like to assist you, but my first

obligation is to the owners of my bank—as well as to
its other depositors."

Luke walked slowly down the stairs. Thyestes awaited
him with his hat and gloves at the foot of the stairwell.
He placed the gloves upon Luke's palm and held his
hat for him. Inwardly, Luke grinned. A man could get
used to service like this, it could be habit forming.

"I tell Miz Scroggings you ready to leave," Thyestes
said.

Luke nodded and thanked him. Thyestes limped into
the sunroom and after a moment followed Lorna out
into the foyer. Thyestes went around them then and held
open the front door. As they passed through, he said,
"Good day, folks. We do hopes you will return soon to
Blackoaks."

Small black boys stood beside the carriage and at the
head of the shafts, holding the horses. One of the urchins
helped Lorna into the carriage and then ran around behind
it to assist Luke up. They stood waving as Luke headed
the carriage around the curve and out the tree-shaded
lane.

Lorna exhaled heavily, glancing back over her shoulder.

"What's the matter?" Luke asked.

"Nothing." She turned, settled in the seat, holding the
metal railing. Then after a moment she shrugged and
said, "Two or three years ago, I'd have traded my soul
to be invited out here to Blackoaks. Looks like it's too
late, the party is over by the time I made it."

Luke laughed without mirth. "The party is over out
here, all right," he said. "The party is really over."

5

It was worse than Ferrell had believed possible. He
came along the trace, following the rambling fieldstone
fence that toppled and crawled and climbed for two miles

before he reached the huge fieldstone gates. From out here there was little hint of the destruction, the stench of dead animals, the filth of shattered structures yet to be cleared away. The big old house looked solid and secure and unassailable, as he remembered it. He came up the driveway, seeing the little black boys in their starched suits running to meet the buggy. He tossed pokes of candy to them. They stopped, grabbing up the small bags at the side of the lane and he rode on ahead of them. At the entrance to the circular drive, he hesitated and stared at the devastation, incredulous. He had thought it would be bad. But he had been unable to imagine such total destruction. Everywhere were the black, gutted reminders of the uncontrollable fires, the rioting, and the senseless slaughter of animals. Where the black craftsmen had worked in their shops, only charred hulks remained. The beautiful old barn, which had seemed so huge and so secure during afternoon rainstorms in his childhood, was gone, the last trace raked away. He felt sick at his stomach.

Slaves tagged in his wake as he inspected the loss and destruction caused by the fire. The blacks caught at his hand, wept, shouted hallelujahs, wailed hosannas, fell to their knees to pray in thanksgiving. He grinned and asked if they didn't think they were overdoing his welcome home just a mite. No matter how good he looked to them, this wasn't the second coming. He had brought no miracle cure for all they had lost. This would only come with hard work, endless, back-breaking labor. They would work for him, they shouted. They cried louder and pleaded with him never to leave Blackoaks again. Aside from this effusive welcome, the inspection tour sank him into despair that was little alleviated by the long hour he spent with his mother and Neva in his mother's private bedroom suite. Miz Claire seemed to have lost touch totally with reality. But Neva had been with her so much she'd begun to believe the things his mother said. It was a difficult hour. He felt exhausted and lower in spirit than ever when he went down the stairway and found the door to his father's old office locked.

"I fetch the key, Masta," Thyestes said.

"The hell with that." Ferrell drew a deep breath, trying

to control the rages building in him. "I told the bastard to stop locking this door." He lifted his boot and drove his heel sharply against the door just below the brass knob. The door sagged slowly open.

He was almost sorry he'd opened this door. It was like prying open the lid of Pandora's box. Styles had left an incredible mass of papers littering his desk top in the confusion of the revolt, the fire, and his physical assault (or the "I-like-you-so-much-better-than-any-woman-I-ever-knew" stroking, as they called sodomy in the seminary).

He read the bad news with a sinking heart. It was all there: the overwhelming mortgages, the heartbroken little suicide note from Kathy, which Styles obviously had never gotten around to destroying and which Ferrell now crushed in his fist, the unpaid bills, the application for a new loan, the whole sorry history of Styles's ineptitude and failure.

Armed with evidence enough to convict Styles of criminal mismanagement, Ferrell mounted the stairs. He walked along the corridor reminding himself to remain calm. The important consideration was that he was taking over. Violence and vindictiveness would make him feel better but would settle nothing in the long run. All that was important was that he was home to take over management of the farm immediately.

He rapped on the door. He was certain Styles had heard from the servants that he was home; he was equally sure that Styles anticipated a visit from him. Nevertheless, Styles let him rap four times before he finally hobbled to the door, supported on a cane, and admitted Ferrell to his room. Ferrell forced himself to overlook this, too.

Styles was freshly shaven, smelled sweetly of an unpleasantly effeminate cologne. He wore a white shirt with lace cuffs and front, a pair of pale blue linen trousers and boots with heels to insure he'd be at least two inches taller than his brother-in-law. Of such minutiae are the small advantages gained by the spiteful and the supercilious perverted whose most jaundiced hatred is always reserved for males unsympathetic in their attitudes. God knew he'd seen enough of this at the seminary. Too much. His being of the heterosexual persuasion had been the blackest mark against him in the unwritten records of the society. But, until he had understood the majority of his brothers at the seminary, he had never truly understood Styles. Now, at least, he understood him and the malicious little cruelties the man was capable of.

Styles bobbed his head in unsmiling greeting and walked with some obvious grimacing to a wing chair in which goosedown pillows reinforced the seat cushion. He let himself down carefully into his chair, clinging to his cane and watching Ferrell with overt malice.

Ferrell saw that no dialogue would be initiated unless he named the topic. He smiled crookedly and said, "I thought I should tell you, Styles, I have left the seminary. Permanently. I have returned home."

Styles shrugged. "What do you want me to do?"

Ferrell laughed without humor. "I don't want you to do anything, Styles. I think you've done enough. More, I believe than a less-qualified man could have done in five years."

Styles's head tilted. Rage flared in his chilled blue eyes. He stared along his patrician nose at Ferrell. "I sincerely hope you're not going to blame me for the slave uprising?"

"I'm going to try not to. The fact is that you did little to prevent it, much to foment it. I'm afraid your treatment of the slaves was cruel and unusual. They didn't strike at you, Styles—"

"Didn't they? They burned my barns, shops, killed my animals, and almost killed me."

"They struck *back* at you, Styles. I'm sorry. I've been home only one day. But that's perfectly clear."

"I offer no apology for my actions."

"I'm not looking for apologies. You protested your innocence concerning the rioting. I merely tried to point out your guilt."

"My guilt!" Styles started from the chair. He gripped the cane fiercely. His voice shook. "I don't have to endure such insults from you or anyone. Five men hanged for that revolt. Five—out of two hundred. Five malcontents out of a population of two hundred blacks. I'd say that absolves me of any guilt."

"Five men rose to strike back at you, Styles. The others

stayed in their cabins, or near them. They refrained. They let those five men bring you their message."

Styles shrugged. "Is that all you have to say?"

Now Ferrell did laugh. He shook his head. "I'm afraid we've just begun. As I said, I have returned from the seminary. I have left the Church. I am assuming management of this farm."

Styles's face paled. Then he tilted his head and laughed. "You bastard," Styles said. "All right. I can't fight you. I won't. Take it over—what there is left." He laughed again.

"I believe there's a power of attorney which you persuaded my mother to sign over to you. I'd like that back."

Styles hesitated. Then he laughed again, his mouth twisting. He got up, walked painfully with his cane to the chiffonier. He shook out a small ring of keys, unlocked a drawer, and drew out a folded paper. He went back to his chair and tossed the paper at Ferrell's feet. "Take it. I suppose this is the gratitude I can expect from a boor like you for all I've attempted to do for this farm." His eyes brimmed with tears of self-pity. "I had all the responsibility. I was left with all the obligations when you ran. It's not my fault I failed. Cotton crops bad. Negroes in revolt. Debts left by your revered father. I never had a chance."

Ferrell took up the paper, glanced at it, and tore it up. "I suppose not," he said. "You'll forgive me, Styles, if I don't weep with you. I can forgive you what you've done to this farm. Your incredible incompetence is forgivable. But I can't forgive you for what you did to my sister. I won't try to do that. As far as I'm concerned, that's unforgiveable . . . . Now, the sooner we conclude our business together, the more secure you're going to be."

Styles raged with laughter salted with tears. "Secure! How secure do you think *you're* going to be? You're going to take over this farm. Hell, what do you think you can do? What can anybody do? It's too late. There are mortgages overdue. If you sold off everything—including every slave—to meet the debts and mortgages against this place, you might end up with this house and the land it sits on."

Ferrell shrugged. "Then we'll have to find some other way, won't we? . . . I think we'll begin by persuading you to return every dollar in your personal accounts wherever they are—back into the Plantation account."

"You go to hell. You can take me to court if you like. But you'll have to prove I've stolen anything." Styles stood up, leaning on his cane. His face was pallid, muscles rigid.

Ferrell trembled with the overwhelming need to hit Styles. He stared at that sharply chiseled face, the small, tight lips, the pretty features, the thick eyelashes, wanting to drive his fists into the visage. He forced himself to calm down. Funny as hell, two men could argue about everything except money without coming to blows. To hell with it. He knew better than to hit Styles because he knew if he touched him once in rage, he'd kill him.

He managed to smile. "No, Styles. I'm not going to let you legally rob this estate blind. I'm sure that money is in your accounts with no evidence that it ever belonged to this estate. However, we both know you've embezzled every penny of it. We're not going into court . . . . You're going to return that money—voluntarily—or you'll regret every cent you spend."

Styles met his gaze levelly, straightening so that he gazed down at Ferrell. Ferrell's gaze did not falter. He merely waited. Suddenly, Styles retreated a step and burst into tears. "All right, damn it. Take it. I'll write you a draft."

Ferrell bowed him toward the mahogany secretary. Styles, crying softly, limped across the room. He scribbled a draft against his account at the bank in Mt. Zion, threw it at Ferrell. Ferrell picked it up, folded it, and put it in his pocket. He said, "I wish it were possible to thank you for what you've done to this farm in two years . . . . You better consider my gratitude expressed— when I didn't kill you."

"Damn you," Styles sobbed. "You son of a bitch. You powerful Baynard. Well, we'll see . . . we'll see . . . You can't save this place . . . . nobody could. So take it—take it all, damn you, and go to hell."

Ferrell gazed at Styles a moment, and then walked out.

Styles stood for a breath's length staring at the open doorway through which Ferrell had walked. His hands trembled. He cried openly, tears streaking down his cheeks. All the hatreds and frustrations building in him since he was a child of four, kicking and screaming on his nursery floor at Winter Hill Plantation, boiled up and erupted from him.

He sobbed. He heeled around, throwing the cane malevolently. He hobbled, half-running across the room. He threw himself upon the mattress, sobbing. "I want Perseus," he wept. "I want Perseus . . . send Perseus to me . . . ."

6

It was past noon when the twice-weekly train pulled into the Mt. Zion depot. Summer rains had swollen rivers, creeks, and swamplands, eroding railbeds and weakening railroad trestles. The train moved forward only slowly and with breathless caution. Strong men wept. Women rode with faces pressed into the shoulder of more stalwart companions or with their eyes tightly closed, their lips moving in incomprehensible prayer. An elderly man kept saying loudly that he'd tried to tell people these ungodly, newfangled contraptions would never be safe. If God had wanted man to fly along steel rails at twenty miles an hour, God would have invented the steam engine instead of the horse. God's message was clear.

While he awaited the delayed approach of the train into Mt. Zion, Hunt Campbell finished off the second quart of the whiskey he'd bought in Atlanta. In deference to the temperance convictions of the Christian ladies on the train, Hunt tried to hide what he was drinking. He poured the liquor surreptitiously into a cup and then sat sedately sipping it.

He smiled sourly. It was difficult, almost impossible, for strangers to detect that he was drunk. One had to know him well to spot that moment when his charm hardened into insolence, when he became disdainful, faintly sarcastic, slightly imperious, and more than usually condescending. He didn't particularly like himself drunk, but he detested the sober Hunt Campbell, the blue-belly, the humorless pedant. The accomplishment he despised most in his flawed personality was his ability to consume depressing quantities of whiskey before he reached nirvana of oblivion. And yet he could not desist, he would not. Drunk, he could live inside his own skin. Sober, he could not. It was that simple, that heartbreaking.

He stepped off the train upon the familiar platform. He saw a few faces he vaguely recognized without pleasure. The station, town, and countryside looked shabbier even than he remembered, hot and squalid. None of the town rowdies gave him a second glance in his rumpled twill trousers, unmatching, unpressed jacket, and cheap cotton shirt. He was rumpled, sweated, more than a little drunk. He was barely a distant, unacknowledged relative of that haughty young New Englander who'd minced off this train two years earlier, defiantly attired in pince-nez, top hat, and morning suit, straight from Harvard yard.

He shook the thought from his mind, unable to endure the irrelevant any more. He took up the squashed carpetbag he'd carried under his train seat primarily as depository for the libation that made possible a journey in his own company. His own nearness filled him with loathing, with a weariness of mind and soul—if any. He detested not only what he had become but what he had always been. He no longer tried to deceive himself. Everything inside the rumpled, sweated man pushing his way through the rapt crowds lining the station platform, everything, every lack, every weakness had been there in his halcyon years as one of the sharpest, deftest wits of Cambridge.

Oh, Christ!

He walked, listing only slightly, along the sun-tortured street to the livery stable. He argued with the hostler who demanded a five-dollar deposit for a rented horse and rig—three and a half to be returned if he got back to the stables, with horse and buggy in good shape, before sundown.

He drove along Birmingham Street, passed the notions store where he had first let Kathy know how deeply he cared for her—or "how badly I want you in my bed, at least temporarily." The swinging doors at the tavern beckoned like the wink of a whore. He dragged his sleeve across his mouth but slapped the reins upon the rump of the aged horse and drove on out of town.

He found the lonely ride from Mt. Zion to Blackoaks the least pleasant leg of his journey. He sweated profusely. He wished to hell he were in hell—anywhere but on this mission. God knew it could have no salubrious outcome—neither healthy nor wholesome. This no longer mattered. He asked nothing for himself but some small atonement for his heinous crime against Kathy. It well might be that Kathy would refuse to see him, that Styles Kenric would put a cartridge ball in his head and he would be beaten and driven off the place with the dogs at his heels. None of this mattered either. He had learned one truth. He could no longer live with his devastating guilt. The truth was, he missed Kathy so bitterly that he found life without her intolerable. There was no chance that he could have her again. But he could say to her how deeply sorry and ashamed he was, how reprehensible and vile he knew himself to be. Inside, he admitted his grievous misconduct all along. The difference was that now he wanted to say it aloud to Kathy and pray for her forgiveness.

His hands tightened on the lines. Or did he secretly hope only for one more glance at that fresh, lovely young golden face, no matter what it cost him—even, as was likely, if Styles killed him? The hell with that. He didn't look that far ahead into the future.

He exhaled. There remained only the moment when he would look on Kathy again and ask forgiveness. He had found life worse than tasteless without Kathy. His need and loneliness had begun the first hour he got beyond the limits of the tormented Crescent City. You could always go back to Shakespeare to find the precise words for your agony—"absence from those we love is absence from self—a deadly banishment."

A deadly banishment. He had been half-alive wandering through exile without her. What use a happy thought without her to share it? What good a bed without her beside you in it? What sense in food without Kathy there to give consuming it a motive?

His eyes brimmed with tears. He had thought he'd missed his cousin's wife after he'd fled Addie's clinging arms under threat of death. How quickly he'd forgotten her—soon after they parted nothing could have driven him back to Cambridge or to Addie. La Rochefoucauld had said it for him, "Absence lessens moderate passions and increases great ones, as the wind extinguishes the taper, but kindles the burning dwelling."

Hell, six years in Harvard, and all he could do was quote from the classics to define his inner agony. Filled with self-hatred, he slapped the reins across the horse, hurrying toward Blackoaks.

He slowed when he turned the rental rig in between the huge fieldstone gate posts. His hands tightened on the reins, the horse slowed, and he felt locked in terror. He looked outside himself for courage; there was none inside. But this time he begged courage not to face physical abuse, but to find the strength to look a beautiful girl in the eyes and speak his guilt until she finally saw into him—where he shriveled in hell.

He watched the small lookouts race down the lane toward him, but he waved them away from the rig. "I won't be staying," he said. "I won't be staying."

His eyes filled with tears, but these he recognized as internal weakness, and he blinked them away. This lovely old place! How little he had understood its unique beauty, its singularity in all the world—never seen before and never seen again. A place of calm, serene loveliness where gentle people asked first that you find comfort and peace and pleasure.

Then, as he turned in before the manor house, his gaze crossed the destruction, the charred barns, crafts shops, stables, and outbuildings. Nothing remained but black framing. He shivered, deeply shaken.

He got down from the wagon, dropped the hobble iron, went up the steps and crossed the veranda. He straightened his jacket on his shoulders, brushed at his shirt and trousers front, scrubbed at his cheeks with his sweated hand. He rang the bell and held his breath, waiting.

The door opened and Ferrell-Junior stood there. For an instant in time, they stared, wide-eyed with shock at each other. Hunt had expected Thyestes, Styles—anyone but Ferrell. He had words for all the rest of them, even Styles—"Please let me speak for five minutes with Kathy before you kill me. Please."

Ferrell said, "Hello, Hunt."

Hunt nodded, swallowed. "I know I've no right, Ferrell. But I want to speak to Kathy. Please, before you say no. Listen to me. For God's sake. I am in hell. I hurt her viciously, and I cannot live with that guilt. I ask nothing but to tell her how sorry I am. Please. Please . . . . "

Ferrell frowned, staring at him. "Hunt, don't you know? Haven't you heard? Kathy is dead."

Hunt staggered back as if he'd been struck in the face. A shudder wracked him. He nodded, feeling somehow that he should apologize, for being in this place, for being alive, for Kathy's death, for thinking his puny guilt and empty-bellied need mattered at all.

Ferrell stepped through the door, leaving it open. He started to speak, but Hunt shook his head, waved his arm, and turned around. He walked unsteadily across the field-stone veranda, faltering as if stepping in a deep hole on the level flooring. He stumbled slightly going down the steps. He made it to the rig. He touched the hand support. He did not climb into the seat because his knees buckled and he sank to the ground sobbing.

Fear that Ferrell would come out to him, speak to him, offer kindness, spurred him. He pulled himself into the seat and snapped the buggy whip across the rump of the horse. It lunged forward, going around the circular drive and turning into the inclined lane between the sharply etched trees.

Before he reached the gates, Hunt looked back one final time. Ferrell had returned inside the silent house and Hunt found all doors to the old pleasant world closed.

He tried to think where he would go, what he would do. But he could not care. It did not matter; the road, like his life, stretched bleak and empty before him.

7

Ahma and Moab ran.

They lost all sense of time, of fatigue, of hunger. As she jogged beside Moab on lonely country roads, she tried to remember only to keep the sun at her right in the morning, over her left shoulder in the hot, eternal afternoons. Neither of them had any idea how many miles they had traveled; they were afraid to know how many had been spent, traveling lost and in circles.

They ate where they could. It was summer and black-berries were plentiful. After a while the taste of the berries palled. Moab killed a rabbit with a rock, but they were afraid to cook it after they had skinned and gutted it. Neither of them could eat it raw.

On that empty-bellied morning when they finally awakened ravenous with hunger, and willing to risk a fire, they did not get close enough to rabbit, squirrel, or bird to make a kill with a rock.

"Hell with it," Ahma said. "Jus' don't think about being hungry. Think about free. That's what lies up there ahead of us, Moab. Free."

They plodded the roads, too tired to talk, too hungry to think. They paused frequently to listen for approaching wagons or carriages from either direction. When they heard the rumbling in the ground that signaled the approach of a horse and rig, they hid in the underbrush until the vehicle rolled past. Sometimes it was the slave patrollers, sometimes a family dressed up and headed on some mission, sometimes a farmer carrying produce to the near-est village.

A few times they were almost overtaken when a horse-man riding alone came upon them over a ridge, around a bend, through a copse of trees, silently and suddenly. At such times they simply parted, running, one on one side of the road, deep into the underbrush, the other on the far side.

They would wait a long time, then steal cautiously back to the road. But they knew they had been seen. If the horseman didn't wait in hiding for them, he was sure to report them to the nearest slave patrol, sheriff's office, or farm.

"We diff'rent-looking niggers," Ahma told Moab. "We don't pass nowhere unnoticed."

"Yeah. I beautiful—and you big," Moab said.

"We ain't black enough. We ain't plain enough. People look at us and we jus' different enough, they remembers."

"Anybody remembers when a king passes by," Moab said.

"If big talk made a big man, you'd be king," Ahma told him. "You so big and great—why ain't we eatin' better?"

"This here ain't my regular kingdom," Moab told her.

The nights were bitterly cold and, even in the loneliest stretch of forest, loud with disturbing sounds. After the first night, they covered themselves with both jackets and lay close to keep warm. Moab's head spun when he was pressed into the incredible depth of Ahma's breasts. He found sleep difficult, even after having kept up with her long strides all day on an empty stomach left him exhausted.

The scream of a panther chilled them. "They don't attack people," Ahma said. "That jus' scare talk."

"I heard of a man's body they found, ripped by a panther . . . . Panther attack if he big enough." Moab's hand closed on the handle of Blade's knife. "They scare the shit out of me . . . not the panther . . . that terrible screaming. I'd rather have 'em jump at me than scream at me."

"Go to sleep. No scream gone hurt you. We got enough to worry about without you carryin' on about a panther screaming."

"It keeps me awake."

"Think about something else."

"*That* keeps me awake, too."

She hit him, but she laughed. But after a few moments he heard her muffled sobbing. He sat up, cradling her in his arms. "Don't," he whispered. "You cryin' upsets me more'n the panther screaming."

She struggled to free herself, but he held her tightly. "It's all right. I was just thinking about Blade. The way I miss him. How I never gwine see him again—this side of Jordan."

"You reckon they is a life after we dead?"

"They must be. The life I had ain't no reason for livin'—if that's all there is . . . . Maybe someday, when I dead and left this world, I find Blade again. Till then, I dead. I dead inside."

"Oh no, Ahma . . . . What about up north . . . . when we free? When you had yore baby—and it born free? Don't be dead, Ahma."

"I tired. I don't want to live."

"I'll make you want to live, Ahma. I take Blade's place."

She laughed now, a fragmented crying sound. "You? You jus' a boy. You ain't never man enough to take Blade's place."

His arms tightened on her. "I will be."

When he was certain Ahma was asleep, Moab got up, carrying only his knife, and stole stealthily out to the road. He walked back along it to the farm they had passed just before nightfall. The place was dark and silent. Moab went out to the rim of the plowed field, followed the thick wall of trees, coming into the chicken yard from the rear.

The chickens, disturbed on their roosts, clucked and cried out sleepily. Moab caught a pullet, wrung her neck, and then stood silently, waiting for the other fowl to settle down. Nothing happened at the farmhouse. No light showed, no one appeared to be stirring.

Holding his breath, he tucked the chicken head under his belt and stepped out of the fence-enclosed pen. As the door closed behind him, the dog growled for the first time and attacked. "Oh shit," Moab whispered. The dog was amaziingly well trained in silent attack. The animal went for his throat. Moab managed to throw up his left arm to shield his neck. The mastiff's huge mouth clamped down on his arm, slashing.

Moab felt as if his left arm were being ripped from its socket. The dog reared back, jerking and tearing with those sharp teeth. Moab set himself to keep from being jerked off his feet. That dog got him down just once, he was a dead chicken thief.

He managed to close his hand on Blade's knife by shutting out the agony from his mind. The dog pulled him forward so he staggered. Perfectly trained, the dog released its grip on his torn and bleeding arm and went again for his jugular. The snarling animal lunged in for the kill. Moab drove the knife as near to the animal's heart as possible. The big dog seemed to halt in midair, to whimper in mortal pain and slump to the ground.

Moab waited for nothing else. The chicken battering at his hip, his arm held bleeding at his side, he raced across the plowed ground, heading for the road.

Ahma was awake, sitting up, tense and in rage, when he returned. She looked at his savagely torn arm and forgot her anger. She took off her underclothes and tied up the wound as well as she could.

"I got us a chicken," Moab said finally. "But I think we better run. Them folks might despise losing a chicken, but they going wild with hate when they finds that dead dog—likely, he the smartest one in the family."

By late afternoon, Moab was in fevered pain. Ahma found a small rise, hidden by reeds, on the bend of a creek. She brought boughs and made a bed for him. While he slept, she looked for herbs the Seminoles had used against wounds and snakebite. Frustrated, she found nothing.

She returned and sat close to Moab, holding his arm. "Don't carry on, Ahma," he said. "I been dog-bit before. I jus' feel a little woozy, that's all. I be fine by morning."

"We ain't goin' nowhere in the mornin'."

"The hell we ain't. I ain't stayin' no one place long enough for the slave patrollers to pick up our trail. I ain't told you before—an' wouldn't tell you now 'cept I feel sick—I bad scared of them patrollers."

She laughed and soothed his forehead gently with her hand. "Them damn patrollers. They don't scare me. They don't find you. You got to find them. You got to git so scared in your guts that you go find them, without knowin' you mean to."

"Well, that's what I don't want to do."

She finished off the last drumstick, chewing it loudly. "I run before. Patrollers never got me. Never will." She laughed, feeding him a hunk of the chicken. "Hell, I outrun them patrollers every night, boy, in my dreams."

"Just the same, we movin' out in the morning."

They splashed in the creek in the false dawn, found blackberries, which tasted better after a brief diet of chicken roasted without salt. They started along the road. By midafternoon, Moab's fever subsided. He insisted they walk faster. "Hell, it's a long way north, Ahma, and I in a hurry."

Ahma laughed. "It's up there, boy. Don't you worry. It's up there, somewhere, ahead of us."

They crossed bridges, they skirted villages, they hid when wagons approached. They plodded north. Ahma said, "I worry. About me. I was all wild. Crazy inside. Till Blade quieted me . . . . Now Blade dead. I get full of hate again—I go wild . . . . "

"You don't think about that," Moab said. "You just keep thinking about us gettin' free."

"Wonder how far we come?"

"I don't know. But I keep looking for the North Pole."

She shivered. "We ain't come all that far. I don't know how I know—but it's a feeling in my bones . . . . I know."

They stopped soon after dark. Both were exhausted. Moab's left arm throbbed steadily, and they had to keep washing the caked blood from the binding cloths.

Moab wanted to go back to the nearest farm and steal another chicken. But Ahma struck him across the head. "You crazy? Ain't you had 'nuff dog bites? What you want now? Some white farmer to shoot you?"

"I'm hungry. I know you're hungry. You a big girl. Big girls are always hungry."

"You gone keep talking about how big I am 'till I take a pine knot to the side of your head." She touched his hand. "We gone do something tomorrow we ain't done before. We gone beg some food at some house . . . . We gone beg first. They don't give it to us, we gone take it."

"Oh, hell," Moab said. "Looks like we need Blade bad."

"Amen," said Ahma.

They spread the jackets. The chill of the night, their hunger, the pain in Moab's arm, Ahma's cosmic sense of loss, made them cold to the marrow of their bones. Ahma drew him close. He could feel the way her breasts gave under the pressure of his body, as if he would drown in their depth. The outline of her *mons veneris* burned his leg. Even the soft touch of her hands aroused him. He grew hard. He tried to control it because he knew the rigidity must be instantly apparent to Ahma. It was. She said, "You might as well forget that, boy."

He tried to laugh. "Gettin' a hard-on is easy, forgettin' you got one on is something else."

"You close to me as you gone git."

"What you savin' it for?"

"I'll think of something."

"Lawdy, Ahma. Jus' think. Tomorrow we might git shot by some fool white slave patroller. You gone die without ever knowin' the wonder of having Moab pushed up inside you?"

"I tole you. Go to sleep, boy. It's gone be a long day."

"Hell, it's gone be a long night."

As the sun crested the next day, they reached a fork in the roads. One sign pointed west to Reform. Moab read the words slowly but accurately. "We best go that way," Ahma decided. "The road run kindly north. And maybe we find a house near the town where the folks will give two pore niggers some side meat and clabber."

"Ask for some corn pone," Moab said without much hope.

"When you beggin' you take what you can git."

They'd gone less than a mile on the road to Reform when they saw an unpainted slab-sided shack on a few acres of unpromising land. A white woman, thin, emaciated, her lank hair caught in a bun at the nape of her neck, came out on the steps to stare at them. She said over her shoulder, "Paw. You best come out here."

The farmer appeared, thinner than his wife, his huge, bony hands clasping a gun. "What you people want?"

"We hungry," Ahma said.

"You niggers runners?" the man said.

"Laws no," Ahma said in her most servile tone. Moab bit back laughter at her obsequious voice. "We on our way back to our plantation—"

"We live yonder, beyond Reform," Moab said.

"You one of Colonel Slaughter's niggers?" the man said.

Ahma seemed about to nod in agreement, but Moab spoke quickly. "Naw, suh. Some little beyond Colonel Slaughter's place."

"The Redfields," the woman said from behind the man. "Must be some of them triflin' Redfield niggers."

"Yes'm," Moab touched his forehead and kicked some dirt with his toe. "We from Redfield's. On our way home. Know the massa be most obliged if'n you could feed us a little side meat and clabber—"

"An' some corn pone, if you could be so kind," Ahma said. "We been travelin' a spell . . . . This here triflin' nigger is my brother."

"That right, Masta. Me and Sister, we on our way to the Redfield's yonder—beyond Reform."

"We can spare a little something," the woman said. "Likely old Redfield will send over some food or pay if we do."

The man shrugged. But he went on standing, his sun-bleached blue eyes watching every move they made. Ahma and Moab retreated to the shade of a chinaberry tree. They sat on the ground, waiting. The woman brought the tin plates piled with greasy meat and corn pone. She poured clabber into tin pails.

The husband sat on the top step of the stoop and watched them eat. They grabbed ravenously at the food, stuffing it into their mouths greedily. He leaned forward. "You sure you ain't runners? I never seed Redfield niggers that hongry."

Ahma looked up, tried to speak, but her mouth was too full. She could only shake her head from side to side vigorously in denial.

The man got up. He walked slowly across the yard casting a lean, limber shadow in the lifeless sand before him. He gave them a cagey smile. "You ain't runners, you got passes. Let me see yore passes."

Moab began nodding in agreement, smiling and trying to speak even before he could swallow the mouthful of food. The farmer frowned, watching him. The woman came to the edge of the stoop and stared.

"Yes, suh. You right. We should of let you read our pass first thing we come in here. You right, suh." He fought into his jacket pocket and brought out the letter of reference Styles had written for Blade's journey to New Orleans. He unfolded the paper and extended it to the farmer.

Holding his gun by the butt, ready to react to any tricks, the farmer reached out and took the sheet of paper. The man moved his gaze across and up and down the paper, returned it. He studied them knowingly. He nodded at last and said, "Oh, well, its all right. Long as you got a pass."

"Yassuh, Massa gwine be mos' beholden to you—and your kind lady—for this good food. Sister and me been travelin' a fur piece."

Ahma finished off the greasy meat and mopped at the bottom of the plate with her corn pone to get the last drop. "Powerful satisfyin' food, ma'm," she said. She bobbed her head and smiled shyly.

Moab could not hide his grin as they loped along the road again, going toward Reform. "Feel better with yore belly full?"

"Why you grinning, Nigger Boy? We ain't free yet."

"No. But we's a lot closer." Moab did a little dance in the middle of the dirt road. "I knowed that white trash was bluffin' us. Knowed he couldn't read. I held that there letter out to him, upside down! I could read it, but no way he could. And he stands there an' preten's he readin' it."

He laughed, putting his head back.

Ahma's voice raked at him. "Just be careful, boy. Just don't git so smart you gits us shackled and jailed."

They'd gone less than two miles when they heard the yelping and baying of hounds behind them, the thunder of fast-ridden horses' hooves shaking the earth beneath their feet.

"It's us they after," Moab whispered. He didn't even know why he whispered. He saw the forest not as a place to hide but as a wall too high to climb. In his mind he saw the posse riding into the farmer's yard. Somebody had described Ahma—nearly six feet tall, with full tits, crisp black hair, long legs. "Oh, hell," the farmer was nodding, pointing and fuming, enraged.

"Dogs," Ahma said. She was running and looking back over her shoulder at the same time. "They lots harder to shake than slave patrollers."

"Let's take to the woods and run," Moab said.

"We need more'n woods," Ahma said. "We got to get a river or stream. And fast. Makes no difference which direction it take us. It's the only way we stop them dogs."

They left the road, running west. Their main hope at the moment was to avoid the village of Reform. They wanted to stay away from people—white or black—until they made a river, creek, or swamp.

The world was no longer silent, no longer haunted with unexplained sounds—the noises they heard without relief were the ominous howling of the dogs, the baying that told the hunters plainer than any words could have that they were hot on the scent of the fugitive blacks.

But Ahma's own senses were sharply developed, too, by her fight for survival in the long flight south to Florida, life among the Seminoles, the pursuit of the U.S. Army, her savage desire to stay alive. "I smell water," she said. She waved her arm south and west, and flung herself forward, running. She did not look back. Breathing through his mouth, Moab followed. The baying of hounds spurred him forward.

They topped a rise, and below them in the distance, Moab could clearly discern the strange blue-green that promised wetlands, a swamp or creekbed. He ran faster. They came into the lowlands, slowed in the mud, plodding.

"Keep moving, boy," Ahma said, breathless. "Mud don't slow hounds. It slow horses and men. But it slow us just as much."

They plodded forward. The ferns grew taller, the jungle thickened, and the mud became soupier, deeper, harder to cross. Ahma caught his hand and gripped it hard. Together they struggled forward. It was some moments before they realized there was silence behind them and had been for a long tense time, now.

"They stopped," Moab said, slowing.

"We ain't. You keep moving. Up ahead somewhere is a creek. We float with it. We cross it. We float. We cross back. But we keeps moving."

"They stopped," Moab said again. But before he could get the words out, the baying rose again, louder and nearer, south of them.

"White bastards," Ahma said. "They knows this country. They think we headin' for high ground." She turned again and threw herself into the morass.

They plunged through fern, vines, and thickly matted willows into a small creek. It was less than twelve feet wide, but it was black and deep. Ahma jumped in, letting the current carry her. Moab hesitated, his old fears of snakes locking him for the moment. Then he dove out as far as he could, swimming after her.

She floated, turned sputtering. "You good boy, Moab."

The creek widened, the land on both sides dried, and to Ahma's horror, she saw they had floated out of the swamp. Ahead, there was likely a river. But she had the fatal certainty that the hunters and their dogs had blocked that passage.

"Yonder," Moab whispered.

He caught Ahma's hair and swam into the thick willows that cascaded out over the banks of the creeks. She swam with him. He caught the dangling limbs and pulled them in under them. They clung to the clay bank, shivering, only partly with cold.

The dogs yelped, straining at their leashes. Concealed behind the green tracery of the willows, Moab and Ahma watched the five riders approach on the opposite creek bank. They rode directly toward them, the yelping rising to a frenzy.

Moab clutched Ahma's arm. "Hit's that Masta Gil Talmadge," he whispered. "And there's that Masta Link Tetherow—oh, Gawd, would he like to git me in his gunsight. And one of them Winterkorn men and Masta Walter Roy Summerton. Don't know the man with the dogs."

"They coming right at us."

Moab closed his hand on her arm. "An' that Gil Talmadge—he follow us ever step to hell. We got to get out of here, Ahma."

"That sound just fine. But how you plannin' to do it?"

"They ain't but one way. We climbs back up on that shore, and we runs—back into that swamp."

Ahma clutched his arm. "We run yonder, Moab. That's where the river is. Where the river is we got a chance to move—faster."

"All right." He shrugged. "Climb up this bank. Stay low—and run. Stay bent low to the ground . . . . You go first and I follow you, 'cause you know where you goin'."

Ahma looked at him and laughed, a bitter sound. "I goin' to hell afore I go back to slavery."

"An' I with you. Save me a place near the fire."

She turned, smiling in a strange way. She grabbed him fiercely to her and kissed him. "Someday you be a man big as Blade—then I really kiss you."

"Then you has to stand in line."

She squeezed his hand one last time. "I be there, Moab." She turned then and scrambled up the bank. The weeds and trees were sparse on the bank. Moab, scrambling up behind her, heard the man yell, spotting her. He came up on the level ground on his knees. Over his shoulder he saw the gun jerked up in Gil Talmadge's arm. Ahma was running, bent over, toward the thicker growth. Sick, he saw she wasn't going to make it. "Hit the ground," he wailed at her.

She plunged forward. But she was too late. Gil Talmadge fired. In a wild agony, Moab saw Ahma struck and driven forward. The firing was turned on him, but he rolled into the underbrush and scrambled on his knees toward the place where Ahma had fallen.

Behind him he could hear men, dogs and horses plunging into the water to ford the creek. Holding his breath, he jumped up and ran. Ahma had pulled herself into the thick underbrush. She held her right leg extended. She was bleeding.

But when she saw him she struggled up. She caught his hand, half-leading him, half-supporting herself, going deeper into the dark growth of cypress that promised the river beyond. Running, she struck a tree and staggered. He saw that she was only half-conscious, running simply on her terrible need to be free.

He caught her against him, supporting her weight. He kept moving forward. The dogs came up the clay bank behind him. He kept crashing deeper into the fern and vines. The dogs' yelping got a frustrated sound. There was delay while horses and men fought their way up the steeply inclined bank.

He pushed through a wall of vines, mosquitoes smoking upward in the millions, protesting, clouding out the sky.

He slapped away the clouds of mosquitoes and, half-carrying Ahma now, he stepped forward, managed to catch his balance to keep from falling over a twenty-foot embankment into a river. "Ahma," he whispered, exultant. "The river."

"Go on," she whispered. "Jump. Float with it. Let it take you—fast—far as it can. Keep running, Moab. Keep running."

"You crazy. You're going with me."

"I can't, Moab. I only slow you down . . . . I learned from them Indians . . . when you fall—you through—they have to leave you there."

"I ain't no fuckin' Indian." He took her up in his arms, feeling as if his left arm would break under her weight. He staggered forward to the brink of the embankment, took a deep breath and jumped.

The impact when he struck the water feet first jarred Ahma out of his arms. As he went under the surface, he was already fighting in panic to find her. He came up, spitting, looking around. She was floating, loglike on the current. He swam after her. He caught her hair, pulled her to him. Turning her so her head rested on his chest, her face above the waterline, he swam in a long sidestroke, using the force of the current to carry them along.

The river dug its way through the swampland, wound out into high ground. Ahead, Moab saw a single-wagon bridge spanning the water. He kicked and pulled himself in under its shadow. He pulled Ahma up on the bank and sagged beside her, gasping for breath. He heard a wagon approaching. He went tense. Pulling himself up, he pressed his face hard against a brick support, staring. It was not the posse. It was a white man wearing a shapeless black hat and a fat black boy on the seat beside him in a flat-bed wagon. He sank back to the water's edge and lay still while the wagon rattled across the bridge plankings above him. Then it was gone. "It's all right, Ahma. They gone."

She didn't answer. He bent over her. She was unconscious.

8

Moab stared around him helplessly. The black river slid past as it had done forever, surface smooth and unbroken, hurrying, unconcerned. Trees banking the far shore rose against the afternoon sky, a thick wall that seemed to press in upon him. The silence was oppressive now that the wagon had rattled across the narrow bridge and along the road. He considered running after the wagon and begging for help. He knew better. There was no one he could trust to help Ahma—except himself.

Some of his panic abated at this thought. He did not know what to do, only that he had to do everything he could. He began by clearing out the space in close under the bridge base. This stone and mortar foundation was thick, sunk into the roadbed with side wall supports more than a foot thick extending four or five feet toward the waterline.

He cut pine boughs and covered them with willow boughs, making a bed for Ahma against this enclosed bridge footing. Working, his mind cleared. The fear that had locked his thinking into one helpless groove lifted. He stopped defeating himself by continually fretting on "how" he would help her. Now he could decide "what" he could do that might save her.

He began by lifting her carefully in his arms and moving her from where she sprawled unconscious in the mud to the pine-bough bed against the bridge base. He removed both his coat and hers, wrung them out, and placed them over her.

Now he faced the problem of the bullet in her thigh. He shuddered—blood poisoning, gangrene, or loss of blood all threatened her life. That bullet had to come out. Blade's sharply pointed, razor-honed knife was a perfect surgical instrument. He stared at it, troubled. The knife had to be heated. It should be white-hot so that the knife itself would not kill her.

He prepared to remove the bullet from Ahma's fleshy upper leg. He turned her face down on the boughs. Thank God, she was unconscious! He lifted her tattered skirt above her hips. Even in this panic-ridden moment, he was conscious of the acute stirring in his loins at the firm roundness of her buttocks. They smiled goldenly nude up at him.

He got up and ran along the bank on both sides of the road gathering sticks for a fire. He had built a small pyramid of slivers and kindling before he admitted he could not risk a fire. No sense saving Ahma's life if his smoke and fire brought Gil Talmadge, his guns, and his hounds.

Hunched on his knees, he looked around, frustrated, sick. Finally, he crawled to the stone base of the bridge. Finding a nick in a large flint rock, he worked the knife furiously back and forth in it until friction sent sparks flaring and the knife blade was too hot to touch.

He bit his under lip, held his breath, and sliced the

501

flesh back and forth across the blackened, torn bullet hole. Fresh blood spurted, and he hesitated for a long, indecisive moment. Determined, he pressed the knife blade into the bullet hole until metal touched metal. He'd found it! Wincing, biting back the bile that rose up in his throat, he probed with the knife point, loosening the cartridge ball and manipulating it slowly and awkwardly upward through the blood and pulpy flesh. He caught the small missile with his finger, pulled it out. He held it a moment savagely in his fist. Then he threw it as far as he could into the river. The splash was sharp in the forest stillness.

He knelt over the wound, pressed his mouth against it and sucked at it. He spat out the blood, sucking again and again. He had no idea what constituted a clean wound. He just kept sucking and spitting until some instinct in him was satisfied that no poison remained in the incision.

He took off his shirt, tore it into long strips, and bandaged the wound. It seemed to him after a long time that the bleeding lessened, then slowed to a faintly spotting red seepage.

He sank back, exhausted. Ahma stirred, whimpering. She opened her eyes, stared up at his face inches above hers. Her face burned with fever. She shook her head wildly. "You still here, nigger boy? You git on down that road . . . . I doan want you hanging around here."

He opened his lips to answer, but she sank into unconsciousness again. He stayed a long time crouched over her. If he had known a prayer, he would have muttered it. He said nothing. For the first time he thought about the hounds. He had not heard their baying for more than an hour . . . .

It grew dark. Night smoked in along the silent river, matching, blending, and fusing the black of the water to the high banks and towering trees. The darkness lowered in on a chill wind. The support walls offered protection, but, bared to the waist, Moab shivered with cold. He hugged his arms across his chest and tried to get warm by thinking about Miz Florine sinking to her knees for him. But that world was gone, and he could not go back, even in his fantasies.

He touched Ahma's forehead. She was fevered, dangerously hot. He dampened a hank of his torn shirt, wiped her face, dripped water on her parched lips.

She stirred, crying out. At first, he thought she was recovering consciousness again, but as she cried out, he realized she was yelling in delirium.

Ahma wept, rolling her head back and forth. "Don't, Massa, no! Oh, please don't, Massa. I cain't, Massa . . . . I a little girl, Massa . . . . Mah mammy tole me to tell you that—I jes' a little girl . . . . Mah mammy say I jes' six years old, Massa . . . . I six, Massa . . . . I cain't take that great thing, Massa . . . . Oh, Gawd, Massa, you gwine split me daid . . . ."

She cried for Blade. "I need you, Blade . . . . I got nothin' . . . . I got nobody without you, Blade . . . . I got no life without you . . . . I jes' a crazy black girl . . . with her head all buzzing with craziness—without you. Oh, Gawd, Blade, I need you."

She raged at Moab, berating him. "Git away from heah, nigger boy! Ain't you got pretty good sense? . . . You stay with me . . . they gwine git you . . . . Run, Moab . . . . Run, boy . . . run north . . . ." She wailed and he tried to comfort her, knowing she was oblivious to him in her delirium. He held her against his chest, whispering. She sobbed. "Oh, you goddamn stupid nigger." Then she grabbed him and held him close, rocking, crooning, as if he were her baby.

Moab laid her down on the pines. He damped more cloths and held them on her fevered forehead until they steamed. His eyes filled with tears and spilled along his cheeks. He talked to her, babbling, knowing she didn't even hear him. "You gwine be all right, Ahma . . . . No more white massa . . . no more hurt . . . . we gwine make it, Ahma . . . . I don't know how in shit we gwine make it, but we gwine . . . . "

All night long he crawled between her bed on the boughs and the waterline to carry cool cloths to fight her fever. He forgot fatigue. He was thankful for something to do as the blistering cold settled in after midnight. Sometime in the darkest hour before daybreak, Ahma's fever broke and she sagged into deep, exhausted sleep. Her breathing was loud, but it was regular, and Moab grinned even though he felt lost with nothing to do but wait.

Slivers of the pink dawn sky lightened long strips of the river. Ahma stirred and Moab crawled close to her. She opened her eyes; they were weak, wan. She tried to smile. Her voice raked him. "What you doin' in this cold an' no shirt on, nigger boy?"

"I'm all right."

"You ain't gwine be all right till I out'n your way."

"I got no reason to do anything without you, Ahma."

"Hell. You jes' a boy. You got your whole life—up north—free."

"I'm as old as you are. Maybe older."

"Hit different with a girl. I a woman. A growed woman. I also cain't run—I cain't even walk. You gwine leave me and save yourself, or I'll kill myself to git out'n your way."

"Damned if you'll kill yourself after I worked so hard to keep you alive."

Her eyes brimmed with tears. "I thank you, Moab . . . but I daid . . . . I don't want to live—"

"You gone want to. You gone have a good life—right in this world you hate so bad . . . . Give me a chance, Ahma. Give me a chance."

"That's what I tryin' to do, you stupid nigger. You promise me you leave. Now. Or I swear I kill myself."

He laughed at her. "No, you ain't. If you gonna die anyway, you might as well lemme pester you to death—"

"You bad—"

"You gonna die, you might as well die the good way."

Ahma smiled in spite of herself. "You really kinda pretty, boy," she said. "Don't ever git the idea you be the man Blade was, but you kinda pretty."

"I hung good, too," he said.

"I hope so." Her voice sounded choked with tears too deep to shed. She drew the backs of her fingers across her tear-filled eyes. "You better be hung real good—you expectin' to kill a big girl like me—with something like that."

He kissed her lightly. "I do my bes', Sister Ahma. I do my livin' best."

She clutched his hand and pressed it tightly. "Cain't ask no more than that."

The sound came suddenly. It was like thunder in the earth. The plankings of the bridge rattled faintly. "Horse," Moab whispered. "Horse and wagon."

"Run, Moab," she pleaded.

He covered her mouth with his hand. "They can't see us down here. Lie still, they pass."

They lay breathless, waiting. The wagon lumbered around the bend and upon the bridge. Moab got to his knees, crawled to the walled supports. He watched the wagon roll east across the bridge. He frowned. "It's the same white man and fat black boy that went past yesterday."

He came back to her, exhaling heavily. "I try to find us something to eat. Berries. Hickory nuts maybe."

Now, her face stricken, Ahma reached up and clamped her fingers over his mouth. "Listen."

Moab sweated, straining to hear. But there was no sound. The wagon and horse no longer sent back vibrations to rattle the bridge plankings. He heard nothing. In fact, the silence was fiercely ominous. He gripped Blade's knife in his fist.

"Don't hear nuthin'," he whispered between her fingers.

"They comin' back." She barely spoke, sitting up. "They walking—cattin' back across the bridge."

He listened, but he heard nothing. Sweated, unable to sit and wait to be jumped, he got to his feet, set himself just inside the right support wall. Now he heard the catlike tread of the two men on the bridge. They came off of the plankings, and he set himself, knife held low, ready to rip upward.

Helpless, Ahma cringed against the wall.

The white man appeared first. He was too smart to come around the support where Moab could have jumped him. He walked several feet away from the bridge. He stared in at them from beneath his floppy brimmed black hat. "Now, take it easy, boy. You ain't goin' to git hurt."

"Nobody goin' to take us back, Mista," Moab said. He

came away from the wall, crouched, the knife low. It occurred to him in a confusing flash that wasn't a complete thought—the man was unarmed. The hell with that. He was falling for no white tricks.

He stepped forward. The white man held his ground, but he was shaking his head. He spread his hands to show he was unarmed.

"Git out, Mista, or I kills you—"

"Moab, don't!" At the familiar male voice behind him, Moab shook visibly and heeled around.

He and Soapy stood, locked, in tableau, staring at each other. Tears streamed down Soapy's face. "We prayed it was you, Moab," he said. "We been prayin' it was you."

Moab retreated, putting his back against the stone support.

"We seen you yesterday," Soapy said. "But we feared you'd stay in the river. We went down to the next bridge, hoping to head you off."

Moab could not speak, he merely shook his head.

Soapy said, "We wants to help you, Moab. You and Ahma."

Moab licked his tongue across his lips. "Who that white man?" he asked.

Soapy laughed. "That Masta Ben Johnson. Masta Johnson don't want you to go back," Soapy said. "He he'ps niggers run no'th to be free."

"Why you want to help us?" Ahma said to the colonel.

The colonel shrugged. "I don't believe in slavery. I don't believe any man has the right to enslave another . . . . "

"Colonel keeps them thoughts pretty quiet around Mt. Zion—if people there could prove he helps niggers go through the underground up north, they burn him out, jus' like they burned pore Miz Jahndark and her baby." Soapy laughed. He was a genuine converted disciple of the colonel's. "Colonel gonna help you-all. Ain't you, Colonel?"

"I'm going to try," the Colonel said.

"Don't want no white man helping me. Never yet seed a white face I could trust," Ahma said.

"You can't stay here," Colonel Johnson said.

"Colonel Johnson could help you, Ahma," Soapy pleaded.

Ahma shook her head. "I don't trust no white man."

The colonel spoke softly. "You got to trust somebody. Nobody can make it all the way—without help. White or black. And you got to learn that the color of the skin don't make the difference . . . . Till you learn that, you're nothing, no matter how free you get."

Ahma sank back against the wall, watching them warily.

"If you'll come with me, we've got some time," the colonel said. "I don't know how much. I sent Talmadge and his posse downriver looking for you . . . . They may have turned to start back by now."

"Where you plan to take us?" Ahma said.

"To Memphis, Tennessee," the colonel said. "It's an open wagon. It's a long trip. There's a lot of risk. I can't promise anything—except I have not failed yet. I don't mean to fail this time."

"What happens to us in Memphis? That ain't free land."

"No. You've made it into Mississippi. We go north to Memphis. There, I'll put you on a vegetable boat to Cincinnati. When you walk off that boat in Cincinnati, you're free. We travel—you three my slaves—to Memphis. We try to get you to a doctor. You act like my slaves . . . . Once you're on the boat, you won't be questioned. The boat is never stopped or searched."

Moab said, afraid to believe, "You comin' north with us, Soapy?"

Soapy shook his head. "I gwine stay with the colonel a while. He'pn' him free niggers."

Colonel Johnson studied Ahma, troubled. "Well? How about it? Will you trust me, Ahma? You got nothing to lose. Those men and their dogs will be back. You can't run . . . . There's a chance I'm telling you the truth."

Moab nodded. "Listen, Ahma. I believes Colonel Johnson . . . . I heard old Masta Talmadge cuss him plenty and swear he'd hang the colonel if'n he ever got proof the colonel was transportin' runaway blacks north."

"I'm not promising you a heaven, Ahma," the colonel

said. "Not even a heaven on earth . . . . You'll find people—white and black—pretty much alike wherever they live. They are the sum totals—the victims of their own ignorances and prejudices . . . . north or south, you're going to run head-on into prejudice—and hatred . . . . But in the North, you'll be free."

Ahma nodded. "We go with you."

Colonel Johnson smiled and exhaled heavily. "We better get to hell out of here, then . . . . Soapy, go bring our wagon."

Ahma touched her slightly swollen belly where life had begun, an embryo in her womb. Her eyes brimmed with tears. Then, after a moment, she laughed uncertainly, but hopefully. "I gonna be free . . . . Thank Gawd, I gonna be free . . . . An' my son, he gonna be *born* free. He gonna be born *free!* . . . . An' when he born—up north there—I gonna hold him in my arms and start telling him that first day that he is *free!* By Gawd, he *will* be free! He gonna be *born* free, and I gonna call his name Blade."

BESTSELLERS

☐	BEGGAR ON HORSEBACK—Thorpe	23091-0	1.50
☐	THE TURQUOISE—Seton	23088-0	1.95
☐	STRANGER AT WILDINGS—Brent	23085-6	1.95
	(Pub. in England as Kirkby's Changeling)		
☐	MAKING ENDS MEET—Howar	23084-8	1.95
☐	THE LYNMARA LEGACY—Gaskin	23060-0	1.95
☐	THE TIME OF THE DRAGON—Eden	23059-7	1.95
☐	THE GOLDEN RENDEZVOUS—MacLean	23055-4	1.75
☐	TESTAMENT—Morrell	23033-3	1.95
☐	CAN YOU WAIT TIL FRIDAY?—	23022-8	1.75
	Olson, M.D.		
☐	HARRY'S GAME—Seymour	23019-8	1.95
☐	TRADING UP—Lea	23014-7	1.95
☐	CAPTAINS AND THE KINGS—Caldwell	23069-4	2.25
☐	"I AIN'T WELL—BUT I SURE AM	23007-4	1.75
	BETTER"—Lair		
☐	THE GOLDEN PANTHER—Thorpe	23006-6	1.50
☐	IN THE BEGINNING—Potok	22980-7	1.95
☐	DRUM—Onstott	22920-3	1.95
☐	LORD OF THE FAR ISLAND—Holt	22874-6	1.95
☐	DEVIL WATER—Seton	22888-6	1.95
☐	CSARDAS—Pearson	22885-1	1.95
☐	CIRCUS—MacLean	22875-4	1.95
☐	WINNING THROUGH INTIMIDATION—	22836-3	1.95
	Ringer		
☐	THE POWER OF POSITIVE THINKING—	22819-3	1.75
	Peale		
☐	VOYAGE OF THE DAMNED—	22449-X	1.75
	Thomas & Witts		
☐	THINK AND GROW RICH—Hill	X2812	1.75
☐	EDEN—Ellis	X2772	1.75

Buy them at your local bookstores or use this handy coupon for ordering:

FAWCETT PUBLICATIONS, P.O. Box 1014, Greenwich Conn. 06830

Please send me the books I have checked above. Orders for less than 5 books must include 60c for the first book and 25c for each additional book to cover mailing and handling. Orders of 5 or more books postage is Free. I enclose $_____ in check or money order.

Mr/Mrs/Miss_____

Address_____

City_____ State/Zip_____

Please allow 4 to 5 weeks for delivery. This offer expires 6/78.　　A-14

Thomas Tryon

THOMAS TRYON, actor turned author, has chilled reading audiences with his tales of the supernatural.

"He writes with an often hypnotic power and invention." —RICHARD R. LINGEMAN, *NEW YORK TIMES*

☐	CROWNED HEADS	23199-2	2.25
☐	HARVEST HOME	23496-7	2.25
☐	LADY	C2592	1.95
☐	THE OTHER	22684-0	1.75